THE TALL CAPTAINS

THE TALL CAPTAINS

BART SPICER

CUTTING EDGE

ISBN-13: 978-1-952138-12-6

Published by
Cutting Edge Publishing
PO Box 8212
Calabasas, CA 91372
www.cuttingedgebooks.com

TO MY WIFE
BETTY COE SPICER
... the kindest cut of all.

FOREWORD

On a bleak morning in September 1759, two legendary commanders led their desperate armies to a brief, decisive battle outside the walls of Quebec. By nightfall, the once-great French empire was doomed; the new British empire consolidated. But with the danger of invasion from Canada thus removed, American colonists were freed from their dependence upon British arms. The Revolution was still fifteen years away, but its seed was planted on the Plains of Abraham.

This book is concerned with the last days of the French in Canada, with the soldiers who fought the battles, with the farmers and townsfolk who endured, with the politicians who plundered the colony. The amounts stolen may seem incredible, but they are not exaggerated. Basically, this is a work of fiction, but the structure and the facts are historically sound. If the reader wishes to separate historical characters from the fictional, he may assume generally that the duMaine family and those others met on board the *Frelon* (except for the King's investigator) are imaginary.

For clarity, the modern form of many place names is used here, as is the metrical system which was not officially adopted until some years later.

CHAPTER ONE

Duncan Crosbie slumped low in the padded chair and lifted his chin for the surgeon's inspection. The small cabin was very quiet, with only the soft creaking of ship's timbers to blur the surgeon's mumbling comments. Crosbie felt the old man's fingers prodding his face and he closed his eyes before the black-rimmed fingernails came into view. The thin reek of stale wine on the surgeon's breath made Crosbie gulp nervously.

He clamped his mouth tightly and sat without moving, forcing from himself a patience that would never come easily. Silently, savagely he cursed the wild intemperance that had already checked his career, a career barely begun but now seriously hampered. And all through his own damnable, foolish behavior, Crosbie admitted to himself. He need not be here now, wallowing across an endless sea in a clumsy old transport bound for the ends of the earth. But it had been impossible for him to sit idly in garrison at Toulon, busy only with the dull routine of defense while other officers with far less energy and ability were already veterans, had seen real service against Cumberland or Frederick of Prussia. In those days he had been a favorite of the elderly Colonel commanding the artillery at Toulon and the Colonel was a soldier whose good opinion came slowly. Himself a child of the Paris gutters, the Colonel had risen in fifty years through the ranks of an army in which promotions usually went only to wealthy sprigs of noble families. He had suffered through the days when artillery officers were denied military rank, being classed as mechanics, less acceptable than even the engineers.

But the Colonel had been among those who had forced recognition and now he shared equal position with the gentlemen who commanded the Horse and Foot. The Colonel guarded his authority jealously. Any criticism had to originate with him or it assumed the guise of insubordination. Crosbie had known all that, welcomed it in fact, for the Colonel's rigidity had placed all junior officers on a common footing and only in such an atmosphere could Crosbie hope to rise, hindered as he was by a lack of wealth or family influence.

And knowing all that, Crosbie had thrown it away. And for what? Even now Duncan Crosbie found it hard to believe that he had been idiot enough to try to impress the Colonel's daughter with his military talents. Even a first-year cadet knew how bootless it was to discuss artillery technique in the hope of dazzling a pretty girl. But Crosbie had driven ahead, intoxicated with his own ideas, boring that lovely maiden with his extravagant praise of Prussian artillery. And this at the Colonel's dinner table with the Colonel aghast, his ruddy face turning bright purple as Crosbie expounded his private notions with juvenile fervor. Inwardly Crosbie shrugged. The next day he had applied for transfer to one of the new units then forming at Toulon for service in Germany. He had even prepared the way for his acceptance as sous-lieutenant with an artillery battalion. But the Colonel's blazing indignation could not be cooled by a routine transfer. He demanded a far greater punishment for insubordination. So Duncan Crosbie now belonged to no unit. He had been sent away, almost banished to the army defending the wilderness settlements of New France, to serve under a former infantry officer of scholarly tastes and no particular reputation. Crosbie would never have the chance now to fight his guns against Frederick in the great battles where glory and advancement could be expected even by a junior officer with no influence at court. Instead he would fight naked savages and untrained farmers, if he fought at all. He couldn't logically expect to see a gun larger than a six-pounder. He would rot in the wilderness with no least hope of promotion, never using the talents that plagued his imagination. And all because of his own thoughtless, headstrong stupidity. His large hands clenched on the arms of the chair in a convulsive grip.

"...most fortunate, young man," the surgeon muttered. "You were almost the very first to contract this peculiar rash. But your face will be fresh and clear long before we land. Others are not so fortunate. When I think of the noble Comte and ..."

"Yes, yes," Crosbie said irritably. "I've had this good fortune for nearly a month now. Is it finished?" He brought up a bony hand and touched the greasy gunpowder-and-brandy paste that coated his jaw. Under it a soft pliant beard bent easily.

"With extreme care," the surgeon said. "With delicacy, you understand, you might venture to shave. But I must caution you against breaking the skin, for then ..."

Crosbie pulled away the soiled cloth that draped his neck and straightened in the chair. "I'm grateful, monsieur," he said quickly. "If you will excuse me?"

"All eagerness to see a clean face, are you?" the old man growled. He moved back a few steps and settled himself on the edge of his bed, one hand tweaking gently at his pointed beard. "Why are you young military gentlemen so enthusiastic about shaving, eh? Can you tell me that?"

Crosbie made an aimless gesture with one hand. "I hadn't thought about it, sir," he said easily. "The great Alexander started the habit, I understand. We keep it up because it tends to reduce the chances of disease when large numbers of men are held in a small area."

"Very plausible," the surgeon grunted. "Well, permit me to offer my blade. I confess I am also curious to see what sort of face lies under that villainous beard."

Crosbie accepted with undisguised pleasure. The cramped compartment he shared with the other junior officers and cadets was entirely lacking in amenities. The surgeon's tiny cabin was luxurious by comparison. Set securely in a fitted chest against the wall were a shallow metal basin and a matching jug of water. Moving with the caution that a month on shipboard had taught him, Duncan Crosbie slipped from the chair, flexing his knees and keeping his neck bent low to avoid cracking his head against the beams. He poured a small pool into the bowl and dabbled his fingers at a tablet of soap that smelled of tallow. He washed his face several times, spilling the filthy water into a slop pail set in a gimbal on the floor. When the water rinsed cleanly from his face, he picked up the surgeon's razor.

"Merde!" the surgeon mumbled, almost to himself. "The young bull has a beard as white as Methusaleh's."

Crosbie ducked to squint into the polished steel mirror. His hair was the bright red he remembered, slightly bleached to a paler tone on top where the sun had touched it. But the new beard and mustache were almost colorless, faintly pink where the hair was thickest. To Crosbie's eye, accustomed to the heavy dark beards of the Frenchmen around him, it seemed a childish, freakish sort of beard that made him embarrassed to look at. As long as it had been covered with gunpowder paste, the beard had been thick and strong, a warrior's beard, but this … this …

Quickly Crosbie spread soap across his chin and brought the razor into position. He stroked the blade down his cheek with a precision rare in one whose hands seemed too large and clumsy for anything smaller than a broadsword. The beard came away easily and the face he saw was at least familiar, though no more attractive than usual. He was too big. That was the final, ruinous judgment. To be outsized at eighteen is, to a sensitive adolescent, to be damaged. And Duncan Crosbie's massive body, large hands and feet were considered grotesque among men who admired a neater structure, and that unfashionable red hair was the ultimate clownish touch. Crosbie's mouth compressed thinly as he stared into the mirror. It was his face and while no one had ever admired it, neither had anyone cared to offend its owner too openly. He turned to thank the surgeon.

"De rien," the old man said, raising a negligent hand. "There was a time when the chirurgien was also the barber. Mindful of my honorable tradition, I can at least lend a razor."

Crosbie thanked the old man again and once more agreed that he had been fortunate to be cured so easily of that disfiguring rash which had swept among the passengers. Duncan Crosbie closed the flimsy door quietly and walked along the dim corridor toward the companionway that led up to the quarterdeck. With the forgetful ease of long habit, he propped his left hand under his belt, leaving his thumb free to rub lightly over the hilt of the Scottish dirk he always wore under his sash.

On either side were the ranks of tiny compartments designed for important passengers and straight ahead was the great cabin which occupied the entire stem portion of the ship. Normally this was the sacred province of the captain, but for this voyage it housed Madame la Comtesse de Boyer and the four other ladies of rank who were journeying to New France. Through its closed door came the high clear ripple of feminine voices. Riding insistently over the light murmurs, the ship's bell rang with a strident tone, calling the new watch to the deck. Crosbie paused at the foot of the companionway until the rapid patter of seamen's feet faded to silence. Then he climbed to the quarterdeck.

The quarterdeck was nearly deserted now for at four o'clock began the long and complicated procedure of feeding the passengers and even officers had learned to be prompt if they hoped to eat. But in the long month when his face had been smeared with gunpowder paste, Crosbie had learned to avoid the other travelers. He and the other afflicted gentlemen had formed the habit of dining separately, at odd times, and of exercising when the decks were deserted.

The ship was laboring heavily on the starboard tack, her yards hauled back nearly chock-a-block by the braces. But the long forward tilting, the wallowing arcs of ocean travel had smoothed away into an easy gliding motion that felt strange after the long Atlantic passage. For a long month the *Frelon* had fought through black wintry seas, holding high to the northern route, hoping to evade the English ships that blockaded Louisbourg and threatened the French convoys. Twice the *Frelon* had put about and run, each time saved only by the heavy weather that reduced visibility to a matter of a few mètres. But now that the mouth of the great river had been reached safely, the danger was past. The English might lord it arrogantly at sea, but on land it was a different story. Crosbie itched with impatience for the end of this dreary depressing voyage, for an end to being cooped in this leaky old ship that couldn't even make a pretense of disputing English command of the sea.

An icy wind swept across the deck, burning his newly shaven face. It smelled strange to him and Crosbie turned to look toward snow-peaked mountains glimmering far away in the lowering dusk. It was the fresh keen scent of snow that made his nose tingle so oddly. Crosbie breathed in deeply. Now the end was in view. The St. Lawrence was fifty leagues across at its mouth and even now, some eight hours after landfall, Crosbie had no sensation of the closeness of land, except for those shining mountains outlined against the sky. A few days more and the *Frelon* would drop anchor off the rock of Quebec.

"The Seine of the New World," a solemn voice said beside him. A hand indicated the great river.

Crosbie turned to a position at the railing beside the stout young man in the coarse grey robe of the Récollet friars.

"The Seine, is it, Mathieu? And will Quebec, that wilderness garrison, be our Paris?"

"You are never serious, Duncan," the young friar said in a deep, measured voice that came from trying to seem older and more solid in the eyes of his seniors. "Let us then call it the Loire of the New World. For Paris is the city of the world. There can be only one Paris."

Crosbie smiled. "You Parisiens. Even holy orders cannot shake your sinful pride."

The young friar bowed his head in a brief silence. "A proper rebuke," he said contritely.

"I made a clumsy joke, Mathieu," Crosbie said quickly. "You are too solemn, my friend."

"Yes, I have no humor. It is very trying for my friends." The round face of the friar creased in quiet laughter. "But I have not complimented you upon your recovery. How very strange you seem without that barbarous beard. Is your strange malady completely cured, then?"

"Let us pray, Brother Mathieu," Crosbie said lightly.

"The Comte de Boyer will be in a rage when he sees you have recovered while he and the other gentlemen are still …"

"The noble Comte will never compare himself with a mere sous-lieutenant," Crosbie said bluntly. "Nor would the other gentlemen."

"No bitterness, please, Duncan," Brother Mathieu said softly. "These gentlemen may occupy positions which you feel they do not deserve. But your chance will come, my friend. Are you not already entering upon a new life, with fresh opportunities for …"

"Please, Mathieu," Crosbie broke in testily. "I confess my human failings. These fumbling idiots offend me. I admit it. Now give over."

"But in New France you will …"

"In God's name, Mathieu! I'm an artilleryman. I understand guns, but who needs my knowledge here? When are guns larger than muskets ever used against naked savages?"

Brother Mathieu shook his head and groaned softly. "Such arrogance I must protest."

Crosbie's voice hardened with the anger of frustration. His bony forefinger prodded at the young friar's robe. "Can't you see, Mathieu? And right at this moment every gunner in Europe is testing new ideas in the field. Frederick of Prussia is making the world respect his cannon. He understands gunnery. And so do I. I could do much ... I have ... I have ideas that could ..."

Crosbie turned his face abruptly from Brother Mathieu and stared blindly out at the shadowed mountains. "But I will rot in a wilderness," he muttered in bitterness. "While others who understand nothing ..."

"No, Duncan," Brother Mathieu insisted firmly. "Not you, my good friend. But you must learn restraint. Even Alexander served a period of apprenticeship."

"Don't mock me, Mathieu," Crosbie said quietly. "I'm not diseased with ambition. I merely want a ... a chance ..."

"It will come, Duncan. Your chance will come in New France."

Crosbie's restless hand smacked solidly against the gilt railing. "The future of New France will be decided in Europe," he said flatly. "It has always been that way. America and India are the prizes won by victories in Europe."

"If victories were won in America, that might affect the decision, don't you agree?"

Crosbie shrugged. "Possibly," he agreed in a weary tone. What was the merit in trying to explain? Brother Mathieu was a scholar and a man of God, but to him one soldier was much the same as another. How could Mathieu understand that European campaigns were commanded by the great generals, especially those against Frederick? The war in Canada was nothing in comparison. Promotion and honors would come easily to soldiers in Europe. Only a niggardly share would ever reach Canada.

"You will find much to admire in your new commander," Brother Mathieu said in a brisk voice, tempting his friend from somber reflection. "Montcalm is ..."

Brother Mathieu's voice died in a gasp. A flailing length of tarred rope slashed hard across his face. Crosbie bellowed angrily and spun on his heel, one great hand stabbing out toward the squat sailor beside him.

The sailor swung his rope forward and down with the full force of his thick arms, striking with vicious precision at a scrawny boy who huddled by the railing, one hand lifted ineffectually to ward off the stinging rope. Fat gouts of blood flowed from his nose, dribbling onto a torn shirt. The sailor recovered, brought his rope up again and once more the end whistled dangerously close to Brother Mathieu's head. Crosbie snatched at it swiftly, ignoring the stinging impact on his palm. He heaved hard, bringing the short heavy sailor stumbling back toward him.

The sailor let his rope slide free and twisted himself desperately, trying to avoid a hard fall to the deck. His wide, flat-featured face turned toward Crosbie just in time to meet Crosbie's hand. The impact was as sharp as a pistol shot. The squat sailor slumped to the deck, shaking his head and growling incoherently.

"Take care how you swing your hungry rope," Crosbie said angrily. He touched Brother Mathieu's sleeve. "Did this pig ..."

Brother Mathieu touched his torn cheek gingerly. A thin smear of blood coated his fingers. He glanced dazedly up at Crosbie, then shouted in warning. "Duncan!"

As he pivotted, Crosbie lashed out with the tarred rope, knowing he'd been foolish to give the sailor any advantage. The heavily wrapped butt of the rope lash smacked soggily against the sailor's head, sending the sailor down to one knee. His knitted cap went sailing across to the mast.

The sailor was motionless for a brief moment. He wiped a greasy hand over his ear and stared unbelievingly at the scarlet smear of blood. "Sale bête!" he snarled. His wide face twisted in shocked fury. The mark of Crosbie's hand stood out like a livid welt across his twisted mouth. He slid a short sailor's knife from his belt and pushed up swiftly from the deck, holding the blade low as he lunged at Crosbie.

The tall young Scot pushed away from the railing, slipping aside to avoid that first clumsy rush. He freed his jeweled dirk from its scabbard and swirled to face the sailor who now leaned heavily against the railing, sucking in air with deep angry gulps. He had fought clever young gentlemen before and he knew he could not win against an officer's sword. But this young gaillard wasn't wearing a sword; he should have been safe enough. But where had that huge boy found such a knife? Who had ever seen a blade like that before? It made three of his knife and it dazzled the eye with a gay sparkle of gems in the hilt. The sailor backed a cautious distance along the railing. He paused there and the ship's captain shouted angrily, adding his commands to Brother Mathieu's pleas.

The sailor shifted hesitantly from one foot to the other. Crosbie padded forward, surprisingly agile for a man of his height. His dark-steel blade flicked back and forth rhythmically, throwing glints of reflected light. The sailor lifted his knife slowly, choking down the terror that rose in his throat. This young devil was out for blood! He edged aside a step, then jumped back as Crosbie countered quickly. He dashed into the ring of curious passengers, seized the first arm he saw and swung around, twisting a tall, dark-haired girl into Crosbie's path.

Blindly, Crosbie caught her with his free arm, never once taking his eyes from the sailor. The passengers parted to a safe distance. Crosbie supported the girl until she regained her balance, then he pushed her easily toward Brother Mathieu. She said something in his ear, but Crosbie was too concentrated to hear.

He advanced one swift stride, shifting to present only his long arm as a target to the sailor's knife. His right knee bent slowly as he inclined into the sailor's terrain, blade first, thrusting, probing, moving always, up and down, in and out, with the sailor's fascinated gaze following the darting blade.

The sailor swept his knife up and around in one desperate slash, hoping for Crosbie's arm. The young Scot recoiled to let the blade go by. Then he shifted forward again, growling deep in his throat. With a hoarse shout, the sailor flung his knife down suddenly, sticking its point in the weathered deck. He shoved passengers aside, clearing a narrow aisle along the railing. He ran with swift, scuttling strides toward the companionway that led down to the ship's waist. His soft-soled shoes pattered lightly on the treads. Then he vanished below-decks.

Crosbie swept one hand low to retrieve the sailor's abandoned knife and straightened, bracing his back against the railing, holding both knives easily in his right fist. Beside him Brother Mathieu was saying something in a thin, excited tone, but Crosbie bent all his attention toward the ship's captain, a thin sour man of mature years whose seedy black uniform was a sharp contrast to the gaudy clothes of the army gentlemen clustered eagerly around him.

The captain glared tightly at the young Scot. After a long silent moment, he gestured vaguely and turned to Brother Mathieu.

"What caused this, monsieur?" he demanded.

Crosbie said nothing. Brother Mathieu explained volubly, his tone harsh with strain. "... and Monsieur Crosbie sought only to defend me. You yourself saw your sailor attack him. With a knife! What sort of monsters do you employ..."

The captain snorted in sour disbelief. "I saw the sailor," he said. He nodded twice, as if Brother Mathieu had settled a confusing problem. He glanced at Crosbie and spoke in a voice of brisk command. "My crew answers only to me, monsieur. If a man must be disciplined, I alone will punish him. Is that clear?"

Crosbie held his gaunt face perfectly straight and he bowed politely. "Perfectly clear, sir," he said soberly. It was a small price to pay, he thought. The captain's displeasure might have been far more severe.

The captain nodded abruptly and returned to his post beside the helmsman. The few passengers still on deck maintained their silence. Crosbie relaxed. He slid his dirk into its sheath and offered the sailor's knife to Brother Mathieu.

"A souvenir, Mathieu?"

The young friar shuddered. "Duncan, you should not do such things." He drew in a shaky breath. "You endangered your life. For what? What of the future you..."

Crosbie shrugged irritably. Good judgment always came too late when it came at all. In his whole life he could remember no instance in which he had acted wisely. If he had, he would not be on this leaky old ship now. He tried to smile at Brother Mathieu, pretending a light-heartedness he was far from feeling. Casually he tossed the sailor's knife up and down on his wide palm, absently admiring the precise carving along the walnut haft and the light easy balance of the short blade.

Brother Mathieu's hand touched his sleeve, turning him slightly, directing his attention to the far side of the quarterdeck. There, with her wide pale green skirt swept casually across the dirty boards, was the dark-haired girl he had caught when the sailor threw her in his path. She was stooped with a thin, fair-haired boy close to her, holding him tenderly while she mopped away the gushing blood that still streamed from his nose. The boy's enormous dark eyes watched her closely, but he said nothing.

Crosbie crossed the deck. He scooped up the boy's faded red stocking cap and winked amiably when the large dark eyes turned toward him. He rammed the cap over the boy's silky hair. The girl glanced up, an incipient smile on her lips. The pleasant expression was wiped away abruptly as though it had never existed. The girl's eyes were as large and expressive as the boy's, but they held only contempt, tinged with fear.

She slipped her blooded handkerchief into the boy's hand and came erect, one hand sweeping back a soft ringlet of dark hair that had draped across her throat. Then she brought her hand forward swiftly, smacking it across Crosbie's face with a sharp crack. The young Scot stepped back in bewilderment.

"You...you French bully!" she stormed. "If I were a man, I'd...I..." She swept forward furiously, eyes blazing. "Get out of my way, you…you…" Her voice cracked with tension. She stamped one foot.

Crosbie moved back another stride, silently. His eyebrows pulled together in wonderment. What a splendid sight she was. But why in God's name was she raging at him? He hadn't done…

The girl turned abruptly away, her back straight and stiff, expressing her disgust as clearly as the words she had used.

Crosbie glanced curiously at Brother Mathieu. The pudgy young friar closed his gaping mouth with obvious effort. He shrugged. A thin hand clutched Crosbie's arm and he looked down.

"Thank you, monsieur," the boy said in a timid voice.

"Eh?" Crosbie; growled. "Thank me? For what?"

"I was…" the boy gulped nervously and pointed his finger vaguely at the deck. "I was he…"

"My God," Crosbie snorted. "I wasn't…"

Something stopped him before he could say that he hadn't interfered merely to help a ship's bound-boy. Those worshipful dark eyes choked off his explanation. If the boy wanted to think that Crosbie was an admirable soldier full of wisdom and justice, what was the harm in that? The girl had blamed him for something he didn't understand. Now the boy was thanking him. So Crosbie said nothing more. As the boy lowered his head, the young Scot could see the shredded shirt pasted to his scrawny back with stipplings of blood. The nosebleed had abated now, but there was an angry welt that circled the boy's neck like a poised snake and Crosbie felt a quick rage. He had not intended to help the boy; he hadn't even looked at him, but now he was fiercely, exultantly pleased that he had fetched the squat rope-wielder a good clout and scared him livid. He was sorry that he hadn't done more; a period of blood-letting would probably improve his manners, Crosbie thought. He dropped a hard hand on the boy's head and ruffled up the pale silky hair.

"Put on your cap, boy," he said gruffly. "What's your name?"

"Denis, Your Honor," the boy said, with an awkward attempt at a bow. He crammed the soiled cap down over his ears, and as the hair was pulled back Crosbie could see the thin starved face, the high beaked nose and the sharp chin, the broad nobbly child's forehead and the widely spaced brown eyes. When he touched the boy's shoulder, the bones felt tiny, like bird bones, but what flesh there was to cover them was hard stringy muscle.

"I'm not Your Honor, Denis," Crosbie said. "My name is Duncan Crosbie and you may tell that forecastle riff-raff that we are good friends and I'll carve the next man who takes a rope to you again. Or better yet, you carve him yourself. Here." Deftly Crosbie tucked the sailor's short knife into the boy's belt.

"Yes, Your…monsieur," the boy stammered. He retreated slowly, obviously hating to leave, but eager not to be a nuisance. He backed to the opposite railing and then turned aside, facing forward, but still able to watch Crosbie out of the corner of his eye.

"You have made a conquest, Duncan," Brother Mathieu said pleasantly. "It comes so easily for you. That boy will always…" He broke off as he observed Crosbie's impatient shrug. "Sometimes," he said soberly, "I think you run from approval."

"Give over, Mathieu," Crosbie insisted. The expression in the friar's eyes mirrored that of the young boy. It made Crosbie strangely uncomfortable, as if he had accepted a reward he had done nothing to earn. "Who was that girl?" he asked abruptly. "What was she so angry about?"

Brother Mathieu shook his head. "She is of the Comtesse's party, but I am not sure of her name. And I have no idea why she…But wait! Possibly she saw only that the sailor was trying to run and you hot in pursuit like an avenging Fury. So she might suppose…"

"That I started the brawl," Crosbie said. He lifted his big shoulders in a casual gesture of dismissal. "You were warning me of my new commander when we were interrupted. What do you know about the aged nincompoops who command in Canada?"

The pudgy young friar drew himself stiffly erect. "Montcalm is but forty-five," he said crisply. "And I can assure you he is no nincompoop. I must advise you that I am related to the Marquis de Montcalm and therefore I cannot..."

"Peace, peace," Crosbie said quickly, smothering a gust of laughter. "I meant no offense to your kinsman, but..."

"Montcalm is not my kinsman, but he is married to my mother's sister and I am..."

"And you are determined to protect his good name if you have to challenge half the army. Very well, monsieur, I withdraw. I know very little about Montcalm, as a matter of fact. What about him excites your enthusiasm?"

"Montcalm has been a soldier since he was fifteen," Brother Mathieu said admiringly. "He was a captain at seventeen; a colonel at thirty. For ten years he was a Brigadier before he was promoted to Major Général and commander of the King's troops in Canada. Merely as a soldier, therefore, he is more qualified than most..."

Crosbie's upraised palm was signal enough for Brother Mathieu. The stern, lecturing tone dwindled and the young friar blushed solidly. "I must ask your pardon, Duncan," he said in a hesitant voice. "I was... carried away by..."

"I hope you will champion me as strenuously, Mathieu," Crosbie said lightly. "Your defense of Montcalm is very reassuring. I knew that most Governors of New France were naval officers floated ashore to their reward. I assumed the army commander would be no better. Tell me more about him."

"I must confess I have never seen Montcalm," Brother Mathieu said with obvious embarrassment. "I know of him only through my aunt."

The young friar glanced away in confusion as if he had made a shameful admission.

The friar's embarrassment was so evident that Crosbie shifted the subject. "And what of this great river, Mathieu? How far to Quebec from here?"

"I...I disremember," Brother Mathieu said faintly. "This stretch may be navigated, though it is hazardous. Above Quebec, however the river narrows sharply and from there to Montreal, the channel is difficult to find. From Montreal to the lake, only small boats may be used because of the rapids. Beyond the rapids one reaches the enormous lake of Ontario, as it is called, where ships have been built. From Ontario, a line of four other great lakes stretches across to the west in a curve like a glittering necklace around the throat of New France."

"A very pretty similitude," Crosbie said.

In the center of the quarterdeck, a hinged skylight studded with thick panes of opaque jealous-glass swung upward and was propped open. Crosbie and Brother Mathieu turned to look down into the cabin below. Warm air scented with whale-oil smoke from the lamps, drifted upward in a solid visible sheet and was whipped to shreds by the cold wind. Gradually, the dim, upturned faces in the cabin became visible. Crosbie recognized none of them.

"The Comtesse is entertaining this evening," Brother Mathieu said in a low voice. "I had nearly forgotten. I must pay my respects. Will you come with me, Duncan?"

Crosbie shook his head, still looking down into the great cabin. "I have not been presented."

A flushed and radiant woman's face rose abruptly toward the gaping skylight, laughing into the fresh breeze. She was obviously standing on a stool or chair and her eyes were on a level with the deck where Crosbie stood. She glanced up casually at him, her eyes widening as she craned her neck to see his face. The laughter seemed directed at him now, Crosbie suspected, though the smile that followed was damnably inviting. She stepped down. Crosbie averted his eyes politely as a brilliantly dressed elderly lady took her place.

"Don't let me detain you, Mathieu. I must go find the steward before he disposes of my dinner. Possibly you will have time tomorrow to tell me more about Quebec and your..."

Denis, the ship's boy, slipped smartly away from the railing to avoid collision with a liveried footman who slithered across the deck unsteadily. He bowed clumsily to Brother Mathieu, almost lurching into the rigging as the ship wallowed sluggishly in the trough of a wave.

"Madame la Comtesse requests the pleasure of your company in the great cabin, monsieur," the lackey said, speaking with pained deliberation as he struggled to keep his balance.

"Yes, go along, Mathieu," Crosbie urged. "I'll just..."

"And Her Excellency most particularly requests that you present this young officer, if he finds himself free to attend."

Brother Mathieu laughed softly. He shifted to glance down at the open skylight. Through it he could discern the bright cluster of feminine faces lifted upward. Nearby Denis watched unobtrusively, holding the girl's handkerchief cautiously to his nose, his narrow chest expanded mightily as if he too had been honored by an invitation to the Comtesse's entertainment. His eyes never left Crosbie.

"Another conquest, Duncan," Brother Mathieu said quietly. He smiled briefly at Denis, then touched Crosbie's arm, urging him toward the companionway. "Come along. Madame la Comtesse could be very helpful to you in Quebec. And, also, she alone is able to set an adequate table on board this depressing ship."

CHAPTER TWO

As Duncan Crosbie stooped to pass through the doorway and into the ship's great cabin, he paused behind Brother Mathieu, awed and somehow shocked at the dazzling scene. Four ladies stood grouped in an arc under the skylight and some dozen gentlemen, gaudy as Spanish peacocks, postured elegantly, leaning on the two large cannon that faced the stem, idling near a long, linen-draped table covered with silver that sparkled in Crosbie's eye. One powdered dandy entered from the narrow door of the stem gallery and latched the panel with finicking precision. None of the gentlemen wore uniform, though Crosbie was sure that all held some sort of military rank. His shabby dark blue and scarlet artillery coat was not his best, nor were the dark kerseymere breeches and cotton thread stockings, but even in his dress uniform, wearing silken small clothes, with his silver-gilt buckles clipped to his shoes, Crosbie would have been a drab sight by comparison. He could feel a quick surge of heated blood coloring his face and he knew it would be glowing like a red lantern any moment. Those posturing monkeys were even wearing smallswords, he noted incredulously. On board ship, where a momentary lurch could result in a broken leg, these fools permitted swords to dangle, merely to add to the danger. Nervously, Crosbie touched the hilt of his heavy jeweled dirk. He rubbed his broad thumb over the carved carnelian wolfs head that was the Crosbie signet. And he waited stiffly for Brother Mathieu to present him.

The regally beautiful lady in scarlet satin must be the Comtesse, he thought. It was she whom Crosbie had seen through the skylight. Brother Mathieu addressed himself first to her and though she spoke with warm condescension to the young friar, her fine dark eyes remained on Crosbie. His hand tightened on his dirk and he strove for an impassive expression. He could do nothing about the hot flush on his face, but at least he could ignore it, refuse to let a constitutional clumsiness put him out of countenance. He had small experience with fine society.

"...and your gigantic young friend?" the Comtesse was saying.

Crosbie stiffened. A dull roaring in his ears made words hard to distinguish. The lady of the magnificent eyes was indeed Madame la Comtesse de Boyer. Two other ladies with haughty manners were introduced in a confusion of syllables that Crosbie barely heard. Three times he bowed and three times he thrust forward a tense leg and swept the floor with his battered hat. Each time he could feel his hair brush against the low beams, but not once did he permit himself to look up or to flinch. Wisely he remained directly under the skylight which afforded him almost enough room to stand erect.

Of the gentlemen, Crosbie previously had met only the pre-ternaturally thin Canadien, Michel Colbert, who was some sort of functionary of the government of New France. What sort, Crosbie did not know, but it was a position that Monsieur Colbert felt elevated him far above any sous-lieutenant of artillery. The gentlemen ogled the young Scot with undisguised amusement, bowing politely enough, but gaping all the while and tittering at his preposterous height and his unappetizing red hair... "quite like a Venetian whore's, my dear friend. Honestly earned, no doubt..." Crosbie let none of his natural resentment show in his expression. Groups much like this controlled the destinies of soldiers in all countries, and the higher a soldier hoped to rise, the more he must devote himself to ingratiating himself with the true rulers of his world. Smilingly, Crosbie denied himself the right to resent the giggling slurs of the gentlemen.

"...such good fortune to espy such a gallant figure," the Comtesse went on, putting her hand softly on Crosbie's arm. "How is it we have not seen you before, monsieur? Have you been in hiding?"

Crosbie's elbow clamped hard at his hat and he attempted a light-hearted shrug. "Until today, madame, I was among those gentlemen who withdraw from public view. An unfortunate rash that..."

"That loathsome...ugh..." the Comtesse shivered dramatically. "My poor Comte is also tainted, as you may know. I refuse to see him so long as he wears that villainous black mud on his face."

"A distressing sight for a lady's eyes," Crosbie agreed. "It may be some consolation to you, madame, to know that the surgeon's black paste has cured me and will surely help the Comte."

"Poor Armand," the Comtesse sighed. "We shall pray for his recovery..."

A thin finger touched her bare arm in a swift, intimate gesture. She turned suddenly, bright eyes flashing angrily. Monsieur Colbert, the slim Canadien, spoke quickly.

"Your forgiveness, dear madame. I could attract your attention no other way and I have been eager to join your conversation with this gentleman."

The Comtesse inclined her head regally, silently. In her scarlet gown, Crosbie thought she had an exciting, glittering beauty, heightened by the towering court wig that tended to diminish her bold features.

"Another young gallant come to Canada to seek his fortune, isn't it?" Colbert asked with a sly grin.

Crosbie stiffened. "To serve his King, monsieur," he said coldly.

"Of course, of course," Colbert agreed quickly. "All of Canada is the King's. But command of even the tiniest outpost can make an officer reasonably wealthy in three or four years. So why should you not anticipate..."

"My commission is in the artillery, sir," Crosbie said, breaking through Colbert's clever light voice.

"But that needn't be a handicap," Colbert insisted. He swayed with the movement of the ship and possibly from wine. "Don't you know that the Chevalier LeMercier, commandant of artillery at Quebec, came to Canada twenty years ago as a penniless sergent? Today he commands at least a million francs, probably much more by this time."

"I do not know the gentleman..." Crosbie began harshly.

"You are a fool, Michel," the Comtesse snapped. "You repeat vulgar gossip like a Breton fishwife. The Chevalier LeMercier is an honorable soldier. Need I warn you that he is in my brother's confidence?" Her chin rose imperiously and she stared directly into the eyes of the knife-thin Canadien. Then more softly she said, "Your tongue runs away with you, sir. You will discourage our young friend before he has even seen Canada. And," she glanced quickly aside, flashed her darting smile at a quiet man standing silently near Colbert. "And you will give Monsieur Tremais the most appalling ideas of life in Quebec."

Colbert stepped back, almost stumbling. His thin mouth snapped shut and he turned abruptly to the quiet man.

"Monsieur Tremais," he said in a sour voice, "the silent watcher, the Ministry's own..."

"Investigator," the quiet man said bluntly. "Was that the term you were about to apply, sir?" There was that in his tone that compelled Crosbie's attention. Clearly much more was being said than the words could convey. Colbert was wary, almost frightened and he covered his alarm with sneering deference. But most interesting was the Comtesse's tight watchfulness as the half-drunken Colbert curled his thin lip at Tremais.

"My brother," the Comtesse said quickly, "will be most happy to welcome you to Quebec, monsieur. Your report to the King will do much to quiet the foolish rumors so current about Canada. Sometimes colonials rather enjoy shocking the sedate folk in Paris. Our careless raillerie has come home to plague us. You will do us a great service, monsieur."

Tremais smiled thinly. "It is my wish to see conditions as they are, madame. I look forward to meeting your distinguished brother."

"With pleasure, I hope?" the Comtesse said, nearly making a demand of it. Her face lighted charmingly and impulsively she gripped the quiet man's sleeve.

"As you say, madame," Tremais said easily, "with pleasure. And now I must retire. My regrets, dear madame. I have much to attend to before we reach Quebec." He lifted the Comtesse's hand, kissed it with the light grace born of long practice. He bowed his farewells. Crosbie was not sorry to see him go, nor was Colbert. The thin Canadien turned once more to Crosbie, his lip curled again, but the Comtesse forestalled him.

"No, Michel," she said flatly. "Go amuse Brother Mathieu with your tales of the savages. Monsieur Crosbie will escort me to the table."

Colbert began a protest, but something in the Comtesse's expression silenced him effectively. He bowed unsteadily and backed away.

The Comtesse led Crosbie toward the long table, thrust a plate in his hand and piled it high with small, dainty bits of food, tiny pastries that hardly made a bite, rolls of meat shaved to an incredible thinness, dabs of ragoût, tiny fish cooked whole with even the heads still on them. The Comtesse poked her fork disdainfully at her plate, apologizing for compelling her guests to dine from a buffet and such uninspired food, too. Crosbie murmured and tried with no success to eat politely and slowly. It was all very well for the Comtesse to disparage her dinner. But she had no way of knowing how delicious it all was to a young man of large appetite who has lived upon weevilly biscuit, cheese that tasted of tar, ragoûts made of ingredients no one dared investigate, with sour thin wine or water flavored with poor brandy.

The Comtesse pressed him with wine and even drank a glass to him—a heady compliment that made him gulp hastily. Again and again his plate was replenished by the Comtesse who seemed to enjoy watching him eat. At least a bottle of wine had accompanied the food and when Crosbie refused a third portion of jellied fruits, the Comtesse poured him a brimming goblet of fine brandy.

"It is vastly comforting to see a Frenchman eat with the gusto of a Canadien," she said in obvious approval.

"I'm a poor Frenchman, if the truth be known, madame," Crosbie admitted. "I was born in Paris, but I soon formed the habit of thinking of myself as a Scot."

"Ah, yes," the Comtesse smiled. "But surely not after the Treaty of Aix-la-Chappelle?"

"That altered everything," Crosbie agreed. "I was eight then and I can remember the day the Scots were told that the King of France had agreed to expel Prince Charlie and his people in exchange for the return of the fortress of Louisbourg. Those Scots who chose to stay in France were offered commissions. Many did stay, but many more left with their Prince."

"I can understand it must have been a frightful blow," the Comtesse said quietly. "To us of Canada, it was important, too, for Canada cannot live without Louisbourg." She touched his large hand with a swift, warm finger. "And you, at eight, decided to stay in France, did you? I am very glad."

"My father was killed in the '45, madame. The King granted my mother a small pension, so we remained to become Frenchmen."

"Do I detect a note of bitterness in your voice when you speak of the decision made for you?"

"Not at the decision, madame. Never that. But I cannot speak easily of Scotland, or of Craigsmuir that was once our home, or of the German pigs and their English armies that have …" Crosbie gulped at his brandy. "If I had no other reason for liking the

French, madame, I would love them because they fight against the English. That alone would be reason enough for me. And ..."

"And there are other reasons as well, I hope?"

Crosbie wiped beads of moisture from his forehead. The cabin, large as it was, had become unbearably close. The skylight above his head was shut again and Crosbie looked at it longingly. Food and wine and now the brandy were all heating his blood dangerously, he felt. And worst of all, warmest of all, was the presence of the Comtesse at his elbow, gazing at him with large brilliant eyes, approving what she saw, admiring him as he secretly felt he deserved to be admired.

"You poor boy," she laughed. "Are you stifling, too? Wait one moment."

The Comtesse stepped aside to speak to a liveried footman near the door. Crosbie finished his brandy and surveyed the chattering collection of fashionable people around him. The noise was almost a solid blur, but he was long inured to French gabble, though he would never learn to enjoy it. With the studiously casual eye of a young man who has never had money enough for fine clothes, he compared the gentlemen's costumes, mentally putting a price on each. Those crystal buttons on a mulberry satin coat would not have sold for a centime less than twenty francs each, a whole louis d'or for one button. And Crosbie had in his pocket just twelve such coins, his entire wealth except for his meager pay. Even if the day should come when he too could afford such extravagant sums for clothing, he would always remember the long poverty of his early life, and the pleasure would go as remembrance returned. He turned his head warily to avoid a hanging silver lamp that smelled warmly of scented oil. The Comtesse came toward him, merely nodding to gentlemen who hoped to intercept her. Behind her trailed the liveried footman and a ...

Crosbie stiffened. The girl he had seen on deck, the tall, dark-haired beauty who had stamped her foot and called him "bully." She held a softly billowing fur cloak in both hands. As she helped to drape it across the Comtesse's shoulders, her wide green eyes lifted to Crosbie, bright and contemptuous. The young Scot bowed in red-faced confusion.

"Thank you, Céleste, my dear," the Comtesse murmured. "You have met our new friend, Monsieur Crosbie?"

Céleste, Crosbie repeated to himself. Foolishly he stared at her, seeing the sharp scornful glitter that made her eyes almost metallic. He cleared his throat loudly, struggling for a pleasant phrase and cursing his clumsy tongue.

The girl totally ignored the Comtesse's introduction. A brief, sharp glance flicked at Crosbie's face, insulting as a slap. She turned away silently as the Comtesse pulled Crosbie toward the door that led onto the stern gallery. The door swung open and Crosbie followed the Comtesse outside. The waiting footman latched the glass door and stood firmly in place, his broad back obscuring the view Crosbie had of the great cabin. Beside him the Comtesse drew in a long slow breath and let it out in a sigh of contentment.

"How delightful is the air of Canada."

Crosbie cudgelled his slow wits for a gallant observation.

"You will find everything different here," the Comtesse said, leaning far out to look down at the glowing wake of the ship in the dark water. "Very different from France. A young officer can be confused very easily and find little profit or enjoyment, if he remains too French. It is wiser to ..."

Overhead a shrill whistle blasted the stillness and the ship's crew swarmed into the rigging as the watch-officer bellowed his orders. Far forward a heavy chain clanked heavily, then ran out with a brisk clatter.

"Anchoring?" Crosbie wondered aloud.

The Comtesse nodded. "The river is treacherous even by day," she said easily. "And the channel markers have been removed so the English cannot follow them to Quebec. So it is necessary to anchor at night." She eyed Crosbie over her shoulder. "You truly know very little about Canada, eh?"

"Very little, madame. I've looked into Charlevoix…"

"Books!" she said with a contemptuous gesture. "One learns nothing from books. My brother often says that officers newly arrived from France are entirely useless until they have spent at least a year in Canada."

Crosbie stifled his momentary anger. "Your brother is a member of the government, madame?"

The Comtesse laughed and tapped his arm gently. "My brother is the government, monsieur."

"The Governor?"

"No, no, not the Governor. The government. Monsieur le Marquis de Vaudreuil is the King's Governor. My brother is Intendant."

Crosbie made a noncommittal sound deep in his throat.

"You do not know what that means? The Intendant?"

"I regret…"

"It is no matter. An Intendant can be a meaningless official, unless he has talent. It is often so in France. He is, en bref, the administrative officer of government. The King uses the office of Governor to reward courtiers of merit. Since the Ministry of Marine manages France's colonies, most Canadian Governors have been retired Admirals who knew nothing of colonial policy. So the Intendant is in essence the government."

"And so it is with your brother?"

"My brother is François Bigot," the Comtesse said proudly.

Crosbie bowed, as if impressed. He had never heard the name before, but he would not admit his ignorance. "The Governor is to be congratulated."

The Comtesse made a brisk gesture. "His Excellency is no fool. His father was Governor of Canada before him and he was born in Canada, as was my brother. Together they function in harmony. Only the French…" The Comtesse's words dwindled softly to silence. Possibly she had been close to indiscretion, Crosbie thought. Or merely bored with the subject. "You must let me sponsor you in Quebec," she said suddenly, and again her hand touched Crosbie's sleeve with firm pressure.

"An honor, madame," Crosbie said in a tight voice that almost escaped his control.

"It will give my salon much éclat to have such an enormous soldier in attendance."

"I…"

"Un beau gars." The Comtesse's hand slipped down to Crosbie's wrist.

"But, I am…"

"À l'oeil clair," the Comtesse said softly, "À l'air résolu." She laughed with an odd catch in her voice and her hand tightened hotly on Crosbie's.

"And then we shall have to find you a wife," she murmured. "A sweet young child with an enormous dot." Her free hand rose to touch Crosbie's cheek with a gentle stroking motion. "Would you not enjoy a huge dowry?"

"I have no wish to marry…" Crosbie said in an uncertain tone. He gripped the railing tightly.

"Of course not, but a well-endowered wife is a necessity for a poor young soldier. We shall find…"

"But I cannot love on order, madame," Crosbie protested.

"Love? I speak of marriage, not love." The Comtesse drew back briefly to look up at Crosbie's solemn expression, then with a small secret smile, she came close to him again. "It is most improper to seek love in marriage," she laughed. "If I had held such silly notion, I would now be Madame Carpentier, a well beloved but very poor housewife, instead of the Comtesse de Boyer. That is, if I had not remained Fleur Bigot all my…"

"And you do not regret the loss of love?"

"I lost nothing, my dear boy. Gaston Carpentier was my constant, devoted lover until he was killed at the Détroit some years ago. You remind me greatly of him." The Comtesse stroked a finger along Crosbie's mouth. "You have the same bold stance, the same gusto. And you are almost as handsome, too."

Crosbie took an involuntary step backward. The Comtesse's hand closed over his. "Your husband..." he stammered. His strained voice choked off in a surge of embarrassment. You'd think he'd never been alone with a beautiful woman before, the way he mumbled of husbands.

"Armand?" the Comtesse said with a mild surprise. "Armand is the soul of jealousy, a Frenchman first and last. He suspects all Frenchmen. He has even challenged some perfect innocent gentlemen. But he cannot bring himself to regard Canadiens as possible rivals. It is amusing at times."

Something in the Comtesse's cool mockery chilled Crosbie, but no young man at eighteen is concerned with protecting foolish husbands. The warmth of the Comtesse's body close to him was making a red haze dance in his mind. Slowly his hand searched under her cloak at the waistline, circled the softness and brought it closer. Only the brilliant sparkling eyes were visible. For a flickering moment, the Comtesse rested fully against him, one hand caressing his cheek.

"We must return," she said abruptly, pushing back. She tugged the heavy fur cloak tightly around her shoulders and smiled at Crosbie's bewilderment. "Dear boy," she whispered softly. "The ladies will remain for an hour of conversation after the gentlemen leave tonight. Then I shall be alone. Quite alone. For all the night. Be very quiet when you come. Tap very softly."

Before Crosbie could appreciate fully what she had said, the Comtesse opened the door to the great cabin and stepped inside.

The great cabin was still crowded. The richest coats, the highest wigs, the most insistent gallants surrounded the girl named Céleste. Crosbie felt a sudden, surprising surge of regret that in her eyes he was a brawling ruffian, a swaggering bully. Then the Comtesse turned smiling to him and Crosbie took his eyes from Céleste.

CHAPTER THREE

No prowling cat could have moved more quietly than Duncan Crosbie along the dim corridors of the creaking transport. And when he tapped at the door of the great cabin, only an alert ear could distinguish that sound from the gentle groaning of the anchored ship. The clicking of the door latch was an explosion in the stillness, but Crosbie was inside before anyone could have seen him. The sudden roaring pulsation within his head drowned completely the sound of the door closing, locking behind him.

That had been ... how long ago? Two hours? Three, possibly. Each hour the ship's bell had sounded softly, but Crosbie had not been attending. Not with the perfumed distraction of the Comtesse's hair resting on his shoulder, the silken rustle of the loose robe she wore, the soft murmur of her voice. He could not remember what they had talked about—whispered about, rather. But it had been filled with promise, intoxicating promise that made the small drab world of the *Frelon* seem a very different world indeed. He did not see how it could be anything but a dream, being here, holding the vivid Comtesse in his arms, hearing the intimate softness of her voice. If it was a dream, he told himself fervently, may nothing wake him from its delights.

Beyond the Comtesse's head, glossy in the faint glow of a night-light, Crosbie could see the shiny brass lock and hasp on the door leading to the adjoining cabin. One of the other ladies was using that. Crosbie had a sudden, chill thought. Where was the Comtesse's husband? A distressing business, this, Crosbie told himself, knowing his own hypocrisy. He had no desire to introduce, even in thought, the pinched, withered countenance of the Comte de Boyer.

What a strangely mis-matched pair this warm, lovely Fleur and the wizened, waspish Comte. What a waste and how foolish it was that she should be so stifled, thwarted...

The Comtesse whispered something and Crosbie abandoned his aimless thoughts as a wild surge of excitement rose high within him. What a magnificent creature she was!

"... very different," she was murmuring softly. "In Quebec, we will have no need to skulk in dark corners. There, I am mistress. Ah, my lovely giant, I cannot wait to take you walking along the allée in the Palace garden. We will ride out to the Cataract of Montmorenci for a pique-nique, and then you will know how beautiful Canada can be for those who deserve its beauty."

Crosbie pulled her tightly against him. Her hands touched feverishly at him and the young Scot felt hot desire mounting swiftly. Then, abruptly, the Comtesse stiffened in his arms, lifting her head quickly.

At that moment, Crosbie heard it, too. A light scraping sound in the corridor outside. And then a sharp, penetrating tap at the locked door.

"Fleur!"

The Comtesse came erect in one smooth motion, looking at Crosbie with eyes that gleamed brightly in the dim light.

Again the soft demanding whisper sighed outside the door. "Fleur!"

Crosbie felt a sudden bleak chill in the cabin. What came next was momentarily close to panic.

"Armand?" the Comtesse asked in a sleepy voice. Her tone was just right, Crosbie thought admiringly. How could she do it? In your mind's eye, you could almost see her awaken, lift herself slightly on her elbow, peer drowsily at the door and speak with a voice that blurred with sleepiness.

Swiftly Crosbie slid across the floor to snatch up his neck-cloth which the Comtesse had pulled free in a tender moment. That was the Comte de Boyer outside, he told himself, and the Comte alone, of all people on board, could demand entrance if he dared face the wrath of his Comtesse. Crosbie knew that discovery here might well be disastrous, for himself and for Fleur.

The Comtesse moved slowly. Deftly she knocked a silver comb to the floor and then shuffled her slippers crisply, all sounds designed to keep the Comte from a growing impatience. Her large eyes stared at Crosbie, stricken.

"Ciel!" she whispered. "It is Armand! What can we ..."

"I'll have to leave," Crosbie breathed. "How?"

With a unison touching in its hope, both looked upward to the skylight. It opened onto the quarterdeck. Escape might be possible if ...

"No," the Comtesse whispered in a taut murmur. "The ship's officer always stands just beside it. That would be as bad as ..."

As bad as being caught right here, Crosbie finished silently. And so it would. The news would reach the Comte in a matter of minutes. Crosbie glanced in apprehension at the locked door and drew a long breath deep into his lungs. His lifted head brushed against the glass of the skylight. There was no way out. Only the door and the skylight, nothing more.

But no! With the keen eye of desperation, Crosbie saw a solution. Quickly, he grasped the Comtesse's arm, pulled her with him toward the narrow door opening onto the stern gallery.

"Lock this behind me," he whispered urgently.

He could see her nod. Behind them, the Comte rapped again, more insistently. Crosbie opened the narrow door silently, edged through and closed it, holding it shut until the Comtesse could secure the latch. He stood there shivering, not daring to move. The Comtesse's long silken robe swirled with dim lustrous shadow in the cabin. She passed from Crosbie's sight as she went to open the door to her husband.

The stern gallery was short and narrow, designed to give the ship's captain a breath of air out of sight of passengers or crew. The high stern of the ship soared overhead. On either side was gilded carving that secured the railing. Below was the water, shining coldly by starlight.

Crosbie shuddered with a sudden chill. He clamped his teeth hard to keep from chattering. He had thought it so very clever to wear only smallclothes and thin shoes when he came visiting tonight. In such garb, he might have appeared to be heading for the necessary-room if anyone had noticed him leaving his hammock. It had been a clever notion, but its cleverness was disastrous now. He could easily die of exposure on that stern gallery.

Sharp angry tones carried clearly to him from the cabin. A dazzle of light almost blinded him. The Comte had brought a lantern with him, apparently—and suspicion as well. That was not a husbandly greeting, not a bit of it. Crosbie edged closer to the glass door and peered cautiously into the cabin. One glimpse was enough. In the Comte's thin nervous hand was a long gleaming rapier. Crosbie recoiled to the far corner of the gallery.

What a blundering fool he was. There would not even be a chance to fight. Crosbie clenched the railing hard and glared down at the water below. No escape there. He would be heard if he leaped overboard. There was no escape anywhere. This foolish disaster could be the end, not only of his career, but his life.

In the cabin, the Comtesse shrieked thinly. Crosbie heard a scuffling struggle, then a solid thump on the floor.

The young Scot was nearly sickened with rage and self-contempt. For a brief insane moment he felt a passionate hatred for the Comtesse who had seemed so enchanting only minutes before. But he knew that the fault lay with him as much as her. Crosbie shook his head angrily and bared his teeth in a tight, wolfish grimace. Caught he might be, caught like an awkward farmboy, but he'd be damned if he would give up before he was compelled to. The only hope he could offer the Comtesse—or himself—was to get away, unseen. If that meant diving down into the frigid water, then he would do that and manufacture an explanation afterward.

Determinedly, he braced himself against the gilded molding and stepped up onto the gallery railing. The quarterdeck was no great distance overhead, but that haven was far beyond Crosbie's reach, patrolled as it was by the watch-keeping officer and the helmsman.

But God be thanked for the Frenchman's love of decoration, Crosbie breathed. Overhanging the stern gallery hung an ornate gilded shield, jutting out to protect the gallery from direct sunlight. Carefully Crosbie raised himself up on the tips of his toes and gripped the larboard strut. Alternately pulling and shoving, he tried to estimate its stability before trusting it with his full weight.

The Comtesse screamed and the door to the stern gallery rattled under a heavy hand. Crosbie had no more time to waste. Desperately he launched himself upward, kicking strongly away from the railing, holding the strut with his right hand and swinging free, groping upward with his left hand for the quarter-deck railing.

He came up too high and too forcefully. His left arm rammed through between the posts of the railing almost to the shoulder and his head cracked against the gadrooned border just below. Dazed, Crosbie let go his right hand and shifted to a grip around two posts.

He dangled there in the cold darkness with only the harsh murmur of the river beneath him. Now that he was outside the ship, he could hear the wailing song that wind made in the taut rigging overhead and the incessant creaking from the ship's timbers as it protested against the anchor cable. A wooden ship was never quiet, and tonight Crosbie blessed the constant noise that would help to smother any sound that he made. Slowly he swung himself from side to side, then kicked away from the side of the ship and heaved himself on top of the shield that covered the stern gallery. He pushed and squirmed until he was stretched out full length. Then he let go his grip on the railing and trusted himself completely to the gilded wooden shield. It creaked alarmingly under his bulk.

The cabin door burst open with a sharp report of broken metal. A wide beam of lantern light shone out over the stern of the ship. Crosbie could hear voices from below, strangely muted and distorted by his protecting shield. They held an odd quality, he thought, a depth of surprise. Probably because the Comte had not found anyone in his wife's cabin. Now if only Crosbie could get back to his berth unseen, the Comtesse would be safe. But sudden voices from the quarterdeck above made his pulse pound with apprehension. If that deck officer grew curious about the commotion in the great cabin and came back to eavesdrop, he could not avoid seeing Crosbie stretched flat on the gallery shield. Crosbie forced himself to lie perfectly still. Any movement would be perilous. If it didn't attract attention from the deck officer or the Comte, it might still force the flimsy shield loose from its mounting and send Crosbie plummeting into the river. Crosbie lay in a fever of impatience, but he did not move. He was cramped with cold and tension. Already his fingers were turning numb.

The muffled voices from below rose to a renewed fury as the Comtesse shrieked of insult. The stern gallery door slammed shut, then sagged open again. Lamplight and angry tones drifted out.

Overhead on the quarterdeck, an annoyed voice snapped out an order Crosbie could not hear. But the footsteps that approached the stern were clearly audible. A ship's dark-lantern threw its concentrated beam directly on him with an impact that felt like cold water to Crosbie. He stared blindly, unbelievingly, up into the glare. He cursed with savage calm and reached up for the railing. A thin hand pushed him away quickly. Then a young, strained voice called out, "No, monsieur. It is from the great cabin below."

The annoyed voice answered and the lamp was withdrawn. The footsteps retreated toward the binnacle and the dark-lantern returned to its place beside the compass.

Crosbie stared blankly up at the sky, his eyes still dazzled by the lantern. That young boy's voice belonged to Denis, he told himself. And he breathed deeply with relief at the thought. And the boy would help him, Crosbie was sure.

It seemed hours later to Crosbie's impatient mind when the ship's bell tapped out a staccato report. Crosbie tried to count the tinny sounds, but he soon fell behind. He wasn't sure if this signal called for a change of the watch, but he flexed his numb hands, tensing himself for quick movement. When a cautious hand reached out of nowhere to tap his shoulder, Crosbie was ready.

He pulled himself stiffly to a sitting position and clutched at the solid railing. He swung himself quietly up and over, dropping down to the deck without a sound. An odd furry object was shoved into his hands. A naval cocked hat! Crosbie clapped it to his head and took the voluminous cloak the boy handed to him. He draped the thick cloth around his shoulders and shivered with the sudden warmth. Quick fingers unbuckled his shoes and Crosbie promptly stepped free of them, letting Denis tuck them under his arm. He could see nothing in the bleak wintery darkness, but all around him were crisp decisive movements, the formal sounds of a changing watch. Shoes scraped on ladders, men muttered with thick, sleepy voices. Now, if ever, was his chance. Crosbie stepped briskly forward and cannoned into Denis, sending the boy sprawling.

A sailor cursed drowsily at the noise. Denis scrambled to his feet.

"I'm all right, monsieur," he whispered tensely. "But please crouch down. Please! You are too tall!" His voice cracked, to a thin wail.

Crosbie crouched, bending his knees under cover of the enormous boat cloak, feeling excessively foolish. The boy tugged at the cloak, leading Crosbie forward and placing the young Scot's hand securely on the companionway railing. Gratefully Crosbie eased himself silently to the waist of the ship. Denis pattered down the ladder behind him, whisking off the cloak the moment Crosbie reached the deck. Crosbie pulled off the hat and Denis snatched it quickly. The boy disappeared into the darkness, his shoes beating a frantic tattoo on the boards.

Crosbie leaned against the midships bulwark briefly until his pulse relaxed to a normal cadence. No one could dispute his right to be here, but it would be far better if he weren't seen at all. He had come this far only because of Denis's quick thinking, and Crosbie sobered quickly when he realized that he had very likely been shielded in the captain's cloak and hat. If Denis had any trouble returning them...

Crosbie slipped forward along the deserted deck. He saw nothing, met nobody. But he did not relax his wariness, nor even breathe very deeply until he had reached his hammock and rolled himself up into it. Then a gusty sigh almost exploded from him. Duncan Crosbie lay in the darkness and laughed silently, holding a blanket wadded to his mouth to stifle the sound of mirth that was close to hysteria. The ship creaked and groaned softly all around him, soothing and gentle as maternal song. Ultimately, long after, Crosbie slept.

CHAPTER FOUR

Duncan Crosbie came on deck with the other passengers when word was shouted through the ship that Quebec would soon be in view. Despite the early hour, the quarterdeck was already crowded with officers. Midships, troops and sailors milled in excited curiosity. Crosbie worked through the crowd until he could see the densely wooded hills that lined the river in low jagged parapets on either side. Ahead, the river disappeared around a bend.

He wondered where the Comtesse—Fleur—was this morning. He had not seen her for three days, but she had been much in his thoughts. Heart-pounding thoughts they were, too, when he remembered that night and the warmth of her touch, the exciting fragrance of her hair.

"Today begins the great adventure, Duncan," a solemn voice said at his elbow.

Crosbie nodded. "For both of us, Mathieu."

"I must ... I must ask you not to address me publicly in ... in such an informal manner, Duncan," the young friar said ponderously. "Despite my years, I am ..."

Crosbie shouted with a sudden gust of laughter. For three days he had lived in an agony of apprehension, awaiting some sort of reprisal that never came. Brother Mathieu's preposterous sobriety was comic relief that washed away Crosbie's dour tension completely.

"I shall not forget again, my dear Brother Mathieu," he said between gasps of laughter. "I deserve your correction."

"You are young and foolish," Brother Mathieu declared sadly. "I am about to embark upon a career of dedication for the Holy Church. That must never be forgotten, even in the most joyous moments."

"I will restrain my foolishness, dear friar. And I wish you well in your career, in return for your blessing."

"You have that, as always," Brother Mathieu intoned. Sketchily, he made the sign of the cross with two raised fingers. Then his stiffly solemn face moved uneasily to a smile. "Benedicite, my good friend."

Slowly the ship began the long turn to starboard. Flattened sails roared like cannon overhead as they responded to the lash of wind from the hills. The ship's way carried her forward and she rounded the bend slowly. Then the maître d'équipement bellowed for the men to let out the main sheet for added impetus. The ship settled to its new course, close-hauled.

Ahead the river seemed to divide into two and Crosbie craned his neck to get a good view.

"That should be the Île d'Orléans," Brother Mathieu said at his side.

Crosbie glanced down quizzically. "But you cannot see, can you, Brother Mathieu?"

"I cannot see, but I have studied the map closely," the young friar said firmly. "This island lies in the channel six or seven leagues from Quebec."

"You have studied well," Crosbie said pleasantly. "Tell me, which channel shall we follow to Quebec?"

"Either will serve," Brother Mathieu answered promptly. "The northern channel may be safer, since it is scoured by the Falls of Montmorenci, and would not become silted as easily as the southern route."

"Excellent," Crosbie smiled. "What is the Montmorenci? A river?"

"A small river, yes. But it strikes the St. Lawrence in a cataract some eight mètres high. An inspiring sight, according to all reports. We shall see it soon. Or rather, you will see it. Look to the right as we come abreast of the island."

The tide was almost at its height as the ship worked its way around the long island, and the channel was never apparent to Crosbie's untutored eye. Marshy tidal flats, both on the island and the mainland, were shimmering under a glaze of water. Then, as the ship began a slow turn to larboard, Crosbie saw the huge foggy spray of the Falls of Montmorenci.

"Most impressive, Brother Mathieu."

"In just a moment, you should catch your first glimpse of Quebec as we round the island." Brother Mathieu beamed up at his tall friend, enjoying the odd position of describing sights which he himself could not see. Seldom had his reading stood him in such good stead.

Ahead was the mouth of another river in the distance beyond the Montmorenci. That would be the St. Charles, the river that formed one flank of the Quebec bastion. Through gaps in the trees along the river he could see outlines of square stone buildings, sharply white in the misty morning light. He craned his neck and just as he was stretched to the limit, a stumbling officer sent him staggering into the crowd. Crosbie recovered his footing, muttered mingled curses and apologies to all sides.

The minor disturbance had been caused by new arrivals crowding the quarterdeck, bowing ceremoniously to the shabby ship's captain. The captain's bow was obsequiously low and Crosbie knew without looking that the female passengers had come on deck. Gentlemen squeezed themselves even closer to allow the four ladies a clear space at the rail. Madame la Comtesse swept past Crosbie, nodding with guarded politeness as he stepped back. When the ship fell off in the trough of a tidal surge, Crosbie held out a rigid arm to help Mademoiselle Céleste retain her balance, and was rewarded with a brief, cursory smile. Behind the ladies came the aging Comte de Boyer, clean-shaven now, with a great clot of powder-covered blood under his chin and a curiously mottled texture to his skin, rather like cheap marble. Crosbie suspected that the Comte had shaven too soon, inviting a return of the mysterious rash that had infected the ship's passengers. But the Comte could not be expected to appear publicly with his scraggly beard slathered with black gunpowder paste. Crosbie's dark uniform received a faint sifting of hair powder as the Comte nodded frigidly to him.

Crosbie stepped slightly back toward Brother Mathieu.

"Can you see, Duncan?" the young friar demanded. "Is Quebec in sight yet?"

Crosbie wheeled to face forward. The great basin before Quebec was open to his view but the river fog that was apparently a daily nuisance blanketed the town in a soggy white shroud.

"The fog is still too thick, Mathieu," he said.

The rising sun lay warmly on Crosbie's back despite the chill wind. As he spoke, a sparkling glimmer danced high above the town.

"What, Duncan? What do you see?" Brother Mathieu, his sedate composure forgotten for the moment, tugged at Crosbie's sleeve.

Crosbie smiled. "I thought I caught a glint of something, but it is too high. Almost..."

"The Cathedral stands at least a hundred mètres above the water, Duncan. The spire should be visible."

The ship heeled in a strong gust that blew against Quebec. Together with the sun that grew steadily warmer, the wind began to clear the morning fog. Slowly, the blocky outlines of the buildings on the rocky cliff became clearly visible.

The Cathedral spire loomed through the haze. Crosbie, with his professional eye for fortifications, noted the high ledge of parapet to the left. That high point would be Cap Diamant, he knew. The bold precipitous cliff fronting on the St. Lawrence was revealed by the sunlight, and later, the easier slope that fell away to the right toward the St. Charles. Far beyond lay a solid bulwark of snow-capped mountains. Brighter sunlight found misty wet slate rooftops and bounced dazzling reflections. Crosbie shielded his eyes, eager for his first glimpse of Quebec's famous fortifications.

"I can see the palisade of Cap Diamant. Looks very substantial. I think I make out three batteries along the cliff. Is that right?"

"The map shows three," Brother Mathieu announced. "And a second row of three along the strand."

Crosbie whistled appreciatively. Six batteries well served could make the anchorage a hell of shot if the English tried to attack Quebec. He staggered slightly against his friend as the ship rounded to and dropped anchor. Brother Mathieu found a thin aperture in the crowd. He slipped up to the railing.

"The largest building in the Upper Town is the Chateau of St. Louis. That great ugly stone building with the steep dormer roofs, on the very edge of the cliff. That is the seat of government for Canada."

Crosbie nodded. He was more interested in the batteries that guarded the city.

"And beside it," Brother Mathieu pointed out, "is the Church of the Récollet friars. That is where I shall be stationed while I remain in Quebec."

With a sudden burning intensity, the rising sun destroyed the fog that draped the city, and all the buildings leaped into view, glistening damply, glossy in the sunlight. From the squat construction along the river, curling away out of sight on either side, the city rose to the sheer cliff along narrow twisting cobbled streets, with no two houses on exactly the same level. Crosbie could make out a wide Market Square opposite a church in Lower Town, and his gaze traveled upward from there, picking out the batteries easily now. It was all a surprise to him. No matter what facts Brother Mathieu had offered during the journey, Crosbie had retained his original idea of Quebec as a wilderness outpost, a squalid stone fortress surrounded with forests, garrisoned with savages. He was not prepared for a city that looked like an illustration from a child's book of faery tales.

"It takes the breath, eh, Duncan?" Brother Mathieu said quietly. "I was prepared for a fortress, but not … not for beauty." His expression was awed and somehow shocked, as if he suspected that Quebec's unexpected beauty was slightly improper.

Small boats danced out from the wharfs of Lower Town. The central battery began a slow salute, booming in ragged sequence that made Crosbie frown with professional irritation. Nothing as undisciplined as that salute would ever have been tolerated at Toulon.

Slowly the crowd thinned as passengers retired to collect their luggage. The Comtesse and the ladies with her had perilously lowered themselves down the narrow companionway to the waist of the ship and were standing expectantly near the entry port, huddled in voluminous fur cloaks.

Crosbie noticed a ship's longboat manned by twelve oarsmen sweep away from the wharf and overtake most of the smaller craft in a race for the ship. The maître d'équipement bustled to the entry port with a crew of sailors carrying a rope-and-slat ladder which was tossed over the side.

Crosbie moved forward, halting at the forward rail of the quarterdeck where a small brass swivel gun was mounted. He wanted to join the Comtesse and her party but he thought it wiser to wait. If the Comtesse wanted him she would make some sign. Casually he twisted the tompion out of the muzzle of the swivel gun and ran a finger around the bore. The finger was coated with rust when he withdrew it. Not even the faintest trace of protecting oil. Crosbie glanced around in disgust, intending to attract the captain's attention to the sorry condition of his armament. But a belated caution stopped him in time. No commander would ever thank a junior who observed his shortcomings. Crosbie screwed the tompion back in place.

Brother Mathieu edged closer. "And where will you be stationed, Duncan? At the Fort St. Louis, I suppose?"

Crosbie shrugged without taking his eyes from the Comtesse as she stood regally beside the entry port. "Don't know," he growled. "I'll report to somebody, probably your cousin's aide-de-camp and then go where I'm sent."

"Général Montcalm is not my cousin," Brother Mathieu said in shocked tones. "You really must not say so."

Crosbie winked solemnly. "It shall be our secret, eh?" he said, deliberately misunderstanding. "I'll not mention your exalted connections to a soul. Never."

The long-boat swept in toward the dangling ladder, oars leaping upright as it touched against the ship. A burly man in a heavy black cloak and a broad laced hat reached for the ladder as the Comtesse and the ladies shrieked words of welcome that were torn to nothing by the driving wind. Behind him came three brisk young men, all warm covered against the weather.

Crosbie swung himself lightly down to the waist, posting himself near the Comtesse. The man in the laced hat was clearly a personage of some importance, judging from the manner in which his three young men collected around him, almost like a royal bodyguard. The one nearest Crosbie was a slim sleek man with thin perfect features and a half amused smile. He arched narrow black eyebrows in obvious inquiry, holding Crosbie arrogantly with his pale bleak eyes. Crosbie nodded stiffly, not moving from his position. At that moment, the Comtesse caught sight of him towering over the others on the maindeck.

She thrust out her arm in a quick imperious gesture. "Monsieur Crosbie," she called.

As Crosbie approached, shifting aside the amused young man with the sharp, perfect face, the Comtesse turned with the burly man to face him. "Monsieur, I present to you Monsieur Crosbie, our gigantic gallant. He has quite captured all hearts. Poor Céleste is completely distracted..."

Crosbie lost the remainder when a gust of wind snatched the words from the Comtesse's mouth. He thought it just as well. Even now it was difficult to make his sketchy bow to the burly man. That damnable red confusion was coloring his face again. He could feel the hot flush even with the chill wind blowing.

"...Monsieur Cadet, my brother's colleague and Commissaire-Général," the Comtesse was saying. Crosbie sharpened his attention. A Commissaire-Général could make a fortune even in peace-time. During a war, his profits would be limited only by his appetites. The burly man nodded with surprising warmth, a broad smile wreathing his wide, slightly flat face. He bowed in response to Crosbie, displaying an enormous spread of shoulder, heavily muscled and thick as a butcher's.

"Madame la Comtesse wishes me to invite you to the reception that Monsieur Bigot is giving this evening," Cadet said pleasantly in a gruff voice. "We are always pleased to welcome officers newly from France. It will be convenient for you to attend?"

Crosbie gulped nervously and murmured something that seemed to satisfy Cadet.

"Splendid! That's settled, then. And now, if you will forgive me, I must escort Madame la Comtesse and her party to the Governor. Until later, monsieur."

"Until later," Crosbie echoed.

The Comtesse flashed a brief sparkling smile. "At the Intendant's Palace, monsieur," she said briskly. "Anyone can direct you. Come early. My brother will be most happy to have a private moment with you before the others arrive." She tapped his arm lightly in farewell.

Clumsily Crosbie bowed. The Comtesse was assisted to the ladder. And he leaped quickly to offer his arm to help Mademoiselle Céleste. Gravely, the young girl shook her head.

Her eyes were sober as she looked up at him, somehow sympathetic, almost pitying. He stepped back as she swung down the ladder.

He trod heavily on the foot of the silent, amused young man. Quickly Crosbie pivotted to make his apology.

"No harm done, cock," the young man said tonelessly, in a strongly inflected English. "Never bother with apologies when you're riding the big horse in the parade."

There was apparently meaning in what he said, but it escaped Crosbie. From the insolent gaze, Crosbie assumed the reference was uncomplimentary. "You'll be Irish, from the size of the tongue in your head," he said stiffly in English. "And a clown, from the sound of you."

"Irish, I am," the young man said, the mocking half smile not the least disturbed. "A clown, no. And before you're tempted to a stronger term, let me advise you there's a captain's uniform under these bulky furs, and a sword that goes with it."

Crosbie nodded, taking the warning as it was offered, merely to avoid the chance of an unnecessary quarrel. "We shall be meeting again, captain," he said easily. "Privately, perhaps."

The Irish captain let his bleak eyes run up the length of Crosbie slowly, almost contemptuously. "Seamus O'Neill prefers crowds," he said in a faintly amused tone. "But we'll meet, cock, never fear. As long as you're near Cadet, I'll not be far off."

Crosbie stepped away, feeling baffled and annoyed at the light mocking challenge in the captain's voice. But there was nothing he could properly take exception to in the words themselves. Changing the subject with an awkward insistence, he said, "Possibly you could direct me to the Général's headquarters, captain?"

Captain O'Neill stroked his thin powdered chin. "Montcalm, is it?" He stared thoughtfully at Crosbie. "Would you be cleverer than you look, I wonder?" He made a quick, precise gesture with one hand. "No matter. You'll find His Excellency at the Fort

St. Louis in Upper Town. I wish you a good day, sir." With swirling arms billowing his cape, the Irish captain offered a flawless court bow and briskly stepped over the railing to the rope ladder.

Crosbie stood quietly, watching the long-boat below as it edged away from the ship and swiftly pulled for the docks of Quebec.

Brother Mathieu padded softly beside Crosbie and looked down at the crowded boat. "You have found new friends quickly, Duncan," he said with a faint smile. "Madame la Comtesse can be extremely helpful to you."

Crosbie nodded soberly, still watching the boat. A frigid blast made him shiver slightly.

CHAPTER FIVE

The afternoon was well advanced before Duncan Crosbie was able to disembark from the *Frelon*. Passengers of greater importance had gone ashore earlier and a half-company of infantrymen labored on deck unloading stores from the crammed hold.

Bells from the many churches of Quebec had rung in celebration. Clearly, the *Frelon*'s arrival was a matter of first importance for Quebec. Crosbie waited patiently, well accustomed to the delays that came to every junior officer, until a boat was available.

He sought out the ship's boy, Denis, finding him sitting cross-legged in the passageway outside the captain's cabin, sewing industriously on a shabby uniform coat, using a huge needle that was longer than his palm. Crosbie stooped beside him, resting lightly on his heels.

"I'll be going ashore now, Denis," he said with a broad smile, "But not before I've thanked you properly for …"

The boy flushed a painful red and Crosbie went on quickly, pretending not to notice.

"You saved my worthless neck a few nights back," he said with quiet sincerity. "I'll not try to thank you for that. Among friends, a handshake is enough, eh?"

Denis dropped the needle and clasped Crosbie's enormous hand with a quick grip. He nodded and gulped nervously.

"Good," Crosbie said. "And I'll ask you to accept this and buy something to remember me by." He dropped one of his few precious louis d'or into Denis's hand and folded the boy's fingers over it.

"Not as a payment, you understand," he said severely, "but as a gift from one friend to another."

He rose carefully to his full height, keeping his head bent in the narrow passageway. He bowed with formal grace. "Au revoir, bon ami," he said.

Speechlessly, Denis looked up at him, his expression strained and agonized as he fought to hold back any unseemly emotion. Stiffly, he nodded. "Au revoir," he said in a tight croaking voice. "Au revoir, bon ami."

Quickly, Crosbie stalked away, one hand toying with the coins remaining in his pocket. He went up on deck and waited in line for a seat in one of the boats.

The docks, the streets and the Market Square of Lower Town were full of townspeople. They greeted all new arrivals with impartial approval, goggling at Crosbie's great height. Demure chaperoned girls whispered softly to each other as the young Scot strode by, and a small mob of boys raced along beside him. The steep climb up the narrow zig-zag street to Upper Town soon discouraged them and Crosbie was left alone.

He leaned well forward, understanding now why there were only a few carriages in Quebec and those few drawn by horses bred more for labor than elegance. Behind him a strong wind blew his cloak. He removed his hat and clamped it safely under his elbow as he plodded up the cliff. A faint cloud of hair powder drifted before his eyes. The half hour of finicking work in dredging his thick hair with white powder would go for nothing unless he could get out of the wind. He held his dress sword carefully aside and made all the speed he could up the cobbled incline to Upper Town. His light buckled shoes pinched painfully in between the rough cobbles. On the crest, Crosbie ducked quickly into the lee of a high church wall and adjusted his uniform properly.

The great square of St. Louis was nearly abandoned. Crosbie turned toward the gates of the Fort St. Louis.

Sentries came wearily to attention as he passed through, but the usual drummer boy was absent. Since the arrival of the *Frelon* had upset the routine of all Quebec, it was safe to assume that it had also increased activity at Montcalm's headquarters.

Inside the reception hall were some two dozen officers; most of them splendidly uniformed in the infantry white with glittering accoutrements. Near the door was a rotund captain in pale blue. The uniform Crosbie recognized as the regiment of Béarn. The others were new to him. He skirted the room slowly, uncomfortably aware of the curious glances directed toward him, feeling doubly conspicuous, not only because of his great height, but also because of the sombre dark-blue-and-scarlet uniform he wore, a dreary note contrasted with the sparkling infantry white.

A corridor carelessly guarded by drowsy sentries led away from the far side of the reception hall. Along it, Crosbie could see partially open doors that apparently opened into the offices of the Général's staff. At the rear, finely carved double doors were firmly shut and blockaded by two rigidly erect soldiers. Crosbie worked his way toward the hallway.

What he hoped to find was a reasonably sensible adjutant who would accept his orders, assign him to quarters, and report his arrival to the Général. He knew that was too much to expect, though. An unassigned officer presented a problem, which staff officers might wrangle over for days. And Crosbie suspected that of all the officers who had sailed on the *Frelon*, he alone belonged to no specific unit. Boldly, he pushed back the door of the first office and stepped quickly inside.

He paused in blank astonishment. The walls of the room were panelled in blue-and-rose brocade that exactly duplicated the colors and pattern of the huge silky carpet. Two tiny gilt chairs were fatly upholstered in the same brocade and placed directly before a long carved and gilded table that stretched nearly from wall to wall and was piled with a disordered mass of papers. Behind it, seated in a deep gilt fauteuil was a young man wearing some sort of uniform. He had removed his coat and Crosbie could not guess his rank. He was precisely framed between two windows that offered a fine view of the southern bank of the St. Lawrence. Crosbie assumed a rigid stance in front of the table. He could see only the top of the officer's dark unpowdered head that was held in support by thin, long-fingered hands.

"Sir," he began.

"See Estére if it's about supplies," the officer said in a quick sharp tone. "Next room."

"It's not..." Crosbie coughed nervously at the tightness in his throat. "I'm reporting for duty, sir."

"Very good. Excellent. Welcome to Canada. Regimental commanders are attending in the reception chamber. You will find..."

"I have no regiment, sir," Crosbie said in a tone that rose to a bellow with exasperation.

Slowly the officer at the table fumbled among his papers, found a bedraggled quill and laid it meticulously to mark his place. Only then did he glance up at Crosbie.

"Mille tonnerres!" he said mildly. "An artilleryman! And where did you explode from, monsieur?"

Crosbie forced a smile for the feeble joke. The man at the table was younger than Crosbie had thought. He was solidly built, smoothly shaven and carefully dressed even if he didn't trouble to powder his hair as regulations required. His eyes were reddened with strain, but he offered Crosbie a pleasantly quizzical smile that erased all memory of his previous peremptory manner.

"I am ordered to present myself to His Excellency, the Général," Crosbie said formally. He held out his orders.

As the officer flipped open the folded paper, he riffled through the mass of papers, found a small silver bell and tinkled it slowly while he read Crosbie's orders.

Before he had finished, a fist tapped smartly at the door. Someone entered without waiting for a response.

"Estére," the officer at the table said without looking up. "Will His Excellency be free today?"

"Most unlikely, sir. He is closeted with the Brigadiers. The *Frelon* brought dispatches that..."

The man at the table waved a brief dismissal, folded the paper tidily and returned it to Crosbie.

"You offended someone, eh?" he smiled abruptly.

Crosbie lifted his chin higher and he stared with silent challenge. No matter what his rank, the man at the table had no right to ask that sort of question.

"Ah, yes. Well, I hope it was not royalty. You are surprised I ask. Don't be. We have asked for artillery officers for three years without receiving a single one. And now you are sent casually to us. Even so, you present a problem, monsieur."

Wisely Crosbie held his tongue. He waited silently.

"Artillery in Canada is peculiarly the province of the colonial regular forces. The King's Lieutenant for Quebec and the commander of artillery of the Troupes de la Marine are the gunners here. So now we are given an officer of the regular establishment, and what are we to do with him? Quebec belongs to Monsieur de Ramesay, the King's Lieutenant. And you belong to Montcalm. So you see."

Crosbie shook his head. "No, sir, I don't..."

"Precisely. It is a problem that merely takes on added confusion with explanation. There is little communication between Canadiens and French here in Canada. Little communication and less love. So you are a problem. Just as I am." Suddenly the young officer grinned widely, displaying startlingly white teeth in an infectious laugh that brought an immediate response from Crosbie. "Yes, I too. I was a dragoon officer once. Now," he shrugged lightly and touched the mass of papers on the table. "Now I am something that defies definition. And so will you be, I suspect."

Again, he lifted the small bell and rattled it briskly. "Let me, however, welcome you most sincerely to Canada, Monsieur

Crosbie. You need not fear for employment, though I confess I have no idea at this moment what your work will be. Ah, Estére," he said interrupting himself as the door opened. "I am giving Monsieur Crosbie to you. Have someone arrange for his billeting, assign him temporarily to the headquarters staff and see his baggage is assembled. And now, Monsieur Crosbie, I leave you to Estére, the Général's esteemed military secretary. I suggest you settle yourself, discover Quebec and present yourself here in the morning, when we can explore your future."

Crosbie, overwhelmed by the flood of directions, could only bow in helpless silence. He found himself outside with the quiet, wizened little secretary who was called Estére.

"Who was that?" Crosbie asked foolishly.

"Captain Bougainville," the secretary said politely. "He is aide-de-camp to the Général and ... and something more."

"Yes," Crosbie agreed. Clearly the brisk young man was something more. Patiently, he followed the stooped figure of the secretary as he led the way through the stone corridors of the Fort St. Louis.

CHAPTER SIX

Duncan Crosbie stood high on the outer lip of the gun battery, one foot braced squarely on the barrel of the immense cannon that poked through its embrasure toward the wide ship basin below Quebec. He shivered in the hard wind and pulled his wide cloak together at the neck. It was already past the middle of May, but Canada showed few signs of Spring. Even the lowering sun bright on his back brought no warmth, but it did throw huge grotesque shadows forward over Lower Town, bringing dusk a full hour earlier to that part of Quebec that lay on the eastward slope of the rock. Judging by the shadows it must be nearly six o'clock, he warned himself, and he was bid to the Intendant's reception this evening. But even knowing time was short, he was strangely unwilling to break off his aimless contemplation of the broad river.

For two hours he had been wandering through town, searching out the artillery installations and inspecting them with cold professional interest. Gunners on duty had eyed him curiously but none had offered comment. It was as if Crosbie had somehow become invisible. And his morbid sensitiveness enlarged upon this feeling until he had made himself thoroughly self-conscious. He knew the loss of confidence that always attended these spells of unhappy awareness and he tried to fight it off.

Irritably he kicked at the gun and glanced down, surprised to see a large fleck of scale break away from the barrel, leaving exposed a shiny patch of untarnished bronze. The cannon very badly needed scaling, he observed; it must be quite an ancient piece. Casually his eye ran down toward the breech, noting the scrolled carving in Latin script that circled the gun. He stared unbelievingly at the vent-hole and after a moment got down to examine it closely. The opening was a full inch in diameter, instead of a tiny aperture. The old cannon should have been fitted with a vent bushing long ago; as it was, at least half and probably more of the explosive charge would be dissipated through the gaping vent, instead of serving to drive a projectile forward. The whole thing was preposterous, Crosbie told himself. Very likely this old gun was in retirement, left here only for firing formal salutes, and never intended for serious use in Quebec's defenses. Slowly, he walked down the long line of heavy siege pieces that lined the battery, pausing briefly at each. At the end, near the far entrance, he stopped, staring blindly at an untidy gunner in a soiled uniform who half lounged against the entry. Although Crosbie was not really aware of him, the soldier gradually shifted to a more military posture. He adjusted his loosened neckcloth. The gunner's movement brought Crosbie back to a realization of the time and his engagement at the Intendant's Palace. Vaguely he nodded to the sentry and ducked to go out through the gate.

He walked past the wide stairway leading to the Château of St. Louis, where the Governor conducted his business, and continued along toward the Palais Gate at the northern end of the town. From the street, he could occasionally see stretches of the great wall that guarded Quebec from attack along the Plains of Abraham. Both the structure of the wall and its quality seemed to vary greatly, being very low in some places, high enough but thin in others. He moved briskly past great stone barracks where off-duty troops were lounging in disarray, ogling passers-by and calling out ribald greetings to the pretty girls. He went by several churches, bowing politely as priests saluted him. The incredible variance in elevation was a constant surprise to him. Not one spot seemed on the same level as another. Beyond the wall, toward the west, the land sloped regularly in even undulations, but the area enclosed by Quebec's walls was precipitous beyond belief. There probably was no level space in town large enough for a tennis court, if there were any people in Quebec with a fondness for the King's favorite game.

From the Palais Gate outside the walls, the ground dropped smoothly to the tidal flats along the St. Charles river. This was the suburb of St. Roch where the Intendant's Palace was located. Crosbie had no need to inquire for directions. Three streets crossed in a wide plaza near an enormous building of blue-slate rock. It must have been all of a hundred mètres long, Crosbie estimated, and possibly a third that wide, a noble structure even for France. Quebec was full of surprises for him, none so consistently surprising as the solidity and size of the stone buildings.

The Intendant's Palace rose for two stories, with two wide flights of stone steps up to the entrance where guards stood rigidly on duty. Crosbie halted a moment to pull his cloak into position, settle his hat. Then he mounted to the door.

The sentries did not move; his uniform guaranteed entry. Another soldier was posted inside to swing the door open. He remained close to take Crosbie's cloak and hat. The hat was dusted expertly with a silken square and tucked snugly under Crosbie's left elbow. The soldier flicked at the plain silver hilt of Crosbie's dress sword, paused to shine the ornate jeweled dirk that he wore always under his sash. The soldier knelt for a brief moment to brush the dust from Crosbie's buckled shoes. When he rose, he retreated silently until his shoulders touched squarely against the wall. Only then did the dazed Crosbie notice that there was a line of a dozen soldiers, perfectly uniformed, waiting in erect silence to assist other visitors to make a proper appearance. Crosbie moved down the long hallway, slightly bewildered by the magnificence of his reception.

Two powdered footmen swung double doors wide and Crosbie entered a vast room whose high ceiling rose to a gilded dome overhead. The walls were sheathed in gilt-rimmed marble, the floors polished to a perilous waxiness. At the far end, a gallery supported on gilt brackets protruded out above the room. That would be for musicians, Crosbie guessed, but he could not imagine the purpose of the wide balcony that ran the width of the room just above the gallery. A rotund butler greeted Crosbie, cocking his red face up and asking softly for Crosbie's name. He then wheeled and bellowed it into the nearly empty room beyond. Hesitantly, Crosbie moved forward.

"Welcome to Canada, cock," a light amused voice called out. Crosbie swerved.

In a wide embrasure between two curtained windows, Captain Seamus O'Neill lounged in a gilt ballroom chair with his feet propped high on another. Slowly, O'Neil dropped his feet, kicked his chair back and came erect. He drew a huge lace-edged handkerchief from his sleeve and dusted hair powder off the black facings of his uniform. "Annoying," he drawled tonelessly, burlesquing the fatigued tones of a court dandy. "Damnably annoying how powder will cling to everything but one's hair. I really shall have to design a more practical uniform for His Majesty's troops of marine." He tucked the handkerchief into his sleeve deftly. "The big wig sent me to meet you, cock. He'll be busy for a while, but he'll come when he's free."

"Who?"

"Le grosse perruque," O'Neill said in a heavily accented French. "The big wig. Monsieur François Bigot, Intendant of all Canada."

"Thank you, captain," Crosbie said stiffly. He could feel the criticism underlying O'Neill's light manner. Captain O'Neill might consider his own position was secure enough for that sort of casual mockery, but Crosbie was not willing to jeopardize his future for the dubious pleasure of a witticism, however mild. To change the subject, he said, "Why is it you persist in speaking to me in English, sir?"

O'Neill lifted one thin eyebrow. "Are you not a Scotty, now? Or am I..."

"I am a Scot," Crosbie growled, "but one born in France. If you will not speak French, why not use Gaelic. Surely that should be our common language, rather than English."

O'Neill's face reddened slowly to a violent contrast with his white wig. "I have no Gaelic," he muttered. "And damned little French. My father had not the sense of yours. Instead of France, he chose to go to the American colonies after the English routed Phelim O'Neill."

Crosbie held his month straight in spite of the temptation to laugh at the posturing Irishman. "But we arrived at the same place, sir, whatever route we followed." Silently Crosbie congratulated himself on the unusual tact of his comment.

O'Neill half turned away, took one stride, then motioned petulantly to Crosbie. "Come along, cock. We'll go find a drink whilst we're waiting."

O'Neill passed through a small doorway into a gloomy corridor hung with dark tapestry. Narrow doorways were flanked with gilt flambeaux and some were guarded by sentries. O'Neill darted quickly around a corner and clattered up a winding staircase. Then he threw open a door and moved aside with a faint smile.

Crosbie caught his breath as he glanced inside. The great chamber was bright with dancing light from chandeliers high on the ceiling, warm from the heat of two fires that blazed from either side of the room. And all the light and warmth seemed reflected in the bright jewel tones of an enormous carpet that filled Crosbie with envious admiration. The furniture was delicate gilded wood, brilliant velvet padding, light graceful tables and buffets and, centered in front of the near fireplace, a simply built table of unusual height with high sidings and a top of red baize. Of the dozen gentlemen in the room, only one glanced up when O'Neill ushered Crosbie inside. After a long, amused scrutiny of Crosbie's height, the gentleman nodded and turned away.

Dazed, Crosbie stared at an immense painting depicting some tragic allegory involving naked females of great size. He waited for O'Neill to indicate the next move. His bewilderment was masked determinedly behind a stern, dour expression.

"This is our lieu de réunion," the Irishman said. "A place of retirement and relaxation. A little wine, a game of cards, good company, if you can stomach these gentlemen and …" he shrugged lightly and indicated the gilt doors, "… a secluded nook for gentle dalliance." He dropped languidly into a wide velvet chair, stretched his thin legs to the fire and pointed negligently at a chair nearby.

Gingerly, Crosbie tucked his sword between his knees and sat stiffly upright. Never in his life had he seen anything to compare with this magnificence, but he would willingly have died before admitting it. He placed his hat on a small table beside his chair and covertly glanced at the gentlemen on the far side of the room.

"They, too," O'Neill said in a disinterested voice. "All here await the convenience of the Intendant. The *Frelon* carried a cargo of great profit. The wolves want their share—and somebody else's, too." His tone was lightly contemptuous, but Crosbie was aware that he spoke with a softness that would not carry across the room.

O'Neill leaned back in his chair, snapping his fingers for a liveried attendant. "A glass of wine with you, sir," he said. "This feathery confection on the table is the famous gâteau d'anis, a cake all Canadiens regard as the summit of delight. As for me, I cannot stomach sweets, unless it be a good Madeira."

Crosbie accepted the cake gratefully; his last meal had been soup and bread on board ship long hours ago. O'Neill poured two brimming glasses of wine.

"I don't believe so many of Canada's wealthy men have been gathered in one room for years," O'Neill said mildly, holding his glass high and squinting through it. "The *Frelon* must have had gold ingots in its hold. You seldom see Monsieur Varin here in Quebec, for example. He is Deputy Intendant for Montreal and a rare scoundrel, though a hard-working one, I must admit. And Monsieur Le

Verrier is not often here, either. He holds some military rank, but it escapes me at the moment. He made a fortune as commandant of Fort Michilimackinac, but then he's Bigot's step-son."

Crosbie took a sip of heavy sweet wine that almost choked him. Apparently there was no way he could halt O'Neill's dangerous slanders, but at least he could pretend complete deafness. The Irish captain chuckled with light malice as he noted Crosbie's embarrassment. "Then there's Brassard Descheneaux. He's Bigot's secretary, so he earns what little he steals. But for a rascal who began life as a shoemaker, he manages fairly well. Beside him, the pompous toad with the scarlet face is Monsieur Breéard. He is naval comptroller. Need I say more?" O'Neill raised thin eyebrows.

"Nothing more, Captain O'Neill," Crosbie declared flatly. "These gentlemen would hardly appreciate …"

"Gentlemen?" O'Neill said with toneless mockery. "I can assure you, sir, there's not a man present who's not the base-born creature of our noble Intendant and I include the clever Monsieur Cadet, who was a bankrupt butcher when Bigot rescued him."

"That will do, sir," Crosbie insisted. "I don't know these gentlemen, but …"

"No, you don't know them," O'Neill said, holding his cold grave face carefully inexpressive. "But I do." Abruptly, he offered a thin smile and lifted his glass to Crosbie. "Your sensibilities do you credit. But nothing I have said is a secret. I was about to point out one other whom you will want to meet. That great beefy fellow sitting next to the little hunchback. You'll recognize his uniform."

The uniformed officer was by far the most soberly dressed of all. His somber blue coat was the same that Crosbie wore, but his scarlet facings were glossy silk. Across his huge chest ran the diagonal pale blue watered silk ribbon of the Order of St. Louis.

"… the Chevalier Le Mercier, who commands the artillery of Canada," O'Neill went on. "Also a man of extreme wealth."

As if he had overheard O'Neill's low voice, Le Mercier wheeled slowly around, looking directly at Crosbie. He muttered something to the gaudy little hunchback near him and pushed up to his feet, moving with ponderous slowness.

O'Neil lifted one hand slowly, then swept it down toward the floor in a sketchy parody of a court bow.

"Your servant, Monsieur le Chevalier," he said in a light amused tone. "May I present a young colleague? Monsieur Crosbie, the Chevalier Le Mercier."

The broad-faced officer glowered down at O'Neill. "You joke too much," he grunted thickly, speaking in a thick Breton accent.

O'Neill's face was an expressionless white mask. "I spend too much time with buffoons, monsieur."

Le Mercier's face darkened to a purplish cast. "You are sometimes useful, Captain O'Neill, but you may not always be useful."

O'Neill smiled politely. "I'll remain useful as long as I'm never frightened by clowns, monsieur," he said tonelessly.

After a long taut moment, Le Mercier turned away from O'Neill, shaking his head like an angry bear. He nodded heavily in response to Crosbie's bow.

"I'm honored, sir," Crosbie said formally.

"Yes, yes," Le Mercier said in an absent tone. "You are the young giant my sergents speak about, are you? Inspecting my batteries like a visiting général, asking no one's permission." Abruptly, he smiled, a quick startling gash across his heavy features. "Sit, sit," he said quickly.

Le Mercier took a chair across from Crosbie, settled himself carefully. "We need more officers of artillery here," he said, heavily pleasant. "Tell me what you think of our installations."

Crosbie seated himself warily. "I've had only a brief..."

"Arrived on the *Frelon* this morning," O'Neill broke in easily. He reached forward and flipped up the lid of a vieuxlaque box on the table.

"Yes, yes," Le Mercier raised a broad red hand and let it fall again. "If all Canada could be as easily defended as Quebec, we could all retire, eh?" He laughed deeply in his throat. "A child with pebbles could hold Quebec. And with cannon…" Another hand rose and flipped away the problem in a lordly gesture.

Maliciously, O'Neill chuckled. "I'd hate to be the man who fired one of those worn-out guns," he said. "More dangerous to the gunner than the gunned, I should say." He took three packs of cards from the box and closed the lid with a brittle snap.

Le Mercier growled savagely, "No ship could live an hour before Quebec unless I spared it."

Casually, O'Neill milked two packs together, rippling the cards with quick fingers. One slipped to the floor and Crosbie bent to retrieve it. The card was far superior to anything he had ever used, a heavy linen square, starched and waxed, block-printed in bright colors. O'Neill took the card from him and without looking up, began to merge the third pack with the others.

"Why don't you ask the neutral observer?" O'Neill's calm eyes were blank, remote, measuring the angry Chevalier.

Le Mercier forced his thick lips back in a strained grimace. He stretched forward and tapped Crosbie's knee with a ponderous gesture. "We gunners understand these things, eh?" He exploded in a gust of brandy-scented laughter, then settled back and watched Crosbie with a flat, unblinking stare.

Silently, Crosbie cursed the mischievous Irishman whose mockery had forced him into such a position. Obviously, he couldn't tell this wild bull of a commandant what he really thought of Canada's artillery defenses, not if he hoped for a career in Canada. And he had absolutely no intention of saying that he approved what he had seen. Only a fool would allow himself to be pinched between two impossible alternatives, and just then Crosbie was sure he was one of God's own anointed fools. He shifted uneasily in his chair.

"A game of baccarat-à-deux, Monsieur le Chevalier?" O'Neill asked with a casual mockery.

"I was waiting to hear this young gentleman's opinion," Le Mercier said stiffly. His reddened eyes never left Crosbie's.

"I've had small opportunity, sir ..." Crosbie began.

"Yes, yes." Le Mercier lifted his hand in obvious demand.

"The guns sited in the battery near the Château are all in need of new vent fittings, sir, as you are doubtless aware, and ..."

Le Mercier's face hardened and O'Neill chuckled softly as both waited for Crosbie to continue.

The entrance behind Crosbie swung open, effectively interrupting the young Scot. O'Neill leaped to his feet, letting the triple pack sift to the table. Le Mercier glanced up, immediately clapped his hands to the arms of the chair and struggled to his feet. Crosbie turned to look over his shoulder and tried to rise at the same time, managing to tangle himself so awkwardly that he was compelled to grab his chair for steadiness.

The Comtesse de Boyer smiled warmly and offered her hand, holding it forward and waiting while Crosbie struggled for balance. At length he was able, hotly flushed with embarrassment, to take it and bow low.

Behind the Comtesse, a diffident retinue of ladies stood on the stairway landing patiently. Crosbie noticed Céleste among them and he tried to ignore her serenely contemptuous stare. The Comtesse clamped warm thin fingers around his hand with quick, knowing pressure. Gently, she turned him toward the squat ugly man who stood smiling beside her.

"This is the remarkable young gaillard I mentioned, François," she said with brisk clarity. "May I present Monsieur Crosbie? My brother, sir, Monsieur François Bigot, Intendant of New France."

CHAPTER SEVEN

In later years Duncan Crosbie was to hear much of the strange man who served as thirteenth Intendant of New France. François Bigot attracted violent partisans who denied all criticism, no matter how damning the evidence, and even more aggressive enemies who denied Bigot any shred of decency. And always to Crosbie at such moments came the memory of his first sight of François Bigot in the doorway of his lieu de réunion, with his regally magnificent sister on his arm, his ugly mottled face crinkled into a warm smile, his eyes admiring Crosbie's great height, his manner radiating a force of attraction that was compelling as a magnet is to steel.

At eighteen Crosbie had met few men of unusual charm and those few had not felt a sous-lieutenant worth much attention. François Bigot, however, welcomed him as if Crosbie's arrival completed a perfect day.

Bigot's was a flat-featured, broad peasant's face. Only his eyes—brilliant and compelling as his sister's—were memorable. And his clothes were atrocious for a man of his figure. His white court wig brushed low to the shoulders of a tight white satin coat elaborately frogged in gilt. His smallclothes were of the same cloth, marked with golden fleurs-de-lis on the waistcoat over which a flood of Valenciennes lace spilled luxuriously. Even his wide flat shoes were white satin, the heels set preposterously with brilliants around the welting. He wore a tiny toy of a court sword at his belt, its hilt scrolled with gilt and capped with a huge diamond. And all this apparent elegance was set at nought by the bulbous stomach that protruded solidly, forcing his clothes grotesquely from their proper lines. Even his feet were poorly shaped for his shoes, for obvious bumps distorted the smooth satin. The end result should have been clownish. Why it wasn't, Crosbie could never determine.

François Bigot rocked back on his heels to look up at the young Scot and he chuckled softly as though the disparity in height was a secret joke to be appreciated only by Crosbie and himself.

"My sister tells me she is indebted to you for relieving the tedium of her long voyage," Bigot said in a quick facile voice that was slightly hoarse. "I also am grateful. Fleur is our one prime delight in Quebec. It would never do to let boredom's grisly face show itself near her. I believe she plans…"

"Monsieur Crosbie will be required to dance attendance for a few weeks more," the Comtesse broke in smoothly. "Then we must see to a wife for him. Someone wealthy, François. You know many such."

Bigot's smile faded slightly, then returned in full force. "Indeed, many such," he agreed. "So many young ladies of Canada lose their hearts to gentlemen from France. Apparently our Canadian gallants are too … crude. Normally I am opposed to such notions, but I can see clearly that Monsieur Crosbie is no powdered popinjay. A young man of parts, I should say."

Crosbie bowed. "Your Excellency does me too much credit," he said stiffly.

"Nonsense," Bigot insisted. "And in any event, one should accept all the credit available, eh." Jovially, he tapped Crosbie's arm and laughed quickly. "And all the profit, too."

Crosbie was aware that everyone was watching him and he could feel that damnable, betraying flush reddening his face. The Comtesse took her brother's arm again with a brisk movement and signalled him by the pressure of her hand.

"Well, we must leave all that for a future discussion, eh?" Bigot turned slightly, addressing the assembled gentlemen. "I am commanded by Madame la Comtesse to demand the presence of all gentlemen for the dancing in the ballroom. We shall permit one brief hour for lamentation. After which no excuses will be tolerated."

A chorus of laughter followed the Intendant's announcement and most of the people pressed forward, eager to accompany Bigot. The movement of the crowd pushed Crosbie against the Comtesse who smiled and whispered something inaudible. Swiftly she thrust a folded paper into his sash and let the general exodus move her to the open door. Céleste stood aside to let the Comtesse leave first. Her eyes regarded Crosbie thoughtfully. He glanced at her and Céleste smiled, a brief, meaningless smile of politeness.

With an unbelieving gesture, Crosbie felt for the paper. As his finger touched it, a belated warning sounded in his head. He withdrew his hand quickly. He suspected that Céleste had seen the Comtesse slip the note to him. For some reason, that thought was irritating.

Beside him was the knife-thin Canadien, Michel Colbert, watching Crosbie.

"You move in exalted circles now, monsieur," he said with his habitual faint sneer. "For a new arrival, you have conquered swiftly."

Crosbie understood nothing of what the Canadien meant and very little of what had been implied by Bigot, though it was clear that he was supposed to find a meaning beyond the words themselves. Freezing his expression in tight control, he bowed formally to Colbert.

Colbert stretched to one side and touched the arm of a short white-uniformed officer.

"Let me present Monsieur Crosbie, sir," Colbert said in an obsequious tone. "He is our Intendant's newest favorite, I should say. This gentleman, sir, is Major Hughes Péan."

Crosbie bowed to the short officer and received a curt nod in response. The black troupe de la marine facings of Péan's uniform were spotted with spilled wine, and the major's face was dangerously flushed. He did manage a comment, in a sneering tone that was a match for Colbert's.

"A bit large for a pet. We'll need a larger kennel."

Colbert giggled nervously, darting a wary glance at Crosbie and moving quickly between him and Péan, urging the short officer away.

Crosbie blinked his eyes. Only by that did he display any of the turmoil inside him. A cold fury touched his mind and he ached to snatch the diminutive major by the scruff of his sodden neck.

"The dogs are barking, eh, cock?" O'Neill eyed Crosbie with quiet speculation. In each hand he carried a full wineglass. One he offered to Crosbie.

"What ails these people?" Crosbie growled. He took the glass and gulped at it gratefully.

"Bigot mentioned profit," O'Neill said. "Everyone is afraid you may take the share they had hoped for. Pay no attention to them. They snap just as nastily among themselves. Dogs, the lot of them, and not a thoroughbred in the pack." O'Neill picked up a pair of dice from the rim of the table, flipping them lightly against the far side, scooping them up without looking when they bounced back.

A thick sourness nearly closed Crosbie's throat. "I've no stomach for such talk," he said heavily. "You'll oblige me, sir, by..."

"Not another word," O'Neill said willingly. He held out his cupped hand in a swift motion. "A round of hazard, cock? We'll not be expected below for another hour."

Crosbie shook his head. "I have no knowledge of hazard, sir," he said slowly. "And no..."

O'Neill cut him off with a flat gesture. "Hazard is a complicated game, but the dice are amiable creatures. We'll have a small bout with Venus and The Dog, shall we? Merely the highest score. That is simple enough, isn't it?"

"Simple enough," Crosbie admitted. "But…" Awkwardly, he put down his wineglass, watched as a hovering servant promptly filled it again. O'Neill tossed off his drink, accepted another and deftly spilled a fistful of golden louis-d'or into the baize table. "One louis?" he offered in a blank, disinterested tone. He rolled the dice the full length of the table, making them bounce from the far board and return almost in front of Crosbie. The nearest displayed a two uppermost, the other a three.

Five, Crosbie thought. That shouldn't be hard to beat. He fumbled under his sash for his waistcoat pocket, touching the folded paper there and shifting it slightly as he withdrew his flattened purse. Any loss tonight might mean serious embarrassment. Slowly, he brought out two louis, dropped a single coin beside O'Neill's, retaining the other. He picked up the dice.

They were small silver cubes inlaid with lacquered stars for pips. Coldly they lay in Crosbie's hand, as cold a chill as he felt at the prospect of losing. Several lounging officers drifted closer, attracted as all idlers are by a gambling bout. Abruptly Crosbie hurled the dice along the table.

"Fichtre!" O'Neill muttered.

Crosbie relaxed with a faint sigh. He glanced down at the five and six that seemed to shine beautifully against the red baize.

"Eleven," O'Neill acknowledged. "You had no need to sink me, cock. Let's wager both this toss, eh?" Without waiting for Crosbie to reply, he flipped two coins from the loose mass before him and made them chink musically against Crosbie's winnings. Gratefully Crosbie slipped his second coin back in his pocket, resigned to losing the one on the table, and hopeful that he could withdraw after this wager.

O'Neill held the dice tight in his hand as if to warm them. After a long deliberate pause, he rolled them swiftly along the table. Crosbie watched the Irishman's face.

"Seven," O'Neill said calmly. "The seven magical daughters of Tara." He flicked the dice toward Crosbie.

Before Crosbie could throw, someone spilled a rattling mass of gold on the table, purposely matching O'Neill's stake.

"The next one with you, sir," O'Neill agreed. "But we are now waiting for Monsieur Crosbie's throw."

This, then, would be all that he need bet, Crosbie realized. Win or lose, there wouldn't be too much alteration in his fortune. With a definite sense of relief, he cast the dice against the far siding and watched them roll and spin to a full stop. A double four gleamed up at him and Crosbie scooped up the four louis as O'Neill smiled politely with his thin pale lips. Then the dice passed from Crosbie to the newcomer whose purple satin sleeves were all that Crosbie noticed.

With attention diverted from him momentarily, Crosbie thought it safe to look at the paper the Comtesse had slipped into his sash.

"Be at the garden entrance to the Palace just after the midnight guard is posted," the note read.

Impassively, Crosbie refolded the paper and tucked it securely under his sash again. He was exultant. The fiasco on board the *Frelon* had not destroyed him in the Comtesse's regard, as he had feared. He recalled the enigmatic watchfulness of Céleste and again he felt sure that she had observed the Comtesse pass the note to him. He put the thought out of his mind; somehow he didn't want to think of Céleste just now.

The purple-sleeved gentleman beside him nudged Crosbie meaningfully, bringing the young Scot's attention back to the table.

"Oh, my turn, is it?" he said in confusion. "Very well, monsieur. Match that." He hadn't glanced at the table since he had taken out the Comtesse's note, but in his present state of mind, he didn't mind wagering a few louis. Lightly he tossed the dice, flicking them up against the backboard and smiling as they rolled to a stop. A four and a two, merely six. Crosbie scooped them up and placed them before the man in purple sleeves. He took four louis from his side pocket. "I'll wager ..." he began.

"Wager be damned," O'Neill said with faint amusement. "You've already wagered. And won."

Beside Crosbie, Purple Sleeves muttered angrily and the aghast young Scot looked down at the pile of golden louis-d'or that lay on the red baize before him. What in God's name had he done? Never in the world could he have paid such a wager if he'd lost. What mad behavior was that, to accept a bet without even knowing the amount? Unbelievingly, he touched the mass of coin.

"You rolled against a five," O'Neill said in his bleak voice, "and won. Will you take a hundred louis of mine that you can't win again?"

Numbly Crosbie nodded. What did it matter? The money wasn't his by any shadow of right. He had easily a hundred louis in front of him, possibly more. That amounted to … two thousand francs! He'd never had so much money at one time before.

He let O'Neill take the dice and drop his wager on the baize top.

"What is this?" Crosbie asked, touching the stack of paper slips that O'Neill had wagered.

"Hundred-franc ordonnances," O'Neill said. "Twenty of them. Right?" He threw the dice swiftly, making them spin crazily across the table. A double six appeared and O'Neill smiled thinly.

"Ordonnances," Crosbie echoed. He picked up one of the papers, saw the confused welter of signatures, the engraved figure "100" in each corner and put it down again.

"Never you mind what they are," O'Neill said bluntly. "You'll never own those, cock. You don't hope to beat a twelve, surely?"

"No," Crosbie said absently, picking up the dice. "But what are …"

"Monsieur Bigot has issued them to help Canadien trade," O'Neill explained, with that clear contempt he always displayed when he mentioned Bigot. "He redeems them every Autumn, so you needn't worry whether they're good or not. Now throw the dice."

Crosbie hurled the dice quickly, still staring down at the stack of paper ordonnances while the dice wobbled across the table. What sort of man was Bigot, he wondered. He lived in a palace; he controlled a vast colony; he commanded a private army; he issued his own money. All these were prerogatives of kings. King François Bigot, he thought wildly.

"A twelve!" someone shouted.

Loud commentaries from onlookers drowned O'Neill's comment. The Irish captain took the dice again, nestling them for a moment before throwing them. A faint tinge of red showed under his cheekbones. One die stopped immediately with a six uppermost, while the other spun in a tight endless spiral. No one spoke during the tense moment. Finally the second die wobbled to a stop, showing a single pip.

"The lucky seven again," O'Neill said in a seemingly disinterested voice.

"Aye," Crosbie growled. He was fast tiring of O'Neill's theatrically controlled manner. Was he afraid to show his true feelings? Crosbie picked up the dice and glanced briefly at the magnificent stake awaiting the winner. Slowly he swung his heavy arm forward, clicking the dice against the table. They bounced briskly from the board and rolled quickly dead almost at once, showing a twelve. O'Neill tapped them away from his sight, pushed the money toward Crosbie.

"Never an O'Neill with such cursed luck as Seamus," he said with a faint smile. "You've a small fortune there, cock."

The dice passed to another pair beyond O'Neill who promptly exhausted their funds in the swift game. As the dice moved slowly along the table, O'Neill brought two glasses of wine and drank with Crosbie.

Something distracted his attention briefly as he stared beyond Crosbie. A tight smile twisted his small even features. "I was going to ask you," he went on, "what it was you'd almost said to Le Mercier about his cannon?"

Crosbie drained his glass and felt a sudden recklessness compounded of his winnings and the wine. He shrugged elaborately.

"Merely that the guns of the Château battery are not capable of firing a single aimed shot," he said flatly.

A dull agonized roaring boomed in Crosbie's ear and he wheeled to look directly into Le Mercier's furious red face.

"Fool!" Le Mercier bellowed. "You will retract at once. At once, monsieur! You hear me?"

Hotly, Crosbie cursed his undisciplined tongue. This was a situation of O'Neill's making, he realized. The sleek Irishman must have seen Le Mercier before he asked his ruinous question. Well, the fat was in the fire now. Either he would retract, or he would ruin himself in Le Mercier's opinion. For a brief, hopeless moment, he tried to convince himself he should retract, but the moment passed quickly. "I am sorry I spoke so harshly, Monsieur le Chevalier," he said quietly.

"You will retract, sir," Le Mercier demanded with drunken severity. "You have slandered my command. You have lied …"

"No, sir," Crosbie said bleakly. He grew aware of the breathless silence in the. room. "I did not lie."

"The Château battery," Le Mercier roared, "is the finest …"

"The Château battery is out of action," Crosbie said coldly. He heard the flat uncompromising words and desperately wished there was another way to say the same thing. "Almost all the guns are unbushed, sir," he said. "All badly need scaling. Not one could be fired accurately at this moment. If you tried, most of the shot would land in Lower Town."

The assembled gentlemen drew in a low collective breath and Le Mercier's rage soared as he fought for words.

"You have round-shot in ready garlands beside each piece," Crosbie went on, feeling as a man must feel when he confesses to murder and knows the executioner is waiting outside. "All the shot have rusted together into a single mass. Not one is serviceable. And the supply of powder in the magazine is …"

Hard hands clamped around his arm, pulling him back toward the door. Angrily, Crosbie glared over his shoulder. Bougainville, that was his name, the captain at Montcalm's headquarters.

"You young fool," Bougainville whispered sharply. "Be silent."

"That man is mine," Le Mercier bellowed. "I want him for ..."

"This gentleman," Bougainville said calmly, "is a member of Général Montcalm's official family." His voice rose crisply over Le Mercier's barely coherent fury. "Complaints must be addressed to the Général."

Briskly Bougainville pivotted on his heel and pushed the dazed Crosbie before him. Bougainville pulled the door open and rushed Crosbie through.

The door opened again and Bougainville wheeled swiftly.

"No duels, cock," Seamus O'Neill said, faintly smiling. "I brought the lad's hat and his money."

Bougainville snatched Crosbie's belongings from O'Neill. "Sir, I hold you responsible for what happened tonight."

Bougainville's harsh tone sliced the smile from O'Neill's face. Involuntarily, the Irish captain took one step back.

Crosbie, urged by Bougainville's hand, moved past O'Neill and down the stairs.

"Thank you, sir," he said thickly. "I ..."

"Never mind," Bougainville said in a flat tone. "That man, O'Neill, is composed entirely of malice. He indulges what he terms his 'humor' until someone corrects him."

"But, I ..."

"Think of yourself, if you must worry. Pray that Général Montcalm is willing to accept you as a staff officer. If he isn't, you may find yourself at Le Mercier's disposal. But in fact, you may have solved your own problem," Bougainville added with a bleak smile. "I think I know now how you may serve best. Come see me early in the morning. I'll take you to the Général. Now, let us join the ladies, Monsieur Crosbie. And for Heaven's sake, put away that indecent sum of money."

CHAPTER EIGHT

At dawn, Crosbie awoke restlessly after the first light had penetrated the tiny window of his sleeping cubicle in the Fort of St. Louis. He rolled out of bed and fumbled for the jug of water that stood on a table. He drank deeply, spilling a chilly stream down his naked chest. The water was somehow unable to soothe the violent thirst that burned in his throat. Momentary dizziness struck him. Too much wine the night before. He stood before the open window, breathing deeply, smiling as he remembered his first night at the Intendant's Palace.

The guard near the garden gate of the Palace had obviously been instructed to expect him. And inside, a fat, merry-eyed woman was waiting to lead him through the garden, along dark passages to a lighted doorway where she magically vanished and the lovely Comtesse de Boyer mysteriously appeared, as if in a well-managed play where the characters are always coming and going with bewildering rapidity.

From midnight to four, when the guard was due to change again, passed with breathtaking speed. There had been much talk, broken incoherent whispers for much of the time, but sharp and crisp enough during the last few minutes of Crosbie's stolen time. He was strangely vague about just what had become of two hundred of the louis-d'or he had won at dice. It had gone toward "a small investment in the Intendant's newest financial venture," whatever that might be. He had no particular concern about the money. At least a tenfold increase was assured, Fleur had said, but the money had come so accidentally to Crosbie that its loss was no more real than its presence. And he still had nearly fifty louis remaining in his distended purse. The permission to invest which he had signed and left with Fleur might make him a rich man soon, but at the moment Crosbie could imagine no greater riches than his fifty louis—and the Comtesse.

He wiped his face and chest with a damp cloth, put on his breeches and slipped into his shoes. He would have to wear the same uniform again today, until he had a chance to unpack his boxes.

His shoes made a hollow clatter in the corridor, not quite drowning out the deep rumbling snores that issued from the chambers where brother officers were still sleeping. There was a particularly cold loneliness that came to the first man up each morning, and so far Crosbie had found no French soldier who rose as early as he did, except for cooks.

He moved quietly down to the necessary room, then sought out the stairs that should take him to the kitchens below. The warm scent of cooking food, the small busy sounds, made an easy target. He entered the low-ceilinged room where two cooks sat hunched at a table, bent low over steaming bowls of coffee.

Crosbie nodded pleasantly, and knowing the ways of army cooks, asked no permission as he poured a mug of coffee for himself and tore away an immense gobbet of freshly baked crusty bread. He settled himself lightly on an open window-sill and bit lustily into the steaming loaf. His window looked out onto a tiny garden. Already a thin patch of watery sunlight illuminated a corner and there a white-smocked barber bent over a muscular man in shirt sleeves who sat comfortably in a withe-and-rawhide version of a barber's chair. Crosbie sipped his scalding coffee cautiously and chewed his bread. That would be a regimental barber out there, he thought, and it would do no harm if he were shaven properly and had his hair dressed and powdered before he was presented to Général Montcalm for the first time.

The barber glanced around curiously as Crosbie approached. The man in the chair opened one eye. Crosbie waggled his chunk of bread in salutation.

"Carry on," he said amiably. "I'll wait till you're finished. I am to see the Général this morning, so I'd best be well shaven."

The relaxed man in the chair nodded pleasantly. "Come, Jeannot," he said in a quick light tone. "You must not make this gentleman late for his appointment. Not a word, sir, it is no trouble to me," he said to Crosbie. "I too have an early appointment."

Deftly the barber wiped away the last of the lather with a cologne-drenched napkin, briskly rubbing until the man's ruddy skin glowed brightly. He then pulled away the protecting bib and assisted the man to his feet.

"Be seated here, monsieur," the man said to Crosbie. "And Jeannot, see that you do your very best for this gentleman."

Crosbie gulped down the last of his coffee and crammed the heel of the loaf into his mouth, chewing hard as he settled himself gingerly in the small chair.

"It was not constructed for a man of your size," the man said with a faint chuckle. "For, in truth, there must be only a few men of your size." He adjusted a tightly pinned linen cap that had slipped to the side of his shaven scalp.

The barber first unwrapped Crosbie's queue, draping the twisted ribbon around his neck while he combed Crosbie's long red hair out straight. He eyed its length thoughtfully and snipped off several inches. Then he brushed it, pulled it back with a pressure that brought tears to Crosbie's eyes, wrapped the ribbon hard, forming a club-like pigtail. Using the same bowl of warm lather he had prepared for the first man, the barber soaped Crosbie's face and began to shave him. Crosbie could feel the blade scrape cleanly as the barber stretched the skin and tweaked his nose from side to side to permit the razor to reach all of the pale stubble that grew on Crosbie's face. It was a very quick shave,

Crosbie thought, as he felt the sting of the cologne-soaked napkin on his cheeks.

Still winking from the cologne, he saw the barber's first customer standing a few feet away, balanced easily, holding a thin blade in his hand in the 'on guard' position. As Crosbie watched, the man lunged swiftly, his left hand swinging back in beautiful rhythm to maintain his balance as he darted the point of the sword at a shred of bark hanging free from a small tree. The point passed a short distance below the bark and the swordsman recoiled instantly. He stabbed forward again, spearing the bark exactly.

"Bravo, monsieur," Crosbie said politely. He bowed slightly and turned to the barber again. "Do you have your powder dredger here? I think that for the Général..."

"I can assure you, monsieur," the first man said quickly, "that the Général prefers his young gentlemen not powder except for formal parades."

"In that case," Crosbie shrugged, "no powder. Call at my quarters, then, and I'll find a piece of silver for you. This was an excellent shave. And very quick, too."

"Let this be my honor," the first man insisted. "And we would not want to spoil Jeannot with too much money. Eh, Jeannot?"

"As Your Excellency wishes," the barber murmured easily, polishing his razor carefully.

Your Excellency!

Crosbie's mouth fell slightly open. He forced it shut with an angry click. Again, he thought savagely. Once more he had done his stupid best to destroy a situation in which success might have followed silence. Would he ever learn, ever?

"My humble apologies, Your Excellency," he said simply. "I did not..."

"Nothing," Montcalm insisted pleasantly. "Most amusing, I assure you. It has been some years since a subaltern has addressed me simply as a brother officer. Truly, I am flattered.

But in repayment for the services of my excellent Jeannot, I shall insist you give me a bout with the épée. My usual companion has not yet torn himself from his warm bed. And truthfully," he glanced up at Crosbie, straining to meet his eyes, "truthfully, I am consumed with curiosity to see what advantage your great height gives you with a sword."

Crosbie stood frozen, still shaken and slightly horrified at his own lack of tact. His Général stood there, smiling easily at him, a solidly formed man with a round muscular face whose expression indicated no serious disapproval, but still Crosbie could not manage to return the smile.

"Come now," Montcalm insisted. "Are you familiar with this blade?" He thrust out the simple steel hilt of an épée and tapped with it at Crosbie's chest.

Montcalm's friendly smile and the fact that he, too, was dressed simply in breeches and shirt with the collar tucked under, did much to reassure the young Scot. Dutifully he accepted the épée and swung it once through the air to test its balance. On the tip was a small pointe-d'arrête, a button with three short thin needles protruding forward. Crosbie glanced at his Général.

"I prefer the pointe-d'arrête to a flat button," Montcalm said. "It gives the illusion of danger that should always be present in swordplay. With it, one is never tempted to toy with the blade."

The tiny points could tear a sizeable gash in human hide, as Crosbie well knew, but what concerned him most was the fate of his best shirt. It could be shredded if the Général was an expert fencer. But there was no possibility of mentioning that. Slowly, he placed himself in readiness.

"One moment," Montcalm said brusquely. He clamped his épée between his knees and stripped his shirt off overhead. "I am no extravagant young subaltern," he laughed. "I do not care to ruin my shirts. They are much harder to replace than one's hide, eh?"

Crosbie grinned widely and followed the Général's lead. With both shirts hung side by side, he profiled against Montcalm.

The Général seemed to be larger without his shirt. He had a deep chest and the strong sloping shoulders that usually went with it. His biceps were hard and corded, with prominent veins.

Crosbie assumed the routine classic profile, balanced easily, with his blade offered from a bent arm. There was a peculiarly awkward posture that would give him an added advantage from his height, but it did not seem proper to adopt it against the Général, particularly not when Montcalm himself stood ready in formal fashion. With the familiar ritualistic sweep, they saluted and touched blades lightly.

"À nous deux," Montcalm said formally.

The Général's blade swept around in a disengage to the outside and Crosbie shifted his hilt to counter. The double feint was enough. Montcalm disengaged again, delicately flicking his épée first to one side, then the other, threatening always. He was clearly inviting Crosbie's attack, but the young Scot saw no point in obliging him. There was a point of impatience which some duellists reached early. It made them especially vulnerable and Crosbie was willing to wait to see if Montcalm would extend himself too quickly.

The swift taut feinting went on, seeming endless to Crosbie. Always Montcalm's blade was in motion, disengaging quickly, beating and re-engaging without the tell-tale elbow and shoulder motion that betrayed so many swordsmen. Crosbie himself tried one feinting lunge, sliding his right foot smoothly forward a few inches, advancing his blade slightly, prepared to go in low. Like a snake's tongue, Montcalm's épée slipped over his, aimed directly for the throat. Only the fact that his lunge was merely a feint saved Crosbie. Somehow he had warned Montcalm, some small movement had indicated the coming lunge. Warily now, Crosbie returned to his waiting tactics.

He straightened his elbow slightly, making it just that longer a distance for Montcalm to travel before reaching his body. Crouched like a coiled spring, continually alert to lunge or parry,

Crosbie felt the tension build within him. As an experiment, he adopted the Italian trick of beating, seizing the initiative now that he was sure that Montcalm was waiting for him to attack first. Softly at first, then with increasing force, he beat his blade against the Général's. Crosbie's heavy wrist was the size of a normal man's forearm and his hands were tireless, so that the steady beat-beat of the blades was not the disturbing shock to him that it was to the Général. Ultimately, the beating would cramp the supple wrist and forearm muscles, making them slow to respond when the attack came. Constantly, Montcalm tried to disengage his blade, but each time Crosbie forestalled him with that pounding, numbing beat. Wryly, the Général grinned, pulling his lips back tight over startlingly white teeth. Anticipating Crosbie's beat, he dropped the point of his blade and darted it forward. That was Crosbie's moment. He deflected Montcalm's blade with the pommel of his épée and riposted swiftly. But not swiftly enough. With a sudden shuffling of his feet, Montcalm retreated just that necessary distance to safety. He regained his position and shook his head happily, grinning now with the true pleasure of a swordsman who has found a challenging opponent.

Again Crosbie resumed the beat and again Montcalm tried to elude his blade without once exposing himself to a telling thrust. Crosbie gradually straightened his right arm even further, extending the distance between him and the Général. Montcalm stepped back momentarily, amazed at Crosbie's reach. Then, without a word, he resumed his stance. There was no warning when he leaped forward, crossing with his left foot before he swooped into a low lunge, the first quick step furnishing just the extra distance he required. Desperately Crosbie swung his blade low, knowing as he moved that he had lost control. He felt Montcalm's blade tick against his, and in the next moment came a brief fiery pain. The three tiny points had stabbed into his leg just below the knee, a fine crippling wound if the blade had been naked.

Crosbie stepped back, briefly pleased that he had not worn stockings that morning. Montcalm's damned pointe-d'arrête would have laddered his best silk hose. Quickly, he saluted the Général and fell back into position when he saw that Montcalm was waiting.

"A splendid touch, sir," he said softly, crossing blades again. "I was helpless."

Montcalm shrugged. "A move of desperation. It deserved to fail. It nearly did."

Silently they resumed the cat-and-mouse tactics, feeling each other out, Crosbie hopeful that Montcalm might be exhilarated enough to risk another lunge, Montcalm watchful and wary, knowing that the unusual arm-length of the young Scot was a hazard that called for close planning. Crosbie crouched slightly, extending his arm again, sticking his rump out awkwardly, but gaining another precious few inches on Montcalm. He beat his blade again, increasing the force each time until steel was clashing constantly. Montcalm stepped clear for a moment, shifted his grip and returned again, only to feel that incessant, numbing beat that was freezing his arm. He could not long maintain himself in condition to riposte if his muscles cramped, nor could he easily attack across that unusual space that separated him from Crosbie's body.

Crosbie could see the faint frown that grew deeper above Montcalm's smile of concentration. Something would happen soon, he felt sure. The Général could not accept this position unless he accepted ultimate defeat. He would have to do something and Crosbie was deeply curious to see how the Général would solve the problem. He increased both speed and force of his beat, drumming swiftly against the Général's blade.

In his own mind, Crosbie suspected that Montcalm was primarily concerned with the numbing effect that constant beating was having on his swordarm. He would probably not be expecting an attack, for Crosbie held a decided advantage as matters stood now. So this, if ever, was Crosbie's moment.

Gradually, he shifted to the right, letting his épée assume a sharper angle, but never easing the beat. Swiftly he stabbed forward in a high thrust for the shoulder.

Montcalm recoiled like a spring winding down upon itself. As the point sought him, he seemed to move just that meager distance before it. He sprang back and down, ducking under Crosbie's blade. The barbed pointe-d'arrête slid dangerously past the Général's face, plucking his tight cap away neatly, leaving only a faint hairline scratch on Montcalm's shaved head.

Crosbie stepped back, aghast at the thought that he might easily have blinded his Général.

Montcalm laughed with obvious relief. He bent to retrieve his cap, tossing it lightly in the air as he swept his blade up in a cavalier's salute to the young Scot.

"I am happy to have that drumming at an end," he said. "My arm will ache for days, I expect." A thin trickle of blood worked its way along the edge of his shaven poll, giving him an oddly raffish appearance as he stood smiling happily at Crosbie, breathing with deep slow inhalations. "Only Captain O'Neill of the Intendant's troops has given me such a difficult bout. But compared to you, Monsieur O'Neill is merely a trickster, accomplished in certain sly attacks. We must match you two one day. It should make a contest worth seeing."

From the doorway behind the Général, two officers appeared abruptly, marching in brisk cadence into the garden. The leader, a broad, hard-faced man, was dressed like Montcalm in a light shirt, wigless with a tight cap wound turban-wise around his shaven head. Behind him Captain Bougainville, immaculate in a fresh uniform with a dazzling white military wig, kept step with him, one meticulous pace to the rear. Montcalm spun on his heel and swept his épée up in a casual salute.

"Ah, Dalquier," he called pleasantly, "you are too late to save me from humiliation. This young gentleman has already wrought havoc with me."

"My apologies, Excellency," Dalquier said tightly, bowing with a stiff motion. "My stupid orderly forgot to ..."

"Nothing, nothing," Montcalm said quickly, waving away the apologies. "I shall approach our bout this morning with a new caution, however. Now, my good Louis, what brings you here this early?"

Bougainville snapped to attention and bowed, hat clamped under his elbow. "You Excellency suggested ..."

"Ah, yes, your undiplomatic gunner who must be rescued from Le Mercier's wrath. I'd nearly forgotten. Well, bring him out, Louis. Let me see this paragon of indiscretion."

With a gesture of confused helplessness, Bougainville indicated Crosbie standing silent near the Général. "Your Excellency has already met ..."

"This young giant?" Montcalm pivotted to face Crosbie. Thick eyebrows pulled down vigorously into a straight line, the full smiling mouth tightened. "You are the officer who insulted the Chevalier Le Mercier?"

"Sir, I ..." Crosbie began clumsily.

"Answer me, monsieur," Montcalm demanded.

"Yes, Your Excellency," Crosbie said simply.

"Precisely what was it you said about the commandant's precious guns? Specifically what?"

Crosbie raised both shoulders and let them drop. "That the guns were fouled by time and needed scaling. That the vent-holes were enlarged beyond further use, and ..."

"Good Heavens!" Dalquier said in a shocked tone. He glared at the miserable young Scot. "What else?"

"I said that the guns would probably not be able to carry beyond Lower Town, sir," Crosbie admitted unhappily. "The furnace for heating shot is also inadequate with no coals on hand and no handling tongs or carriers to move the hot shot to the guns. And I told him that the round-shot garlanded near the guns have all rusted into a solid mass."

Montcalm slowly placed both hands on his hips and stared at Crosbie. "Nothing more?" he asked, seemingly incredulous.

"I think I may have said something about the powder supply, mon général," Crosbie confessed. He stood stiffly, teeth clenched hard, determined not to display any of the despair he felt.

"And what of the powder, monsieur?" Dalquier insisted. "Out with it! Don't make His Excellency drag the facts from you."

Helplessly, Crosbie said, "The combined broadside of that battery would be more than four-hundred-and-fifty pounds of shot, English measure. To fire one salvo, then, some one-hundred-and-fifty pounds of powder, English measure, would be required. The poudrière of the Château battery contains powder enough for one salvo, but not enough for two."

Silently, Montcalm looked at Crosbie. The young Scot pressed his elbows hard against his ribs to hide the nervous flutter of his tense muscles.

"What," the Général suggested in a deceptively mild tone, "what do you think is the reason for this condition you report?"

Crosbie relaxed slightly. The Général had offered him a way out. If Crosbie were now to ascribe a flattering, or even a reasonable explanation for the battery's condition, then some of the harm might be softened. But how could he...

"I know nothing of the situation here, Your Excellency," he said miserably. "No explanation comes to my mind, but..."

"And how did the Chevalier Le Mercier receive your observations?" Montcalm demanded with an odd twitch at the corner of his mouth.

"He was... displeased," Crosbie said.

"Displeased!" Dalquier choked and had to cough heavily.

"Displeased!" Montcalm echoed with a roar of laughter.

Bewildered, Crosbie glanced quickly at Bougainville, saw that he too was trying to stifle a laugh.

"Displeased! My sainted memory of Heaven! Displeased! The Chevalier spent two hours last night advising me of his displeasure in a voice that rocked the fort," Montcalm laughed. He flipped his hand, gesturing for Bougainville. "Take this indiscreet young man away, Louis, and put him to work. Try to teach him at least enough sense to stay far away from Le Mercier."

Bougainville took the dazed young officer's arm and led him unprotesting from the garden. "You have put the Général in a rare humor," he said softly. "I've seldom seen him so boisterous. Of course, he despises Le Mercier, so I expected him to champion you, but there is more. I suppose it's due to your good sense in giving the Général a good bout this morning. He greatly dislikes opponents who don't try their best with him. You showed a certain tact there, my boy."

Crosbie shook his head. "I have no tact," he said with bitter sureness. "You should know that."

"Come now," Bougainville said soothingly. "You are safe from Le Mercier. There's no need for you to be sour. Your face is as dour as Dalquier's."

"Who?" Crosbie said with no interest.

"Colonel Dalquier," Bougainville said, opening the door to his office. "The gentleman you met in the garden with me."

Bourgainville pushed Crosbie into a deep chair and went himself toward the big windows at the end of his room where he stood staring out over the river. "Poor Dalquier's Béarn regiment mutinied a few months ago at Montreal. They'd had nothing but horsemeat for food and precious little of that. Food becomes very important to troops in garrison, as you may know. It was really not a serious mutiny, you understand, but Dalquier is consumed with chagrin."

Crosbie nodded glumly. Chagrin, he thought stupidly. It seemed a gentle word to use. Crosbie would have felt like killing himself if mutiny had exploded in a command of his.

Bougainville turned and sat on the windowsill. "The Général has had to rely on the Chevalier Le Mercier's reports of our artillery defenses here," he said briskly, all business now. "Lacking an artillery aide, we had no other recourse. You will now prepare a second report, for the eyes of the Général alone. You will consult no one else, report nothing you have not seen for yourself. Understood?" Without giving Crosbie a chance to reply, Bougainville went on. "This report must be finished quickly. Within the week. The army marches next week and before that I must attend a meeting of our Indian allies. I will want you with me."

"I?" Crosbie growled. "But I know nothing of ..."

"I don't require your advice," Bougainville said flatly. "The Indians are all children, dirty murderous children. They are impressed by many childish things. Among them, a man of unusual size is regarded with awe. Your mere presence should be helpful." Bougainville smiled thinly. "And just now we want the Indians to feel somewhat in awe of us. They are very difficult to manage always and lately they have become worse."

Crosbie found no words. New and startling changes seemed to flood his life in the brief time he had been in Quebec. The artillery report was merely a routine assignment. But Indians! And also in the back of his head was a growing anxiety that developed from the obvious distrust and contempt between the French and the Canadiens. It was particularly disturbing to Crosbie whenever he thought of the Comtesse de Boyer. What would Fleur think if ...

"It will not be easy ..." Bougainville said softly, speaking almost to himself. "We will probably find the Indians have become unmanageable. But we must have them. We must."

His voice held a quality of distress that silenced Crosbie for the moment.

"This wretched country," Bougainville said, "this terrible land. But it is always the soldier's lot, eh?" He lifted his head and seemed to shake himself. "Always wars are fought in miserable pockets of the world, is it not so? Here we have no cavalry and could not use it if we had, so we must depend upon these filthy indigénes if we are to know what the enemy is doing. The Indians are our cavalry." Bougainville prodded at the drawstring of his wig as if it were chafing him. "The Général cannot force himself to speak to the Indians, not since their atrocities at Fort William Henry last year. So we must do our best alone, Monsieur Crosbie."

"Yes, sir," Crosbie said stiffly. "Will we leave soon?"

"Soon," Bougainville said with quickening interest. "Montcalm marches south to intercept the English commander, Abercrombie. You will see a battle, young man. Abercrombie will have twenty thousand men, possibly more. We will be fortunate if three thousand effectives are available. Yet we will win. As always."

Crosbie whistled softly. The depressing odds actually seemed to cheer Bougainville. The captain stirred from his uncomfortable perch and moved to his chair.

"Where will we fight, sir?" Crosbie asked eagerly.

"At Carillon, possibly," Bougainville said, smiling faintly. "You do not know of it? Surely you have heard … Ah, well," he shrugged. "One hopes for too much. Let me show you briefly."

Crosbie leaned forward as Bougainville drew a blank sheet of paper from a pile and dipped his quillpen. With quick, deft strokes, the captain sketched a rudimentary map, emphasizing three points with dark circles.

"From our northern position," Bougainville said crisply, "we look south to the enemy. At our extreme left, guarding the mouth of the St. Lawrence, is Louisbourg, the most powerful fortress in America. On our other flank, is the most vital western position, Fort duQuesne, with its line of smaller forts that guard the Ohio valley and the Great Lakes. Between them lies the bastion, the heart of Canada, Quebec and Montreal. We can be attacked at any point. Let me show you what the English have planned for us."

Bougainville drew a broad arrow slashing toward the fortress of Louisbourg. "The English have a new Prime Minister now, Mr. Pitt. And Mr. Pitt has a new general. That is Amherst. With him will be the three best Brigadiers in the

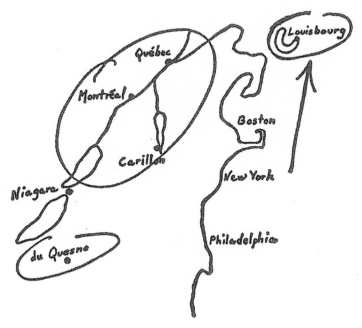

English army, also chosen by Pitt. Amherst will have some twelve thousand men to assault the Chevalier de Drucour who defends Louisbourg with three thousand. That is a situation full of peril, as you can see. But we can spare no more men for Louisbourg. It must hold."

Bougainville chewed the tip of his pen briefly, watching sharply as the young Scott nodded his understanding.

"Now, at the other end of Canada, at duQuesne, where our small handful routed the Englishman Braddock just three years ago, we have a different problem. Mr. Pitt is mounting a massive attack to the west with some seven thousand soldiers under the Brigadier Forbes. And Forbes is not a fool as Braddock was. He will not throw away his victory, nor will he even be compelled to fight very hard. De Ligneris commands at duQuesne with a thousand men, including Indians. He will obstruct Forbes as long as possible, then withdraw. We can only hope that Forbes will not reach duQuesne this year. If he does, the fort is lost. DuQuesne is not defensible against formal assault."

Bougainville drew in a long slow breath. Crosbie watched him, fascinated.

"There remains our central position, the bastion. It can be approached from the east, if Louisbourg falls; from the west if duQuesne is taken, or from the south, following the water route of Lake Champlain and the Richelieu river. Against the three attacks we expect, we will hold at Louisbourg, delay at duQuesne, and advance from the center against Abercrombie, which is doubtless the stupidest general employed by the English. However, the clever Mr. Pitt has given him his very best Brigadier, the young Lord Howe, as, his second-in-command. Against Abercrombie, we will take our station at Carillon. We may fight there. But we have several choices. I would prefer the position at the Île aux Noix, a low island that lies at the northern outlet of Lake Champlain. However, the Général has not yet asked for my advice. I expect we will stand at Carillon. This is the site called Ticonderoga by the English, but since they will never command there, we may as well go on calling it Carillon."

Bougainville leaned back and chuckled at Crosbie's frown. "All that is too much to absorb at once," he said amiably. "Take the map and study it later. Now, excuse me, I must see to the muster rolls. And you, sir, will be extremely busy in the short time you have to complete your report."

Crosbie nodded at Bougainville's clear hint. He rose slowly. "My thanks for the explanation, sir," he said. "I had no clear view of the situation until now. And I have also to thank you for ..." He made a confused gesture with one hand. "I have much to thank you for," he concluded lamely.

For a long quiet moment, Bougainville sat looking up at Crosbie. Then he came to his feet. "We are all soldiers here, monsieur," he said in a flat, formal tone. "No officer of Montcalm's will ever be left to the mercy of any Canadien. If you do your full duty, no other thanks will be expected."

Bougainville came around his table, moving in slow steps, not looking away from Crosbie. "Do I speak brusquely, monsieur? Recall, then, that we are at war and there are many strange tensions here."

He poked his finger at his wig again and waited for Crosbie's response. The young Scot cleared his throat with a harsh cough.

"I could not possibly find offense in anything you have said, monsieur."

"Excellent," Bougainville smiled. "There is one thing more. And do not take offense at this either, if you please. I would remind you that in many ways Quebec is a small village. One's comings and goings, one's private engagements, all are common knowledge. There are few secrets here. Officers in Quebec live in a tiny community and gossip is the prevailing joy of all Canadiens."

Briskly Bougainville brought up his hand, palm open. "Please do not glower at me, monsieur," he said placidly. "You are thinking that your private life is none of my concern. I agree. It is not. And I do not want it to become my concern. I shall say nothing more. My intention was to alert you to the situation. And now, sir ..."

Crosbie bowed in stiff unison with Bougainville. The young Scot stamped out of his office, his jaw hard, his mouth clamped shut against the angry words and the hot fury that welled within him. Bougainville had skirted a perilously thin line between legitimate concern and outrageous interference. There had been no concrete statement for Crosbie to seize upon as the basis for offense, but the meaning was clear, the intent obvious, even to Crosbie, and he burned with a young man's bewildered resentment.

CHAPTER NINE

For the first few days, time passed quickly for Duncan Crosbie. He was too busy to be conscious of his loneliness. Having no one to guide him about Quebec, he managed to lose himself in the narrow crooked streets with surprising regularity as he searched out the artillery batteries that guarded the city. When lost, he found a point from which he could see the ships at anchor in the river basin and took his departure from the *Frelon* that was stationed directly off the wharf from the Market Square, but a few days later, the *Frelon* dipped her colors in salute and sailed sluggishly downriver, leaving Crosbie with a strange feeling of desolation, as if that wallowing old transport had been his last link with his early life in France.

He learned something of normal life in Quebec during those lonely days and what he saw brought him back to his quarters at night with a sombre, withdrawn attitude. For only in high official circles was there ease or comfort for Canadiens. A wide, incredible disparity separated the Intendant and his favored few from the townsfolk of Quebec who endured cold and semi-hunger as a routine affair, taking all hardships with smiling confidence that Crosbie admired—and envied. Their quiet determination made them somehow akin to Crosbie's Highland forbears.

Every inspection trip that Crosbie made was overseen by two taciturn sergents assigned by the Chevalier Le Mercier. Neither of them attempted to interfere, nor did they help him, not even to locate the batteries. The three along the waterfront were not difficult to find, but those along the brow of Quebec's cliff had been hidden by an expert. Their names gave Crosbie the hint he needed, for the Château, the Clergy and the Hospital batteries obviously were named for noteworthy features nearby. Those along the strand were called the Royal, the Dauphin and the Queen's batteries. When he had located and inspected the six city installations, Crosbie took a small revenge on the sergents by leading them on a tour of the western wall, obstensibly examining the cannon, but actually following the precipitous route at a pace that would have foundered a young mountaineer. At day's end, both sergents collapsed at a convenient wineshop and no urging of neglected duty could have moved them another step. With a contented grin, Crosbie strolled down the steep zig-zag path to Lower Town.

When Bougainville had warned him of the constant supervision he might expect in Quebec, Crosbie had immediately decided to find quarters outside the Fort St. Louis. He had been annoyed to learn that permission must come from Bougainville and later he had been irritated by that officer's veiled amusement at his request. But now all that was easily forgotten in the privacy of his large room in the Lion d'Or with its narrow window that overlooked the Market Square of Lower Town.

Here Crosbie felt that he had joined the normal life of Canada. From his window he watched housewives bartering at the stalls for what slender provisions were available. And just beyond the market, on the nearby wharf, landed the sailors from merchant ships and men-of-war. The large common room of the Lion d'Or was the favored rendezvous of the boisterous bearded men who trapped furs in the unknown lands far to the north. These above all delighted Crosbie, appealing to the wild romantic streak that was a prime factor in every Scot ruined by his wild romantic Prince.

For three nights he had been roused from sleep by the raucous shouts, the furious fights that flared in the common room, but still he remained enchanted by the swaggering voyageurs who made the night hideous with their barbarous revels and never seemed to require sleep.

From his window, more than half the people he could see were wearing the sombre garb of the clergy. Quebec was truly a city of priests, with the Jesuits ranking first in prestige due to their success with the Indians, and the Récollet friars first in affection, as was only fitting for the first order to bring the Cross to Quebec. A life-and-death struggle for supremacy was being fought between the Jesuits and the Sulpicians, but it was seldom reflected in the routine of daily existence. The Sulpicians ruled in Montreal; the Jesuits in Quebec. Both contested for the King's favor. The townspeople of Quebec cared little which religious order controlled in Canada; such concerns were as removed from their lives as the outrageously extravagant world that surrounded François Bigot and his friends. Neither the Intendant nor the Church were Canada; there was something more, Duncan Crosbie realized. He had not yet learned enough to understand what it was.

When the path leveled along the strand of Lower Town, Crosbie strode along more briskly, eager to get to his room and find something to drink. He'd been a fool to leave the fort, he told himself. At first the new quarters had brought a welcome sensation of freedom, but gradually his loneliness had increased. At the fort were billeted the young officers who could have shared a certain companionship with him. One day Crosbie had called at the Church of the Récollets to find Brother Mathieu. The young friar was undergoing a required week of 'retirement and contemplation' before starting his missionary assignment. In no period of his life had Crosbie been so sharply aware of his loneliness. Even though the Intendant had warmly invited him to visit the lieu de réunion whenever he found a free evening, Crosbie suspected that he would be well advised to wait for a specific invitation. As for the Comtesse—nothing. Not a word. No message. Once he had caught a vagrant glimpse of Céleste as she whirled by in a gilt calèche. She had smiled at him, that reserved smile that meant nothing.

Crosbie banged open the door of the tavern, walked through the long common room and went directly up the stairs. Each evening he shaved and put on his best uniform, holding himself in readiness for a summons that had not yet come. And later, each evening, he had stripped off his fine coat, attired himself more suitably, and stamped down to the common room to dine alone.

Of his assignment, there remained only the actual writing. After he had finished that, he would be without employment until Bougainville sent for him. He dreaded being alone in Quebec with nothing whatever to do with his time.

With his thumb on the latch of his door, Crosbie paused and glanced back over his shoulder. At the foot of the stairs, his landlord shouted up to him.

"Monsieur, monsieur," he called. "One moment, please."

"What is it?" Crosbie waited.

"These men, monsieur. They wish to …"

A thick-bodied caporal pushed past the landlord and ran heavily up the stairs, followed by two slovenly soldiers, all three wearing the black facings of the Canadien regulars, the troupes de le marine.

"This tavern is being searched, monsieur," the caporal barked in a high, determined voice. "A runaway bound-boy is hiding here, we think, and …"

Crosbie yawned. "What is that to me?"

"Your room," the caporal went on forcefully, using his full lung power as he might on a parade ground. "It was locked, monsieur, and the landlord refused to open it. Therefore, we must …"

"Don't bellow at me," Crosbie said flatly. "I know nothing of any bound-boy. I locked my room to keep people out of it. I'm pleased to find the lock is effective."

"I must search, monsieur," the caporal insisted loudly.

A bright anger came to Crosbie, replacing his boredom with a tingle of excitement. The young Scot released the latch, turned deliberately to face the caporal, one large hand dropping casually to the hilt of his dirk.

"Is the light clear enough for you to see my uniform, caporal?" he demanded quietly.

"Yes, sir," the soldier answered. "But I must..."

"I tell you I know nothing of this boy," Crosbie went on, moving closer to the caporal. "Do you doubt my word?"

The caporal shifted his musket nervously and for the first time he looked at Crosbie with the eye of a fighter. "The...the Governor's orders, sir," he said hesitantly. He glanced over his shoulder for his two men. "I must..."

"You will not," Crosbie said flatly. "These are my quarters. Only His Excellency, Général Montcalm may enter without my permission."

"Sir, I..." The caporal swallowed heavily. Then he planted both feet firmly and brought his shoulders up high. His tightly clenched hands betrayed his inward tension. "I must insist."

Crosbie nodded. He bent forward slightly so that he could look directly into the caporal's eyes. His voice was very quiet. "Try it," he almost whispered. "Try to get in."

For a frozen moment, the caporal returned Crosbie's stare. Then he shook his head, growling to himself. He stepped back one pace and bumped into one of his men. Relieved, he turned to snarl at him. Then, safely separated, he addressed Crosbie in a wheeling voice. "Sir, as an officer, I appeal to you..."

Crosbie smiled grimly. "Earlier such an appeal would have succeeded. It is too late now." He remained balanced lightly, ignoring his sword as he usually did, gripping his jeweled dirk, not taking his eyes from the caporal for a moment. He stayed there immobile until the three soldiers stamped back down to the common room again. The landlord shrugged heavily, winked, and followed them. Then Crosbie let out his pent-up breath with an explosive sigh and shook his head at his own foolishness. Crosbie was in no frame of mind to endure a caporal's bullying, no matter how firmly authorized. There might be trouble later because of his behavior, but right now Crosbie felt much better, far less bored and lonely. He unlocked his door and went through, being careful to throw the latch and secure the door behind him.

He stopped just inside, bewildered. The room had been altered drastically. Both of his cowhide trunks had been unpacked, the clothes and equipment stored tidily on open shelves against the wall. A pile of soiled linen had been removed from a dark corner, had been washed, starched and ironed. Crosbie could see his shirts and neckcloths hanging in a rigid row, with starched jabots standing delicately stiff. His dress uniform was laid out across the bed, shoes gleaming with polish.

A tousled fair head shoved out from under Crosbie's bed, one brown eye visible to him. The eye focussed on Crosbie, then with a brisk scramble, a thin scrawny boy crept out and stood erect, silent and just a little defiant.

Swiftly Crosbie wheeled to the door, thinking of the caporal. He tested the latch, opened the door and glanced briefly out into the empty hallway. Then he locked the door again.

"You, Denis?"

"Oui." The boy braced his shoulders stiffly. A faint trickle of blood ran from one nostril as Crosbie watched.

Crosbie handed him a clean napkin. "Are you this runaway bound-boy..."

"Oui." Denis swabbed at his nose incuriously, as if this errant nose-bleed were a routine matter. His eyes never left Crosbie.

The young Scot dropped his cloak and hat on the table. Quickly Denis snatched them and draped them over a peg near the door, Crosbie fumbled for the tinderbox and again Denis forestalled him, striking a light dexterously and applying the flame to four candles spaced about the large room. The boy drew out the only comfortable chair and held it until Crosbie sat. Then he darted to the windowsill for a bottle and glass. He poured a brimming glass of brandy and silently took position behind Crosbie's chair, keeping the napkin close to his nose in case of further nervous bleeding.

Incredulously, Crosbie tasted the brandy. It was a far finer vintage than he had ever bought for himself. Denis offered him a new clay pipe with an enormously long stem. The boy held the tinderbox ready, his eyes pleading. Crosbie put the pipe in his mouth, drew in deeply several times, then blew out a long gusty streamer of smoke. He sat back and half turned to see the boy clearly.

"All this," he said quietly, "you did all this?" He waved the pipe-stem at the refurbished clothes stacked around the room.

"Oui."

"The landlord let you into the room?"

"Oui."

"Because you told him ... what?"

"That I was your ... personal valet." The boy adopted a rigid stance, a parody of military stiffness.

"And the brandy? You bought that? And the pipe and tobacco?"

"Oui. Of the money you gave me on the ship."

"Why?"

"Because ... because ..." The boy's voice cracked and he gulped desperately, bringing the nervous squeak under control quickly. "Because we are friends."

Crosbie nodded soberly. "Naturally," he said evenly. "But another time, you must be more sensible. Only générals drink brandy of such quality. My thanks, bon ami."

"It was ... nothing ..." Denis said, speaking in slow bursts that gave him a greater sureness. "My pleasure ... entirely ... bon ami."

"Then sit, Denis. Sit and have a taste of the fine drink with me. Or I imagine you are too young for brandy, are you?"

"No, sir. But it would not be fitting for me to sit."

"No?"

"No, sir," Denis said flatly. "A personal valet does not ..."

"And what about a personal friend?"

Denis regarded Crosbie seriously and the young Scot found something disturbing in that steady gaze. Then the boy smiled. And Crosbie grinned in response, the grin spreading over his gaunt face.

Then, abruptly, Crosbie sobered. Denis presented a problem that he wasn't at all sure he could solve.

"You did run away, Denis?"

The boy nodded silently.

"You were properly indentured as a ship's boy?"

Denis nodded again. His mouth pinched in tensely.

Crosbie chewed thoughtfully on the pipe stem. The boy would be liable to arrest all his life, unless he served out his indenture time or bought himself free. There was no chance of buying him free, since his legal master had left when the *Frelon* sailed for France. There was nothing he could do. Unless ...

He glanced up sharply. "How old are you, Denis?"

"Fourteen, I think, monsieur."

"My name is Duncan," Crosbie said absently. "Fourteen, eh?" He eyed the boy carefully. Damnably thin, he was, with pipe-stems for arms and twigs for legs. No meat on him anywhere, but a fair length of bone and a fine way of carrying himself. In time he would do. But now?

"Well, there's no hope for it," he said with finality. "You'll have to enlist. I'll have you signed on tomorrow." No civil author-ity could touch a soldier. Denis would be safe from arrest in the army.

"As ... as your ..." Denis hesitated, not daring to pose the question.

"My personal valet," Crosbie said. "I am authorized one, though I've never exercised the right before. Now be very careful not to let anyone see you tonight. Don't put your nose out that door until I say the word. And tomorrow, you'll be collecting sixteen francs a month as a soldat and you'll have a new lot of troubles. Understood?"

"Perfectly, sir."

Crosbie sipped at the fine brandy again and drew in a lungful of pipe smoke. "In my quarters, we will behave as friends should. On parade or elsewhere, we shall be very formal. But not at home. Understood?"

"Perfectly ... Duncan." The boy smiled, relaxing so obviously that he seemed momentarily off-balance. He propped himself against the table, and giggled; a boy's tight nervous giggle that was mostly a reaction from the terrible tension he had been living with. Crosbie pretended not to notice. He rose, drank off the remainder of his brandy and began to undress.

Crosbie sluiced himself quickly with cold water, accepted the towel that Denis held ready. The boy then soaked a napkin in cologne and Crosbie wiped his chest vigorously, nostrils flaring at the pungent odor. He sat to roll on his long silk stockings, then slid into the extremely tight breeches of his dress uniform. Denis knelt to cinch the stockings taut and locked the knee buckles securely. Crosbie adjusted his shirt, turning back the cuffs, tucking the collar under. Then he sat again and Denis draped a cloth over his shoulders, sliding a basin along the table until it was under Crosbie's inclined head. Denis dredged the hair powder from the huge box on the windowsill, sifting it onto Crosbie's red hair, working it in with one hand as he spilled more powder. Finally, the boy put down the dredger, wiped his hands and pulled Crosbie's whitened hair tightly back, tieing it with a fresh black ribbon. Denis flicked away the protecting cloth, pulled out Crosbie's collar and fitted the neckcloth, folding and knotting it skilfully. Crosbie rose to button his waistcoat. He slipped into his coat and adjusted his sash, being careful to slide his scabbarded dirk into its customary position. Crosbie pulled down his starched lace cuffs and went to regard himself in the steel mirror pinned beside the window. He nodded once, regally, and Denis laughed.

Crosbie remained at the mirror, admiring his best uniform. The new gold buttons he had purchased only yesterday with a portion of his winnings. They made his sombre coat far more sumptuous, Crosbie thought. He moved back to catch the glint of his new gold swordhilt. True, he still owed its price to Quebec's leading fourbisseur, but the debt did not disturb him as it would have only a few weeks earlier. The new hilt was far more appropriate to a dress uniform than the plain silver one he had worn before. Crosbie turned happily, this way and that, enjoying the glitter, enjoying even the light amused laughter from Denis. He tossed back his lace cuffs with a dandified gesture and bowed extravagantly low to the boy.

Denis applauded softly. "Magnificent! Such a size!"

And now that he was dressed like a strutting peacock, what was he to do? On previous evenings, he had waited a reasonable time, then changed to a workaday uniform and gone down to the common room for his solitary dinner. But he didn't want to change tonight. Something in Denis's silent admiration made him feel more competent, easier and surer of himself as he was now.

"I'll go down to dinner," he said abruptly. "You stay here and be quiet. I'll bring something for you when ..."

"No need, Duncan," Denis displayed a long loaf of bread and a heel of sausage. "I am content with this. Shall I ... shall I wait up for ..."

Crosbie saw the boy gulping to restrain a yawn. "Usually," he said soberly, "I shall expect you to wait up for me, but tonight is not usual. Take a blanket from the bed, and the pillow. Good night, Denis."

Denis bowed awkwardly. "Good night, Duncan."

Crosbie locked his door carefully behind him and clattered down the hall.

The broad low common room was lighted brightly with cheap tallow dips that swung overhead from brackets set in the beams. A vagrant finger of light flared occasionally from the great fireplace at the far end near the long table where the landlord served his sparse meals. Through the rest of the room, dozens of rough tables and chairs were scattered informally, gathered as the size of various parties required. The largest group present when Crosbie entered was collected near the fireplace, all of them intent upon a short, bull-throated man with a bushy black beard who was narrating an amorous adventure whose telling demanded much waving of the arms. Crosbie approached them, ignoring the gradual hush that settled over the room. He took a chair at the far end of the big table, facing the group of voyageurs.

Glumly, he accepted a plate of food and ordered a bottle of Bordeaux to accompany it. His voracious young appetite was always on call, but even as he plied his two-tined fork swiftly, he found the strange food vaguely repulsive. He gulped from his glass and broke off a section from the loaf of bread before him. It, too, was odd in color and texture, but rather appetizing for all that. He glanced curiously at the landlord's wife who was hovering anxiously nearby.

"A ridiculous bread, Your Honor," she exploded, glad of an opportunity to explain. "All wheat is now exhausted until more arrives from France." She lifted wide reddened arms and flapped her hands alarmingly close to Crosbie's bottle of wine. "This frightful winter, monsieur. You cannot imagine the hardship. All food is at an end. Wood is scarce and coals almost unheard of. It is this war," she confided shrilly, "this endless war that..."

With heavy shoes pounding on the floor, the landlord crossed the room and placidly smacked his Wife's bottom with a clout that sent her reeling toward the kitchen.

"A good woman, monsieur," he said in a low, pleasant growl, "but she will talk. The food is vile. That is the truth. We can do no better."

Crosbie nodded. A sensible man, the landlord. "And what," he asked curiously, "have you served me tonight?"

"That is sagamité, monsieur, a dish we copy from the Indians. A kind of pudding made of ground maize. With it I have put bits of ..." he glanced unhappily at Crosbie, then away. "... horsemeat, shredded finely and sautéed. Just so. It is all we have."

Crosbie swallowed heavily.

From the table opposite, a thick voice rumbled, "The Intendant, Bigot, has young carrots grown in the cellars beneath his bakery. Even in winter, his food is magnificent."

The landlord shrugged. "This one," he said to Crosbie, "cannot comprehend that a grand seigneur lives in a different manner from a simple man. This one is of the north, you comprehend. Little better than a savage himself."

Crosbie took another sip of wine and bit off a piece of the heavy bread.

"The bread is mostly oats now," the landlord explained. "Only a little wheat is ..."

"Bigot has so much wheat, he feeds it to his chickens," the rumbling voice added insistently. "And he never lacks for the best flour, either. You are a sheep, landlord."

The landlord chuckled mildly and moved away, leaving Crosbie to his wine. A saucer of some sort of pudding that smelled vaguely like the tallow dips overhead was placed before him. Casually, Crosbie pushed it aside and poured himself another glass of Bordeaux.

"Our pretty beau can't stomach the stuff," the rumbling voice said sneeringly. "Too greasy for you, beau?"

Slowly Crosbie lifted his eyes, recalling how superciliously Bougainville's eyebrows had slanted when he was amused, and trying to copy just that expression. Silently he stared at the wide bearded man who stood on the opposite side of the table, one huge brown fist knotted and supporting his weight as he leaned forward.

Crosbie lifted his wineglass and squinted through it toward the tallow dips. He sipped it.

"Well, speak up, pretty beau," the wide man growled. "What are you, a dolly?"

Crosbie lowered his glass and a wild flare of excitement rose inside him. "What are you," he asked bleakly, pretending to see the bearded voyageur for the first time, "A carnival dancer?"

And the gaudy clothes were just spectacular enough to bear out Crosbie's suspicion. From the red silk tasseled cap down to the high beaded moccasins knotted with red silk laces, the bearded man was a shaggy bear in mating plumage stolen from a game cock. But the width of his shoulders, the size of the fist lying before Crosbie, belied any effeminate suggestion. Taunting laughter floated from the next table and the bearded man colored with rage.

Crosbie leaned back, one hand touching the hilt of his dirk. As usual, he forgot the newly gilded sword that hung at his belt. The bearded man came stiffly around the table, moving with ominous deliberation, rumbling softly to himself, almost crooning. Crosbie watched him tightly.

A startling clatter of horses' hoofs outside broke the hard concentration of the common room. The door from the Market Square was thrust open.

Two white-uniformed soldiers entered briskly, stepping aside to clear a path for the officer behind them. Crosbie glanced up curiously and the squat bearded man stalking him froze in position warily, waiting to evaluate the threat posed by the new arrivals.

"Ah, Monsieur Crosbie," Seamus O'Neill said in his hard, flat voice. "The Devil's own time I've had tracing you." The Irish captain glanced around with unconcealed distaste. "And a filthy sty it is that you've chosen."

He approached Crosbie, pushing arrogantly past the bearded voyageur as if he weren't present, sure of his protection by the two soldiers who followed him closely. He balanced himself precisely before Crosbie, booted feet spread wide, both hands tucked into his sash.

"I must speak to you alone," he said tonelessly. "A matter of urgent business."

"What business do we have, captain?" Crosbie asked suspiciously.

"Come over here," O'Neill said flatly.

He urged Crosbie to his feet, pulled him into the far corner of the common room. His thin face was cold, white, expressionless as a cameo.

"Concaire!" he snapped. "Bring me the desk."

A soldier advanced smartly and presented O'Neill's traveling desk, a small polished cherry box with brass corners. Promptly the soldier withdrew out of earshot. O'Neill placed the desk on a table, unlatched the lid and raised it, taking out two crisp sheets of paper.

"The Commissaire-Général has instructed me to purchase your grain," he said in a flat, business-like voice, "for a price of ..."

"My what?" Crosbie asked quietly.

O'Neill looked up. He snorted with thin amusement. His pale blank eyes watched Crosbie tightly. "I thought so. You actually didn't know, did you? They didn't even bother to tell you, eh, cock?"

Crosbie eyed O'Neill resentfully. Something warned him not to give the Irish captain any advantage, even if Crosbie was forced to pretend he knew what was going on. He shrugged easily. "Didn't they?" he said mildly.

O'Neill's features were carefully inexpressive. "The cargo of the prize-ship Brittania which you and a syndicate of investors have purchased will in turn be purchased by the Commissaire-Général. At least, the wheat will be. Your share of the re-sale is forty-seven thousand francs." Crosbie's impassive face showed no response; O'Neill went on. "This is the agreement you must sign. And this," placing the second sheet on the desk, "a receipt for your money."

Again O'Neill invited comment and again Crosbie eyed him stonily, hiding the leap of exultation that swept him high. Forty-seven thousand francs! It was incredible. He had kissed his two hundred louis good-bye when he gave them to the Comtesse and signed the investment agreement she had offered him. The money, recently won, seemed ephemeral; its loss was not real. But now...

Crosbie took a quill from O'Neill's desk and tested its nib carefully, scraping it with his thumbnail and then dipping it in the flask of ink O'Neill held ready. With fast driving strokes, Crosbie twice signed his name and accepted the paper O'Neill handed to him.

It was an order signed by François Bigot for forty-seven thousand francs to be paid upon presentation to the Intendant's treasurer. Lifting his eyebrows, Crosbie folded it and tucked it lightly in his sash. "I should have preferred gold," he said casually.

O'Neill laughed in a harsh, humorless tone. "Don't overdo it, cock," he said with light contempt. "There isn't a million francs in gold in all Canada. Send the ordonnances to Paris if you want to bank your money." With a wide gesture, O'Neill brought out a thin silver snuffbox and flipped the lid. "Pinch of coarse rapee?" he offered. "Vile stuff, but I'm just a poor soldier. Nobody ever gave me thousands of francs for nothing. But you'll be able to afford the finest Brazil snuff now, so I suppose you won't..."

"Thank you," Crosbie said stiffly, "I do not snuff." He ignored O'Neill's sour comments. A few days ago he would have felt the same himself, though he hoped he would have had more sense than to say so. He bowed to the Irish captain. "Thank you for your courtesy in coming here, monsieur."

"And that's all? 'Thank you Seamus O'Neill, and now go home.' Is that it? Don't you even offer a taste of brandy?"

"My apologies, sir." Crosbie spun on his heel, shouted for the landlord to bring out his best brandy. He led O'Neill back to his table and both of them brushed by the squat bearded voyageur who was still waiting where O'Neill had shoved him, as if for him the world had been arrested and would resume its motion only when the big young Scot was alone again.

Deftly O'Neill poured two glasses, gave one to Crosbie and lifted his in a silent toast. He tossed it off and slammed the glass to the table. "You've nothing more to say?" he asked, tonelessly insistent.

"I must repeat my thanks," Crosbie said ambiguously.

O'Neill snorted. He nodded quickly and stalked toward the door. He stopped abruptly. "Your Général despises tavern brawlers, Monsieur Crosbie," he said in a lightly amused tone. "You are fortunate my arrival saved you from that predicament. His Excellency is quite capable of throwing you in prison for demeaning the uniform."

Crosbie glanced swiftly at the glowering voyageur beside him. Then he laughed. "My thanks again, captain," he called out. "Though the truth is there would have been the briefest brawl you could imagine."

O'Neill smiled politely with his thin pale lips. He turned and this time left the tavern. From the quiet room, Crosbie could hear him mount with his escort and clatter away along the cobbled street.

"And now, my fine high-necked beau..." the bearded man snarled.

Disdainfully, Crosbie sat in his chair, lifted his glass of brandy and sipped from it. "Landlord," he said loudly, "advise this... fellow that I am an officer of the King. He attacks me at his peril."

Crosbie was secretly delighted at the utter silence that fell upon the room. Hardly anyone seemed to breathe. In the deathly stillness, he refilled his glass. Then the bearded man roared incoherently. Wide hard hands snatched at Crosbie's neck. But the young Scot had slipped quickly aside, rising to his feet and standing with his back to the table. His broad dirk slid from its jeweled scabbard with a soft swish and Crosbie jabbed it at the man's throat, stopping only when his point had pinked the skin. "Now go back to your seat, monsieur," he said in a hard quiet tone. "Another word and I'll slice your neck."

Hot reddened eyes glared at Crosbie. A warm winy breath panted heavily. Then the voyageur blinked his eyes and stepped back with a surly grunt. He retreated around the table slowly, watching Crosbie's dirk.

"Next time, I'll have a knife, too," he snarled.

"Next time I'll have you whipped through the streets like a common rogue," Crosbie said pleasantly, returning his blade to its sheath. He sat again, breathing deeply from excitement.

The rotund landlord bent obsequiously at his shoulder to whisper. "These men are like beasts, Your Honor," he said softly. "When they first return to the city, you understand, there is no restraining them. They even fight for enjoyment, if Your Honor can imagine such a thing!"

Crosbie shook with easy laughter. If he could imagine such a thing! What better reason for fighting?

"Truly, monsieur," the landlord persisted. "They are not men such as you are accustomed to. If Your Honor would care to withdraw to your room, I have some cinnamon and with brandy and a drop of hot water, I could make a drink that..."

"No. Certainly not," Crosbie said flatly, sipping from his glass and refilling it. "I'll not be chased to my room. Now be quiet, landlord. Take your ruffianly friends a bottle of brandy with my compliments. And leave me in peace."

The landlord wrung his hands silently and moved around Crosbie's chair to speak to the group of voyageurs at the other table. Crosbie leaned back contentedly, making sure that none of the burly men at the opposite table could stir without his notice. Beyond that he ignored them and gave himself up completely to rosy dreams of wealth.

He was a rich man. That was a heady thought. For all his life, Crosbie's father had been a soldier dependent upon his pay and his whimsical Prince. Never had there been a financial competence for Crosbie—until now. With forty-seven thousand francs, he could buy a small estate and retire. Or, more appealing yet, he could purchase advancement in the army. If he wrote now to Paris, he might be able to find a captain's commission for sale. Possibly by next year, he would command a battery in the field against Frederick or the Duke of Cumberland. His pulse pounded wild with anticipation. A new world was open to him now. The long dreary years of penny-pinching were behind him. It would be genuine gold lace now, and the very finest silk and the best horses. Gold spurs, if he wished. Nothing was impossible.

Crosbie's warm and colorful dreams were shattered when a thick iron poker crashed onto his table. He glanced at it absently, then realized that it constituted some sort of challenge. The poker had been bent into a complete circle. It would take an enormously powerful pair of hands to bend that good poker, Crosbie thought. He put his glass down and drew the iron circle closer. It was solidly coated with hard-baked flaking soot. Lifting it with two fingers, he carried it around his chair toward the table where the voyageurs sat over their drinks.

Crosbie strode in silence. All faces turned to him, but no one spoke. Clearly, the others were remaining neutral; this was strictly between Crosbie and the bearded man. The young Scot lowered the bent poker to the table and dusted his fingers together. Then, with a darting swiftness, he snatched the red silk cap from the bearded man's head and used it to grip the poker, retreating just far enough to be out of reach. With the sooty poker well wrapped, Crosbie gripped it hard in both hands, pulling mightily. Gradually the poker began to straighten. Crosbie clenched his teeth and his neck thickened with strain until it nearly tore his lace stock free. Someone at the table grunted in sympathy. As the poker lost its curve, Crosbie relaxed and shifted his grip, placing the arc against a chair back and leaning forward, pressing now rather than pulling. In that posture he could use his weight to advantage and the poker came straight slowly. It still had a noticeable kink in it, but there was no trace of the full circle. Crosbie held it in one hand, tossed it on the table where it slid into the bearded man's lap. Crosbie wiped his hands on the gaudy cap and dropped it to the floor.

"You children must not destroy the landlord's property," he said lightly in a falsely paternal tone, hiding his struggle for breath by speaking in short phrases.

Howls of raucous laughter followed Crosbie back to his table. Most was directed against the bearded man. Crosbie did not look around. There would be another move, he knew, and it would come very soon. Briefly he felt exhilarated at the prospect, but only for a moment. It might be permissible for an officer to defend himself if assaulted, but to invite a brawl was another matter. Especially after he had twice been warned. It was a serious business.

Rolling wheels outside attracted a surprised attention. Only a few carriages existed in Quebec and even those were almost never seen in Lower Town by night. Small bright riding lights cast a sombre glow through the smeared glass window of the tavern. The carriage ground to a halt.

Immediately Crosbie moved toward the door, positive that the carriage had called for him. "Ho, landlord," he shouted exuberantly. "Bring my hat and cape." He strode briskly through the door in time to see Mademoiselle Céleste descending the narrow steps of a gilded coach.

He leaped forward, brushing aside the footman and offering his arm.

"Monsieur Crosbie," she said in a pleased tone. "I am so happy to find you. Captain O'Neill said you were here, but..." A vague shadow of a frown, a meagre gesture were enough to indicate how unsuitable she thought the tavern was for a young officer's quarters. "I am bid to ask you to sup at the Palace. His Excellency and Madame la Comtesse…"

"And you?" Crosbie broke in, greatly daring in the new confidence that came with his new wealth.

"And I, also, monsieur," Céleste said calmly, half smiling, her eyes bright in the dim light.

"Say no more, mademoiselle," Crosbie said briskly. "I shall find my hat and return at once."

He bowed hastily and stepped back inside the common room, seeking the landlord.

The squat bearded man snatched suddenly at Crosbie's wrist, hauling him well down into the large room, stepping in a fast, prancing circle, swinging the young Scot helplessly around. He released Crosbie abruptly, sending him staggering away to crash solidly against the stone fireplace.

Crosbie silently cursed his own carelessness. One faint smile from Céleste and all sense seemed to depart. He should never have turned his back on the bearded man, once having challenged him. Crosbie felt for his dirk, then noted that the short voyageur stood waiting, barehanded. Crosbie dropped his hand.

The bearded man approached in a low crouch, both arms extended, hands hooked to grab Crosbie. He moved forward in short shuffling steps, always well balanced.

Quickly Crosbie ran to one side, pivotted and reversed direction. His second turn confused the voyageur and for one moment, he was off balance. Crosbie slashed at him viciously with the flat of his hand, using its edge like an axe against the man's neck.

The heavy squat man moved back, dazed, but still dangerous. Savagely, Crosbie rushed forward. And slipped.

One shoe slid away in a pool of wine, bringing Crosbie's knee crashing to the floor. The impact numbed him briefly and he glanced up to see the squat man darting forward.

Crosbie ducked lower, heaving his shoulders against the man's legs. With both hands, Crosbie seized him just below the knees. Then he rose with a surge, shouting hoarsely.

The squat man was a solid weight, but he came off the floor like a child. Crosbie had no maneuver in mind. He merely rose with the man who was still upright. As he came up from his low crouch, Crosbie heaved, thrusting mightily and sending the man straight up overhead. With a splintering crash, his head struck the ceiling. As he began to drop, the bearded man grabbed at a beam, supporting himself precariously, his feet a good two mètres off the floor. Dangling there, he swung slightly and in a desperate lunge, managed to slip his right hand over a second beam. And so he hung, arms spread wide, secure enough for the moment, until he should drop to the floor where Crosbie waited.

The young Scot seized his chance. He picked up his bottle of brandy and tossed it precisely upward. It sailed just to the squat man's face, forcing him to let go with one hand to ward it off. In stopping its upward progress, he forced a great slosh of brandy out of the bottle. It showered his face completely and a deafening bellow of laughter went up from the men below. The squat bearded man dangled by one hand, clutching the bottle in the other, blinking down with the drunken solemnity of a Barbary ape.

Crosbie snatched his cloak and hat from the landlord and left the tavern quickly, slamming the door behind him.

Céleste smiled softly at him from the carriage. "Your party sounded so gay in there," she said. "Your friends will be sorry to see you leave."

Crosbie leaped in beside her and the footman raised the steps and closed the door.

"I don't think so," he said solemnly, breathing deeply and laughing inwardly at the thought of the dangling voyageur. "Though some of them may wish I had stayed. It is barely possible."

CHAPTER TEN

The wild exhilaration stayed with Duncan Crosbie all the way to the Intendant's Palace. In the dark, scented interior of the great coach, he lay sprawled back happily, talking with the garrulity that comes occasionally to a normally taciturn man, and is all the more remarkable because of its rarity. Beside him Céleste sat poised on the velvet seat, her features deeply shadowed except for flickering highlights picked out by the coach's riding lights. Crosbie could dimly see the amused curl of her full mouth, the dancing humor in her eyes.

"I had almost given up hope of seeing you smile at me," Crosbie said, determined to push his advantage, even for that brief moment. "I thought you would never learn the truth about…"

"Brother Mathieu told me everything, monsieur," Céleste said soberly. "I was in error. I saw only that … that poor little boy, and I…" She drew in a long uneven breath. "That boy! Did you know he has run away from the *Frelon*? The town-major's guard is searching for him. But, I … I am sorry, monsieur. I should have known…"

"Nonsense," Crosbie insisted. "I must have been a grisly sight at that moment. I have often tried to explain, but always those twittering gallants have surrounded you whenever…"

"Monsieur, those gallants are good friends," Céleste said in quiet reproof. "And I am companion to the Comtesse. I am not always free to do as I wish."

"Surely the Comtesse would not object if you…"

Céleste laughed sharply, an edge of bitterness clear in her tone. "Madame la Comtesse would be monstrously displeased to think I had found favor in your estimation, monsieur. And her displeasure would probably be extended to you. She insists that you are the image of her lost childhood lover. But she could not endure the sight of you if your devotion wavered in the slightest degree."

Abruptly Crosbie sat upright, sobered at the implications Céleste was suggesting. The accursed wave of self-consciousness swept over him and his mind stumbled in confusion. The girl's features seemed flushed and rather tense, no longer amused. Duncan Crosbie cleared his throat harshly.

His voice was low and strained. "This is difficult for me to say," he began hesitantly. "I have no gift for words. But you must believe me when I say that I do not think of the Comtesse in the same way I think... of you. It may be difficult for you to understand, but sometimes a man may respond to a ... clever and sophisticated woman without ..."

"You think I don't know?" Céleste broke in hotly. "Do you think I have not seen a dozen Monsieur Crosbies come and go? Come with a high chin and swaggering insolence, and go with broken spirits?" Céleste moved into the deep shadows. "I knew one of them. A nice boy. A friend. Now ... now, I cannot bear the sight of him."

Crosbie shook his head stolidly, knowing he was out of his depth when he tried to discuss a complexity he would never understand.

"I am not ... those men," he insisted. "I don't ..."

"You don't know!" Céleste almost wailed. "You don't understand. You shouldn't be involved with such ..." She choked abruptly into silence, as if a mental warning had sounded.

"In such ... what?" he demanded irritably.

Céleste moved indistinctly in the dark coach. "Never mind," she said tonelessly. "I could never make you understand without ..."

The carriage rattled to a halt outside the Palace entrance. A double train of footmen ran down the staircase, holding flaming torches high. The sudden illumination bathed Céleste's face in a rosy flush and quickly she dropped her head, covering her eyes. Crosbie touched her arm gently.

"I am very sorry," he said softly. "I had hoped that we might ..."

Céleste brought her head up in a proud movement. She smiled, a brightly formal smile as sad as summer rain. "Be very careful," she said, almost whispering.

The door of the coach opened soundlessly and the footman pulled the steps into position. Crosbie backed out first, then held his arm for Céleste. He led her silently up the long staircase, supporting her trembling fingers on his wrist. He paused briefly to rid himself of his cloak and waved away the servant who wanted to whisk at his uniform. Céleste moved down the wide hallway and stopped near a closed doorway that led into the ballroom. As he joined her, Crosbie could hear the faint frail notes of a harpsichord playing softly with several muted violins sighing in the harmonic background.

"Madame la Comtesse has invited some ladies of Quebec to a musical evening," Céleste said in a brisk, impersonal voice that carried clearly down the hall. "But the Comtesse will not have stayed for long. I will find her in her withdrawing room and tell her you have arrived. Will you join the ladies, or would you prefer ..."

"I've small ear for music, mademoiselle," Crosbie said politely. "I would prefer a moment alone with you, if ..." As Céleste shook her head in sudden, silent alarm, Crosbie went on blandly, "I'll just take myself up to the lieu de réunion, if I may," he said in a clear flat tone.

Céleste smiled with evident relief at Crosbie's quick understanding. Apparently, she urgently wanted the servants to notice her casual, impersonal attitude toward Crosbie.

"Until later then, monsieur," she murmured, sweeping low in farewell as Crosbie bowed.

Crosbie remained where he was until Céleste had vanished down the corridor. The girl's behavior was damned odd, he thought, as if she knew of something horrible that was about to happen. Crosbie's high spirits made it impossible for him to accept the possibility of impending disaster, but Céleste had been very serious. Well, he would be careful. And any misguided soul who thought he was merely the Comtesse's pet poodle would discover his error very promptly. His chin rose in defiance. He moved along the corridor, skirting the ballroom, using the narrow, dark hallways that led to the Intendant's gaming rooms.

Hundreds of candles flared from the crystal chandeliers. A soft wave of heat drifted from both fireplaces. There were at least two dozen gentlemen present tonight and six or seven footmen who stepped carefully among them with wrapped bottles of wine poised for an empty glass.

All were huddled intently around a small table in the center of the room. Only a few glanced up as Crosbie entered and of them only one made any sign of recognition. Captain Seamus O'Neill slipped out from the crowd and approached Crosbie, his thin sharp features flushed slightly with wine. He bowed to Crosbie.

"The Comtesse told me to look out for you," he said, his normally toneless voice heavily inflected now with drunkenness. "Forgot to be at the door." He indicated the table with a quick gesture. "The play is too exciting. His Excellency..."

Soft sibilant warnings from the watching gentlemen reached O'Neill and he lowered his voice.

"...enormous stakes," he confided slyly. "He and Cadet are..."

Malicious pleasure was vivid in his sharp face. He winked wisely and sketched a series of motions as if dealing cards. Then he pointed toward the tight circle of onlookers around the table.

A footman offered a tray of filled wineglasses and Crosbie accepted one.

A thick, wine-hoarse voice snarled from the table. Crosbie could hear the word, "double" and then a deep murmur went up from the assembled gentlemen.

"Great God," O'Neill whispered. "Bigot's doubled the stakes again. He's already down fifty thousand or better."

Crosbie rose to the tips of his toes. In that position he could look over the heads of the watching men. His view showed him the back of the Intendant's head with its high white wig, and the florid, befuddled face of Joseph Cadet, the Commissaire-Général. On the table lay a great mound of cards together with scraps of paper on which wagers had been written. Bigot was banker for the game, and he was losing seriously. Cadet's expression was gleeful, exultant. He slapped down two cards to make an eight and chuckled as Bigot scribbled another paper acknowledgment. The play was fast, without pauses or hesitations. Crosbie could easily have followed the fall of the cards by the murmurs that drifted from the crowd around the table. Though they might have been close friends of Cadet, all were eager to demonstrate their distress whenever Bigot lost a hand. And Bigot apparently was losing consistently.

O'Neill said in a thick voice. "It's a question of memory from now on. If Bigot can remember every card played so far, he has a chance, if not..." He shrugged. "Cadet wins again. As usual. I'll wager I've seen Cadet take more than..."

Slow deliberate footsteps moved limpingly up the narrow staircase and O'Neill glanced around curiously. His mocking expression turned to quick excitement. He pivotted, touched a man's arm briefly, then straightened stiffly and marched directly to the door. He swept his right hand to the floor as he bowed. In a hard, rasping, parade-ground voice, he called out, "Your Excellency!"

Crosbie, taking his cue from O'Neill, bowed politely, keeping his head reasonably high to see who it was that merited such attention from the cynical Irish captain. Behind him he could hear a sudden scuffling of feet, abrupt crisp sounds as the assembled gentlemen disposed themselves to bow.

The man who posed in the doorway was taller than O'Neill, still slender except for a small hard swelling at his waistline. His face was long and narrow, the eyes enormous and ringed with thick dark lashes, the chin long, tapering to a point that seemed to wobble uncertainly as he spoke. His face must have been almost beautiful once, and even now, the remnants of that beauty gave him a startling distinction. He wore a magnificent silky white court wig and he was dressed with the same sort of excessive splendor that Bigot found so appealing. His small-clothes were shimmering pale blue satin, and his red-heeled shoes were covered in the same fabric. The glittering gold buckles at knee and foot were set with small faceted sapphires. His blue waistcoat was embroidered with tiny gold fleurs-de-lis and the same figure decorated the pocket flaps and cuffs of his bright blue velvet coat. Over all was draped the pale blue ribbon of the Order of St. Louis. Although he had never seen him before, Duncan Crosbie knew this was the King's Governor.

Languidly, the Governor raised a long plump hand. "Gentlemen, gentlemen," he said in a wheezy tenor voice. He flipped his hand in a gesture of dismissal and walked into the room, treading warily as though his feet ached. He headed straight for the table where Bigot now stood to face him. "François, my dear friend," he said. His narrow face broke from its frozen cast and the Governor smiled warmly, patting Bigot's sleeve.

"Your Excellency honors us," Bigot said.

"Nonsense," the Governor insisted cordially. "I have brought you a small present fetched from Paris on the *Frelon*." He clapped his hands, two slow solemn explosions.

Two of the Intendant's liveried footmen edged into the room, carrying between them a stout wooden crate.

The crate was eased to the floor. Wooden sides fell away from a large black velvet case that showed wide golden hinges at the corners. The Governor directed the servants to place the velvet case on the table and then waved them away.

The Governor bent fussily, turning the velvet case until the clasp faced the Intendant.

"Now, my good friend," he said eagerly, "open it."

Bigot reached out with one hand. A fat cluster of diamonds winked from his little finger. He flipped the catch and lifted off the top of the case. All four sides fell away, disclosing a glossy white wig mounted on a bulbous velvet stand the general size and shape of the Intendant's head. The lustrous texture of the court wig shimmered like new silk.

"Ciel!" Bigot whispered. "How magnificent!"

An answering chorus of murmurs approved his opinion. And although he had never given much thought to formal wigs, Duncan Crosbie recognized this as a special product, representing not only a serious financial outlay but also a considerable time in the making. The Governor's gift was distinguished to the point of ostentation.

Gently Bigot stroked the soft curling roll that swept high from the forehead of the wig. "Such a quality," he said admiringly.

"You must thank our good St. Luc de la Corne, my dear François," the Governor said in a high, twittering tone. "For it was he who supplied the proper scalps. Heaven knows hair of such fineness is simply not available in France these days. Only a Canadien gentleman can find the material for a wig of this degree." With a complacent motion, the Governor lightly touched the bottom curls of his own wig. "Splendid, eh? It was made by my own Perrier. I would allow no other hand to fashion a wig for me."

Bigot nodded his gratitude and a murmured chorus echoed him. Crosbie clenched his mouth firmly, fighting against the sudden sick bitterness that choked his throat. He stepped back toward the doorway and O'Neill joined him on the landing outside.

"It was really a ... scalp?" Crosbie asked hoarsely.

"Torn from the head of a woman who must have been a beauty, I'd say, judging by the way she pampered that long silvery hair." The Irishman's voice was cold.

Crosbie grunted heavily. What kind of a man would want such a grisly trophy around him?

"I knew a girl once, in Pennsylvania," O'Neill said, almost to himself. "Her hair was like that. It would fall below her waist when she let it down." He twisted his mouth bitterly. Then he bowed abruptly to Crosbie. "Shall we join the ... gentlemen?"

Crosbie halted just inside the door. O'Neill moved steadily forward, detouring around the crowd that hemmed Bigot and the Governor. The conversation had taken a new turn, he soon realized, but he made no attempt to listen. He stood alone at the door, his physical isolation serving to emphasize the loneliness within him. Sooner or later, something always arose to put him at variance with the Frenchmen among whom he worked and lived. It was only an accident of history that had made a French soldier of him. At times Crosbie was dourly sure it was a monstrous perverted joke the gods were playing on him. He stood silently with folded arms.

A flat painful silence had fallen and Crosbie turned curiously to look at the table where Bigot sat with the Governor. Two elegant gentlemen edged slowly away from the group and retreated toward the open door, seemingly apprehensive.

"I asked what response to your request, Excellency?" Bigot's smooth warm voice said in a demanding tone.

Crosbie could see both pale hands fluttering on either side of the Governor's head. Apparently he had shrugged.

"Of course," Bigot laughed. He leaned back and bellowed heartily. "Do not trouble to be diplomatic, my dear Marquis," he said pleasantly. "I know you would spare me pain, but all here are my friends. You may speak freely." Bigot looked around quickly, then added. "I see seven Chevaliers of St. Louis present in this room. And all of them elevated because of my recommendation. But when you apply for a patent of nobility for me, it is summarily…"

"By my recommendation," the Governor broke in sharply.

"Exactly so, Your Excellency," Bigot seconded. "I have so long regarded us as a single entity that I no longer make a proper distinction. Few administrations are so smoothly operated as ours, my dear Marquis."

"I know that to be true, François," the Governor said, mollified now and eager to soothe Bigot. "But I fear that the sly reports sent to Paris by Général Montcalm have poisoned the court against you."

Bigot waved expansively. "The Général does his small best," he said lightly, "but surely there must have been a better reason for rejecting…"

"A certain constant reference was made to rising expenses," the Governor said diffidently. "The Ministry does not understand that…"

"That I must house and feed seven thousand troops," Bigot said flatly. "That I must feed and protect her own people. That I must hold men in the militia when they should be home growing the food which we must now bring from France. This Canada is a prize worth holding, Your Excellency. It may cost us dearly to hold it against the English, but we will hold it, no matter what the cost."

Quickly the Governor applauded and the gentlemen grouped closely around him joined in a clattering salvo. Flushed, Bigot looked around fiercely, then relaxed to smile and nod at his friends.

"I know that Canada is dear to you, François," the Governor intoned pompously. "You may have jeopardized your rightful promotion by your faithful devotion. I know you count that small loss."

Bigot laughed again. "I would prefer my devotion be recognized with suitable rewards," he said briskly. "Possibly next time you should ask merely for a patent of nobility of no rank. At least I may be Monsieur de Bigot, eh? That would be something."

"I ..." the Governor stumbled. "François, I ... I did ask for ..."

"And it was refused?" Bigot came to his feet in a furious rush. "Refused? A patent of no rank?" He swung viciously at the preposterous towering court wig on its stand, clouting it into the crowd around him. "Refused? God damn that whore Pompadour! She has done this to me!"

Bigot's abrupt change from easy laughter to uncontrolled rage caught everyone gaping. Even at his removed distance, Crosbie took an involuntary step backwards.

"She has done this!" Bigot stormed. "And I listened to her. 'Be patient, François, I shall never forget you, nor what you have done for me.' God damn her, I say! I'll wait no longer while she tickles that slobbering old fool with plump young girls. By the sainted Virgin, I swear that bitch Pompadour has had her last bribe from me. Expenses are rising in Canada, are they? They'll rise no more. We'll save millions by cutting off Pompadour. We'll see how that slut enjoys herself without my money. No more, I say! Let her pay me now!"

"In Heaven's name, François," the Governor screamed. "Be sensible. Madame la Marquise de Pompadour is your good friend, as I am. She will ..."

"She will answer to me," Bigot roared. "I swear it. By everything holy, I'll see that cheating slut begging for crumbs again. She'll remember François Bigot then. Remember when she was merely Jeanne Poisson and the friendship of a Bigot of Bordeaux was something to treasure. She'll remember then and I'll spit in her raddled face! By the gentle Jesus, I'll see her ..."

A timid hand plucked at Crosbie's sleeve, then tugged, urging him the last step that brought him to the landing outside the room where the Intendant's hotly furious voice still poured in full flood.

"Céleste," Crosbie said softly. "This is no place..." He stopped, letting the words dwindle to silence as he noticed the ladies standing behind Céleste. "Madame," he said politely, bowing low.

"That is my brother?" the Comtesse asked crisply. "Has the Governor told him of..."

"A refusal," Crosbie finished when she hesitated.

"That fool," she said viciously. "I told him to wait until I could... And with Monsieur Tremais in the same room, making note of every word he says! But come, Monsieur Crosbie, you must not remain in that room. My brother hates the people who see him in one of his rages. He can never endure them afterward. Come with me." She turned imperiously, pushing her retinue before her. Crosbie followed more slowly, looking to Céleste for a clue to the Comtesse's strange behavior. But the girl only frowned thoughtfully, her steady, measuring gaze never leaving the Comtesse.

At the head of the stairs, the Comtesse paused, sending her ladies on ahead. She waited for Crosbie to come up with her. She halted him with a jeweled hand hard against his chest.

"You may not stay to supper," she whispered urgently. "My brother will be in torment tonight. He will entertain, as always, and only a few people will see how he suffers. When they have gone he will rave and smash and scream with his anguish. You must not be here on such a night, or you may be smashed also." The Comtesse forced a wan smile. "My poor François. Why will he torture himself for such silliness? He so desperately wants noble rank. Heaven knows he has earned it time and again. But that... that woman refuses. Always she refuses. I have warned her it is dangerous to deny him the honors he deserves, but Pompadour is another who cannot endure those who saw her in bad days. She will never, never..."

The Comtesse bit at her lower lip with a look of such torment that Crosbie instinctively reached out toward her. She dropped her head briefly and drew in a long shuddering breath.

"Forgive me, dear giant. I am so distressed for ..." She glanced up at him sharply. "Tell me, did Monsieur Tremais seem to pay unusual attention to what happened tonight?"

Crosbie shook his head slowly. "I did not notice him in the room, madame," he said softly.

The Comtesse nodded. "Now I must send you home, dear boy. And I had such hopes for tonight. I had a young girl for you. My brother was to have presented you to her, with his liveliest compliments. But all that must wait. I dare not ask him ..."

"But I ..." Crosbie shut his mouth with an audible snap.

"Do not be foolish, dear heart. The girl is the only child of a great seigneur. A good three million francs evaluation for his estate. An excellent dowry, eh? It would be a perfect match for you."

Crosbie tried to mask his shocked resentment, but the Comtesse only smiled.

"Did I not promise you a rich wife? I have found a prize for you. And now that you have some small fortune of your own, your suit will be received with approval, I am sure, provided my brother adds his good offices. But now we must wait ... for some time, I fear?"

"Good," Crosbie said cheerfully. "The longer the better."

The Comtesse tapped his chest in mock-reproof, but her magnificent eyes commended him warmly. "But now you must leave."

"But later," Crosbie urged softly, drawing closer to the warm scented lady whose eyes invited him closer. "Later?"

"There can be no ... later," the Comtesse said, laughing. "You will have only a short time as it is. You are to leave at dawn with Monsieur Bougainville to visit the savages at home. Louis said you will have much to do before ..."

"I do?" Crosbie managed a short, jerky laugh. "Good God! I haven't heard a word. Why..."

"Louis Bougainville was going to call on you tonight," the Comtesse replied. "Doubtless he left a message when he found you gone."

Crosbie nodded. He did see. There was a report, still unwritten, which would have to be sent to the Général before dawn, if he was to leave then. The few hours he had left would be barely enough. There would be no time for sleep, and no time for...

Regretfully, Crosbie bent low over the Comtesse's hand.

"Return when you can, monsieur," she said softly. "I shall guard your mademoiselle until then."

"And my love?"

"And your love, dear giant," she whispered.

CHAPTER ELEVEN

When the first grey light began to seep through the small panes of scraped horn in his window, Duncan Crosbie was still wearily composing his report to Général Montcalm. Before him the table was littered with crumpled paper. A small pool of thin greyish ink glittered by candlelight in the well made from a horse's hoof, and beside it was Crosbie's dirk rammed into the tabletop where he could easily reach it when he needed to freshen the nib of his quill. A small mound of quill shavings surrounded the blade. Irritably, Crosbie blew them onto the floor.

He dashed his pen into the ink and scribbled quickly, finishing the report in a frenzied effort. It was understandable, he thought, with the facts clearly stated. If his comments ever reached Paris, several local reputations would surely suffer; and if it were seen in Canada, Crosbie knew he could expect nothing happier than a challenge. Yet Crosbie felt certain in his own mind that neither extremity had shaped his opinions. This report detailed what he had seen, nothing more. Its recommendations were sternly worded, but no more so than the situation warranted. He was willing to stand on it.

He folded the paper, softened a blob of sealing wax in the candle's flame. When the wax was in place, he worked his dirk free from the tabletop and reversed it, imprinting the Crosbie wolf's-head on the warm wax. He turned the report and addressed the front in a meticulous hand to Son Excellence le Général le Marquis Louis-Joseph de Montcalm-Gozon de Saint Véran. It was done. Stiffly, Crosbie rose and stretched wide.

He lifted one foot lazily and rapped his shoe against the bed where young Denis lay quietly asleep. The bed rocked high. Denis came awake abruptly, and offered a wide, unhesitating smile when he remembered where he was.

"Good morning, monsieur," he said happily.

In a matter of minutes, water was presented and a towel laid close by. While Crosbie soaped himself and snorted into the shallow basin, Denis dashed down to the tavern kitchen and returned with a steaming canister of hot water for shaving. The boy had worked up a foaming lather by the time Crosbie had stropped his blade.

Refreshed and clean, Crosbie began to dress. He shook his head when he saw the uniform that Denis had laid out for him.

"That is my best coat, Denis," he said. "We will reserve it for important occasions. Today I need a field uniform. The heavy doeskin breeches, the rough coat. Cotton-thread stockings, not silk. And remove the gold buckles from my shoes."

When he was completely dressed, he tucked his dirk under his sash, stringing its scabbard on a thick rawhide thong for safety.

"You stay here, quietly," Crosbie said in a flat, commanding one. "I'll have some breakfast sent to you. Dress yourself and be ready to leave when I send word. Understood?"

Denis snapped to attention. "Perfectly understood, monsieur." He ran to pull the door open, standing stiffly beside it as Crosbie stamped through.

In the common room of the Lion d'Or, Crosbie shouted for the landlord to bring him his breakfast. His long jaw felt raw from close shaving and his eyes were inflamed and gritty, but he knew a tot of brandy and a steaming mug of coffee would set things to rights. And the prospect of action was alone a great stimulus to Crosbie.

Horses clattered on the cobbles of the Market Square outside and Captain Bougainville arrived in the common room at the same moment the landlord shuffled in with a loaded tray.

"Excellent timing, Monsieur Crosbie," Bougainville called out cheerfully. "Hot coffee. I will gladly join you in a mug and then we must be off."

Captain Bougainville, as always, was the perfect model of a soldier on parade. His white uniform was as pristine as his short military wig, his shirt ruffles and cuffs stiffened with just the faintest film of starch. His leather accoutrements were glossy and his metal buckles and buttons sparkled. He regarded Crosbie with the clear gaze of a man who has had a sufficiency of sleep and sees the world as a pleasant place.

The young Scot dourly returned Bougainville's glance, conscious of his worn uniform, his frayed linen, his unpowdered red hair. Never would he be able to emulate the easy grace and competence of Louis Bougainville.

Bougainville poured out a wooden mug of coffee, proffering it with a smile that did much to erase Crosbie's self-consciousness.

"Let us drink to a successful mission, monsieur," Bougainville said pleasantly. He spilled a large dollop of brandy into Crosbie's mug and then gave himself a much smaller amount. "I cannot stomach spirits early in the morning, much as I enjoy the effect." He lifted his mug in salute to Crosbie.

As they stood amiably together sipping their coffee, Bougainville casually touched Crosbie's report, shifting it on the table so that he could read the superscription. "I will have this delivered to the Général when my orderly returns my horse to the fort." He smiled abruptly at Crosbie. "You have been all night slaving at this magnum opus?"

"Most of the night," Crosbie admitted.

"Well, it matters little. You will have a restful day with nothing to do but sit very still in a canot. Though that is not always as restful as it might seem. Your valise is packed?"

"Not yet, sir," Crosbie said quickly. "I have one matter that needs attention. If you could help ..." Crosbie turned to bellow for Denis. The young boy scampered down to the common room and braced himself before them, hands rigidly beside his legs, his thin chest expanded incredibly as he strained for a soldier's posture.

"Be at ease," Bougainville said automatically. "What..."

"My personal servant, captain," Crosbie said stiffly. "Can you enroll him this morning?"

"I..." Bougainville laughed suddenly. "And why should the recruitment of a servant be so urgent, monsieur?"

"It's that or prison for the boy," Crosbie said bluntly, knowing instinctively that a direct appeal would do better with Bougainville than sly evasion.

Bougainville nodded. "I assume you would rather I asked no questions about him?"

"No, sir," Crosbie said flatly. "Ask what you will."

Bougainville smiled briskly. "Excellent." He pivotted and walked to the door where he called to someone out of sight. Then he came back to Crosbie.

"Since my orderly is to return directly to the fort, he can take the boy with him," he said. "I'll send a note."

Denis looked at Crosbie, his eyes wide with alarm. A thin nervous trickle of red appeared at his nostrils.

Crosbie gave Denis his handkerchief to stem the nosebleed. "Everything is all right, Denis," he said gently. "You'll go with the captain's orderly and be enrolled on the muster lists. Draw your uniform and return here to wait for me. Understood?"

"Perfectly, monsieur," Denis said through stiff lips. He touched the handkerchief experimentally to his nose. His eyes watched Bougainville warily.

Bougainville's orderly, a rotund little caporal in a glaring white uniform strode briskly into the common room.

"Martin," the captain said. "Give me my writing case." He sat at Crosbie's table, waved the young Scot to a chair and leaned back. The caporal left the room silently.

"And what is our new recruit's name?" he asked pleasantly, smiling at Denis.

"Denis, monsieur."

"Excellent. You are named for France's patron saint, eh? And the family name?"

Denis glanced helplessly at Crosbie. He faced Bougainville again and shook his head. A fat wick of pale silky hair fell forward across his face.

Crosbie stretched across the table for his coffee mug. "What was the family that raised you, Denis?" he asked quietly.

Hopefully, Denis said, "Rocher, monsieur."

"Good enough," Crosbie said. "Rocher is what we will use, then. Or shall we make it duRocher, eh, captain. A touch more distinctive, would you say?"

Bougainville nodded his laughing agreement. "No question. Denis duRocher. And what age?"

"Fourteen," Crosbie answered.

Bougainville's caporal entered again, opening a traveling desk as he crossed the room. He slid a sheet of paper before Bougainville, pulled a quill loose from its slot and flipped up the lid of an ink-pot. The captain dipped his pen and wrote quickly in tight, rounded characters. He sanded the sheet, folded it and gave it to the caporal together with Crosbie's report. "Deliver both immediately," he said. "And stay with the boy until he is finished with the formalities. And see that he is given his sixteen-franc bounty for enlisting. Don't let the sergents steal it for wine."

The caporal saluted briskly and took Denis's arm, walking with him to the door.

"I hope he will be as useful to you as my good Martin is for me," Bougainville said easily. "And now, monsieur, if you will get your valise..."

Bougainville waited for Crosbie outside the door. They sauntered slowly along the street toward the river, pleased with the fresh coolness of early morning.

"You have never been a passenger in a canot before?" Bougainville asked. When Crosbie agreed that this would be his first experience, Bougainville went on, "Then I should warn you that you will have a choice of only two postures. You may crouch and bend your knees over a thwart, or you may sit with your legs extended under several thwarts. But whichever you choose, you will soon swear you were wrong, for muscles can cramp with excruciating pain after long hours, and in no circumstances may you shift position. These canots, you will see, are made of slim branches of green wood with a delicate skin of bark pasted together to form the hull. It seems fragile, but actually it is very strong. However, a man of your great length cannot possibly enjoy a trip by canot. As for me," Bougainville added with a quiet chuckle, "I suffer mostly in my behind."

As they rounded a corner and stepped onto the wharf, Crosbie could see two canots waiting for them. One lay off the wharf some distance, already fully manned. The other was held against the pilings by several men while others lounged about the stone wharf. Bougainville pulled off his hat and waved it in a wide circle. At his signal, the canot hovering off-shore immediately straightened from its aimless circle and headed into the western channel, ten paddles rising and falling rhythmically with glittering sparkles as water fell from the blades.

"That one is a canot-du-maître," Bougainville said. "It will carry a stupendous load of supplies, some three ship-tons, as well as its crew. An odd shape, is it not, with those great swept-up ends. Rather like the skates that children use on the ice in Holland. St. Luc de la Corne precedes us with three bullocks and much brandy for the feast tonight. They will paddle without stopping all day, but we, as befits the representatives of the Général, will go slowly, being careful not to arrive until all is prepared for us."

A wide bearded man leaped to the wharf from the canot and approached Bougainville in a series of odd little bows, pulling a soot-streaked red silk cap from his wild hair as he came nearer.

"This is Le Singe, the voyageur chief," Bougainville told Crosbie. "I dare say you know how he came by that name?"

The wide burly man laughed heartily and turned squarely to face Crosbie. Le Singe meant The Monkey, Crosbie translated mentally, but this man was not malformed that he could see. The shoulders were wide, the chest massive with solid muscle, but the arms did not dangle to any unusual length. Then why...

"The pretty beau does not remember me, eh?" Le Singe growled pleasantly. "I hung so long last night from the rafters that my crew thought I had grown to the wood. Hell's own happy time they had, with their misbegotten advice." Le Singe walked completely around Crosbie, staring admiringly at the young Scot. "But by the sacré balons de l'évêque, I cannot see where the strength came from to throw me high against the ceiling."

"None of your blasphemy, Pierre," Bougainville said easily. "Are we now ready to depart?"

"One moment, captain," the voyageur chief said, pulling on his stocking cap and cinching his scarlet sash. "I'll just load these valises..."

Bougainville pulled Crosbie aside. "Le Singe chooses to regard you as a friend," he said quietly. "Try not to alter that view. He could have resented your treatment of him last night, but it has won him a nom-de-guerre that he rather enjoys, so he is charmed with his memories. I shall not," Bougainville went on more sternly, "say anything more about the Général's opinion of tavern brawlers. It may be that you did not understand. There must be no more of it."

Crosbie nodded, thanking his vagrant luck. Last night could pass into the forgotten past with small loss to anyone.

Gingerly, Crosbie lowered his solid bulk into the canot, his back against a pile of baggage and his legs underneath three struts. Bougainville swarmed quickly down from the wharf with Le Singe and perched on a thwart just behind Crosbie. Le Singe pushed off and six paddles dipped in unison.

Curiously, Crosbie fingered the fabric of the canot, laying his palm against the springy bark and feeling under it the silent cold pressure of the river. The nearest shore looked terribly far away to Crosbie's measuring eye. And the river would be deathly cold.

"This," Bougainville said, "is a demi-canot. It is not intended to carry heavy freight. Still it does well, eh, with nine of us and nearly a ton of baggage and presents for the Indians."

"Presents?" Crosbie echoed.

"Presents for the childish Indians," Bougainville said. "If we should arrive without presents, they would not be able to remember who we are."

"Will there be many of them at the feast?"

"Who can say?" Bougainville snorted. "Of all caprice, Indian caprice is the most ... capricious. If a tree fell in the forest last night, possibly they all went home. If a comet should appear, they will surely hide in their hovels. But I expect from fifty to a hundred chieftains. Each will bring several lesser chiefs. The total may vary from two hundred to two thousand. But this is a council of chieftains. It is not meant for mere warriors."

"Indeed," Crosbie muttered politely His interest in Indian affairs was rapidly dwindling as the canot surged in a gentle rocking motion through the water. The rising sun grew gradually warmer on his back. The long sleepless night was beginning to take its toll and Crosbie nodded with drowsiness.

Bougainville's light, quick voice continued with his instruction on Indian history, recounting his own experiences as Montcalm's ambassador to the Indian nations. His voice barely reached Crosbie's consciousness and Bougainville's stories merged weirdly with sleepiness to create an effect rather like a pastoral dream populated by painted, howling savages.

Hours later the crew backed water vigorously and slid the canot gently to a mooring along the north bank. Crosbie awoke with a start. He blinked dazedly as two paddlers leaped into the water and ran the canot up onto the sandy strand. He placed his hands on the gunwales ready to heave himself upright. He was stopped by Bougainville's hand on his shoulder.

"You will not be able to walk, my friend. Sit quietly and let Le Singe help you."

Between them, Bougainville and the voyageur chief pulled Crosbie backward by his arms, sliding him free of the struts. Crosbie could not bear his own weight and Le Singe was compelled to lower him, placing him with his back to a rock. He sat there for long minutes, massaging his numb legs, biting his lips as the circulation slowly returned with a maddening minor pain like the stinging rash created by nettles. He could see Bougainville striding rapidly up and down, rubbing his hand gently and cursing in a muttering undertone.

Bougainville shook his head sadly. "We lower the prestige of the King's army, my friend," he grinned. "But truly, a canot is a villainous form of transport."

"For one of my length," Crosbie said through clenched teeth, "it is torture." By holding himself braced against the rock, he could support himself. He began to walk, staggering.

Bougainville took Crosbie's arm and led him up the river-bank toward the small fire that Le Singe had lighted to heat water for tea. A parchment-wrapped bundle of prepared food was lying opened on a flat rock nearby, and a flat leather bottle of brandy had already started its round of the crew, each man throwing back his head and taking a great choking gulp before passing the bottle along. Bougainville accepted the leather flask and swigged quickly, then handed it to Crosbie.

Crosbie gulped down his brandy gratefully, gasping as the raw spirit scraped at his throat.

"Trade brandy," Bougainville said. "It is atrocious to start with and then it is laced with pepper, to give it a certain character. The Indians love it. And so does our noble Le Singe, eh?"

The voyageur chief grinned hugely, displaying a broken tooth on one side of his mouth. He brought the two officers each a cold bird wrapped in a napkin.

Suddenly aware that he had not eaten that day, Crosbie bit lustily into the cold fowl. He was grateful for the large chunk of hard bread. He took two steaming mugs of tea from Le Singe and carried them to Bougainville who had settled himself on a square rock overhanging the quick-running river.

Bougainville tossed the carcase of his duck into the water, and took his mug of tea from Crosbie. "Sit down, monsieur," he said in a thoughtful tone. "There are some things I must tell you."

Crosbie leaped to the rock and sat beside the captain, dangling his legs just above the water.

"First, the matter of your hair," Bougainville said quietly. "The color is anathema to all Indians. Red hair indicates the presence of evil spirits. When we make our second stop, a short distance from the Indian bivouac, you must powder it heavily and be sure it stays white as long as we are with the Indians. Understood?"

"You are serious, captain?" Crosbie growled. "What..."

Bougainville's upraised hand cut off Crosbie's irritated response.

"Indians are children," he said easily. "We must be careful not to offend their ridiculous sensitivities. Also, they have the pride of devils, with as little justification. My second instruction is that you are not to offer violence to any Indian for any provocation whatever, no matter how serious. The blood-feud is a vital part of their lives. So much for the warnings. For the rest, merely stay close to me, bear yourself regally, haughty as an emperor, and say nothing."

Crosbie shook his head and laughed helplessly.

"Does it sound ridiculous?" Bougainville smiled. "Of such is Indian diplomacy constructed. We shall feed them, give them brandy and presents, listen patiently to endless hours of outrageous boasting which will all be patiently translated by St. Luc de la Corne. Then you will have the ineffable pleasure of watching me chant the war-song. That will be all, but it may take two days to accomplish. You will need all your patience."

"I am not a restless man," Crosbie said shortly.

"I have observed your control," Bougainville said. "Except for a sudden flush, you restrain yourself admirably. It may be that nothing will happen, but it is best to know what to expect. Your height will mark you out. The Indians will admire and they will envy. Some local champion may offer insolence. You will ignore it."

"Very well, captain," Crosbie said.

"And let that be an end to formality," Bougainville said pleasantly. "We are too close in years for such protocol. You will address me as Louis when we are in private. And I shall do my meagre best to pronounce your own name at such moments. How does one say it?"

"Duncan?" Crosbie said with a mild surprise.

"Dooncahn," was Bougainville's version. "Ah, well. Practice will give me the necessary nasality. And now, let us squirm once again into our torture chamber for another lap of this wretched journey. All will not be gruesome, Dooncahn, my friend," Bougainville grinned. "After the feast and the speeches, we will be invited to accept a charming, well-greased Indian maiden for the night. Not too bad, eh?"

"Not too bad," Crosbie echoed.

CHAPTER TWELVE

Darkness lay thick along the river behind the demi-canot as it rounded a bend and headed for the populous Indian village along the south bank. The setting sun was low on the water ahead, bouncing dazzling reflections.

At the second halt, a half-hour earlier, Crosbie had pomatumed his red hair thickly and stooped patiently while Bougainville dredged powder over it. Not a trace of natural color was visible now. One of the crew had knelt to wipe his dusty shoes and flick at his worn uniform while Captain Bougainville unwrapped a magnificent black beaver hat, pinned up its cocks, looped on a splendid bordering of gold, and fastened a great white plume with a gold rosette. When he had settled the magnificent hat on his wig, he led the way back to the canot, smiling broadly at Crosbie's wonderment. "It is the Général's hat," he had explained. "the Indians will recognize it and accept me more readily. Such a hat stuns the imagination, eh?"

The crew had resumed the rhythmic hum that helped them maintain their beat. Le Singe began softly to sing and one by one the paddlers joined in.

"*En roulant, ma boule, roulant,*
En roulant, ma boule.
En roulant, ma boule, roulant,
En roulant, ma boule!"

The lilting nonsense-song released spirits long repressed among the crew and obviously they felt all the better for a chance to bellow in time with their paddling. The canot swirled in a long arc and drove straight for the bank.

> "*En roulant, ma boule, roulant,*
> *En roulant, ma boule!*"

Bougainville turned slightly and Crosbie leaned foward to hear what he was saying.

"There will be no opportunity for introductions." The captain indicated a wide plaza in the center of the Indian village. "The gentleman who comes to greet us is St. Luc de la Corne, whom we call the général in command of Indian forces. With him will be other partisan leaders, one with each tribe present. Be sure you remain close by me at all times."

Crosbie grunted his assent and sat back.

As the canot swept forward, he could see the village distinctly. It perched on a bare stretch along the bank, in a space about two kilomètres long, and every bit of that area was crowded with domed tents made of bark or skins. The tents were grouped with no order, but in the cleared center a tall red-painted post stood alone. Here were gathered the Indian leaders, well over a hundred men. If there were any women in the bivouac, they were keeping out of sight. A score of bare-chested young warriors wearing only skin-tight leggings and flapping breechclouts dashed up and down, trying to anticipate the canot as it approached. Older men stood in dignity, arms folded, faces impassive. Most of them were draped in army cloaks or gaudy blankets woven in rainbow hues. A small cluster of informally uniformed Frenchmen waited apart, near to the stand where Bougainville would make his landing.

The young men waded out to ease the canot to shore. Bougainville reached forward when it came to a halt. Gracefully, he placed his arms around the necks of two warriors and swung himself lightly to the dry sandy riverbank. Crosbie followed his lead, gripping two slim, slippery bare shoulders and muscling himself up and out of the canot. Both young Indians grunted with surprise, gobbled something to each other. They staggered through the shallow water and managed to deliver Crosbie without wetting his feet, but it was a near thing. They had not been prepared for such a weight.

Bougainville placed himself stiffly on the bank, facing the waiting chieftains. His ornate laced hat caught the dying rays of the sun and blazed gloriously. The high white plume danced in the light breeze. Betraying none of the stiffness of his muscles, Crosbie strode to a position one pace to the rear, on Bougainville's left.

The chieftains remained immobile. From the knot of uniformed men came a tall thin man with a dark, saturnine face. He wore a fine white infantry uniform coat but below it he was dressed in soft white leather leggings fringed and beaded luxuriantly. He doffed his plain cocked hat and bowed formally to Bougainville, who lifted one hand negligently, as if a return salutation would have been too great a condescension from Montcalm's representative. Up to join him came a short heavy Indian with a fine large nose like a hawk's. He wore a dark cinnamon silk coat, a blue neckcloth with silver spangles, a red satin waistcoat and white silk breeches that were soiled with grass stains at the knees. Large brass ear-wheels hung from each lobe and dangled almost to the shoulder. Hatless, he bowed clumsily in comical imitation of the Frenchman.

"Monsieur St. Luc de la Corne," Bougainville said in a low voice. "We are pleased to see you."

"I bid you welcome monsieur," the uniformed officer said stiffly. "Permit me, monsieur, to present Le Bâtard Espagnol, who will serve as linguister, if that is pleasing to you."

The short Indian bowed again with even less grace. Crosbie heard Bougainville smother a chuckle as the captain again lifted a hand in casual greeting. The gaudily dressed Indian who called himself The Spanish Bastard moved slowly to a position behind Crosbie. One at a time, the remaining French officers, all of whom wore some semblance of uniform, came up to Bougainville, were presented, and bowed. The names rippled smoothly: Marin, Langlade, Niverville, Longis, La Plante, Hertel, Lorimier, Sabrevois, Fleurimont, Herbin. Each moved to the rear, leaving Bougainville standing alone at the head of a considerable procession as he moved directly toward the tall, red-painted post in the center of the Indian village. The sombre waiting Indians parted slowly, leaving an aisle. Bougainville marched forward erectly.

Just in front of the painted post was a large chair, cobbled together of stout branches and completely covered with animal skins. Looking neither right nor left, Bougainville stopped and pivotted smartly. A brief gesture directed Crosbie to move behind the chair. The young Scot placed himself rigidly. The other officers grouped themselves nearby. La Corne stayed in front, standing in what would have been the chamberlain's post if this were a true court levée. Beside him the squat hulking figure of Le Bâtard Espagnol hovered. Regally, Bougainville lifted his chin, gazed slowly, almost insolently around at the silent, standing chieftains. Then, deliberately, he seated himself.

Obviously, that was the signal, Crosbie realized. As Bougainville relaxed, the silence was broken. From the tents, Crosbie could hear routine domestic noises that indicated a meal was being prepared. Somewhere in the distance a child squawled briefly before being muzzled by a maternal hand. Young warriors on the outskirts of the crowd gave out a lusty series of hoarse shouts and fired off muskets in a rippling feu-de-joie. Two of the demi-canot's crew, together with Le Singe, shouldered through the Indians, bent low under the weight of heavy sacks. They eased them to the ground in front of Bougainville. Then a short, aged Indian, whose bulbous paunch was cloaked with a bearskin, waddled forward toward Bougainville's chair. Crosbie stared in fascination at the wide band of vermilion that ran across the chief's nose and cheeks, and at the long, grey-streaked greasy hair that fell almost to the Indian's waist.

The chief held himself as straight as his rotund shape would permit when he addressed Bougainville in a series of deep guttural gurgles and grunts that Crosbie could not believe constituted a meaningful language. Bougainville sat quietly staring into the chief's eyes as long as he was speaking. When the Indian finished, Bougainville turned to La Corne. That officer signalled to Le Bâtard Espagnol for translations. La Corne dropped his hand casually to Bougainville's arm and let it rest there lightly. Le Bâtard inclined forward obsequiously and said, in a high nasal French, "The noble chieftain, Ganwho, council chief of the Ottawa, greets Le Petit Onontio and through him, Le Grand Onontio who protects his Ottawa children, and sends them many presents from his great storehouse of treasure in France. The chief Ganwho sees the hat of power upon your head and his heart is exalted to know that he and Le Petit Onontio are brothers who serve the same father and that they shall always follow the laws of Le Grand Onontio so long as the waters shall flow through the river before us. So says Ganwho."

Crosbie glanced down at Bougainville and at that moment, he noticed that La Corne tightened his grip significantly on Bougainville's arm. Bougainville paid no heed, apparently. He stared directly at the chieftain Ganwho.

"Tell the chieftain Ganwho of the Ottawa nation that Le Grand Onontio has turned his face half away from Ganwho, his son. So does Le Grand Onontio on his golden throne in France show his displeasure at Ganwho's faint heart. Let Ganwho search his spirit for the true path. Let Ganwho deny the voices that cry for peace in the mocking tones of cowardly women. Tell Ganwho that Le Grand Onontio has not turned his face entirely away. Le Grand Onontio will wait to see if Ganwho can find again the fierce spirit of the warrior-chieftain who defeated the Englishman Braddock many moons ago. Le Grand Onontio will wait. But not for long. Tell Ganwho what Le Grand Onontio has said."

Bougainville pointed a finger toward Crosbie, indicating a large leather pouch open at his feet. Crosbie offered the bag and Bougainville thrust in his hand and extracted a small, gold-hued medal hung on a thin metal chain. Bougainville handed it to Ganwho with a disdainful gesture, then lifted his hand for Le Bâtard to translate what he had said.

There was little need for translation, Crosbie observed. A rising murmur had grown while Bougainville was still speaking. During the period of formal translation, reactions were voiced in louder terms. All understood the snub delivered by Bougainville. Apparently the elderly chieftain had not supported French policies when he spoke in his tribal councils. Though how Bougainville knew that, Crosbie could not imagine.

Ganwho accepted the small medal and hung it around his neck under the fur cloak. He listened impassively to the thin voice of Le Bâtard, and when the grunting and gurgling had ended, he eyed Bougainville balefully for a long moment. Then he turned silently and moved back into the muttering crowd.

He was succeeded by a younger chief, a mature, stalwart man who wore a French army cloak shoved back off his bare shoulders. This Indian had immense presence. He stalked arrogantly up to Bougainville's chair, cast one curious glance at Crosbie, then lifted one hand slowly in salutation to Bougainville. His voice was low with a lilting quality that was pleasant to hear. He was very brief.

Le Bâtard translated hesitantly, watching the chief tightly, as if fearful that he would be corrected violently for any error. Then Crosbie looked down at La Corne's hand again, saw one finger rise and fall several times, tapping Bougainville's arm. So that was the signal, he thought. Only La Corne, the partisan leader, would be able to judge the value and capacity of each chieftain. A signal of approval or disapproval would be all that Bougainville would need. Very likely the only issue to be determined was the simple one of peace or war. The tight grip to indicate the pacifists, and the light quick tapping for the fighters. So Bougainville, without previous consultation, would know exactly which chiefs to greet warmly as friends of the French.

"The great war chief Pontiac, greets his friend, Captain Bougainville who speaks for Général Montcalm," Le Bâtard said carefully. "Pontiac and his warriors await eagerly the call to fight against the English. Pontiac is a Frenchman, born a Frenchman, will die a Frenchman. No single Englishman will ever be permitted to set foot on his land."

Bougainville smiled broadly, warmly, at the solemn Pontiac. His finger directed Crosbie to a second pouch from which Bougainville extracted a heavy golden necklace made up of small medallions and a pendant showing the carved profile of Louis XV. Bougainville himself draped the necklace carefully over Pontiac's head. He motioned Le Bâtard to listen carefully as he spoke with a loud voice that carried clearly to the entire crowd of Indians.

"The name of Pontiac, the true friend, is spoken with true affection in the halls of Le Grand Onontio in France. Of all the great warriors who support the banners of Le Grand Onontio, none stands higher than Pontiac. I bring the personal greetings of Le Grand Onontio to his true son, Pontiac."

Pontiac regarded Bougainville calmly, his thin mobile features shifting for a flickering moment in a faint smile. It almost seemed possible to Crosbie that the chief had winked at the foolish language he and Bougainville were required to use. He stood easily while Le Bâtard translated. The assembled chieftains muttered again, this time the general tone being one of pleasure and approval. Pontiac pulled his cloak together with an imperious gesture and strode through the crowd.

As he had begun, so Bougainville progressed for several tireless hours, greeting each chieftain as he was presented, rebuking some, complimenting others. None was saluted with the great warmth that Bougainville had displayed toward Pontiac, nor was any chief dismissed as cavalierly as the portly Ganwho. Bougainville followed La Corne's signal in each case. Bougainville carried off the formal audience with great style, handing out presents with a lordly hand. The matter of presents occupied Crosbie's curiosity for a time. It was entirely one-sided. One gave presents to the Indians at such a meeting, but never received any token in return, save the all-important expression of fealty and obedience. It was an excellent trade by any judgment.

When the last of the young warriors had been presented to the Général's representative, Bougainville rose slowly and stood erect just in front of Crosbie. With a full sweeping gesture, he removed his magnificent hat. He turned to hand it to La Corne and with that transfer of the Général's hat, all formality disappeared. One of the Frenchmen whisked away the great fur-covered chair. Another carried the laced hat away to safety and Bougainville, trailed closely by Crosbie, walked toward the far end of the plaza where several large fires were shooting long tongues of flame up to the dark sky. A heavenly odor of roasting meat swept over them as they were ushered to a clear area near the central fire.

Crosbie stood stiffly while Bougainville seated himself on a mound of blankets heaped near the fire. Then he crossed his long legs and eased to the ground. Kneeling before the fire were seven or eight aged Indian women, busy with chunks of spitted bullock roasting in the embers. The fragrance was tantalizing to Crosbie and he was forced to swallow frequently as he waited to be served.

Bougainville leaned to one side and spoke softly to La Corne who shook his head to reply. "There is no hope for it, monsieur," La Corne said quietly. "They insisted the brandy be opened the moment we arrived. But we did manage to water it well. Not many are drunk yet."

La Corne in turn inclined sideways to whisper something to one of his partisan officers. The officer moved around the glowing fire and returned shortly with both hands clutching a collection of wooden and metal mugs. La Corne passed one to Bougainville and another to Crosbie.

The brandy may have been watered, but the fiery bite of pepper added to it brought tears to Crosbie's eyes. Bougainville tasted it warily and smiled thinly at La Corne.

One of the canot crew bustled up from the riverbank with a rawhide valise which he opened on the ground before Bougainville. He removed a tall clattering stack of metal platters and immediately went to the fire where the meat was roasting. Deftly, he carved thick slabs, one to each platter, and passed them to the seated officers.

Bougainville balanced his platter on his knees and brought out a thin wooden tube which when pulled apart proved to be a sheath for a thin knife and fork. He applied himself to his cut of roast.

Crosbie and most of the others managed with knives and fingers. Crosbie's dirk sliced through the tough meat easily and its point served to convey morsels to his mouth. He cleared his platter quickly and accepted a second cut. Even so, his keen appetite drove him to rapid eating and his empty platter was put aside while most of the party were still busy with the stringy roast. There was another course going around, a dish that resembled a pudding, which partisans and Indians alike ate with their fingers. Crosbie refused the bowl when it came to him. He was curious about it, but he would have to be extremely hungry before a communal dish would attract him.

The brandy mugs were filled again and again. From the Indians seated around them came boisterous shouts, swift gobbling comments and wild bursts of laughter. Crosbie had heard somewhere that Indians were more phlegmatic than English generals, but certainly this collection was as animated as a company of Gascon musketeers.

Crosbie stabbed his ornamented dirk again and again into the sandy soil to clean the blade and returned it to his scabbard. He leaned back silently to watch the Indians near him.

He had become the object of serious curiosity by many of the younger warriors, probably because of his size, he suspected. One of the three closest to him had assisted him from the canot. Very likely his report of Crosbie's weight had caused some minor dispute among them. But the atmosphere seemed amiable enough, Crosbie thought.

The tallest of the three warriors snatched a bottle from one of the others, held it up and drank deeply, then tossed it away empty. He stooped to pick up something and then approached Crosbie, moving with stiff-legged strides. His face in the firelight was almost vermilion. He was painted with only a thin band of black across his nose and cheekbones. As he came closer, Crosbie could see that all his facial hair had been plucked away, even his eyebrows, and all that remained of his hair was a bristly roach that ran from forehead to neck in stiff formality. Because of its hairlessness, his head seemed enormous, his eyes sunken, lost in shadows and somehow disturbing because they were not visible. A short distance away, he stopped and held out a soft bundle toward Crosbie.

The young Scot glanced at him warily. The Indian grimaced and nodded with vigorous intensity. Apparently, the bundle was for Crosbie. Gently, being careful not to move abruptly, Crosbie reached out one hand. The bundle was some sort of fur, three fine skins threaded together at the necks with a rawhide thong. Crosbie held the skins to the light. The fur was pale and shimmery in shades that varied beautifully from deep brown to a silvery sand color. He had never seen anything like them before and he spread the fan of skins wide on his knee.

Bougainville whistled softly behind him. "What did you pay him for those?" he asked sharply.

"Are they valuable?" Crosbie turned his head to address the captain.

"They are stone martens," Bougainville said dryly. "Rare and valuable. The Général is collecting skins for his. Marquise. He would be very happy to purchase..."

Bougainville's voice broke off abruptly as he saw the tall warrior swoop toward Crosbie. While the young Scot had his head turned, the Indian swiftly snatched at the hilt of his jeweled dirk, slipping it from its scabbard and retreating lithely across the fire. Crosbie dropped the furs and leaped to his feet, roaring with outrage. Before he could take a step, both Bougainville and La Corne seized his arms.

"Don't move!" Bougainville snapped. "You can't..."

"My dirk," Crosbie said excitedly, striving for composure and failing miserably. He heard his voice crack with tension as it had when he was only fourteen. "That drunken clown stole my..."

"An exchange," La Corne said in a soothing tone. "He gave you three martens for the knife. And the skins are worth more than..."

Crosbie drew in a deep breath. Across the fire, the three young Indians cavorted, the tallest holding Crosbie's jeweled dirk high where its dark-steel blade reflected bright flickers. Crosbie shook his head and spoke more quietly, trying to explain. "It is my family dirk," he said in a strained voice. "The hilt carries my family signet. I would never exchange it for..."

"Then why did you accept the martens?" Bougainville demanded sharply.

"But I didn't know!" Crosbie's voice rose in growing anger.

"Well, it's too late now," La Corne insisted. "The trade has been made, even if you didn't know what you were doing."

"It's not too late," Crosbie said flatly, a cold rage replacing the first hot flush of anger. "He'll not have the dirk." Almost without effort he threw the restraining arms aside.

"Wait," La Corne bellowed. "You'll insult the Indians if you…"

Crosbie took La Corne's shoulder with one large hand and shoved him aside. He'd insult every Indian alive, if necessary. The dirk had an importance none but a Scot could appreciate. There was no point in trying to explain further. A reigning king would as gladly give up his scepter. The dirk alone remained to Crosbie of his family, of the forfeited lands at Craigsmuir, of the lost country and the defeated Prince.

With a flash of insight, La Corne recognized Crosbie's determination, realized that only force would deter the young Scot who towered furiously over him.

"Wait!" he called again, desperately. He pivotted quickly, shouting across the fire, gurgling and gobbling like an Indian born. He gestured widely, shaped fantastic forms with both hands, talking loudly and forcefully all the while. His intensity caught Crosbie and the young Scot stopped short, willing to accept the dirk as a result of parley, if that were possible. How it was returned mattered little to him, so long as he had it.

Bougainville came beside Crosbie again, his face a cold mask. "La Corne is saying that the dirk is your family totem, your private magic," he said in a low voice. "Then… something about it carrying the spirit of your fathers." Bougainville shrugged and let his breath out explosively. "Let us pray that the drunken young warrior will return it. If not…"

La Corne listened to a taunting reply from the Indians. Even Crosbie, totally ignorant of the language, understood how contemptuously La Corne's request had been denied. A hard hot flush mottled Crosbie's face. Bougainville snatched at his arm again.

"It is too late for that," La Corne said bitterly. "Let the fool go. Too many here understand French, so the damage is done."

The Indians across the fire hooted and screamed, prancing high-kneed around the fire.

"You must withdraw ... or fight him," La Corne told Crosbie. "What he has just said about you is beyond apology."

Bougainville glanced quickly at La Corne, stared for a bleak moment, then shrugged wearily again. "Fichtre!" he almost snarled. "Can you then limit it to a personal quarrel between two young fools?"

La Corne nodded soberly. "It stands just so," he said quietly. "A personal duel."

Crosbie shifted his shoulders irritably. "I'll have the dirk, if I have to fight every ..."

"Be silent, you young idiot," Bougainville scowled. "This warrior is sure he can defeat you. Apparently he is the local champion. Can you wrestle as the Indians do?"

Crosbie shook his head. "I know nothing of these games."

"He will be greased," Bougainville said sharply. "You will not be able to hold him."

Crosbie's mouth was a grim slit. He brought up both large hands and hooked them tensely. "I'll hold him," he said softly. He pulled in a long slow breath, looking across the fire where the three young warriors had been joined by a great number of older chieftains. The shrill excited yelpings increased in volume. "I'll hold him," Crosbie said again, almost to himself.

"Do you know anything of the way of fighting à l'anglaise?" Bougainville demanded, "with the clenched fist in the fashion they call la boxe?"

Crosbie shook his head angrily. "I have no tricks. I'll need only to get my hands on him."

"Be silent one moment," La Corne snapped. He spun again to face the Indians and again spat out a long string of grunting gibberish that Crosbie did not try to listen to. La Corne stooped to pick up the marten skins that Crosbie had abandoned. With them in one hand, he stalked around the fire, holding out his empty right hand to the tall young warrior.

A lengthy colloquy followed between La Corne and the young warriors, joined by the elder chiefs. Crosbie shifted impatiently. All this damned nonsensical gobbling and chattering was vastly annoying when he wanted to snatch the dirk and have done with it.

Bougainville's hand gripped his arm tightly. "If you lose," he said in a low, worried tone, "you lose both knife and furs. Do you realize that?"

"I care nothing for the furs," Crosbie growled.

"You lose both," Bougainville repeated, "if you lose."

"I'll not lose," Crosbie said simply. "As long as I'm alive, I'll have the dirk."

The cold clear statement fell upon Bougainville's ears with the sure impact of doom. He completely believed that Crosbie would win or die fighting the young warrior.

"You are a prime young fool," he said unsteadily. "I wish you well. Now…" His fingers flipped open buttons and stripped coat and waistcoat from Crosbie's shoulders. "Your cravat as well," he insisted.

Crosbie tore his neckcloth free and let it drop.

Across the fire, the argument wore to a solution. The young warrior suddenly drew back his arm and hurled the jeweled dirk. It revolved once in the air and struck point first in the red-painted post. La Corne walked slowly to the post and deliberately draped the three marten skins over its hilt. A lusty chorus of gobbling shrieks went up from the watching Indians who quickly cleared an open area around the post. The young warrior leaped into the clear alone, stamping stiff-legged at the ground like a fighting cock, tossing his head fractiously, eager for Crosbie to appear.

The young Scot did not make him wait. Bougainville slipped aside with a final reassuring slap on his back and Crosbie moved forward in measured strides as if he marched to slow music.

The young Indian sidled forward, quartering across Crosbie's front, offering his left wrist tantalizingly. Crosbie noted the solid, easily moving muscles of the warrior's shoulders. A thin puckered scar trailed across one shoulder, down across the chest almost to one nipple. The Indian poked his left hand farther out, fingers stiffened, and Crosbie snatched at it hungrily. He clamped down hard and yanked. He nearly went flat on his back as the Indian's wrist slid greasily out from his grip, as if he had tried to grab at quicksilver.

A hooting shriek of mocking laughter erupted from the Indians. They called out thin shrieking encouragement to their champion. Crosbie shook his head stolidly and moved forward.

The Indian darted close enough for Crosbie to lunge at him. Then the warrior slipped sideways to the ground, lashing out with his feet and twisting suddenly. Both legs clamped around Crosbie's knees, one smacking him hard from behind, bending his legs and bringing him to the dusty ground with a dull thud. The Indian rolled quickly, forcing Crosbie's legs high behind his back, applying damaging pressure. Crosbie spat out a mouthful of sand. He muscled himself up with both arms, denying the pain of the leg clamp, slowly forcing the Indian back by sheer power. Lithely, the Indian broke free and rolled to his feet.

As Crosbie brought his aching legs under him, the warrior slashed at his neck, using the side of his wrist like a club. Pain flared in Crosbie's head. He slumped again, lifting both arms to ward off another blow. Gradually he struggled to his knees, then to his feet.

The Indian warrior lounged contemptuously on the far side of the painted post. Crosbie lurched forward, arms reaching, hands shaped into claws.

The Indian leaped aside, then clutched Crosbie's left arm. He dropped to his knees and twisted back, bringing Crosbie down over him. The Indian pulled up both legs and kicked, sending the young Scot slipping up and over. But this time Crosbie was willing to concede the Indian's superior speed and agility. He wanted only to get a firm grip on the slippery wrestler. He gave with the Indian's thrust, dropping solidly to the ground, hoping to tempt the Indian closer. The Indian pounced high, coming down with his knees on Crosbie's back, grabbing a double handful of Crosbie's long powdered hair. A white cloud drifted over Crosbie's face as the warrior heaved, trying to bring Crosbie's head back. The young Scot growled deep in his throat and lunged heavily, throwing himself over backwards. But somehow the greased Indian slid out from under. He had regained his feet before Crosbie was able to shove himself up from the ground.

Savagely, Crosbie lurched upright, sweeping his right arm in a hard arc, hoping to catch the warrior as he rose. He felt the impact all the way to his shoulder. He had caught the Indian's head solidly. The warrior shuffled quickly back, wary now that he had felt Crosbie's strength.

Crosbie came raging in, eager to follow up any advantage he might have. He followed the Indian who retreated cleverly, skipping away from Crosbie's bull-like charges. Crosbie swung his arm again, this time aiming for the body, and he grunted with satisfaction as he caught the elusive Indian heavily in the ribs. The warrior slipped and fell, doubling his legs as he went down. He lashed out with both feet and drove Crosbie's legs aside. The young Scot smacked against the ground, dazed at the impact. The warrior rolled up, leaped again on Crosbie's back. Crosbie exploded furiously under him, twisting, snarling savagely as he tried to turn to face the Indian. Through the dense cloud of dust and hair powder, he could see little, but when he noticed the puckered shoulder scar in front of his eyes, Crosbie brought his head up smartly, catching the Indian's jaw with a butt that snapped the warrior's mouth shut.

Separated now, Crosbie could see a thin trickle of blood in the corner of the warrior's mouth. Crosbie ran forward in a headlong, clumsy rush, both arms extended wide to trap the Indian. He lurched to the right just in time to lock his hand tightly around a wrist. And this time his hands were thickly coated with sandy dirt. The grip was not broken.

Crosbie stood where he was, breathing with a slow rasping sound, his long heavy legs braced awkwardly apart, holding the squirming Indian wrestler with just one hand, not even trying to pull him closer yet. He gripped the warrior easily, knowing with deep contentment that his turn had come. A strange silence fell among the hooting Indians who ringed the painted post, and over the faint murmurs came the hard raucous voice of Le Singe, the voyageur chief.

"Throw him into the trees, pretty beau," he bellowed.

The Indian twisted fiercely. He drove straight at Crosbie, dropping to the ground as he came closer, hoping to pull Crosbie down and throw him overhead. Crosbie snatched at the Indian's free wrist, missed and was hauled down to his knees. The warrior could not exert enough leverage to move him further. Crosbie stretched to grab at the Indian's ankle and then struggled to his feet, holding the warrior safely by an ankle and a wrist. He twirled suddenly, spinning the Indian champion out from his body, lurching clumsily as he wheeled in the loose earth. He let go after three dizzying spins, aiming the Indian's hurtling body at the painted post.

The warrior's shoulders smacked squarely against the wood, his head flying back at a wrenching angle. He slipped stunned to the ground and Crosbie leaped forward like a raging bear. He snatched at the Indian's neck and knee, swinging him up clear of the ground and lifting him straight overhead, muscling him up with a harsh grunt. He shouted incoherently as he balanced the Indian in mid-air. High, thin voices shrieked at him, but in his fury, Crosbie heard nothing. He took a giant step toward the post and leaned forward, bracing the Indian's body against the post.

The painted savage face was defiant, the hard black eyes unconquered. Crosbie bent the warrior backwards against the post. The Indian merely snarled at him. Then he shrieked thinly as Crosbie applied more pressure. That was the only sound from him. His thin lips receded as the warrior bit them to restrain another scream. Crosbie drew in a deep breath and laughed at him. He leaned harder.

Rough hands battered at his shoulders. Harsh voices yelled in anger. An Indian clipped him at the knees and Crosbie staggered aside, nearly falling. He was forced to let the young warrior drop in order to recover his balance. As he turned, snarling, Bougainville grabbed his arm.

"You must not kill him!" the captain roared. "Are you mad?"

Several young warriors dragged their defeated champion away from the post. Crosbie put out one hand and braced himself. He tried to speak, but only a dry hoarse rasp was the result. Crosbie ignored the excited talk around him. Stiffly, he pushed away from the post, took two steps around it and lifted the marten skins away from his dirk. He worked the point free gently, then wiped the blade on his soiled sleeve. He held it high in the flickering firelight.

CHAPTER THIRTEEN

In the great domed council tent of the Indian bivouac, Duncan Crosbie stood painfully erect behind the seated Captain Bougainville. A tiny ritualistic fire burned in the center of the tent and around it sat the primary chieftains of the Indian tribes allied with the French.

Bougainville occupied the place of honor, opposite the entrance. St. Luc de la Corne and the other partisan commanders grouped themselves behind him, facing the fire. Only Crosbie chose to stand, his shadow looming monstrously on the sloping wall behind him.

The wide circle of seated chieftains included only the important war leaders. Three or four mètres of cleared space behind them was filled with outstanding warriors whom the chiefs regarded as particularly deserving of the privilege of attending and listening to their solemn deliberations with Le Grand Onontio's representative.

A redstone pipe as long as a man's arm was circulating solemnly along the circle. It had begun with Bougainville, as was only fitting, had proceeded down the right-hand arc of chieftains. It was returned when it reached the empty space before the entrance. Again Bougainville had blown a streamer of aromatic smoke and then sent the pipe travelling down the second arc.

Duncan Crosbie shifted his weight imperceptibly, keeping his arms folded, gripping his elbows when nervous tremors touched his bruised muscles. He was far more presentable now than when he had scrambled in the dirt with the Indian champion, but his appearance would never have gained him admittance to the Intendant's Palace. For one thing, he was bare-legged, his stockings having been destroyed beyond repair in the fight. Beneath his coat, his shirt seemed fresh and neat, though it was a form of fraud. It had been borrowed from Bougainville and had to be split up the back before it would fit Crosbie. From the front, it gave him a respectable air. A pair of Valenciennes lace cuffs spilled luxuriantly down his hands, covering the deep raw gouges of the fight. His face was a livid panorama of bruises, vaguely covered with powder from Bougainville's supply.

By now, some hours later, the Indians had managed to explain away the defeat of their champion. Bougainville translated the explanation to him. In the Indian mind, Crosbie had not won with his own strength. The Indians had seen his heavily powdered hair when the fight began. But at its end, when Crosbie held the warrior overhead like Cyclops hurling his rock, his hair had not been white, but a fiery red, sure proof that his immense frame had been momentarily invested by demons whose power had defeated the Indian champion. La Corne had agreed with the Indian superstition, for it would never have done to admit that a French officer had red hair. At the recollection, Crosbie snorted lightly and for that moment forgot the nagging ache of strained and tormented muscles.

Oddly, Bougainville's anger had not lasted for long. Crosbie was both surprised and gratified to discover that the captain's basic reaction was one of approval, possibly even of admiration. As long as no serious harm had been done to the Indian alliance, Bougainville could permit himself a personal reaction. But if the Indians had threatened to dissolve their war parties and go home, then Crosbie felt sure that Bougainville would gladly have cut out his heart for an Indian feast. Something of the captain's change of attitude may have been due to Crosbie's returning the magnificent marten skins to his defeated opponent, who accepted them with poor grace, only to sell them promptly to Bougainville, who bought them for Montcalm's collection.

Crosbie drew in a deep slow breath. He felt fine, twice as big as life, as if his muscles had grown enormously since the fight. He clamped his mouth hard, striving to hold his expression impassive.

As the pipe circulated, the chiefs began to speak, rising to address the council as the spirit moved them, following no procedure that Crosbie could discern, though there was probably some order of seniority. Either La Corne or Le Bâtard Espagnol leaned close to Bougainville to translate. With the finish of each translation, he nodded his head with great deliberation, staring expressionlessly into the small fire.

At first Crosbie listened eagerly, enjoying the strange flights of Indian fancy, but as the evening progressed, his attention wavered. He found himself thinking vaguely of Céleste, And then his mind shifted to the Comtesse and her warm scented boudoir in the huge gloomy Palace at Quebec. The Indians were beginning to lose their novelty for him and he occupied his mind with casual wonderings until he became aware of the import of the most recent translation.

There was something horrible being alluded to, Crosbie realized, but he couldn't quite understand what it was. Apparently the last chief had referred to the campaign of the previous year against the English at Fort William Henry, bragging of the success of the French and their Indian allies. All that was clear enough, but Le Bâtard hesitated oddly over the rest of it. Crosbie gathered that the English prisoners from the fort had been tortured by the Indians, but he wasn't sure. Then Le Bâtard said in a wavering tone, "The great chief himself killed the English captain and ate his heart before all his warriors and in the sight of the Great Spirit who ..."

Bougainville gestured sharply, cutting off Le Bâtard's blunt report. "Enough of this," Bougainville whispered to La Corne. "I am sickened. We all know what horrors these beasts committed. Spare me the details."

La Corne smoothly took over the translation, summing up briefly the account of an Indian massacre of several hundred English prisoners from Fort William Henry. Though many were returned as had been promised, the French had been powerless to prevent the slaughter and removal of captives by their blood-crazed Indian cohorts. Many Englishmen were later purchased from the Indians by the French, and released, but dozens more had been tortured, some eaten by the Indians. Even as La Corne abbreviated the story, it was horrifying to Crosbie. No wonder Montcalm could not bear to treat with the Indians any longer. He could see Bougainville shudder slightly. Both were relieved when another chieftain got to his feet and began a long, involved harangue.

This was the Ottawa council chief who had been rebuked by Bougainville, Crosbie noticed. What was his grotesque name? No matter. The chief's soft paunch swung from side to side as he pantomimed a slow stalk through dense undergrowth. He lifted his round face to search the skies, shaded his eyes to inspect his surroundings. Then his arm waved forward; he whooped exultantly and joined battle with his unseen foe, striking fiercely again and again with his long-handled hatchet that dangled bright feathers from the butt. The Ottawa won his fight, apparently single-handed. He strutted in a tight circle as La Corne translated.

"The noble chief Ganwho recounts his defeat of Brad-dock," La Corne said dryly, in a voice pitched only for Bougainville. "The potent medicine vouchsafed him by the Great Spirit gave added power to the forces he led, and withered the arms of the English. He omits to mention that Pontiac commanded the Ottawas and Athanase, the Hurons.

"Keen as hounds on the scent of blood, they left the fort with a few Frenchmen..." La Corne's mouth twitched as he added parenthetically, "There were two hundred and fifty French and Canadiens, but let us return to Ganwho's account.

"The great captain led them forward, his white shirt glowing like foxfire in the forest and with him was the boy captain whom all loved. These were Beaujeu and Dumas," La Corne added.

"A whistling bird had brought the news that the English were nearby and Ganwho went forth to offer battle, his spirit clean, his heart pure. Three leagues from the fort, they came upon the enemy, who was following a narrow road that crossed the Monongahela and wound up the hill between two ravines. Here Beaujeu and Ganwho disposed their men, waiting for the moment to strike.

"The English were as numerous as the trees of the forest," La Corne went on. "Actually less than twenty-five hundred. But Ganwho heard the thunder of their trumpets shatter the stillness; he saw the sun put to shame by the dazzle of steel bayonets and gold buttons. The scarlet coats and bearskin hats struck awe in all hearts, but not Ganwho's. Even the long trains of artillery, the white-topped wagons loaded with thunder meant nothing to him. The heavy trampling of many feet came nearer and nearer. Many of the Canadiens ran away." La Corne sneered lightly. "And so they did, the bastards. But not Ganwho with his strong heart.

"The awful army climbed the road, packed tightly in the four mètres between the great trees. No scouts came to investigate the ravines where Ganwho and the great captain were waiting. The powerful new medicine given unto Ganwho lulled the enemy.

"The moment struck and with a roar, the noble Ganwho attacked, slaying hundreds himself, inspiring all who watched with the purity of purpose that has always been Ganwho's gift to his people. So perished the English army, to the man."

Without altering the easy tone of his voice, La Corne added, "I believe the timorous old savage has changed his mind. He will be with us now, otherwise he would not have recounted his only good story. There was much more of it, you realize, that I did not repeat. Ganwho sees himself now as the champion of the French against the English. If you would turn very slowly and nod in his direction, it would have a good effect. He is with us now."

Crosbie noted that Bougainville waited until La Corne had straightened, until Ganwho had resumed his place in the circle. Then, with regal solemnity, the captain looked directly at the aged chieftain, letting his stern expression relax briefly and very deliberately, he nodded. Ganwho's round face beamed in response. Ganwho had just re-lived the great moment of his savage life. He was committed now to making another effort against still another English army that would perish just as surely before the righteous fury of the mighty Ganwho.

Crosbie was full of admiration for the way in which Bougainville and La Corne worked together to create such a solid wall of favorable opinion among the chieftains. Together they were invincible in this delicate sort of backwoods diplomacy. Crosbie could see that the general tone of the council had grown increasingly war-like.

Every chieftain present, saving only the silent Pontiac, had made an oration, usually one that centered upon a magnificently courageous act of the chief's. All this served to establish his staunchness of spirit and his value as an ally who should be pampered with many presents, placated with compliments. More and more the orations were ending with a shrill screech and a wide flourish of knife or hatchet. This Crosbie assumed, was the declaration of war. But God knew they took an interminable time about it. At length, all had spoken. Then Pontiac rose quietly and looked around at the savage chiefs.

Slowly, with a graceful deliberation that emphasized the value of the gesture, he slipped a brass-bound hatchet from his belt and raised it aloft. He froze in that attitude for a long silent moment, dragging out the tension until even Crosbie realized that this was the climax toward which the council had been building all evening. Pontiac swept the hatchet low with a ferocious motion. He shouted something in a harsh, guttural voice and the assembled chieftains bellowed approval. La Corne tapped Bougainville's shoulder and whispered, "War!"

Bougainville came quickly to his feet, standing in place, and with him rose all the chiefs, shouting, shrieking, all brandishing weapons. The captain strode toward the central fire. Then solemnly he proceeded around the circle, gazing directly into the eyes of every chief. When he had returned to his position, he raised both hands over his head and spoke for the first time. His was the startling, controlled voice of an officer who can command a regiment on parade. The deep roaring tone surprised Crosbie.

"Let us trample the English under our feet!" he shouted.

The Indians shrieked approval.

"Let us trample the English under our feet!" Bougainville roared again.

The chieftains made short, shuffling motions, moving forward and back in tiny, tense motion that barely avoided collision. Sharp-edged weapons slashed dangerously through the air. Younger warriors in the background jigged in place ecstatically.

"Let us trample the English under our feet!" Bougainville chanted.

The Indians repeated it after him. Moving in a tight circle around the fire, Bougainville chanted his war-song over and over, tirelessly, his smooth, civilized expression lost in a savage grimace. "Let us trample the English under our feet!"

This clearly was the finale of the council. All the Indians were on their feet, screaming and scuffling like roosters while Bougainville made his circle again and again, chanting the rhythmic war-song that intoxicated his Indian audience.

Crosbie saw that La Corne was watching the Indians closely, shifting positions so that he could see every chieftain separately. When he was apparently satisfied that the fury was mounting in a unanimous upsurge, he moved unobtrusively beside Bougainville and took up the war-song himself. After several more repetitions. Bougainville resumed his place and La Corne continued alone.

"Let us trample the English under our feet!"

In a few moments, another of the partisan officers relieved La Corne in the center. Bougainville took Crosbie's arm and pulled him back against the tent wall out of the crush of weaving, howling Indians.

La Corne followed, putting his mouth to Bougainville's ear. Crosbie stooped to listen.

"...higher than I expected," La Corne was saying. "But too quickly. I am afraid that..." He gestured helplessly and scowled at the prancing chieftains.

"Let us trample the English under our feet!"

"We will give them much brandy," La Corne said, "but even so, I think the enthusiasm may fade. But if you were not here, then no chieftain could retract. You see?"

Crosbie glanced at Bougainville's solemn face. He could understand only a little of the problem, but he saw La Corne's point. The Indian chieftains had committed themselves and their men to an effort in support of the French army. But some wavering chiefs, who were now intoxicated with the prospect of combat, might reconsider by the cold light of morning. However, if the Général's representative had already left, then the chiefs could not alter their decisions without dishonoring themselves. From Bougainville's thoughtfulness, Crosbie realized that the captain considered it a useful safeguard.

"Much prestige was lost when the Governor's brother bungled our winter campaign," La Corne said irritably. "Rigaud should never have commanded that attack. Now the Indians are all depressed and..."

Bougainville made an abrupt gesture. "I think you are right," he said quietly. "Get my canot crew together and have Le Singe collect my property. We will leave as soon as we can safely slip away."

CHAPTER FOURTEEN

Duncan Crosbie climbed wearily up the darkened staircase to his room at the Lion d'Or. It had been daylight for two hours, but the bleak stormy morning did nothing to brighten the gloom. Crosbie halted outside his room to unlock the door. He entered, tossed his hat and cloak on a chair.

Last night Captain Bougainville had spent another nervous hour before the French party had been able to leave. Sitting on a sandy stretch of riverbank with only his cloak for protection did nothing to soothe Crosbie's bruised muscles. And the long hours of crouching in the canot on the return to Quebec had finally stiffened the young Scot so drastically that Le Singe had been required to massage him briskly before he could stand alone. Now the last short climb up the tavern stairs seemed the most trying part of the entire journey.

Inside his room, Duncan Crosbie expelled a lusty sigh of relief. He fumbled for his tinderbox. Crosbie's fingers were too stiff to manipulate the flint and steel deftly, and he ground away a great spray of flint before he managed to strike a light and touch it to the stub of his candle.

A sharp rustling from a dark corner halted Crosbie. He stiffened, then swirled in a tight spiral, all weariness forgotten. His right hand flicked out his dirk and his left swooped toward the candle, dashing it to the floor. Crosbie waited in the darkness, straining to hear the sound again.

"Monsieur? Monsieur Crosbie, is that you?"

Crosbie snorted when he heard that low hesitant voice. In his tiredness he had completely forgotten about Denis.

"Denis," he said thickly. "Denis, my boy. I'm a great gormless idiot. I quite forgot you were here."

He rammed his dirk home and groped along the floor for his candle, lighting it again and placing it carefully on the table.

Denis struggled up from a folded blanket in the far corner. "I was waiting, monsieur," he said drowsily, "but I must have fallen asleep."

"No matter." Crosbie stripped off his coat and waistcoat, draped them over a peg and carefully hung his swordbelt over them. The scabbarded dirk was eased lovingly to the table. "The landlord is at work, Denis. Run down and see if he has something for us to eat." He pulled off his neckcloth and freed his shirt at neck and wrists. "Why were you waiting up for me?" he asked casually.

Denis came erect, shivering. He rubbed one bare foot on the other for warmth. "The priest," he said. "The priest wanted..."

Crosbie stripped his shirt off. "Priest? What priest?"

"Not a priest, Duncan," a solemn voice said quietly. "A friar. I must have fallen asleep, too. What time is..."

"Mathieu," Crosbie growled in surprise. "What brings you here?" He touched Denis lightly. "Get to the kitchen, boy. At least find us some coffee or tea." He sat heavily and kicked off his buckled shoes. "Well, Mathieu, have the good brothers..."

"My visit does not concern the Récollet order," Brother Mathieu said with all his familiar stiffness. He rose from Crosbie's bed, adjusted his grey robe and stood silently, waiting until Denis should leave him alone with Crosbie. He followed the boy, closed the door carefully, then returned.

"I received permission to come here last evening. Your orderly said you would not be back, but I thought it best to wait. I have little time and it was important for me to speak to you." Brother Mathieu touched his lower lip with one finger. "That orderly, Duncan. Haven't I seen him..."

"Don't ask me," Crosbie said crisply. "You wouldn't want to know. Well, what's so important, Mathieu?"

"Isn't he the boy we saw on the *Frelon*? The one who ..."

"He's a soldier of the King, Mathieu," Crosbie growled. "Let it go at that. Now, what is the urgency, Mathieu? Has a girl ..."

"Your levity is as ill-advised as ever, Duncan," the little friar said testily. "If you have rescued that boy from the *Frelon*, I would certainly not condemn you, even if you had broken a law. You are always too eager to hide your goodness, Duncan. But enough of that. The boy is in good hands; I know that. I have come here to warn you, Duncan."

"Warn me?" Crosbie repeated with a smothered yawn.

Brother Mathieu cleared his throat sharply and coughed twice. "You might offer me a glass of something, Duncan," he said.

"My apologies, Mathieu." Crosbie struggled with the laces of his breeches. "There is a bottle of excellent brandy here somewhere." He prowled about the room, fumbling along the windowsill, exploring the shelves. "Well, it seems to be hidden. But here's a bottle of indifferent Burgundy."

Brother Mathieu accepted a glass of wine from Crosbie and sipped at it thirstily. "It is really a very pleasant wine, Duncan," he said in a voice that was clear and steady now. "Far better than the wine the brothers can afford."

"But I've taken no oath of poverty," Duncan Crosbie said amiably. "I buy poor wine because I'm poor." With a sudden rush of memory, he realized that he wasn't poor any longer. The immense sum of money he commanded had actually slipped from his mind. Why he wasn't poor at all! The best wines would soon be a matter of daily routine for him. "I suppose I should say that formerly I was poor," he added, still smiling at the thought that he had forgotten. "I've managed to make a little money lately."

"I have heard," Brother Mathieu said tartly. "All Quebec has heard."

"I doubt if all Quebec knows I am alive," Crosbie laughed.

Brother Mathieu shook his head sadly. "Duncan, you are sometimes very silly. Every house in Quebec has at least one French soldier quartered in it and soldiers gossip, especially about young giants of meagre rank who purposely offend such important men as the Chevalier Le Mercier. And your fantastic brawl with the voyageurs in this vile tavern was a charming scandal, I can tell you. It was through that tale that I knew where to find you."

"Very well," Crosbie said agreeably. "Soldiers gossip, so you knew where I was. But why did you want to find me?" Hurriedly, he added, "Not that you are unwelcome, Mathieu. Never that. But you will admit the hour is unusual, even for spiritual errands."

"This will rank as an errand of mercy," the pudgy friar said solemnly. "Please sit down, Duncan. You must be very serious and hear me out."

Crosbie drew a chair around to face Brother Mathieu. "Now, Mathieu," he said heavily. "Now I am serious. And very sleepy." He rubbed at a painful bruise on his arm.

"First I must say that I regret not having been able to welcome you when you called at the College of the Récollets last week. I have been trying to learn something of the work that will soon be my assignment among the savages."

Crosbie grinned. "I've seen something of the savages recently. They have need of your gentle services, Mathieu."

"I pray that I shall be able to help them," Brother Mathieu said placidly. "In my course of instruction I talked with many local residents who are familiar with Indians. It was through these talks that I first heard of... what I wish to tell you."

Crosbie stifled a yawn. "You are being... ominous, Mathieu."

"I believe the news to be ominous, Duncan. I wish my information were more complete, less vague. But I will soon be leaving Quebec, so I must pass on what I have heard."

Crosbie shuddered slightly in the cool room. The little friar sipped again from his wineglass and Crosbie reached for the bottle, tilting it high in a long draught.

"You have recently received a large sum of money," Brother Mathieu said severely. "I shall not comment on the ethics of your business affairs. You have the money, that is the crux of the affair. In some manner, the money will serve to ruin you."

Crosbie shifted uncertainly, embarrassed for Mathieu. He hoped the young friar was not going to moralize at him. The Church had its views about money. A young soldier had his. They might not be the same, but there was no necessary conflict, that Crosbie could see.

"I first heard you mentioned as one of the Intendant's favorites some days ago," the friar went on sternly. "The townspeople were slightly surprised, for Monsieur Bigot does not usually find Frenchmen very much to his taste. Nor do most Canadiens, I find. Then I heard of the new wealth which you had accumulated through Monsieur Bigot's favor. My informant seemed highly critical. He told me that he was sure you were being paid for some infamous purpose by the Intendant and being paid very well."

Crosbie opened his mouth to object, then closed it when the rotund young friar lifted one hand, commanding silence.

"Later a woman I know, a woman of malicious tongue, insisted to me that you were hired as stud to the Comtesse de Boyer and being paid a handsome fee per leap. These local people, even the women, are given to blunt speech, I have observed. Please do not interrupt, Duncan."

"I didn't say a word."

"You were about to. I could see it in your eyes. I will make no comment on these two statements I have repeated. Both may have no basis save casual malice. The third point, however, was so disturbing to me that I considered it my duty as a friend to come to you at once."

Brother Mathieu's smooth round face was heavy with sorrow as he gazed directly at the young Scot.

"I called yesterday at the..."

A timid rap on the closed door made him break off abruptly. "We must be private, Duncan," he said sharply.

"All right, Mathieu," Crosbie agreed. "Come in," he called.

Denis backed into the room, balancing a wooden tray with a steaming earthenware jug, several ungainly wooden piggins and a warm, newly baked loaf of crusty bread. He slid the tray onto the table before Crosbie and straightened with a triumphant smile.

"Excellent," Crosbie said. He glanced sharply at the boy. "Turn around, soldat," he snapped harshly. "Completely around."

Denis rotated proudly. His fine silky hair was heavily powdered now and held back by a ribbon. The white uniform coat with its violet facings was an atrocious fit. The smallclothes were slightly better, and the high black gaiters glistened with recent polishing. The boy's stock was sharply starched, cutting into the flesh of his throat, forcing his chin high.

"Very good," Crosbie said at length. "You will search out a tailor immediately after breakfast and have that uniform altered to fit. Have the bill sent to me. Now, go have your breakfast in the kitchen. Brother Mathieu wishes to speak to me in complete privacy."

Dennis nodded happily and turned to the door.

Crosbie poured coffee. He tore off a large chunk of bread, took the remainder of the loaf and a piggin of coffee over to Mathieu. "Well, get on with the warning," he said lightly.

Brother Mathieu breathed heavily on the hot coffee. "I was about to tell you of my call at the Intendant's Palace," he said. "I went to pay my respects to Monsieur Bigot and to the Comtesse. I was placed in an anteroom to wait. While I was there, I heard a conversation between two men in the hallway outside. One man mentioned your name, laughing rather contemptuously as he spoke. The other man said that the red-haired giant, obviously meaning you, would no longer be a nuisance, since you had the money now and that would be the end of you. That is actually all that I heard. The tone of voice was truly shocking to me, for it expressed an evil gloating that was clearly ungodly in its passion. I hope you will accept my judgment of that."

"I accept it," Crosbie said with a mouthful of bread. He gulped at his coffee. "Who were the …"

"The first man was a Captain O'Neill who is a soldier of Canadien regulars, the troupes de la marine. The other I knew, since we journeyed from France together on the *Frelon*. His name is Michel Colbert, an extremely thin …"

"I know the man," Crosbie said crisply. "Those were his words? You have actually quoted him?"

"I was very careful, Duncan," Brother Mathieu said.

"What in hell's name can it mean?" Crosbie demanded, coming irritably to his feet.

The young Scot's bewildered annoyance brought a reassuring smile from Brother Mathieu. "This is, indeed, done in the name of Hell," he intoned. "I distrust these men. There is evil about them. You understand why I thought it necessary to warn you."

"Yes. And I am grateful. But what …" Crosbie's broad hand carved a flat gesture in the air. "Well, damn them both," he said harshly. "I'll see them in hell before they ruin me. But what does the money have to do with them? I got the money from …"

From the Comtesse, he finished silently. She had invested his winnings for him. And she was Bigot's sister. Seamus O'Neill was Bigot's man. So, apparently, was Colbert. And Crosbie's new wealth had come through Bigot's favor. Since all belonged to the same group, the threats Mathieu had overheard should be given serious attention. But why had he been allowed to make such an enormous profit, if Bigot planned only to ruin him later?

"I don't understand any of this," he said flatly.

"Be wary, Duncan," Brother Mathieu said soberly. He finished his coffee and returned the piggin to the table. "Put your trust only in God's mercy and be very careful in dealing with evil men. But there are also good men here, men like the Général, and his aide Louis Bougainville who had both befriended and instructed you, I am told." Brother Mathieu smiled. Clearly he considered that the young Scot would be better for instruction.

"Aye," Crosbie agreed. With the memory of the Indian council still clearly in his mind, he added, "I am grateful for that instruction, Mathieu. Captain Bougainville is a man to admire, perhaps a man of real brilliance."

"In more ways than you know, I suspect," Brother Mathieu said slowly. "He was a successful young lawyer and a member of the Parliament of Paris before he joined the army. He served as military attaché with our Embassy in London and while he was there he published a treatise on the integral calculus which earned him the Fellowship of the English Royal Academy. A brilliant young officer, Duncan. Montcalm chose him over much more experienced men when he needed an aide. Bougainville is erratic and somewhat frivolous, I fear, for the dark mysteries of science are simple to him. But he will mature well, I am sure. And France has few men of such immense capacity. You are fortunate to have such an instructor, Duncan."

Crosbie whistled softly. He nodded, genuinely impressed. Bougainville's talents were obvious to anyone, but Mathieu's brief outline of the captain's background showed him why Montcalm's great confidence in his young aide was thoroughly justified.

Brother Mathieu touched his shoulder lightly. "Now I must go, Duncan. I hope my warning will save you from whatever trap these vicious men have planned for you."

Crosbie turned to the young friar who stood belligerently in front of him, soft hands clenched fiercely, his round chin aggressively firm. Mathieu was deeply persuaded of a danger to Crosbie. As a peaceful man, he could not advocate violence, but his truculent air of defiance was designed as an example for Crosbie. If the young Scot needed spiritual guidance, he need only look at Brother Mathieu. Crosbie smiled at the pudgy friar with genuine affection.

"I promise you, Mathieu," he said calmly, "they'll wish they had never been born. Now that you've warned me, I'll see that ..." He let one huge fist slam to the table heavily.

"I am no longer worried, Duncan," Brother Mathieu said staunchly. "But if I can assist you in any way ..."

"I could ask for no stouter champion, Mathieu," Crosbie said. He rose and put one hand on the friar's shoulder. "I owe you something for this warning. Someday I'll manage to repay it."

Brother Mathieu dropped his eyes in confusion. His smooth round face reddened deeply and he fumbled at his plain wooden rosary. Crosbie noted his pudgy softness and wondered again that these signs of physical weakness gave no hint of the indomitable spirit within. Brother Mathieu nodded again, almost to himself.

"Be sure to let me know how it all turns out, Duncan," he said soberly. "I will write when I am settled. And now, I must ..."

"When do you leave Quebec?" Crosbie asked, walking to the door with his friend. "Soon, I take it?"

"Within the next few days. I go first to Montreal, then on across the Lakes to the Détroit. From there I will be sent wherever I may best be used."

"I envy you," Crosbie said sincerely. "It will be a great adventure, Mathieu."

"My single prayer is that I may help these poor indigènes," the friar said, his eyes fixed firmly on the floor. "I have seen many of them lately, squalid, naked heathens who should arouse only pity. Yet ... I find them ... terrifying. They have a natural ferocity that turns me to ice, it is so far beyond my understanding. They are like cruel children who have learned only how to kill. With them, I am always frightened. I pray I will learn to conquer this fear."

Crosbie stared at the young friar. His admission of fear was spoken in a quiet, even voice. Brother Mathieu was afraid but he had looked closely at his fear and found within himself a hope of conquering. "This fear worries me only because I may, through weakness, be tempted to save myself and betray my work."

"The prospect doesn't worry me," Crosbie said formally. At Brother Mathieu's silent direction, he swung the door open and bowed. "Au revoir, Mathieu."

The rotund little friar lifted one soft hand in a sketchy benison. "Au revoir, Duncan. God guide you, my friend." Brother Mathieu slipped through the doorway and walked with quick firm steps to the stairs.

Crosbie eased the door shut. He went back to the table and poured more coffee. Nervously, he wandered to the window. He could see the dim outline of Brother Mathieu's flapping robe as the young friar turned toward the Récollet Collège. A simple man, Mathieu. Crosbie envied him the sureness he felt, even the fear that plagued him, for Mathieu's life would never be frustrated with vague desires, confused ambition. Mathieu was a simple man and Duncan Crosbie by comparison felt old and iniquitous with complex dreams that seemed to lead nowhere.

He turned. His eyes focussed briefly on the wide flock bed in the corner. After a sleepless night, he had been looking forward to a good morning's sleep. Even as he thought of it, he knew there was no possibility of rest for him. Not after the warning Brother Mathieu had brought. Crosbie stripped off his soiled breeches and began to lay but a fresh uniform.

Mathieu had brought the warning. The rest was up to Crosbie and he could think of only one quick, sure way to find out what substance there was to Mathieu's report. Quickly, with irritable, jerky motions, he stropped his razor, his mouth clamped hard into a thin, down-curving line of determination.

CHAPTER FIFTEEN

While Crosbie was dressing, a low muttering thunder rumbled constantly from the river, echoing like a distant cannonade from the Laurentian mountains. Swearing harshly under his breath, Crosbie sat again and stripped off his fine silk stockings, changing them for a cheaper cotton pair, clipping his buckles on the flaps of an old pair of shoes. He stripped the lace and cockade from his hat and unpinned the cocks, anticipating the heavy rain that would soon follow the thunder. He wrapped a thick scarf around his neck and tossed his rain cape over his shoulders. Made of the thick black tarpaulin used to protect cannon in foul weather, it was a favored garment among young artillery officers. His was meagrely decorated with a thin strip of sham-gold lace that had long since worn to a brassy glint, and a shabby velvet collar. Crosbie surveyed his looming figure in the mirror and snorted with no pleasure. A fine villainous sight he was. But then, the apparent villainy might be an asset today.

He stamped solidly down the stairs and out onto the stormy Market Square. Merchants and shoppers were huddled out of sight and as Crosbie stepped outside, great spattering drops smacked on the cobblestones before him. Crosbie hunched his shoulders high, pulled his tarpaulin cape closed. He turned toward the suburb of St. Roch where the Intendant had his Palace.

Many of the stone warehouses and wharf sheds were empty now that the English blockade had almost eliminated shipping from France. The enemy frigates off the mouth of the St. Lawrence were seizing fortunes in prizes every week, forcing the straitened economy of Canada into an even more perilous position. But though they were empty of goods, the warehouses had been found very useful. Here were billeted hundreds of the refugees from the Gaspé peninsula, farmers and trappers who had fled before the English invasion aimed at Louisbourg. Most of the Acadians had remained at home, all of them fearful that the English, if they won, would again round them up and ship them away like black slaves. But many had fled toward Quebec. Penniless, ragged, hungry, they were a serious drain on the limited food supplies of the city. They huddled wherever they could find shelter and prayed incessantly for an end to war. Not for victory, merely for peace. Already they were late for the Spring planting. Another few weeks and it might be impossible for them to make any sort of crop this year. And they knew what that meant. The King of France protected his children, the Church comforted them, but famine was stronger than either. The Acadians had known desperate times before, and now they sat miserably in Quebec, even more fearful of the days to come.

For weeks, the refugees, driven to bitterness and despair, had made the Lower Town a dangerous area by night. But few cared to offer violence to a King's officer. Crosbie pushed on, keeping his head low, his eyes half closed to avoid the pelting rain.

He angled up toward the Palace Gate that would bring him out just opposite the Intendant's Palace. The narrow streets seemed even more narrow; a dense fog had rolled in from the river basin and visibility now was limited to a few mètres at best. Twice Crosbie brushed against buildings he hadn't seen in time to evade. The crooked cobbled streets made movement a hazard and Crosbie stumbled with weariness as he struggled along the uneven paving.

It was a team of horses that halted Crosbie. The tall heavyweight team was harnessed to a pretty gilt calèche that was cramped back in the space between two buildings. The thick-shouldered horses almost blocked the street as they shifted nervously in the hard rain. Crosbie cursed their owner as he detoured to pass in front of them. Whoever left such a fine team out in the cold rain was a fool or a brute who deserved a good hiding. The off horse nickered softly to Crosbie and the young Scot stroked his soft, rain-wet nose as he shoved the team back a step to make a passage for himself. Nearby a muffled gasp drifted uneasily to Crosbie's ear, a shoe rasped on the cobbles. Without thought, Crosbie ducked low and leaped toward the nearest building, placing his back firmly against the wet stone. Under the shelter of his cape, he drew his long-bladed dirk, keeping the point covered for the moment. Several feet scraped on stone and again he heard the muffled gasp, louder now, and more urgent, as if someone were trying desperately to shout through a gagging cloth. Crosbie crouched tensely, not moving.

"Move along, fellow," a voice said quietly. "Just move along. Nothing here for you."

Crosbie was careful not to shift position. In the heavy fog, he was nearly invisible, cloaked as he was in the dark tarpaulin with his head covered by his flopped hatbrim. The shabby velvet collar of his cape grew sodden with rain and a thin icy trickle threaded an uncertain route down his neck and along his spine, touching Crosbie with the chill of panic. Involuntarily, he shivered.

"Move along," the confident voice said again, still held quietly in control.

"Damn the fool," another, lighter voice said with a flat snarl, "let me …"

"Be quiet," the confident man said easily. "Just give him a moment to think. Do you want to be killed?"

"I am an officer of the King," Crosbie said harshly. "What are you scoundrels up to?" He spoke without lifting his head. No gleam of brightness showed in the fog.

"Very well," the confident man said with the impatient sigh of a peaceable man driven to exasperation. "Georges, you can …"

Quickly Crosbie slashed out with his left hand, tossing his cape up onto his shoulder. His broad hard hand slapped the withers of the horse nearest him and the beast reared in alarm, both forefeet lashing out wildly. His teammate responded with a windy snort. The light calèche, brakes locked, was dragged by main force across the narrow street, stopping only when the plunging horses found themselves blocked by the opposite building. The team whinnied and reared, hoofs kicking. And through the uproar of the excited team came a thin scream. Then another, louder and more agonized in tone.

"Henri! My legs! For the love of God! Henri! My legs! God in Heaven, those brutes have ..." the high whining voice blurred in another shriek.

The startled horses had dragged the calèche over someone's legs, Crosbie realized. The long thin screams goaded Crosbie into movement. He slipped to the rear of the carriage and it was that turning that saved him. A heavy dragoon's sabre whipped through the air and smacked with a glancing blow against the stone building where Crosbie had been crouched only a moment before.

The screaming man was pleading for help, scrabbling against the carriage, begging Henri to stop the pain. Crosbie waited, bent low in a frozen arc behind the carriage. To his rear, someone moaned softly, not the injured man this time, Crosbie thought, but he wasted no time in speculation. All his attention was devoted to the man with the heavy sabre. Crosbie had seen nothing after the blade had rasped against the stone in a shower of sparks. He brought the point of his dirk forward, feeling a momentary reassurance from the familiar weight of the jeweled hilt. He waited, hardly daring to breathe, cursing himself for walking into a serious fight that was none of his affair.

Overhead, a steady drip of rainwater touched at the back of his head where he crouched. It came in a solid stream from the slanting roof of the house beside him and Crosbie tried to ignore it. His annoyance stemmed from the fact that the water interfered with the acuteness of his hearing. That steady stream was a damnable...

It stopped abruptly. Something had come between Crosbie and the stream from the roof! Wildly, the young Scot lunged up, stabbing his dirk in a high angle, blindly hoping it would find a target. The blade ripped through cloth with a soft whisper, sliced into flesh, grated on bone, then glanced away. Crosbie's arm was extended almost directly over his head. Desperately, he scrambled aside and backed away from the carriage.

A man grunted in pain. Then the sabre whistled ferociously, crunching into the frail wood of the carriage. That was all. The sabre fell, ringing dully in the wet street. Footsteps sloshed through the full gutters and Crosbie was left alone. He waited for a long tense moment before moving. The injured man continued to whimper about his broken legs, and behind Crosbie there was that same low groaning murmur, the sound that had first attracted his attention. Cautiously, he rounded the rear of the carriage. In two long strides, his shoes touched a soft yielding mass on the ground, lying huddled in an angle of the building.

Crosbie kept his dirk ready as he knelt and explored with one hand. His fingers struck a man's shoulder. Slowly, Crosbie let his hand slide down to the man's wrists. They were bound in front with stout linen cord. Crosbie did not cut the bonds until he first investigated the man's head. When he touched the wadded cloth rammed into the man's mouth, he relaxed his extreme wariness. He pulled the gag free and eased his dirk under the wrist-cord, sawing gently until the strands parted. He took the man's thin arm and brought him up to his feet, letting him lean against the stone building for added support.

"A robbery, sir?" he asked in a strained voice. "Why are you tied like this? A robber doesn't need to..."

"No." The man coughed thinly. "No, not a..."

The injured man was crying helplessly, face down, his thick body seen as a blur against the wet cobbles. Crosbie shifted uneasily. Someone would have to take care of him. Maybe he should be taken in the carriage and ...

A narrow door in the stone building opened inward, flooding a long thin stretch of the street in brightness. Absently, Crosbie stooped to pick up the heavy sabre abandoned by his assailant. A good blade, he noted, an old one, but well cared-for. He sheathed his dirk and dangled the sabre from one hand, still supporting the thin man who wavered unsteadily. The light of a four-branched candelabra fell on the man's sallow face, showing his mouth distorted as he gasped for air.

"Madone, what has happened?" the woman's voice stabbed in terrified demand. "Dear God, is it Monsieur Tremais? Has he ..."

Crosbie turned and the candles illuminated his thin gaunt face. The light danced wickedly along the edge of the sabre. He shifted the thin man around to face the door. The woman screamed.

"Stop that," Crosbie snapped. "This man needs help. And there's another ..." He stopped short in surprise, squinting to see more clearly, "You?" he growled. "What are you doing ..."

"Bring him in. Bring him in," she said quickly in a voice that was thin with strain. She stepped back as Crosbie helped the thin man inside the warm lighted room. Crosbie eased him to a battered wooden chair and turned to face Mademoiselle Céleste.

The girl stood tense, the candles held at shoulder height, throwing dramatic shadows across her face, emphasizing the expression of caution, of ... fear.

Crosbie propped the sabre against a bare well and by doing so, seemed to dispel much of the girl's apprehension. She remained stiffly near the door, eyes warily on Crosbie, but with much of her attention directed toward Monsieur Tremais. The elderly man pushed back his great hooded cape, removed his hat and sat slumped in the chair, breathing in stertorous rasping sounds. Crosbie glanced around the bleak room, wondering how Céleste came to be here so opportunely. Tremais, too, for that matter. It was a cheerless place, sparsely furnished as a sort of office with high bookkeeping stools and sloping tables, a fireplace where a small fire had burned itself out.

Both the girl and Monsieur Tremais were regarding him with obvious question, possibly even suspicion. God knew that he wanted no gushing thanks for having helped this sallow little man, but a decent response did not include such a ... a measuring stare. Crosbie dropped his sodden hat on a wide table and glanced uneasily from one to the other.

"Are you feeling better now, monsieur?" he asked politely.

Monsieur Tremais lifted his chin. His eyes were a hard, cold grey. "How did you come to be here, monsieur?" he demanded.

"Yes," Céleste said quickly, as if Tremais had finally asked the question that burned on her tongue.

"I?" Crosbie said hesitantly. "I was going to ..." His mouth snapped shut in sudden anger. Why should he be required to explain?

Tremais twisted his clenched hands apart and lifted one palm in clear entreaty. "I was attacked today. Robbed, if you will. Both scoundrels were put to rout by you. Very easily put to rout, I noticed. I now ask how it is that you came so fortunately to the scene. Please answer."

Crosbie's face flushed self-consciously as it always did in moments of embarrassment. Tremais watched him closely.

"Were they your men?" Céleste asked in a voice that rasped with anger.

"Mine?" Crosbie's reddened face blazed, but bewilderment left him as the implications of the question became clear to him. He turned directly to Céleste, a furious pounding in his head. "I would challenge any man who said that," he said quietly. "Perhaps Monsieur Tremais would care to repeat the question?"

Tremais did not move. No shadow of expression showed on his pale, drawn face. "Mademoiselle speaks too bluntly, monsieur," he said. "Let me say this, and I speak without rancor, believe me. Mademoiselle and I arranged to meet here privately on a matter of great importance. Upon leaving, I was attacked. And then rescued by you. A question remains to be asked, monsieur. I hope you will accept the question without anger. And answer it." Tremais's body betrayed a growing fatigue, but his eyes were alert, his voice quietly determined.

"I was walking toward the Intendant's Palace," Crosbie said stiffly, choking back the anger that rose hot in his throat. "I had hoped to find Mademoiselle there and ask her advice on a matter of great importance." Crosbie noted that he was aping the stilted phrases of Tremais, but they seemed best designed for this sort of discussion, he thought.

"You will forgive my further inquiry, monsieur." Tremais's tone was serene, confident. "Can you tell me what that problem was?"

Crosbie glanced briefly at Céleste, saw her standing with her chin high and arrogant, eyes stormy. Her suspicion had completely destroyed her confidence in Crosbie and now she regarded him with the same harsh contempt that she had shown that first day they met on the *Frelon*.

"It is very important, monsieur," Tremais insisted.

Crosbie drew in a deep slow breath. "I was told of... some ridiculous plot against me," he said coldly, hearing the words and knowing how foolish they must sound to Tremais. "A friend of mine, a Récollet friar, told me something he had overheard. You may remember him; he traveled with us on the *Frelon*. Brother Mathieu?"

Tremais nodded. "And he said..."

"That two of the Intendant's officers were planning to injure me somehow," Crosbie said with growing heat. God, what idiocy it sounded! "So I wanted to ask Mademoiselle if she knew anything about it," he ended lamely. "I walked from my quarters and found you here. And now, monsieur..."

"One moment, please," Tremais interposed smoothly.

"No, sir," Crosbie said flatly. "I've answered questions you had no right to ask. You needed the answers, you say. Now you may tell me why."

Tremais pursed his mouth in thoughtful consideration. Then he glanced toward Céleste. Crosbie turned with Tremais, just in time to see Céleste shake her head with quick decisiveness.

"I am sorry I interfered," Crosbie said, his voice shaking with anger. "I should have left you to be killed in the street. Then I would have been spared the necessity of killing you myself."

Tremais permitted himself the ghost of a smile. "Please," he said gently. "At my age I do not fight duels, even when I am clearly in the wrong. Believe me, sir, when I say that your behavior, even your youthful anger, is perfectly consonant with innocence. I do not..."

"Innocence!" Crosbie raged hotly. "Damn you, sir. What are you saying? Who accuses me? Of what?" Then he remembered the question Céleste had hurled at him and he glared at the girl. "Do you think I would need two men to help me dispose of this..." he stared balefully at Tremais, "...this gentleman?"

"Were they your men?" Céleste repeated with cold insistence.

"They were not," Crosbie said flatly. "And now you explain your presence here. Why are you hiding in this hovel?"

"Hovel!" Céleste cried. "This is my father's warehouse office."

"Céleste!" Tremais cut in sharply. "Let us remain with the subject. This young man deserves our warmest thanks, unless..." He waved a thin hand in brief dismissal. "Can you tell me something more of this plot against you, sir? The motive that brought you out in this dreadful weather today."

Crosbie glared at the elderly man for a long moment, itching for some sort of action that would relieve his frustrated irritation, but knowing that in Tremais's manner was a depth of serious purpose that he should not question. At length he nodded.

"Recently I made a great deal of money by investing in one of the Intendant's ventures. I don't understand much about it…"

Céleste snorted her contemptuous disbelief and Crosbie stumbled mentally as he tried to go on. "So, Brother Mathieu told me that two of Monsieur Bigot's officers were planning to use that money somehow to ruin me. I don't know what it means. Neither does Brother Mathieu. I thought Mademoiselle Céleste might know."

Crosbie spread his hands simply and Monsieur Tremais smiled his appreciation.

"Thank you, sir," he said quietly. "Now I will explain. In brief, I am Investigator for the King, as you may know. It is no secret. I have been sent to Canada to examine into charges of corruption and peculation in the local government. I have learned much. I met Mademoiselle Céleste here today because she had uncovered evidence that I desperately needed to finish my report for the Ministry of Justice. I received certain documents from her. I put them in my valise, and left. I was then attacked."

"But why do you think I …"

Tremais lifted an astonished eyebrow. "Can't you imagine, monsieur? Really, can't you guess why?"

Crosbie lowered his eyes. Again, the implication was obvious, even to his angry mind.

"I see you can," Tremais went on softly. "Certain evidence implicates you deeply in the greatest swindle of all I have investigated. The sale of the prize-ship Brittania and her cargo. So, you can understand that your … fortuitous appearance here gave rise to certain … questions."

The King's investigator kept his gaze hard on the young Scot. No expression betrayed him.

Crosbie nodded stiffly, his muscles suddenly hardened and unmanageable with shock. "It … it was the … Brittania," he said through lips that were almost unmoving. "Captain O'Neill told me.... some time ago. That part is true. The rest is not. I have never swindled anyone. Never. And I did not ..."

Tremais turned from Crosbie and glanced at Céleste.

"No," she said flatly. "Both Monsieur Bigot and the Comtesse said it was his idea entirely. The Brittania did not arrive in harbor until after he came. And why would he have been given a share of the profits, unless he had really invented the swindle? And how very sly he is, to let me deliver the proof to you, and then set his brutes on you. And then to come himself at the last moment. Being your rescuer, he can demand gratitude from you. So, Monsieur Crosbie recovers the evidence I brought to you, and at the same time, worms his way into your confidence." Céleste smiled bitterly. "Very clever, monsieur, would you agree?"

The girl had delivered her summation with none of the heat that had marked her previous statements. It was as dry, precise and impersonal a tone as Tremais himself might have used. And it was damning. Even Crosbie was impressed with the way in which her spurious logic seemed to destroy him as an honorable man. The young Scot was silent, aghast at the weight of appearances arrayed against him.

"Captain O'Neill speaks of him as the clever man, the brilliant boy with the mind of a born conspirator. O'Neill you know well, Monsieur Tremais. He never speaks admiringly of any ... any decent man."

Crosbie stared, open-mouthed and stupid at Céleste. He, the clever one? He, a man envied and admired by O'Neill, that sharp-eyed, sly Irish captain? All this was fantasy, the very edge of madness. Crosbie could find no words. He simply stared at the girl, with much the same expression he must have assumed when his mother had admonished him as a child. Tremais watched the young Scot closely, smiling thinly to himself. Crosbie turned toward him.

"It sounds so…real," he said. "I can't think what to say. I listen and I'm almost convinced myself. It all sounds real. But it isn't. None of it." The young Scot swallowed heavily.

"An accusation," Tremais said soberly. "And a denial. Both without supporting evidence. I do not think…"

"One moment," Crosbie said quickly, urged by a fleeting thought. "I have been away from Quebec for some thirty hours. And until I left the tavern to walk here, I was never alone in that time. How could I have known of your meeting here with Mademoiselle Céleste? It was pre-arranged, you said?"

"Yes," Tremais nodded. "Mademoiselle and I agreed early last evening that we would meet here this morning. The time was a compromise for both of us. Therefore, you could not have known about it if you were away from the city. However…"

Crosbie's gaunt face settled again into dour lines as the King's investigator paused in thought.

"It is not conclusive," Tremais said finally.

For a long silent moment, Crosbie stared into the small cold grey eyes. He was not innocent—or guilty. Not an enemy—or a friend. He rested, in Tremais's judgment, somewhere in Limbo, a suspended, undetermined position. He could say nothing to sway the man. Crosbie let out a pent-up breath with an explosive sound. He lifted his heavy shoulders wearily.

"We left that injured man lying outside in the rain," he said dully. "Even if he was…"

"Ciel!" Tremais murmured. He pushed free of the chair and hobbled swiftly across the floor, pulling back the narrow door in an excited gesture. "How could we have…"

The light calèche was gone. The candlelight revealed only a few short lengths of heavy cord and a wad of cloth—Tremais's bonds and gag. The steady downpour had long since washed away all traces of blood. Very likely the ruffian who had run away from Crosbie had sneaked back later to find his injured companion and had taken the calèche to carry him away. All that was understandable enough. Risky, but the storm had made enough noise to cover the sounds of escape.

Crosbie stayed inside. Any moment he expected Céleste to produce proof that he had stolen Monsieur Tremais's pretty carriage.

"There is nothing more I can do, mademoiselle," he said heavily, "so if you will excuse me, I will ..."

"What is this?" Tremais shouted. "How could it be? Céleste! Céleste, look at this!" Vigorously, he swung his thin arm high through the air. Suspended in his tight fist was a small leather valise, shiny with rain.

"It couldn't be," Céleste said positively. "It is your valise, but you will find it empty."

Tremais slammed the bag excitedly onto a table and fumbled with the straps. This, then, was the valise in which Tremais had put the evidence he had been collecting, evidence that implicated Duncan Crosbie as well as others. Crosbie stood quietly as the elderly man snatched out a fat stack of papers and spread them across the tabletop.

Irrepressible laughter rose suddenly within him, and looking at Tremais's astonished expression, he exploded, a raucous uproar that shattered Céleste's dignity and interrupted Tremais's inspection of his recovered papers.

"All there?" Crosbie demanded in a choking voice. "All there, Monsieur Investigator? No little scrap missing that I might have swallowed when you weren't looking? Nothing ..."

Tremais brought a thin smile to his lined face. He sat deliberately on the edge of the table and flipped at the papers with one finger. "I suddenly remembered," he said in a tone of soft musing, "how your voice sounded in the street when I heard you say, 'I am an officer of the King.' I felt a great thankfulness. I should like to express that thankfulness now, monsieur. And my apologies."

Crosbie goggled at the sedate, precise little man. Céleste whirled toward him, sparked by a sudden anger. Tremais lifted one hand calmly and halted her.

"I should have remembered earlier," he said warmly. "'I am an officer of the King.' That was your reason for interfering when you suspected violence was being done in the King's realm. For that reason you saved me." Tremais stroked his dry, wrinkled throat with a thin hand. "I, too, monsieur, am an officer of the King." He rose carefully, walked around the table with small finicking strides to place himself in front of Crosbie. Then, with slow and infinite care, he bowed.

The abrupt change was too much for the young Scot. In shock, all amusement left him. The anger had vanished long before, but a deep bewilderment was strong in his mind.

"But why are you so sure?" Céleste demanded.

Tremais straightened slowly, stepping backwards. He resumed his seat. With a minimum of movement, he scooped his papers into the damp valise. When it was secured again, he folded both thin hands on top and smiled faintly.

"The evidence was stolen," he said in harsh, dry tones. "It implicated Monsieur Crosbie among others. For a moment, the evidence was in Monsieur Crosbie's possession—or could have been, if he had known of it, and wanted it. Nonetheless, it was left behind. Purposely left behind for me to retrieve. Why?"

Tremais lifted one hand serenely. "I will tell you, mademoiselle. This valise was on the seat of my calèche, therefore it was purposely removed and placed against the door for me to find. I have no doubt that some scoundrel waited out there to see me find it again. Can you find it in your heart to believe that Monsieur Crosbie was foolish enough to return evidence against himself?"

Céleste's expression was coldly unconvinced, her eyes sombrely fixed on Tremais. She said nothing.

"It is at this moment that Monsieur Crosbie's motive for coming this way, becomes important," Tremais said briskly. "Brother Mathieu warned him of a vague plan designed to injure him. In this valise is the end result of that plan."

"Are you serious?" Céleste asked quietly.

"Completely. Let me put it to you, mademoiselle. If this young officer had not appeared today in such happy circumstances, would you ever have suspected him of real villainy?"

"But the statements of ..."

"Of Captain O'Neill," Tremais said. "Exactly. Only Captain O'Neill seems to have recognized Monsieur Crosbie's 'cleverness.' No one else, apparently, has had such perception. If we eliminate Captain O'Neill's statement from our file of evidence, what have we left? Of course, we still have the statements of the Intendant and the Comtesse de Boyer." Tremais's dry tone gave mystifying dismissal to both the powerful Bigot and his beautiful sister, but Crosbie was too confused to demand an explanation of one minor phase of this whole bewildering mystery.

Céleste moved back, careful not to look toward Crosbie. "Before today," she said in a low, hesitant voice, "before today I had not thought he could be a villain ..."

"Exactly, mademoiselle," Tremais said with brisk satisfaction. "The situation has now taken an intriguing direction. But if I had listened to the urgings of my heart, I would not have needed this physical proof of Monsieur Crosbie's innocence."

Crosbie blinked. Very little of the quick, allusive conversation made sense to him. His most fervent explanations had convinced Tremais of nothing. But merely finding the valise had somehow altered the situation completely. He was now in the strangest position of being proven a thief by the evidence in Tremais's valise, but at the same time, absolved of greater villainy by the mere fact that the valise had not been stolen from the King's investigator. It was difficult to see what he had gained.

"Earlier today," Tremais said with slow sincerity, "I heard him say, 'I am an officer of the King.' Then I knew."

CHAPTER SIXTEEN

The silence of the bleak warehouse room emphasized the tension. Duncan Crosbie held his face sternly in a frozen mask. Céleste stared with intense concentration at the damp valise. The King's investigator sat placidly in his chair, beaming.

Abruptly, Céleste turned toward Tremais. "You have forgotten what Monsieur Colbert said about...the incident on the *Frelon*," she said severely.

Tremais smiled. "I have forgotten nothing. I have Monsieur Colbert's statement in my valise. With it I have several comments made by the Comte de Boyer concerning that strange evening. Also I have talked with many people in Quebec who know both Colbert and the delightful Comtesse. All I lack is a confession from Monsieur Colbert. Even so, I am confident I know exactly what happened that night. And why it happened."

Tremais chuckled softly.

"You are not, my huge young friend, the first eager boy to be forced into an invidious position by a scheming woman of great charm. Nor, I am sure, will you be the last."

Céleste brushed both hands up along her temples, smoothing back her lustrous dark hair with a distracted gesture that was beautiful to see. "I cannot understand what you mean," she said.

"It is clear that Monsieur Crosbie was invited to the Comtesse's cabin for the single purpose of being caught by the Comte. To insure his capture, information reached the Comte through a ship's officer. He was told at the instance of Monsieur Colbert, though I cannot yet prove that."

"But..." Crosbie heard the short, stunned word drop from his strained lips. What was the man saying? Surely he didn't mean...

"Madame la Comtesse has been Monsieur Colbert's friend for many years," Céleste said sharply, "but I have been with her for nearly a year and I have never seen the least sign of..."

"One needs sharper eyes than yours, dear child," Tremais said with something of a smirk. "Colbert has been the Comtesse's lover for several years. When the complacent Comte began to suspect, a convenient scape-goat was found. Please do not frown at me, mademoiselle; the matter is not open to dispute. Monsieur Crosbie met the Comtesse only a few hours before he was... nearly caught. The Comte was told of... events in time to surprise the guilty pair. But somehow our energetic young friend managed to elude capture. I hope you will one day explain how you managed that, monsieur."

"Have I been that blind, Monsieur Tremais?" Céleste's tone was incredulous.

"Our young friend is no clever schemer," Tremais said pleasantly. "If he had just a modicum of the slyness that Captain O'Neill attributes to him, he would not be in this predicament. He was pushed into Monsieur Colbert's place on board the *Frelon*. I am now wondering whose place he has taken in reference to the Brittania."

Céleste darted one anxious glance at Crosbie. He fully expected her to wither Tremais with a further piece of damning information. After hearing them discuss his fiasco on board the *Frelon*, he was prepared to hear complete details of every idiocy he had ever committed. That he had been a fool, he already knew. That he had been a dupe, was news to him. He was not willing to accept it merely because Tremais said so. But Crosbie filed every word away in his memory. The Comtesse alone could answer the questions that had to be asked.

Crosbie shifted his weight impatiently and suddenly Céleste blushed. Her fair skin glowed with a bright sheen that seemed almost painful. She clapped her hands firmly against her burn-ing cheeks.

"Yes, my dear child," Tremais said gently, "I also feel like an ungrateful fool. Monsieur Crosbie has not behaved cleverly, or even sensibly, but he is no scoundrel. However, monsieur," he said to Crosbie, "I will need to know more about this unusual transaction that resulted in such enormous profit to you ..."

Crosbie flicked out his long-bladed jeweled dirk and hurled it point first at the table before him. The gemmed hilt vibrated with the impact. A dull flake of dried blood fell from the cut-ting edge. With the dirk stuck fast in the table, Crosbie reached out one hand and twisted the hilt. A triple-thread loosened and the cairngorm top came free from the dirk. From the secret compartment which an earlier Crosbie had designed, the young Scot teased a tightly rolled sheet of parchment. He tossed it, still rolled, to Tremais. Then he put his dirk together again and eased it from the table. He wiped its dark-metal blade clean on his damp cape, dried it briefly on his coat and sheathed it carefully.

"A magnificent weapon," Tremais said dryly. "No wonder you put both those brutes to rout. But what does it ..."

Crosbie smoothed the paper flat before Tremais. "Forty-seven thousand francs," he growled. "That is my share from the sale of the prize-ship Brittania. I surrender it to you." Briefly, he glanced at the incredible figure. Once before in his life he had owned as much as four thousand francs. Never more. He shoved the curling paper sharply toward Tremais. Then he remembered something. "This is the total, monsieur," he said in a harsh voice. "Of it, two hundred louis d'or represents my investment in this dubious venture. Four thousand francs. I will expect that much to be refunded."

"Merciful saints above us," Tremais muttered. "Even if you had been convicted, monsieur, your fine would not be half so large, I should think. What do you hope to gain by ..."

"I want nothing this way," Crosbie said angrily. "But I hold you responsible, monsieur, for my four thousand francs. Is that clear?"

"Perfectly clear," Tremais chuckled. He rose and picked up his shiny valise. "A few days from now, I shall send for you," he said in a matter-of-fact tone. "I will want a precise statement from you of all conversations that relate to the question of the prize-ship. But that can wait for the moment. Now, dear mademoiselle, I think I should take you home with me until your father can be advised to come for you."

"Home?" Céleste said. She turned from her steady inspection of Crosbie and lifted her eyebrows.

"Obviously, dear child, you cannot return to the Intendant's Palace. He knows you have helped me. Even if no violence is offered you, there can be no further usefulness for you."

Céleste said coldly, "You forget my father is a grand seigneur in Canada. Bigot would not dare to harm him, or me. I will be perfectly safe with the Comtesse. Bigot knows I will bring everything to you. It will be interesting to see what he thinks it important for you to know. And what he wants to keep secret. I can find out."

Tremais spread his thin hands in a gesture of helplessness. "You overwhelm me, mademoiselle. Let me applaud your courage."

"Nonsense," Céleste snapped.

"Why are you doing this?" The blunt question slipped from Crosbie's lips unexpectedly. The words had been formed in his mind long before, but he had not intended to speak them out loud.

Tremais spoke first, in swift, harsh words. "I arrested her brother," he said. "He stole for Bigot. Céleste wants to punish Bigot. It is that simple."

"My brother," Céleste said quietly, "was commander of a small fort. He was a fine boy, brave and good. He, too, thought he was in love with the Comtesse."

And now Crosbie's flaming features were a match for Céleste's. But neither found it necessary to move away or to avert their locked glances. Crosbie fought for words and cursed his stupid tongue that refused to find the right phrase.

"I ... I am sorry," he said lamely. And that was enough.

Céleste touched his clenched hand with a light darting touch. It wiped away all that had gone before, the sharpness, the suspicion, the fear. His bleak young face softened.

"I came to find you today," he said quietly. "I hoped ..."

"I must interrupt," Tremais said briskly, pulling on his sodden cape. "It is time I returned. I will escort Mademoiselle Céleste to the Palace."

"I would be happy to ..." Crosbie began.

"I must insist," Tremais said flatly. "No one, save we three here, know that it was Monsieur Crosbie who beat off those brutes today. We will keep that our secret. He will be our corps de réserve. However, Monsieur Bigot knows that Mademoiselle Céleste and I were together here. Therefore, I shall escort her openly to the Palace."

"But what is the point ..." Crosbie said heatedly.

"The point is that I am an old and wickedly wise man and I suspect that someone waits outside to see who leaves this building. I shall go with mademoiselle. You, monsieur, will remain behind for as long as you are able to restrain yourself. If anyone tries to enter during that time, I suggest a further resort to that incredible dagger. And now, mademoiselle ..."

Tremais turned to the door.

Crosbie put one hand lightly on Céleste's shoulder and urged her around to face him. "He is right, I suppose," he said hesitantly, "but, I wish ..."

Her fingers, smooth and cool, stroked swiftly across his lips in a fleeting gesture. Her smile was the warm radiance he so well remembered. "I have been a fool," she murmured. "Forgive me ... Duncan."

"It's very easy to be a fool," Crosbie said with deep feeling. "But you could never be so great a fool as I have been." He lifted her hand, kissed it gently, then stood back to let her pass.

Céleste picked up her cape and swung it around her shoulders. A deep conspirator's hood disguised her completely. Tremais pulled the door open impatiently. Céleste glanced once at Crosbie, then turned and went out into the stormy street. The door slammed shut as a gust of chilling rain blew into the room.

Crosbie rammed his hat hard on his head, pulled his cape close and leaned forward to blow out the candles. A vagrant draught of air brought a faint reminiscent trace of Céleste's perfume to his nostrils. Softly, he crossed the bare room and took a position where the door would shield him if anyone entered.

The need for sleep swept over him and every tormented muscle of his great body ached with fatigue. He forced himself to stand without moving, giving a possible watcher every indication of a empty room.

Even if Crosbie had begun the day well-rested and alert, he would have been bewildered by the quickly shifting reactions of Céleste and Tremais. He could understand that he had rendered himself suspect by that investment in the prize-ship. But there remained the matter of the missing—and later recovered—evidence. That also had proved something, though Crosbie was too tired to remember just what it had proved. He was no longer suspected of thievery. That much he did realize and he was content to let it rest there.

After a numbing, drowsy hour, Crosbie wrenched the door open and stepped out into the storm. He closed the narrow door softly and made a serious effort to move quietly until he was some distance away from the warehouse. Then he strode along rapidly, eager to reach his room at the Lion d'Or and the warm bed that haunted his thoughts. The storm had eased and the rain fell straight, no longer driving in horizontally at gale force.

Crosbie almost ran to the tavern. A warm yellow light seeped through the smeared windows, as welcome as a lighthouse beacon to the weary, rain-soaked, bewildered young Scot.

Crosbie pushed back the door, kicked it shut behind him and stood inside, breathing the warm, fetid air with delight. His feet squelched nastily as he walked to the stairs; then he stopped as a short, white-uniformed figure sprinted down.

"Denis, what are you..."

"You must come. At once," the boy gasped excitedly. "Monsieur le capitaine Bougainville said I should bring you. At once, Duncan."

Crosbie groaned softly. "Tell me quietly," he said.

"Monsieur Bougainville goes to join Montcalm at Fort Carillon. You are to go with him. Also I!" Denis's thin voice cracked drastically on the last phrase. "Monsieur Bougainville has taken your heavy baggage. He will go to Anse-au-Foulon at three o'clock. You are to meet him there. Monsieur Bougainville has sent horses. One for you. One for your light baggage. One for the soldat who will return with all the horses. And..." Denis gulped, recovered himself sternly. "And one for me!" He flourished Crosbie's fine light musket dangerously in the air. It was the new model called a fusil, light enough so even a young boy could handle it with ease.

"Naturally," Crosbie said heavily. "One for you. Is my baggage ready?" He took the fusil from Denis and propped it against the wall.

"An hour ago, monsieur."

Crosbie ran a large finger under his neckcloth and drew a long slow breath. He thought momentarily of his unused bed upstairs and then forcibly put the thought out of his mind. Tired as he was, the coming journey to Carillon excited him as much as Denis.

CHAPTER SEVENTEEN

Duncan Crosbie climbed with long weary strides up the steep narrow street that zig-zagged to Upper Town. Ahead stumbled Denis, leading his horse and still farther ahead was Bougainville's soldier.

As they entered the level stretch of St. Louis Square, all of them halted for a rest, letting the horses turn tail to the storm while they stepped into the lee of the Château. Crosbie tilted back his floppy hat and wiped his cold wet face. He said, "Who knows the way?"

"It is very simple, monsieur," Denis said eagerly. "Out the St. Louis gate and take the road to Sillery that crosses the Plains of Abraham. When you find a path leading off to the left, follow that. It leads to Anse-au-Foulon, half a league away."

Crosbie led the cavalcade down the street and out on the slippery road.

He rode slowly, not wishing to push the small horse unless it became necessary. Twice the beast slipped and slithered on the glossy surface, but each time recovered his footing before Crosbie had to leap free.

At length they came to the turn-off, a narrow footpath through rolling meadowland. Crosbie held his unwilling horse at a walk, carefully. The path wound to a bluff beside a small stream and apparently disappeared.

Crosbie dismounted wearily, giving the bridle of his mount to the soldier. Denis slid to the ground and ran to unload Crosbie's valise from the pack horse. The soldier took the three leads, and turned without delay, kicking his horse into a brisk walk back along the path toward Quebec.

"I suppose there is a path down to the river?" Crosbie asked slowly.

"Yes, monsieur," Denis said. Crosbie picked up his light bag, slipped the sling of his fusil over one shoulder and stood back as Denis jumped lightly down the path. The boy vanished in the bank of mist and fog. Crosbie sighed and cautiously set himself to follow.

The path was very steep, but it had been used often. Thoughtful men had kicked flat spaces, rather like rudimentary steps, and strewn gravel over them. But the climb was torture for tired bruised muscles. Crosbie plodded dully, his head throbbing. Finally, he reached the narrow, rocky strand where Denis was waiting. He was now standing in a deeply indented cove, the Anse-au-Foulon that Denis had mentioned. The storm lashed the river into foamy white madness. Above him the rocky escarpment stretched for leagues in each direction along the river, the best natural protection that Quebec could possibly have. Crosbie found a dry rock for his valise, put it down and rested himself by leaning against the stone, propped by his short fusil.

"It will not be pleasant on the river today," he said. He regarded the skinny boy. "Are you dressed warmly, Denis? This will be a cold journey, I suspect."

"I am fine, monsieur, fine," the boy insisted. His eyes danced with excitement. This was Denis's great adventure. He was going to Fort Carillon, not as a menial, but as a soldier. No consideration of weather or discomfort could bother him today.

From the solid bank of mist and fog, a hoarse shout sounded booming along the water. Crosbie lifted his head and bellowed in reply.

"À Carillon!" he shouted.

Slowly, the high sharp prow of a large whaleboat protruded from the fogbank, and gradually the entire length of the boat became visible. Captain Bougainville sat forward. With him was the wide burly form of Le Singe. Gently, the crew tossed oars, letting the big boat slide into the cove under its own momentum. Le Singe judged his moment carefully, then leaped ashore, digging his heels hard into the soft mud and holding the boat steady with a hook.

"A good day to you, monsieur," he called out gaily. "Will you embark?"

"With pleasure, my good Le Singe," Crosbie tossed his valise into the boat where an oarsman caught it and lashed it securely. Then he took Denis by the waist, lifting the boy easily and walking with him to the boat. Denis clambered over a roped heap of new iron ramrods, hundreds of them, lashed to the thwarts. Then Crosbie was free to salute Captain Bougainville.

As always, the captain looked brisk and preternaturally neat.

"A thousand apologies, Duncan," he said pleasantly. "I expected to find you asleep this morning. Imagine my surprise to find you had gone out on private business."

Crosbie nodded grimly; private business, indeed. He only hoped it might remain private. He swung one long leg over the gunwale and heaved himself to a seat beside Bougainville. The captain signalled Le Singe who pushed the boat clear of the rocks and leaped in.

"The terrible life of a soldier," Bougainville said mockingly. "I returned to my quarters to find an urgent dispatch which I must take to the Général at Carillon. Also awaiting me was the Général's order appointing you as his artillery aide, so your place is at Carillon."

"Yes," Crosbie said vaguely. "What is an artillery aide?"

Bougainville smiled thinly. "It furnishes you a certain protection."

Crosbie started guiltily. "Protection?"

Bougainville sighed. "Carillon is a fortress. Fortresses have artillery. Artillery in Canada is entirely a provincial concern, manned by Canadien regulars and commanded by the Chevalier Le Mercier who is now at Carillon. Le Mercier is not your friend, but there is no Canadien who would dare abuse a member of Montcalm's official family." Bougainville spread both small hands wide. "Quod erat demonstrandum."

Crosbie held up one huge arm, signalling for Denis's attention. When the boy looked up, Crosbie made a gesture of drinking, cocking his elbow and bringing his thumb sharply back toward his open mouth. Denis bobbed his head understandingly. He brought out the flask of brandy and would have come to his feet, but for the coxswain's quick snatch that forced him back in his seat. The coxswain tossed the leather bottle forward in a long exact arc. Crosbie caught it easily and pulled the cork, offering it first to Bougainville.

"Thank you, Duncan. Most welcome just now." Bougainville tilted his head for a long swallow. "Excellent brandy," he said. "Every bit as good as the Général's." He held the flask lightly in his hand and glanced at Crosbie. "If you had paid close attention, my young friend, you would have been more curious about why the Général appointed you as artillery aide. This is a formal appointment, you realize. It should do much to advance your career."

Crosbie had not paid close attention, he conceded. His mind was still occupied with wild plans for extricating himself from the mess he was in because of the prize-ship Brittania. But now he knew he must put it all behind him, erase it from his mind and concentrate on the serious professional work waiting for him at Carillon.

"You may thank yourself, I would say," Bougainville went on judiciously. "His Excellency could not have heard good reports about you. Therefore we must assume that your report on the status of Quebec's artillery was of such a quality that it overshadowed your many faults." Bougainville grinned abruptly.

Crosbie flushed slightly and lowered his eyes, pretending to fumble with the cork of his flask. Professional compliments were still rare to him. Hardly any superior officer had yet offered much more than a growl of irritation.

"What is the route to Carillon?" he asked suddenly, eager to change the subject from personal matters.

"Upstream to Trois Rivières," Bougainville said easily. "From there we turn south and go up the Richelieu to St. Jean or Chambly, where we may hope to find a sailing craft that will take us comfortably south on Lake Champlain to Carillon. It is eighty long leagues in all, but after we enter the Richelieu, it should not be unpleasant. Not nearly so bad as that Indian canot we took to the savage council, eh?"

Crosbie laughed with Bougainville at the memory. He held out the flask with a flourish, remembering the war-song that Bougainville had chanted for the Indians.

"Let us trample the English under our feet!" he bellowed.

CHAPTER EIGHTEEN

Despite Bougainville's assurances, the journey to Fort Carillon had been actively disagreeable for Duncan Crosbie. Even though the big whaleboat was considerably roomier than a canot, there had never been a boat designed to accommodate men of Crosbie's great height. The brief stretch up the St. Lawrence to Trois Rivières had been sufficient to force his long muscles into rigid cramp.

Trois Rivières stood on the north bank, opposite the village of St. François, stronghold of France's Indian allies who were tightly controlled by their Jesuit overseers. Here, where the river widened in the confluence of other streams, Bougainville landed briefly to pay a courtesy call upon Monsieur Rigaud de Vaudreuil, governor of the province of Trois Rivières. Rigaud, being brother to the King's Governor for Canada, received punctilious consideration.

From Trois Rivières, they left the St. Lawrence, turning south at the mouth of the Richelieu, their tireless oarsmen laboring mightily against the hard current. Rain, thin and cold, hurled directly into their faces by the prevailing winds.

Even after they boarded the small brig at St. Jean and sailed upstream into the wide expanse of Lake Champlain, the rain stayed with them, soaking through cloaks and hats. A flurry of wild wind drove them nearly aground on the low, flat Isle-aux-Noix and Crosbie was given a close view of the site that Bougainville considered the best defensive location in that area. The island sat like a cork in a bottle, plugging the head of the

Richelieu, with nearly impassable swamps on either bank making the lake the only feasible route of approach for an enemy. Crosbie's enthusiasm for the position did not equal Bougainville's, however; the island seemed too easy to outflank by determined assault.

A driving rainstorm had blown them swiftly southward down the lake, obscuring the distant shoreline most of the time. Crosbie spent long hours on the flat roof of the deckhouse, peering for a vagrant glimpse of the land that lay shrouded in a veil of mist and fog.

When the lake narrowed, they could see the square stone outline of Fort Frédéric, which the English called Crown Point, looming on the west bank. In that mountainous swampy country where the waters of Lake Champlain offered the only reasonable mode of transport, the guns of Fort Frédéric controlled all traffic. The brig dipped its ensign in brief salute to the King's majesty, hardly slowing in its wild scudding flight down the lake.

A blunt, square-nosed promontory jutted from the western shore, reducing the lake to a width of some two hundred métres, and there, a bare twenty métres above the water, stood the grey stone bulk of Carillon. It seemed monstrous, shaped with formal European rigidity, far more powerful than Fort Frédéric. In the sharply angled stone bastions, gun-ports were shielded against the storm, but Crosbie's professional eye visualized the plunging fire that could be hurled from the walls to stop any attempt to force the gateway to Canada.

Wild, and lost in the deep wilderness, how did this outpost of the King's empire come by the gentle, village-countryside name of Carillon, Crosbie wondered? The name the English had called it—but would never call it again, Bougainville had assured him—seemed more fitting. The harsh, violent sound of Ticonderoga, its savage, broken syllables, carried an ominous note that suited this forbidding land.

Crosbie stared up, unbelieving, at the splendid stone fortress as the brig edged closer. Its magnificent construction gave it an air of impregnability. Softly, Crosbie whistled in tuneless appreciation.

Bougainville smiled. "Impressive, eh? Designed by the immortal Vauban, no less. Complete with glacis, counter-scarps, covered ways and demi-lunes, in the classic shape of a star, with five bastions. Most impressive, but..." Bougainville shrugged. "It's in the wrong place," he said flatly. His hand urged Crosbie forward as the brig eased into its berth.

Bougainville led the young Scot up the slope into the fort. Left to wait in the anteroom while Bougainville was ushered into Montcalm's office, Crosbie composed himself, uncomfortably aware of his damp, reeking wool coat, and his soggy shoes. He held himself erect, his dipping hat clamped properly under his left elbow, and staring blankly forward, compelling from himself a resigned patience he was far from feeling. Captain Bougainville had presented himself at Carillon with his usual tireless good humor, waving pleasantly to friends who had hardly been able to force more than a surly nod in response. But filthy weather and loss of sleep never seemed to affect Bougainville, Crosbie reflected. The captain remained the same amusing, endlessly interesting man he had been when comfortably in garrison at Quebec. Crosbie suspected that it was his indomitably gay spirits that made him so valuable to Montcalm, and in thinking that, Crosbie did not feel that he detracted from Bougainville's very real abilities. But having someone like Bougainville always on hand would lend all hardships something of the air of a gala pique-nique. God knew he had cheered Crosbie's drooping spirits many times during their wearisome trip from Quebec.

A bench along the opposite wall was solidly packed with regimental officers waiting for the Général's summons. They had received Bougainville's entry with varying degrees of condescension, while dismissing Crosbie with only a casual glance. And even that was denied him now as he sat shivering in his wet uniform, dismally aware of his shabby appearance as contrasted with the white-wigged noble dandies, all of them tacitly agreed not to see him. Crosbie touched the hilt of his dirk, rubbing his broad thumb over the cairngorm seal; and the old familiar magic worked again, giving him a sense of sureness that not even the supercilious young officers could upset.

Bougainville pulled open the door abruptly, gesturing for Crosbie. The young Scot rose stolidly, feeling all eyes upon him. He dragged his wrinkled cloak into position and followed Bougainville into the Général's office.

Crosbie hardly recognized Montcalm, remembering as he did the smiling stocky man who had fenced so cleverly with him in Quebec. Now the Général stood before him, outlined against a narrow window that overlooked the lake, his hands locked behind his back, his features grooved with lines of tension. In full uniform, golden epaulettes glittering, Montcalm appeared larger and taller than Crosbie remembered. He smiled briefly, acknowledging Crosbie's clumsy bow.

Bougainville took position unobtrusively behind the Général, offering Crosbie the soothing reassurance of his steady smile. Slowly Montcalm brought his hands forward and Crosbie could see the long foolscap sheet he held.

"I was interested in this report," the Général said briskly. "That is why you are here. I want you to …" He spun on one heel to glance at Bougainville. "Have you told him, Louis?"

"Non, mon général," Bougainville said easily.

Montcalm shrugged. "Come over here now, both of you." He lifted a finger, directing them toward a wide sepia chart that hung on the wall behind his desk, taking up the entire space between two windows with its meticulous notation.

"You had certain harsh opinions of Quebec's artillery preparations, Monsieur Crosbie," Montcalm said evenly.

Crosbie brought his heels sharply together and thought it best to say nothing. The Général nodded his agreement.

"Very well," he went on. "Now I wish to hear what you would recommend for our position here."

"But, sir..." Crosbie snapped his mouth shut.

"You were saying?"

Crosbie damned himself silently. "The fort, mon général, is magnificently designed. If there are enough guns, I could hardly suggest any useful..."

"I am not speaking merely of the fort," Montcalm said patiently. "We cannot sit here and await attack. If we did, the English would simply lay seige, hold us here and go on to Quebec. Carillon has its function, monsieur, but that is not it. Now attend me, if you please."

One hand stabbed swiftly at the map. "Here are the English, at the southern end of Lac St. Sacrement. They will move north along the lake, take one of two possible routes to approach us at Carillon. The English will have to leave their boats at the northern end of Lac St. Sacrement and attack overland. So much we know. Now then." The Général stretched his arm wide, indicating a position in the center of the map. "Here is Carillon," he said slowly. He traced along the course of a river that connected Champlain with Lac St. Sacrement. Its course ran due west from Carillon, then curved in a slow arc to the south, and then back to the east. "Up the river which joins the two lakes, the English must come. They may choose the well-used path that intercepts the river bend. It requires two crossings, however, which we could easily defend. Or, if they are vigorous and enterprising, they may elect to move along the Indian trail which follows the river, staying on the west bank all the way to Carillon. One of those two routes, they must take. The river itself is too treacherous. So..." Montcalm chewed at his inner cheek thoughtfully. "Here," he said abruptly. "Here. Here and here. Also here. Make a note of the positions, Monsieur

Crosbie. Both sides of the first crossing. Both sides of the second crossing at the sawmill. These two low mountains. And this stretch immediately in front of the fort. Do you have them in mind?"

Dazedly, Crosbie murmured that he understood.

"Good. You will reconnoitre all these sites. Give me your report on artillery requirements for defending each."

Crosbie swallowed heavily. His throat was dry. He had only the vaguest notion of Montcalm's intent, and for one wild moment, objections crowded into his mind. Then sanity returned and he said merely, "Yes, mon général," acknowledging his orders.

Montcalm glared at the chart for a further moment, then wheeled and marched nervously to his wide table. He sat deliberately and pushed forward a sheet of paper, his silver inkwell and a tall tubular rack full of freshly sharpened quills. His hand motioned Crosbie to a chair. "Make your notes, monsieur," he said amiably. "When you are ready, you may ask questions."

Gratefully Crosbie sat, dropping his hat to the floor and tossing his sodden cape onto another chair. He dipped a quill swiftly and scrawled short, sketchy notes. Montcalm meanwhile scanned a voluminous sheaf of papers, then held them over his shoulder to Bougainville.

"You study it, Louis," he said lightly. "If there's anything for me to know, you tell me."

"The engineer's report?" Bougainville asked thinly.

"Yes. One of those verbose affairs that delights Pontleroy's complex mind. Convey my enthusiastic compliments, Louis. We may have need of Pontleroy's best talent soon, so see that he stays in a good frame of mind. Now, monsieur, what more do you want to know?"

Crosbie lowered his quill. He strove for a level tone of voice, the even, uninflected delivery that would be most appropriate to a discussion of professional problems.

"Do any of these locations have preference, mon général?"

"No. Go on."

"Am I to assume that the entire infantry force is available at each location?"

"Yes. What else?"

Crosbie flicked his quill pen. "The purpose of each location, sir," he said quietly. "Defensive or offensive?"

Montcalm suddenly sat back, laughing softly. He craned his neck toward Bougainville. "The great strategic question, eh? Do you know the answer, Louis?"

Bougainville brought one finger sliding slowly up the side of his nose, pushing it hard to one side in a comical gesture. "Yes, I know, mon général," he said.

Montcalm stared at his chief aide soberly, all laughter gone now. His heavy black eyebrows lifted faintly. "I think you may," he said almost to himself. "There will be no discussion, Louis," he added sharply.

"Certainly not, sir," Bougainville replied equably.

"To answer your question, Monsieur Crosbie," Montcalm said, "I do not know the answer yet. Make what assumptions you must. Get the report to me within the week. Sooner if possible."

"Very good, sir," Crosbie said. He returned inkwell and quill stand to their proper positions and watched the Général for a signal to withdraw. Montcalm sat unmoving, regarding the young Scot with a steady, quizzical eye.

"Your Quebec report showed a certain...judgment," the Général said in a sharp tone. "Your opinion was...uncomplimentary. What portion of that opinion was induced by your personal animosity toward the Chevalier Le Mercier?"

"Sir!" Crosbie stiffened with outrage.

"Answer me," Montcalm demanded quietly.

"None, sir," Crosbie snapped. Not even a Général had the right to...

Montcalm lifted one hand casually. "Splendid," he said drily. "The good Chevalier is here at Carillon. He has already delivered to me a report on this subject. I suggest that you do what you can to avoid his company. In any event, I do not want to hear of any … collision. You understand me, monsieur?"

"Perfectly, Your Excellency," Crosbie said stiffly. "Now, if I may be permitted to withdraw …"

"I will tell you when you are dismissed," Montcalm said in a casual tone. "Louis, give me that report."

"At your elbow, Excellency," Bougainville said.

Montcalm smiled thinly, picked up the paper he wanted. "There was a brief reference that I did not understand," he said. "Something about the changing sizes of guns."

"I remember, mon général," Crosbie said. "I reported that several of the permanent batteries have cannon emplaced that vary in the size of bore. It makes for a needless complication of supplies and may …"

"No, not that," Montcalm said. "Something about …"

Emboldened by Montcalm's ready acceptance of interruption, Crosbie broke in again, focussing on the point that was not clear to the Général. "When a gun has been in use for many years, sir, it tends to lose its true bore dimension from the action of time and the effect of much shooting. Many of Quebec's guns must have been taken from warships, I assume."

"But what does that mean?" The Général put down Crosbie's report and leaned forward intently on his elbows. "Are naval guns inferior to …"

"No, sir. Not invariably. Navy ships often carry long-range guns as stem chasers. Those are splendid cannon, often of bronze, but the routine naval gun, which is called a carronade, is made of iron, and designed to fire in broadsides at short range. Carronades are not constructed to the same accuracy as long guns which are used for precise firing. And in a defensive installation such as

Quebec, carronades should never be used in the upper batteries, even if they are in good condition."

"And what should we do with those short guns, then, in your estimation, Monsieur Crosbie?"

"I would first have those I selected sent for re-boring. Then we would have to re-cast the round-shot to their new diamètres and also make new canister containers. Then all those guns should be placed together in one of the lower batteries along the shore where a slight variation would not kill any of our own men."

Montcalm smiled grimly. Then, abruptly, he chuckled. "I was thinking, just then, of the Chevalier Le Mercier," he said pleasantly. "How unhappy that gentleman will be when we return to Quebec. Such an amount of labor I will have for him, eh?" The Général picked up Crosbie's report once again and handed it over his shoulder to Bougainville. "I was also impressed with your thoughts about training the gunners. Have you had experience with that problem?"

"A certain amount at Toulon, Your Excellency."

"And is the state of training so very bad now?"

"I would say so, mon général," Crosbie said flatly. "Most of the men are assigned merely to the artillery units, not to specific guns in specific batteries. Often they change assignments and most of the men have never seen the guns fired. We should have crews permanently assigned to each gun, with a non-commissioned officer to every three or four guns. Then, with long periods of drill and some actual firing practice, I think we would reach moderate efficiency. Also the morale would rise among the men themselves as they understood their work, and in time of attack, that element of morale will be important."

Montcalm rubbed his blue-shadowed chin with his wide hand. "You have a rather positive way of presenting all this, monsieur," he observed mildly.

Crosbie felt his face flush again. "I have given much thought to all these questions, Your Excellency," he said firmly. "I've argued it all out in my head, many times. The words come easily. But only on this subject."

The Général's tired, red-rimmed eyes watched him sharply. Then Montcalm smiled and rose to his feet.

"Welcome to my official family, Monsieur Crosbie," he said warmly. "Louis, you take our young gentleman along with you and see that he is comfortably billeted. Then send him out to do our work for us. Return in an hour. I have a disagreeable problem for you."

CHAPTER NINETEEN

For the remainder of Duncan Crosbie's first day at Carillon, a lashing storm held the fort fog-bound. After Bougainville had escorted him to his quarters, Crosbie and Denis occupied themselves with unpacking, appropriating a small iron stove and enough firewood to ensure reasonable comfort. From a deep recess in Crosbie's trunk, Denis extracted two bottles of excellent brandy, displaying them with a wide flourish that won a grin of approval from Crosbie. When his small room had been set to rights, Crosbie picked up his tarpaulin cape, his flopped hat, and set out for a tour of the walls before nightfall should make all inspection impossible.

Three dozen cannon ringed the walls of Carillon, all of them on small-wheeled defensive mounts that would make them difficult to move should the Général want them employed outside the fort. Crosbie made a mental note to order high-wheeled oaken carts from the smithy. Only a third of the guns were eighteen-pounders, the minimum calibre considered efficient in siege-work, but then Crosbie realized he was applying a European standard of judgment. Here in the wilderness, an eighteen-pounder might be thought as useful as the routine forty-two pounders, in view of the enormous difficulty of bringing guns into action so far from a permanent base. The remainder were twelve-and eight-pounders, all in reasonable condition, but all in need of scaling, with several over-due for new vent fittings. The gun positions were sketchily manned at this hour, but Crosbie noted that at least one non-commissioned officer was on duty with each division of guns and for a Canadien battery, that was all that could be expected. Too, these gunners seemed fairly well-trained and in excellent spirits. Uniforms were always a useful guide to the state of morale in any unit and these red-and-blue artillerymen were presentable enough for formal parade.

On his way back to his room, Crosbie observed wide ranks of regimental tents, pitched in rigid lines all around the fort. Here were bivouacked the thousands of men sent against the English, men for whom no accommodations could be found inside Carillon.

He sent Denis off to find him some dinner, feeling strangely unwilling to join the Général's other aides in the diningroom tonight. His mind was a turmoil of plans, stratagems and complicated time-schedules; he wanted only to be left alone to plod his way slowly and methodically to a solution.

The last vestiges of winter vanished with the next morning. The rain continued, but softly now, pelting warmly against the fort. The air was soft and moist, smelling of greenness and fertility. The storm seemed to have washed away the drabness of winter. Crosbie went back to leave his raincape, wondering at the abrupt seasonal shift. He stuffed a handful of paper cartridges in one pocket and picked up his light fusil. That, with his ever-present dirk, would be all the armament he would need for his inspection.

The sentries at the main gate passed him through, one of them seeming about to speak to him. But one glance at the young Scot's dour, withdrawn expression, and the soldier slapped his musket in salute, silently.

Crosbie climbed in long measured strides up the slight slope of the promontory, heading due west to get an idea of how the land lay. He had not yet developed the veteran officer's knack for visualizing terrain from a map. The low mountain rising to the north and west of the fort was a commanding position. If heavy artillery could be mounted on its crest, Carillon was doomed. Crosbie felt a faint quiver of apprehension as he looked up.

He walked across the promontory along the low ridge that Montcalm had indicated. On each side, the land fell away easily to the river on one hand, to Lake Champlain on the other. As a defensive site, this was very good, except for the fact that an enemy could easily cross the promontory farther west and place his troops astride the narrow path leading north to Fort Frédéric. With artillery, he could then prevent any reinforcements or supplies from coming to Carillon.

From the defensive line, Crosbie turned south toward the river, climbing down to the edge of the water. The opposite bank was a wide soggy morass which no heavily armed troops could hope to pass. Light infantry, possibly, but light infantrymen alone would never harm Carillon. Crosbie groped along the river cautiously, the footing dangerous after the rain. Three small streams ran into the river. Each had cut a fine deep ravine for itself and though Crosbie muttered with annoyance at the nuisance of leaping them, he was inwardly delighted. Those ravines would also impede the passage of an artillery train, requiring laborious bridging at each stream.

Ahead in the shadowed riverbed lay a low stone sawmill just downstream from a lofty falls. A detachment of soldiers lounged in the doorway and under the eaves of the mill. Four sentries posted at the log bridge crossing the quick river snapped to a rigid posture when Crosbie appeared.

Crosbie stopped at the approach to the bridge and turned on his heel, orienting himself again. The mountain he had observed from the fort was now due north of him. Cannon on that peak could easily interdict the bridge, he realized.

One look at the racing river and Crosbie knew that no enemy would be able to approach Carillon by water from the south, not with that boiling falls and three stretches of rock-studded rapids to bar the way. The only logical route for the enemy to take against the fort was overland, intersecting the arc of the river.

That route was visible from the bridge. Crosbie crossed over, acknowledging the slapped-musket salutes from the sentries. A low ridge cut off his view of the sawmill post as he moved south along the path. He crossed the crest and then he could see a second log bridge that crossed the river at the northern head of Lac St. Sacrement. Far to his right, across the arc of the river, rose another low mountain which Crosbie judged would dominate this entire area, if cannon could be sited on its peak.

The dense forest and undergrowth thinned out as the young Scot worked closer to the river. On the northern bank, only a narrow strip of weed-choked meadowland rimmed the stream. Across the river, on the side that Crosbie had already mentally assigned to the enemy, new grass sprang pale from the ancient loam, making a good level base for an encampment. Beyond it stretched a lightly wooded plain that gradually merged with the dark forest.

Putting himself in the position of the enemy, Crosbie could see only two alternatives. First, the English could take the direct and simple route across the two bridges, fighting for every inch of ground. Or they could try to make their way around the arc of the river, delaying battle until they were almost at Carillon's walls. Crosbie knew he would have to inspect that second route before he could anticipate the enemy's decision.

Crosbie crossed the sentry-guarded bridge and strolled through the flat meadow in a long arc across the wooded plain and into the broken ground of the solid black forest beyond.

The commanding mountain directly ahead was blotted from view the moment he entered the dense forest. He fought his way down the muddy ravine of a small stream, up the other side, and found himself ankle-deep in a dank spruce bog. Briers snatched at his clothing and roots half-hidden in ancient mold reached up to trip him. Dripping spruce boughs wiped nastily across his face and tangled with the barrel of his fusil. Thick swarms of black gnats buzzed around him, biting fiercely. The only consolation to

Crosbie was the conviction that this route was clearly impassable to any modern army.

The weary young Scot fought clear of the tangling bog and worked his way back to the edge of the river, following its western bank past the rapids to the mill-race where he reached the path leading to Carillon. This wild land would present terrible problems to an attacking army, Crosbie considered. Though Carillon itself was by no means impregnable, the French could make the enemy pay dearly. With the vigorous employment of artillery, Crosbie figured he might make that cost prohibitive.

CHAPTER TWENTY

In the days that followed, Duncan Crosbie tried to assume the mentality of an English general. He appointed himself commander of the force attacking Carillon and his long weary days were spent walking over and over every possible approach to the fort. He allotted himself ten thousand English troops, a magnificent artillery train, supplies without stint. He maneuvered from every angle, assaulted every plausible defensive position. He took Carillon a dozen times each day. Not once was he repulsed. The fort simply was not defensible against strong, formal attack.

In addition to all the sites that Général Montcalm had instructed him to survey, Crosbie found still another. Directly across the mouth of the river where it emptied into Lake Champlain, was the highest mountain in the area. From its peak even a small field piece could subject the fort to ruinous fire. Given two well-served siege guns and Crosbie would guarantee surrender of Carillon within three days. Here again the enemy was denied a dominating position only because of its inaccessibility. The three low mountains near the fort were alike in their surrounding areas, low boggy morasses and rough, broken ground that would require a carefully constructed road. In a week's time, cannon might be mounted on any of the commanding heights. But in a week Général Montcalm could nullify the value of any height selected. It was not exactly a stalemate situation; the odds still greatly favored the attacking English. But with watchfulness, with alert attention to the enemy's movements, with a successful general's genius for timing and—Crosbie added as a prime element—with luck, Carillon might make such resistance as to destroy the English army's future usefulness. It was an enormous gamble that lay in Montcalm's hand and Crosbie began to understand something of the strains to which his commander was subjected.

Early each evening, the Général called together his regimental commanders, the ranking officers of the Canadien regulars and militia, together with his staff. This council of war had only one subject on its agenda: how best to defend Carillon. Only the professional French officers were wise enough to see any peril in the fort's location, and not all of them. To a man, the Canadiens insisted the fort was impregnable. Always it was the Général's right hand, Colonel the Chevalier de Bourlamaque who brought the conversation back to its professional basis again. Crosbie was constantly impressed with the ease with which de Bourlamaque managed the touchy provincials: an easy attitude of deference, a willingness to listen, followed by a brief and sincere compliment, that was all. Few Canadiens had a fair word to say to Montcalm, but all seemed to admire de Bourlamaque.

The Colonel, a gloomy, taciturn man, was the work-horse of Montcalm's staff, serving as Brigadier. The second-in-command, the Chevalier de Lévis, was currently in Montreal, but was expected at the fort before the English arrived. As a consequence, it was Colonel de Bourlamaque who took on his shoulders most of the onerous detail of preparing the troops for combat.

Duncan Crosbie managed skillfully to avoid a meeting with Le Mercier, despite the fact that he saw the burly red-faced commandant every evening at the officers' council.

When the meeting with Le Mercier came, it was every bit as unpleasant as Crosbie had anticipated. Crosbie had returned to the fort after a fatiguing day spent climbing the low mountain opposite the sawmill. He had hoped to gobble a bite of dinner in the decent privacy of his room and go promptly to bed, but Denis was waiting for him with word that he was bade to dinner in the Général's quarters. His dress uniform, complete with sword, was laid out. Hot water for shaving stood steaming on the table. Crosbie stifled his groans of weariness and slowly dragged off his soiled clothing.

No visible signs of his tiredness remained when he presented himself at the Général's anteroom an hour later, but Crosbie felt that his mind was a bedraggled, sodden sponge. His initial report had been forwarded to Montcalm days before and he expected a sharp questioning period from the Général. He squared his shoulders as the orderly barked out his name.

He entered, blinking in nervousness. Brilliant light struck at his eyes, dazzling him. For a ranking Général, the Marquis de Montcalm lived simply, but the simplest existence for a Général is incredible luxury to a penurious sous-lieutenant dependent upon his pay. The Général's table was laid for a party of six, with triple-branched candlesticks at head and foot. An astounding array of bottles stood ready on an adjacent shelf and the room was redolent of a spicy aroma that made saliva start in Crosbie's mouth. He clamped his elbow hard, holding his hat firmly in place as he bowed low to his Général.

"No formality, I beg of you, monsieur," Montcalm said, smiling. "Please let Jeannot take your hat and come join the others in a glass of Jerez." Cordially, the Général gripped Crosbie's arm and led him across the room toward a wide bank of windows overlooking Lake Champlain. There Captain Bougainville stood with a glass ready for Crosbie's hand. Promptly the captain poured a pale, straw-colored wine into the glass and held it out.

"This wine was sent to me by my dear lady," Montcalm said easily. He sipped delicately from his glass and rolled the wine appreciatively over his tongue. "A Spanish wine of some note. You are familiar with these other gentlemen, Monsieur Crosbie?"

The young Scot had observed Le Mercier's blue-and-scarlet uniform the moment he had entered. Colonel de Bourlamaque stretched his stiff smile slightly wider to welcome Crosbie.

The last member of the party of six was Estére, the Général's military secretary, a self-effacing, wizened little man. It seemed to Crosbie that Estére's smile had a personal meaning for him. Probably something to do with that damned report, he thought, turning to greet Le Mercier, who contented himself with a meaningless grunt, designed to avoid direct offense, but devoid of all pleasantry.

De Bourlamaque extended himself gruffly to smooth over Le Mercier's surliness. He offered Crosbie an open snuffbox, pressing it on him so warmly that Crosbie hardly managed to refuse. "Not to every taste, I know," the colonel said in a hoarse, amiable tone. "Each to his own, eh, monsieur?"

Crosbie agreed willingly. He sipped at his wine, listening to the commonplace comments of soldiers little used to social gatherings.

The Général was a courtly host. Smoothly, he seated his guests, assigned his quietly moving servants their tasks. Crosbie found himself wielding a sharp carving knife, his teeth gritting with concentration as he tried to shave thin slices from a cold ham.

"A suitable task for you, I understand, Monsieur Crosbie," the Général said from his seat at the head of the table. "My good Louis tells me you have a certain skill with the knife."

Crosbie flushed heavily. His slices were as thin as any chef could have managed.

"My father insisted that every gentleman should be able to carve a thin slice," de Bourlamaque growled pleasantly. "But never in my life have I seen neater ones than yours, monsieur. Will you try some of this beef I have haggled apart, or do you prefer the clumsy gobbets of mutton that Bougainville has spoiled?"

De Bourlamaque's bland question brought laughter, and for the first time, Montcalm's dinner party coalesced into a unit. Crosbie accepted enormous servings of everything, suddenly ravenous.

"A glass of wine with you," Montcalm said formally, raising his glass. "Here's to our corpulent opponent, General Abercrombie."

"So long as you do not toast young Lord Howe, I join with pleasure, Your Excellency," de Bourlamaque added.

"A plague on Lord Howe," Montcalm agreed. "He is far too clever, that one. Shall we drink confusion to Abercrombie's Brigadier?"

All joined lustily, even Crosbie who echoed the sentiment without understanding. Lord Howe was second in command of the English army that would soon attack Carillon. Apparently, he was considered the real threat.

Dinner proceeded comfortably. Crosbie had taken a glass or two more wine than necessary, but it served to make the party amusing. At length the cloth was removed. Silver plates of fruits and nuts appeared on the polished board. Fresh glasses were presented.

"My last bottle of crème de Noyeau, gentlemen," Montcalm said, lifting a squat black bottle. "A speciality of my own distillery at Candiac. Let me urge a taste upon you. A rare treat, I can assure you."

Bougainville made a cryptic motion, and one after the other, the officers at the table politely declined. Crosbie caught the obvious hint and also refused. Clearly, the crème de Noyeau was a favorite tipple of the Général. If this were the very last of his supply, it would be doubly precious to him. And Crosbie was well content with the cognac. He cracked a walnut easily between two fingers and picked out the meats.

The moment for toasts caught Crosbie by surprise and he almost stumbled as he untangled his feet to rise for "The King!" Others might be drunk at ease, but not that first, mandatory salute to Louis XV. Montcalm smiled at the gawky young Scot as they seated themselves once more. "Monsieur Crosbie," he commanded.

Crosbie fumbled in his mind for a suitable toast. "I'll give you Carillon, Your Excellency," he said in a loud tone, lifting his glass. "May its bells ring a solemn dirge for English tyranny!"

Montcalm applauded when he had lowered his glass. "A splendid conceit, monsieur," he murmured. "You visualize our cannon as Carillon's bells, eh?"

Le Mercier lifted his glass. "I give you the brave Canadiens who will ring the peal for the English!"

Bougainville replied with a toast to the musical conductor who would select the tune to be played and with that the allusions to Carillon's name were ended. The bottles passed along the table and were replaced by the watchful servants as they were emptied.

"Our last evening at Carillon, gentlemen," the Général said easily.

All casual conversation was silenced as all five officers turned toward Montcalm, knowing more would follow.

"We will move out in the morning," Montcalm said. "The orders will be issued at dawn. The Regiment of Berry will remain at Carillon. De Bourlamaque will command the advance at the Carrying Place, with an outpost at the head of Lac St. Sacrement. The main body will bivouac at the sawmill. So, gentlemen, we begin our campaign. Let me drink success to all of us."

Montcalm rose with lifted glass and his officers stood eagerly.

"There is news then, Your Excellency?" de Bourlamaque inquired hoarsely. "The English are moving?"

"Soon, soon," Montcalm said, seating himself and pouring a slight dribble of crème de Noyeau into his glass. He sniffed it with a deep inhalation. "Magnificent," he said softly. "Yes, the English will move soon. Already they have mustered a thousand boats and rafts for their guns."

"Do we know their numbers yet, mon général?" Bougainville asked quietly.

Montcalm shrugged. "The reports continue to vary," he said. "Monsieur Longis holds the record with his estimate of thirty thousand. The English muster rolls last week showed nearly twenty-five thousand. I think twenty thousand is closer, through many will be left behind to follow later. The odds are much as usual." The Général sipped his liqueur.

Crosbie grunted to himself. Montcalm accepted a figure of twenty thousand as a minimum, which would give Abercrombie the greatest army ever assembled in the New World. Against them, Carillon could gather a scant three thousand and of that number, nearly five hundred would be Canadiens and Indians of dubious value. Yet the Général and the other officers grouped around his table drank their brandies with quiet content, unimpressed by the weight of the force that would soon be hurled against them. The French army had conquered English forces up to ten times their size in the past years. This then was to be considered merely a routine imbalance. Crosbie kept his eyes hard on the Général.

"What would you do, mon général," Bougainville said in a musing tone, "if you were ever given such proportionate advantage against the English? Suppose you had the twenty thousand, and Abercrombie only three?"

Crosbie saw Montcalm's muscular face flatten into sharp planes as the Général compressed his lips. His easy, relaxed attitude vanished. Montcalm's hand coiled into a tight fist against the polished table.

"What I would give for that! Just once. Only for one brief campaign! I would have Abercrombie retreating in a full run from Albany. I would strike him in New York before he could possibly prepare for me. Then north to Boston to destroy Amherst's base, and the war would be over. Like that!" Montcalm's hard fist smashed against a flickering candle, pounding it into a soft smoking blob of wax.

Briefly, Crosbie had a glimpse of the quality that made Montcalm a victorious general. For that fleeting moment, the young Scot understood what torment it had been for Montcalm to sit endlessly waiting, defending when every impulse urged him to attack. The general who is thwarted by inadequate force is a bound Prometheus, damned to a torture that lesser men can never feel.

"How long have we been here now, Louis?" Montcalm demanded. "More than two years, isn't it? Never, not at any single moment since I have commanded in Canada, have we been able to mount a resolute campaign against the English and drive it home. Never. One hundred thousand men could be found to fight Austria, but I came here with only twelve hundred replacements. I sometimes wonder if the King has ..."

The habitual discretion of the veteran officer jumped to the Général's rescue. His bitterly sharp words cut off abruptly, silenced at the very moment he heard himself mention the King. At length he shrugged and barked out a harsh, painful laugh.

"You touch closely at the hidden places, Louis," he said quietly to Bougainville. "I wonder if any of my thoughts are secret from you."

Bougainville managed a light airy gesture with one hand. "It would be unfair, mon général," he said pleasantly, "to give you equality with the English. Poor Abercrombie. As things stand now, he has a slight chance of success, but imagine how he would feel if ..."

The Général laughed, and this time with genuine humor. "You are a bouffon, Louis. I must, by the way, thank you for that amusing English paper you sent me this morning. I have never laughed so heartily."

"The editorial from Boston, eh?" Bougainville grinned. "The classical touch was charming, I thought. 'Delenda est Canada.' Magnificent conceit, these Bastonnais display."

The Général said, "I wish I could understand why the English refer so constantly to our use of Indians. Surely everyone realizes that the English command twice the savage warriors that we do.

Why do the English pretend that only the French send out raiding parties?"

"The English have a genius," Bougainville said lightly. "They are able to ignore the most obvious fact. After a time, they feel that the fact loses validity. This is called English doggedness."

Montcalm joined in the brief laughter. "Possibly the English can forget who slaughtered the inhabitants at Montreal, but I wonder how long it will be before Canadiens forget. Well, gentlemen, it is a great pity to break up such a gathering, but tomorrow will be an active day. Have you any questions before we ..."

Courtesy demanded a negative response to the Général's invitation, but Duncan Crosbie stirred in his chair.

"Sir, I ..." Crosbie plucked at his tight neckcloth. "I was ..."

"Yes, Monsieur Crosbie?" the Général said. "Speak out."

"It was about the field carriages I requested, Your Excellency," Crosbie said hesitantly. "I dislike troubling you, but ..."

"Yes, yes, what is it?"

Crosbie gulped for air, then desperately, he said, "The smiths will not complete the carriages without specific order which they cannot accept from me alone. There is a shortage of wheels, also ..."

"Also, I ordered them not to make the carriages." The Chevalier Le Mercier lurched forward, his flaming face close to Crosbie's. "Cannon are my responsibility and ..."

"Yes, yes," Montcalm broke in impatiently. "I realize your position, my dear Chevalier. I will discuss Monsieur Crosbie's suggestion with you sometime tomorrow."

"But, sir, I ..." Crosbie snapped his mouth shut with belated caution. No sous-lieutenant argued with his général. He should have learned that basic lesson before now.

Montcalm eyed him tightly for a moment, then gestured for him to speak.

"The carriages will take at least three days, mon général," Crosbie said unhappily. "I thought ..."

Le Mercier's great hand slammed down on the table with a resounding crash. "I will be damned forever if I will listen to another wet-nosed sous-lieutenant with his schoolboy notions. Another moment and he'll invent a breech-loading cannon for us."

Crosbie tightened his hands, fighting for restraint. "Monsieur le Chevalier may not have heard that a breech-loading cannon was invented over a hundred years ago," he said heavily.

The foolish distraction upset Le Mercier's chain of thought. He goggled at Crosbie, his dense eyebrows meeting in an abrupt frown. And Crosbie guessed what he must be thinking. Le Mercier had been a sergent of artillery when he first came to Canada. His formal training must have been meagre and he simply didn't know, had never heard of a successful breech-loading gun. In his mind, it was merely the symbol of the ridiculous, as a sensible person might regard the suggestion that a man might fly.

"Nonsense," Le Mercier growled. "Perfect nonsense."

"Schoolbooks have useful information," Crosbie said flatly.

"I share the Chevalier's surprise. I had never heard of a breech-loading cannon," Montcalm said in a mild conversational tone, ignoring the clash between his subordinates. "I should think you artillerymen would be screaming for them until the Ministry of War was deafened. What, then, is their fault?"

Crosbie turned to the Général, keeping his face perfectly straight. "The locking device, mon général," he said stiffly, "is the major problem. It must be strong enough to withstand the explosion in the bore and that means it must be large and heavy. Such cannon are enormous. Also, since the powder-gases tend to escape into the lock, the life of such a cannon is shortened by corrosion. Most of the muzzle-loading guns we use can last for hundreds of years, given reasonable care. Those on Quebec's walls are proof of that."

Montcalm chuckled, carefully not glancing at Le Mercier. He studiously ignored the Chevalier's hoarse growl. "So your breech-loader is no great success, after all."

"The faults are technical, Your Excellency," Crosbie said insistently, warming to the subject. "Every fault can be cured. We need a new metal, an alloy lighter than gunmetal, yet stronger. Then we need a new device for enclosing the explosion, so that not all the force of the powder is exerted against the locking mechanism. These are, in essence ..."

"Preposterous," Le Mercier concluded in a snarling voice. "New metals, new guns. Do you know what we need, monsieur? What we need are men who aren't afraid to fight the guns we have!"

Crosbie's face whitened with anger. "Do you accuse me of cowardice, monsieur?"

Swiftly Bougainville leaned to touch Crosbie's arm. "He spoke in haste, my friend," he said calmly. "I am sure the Chevalier would never ..."

Le Mercier drew in a long complacent breath, pleased to see the effect of his words.

"Will you answer me, monsieur?" Crosbie demanded quietly.

"Gentlemen," Bougainville broke in. "Gentlemen, I remind you that His Excellency wishes to retire. May we not continue this discussion elsewhere?"

Bougainville offered a way out for anyone willing to take it. Crosbie felt his face flushing hotly in embarrassment, but not for a moment did he take his eyes from Le Mercier. He would accept any form of retraction from the Chevalier, but, in honor, he dare not let the matter rest where it was.

"Monsieur le Chevalier," he said, his voice grating with the strain of trying to speak quietly, "has the decision. I will accept an apology," Crosbie said bluntly, "but ..."

"An apology!" Le Mercier bellowed, outrage and brandy fusing in a roaring incoherence. "I'll see you damned ..."

Général Montcalm came to his feet. The other officers rose with him. For a long silent moment, the Général regarded Crosbie. Then he turned to Le Mercier. "There are no cowards in my command," he said crisply. "Do you agree, monsieur?"

Le Mercier moistened his lips and nodded uncertainly. "Of course, mon général. I never thought..."

"Monsieur Crosbie!" the Général snapped. "The Chevalier le Mercier sees no cowards in this room. Is that sufficient?"

Crosbie understood. Only he could make the decision in a matter affecting his honor. Even the général could not interfere beyond this point. Le Mercier's statement was not a complete retraction, but Montcalm seemed to think it could be accepted.

"I regret," he said formally, "that I misunderstood the Chevalier's comment."

Montcalm nodded briskly. "I am sure the Chevalier regrets his comment was capable of misconstruction." His level gaze demanded a response from the befuddled Le Mercier.

The Chevalier lifted one red hand helplessly. "It is regrettable," he conceded.

The incident was over. The officers bowed to the Général and filed through the door, Le Mercier first and Crosbie hanging back. Bougainville delayed also, staying at Crosbie's elbow.

"Monsieur Crosbie," Montcalm said quietly. "The Chevalier le Mercier is not adept with either his tongue or his sword. He can be maneuvered into a duel—and killed, very easily. If you fight with him, I will have you hanged for murder. Le Mercier is a fool. You need not ape him."

Crosbie bowed stiffly.

"There will be fighting enough for everyone very soon," the Général said with the faintest hint of a smile. "Devote your full attention to the English, young man."

Montcalm turned, moving toward a door in the far wall. Crosbie stayed rooted in place, his face blazing. Montcalm opened the door, then glanced over his shoulder.

"Another interesting report, Monsieur Crosbie," he said briskly. "Very commendable. Louis will tell you what I want now. Good night."

Bougainville and Crosbie bowed as the Général withdrew to his sleeping chamber.

Crosbie drew in a long shaky breath. Louis Bougainville shook his head slowly.

"I was worried for a moment, Duncan. The Général detests brawlers. But his dislike of Le Mercier is so great that he let you proceed far beyond the point..." Bougainville shrugged. "Well, I fully anticipated finding you in the guardhouse by this time. You must learn to restrain yourself, my friend."

Crosbie nodded bleakly.

Bougainville smiled easily. "And now to business. Have you met Captain Longis, who commands a troop of Indian scouts?"

Crosbie frowned. "Is he the one with the huge black beard?"

"An enormous beard," Bougainville agreed. "Yes, that is Longis. You are to go with him when the English army lands at the head of Lac St. Sacrement. The Général wants a complete report of the artillery that Abercrombie has available to him. Longis will find a point of vantage for you and I have an old naval telescope you may borrow. Be sure you observe every piece in the English artillery park."

Crosbie nodded. "Are we actually going to fight them?" he demanded tightly.

Bougainville shrugged. "Who knows? If I were in command here, I would retreat. But I am not in command. Montcalm will decide, has probably already decided."

CHAPTER TWENTY ONE

But Montcalm had not decided. During the long warm days while his army lay encamped around the sawmill, the Général held his council every evening as before. The information that came in every day clarified the situation more and more. The exact units, the status of equipment and training, the basic supplies, the armament, all this Montcalm knew of the English forces. He was desperately outnumbered; his position was indefensible. Retreat was the logical solution. But Montcalm remained, offering no hint of his decision.

Crosbie strained eagerly for the moment of action. If the French were to retreat, now was the time to leave. If they were to stand, now was the time to fortify the three low mountains, dig gun positions and emplace the artillery batteries. Crosbie chafed irritably as the time shortened.

An Indian runner brought to Carillon the first definite word of the English advance. Crosbie was sitting glumly beside a small fire near the sawmill. Beside him Denis sprawled happily, toying with a massive issue musket he had found somewhere. Lazily Crosbie reminded himself to send Denis, musket and all, back to the fort before the attack. The boy would object, but Crosbie would make it an order. Denis was far from being a trained soldier. And he was Crosbie's responsibility. He smiled at the boy.

"Denis, have you cleaned my fusil?"

"Oui, monsieur," the boy said promptly.

"Let me see," Crosbie said without moving.

Denis stooped through the entrance of the small tent that Crosbie shared with Bougainville. He squirmed out in a moment with Crosbie's light musket and held it out.

The piece gleamed. Crosbie inserted the nail of his little finger into the bore and twisted. A feathery flake of lead peeled away and he displayed it in his hand for Denis to see.

"Heat the ramrod gently," he instructed. "Don't let it get too hot, and be sure to have a cloth to hold it with. Then run the hot ramrod through the bore. Do that several times until all the fouled lead is melted out. Understand?"

Denis nodded glumly. He'd never even heard of a fouled bore until now. "What does it do? The fouled lead?"

Crosbie returned the fusil. "It makes the ball wobble in flight."

He glanced up as Bougainville approached the fire. The captain sank wearily to a seat. "The English have started," he said slowly. "The first division has already embarked and the rest will leave at dawn. We just received word."

"Do we make a stand here?" Crosbie broke in.

"For the moment. At least until the English land. Then … well, then we will see."

"You mean the Général hasn't decided. Not yet?"

"Not yet."

"What about the guns. Louis, do you realize we don't have a single cannon outside the fort?"

Bougainville took off his cocked hat. "I know, Duncan," he said slowly. "What's more, none of the field carriages you wanted have been made. I don't …"

"But they've got cannon!" Crosbie burst out. "Longis says the English have …"

"Damn you, Duncan," Bougainville said sourly. He threw his battered hat down with a full sweep of his arm. "Damn you, do you think I don't know?"

Crosbie rocked back slightly in amazement. The equable, poised Captain Bougainville never exploded. It must be the tension, Crosbie realized. Bougainville got it all. He lived with the Général, spent every waking hour with him. The strain of waiting would bear more heavily upon Bougainville than anyone else, saving only Montcalm himself.

"What's the trouble, Louis?" he asked quietly.

Bougainville shook his head. "I am stupid, Duncan. I try to anticipate the Général. But I fail. Probably the Lord Howe will try to anticipate him too. And fail as I do. Now let that be an end of it, Duncan. I should not speak this way."

"Why do you say Howe instead of Abercrombie? Is Howe really that important?"

"Important enough so that we know he is the true commander, in spite of Abercrombie's rank. Lord Howe is one of those brilliant freaks, a born commander. And his family is rich and powerful, so that his rise has been fast. Within a year, he will have Amherst's place, mark my words. And luckily for him, Howe is the eldest brother, so he will succeed to his father's wealth and influence. His two younger brothers are almost as talented, but hampered by their brother's fame, naturally. We may meet the youngest one day. He is William, who already commands a regiment of infantry under Amherst at Louisbourg. The other brother I know nothing about. I think his name is Richard. He is a naval officer. A rare collection of talent, eh?"

"Indeed," Crosbie agreed easily.

Bougainville pushed himself up wearily. "Enough of this gossip, my friend. I met Longis on the way here. He will expect you before dawn at the sawmill. And you will be glad to hear that the Chevalier de Lévis is now on his way with a few more troops from Montreal." He yawned wide. "Forgive me, Duncan. I must get some sleep. You, too, my friend. We'll all be up before dawn tomorrow."

"Yes," Crosbie said vaguely. Nothing was further from his mind than sleep. Now, after all the long months of waiting, the English were coming, vast in numbers, superior in equipment and armament. Crosbie shivered, but not from fear. His gaunt young face tensed with excitement as he stared blindly into the fire.

An earlier Duncan Crosbie had spent a night like this before Culloden, resting in the heather with Prince Charlie and his French comrades, waiting for an overwhelming English attack. His father had been much like him, he had been told, so probably he too had felt the same cold grue, and had made himself the same tight-lipped vows of valor, and determined to fight well, and all the time with that same hard icy knot in his throat, that terrible apprehension, not of death, but of displaying the fear that threatened to choke him. The thought of his father was sobering. That Duncan Crosbie had not lived beyond the day of battle. And this Duncan Crosbie could die as quickly as the first. If death should come for him at Carillon, Duncan Crosbie prayed that he might meet it as bravely as his father had, with the defiance that properly became a man.

The young Scot sat unmoving through the warm night. The small fire greyed with ash. Strange animals rustled the under-brush. Tramping sentries called out sleepy orders. The swift river splashed thunderously over the sawmill falls. Duncan Crosbie noticed none of it.

CHAPTER TWENTY TWO

With the bearded partisan commander, Longis, and three painted, stinking Indians scouts, Duncan Crosbie lay hidden on a slight rise overlooking the northern end of Lac St. Sacrement. Below him and as far down the lake as he could see with Bougainville's telescope, spread the English fleet of bateaux and whaleboats, a thousand of them, Longis had counted.

The advance force was composed of a motley collection of green-uniformed soldiers whom Longis identified as rangers, and a number of poorly disciplined men who seemed to be garbed as sailors. An hour earlier, the advance party had pushed back the small unit stationed at the landing by Colonel de Bourlamaque. The French soldiers withdrew across the river, setting fire to the bridge as they crossed.

When the advance force had signalled, the main body of the English army swept in toward the landing place. Crosbie ached for just one canister-loaded cannon to blast into their packed ranks.

The English poured ashore in a steady wave. First, regiments in the blue-and-buff of the provincial levies, then the solid scarlet mass of the English infantry of the line, soldiers magnificent in appearance and discipline, almost as good in combat as French regulars. Regimental bands were the first to land, escorting their color bearers. The blaring martial tunes soared arrogantly through the forest stillness. Flags whipped in the warm breeze, and serjeants counted step as if this were merely another garrison parade ground.

The green-uniformed rangers formed a defensive perimeter within which the regiments were formed, each centering upon a hastily erected headquarters tent where its colors were flown. Between two scarlet regiments, the English staff disembarked in complete security. A vast pavilion of tinted canvas was raised and the large cluster of gold-laced uniforms disappeared inside.

By mid-morning only half of the English army had landed. The ranger companies had relinquished their guard duty to the regulars and had moved forward, out of sight in the dense forest. Off-shore, the remainder of the flotilla waited its turn, with artillery barges leading the long column of supply boats. Crosbie could easily count the guns from his vantage point. He tapped Longis's shoulder and squirmed back from the slight rise, pushing his telescope together compactly.

"I've seen enough," he said briskly.

Longis scratched at his dense black beard, then rubbed his moist fingers across his pale doeskin shirt. He cocked his head as if he were listening intently. Crosbie could hear the regimental music still blaring brassily.

"They have been ashore for three hours now," Longis said thoughtfully. "Those provincial troops in the van were Rogers's companies of rangers. If Abercrombie was going to rebuild that bridge, he would have them out chopping timber. So, possibly..." Longis scowled ferociously at his Indian scouts, grunted something at them. "Tell the Général that I will cross the river. I think the English may be planning to go around the outer arc of the river. I will collect what Indians I can find and cross over, staying just ahead of the English scouts. Then we will be sure what direction they take. You understand?"

Crosbie nodded. If the English hoped to approach Carillon by the shorter route across the Carrying Place, they would have to rebuild the bridge that de Bourlamaque had just burned. Without it, they could not bring up their guns and supplies. Since they had not made a move toward replacing the bridge, they probably intended to follow the longer route, through the tangle of forest on the far side of the river.

"Very well, monsieur," Crosbie said.

Longis grinned. "Bonne chance," he said lightly. He tapped an Indian's shoulder and immediately set out at a quick jogging trot through the underbrush.

Crosbie walked swiftly back along the path toward Montcalm's headquarters at the sawmill. The sawmill bridge was still intact, though several kegs of gunpowder were stacked below to blow it in event of a sudden attack. Four sentries guarded the approach and Crosbie was inspected carefully before being allowed to cross over.

Where yesterday entrance to the Général's office had been a routine matter, today it was a privilege dearly won. Crosbie was stopped on the veranda which served as anteroom to Montcalm's sawmill headquarters. A sentry entered to notify Captain Bougainville. Crosbie propped himself on the stout log railing, looking downstream toward Lake Champlain and the fort of Carillon.

The ground rose sharply from the river and only the upper roof-tops of Carillon were visible to Crosbie, but even so, he was aware of unusual activity just outside the walls of the fort. The regiment of Berry was stationed there as rearguard and every man was busy with something... something like...

"Retrenchments," Bougainville said drily. "Berry is digging a defensive line along the ridge you surveyed."

Crosbie then realized that the activity was orderly and systematic. Trees were chopped, fell, and were dragged aside. Soft moist loamy earth flew high, impelled by Berry's shovels. What had seemed to be frenetic movement now made clear sense.

"Retrenchments along the ridge," Crosbie said quietly. He rubbed his blunt jaw with a grubby hand. "The only clear ground is behind the ridge," he said, almost to himself. "So, to get a decent field of fire forward, you would have to clear the forest.

At least a kilomètre, possibly more. There would be ten thousand trees in that space."

"It comes as a late idea," Bougainville said, keeping his voice too low to be overheard. "We have three thousand men. How long would it take three thousand men to cut ten thousand trees, Duncan?"

Crosbie grinned. He held out a strip of parchment. "Here is the artillery count, Louis. Number and calibres. Now will we move our own guns out of the fort?"

"Please ask for no confidences, Duncan," Bougainville said quietly. "Did you observe the English troops? How did they bear themselves?"

"Like the lords of creation, Louis. They've come to swallow us whole," Crosbie said heavily. "Bands playing stirring selections, the staff officers sitting down to tea in a pavilion while the army gets ready to move forward."

"Forward how?" Bougainville demanded sharply.

"Longis says they will probably go around the outer arc, staying on the west bank. He has taken his scouts out to make sure." Crosbie gestured over his shoulder at the infantry formations near the sawmill. "They will come on us from the west, so quite naturally, we have our men facing south. Very clever."

"Last night I suggested that you might trust to the Général, Duncan," Bougainville said in a harsh whisper. "Now hear it as an order."

Crosbie nodded glumly. The rebuke was justified.

Bougainville smiled abruptly. "We wait for intelligence. When Longis sends a man back with his report, we should know the answer." Briefly, Bougainville glanced at the sun. "Nearly midday," he said. "Even the English will not delay much longer. You wait here, Duncan. I will have work for you soon."

Before Bougainville could return to the headquarters office, a leaping, screaming Indian came into view upstream near the falls. He dropped down the riverbank and ran toward the sawmill. Bougainville walked briskly inside the building and returned almost immediately, wearing the Général's gold-laced hat. The Indian reduced his high-stepping, prancing strides to a sedate, dignified stroll, presenting himself to Bougainville with solemnity. Bougainville raised one arm, very deliberately, in greeting. After a long moment, the warrior produced a strip of paper wound tightly around a short twig and bound in place with black thread. Bougainville accepted it, giving the scout a small metal token in exchange. The Indian wheeled quickly and dashed away toward the tribal bivouac in the forest. His work was done for the day. Now he could spend the afternoon reclining on his couch, regaling the old men and young boys with boisterous lies of his bravery against the English.

Bougainville unwound the message from the stick and held the paper up to the light. Crosbie could see bright beads of sweat standing out strongly on his forehead.

"As you said, Duncan, the English have started around the outer arc. They marched in four columns into the forest, with Longis just ahead of them." Bougainville stared out, as if through determination, his eyes could pierce the dense foliage, level the low hills, and give him a glimpse of the marching English army. "Stay here, Duncan. I will need you soon, I expect." Bougainville returned to the office, taking off the Général's hat as he went inside.

Duncan Crosbie could visualize the route the English were following. The virgin forest with its tangling underbrush and mucky spruce bogs, the fallen trees that lay meshed in a natural abattis, constituted an obstacle that Montcalm himself might have chosen for the English. For a moment, Crosbie looked out at the comparatively easy ground between the sawmill and the area where the English had landed. To come directly across would have required two bridges and possibly several fierce skirmishes, but the advantages were obvious. Only a fool would choose the long way around. A fool, or a man ignorant of the terrain. Abercrombie would have weary, frustrated troops to employ when he came into position against the waiting, rested French army. The man was a criminal idiot, and his much-praised Brigadier, the fabulous Lord Howe, could hardly be better, if he agreed to that ruinous approach toward Carillon. The mere thought of transporting cannon and artillery supplies through that impassable jungle made Duncan Crosbie ache in sympathy with the English gunners. Stupid decisions such as that could lose an entire campaign. Montcalm must be exulting at the news from Longis.

As the afternoon wore on, the army waited. The midday meal was lavish with a plentiful issue of wine. Many of the troops lay dozing in the brilliant sunlight with no more than half of them standing ready. During all that time, the vast English army floundered through bogs, climbed mountains of fallen timbers, trudged painfully through thick underbrush, never able to see the sun, never sure just where they were headed.

After the soldiers had been fed, Général Montcalm sent orders to Colonel de Bourlamaque, pulling him back to the sawmill position. Slowly, with cautious deliberation, the advance troops moved to the rear, crossing the bridge in front of the mill and setting it ablaze. Good engineer troops could rebuild it in a day, but even a day might be a critical period of time. The bridge was thoroughly destroyed; the stone abutments on either bank being knocked down and scattered in the roaring river. Most of de Bourlamaque's men took station facing west in the direction from which the English attack must come, if ever the enemy could fight its way through that terrible forest, and do so with enough energy left to assault the French lines.

After siting his troops, Colonel de Bourlamaque stamped angrily up to the sawmill, grunted a salutation to Crosbie, and banged open the door to Montcalm's office. A moment later, Bougainville came out quietly and latched the door behind him.

Crosbie asked, "De Bourlamaque wants to make a stand? Or to attack?"

Bougainville lifted one eyebrow. "Do not pry, Duncan," he said testily. "The Général and Colonel de Bourlamaque are discussing a question of basic judgment. If they were not gentlemen, I would say they were brawling. I wish Longis would send another report," he muttered in a strained voice. "The Général is taking this delay very well, but I do not have such strong nerves."

A sharp rattled salvo of musketry echoed from the low mountain, seeming to come from all directions. The brisk firing rose to a crescendo, rolling in solid waves of angry noise along the river.

"There's your report," Crosbie said. "I guess Longis didn't stay far enough ahead. Does he have enough men to fight a skirmish?"

"Two hundred or so," Bougainville said.

Crosbie said calmly, "A couple of hundred men should be able to protect themselves. That's no parade ground back there. It's full of places to hide. We'll know what is happening as soon as Longis …"

Three Indian scouts appeared above the falls, not cavorting now, but running with intense concentration. None had muskets, so they must have run in panic. As Crosbie watched, they turned away from the sawmill, dashing madly toward the Indian encampment.

Bougainville glanced at Crosbie with a frightened surmise and the young Scot forced himself to remain where he was, standing solid, showing nothing of the dread that seized his throat with a dry, hot clutch. Indians were known to panic for little reason. A few Indians always ran if the omens seemed wrong. It meant nothing.

A few minutes later a tight knot of warriors came into view on the high ground. They moved in disciplined order, and as they took turns coming down the riverbank, Crosbie could see that they were surrounding a bearded man in a pale doeskin shirt, all of them keeping as close as if they constituted a royal bodyguard.

That would be Longis, Crosbie assumed. The partisan officer leaped down the bank and ran lithely toward the sawmill. He sprang onto the veranda with one bound.

"What's happening, Longis?" Bougainville demanded. "Did you meet..."

"Got lost; ran into them; had to fight to get back," Longis spat out his report in short gasping breaths, fighting for control. "We were all lost. Every man in the forest was lost. Even Rogers was lost. We came through, but... lots of men... killed or captured. We surprised them. The whole English army began to... retreat. Where's the Général?"

Bougainville erupted in low, rollicking laughter. He pulled open the door and preceded Longis into Montcalm's office.

Crosbie could easily understand Bougainville's elation. In a forest like that, a sudden onslaught by an unsuspected enemy, coming from the flank, might very well destroy the English advance march. When troops retreated, or even halted in line of march, the following units piled up on those forward, creating a tangle that only time and genius could unravel. Longis had done a good day's work.

Captain Bougainville came out again briskly, moving along the veranda. Couriers were advised of an officers' council at four o'clock, and sent off with the message.

"You, too, Duncan," Bougainville said. "Be here at four. You can leave now, if you like. There won't be anything more today, I am sure."

Bougainville's hard round face broke into a rapturous grin. "Longis ran into a hornet's nest back there. He was on the far side and had to fight his way through the English advance party. Ciel, what a shock it must have been!"

"I suppose it was," Crosbie said, mystified by Bouganville's behavior. "It had to be something like that. What of it?"

"Longis's unit killed some English soldiers. Longis was right there. He actually saw them."

"Saw what?"

"Lord Howe," Bouganville answered flatly. "Lord Howe, Abercrombie's Brigadier, the only brilliant commander in that entire army." Bougainville shook his head. "One should not exult," he said soberly. "It is not proper. But still..."

"But what?" Crosbie roared.

"Dead," Bougainville said softly. "Longis is positive. He has seen Howe often. He is completely sure. Lord Howe is dead."

CHAPTER TWENTY THREE

Duncan Crosbie was early for the council, but even so, he could hear loudly roaring voices as he entered the sawmill headquarters. Softly, he eased the door open and went in, skirting around the wall to a position behind the Général.

Colonel Dalquier, commander of Béarn, had the floor when Crosbie entered. The young Scot heard only the end of Dalquier's commentary, but he could easily reconstruct the rest. Dalquier wanted to attack the English while they were still floundering in the tangled forest. His large tanned hands clawed the air fiercely as he advanced the proposal.

The Général stood with folded arms, his face carefully bland. He nodded when Colonel Dalquier finished.

"Thank you, monsieur," he said coldly. He glanced quickly around the room. "Now we will proceed to the subject I have placed before the council. Shall we stand at the sawmill?"

Colonel de Bourlamaque was rabidly eager to attack, but willing to consider a delay until the English advanced from the forest. Further, he would not wait. Not a moment. A murmured approval ran through the room.

Crosbie placed his shoulderblades squarely against the wall and listened with slight interest. By now he had attended dozens of councils-of-war at Montcalm's headquarters and the more he saw of them the more they offended his sense of propriety. The councils were the last remnant of the feudal period when independent barons banded with each other to attack a common enemy. Each being too jealous of his authority to relinquish his position to a central command, the barons instituted the conseil-de-guerre. When unanimity could be achieved, such a council made for enthusiastic support from the subordinate chieftains. Lacking unanimity, it induced a state bordering upon anarchy as each commander strove to force his opinion upon the others at any cost and usually at the top of his voice. The council was a serious handicap to Montcalm. Thank God that Abercrombie also had a council to bedevil him. Crosbie surged away from the wall when he heard Montcalm mention his name.

"Explain to these gentlemen why our position here is untenable, monsieur," the Général said. "You appreciate the reason?"

"Of course, Your Excellency," Crosbie said. "That low mountain just west of here commands the sawmill. A single gun emplaced there could enfilade our position. No soldier could live along the riverbank."

Montcalm pivotted again, facing the council. "Our junior member sees the point that has eluded many of you, gentlemen."

"Your Excellency!" The harsh growl of the Chevalier Le Mercier filled the room. "I challenge that officer's statement! It would take a month to emplace even a six-pounder on that mountain. The terrain is impossible."

Montcalm spoke wearily over his shoulder. "Monsieur Crosbie?"

"Two days, mon général," Crosbie said evenly. "Given a thousand men to prepare the ground."

The Général nodded. "And Monsieur Abercrombie has as many thousands as he could possibly need."

"Preposterous, Your Excellency," Le Mercier insisted. "This young fool ..."

"Two days!" Crosbie roared, drowning out the Canadien.

Montcalm smacked his hand hard against Estére's table.

"I accept Monsieur Crosbie's judgment, gentlemen," he said in a flat tone of command. "I trust I do not have to explain further why this position must be vacated."

The officers shuffled their feet. None cared to dispute Montcalm. Not one had previously suggested retreat. All wanted desperately to follow up the momentary advantage gained by the death of Lord Howe.

"The English army remains in their forest, halted in their tracks," the Général went on in a level tone. "Abercrombie has suffered a severe blow in the loss of his Brigadier. I can appreciate that. It is easy for me to understand Abercrombie's dismay. I have only to imagine what a shock it would be to lose my own de Bourlamaque."

The colonel straightened in his pride. The lowering frown smoothed away from his heavy features as the meaning of the compliment struck home. He glared staunchly forward, all umbrage forgotten. His tactical advice might be ignored, but his true value was appreciated by his Général and no soldier could hope for more.

"Unless Abercrombie withdraws within the hour, his army must remain in the forest all night. Obviously, he has given up all hope of immediate attack. But even one night in that dismal swamp will destroy much of the confidence of his troops. So, we are given a space of time in which to reconsider our position. Let us use it to the best advantage, gentlemen."

De Bourlamaque lifted his head abruptly. "We await your command, mon général."

The Général moved over to the open window. He spoke with his face half averted. "We have some three thousand soldiers, gentlemen," he said thoughtfully. "We must find a way to place them so that our full weight can be used. At the same time we must channel the English attack so that Abercrombie can bring only a part of his force against us. Does any of you know of such a place?"

Crosbie completely forgot his altercation with Le Mercier in his enjoyment of the Général's approach. Gently, Montcalm was leading the senior officers into recommending a withdrawal to the retrenchments which the Regiment of Berry had been preparing all day. But the suggestion would initiate with the council, as the minutes would show, not with the Général. Then Montcalm would be free to point out the dangers in even that position, all without jeopardizing his authority or his reputation. It was a masterful maneuver.

The council proceeded as Crosbie anticipated. The defensive line in front of the fort was considered from every angle, and ultimately approved. Bringing such primitive strategists into line with his thinking was difficult work for Montcalm, but one which he had often faced. In all armies the situation was the same. Valor alone was appreciated. Wisdom was usually equated with luck if it was considered at all. Every officer knew of Hannibal; not one could name the commander who had defeated him. A brave fool could—and often did—command huge armies. One such General lay only a short distance away, preparing to attack Montcalm.

"The line of retrenchments is short," Montcalm said, thinking aloud for the benefit of his officers. "But if we build the parapet in long zig-zags, then we could mount our entire force against the enemy. Yes, that will do. Now, gentlemen, what is wrong with that position? How would you assault it? Assume you are Monsieur Abercrombie. What would you do?"

Montcalm's regimental commanders glanced at each other. This was highly unorthodox procedure, they felt. The Général had approved the position, so why consider it further? It remained only to make the site as strong as possible and await attack.

"There is another low mountain south of the fort," the Général said. "It dominates our new position. Also, I invite your attention to the terrain. The retrenchments will run from side to side across the promontory on which stands Carillon. If Abercrombie attacks us, we will be in splendid position to hurt him seriously. But if he goes around, crossing the promontory farther inland and comes out on the shore of Lake Champlain north of the fort, he could then command all movement north along the lake. Then we would be penned on the promontory, completely cut off."

Montcalm let the full weight of his warning sink in before he turned again to look squarely at his officers. None seemed eager to answer him. The Général smiled bleakly.

"We will move back immediately, gentlemen. See that all units are bivouacked before dark. Officers will remain with their commands. Very well, that is all, gentlemen. You may..."

"But, Your Excellency..." Several voices merged into a single interruption.

"Yes, gentlemen?" Montcalm bent politely forward.

"But what if Abercrombie does cross the promontory instead of attacking, mon général?" Colonel Dalquier barked out nervously. "What will we..."

"We will decide that later," Montcalm said equably. "I expect that we would be compelled to attack the English before they could fortify along the lake. Then..." The remainder was obvious. The troops would have to be evacuated to the north by boat.

It was a thoroughly sober group of officers that filed out of the Général's headquarters. Their earlier elation had been buried under an avalanche of unpalatable fact. All respected Montcalm's opinions, and all felt a momentary flare of hatred that he should be right. Maps would be consulted feverishly tonight, each regimental commander hoping to evolve a better plan and all knowing they were doomed to failure before they started.

The Général seemed a man of stone. He stood unmoving, silhouetted against the darkening sky beyond the window. His neat military wig glimmered brightly in the failing light. His eyes were hidden under the shadow cast by his dense, knotted brows. The door closed behind the last regimental officer and Montcalm sighed softly.

Bougainville remained, and Crosbie hesitated, wondering whether he should go or stay until dismissed.

After a long moment, Montcalm forced a smile for Bougainville. "I saw your copy of Thucydides on your table, Louis," he said heavily. "There is a passage..." The Général chewed at his inner cheek gently, then said, "'Realize before you get into it how great are the chances of miscalculation in war.' It goes on to say... 'It is wont generally to resolve itself into a mere matter of chance. Both sides equally have no control and what the outcome will be is unknown and precarious.' The writer was no soldier, but he understood war as none of my officers do. They really believe that ferocious bravery is alone sufficient. God, what I would give for a few brilliant cowards to help me plan!"

Bougainville chuckled easily, breaking the Général's dour concentration. "I offer myself, Your Excellency. My mind may not be overly agile, but I am mightily afraid."

Montcalm laughed explosively, a brief smothered sound that surprised even himself. "You may be frightened now, but the moment the English appear, you will probably dash off and commit some heroic atrocity." The Général caught sight of Crosbie against the dark wall. "And of Monsieur Crosbie, I have no hope whatever. And now, Louis, I am off. You know what to do?"

"Yes, Your Excellency."

"Good. I will be in my quarters. Disturb me if necessary."

Montcalm clapped on his ornate hat and strode briskly out.

"A great, lonely man," Bougainville whispered. "I wish..."

Crosbie shifted restlessly. "Louis..."

"Ah, Duncan. You will be very busy tonight," Bougainville said quickly in a brusque tone. "The guns of Carillon are to be emplaced on or behind the new retrenchments. That is Le Mercier's responsibility, you understand. But you are to observe every detail. If anything goes wrong, try to persuade Le Mercier to take the proper steps. If he refuses, come for me. I will be around the boat landing most of the night."

"Boats..." Crosbie began. A chill dread struck him. "Boats, Louis?"

"Yes, Duncan. We will fight if Abercrombie comes at us in a frontal assault. But if he circles our position, we will have to withdraw."

CHAPTER TWENTY FOUR

Throughout the long strenuous night that followed, the French bivouac was a bustling, cheerful center of vigorous preparation. Crosbie had never before witnessed such willing eagerness in veteran troops. Fat pine torches lighted the entire position forward of the fort as the soldiers ate their dinner and set to work in alternate platoons, half the men resting while the others worked on the retrenchment of chopped trees. And every man sang.

Long before daylight, Crosbie thought he would go deaf from the incessant, tuneless din that soared, full-throated, through the night. Even the Indian scouts were appalled by the noise. Auprés de ma Blonde was the decided favorite during the first hours, giving way to La Delle Lisette when the Béarn regiment went to work. But the tinkling, childlike tune of the soldiers' best loved song was the one most frequently heard as the first streak of dawn lighted the sky.

"Malbrouck s'en va-t'en guerre,
Mironton, mironton, mirontain,
Malbrouck s'en va-t'en guerre,
N'en reviendra jamais!"

Over and over, the inane jingle was picked up as one regiment tried to outdo another in sheer volume. Since the War of the Spanish Succession, this has been the French infantryman's own song. Even the most ignorant man in the ranks could learn the words, or at the very least, follow the simple melody. Crosbie gritted his teeth at the constant rasping as his nerves tensed with irritation. The song died for a brief space, only to rise high again when a waggish soldier offered a revamped version:

"Ackrombie s'en va-t'en guerre,
Mironton, mironton, mirontain."

"Ackrombie" was doubtless a reference to Abercrombie, Crosbie assumed. It didn't scan, but still, it was no worse than singing "Malbrouck" and expecting reasonable men to understand that you meant "Marlborough." The change did nothing to improve the sing-song music, but the troops leaped at the excuse to bellow again. The new version made the rounds quickly. Crosbie held both hands over his ears as he worked.

Of Carillon's cannon, only the eight-pounders were light enough to place along the new fortification. Crosbie supervised the lowering of the nine guns from Carillon's wall, sending the low-wheeled carriages down first, and swinging the ton-weight of the iron guns by block and tackle. He watched carefully as a gun was eased onto its carriage, the trunnions guided into their sockets as the breech settled upon its block and the ropes were slacked off. A sergent snapped down the holdfasts and Crosbie stooped to inspect the aiming mechanism. He trimmed the elevating screw, then rotated the laying screw right and left from zero, watching the barrel's response. He straightened and nodded his approval to Le Mercier who was standing close by.

Another eight-pounder hung just above the stone paving, its muzzle no great distance above Crosbie's head. Gently, he patted its breech. The cool iron was vastly reassuring. Let who would command the Horse and Foot. Enough of these monsters and he could send them all running.

"Magnificent, eh?" Le Mercier's growling voice was oddly diffident. He too stroked the massive breech with a scarred hand.

That casual duplication of gesture established a certain rapport that endured throughout the night. Le Mercier moved back to let the sergent roll the new gun carriage into place and he took Crosbie's arm, pulling him aside.

"Those field carriages you wanted," he said quietly. "The smiths managed to finish one before I could stop them. Maybe we could find a use for it, eh?"

Crosbie's mouth fell slightly open and he was grateful for the gloom that masked his surprise. "But … but, I thought you said …"

"Fichtre!" Le Mercier spat. "You are a gunner. A firebrand, full of words, but a gunner for all that. Before, I was talking for that French Général. But now …" He smacked a beefy hand against Crosbie's back. "Have it rolled out here. We'll see if those smiths know their work."

"Thank you, monsieur," Crosbie said quickly. He spun on his heel before the commandant had a chance to change his mind.

Two infantrymen helped the eager young Scot to roll the new carriage into Carillon's courtyard where he could inspect it by the torchlight. Its high oaken wheels came almost to Crosbie's shoulders, giving the carriage a mobility denied to the tiny-wheeled fortress mounts. Crosbie ran it under a lowering gun and helped guide the cannon onto the bed. He snapped the holdfasts himself and bent to test the aiming devices. When he came erect, his gaunt young face was beaming. Now, by God, now he could show the English how one gun can be made to do the work of two. Frederick of Prussia knew the answer and he had shown the world, but only a few devoted gunners had learned the lesson. Mobility. It was that simple. A gun was an enormous weight. A lazy artillery officer would be tempted to leave it where it was, and hope the enemy would present himself at its muzzle. But Frederick had moved cannon as he moved troops. No enemy knew where to expect the murderous blast of canister through his packed formations. Best of all, Frederick had designed horse carriages not merely to bring cannon onto the field of battle, but actually to maneuver them during combat. A four-horse team, and Frederick had given himself the equivalent of an infantry battalion's fire power with one gun. Crosbie had never seen the Prussian horse-artillery. Few had. As far as Crosbie knew there were no such batteries in the French army now, and none planned. Well, he was far from commanding a horse-drawn battery, but he did have one small gun mounted on a fairly mobile carriage. The battle would prove its usefulness.

All of the eight-pounders were ranked at the gate of the fort, left under guard until their emplacements were completed. Le Mercier had gone ahead to scout the new retrenchment wall. Crosbie helped to roll his newly mounted gun into place with the others, paused to grin again at its great height as it towered above its battery-mates on its new carriage. Then he strode briskly out of the gate, swinging his arms and humming softly to himself.

He found Le Mercier in conversation with Captain Pontleroy, the army's engineer. Pontleroy was pointing along the low parapet which was all that existed of the new fortifications so far.

"...three mètres in height," the engineer was saying. "I will build a banquette behind it for a fire-step. You will observe that the ground slopes forward from the retrenchment in a natural glacis. I will form a dense abattis of fallen timbers there. Now, Monsieur le Chevalier, shall I break apertures for your guns, or do you prefer to raise them above the walls?"

Crosbie eyed Le Mercier apprehensively. If the guns were mounted above the wall, their gunners would be exposed to devastating fire. Fervently, Crosbie hoped the commandant would make the sound decision. He wanted nothing so much as to avoid controversy, if it were at all possible.

Le Mercier stroked his bristly chin. He wheeled to look forward from the wall. With one hand, he chopped off imaginary heights. Then he turned toward Crosbie. "A low platform so that the guns are above that low ridge, eh? Then break the apertures. Do you agree, monsieur?"

Crosbie drew in a relieved breath. "Completely, sir. We have eight guns to emplace. If we cut our apertures at the closed angle of each zig-zag, we will have a good field of fire with only a narrow opening. A slot about..." Crosbie spread his hands just slightly wider than the muzzle of an eight-pounder.

"Exactly so," Le Mercier growled. "I leave it in your hands, young man. One moment! You said eight guns. We brought nine down from..."

"One is in reserve, monsieur," Crosbie said, fiercely determined. "The mobile field carriage makes it..."

Le Mercier laughed in a thick roupy gurgle. "Your own pet, eh? Very well. Make sure the Général approves and I have no objection." He waved the problem aside. "I am going now to dinner. And I will rest for an hour. You will find me in my quarters if you need me." He eyed Crosbie with a hot glare, then suddenly smiled. "Which I doubt," he added, stalking off into the darkness.

Left to himself, Crosbie drove his half-battalion of workmen without rest, laboring himself at tasks most officers would consider demeaning. The long dark hours of the steamy night passed in a blur of fatigue. And his men kept pace with him, toiling beside the grim young Scot, ruefully shaking their heads when he demanded greater effort and got it by doing the hardest work himself. No French soldier could resist the appeal of an officer who worked with them. Every man sang lustily until Crosbie's ears rang with their dissonance.

Forward of the new wall, regiments of soldiers fought to erase the virgin forest, bringing down monstrous trees in thundering crashes. Crosbie led his men forward to collect the heaviest trunks for his gun platforms, adzing them roughly to prevent rolling, and dragging them back to the gun redoubts.

Untrimmed logs framed each embrasure in the wall, a tunnel-like casing through which the gun would peer. Behind each opening, a square platform of heavy timbers was built to hold an eight-pounder. And beside the platform were dug small rock-lined magazines where powder could be stored safely during the battle.

When the last platform and embrasure was ready, Crosbie had the guns hauled forward. Powder charges and priming quills were packed into the magazines and great mounds of canister were heaped beside each gun.

Crosbie left most of the men to rest beside the guns and went back to his field-mounted carriage. He had a battered stone-sled dragged close behind it and in the sled loaded supplies for independent operation. Powder charges, round-shot, canister and grape in equal amounts, a big handful of priming quills, rammers, sponges and reams, together with his dispart sights were stored safely under a protective tarpaulin.

The first streaks of light were visible in the east when Crosbie slumped on the stone-boat and looked at the result of his night's work. The platforms were ready. He had only to bring all of Carillon's guns around onto the western wall so that every one could bear upon the enemy. Then his work would be finished. But the new retrenchment was not yet finished, nor were more than half the trees cleared from the promontory. The work would go quickly with daylight, but surely a full day's labor remained, Crosbie thought.

His fatigue fell away as he gradually became aware of the perilous situation. An attack now would find Montcalm's force completely unprepared. But if attack were imminent, he should be at his guns with full crews ready. As it was, he had no idea where Carillon's gunners were quartered. The only troops in sight were infantrymen.

Impatiently, Crosbie pushed to his feet and stalked hastily toward the fort. Sleepy sentries stared at him dully. He strode into the courtyard and halted abruptly as he caught sight of Captain Bougainville seated at a flimsy table, pouring steaming coffee into his cup. Crosbie's tongue licked at his dry lips. A painful crack opened as he tasted the dust. He swallowed with painful effort.

"Duncan!" Bougainville called cheerfully. "Some coffee?"

Silently Crosbie took the cup and sipped the hot brew, unmindful of its scorching heat. He sighed when he put the cup down.

"We aren't ready, Louis," he said in a bleak tone.

"No," Bougainville said. He offered a heel of bread.

"But, for God's sake, Louis, what if Abercrombie…"

Bougainville raised his hand. "Easy, my friend. Abercrombie managed to collect his army only an hour ago. They are now all huddled together at their landing place. When they are fed, and sorted out, General Abercrombie will probably call a council of war, and sometime this afternoon he should decide what to do." Bougainville smiled easily. "His Excellency is convinced Abercrombie will not be able to advance today."

Crosbie nodded. An army that had laid on its arms all night in that dank forest would be in no condition for immediate attack. But Crosbie felt no relief, merely irritated frustration. He had driven himself and his men to the point of exhaustion and now it was apparent that they might just as well have waited for daylight to finish their work. Wearily, he rubbed a massive, grimy hand across his forehead.

"Go get some rest, Duncan. You've had a busy time."

Crosbie glanced curiously at the captain. As always, he was freshly shaven. His tight wig was powdered and he wore a fresh uniform, the white coat as pristine as his linen. But his eyes were ringed with red, his face scored with the tiny lines of fatigue.

"And you?" Crosbie asked.

Bougainville shrugged. "I merely watched while our boatmen repaired all our bateaux. I was awake, but not very active. Not like you, Duncan. I have heard reports. Do you never tire?"

"Yes," Crosbie said thickly.

"Go to bed, Duncan," Bougainville insisted. "At least for the morning. Here's young Denis looking for you. Let him ..."

Crosbie nodded heavily. A grey haze seemed to obscure his vision. A small hard hand touched his elbow and the weary young Scot stumbled away toward his room.

CHAPTER TWENTY FIVE

Duncan Crosbie awoke to the blare of bugles. He brought up an arm to shield his eyes from the strong sunlight that flooded in through the narrow window. Slowly he opened one eye. The room was cluttered with his equipment, but a space was cleared near the door where young Denis sat, fully uniformed, his hair powdered and clubbed behind his neck with one of Crosbie's ribbons. The boy was cross-legged, his head bowed intently as his untrained fingers twisted and prodded, shaping musket cartridges from a store of powder and shot which he twisted into waxed paper cylinders. Crosbie inspected the product sleepily.

"The paper should be tighter," he said heavily. "You'll see why if a cartridge ever falls apart just when you are trying to reload."

The boy smiled quickly. "I am practicing," he said. He pushed the powder and shot carefully under Crosbie's bed. "I will get coffee."

Crosbie swung his feet to the stone floor and raised himself up with a painful grunt. Every muscle ached and he felt as if his sleep had been only minutes long, though the sun's position proved it was past midday.

Crosbie pulled the ribbon from his knotted hair and dragged a comb painfully through the tangled mat, then bound it tidily again. His long blunt chin was stubby with pale whiskers. He walked toward the window, stroking his razor along a hone, whistling idly. Outside he could see a narrow strip of Lake Champlain with the dense woodland of the eastern shore beyond. Into that stretch coasted a long bateau, packed with white-uniformed

soldiers heading toward Carillon. Those would be the reinforcements the Général was expecting. One man in the prow lifted a
bright brass bugle and blew a screaming note across the water.
Crosbie winced and turned away.

When Denis brought hot water and coffee, Crosbie shaved
and pulled on a fresh shirt. Denis knelt to dust his knee-high
boots as he sipped his coffee. From the routine quiet of the fort,
Crosbie was sure the situation had not changed since dawn.
Apparently the English were in no hurry to assault Carillon.
Crosbie finished dressing, clapped on his hat and strode from the
room, thanking Denis with an amiable buffet on the shoulder.
The boy beamed.

Crosbie walked along the corridor and stepped out onto the
wall that surrounded Carillon. Below he could see the long file of
boats hovering off-shore, waiting their turn to unload.

The young Scot leaned against the breech of an eighteen-
pounder, feeling the warm breeze on his face. He stroked his finger
over the fleur-de-lis molded into the cannon. Just above it, some
learned gunner had engraved the letters, "U.R.R." in enormous
characters. "Ultimo ratio regis," Crosbie murmured. The King's
final argument. Properly served, artillery could be the King's
most potent argument as well, though few monarchs knew that
and even fewer generals. Frederick of Prussia had shown them
often enough, but neither his English allies nor his French enemies
understood the lesson. And even Frederick knew only a portion
of artillery's capabilities. Crosbie pounded his great fist solidly on
the gun. What he would give for a chance! Given a free hand, one
man who understood artillery could change the world in just a few
years. The sharp frustration made Crosbie's fingers clench painfully. If France did not develop that man, surely another country
would. The man would come, and the victories would follow.

Crosbie forced himself to calmness. He had long realized
his own position. In an army where advancement came through
family and influence, any display of merit was not only useless,

it was often an affront. Only incredible good fortune could bring him promotion. Viewed realistically, his future was not hopeful, but he would surely be ruined if he permitted bitterness to reduce his efficiency. Grimly, the young Scot turned his back on the long cannon.

He walked slowly around the wall, heading toward the west gate. Below the courtyard, seated in bright sunlight, was a work-party of several hundred infantrymen busy making musket cartridges. In a hot fight, a plentiful supply of ready cartridges could mean the difference between defeat and victory. With the new iron ramrods copied from Frederick of Prussia, a soldier could fire five or six shots a minute, but not if he had to pour each measure of powder separately.

Crosbie descended the narrow stone steps and came out near the open gate. There his cannon stood ready on its new field carriage, with its supply sled hitched to the trail. Crosbie detoured to run an admiring hand over the fat black breech. The gun was cool and smooth under his fingers.

"Your sweetheart, is it, monsieur?"

Crosbie turned with a quick flash of dismay at the truculent note in Le Mercier's voice. He forced himself to smile in response, determined to avoid any further clash with Le Mercier.

"My Carillon sweetheart," he said quietly.

Le Mercier smiled, a wide, snaggle-toothed expanse that gave the lie to his surly voice. "I like a young man who likes guns," he growled. "Our French Général cannot understand that. He thinks I dislike you. As if I could dislike a man who knows gunnery!"

Crosbie goggled at the hulking commandant. "Very kind of you, monsieur," he said hesitantly.

"Nonsense," Le Mercier insisted. "I can see a splendid future in store for you, my boy. Do you know my gunners speak of nothing else? They say you labored like Hercules last night. Did you really carry the guns into position in your arms?"

"Certainly not," Crosbie snorted. "No man could."

"Well, I wouldn't have been surprised if you had," Le Mercier roared. "The soldiers love an officer who works with them. That is the root of my success, too. I might have known you were no Frenchman."

"I am a Scot," Crosbie said uncertainly.

"Exactly. No Frenchman knows how to get the best out of good men. Well, you have won the gunners. I will expect excellent practice when the English attack." The Chevalier gestured toward the retrenchment. "I will direct the fire of the guns along the wall," he said briskly.

Crosbie nodded, fighting down his disappointment. He had hoped for that assignment.

"You may do as you like with that field gun," Le Mercier went on expansively. "But for the first attack, I want you here at the fort to direct the sergents and gun-pointers. They have wit enough to carry on, but they will need supervision at first. You understand?"

"Yes, monsieur," Crosbie said. At least he would have one gun. "Again, I must thank you for your confidence in me."

"You have earned it," the Chevalier growled. "We began badly. I confess I had no liking for you. We see too many French popinjays posturing around Quebec. But now you have my confidence. Continue to merit it and you'll continue to have it. That I promise you." The commandant tapped his red fist against Crosbie's chest, nodding vigorously. Then he turned away and laboriously began to climb the narrow staircase up to the wall.

Crosbie relaxed his stiff facial muscles and blew out a long sigh of relief. Friendship with Le Mercier might be far more trying than the previous collisions had been. But the Chevalier commanded Canada's artillery and he alone could give Crosbie an opportunity to prove himself in combat. That opportunity was worth any price to the eager young Scot.

CHAPTER TWENTY SIX

Duncan Crosbie stared out the open gate, squinting against the low rays of the afternoon sun. On top of the completed retrenchment, one man stood outlined sharply. That was Captain Pontleroy, Crosbie realized, seeing the scarlet breeches and stockings, and long red waistcoat that made the engineer look like a man of flame as he posed with one hand on his swordhilt. Pontleroy had earned a moment of Satisfaction; his work was nearly finished. The thick zig-zag wall, a full three mètres high, ran the width of the promontory. Forward of the wall, half the garrison's soldiers still worked at clearing the dense forest, but the major portion of the job was finished, as far as Pontleroy was concerned. For everyone else at Carillon, the test was yet to come.

From the rear of the fort, newly arrived reinforcements were marched into the courtyard. The tall swaggering mustachioed veterans in the pale blue of Béarn rested on their muskets as their officers went in to report. Crosbie skirted the voluble soldiers as he stepped back from the entrance.

The lounging troops snapped to attention without orders. Crosbie turned, then doffed his hat in formal salute. Through the open door moved Montcalm, followed by Colonel de Bourlamaque and a tall, elegant young Brigadier who could only have been the tardy de Lévis. The three senior officers strolled easily out the gate, trailed discreetly by a mixed collection of staff and regimental officers. Captain Bougainville detached himself from the group when he spotted the huge young Scot near the door.

"You're looking well, Duncan," he said amiably.

"I'm fine," Crosbie said with quick impatience. "What's happening?"

"Merely a tour of inspection. The Général may want to see you later. Or de Lévis…"

"No, no," Crosbie broke in. "What's happening with Abercrombie?"

Bougainville smiled pleasantly. "He is coming, Duncan. Restrain your zeal, my friend. The English commander took the sensible route this time, cutting off the arc of the river. He has rebuilt both bridges and established headquarters in the sawmill. He has made no move toward the fort yet, beyond a few skirmishes."

"Good," Crosbie nodded.

"Yes, Abercrombie gave us the time we needed. Now we are ready. I must tell you how surprised I was when the Chevalier Le Mercier complimented you to the Général this morning. I was surprised, but the Général, as you may imagine, was struck dumb. An excellent stroke, Duncan. I congratulate you. Can you continue to work with him?"

"I hope so," Crosbie said fervently. "I'll try."

"Hold your temper with a tight rein," Bougainville said quietly. "Stay close to your quarters, Duncan. I may need you this afternoon." He turned, running quickly to catch the Général.

Crosbie resettled his tricorne squarely on his head and watched Montcalm until he passed from sight beyond the hew wall.

"Still moving in lofty circles, aren't you, cock?" The low, hard voice crackled from the open doorway.

Crosbie wheeled to look at Captain O'Neill. The Irishman stood stiffly, his cold, grave face expressionless as a cameo. As Crosbie regarded him, O'Neill's thin pale lips twisted into a faint grimace of mockery.

"I never expected to see you with the army," Crosbie said flatly, his voice deliberately insulting.

O'Neill's even features contracted in a brief frown, but his voice remained as casual as ever. "I was fighting while you were belching with your mother's milk." His pale blank eyes watched Crosbie with faint, slightly contemptuous amusement. "I brought some messages for you," he said in a disinterested tone. "I cannot recall them at the moment. Possibly later. It seems I heard certain threats made, too. But they would hardly interest such a braw laddie, would they?"

The young Scot's fists clenched hard in restraint. Hard knots of muscle bulged along his jaw and his face flushed, but he held himself firmly in check. He forced himself to nod and offered the thin bleak edge of a smile. He'd be damned if he would let this sleek scoundrel see he had stirred him. "You are as kind as ever, Captain," he said heavily. "And as discreet."

O'Neill laughed, a thin chuckle that sounded like twigs snapping underfoot. "I suspect someone has turned you against me," he said blandly. "Just as well, I suppose. I can hardly afford friendship with anyone in such poor favor with the Intendant."

O'Neill watched the huge young Scot with detached amusement, not quite sneering. "I could tell you what is going to happen to you. It would be expensive information, though." The Irishman stepped slightly away to see Crosbie more clearly. One thin white hand toyed with his golden swordhilt. "I could even tell you how to avoid the danger. But that would come even higher, laddie." He cocked an eyebrow inquiringly and waited.

This time it was Crosbie's turn to laugh and his deep hoarse bellow filled the great courtyard. No other reply was necessary.

O'Neill's expressionless face went cold and hard, all amusement gone. "You are finished, cock," he said, quietly positive. "I could save you, if I chose."

"If I paid enough?" Crosbie snorted. "Is there anyone you wouldn't sell for a price?"

"Not a soul," O'Neill said blandly. "Including you. But you are already destroyed. You need what I can sell."

"And your price?"

O'Neill smiled thinly. "Everything," he said mildly. "Transfer the funds you hold in the Quebec Treasury and I will tell you what I know."

"And if I refuse?" A wild, preposterous idea flashed into Crosbie's mind, delighting him with its unholy quality of retribution. Carefully, he kept any sign of elation from showing in his expression. The money he had received from the sale of the prize-ship Brittania had already been surrendered to Monsieur Tremais, the King's investigator. The receipt showing the forty-seven thousand francs on deposit in the Quebec Treasury was no longer Crosbie's. But O'Neill did not know that! O'Neill would willingly buy a bag of wind, if Crosbie presented it cleverly enough.

"You won't refuse," O'Neill said flatly. "What good would your money be when you're in jail for life? And believe me, cock, jail is the best that can happen to you now. Unless..."

The alternative lay clear to Crosbie. The young Scot put a broad hand to his mouth to shade any expression that might give him away. "I'll have to think..." he muttered. "Come to my quarters." Without waiting for O'Neill, he strode briskly off down the stone corridor.

O'Neill turned and trailed Crosbie, his steps quick and soundless as though his thin body were weightless. In Crosbie's small room, he closed the door, bracing it with his arm, standing there stiffly, the perfect oval of his face pale in the shadowed room.

Crosbie loomed huge in the tiny room, propped against the windowsill and O'Neill read into his slumped posture the bleak depression he wanted to see.

"A bit frightened, cock? Just that first little chill, eh?"

"What do you have to tell me?" Crosbie demanded harshly. There was no denying that he did feel a twinge of the fear O'Neill had mentioned. He knew how easy it would be for the Intendant to ruin him, if he wished. But why should he want to? What was Crosbie to him?

"Something comes first," O'Neill said blandly.

"How do I know that you will..."

"You must trust me." O'Neill chuckled easily and the soft sound built into a full-throated laugh. "A difficult position for you, cock. But what can you do? You know whether you need to hear what I know. I think you do, but I can only guess. You actually know, don't you? Will you buy?"

For a long bleak moment, the young Scot looked at the slim captain. Then, silently, Crosbie nodded. He picked up a tiny inkhorn, shook it savagely, and pulled off the cap. He dipped a ragged quill, seized a scrap of heavy paper and scribbled quickly. He signed a huge signature and turned the paper for O'Neill's inspection.

The Irishman reached one casual hand, lifting the paper. Crosbie's dirk slammed hard into the table, skewering the paper. The jeweled hilt wavered with the force of impact.

"Leave it there," Crosbie said quietly.

O'Neill's mouth twitched with faint amusement. "You are far too abrupt with that toothpick," he said evenly. He bent to read the paper. "This won't do, I fear," he said after a moment. "In this you authorize me to collect any and all sums deposited to your account with the Intendant's Treasury, but you don't specify..." O'Neill stroked a thin finger along his powdered jaw. "And what if you should produce the first receipt, the one I gave you? Then there would be no money for me. No, cock, this won't do. Not at all."

Crosbie shrugged. He pulled his dirk free and slid it into the sheath at his left side. "The original receipt is in Quebec," he said truthfully. "This is the best I can offer." He waggled the paper lightly, letting its crisp crackle remind O'Neill of the sizable sum it represented. Or so O'Neill would think.

The Irishman's eyes were calm, remote. "A gamble, is it?" he murmured coldly. "Bien. I'll gamble. Give me the paper."

"When you have told me ..." Crosbie tossed the sheet to the table where it would lie halfway between them.

In the silence that followed, Crosbie wondered whether he would have been willing to sign such a document if it really had represented thousands of francs. That sum could have assured his future in the army or out. But even as he speculated about it, Crosbie knew in his own mind that he would never have given that cold-voiced scoundrel a single franc for his information. He was beginning to regret that he had ever thought of turning the tables on Captain O'Neill. But the prospect of trading the rascal a worthless paper tickled him deeply. He had to fight to keep from grinning as he waited for O'Neill to make up his mind. He would give a goodly sum for one glimpse of O'Neill's face after he discovered what Crosbie's paper was worth!

"Very well," O'Neill said in a brittle tone. "Monsieur Rigaud, the Governor's brother, is coming here tomorrow, possibly tonight. He'll have orders for Montcalm. And he'll bring with him a warrant for your arrest."

O'Neill's quiet tone merely emphasized the force of his statement. Crosbie felt a sudden tightness in his throat.

"...charged with swindling a King's minister. Also with stealing away a bound-boy whose indenture still has some four years to run. That surprised me, laddie. I always thought your tastes were more ... routine."

"Shut your filthy mouth!" Crosbie roared.

O'Neill shrugged. "The second charge is not important but it shows you are such an evil fellow that you'd best be locked up until a court can decide what to do with you. Montcalm will be ordered to put you under restraint and deliver you to Quebec." O'Neill spread his hands wide and shrugged. "That is all, cock," he said briskly. He picked up the paper and turned to the door, pulling it open.

"But what ..."

"How can you evade your just punishment?" O'Neill grinned. "Get yourself killed, laddie. Be a hero. There's no other way out."

The door slammed hard behind him.

No way out! The words repeated themselves in Crosbie's mind. When that warrant was served, Duncan Crosbie was finished. Even if he were ultimately freed, there would be no career for him. Years might pass before he was even brought to trial and by that time, a mountain of plausible charges would probably be added to the first two. He would never be able to clear himself.

The young Scot slumped to a chair. He stared blindly at the stone floor. What was he to do? With a healthy burst of fury, he cursed the fate that had brought him to Canada, that had introduced him to the Intendant's circle in time to serve as scapegoat for those thieves. Compared to them, O'Neill was a shining spirit. He raved inwardly at Tremais and Céleste for betraying him. Even giving up the money had not helped his cause; it made it worse if anything, for now he did not even have the funds to employ lawyers to defend him.

Gradually the rage wore away and Crosbie's first fierce reaction was blunted by a wave of depression. He could find no resource within himself. He had no friends to stand beside him. His family was unknown to most Frenchmen and his honor was now subject to question by the lowest man. What was he to do? What in the name of God could he do?

CHAPTER TWENTY SEVEN

Bleakly Crosbie watched the thin strip of sky through his narrow window. Gradually it had lightened with the coming of dawn and he knew he must soon shake off the dour depression that weighted his spirit. The endless night had seemed to pass swiftly. Denis had slept quietly on his pallet, breathing with soft regularity, relaxed and secure in his mind. But Crosbie's mind had been hag-ridden with a vision of himself, a loud, bombastic child in the deceptive shape of a man, who swaggered to hide his fear, who shouted so that he might not weep. He had indulged in a dream of sudden wealth. Now he had completely destroyed himself.

Stiffly, Crosbie levered himself up from his bed and rose to his feet. He looked at his thin strained face in the wavery, dim steel mirror. Through the night he had lived with a Duncan Crosbie who sickened him. And, he suspected with a rare flash of insight, he had over-done his remorse. This Duncan Crosbie was a man who couldn't even be honest with himself.

But now was the time to put all of this behind him. The day would hold terrors enough. And Duncan Crosbie had a part assigned to him. He would do his best. This might be his last day as an officer of artillery. He could make it a day worth remembering. Maybe he was good for nothing else, but he was a gunner. He knew how to fight guns and today would prove that. He would not leave this room under the handicap of fear and apprehension, for the future. Today would bring a battle; and that battle would be a separate, living time of its own, having no logical place in yesterday or tomorrow. And the Duncan Crosbie who fought today would not be the fool of yesterday, or the dishonored wretch of tomorrow. Crosbie gently stirred Denis to wakefulness.

The boy raced to the kitchen for hot water and coffee. They ate their morning bread without conversation and then Denis assisted as Crosbie put on his best uniform. Whatever awaited him today would be met with proper dignity. Crosbie buttoned the wide scarlet cuffs of his blue coat, teased his silk lace jabot into a billow under his chin. At least he would make a splendid corpse, he thought ghoulishly. With a shock, he remembered O'Neill's suggestion and he snorted in contempt. Death could find any man on a battlefield, but Crosbie swore by Sainte Barbara, death would have to search for him. The end of battle was to live, not to die; to win, not to lose.

He strode along the corridor with Denis at his heels, fingering the jeweled hilt of his dirk. He led Denis straight to the abbreviated battery that guarded the water of Lake Champlain. This would be the only safe post today and it was here that Denis would be stationed. The boy could make himself useful as a spare man for the gun crews; he could be used as a sentry to watch the lake for unauthorized movement. Crosbie gave the battery sergent his orders in a harsh, commanding tone. He tapped the back of his great hand on the boy's chest.

"Bonne chance, Denis," he said quietly.

"Bonne chance, Duncan," Denis said. The boy's lower lip quivered slightly before Denis could anchor it between his teeth. The betraying hint of nervous bleeding was apparent in his nostrils. Crosbie tucked his fine handkerchief inside Denis's coat and marched away before he was tempted to say something more.

The young Scot walked briskly around the walls, inspecting the gunners who would be his especial charge at the onset of the battle. The sergents presented their gunteams with understandable pride. Every man bore himself well, uniform brushed clean, even though powder stains were clearly visible on some of the scarlet facings. Every head had been properly powdered and the butt of a whalebone hairpin protruded above each ear in perfect regimental fashion. Crosbie expressed his complete approval.

He descended the narrow staircase to the courtyard, intending to report to Le Mercier and Bougainville in case there had been a change in orders. He arrived just in time to see the Général enter the courtyard.

Montcalm led his staff at a brisk clip across the stone cobbles. His dark, embroidered coat was dazzling with gold lace. A fine lace spill reached nearly to his waist, held in place by the diagonal pale blue watered-silk ribbon of the Order of St. Louis. Jeweled stars and sunbursts decorated his chest, glittering in the early sunlight. The cocks of his gold-laced tricorne were filled with white ostrich plumes that fluttered as the Général moved through the gate.

Bougainville brought up the rear of the procession. He signalled for Crosbie to take position beside him and the young Scot stepped out quickly, falling into place as the junior member of the staff. More than a dozen officers comprised the group, representing all the branches. Le Mercier and Crosbie for artillery; Pontleroy and Desandrouin for engineers, and Bougainville might be considered to represent cavalry, although there was not a single troop of Horse on the continent. Just behind the Général marched the two Brigadiers, de Lévis and Colonel de Bourlamaque, a mis-matched pair; de Lévis towering slim and dangerous as a blade; de Bourlamaque short, squat and powerful as an old seed bull. Only after he had surveyed the staff did Crosbie glance ahead and when he did, he nearly gasped audibly.

Half the army remained at work felling trees far inland on the promontory, but the remainder were drawn up in parade formation across the entire area, standing bravely before their new retrenchment wall. The white infantry uniforms were a solid bank as the men stood unmoving behind their regimental colors, their coats turned back in blue, green, lilac, yellow. Muskets and sidearms reflected a prismatic dazzle from the sun.

The Général posted his staff at the exact center, a spot carefully measured and marked by a stake. There his flag was grounded. The color-sergent gave it a practiced flip and the huge embroidered banner unfurled to the light breeze. It was magnificent to Crosbie's eye, the field of glossy white silk with the broad fleurs-de-lis of the Bourbons embroidered in heavy gold. At the upper corner, a representation of the Madonna and Child was wonderfully wrought in colored silks and seed pearls. The regimental color-bearers dipped their staves in salute and Montcalm set off swiftly for the far end of the formation, trailing his staff behind as he began his tour of inspection.

There would not be sufficient room for the army to pass in review, Crosbie estimated. After his inspection, the Général would probably dismiss. Montcalm wheeled as he came abreast of the first unit, a mixed collection of Canadien regulars, milita, and Indian scouts.

The tallest warrior wore a captured British major's coat with a silver gorget under it against his bare chest. Except for breech-clout and moccasins, that was his uniform. He smelled rank as a wolf in rut, but Montcalm greeted him warmly, moving slowly but efficiently along the line of massed soldiers.

Faces began to blur in Crosbie's mind before they had finished half the route. Apparently every soldier in the army had determined to present as gallant a picture as possible. Uniforms and accoutrements were spotless. The gunners who stood ready beside their cannon, were not so spectacular in their sombre blue-and-scarlet, but Crosbie was primarily concerned with how they carried themselves. Nothing is more to be dreaded than surly, cheerless soldiers on the dawn of battle. But Crosbie could find nothing but bright, watchful expressions, broad grins covertly smothered, all excellent signs to any officer. The gunners were ready and Crosbie had little interest in the long rigid lines of infantry. Montcalm smiled and bowed his way along the line, complimenting the officers, observing the men carefully.

Then he pivotted from the far end and headed back toward his flag.

One poorly disciplined soldier from Languedoc, Montcalm's home province which had furnished the Général with his most individualistic regiment, lifted his head suddenly and shouted, "Vive notre Général!"

Montcalm hesitated in his stride. Sergents barked for silence. But the single shout had already kindled ready tinder. Eager soldiers repeated the cry. "Vive notre Général!"

Several dozens that second time. But the third was a bellowing unison. Even the sergents gave up then. They and the grinning officers joined in the growing chorus. "Vive notre Général!" The opportunity to yell was a welcome release for pent-up tension and the entire army seized its moment. Montcalm stood smiling gravely.

"Vive notre Général!"

Montcalm raised his right arm slowly.

"VIVE NOTRE GÉNÉRAL!"

Montcalm's hand dropped to his side and the cheers stopped, cut off short as the army realized the Général would reply. The undisciplined bellowing in ranks would have distressed an English general. Even Crosbie instinctively felt displeased. But Montcalm knew his men, knew the incredible fortitude and enthusiasm of the French soldier when he was commanded by a Général he could love as well as respect. Montcalm took three strides forward, and his colors followed. He lifted his wide chin in a proud gesture, surveying slowly the entire length of the rigid, waiting line.

To the silent, expectant troops, he seemed enormous, commandingly tall outlined against the bleak stone of Carillon. His voice was low and vibrant, pitched to carry clearly to the farthest man in ranks. "Pour Dieu et Saint Louis!"

Montcalm waited and the answering roar seemed to shake the ground. He bowed once, low and courteous, doffing his hat and sweeping the flowing ostrich plumes across the bare ground. The Général gestured briefly for regimental commanders to resume command of their units, but the cheers continued until he had withdrawn with his staff to the comparative quiet of Carillon's courtyard.

"A stirring demonstration, mon général," de Lévis said with quiet sincerity. "What enthusiasm!"

"Pray that we may be worthy," Montcalm said soberly. "You understand your assignments, gentlemen? Bougainville, will you ..."

Promptly Captain Bougainville stepped forward, unrolling a chart in his hand. "The order of battle," he said in a voice that tightened with strain. "The Left under command of Colonel the Chevalier de Bourlamaque, composed of La Sarre and Languedoc. The Center under direct command of His Excellency, composed of Berry and Royal Roussillon. The Right under command of Brigadier the Chevalier de Lévis, composed of La Reine, Béarn and Guienne. Regimental commanders have been assigned their posts. The detachments of troupes de le marine are assigned to defend the slope between the retrenchment wall and the river. All other Canadien units are assigned to defend the slope on the Right between the fort and Lake Champlain."

Bougainville went on with details of signals, locations of various headquarters, supplies, special assignments in event of several contingencies.

"Our last information is nearly an hour old," he concluded. "Then the English were forming in order of battle. It is reasonable to assume that they will march to attack our position. But if they should decide to by-pass us to establish a position on the edge of the lake, then the Chevalier de Lévis, with the Right, will attack them at all costs. That attack will be ordered only by His Excellency." Bougainville folded the long sheet carefully; it would be preserved in the army's archives. "A single gun will give the alarm when the enemy begins his advance. The work details will withdraw to their positions. No soldier will fire until another cannon sounds the signal. By command of His Excellency the ..."

"Yes, yes," Montcalm interrupted. "Very well, Louis. Now, gentlemen, if there are no questions, I hope you will all join me in a glass of wine while we have a moment to spare."

Only the two Brigadiers accepted. The others would be too busy in the short time that remained. Crosbie clutched Bougainville's arm as he moved away.

"Have the English brought up their guns, Louis?"

"Not yet, Duncan," Bougainville smiled. The captain's eyes were heavily red with sleeplessness but he showed no other sign of fatigue. "I doubt if they will be able to bring their cannon into play against us today."

Behind them, Le Mercier snorted briefly. "It will be more target practice for us, eh, young man?" His heavy thumb prodded Crosbie's ribs.

The young Scot nodded nervously, watching Bougainville. "Something else, Louis?"

"Possibly," Bougainville said slowly. "The English have carried several bateaux across from their landing place. They may try to rush a flanking party past us along the river. Be sure you are alert to the possibility."

"I will," Crosbie assured him.

Bougainville nodded. "Bonne chance," he said easily. He moved away toward Montcalm's office and Le Mercier draped his thick hand over Crosbie's shoulder. "All prepared, my boy?" he asked in a pleasant growl.

"All ready, sir."

"Excellent." Le Mercier rubbed both hands together briskly, making a dry rasping sound. "I have given you my best guncrew for your peculiar field gun. Be sure you take good care of them."

"I'll be careful, sir," Crosbie said sincerely. He remembered to thank the gruff Chevalier for the new gunmount. Le Mercier waved it away with a flip of his hand.

"I'll be curious to see what you do with it," he growled.

CHAPTER TWENTY EIGHT

The strong heat of the sun fell squarely on Duncan Crosbie's back as he bent low, sighting the long cannon. This was the last gun in the row that faced west from Carillon's walls. Crosbie had aimed each of them himself, manipulating the elevating and traversing screws with delicate precision until each muzzle pointed just were he wanted it. He straightened with a soft grunt and a solid rivulet of sweat poured warmly down his back. His neck was moist and hot, coated with a thin paste of sweat and hair powder. He wiped it away and shouted for the gunnery sergeants.

All the veteran crew leaders gathered close around him.

"I have sighted your guns," Crosbie said, bellowing to make his voice carry the distance of the long wall. "Sergents will observe the aiming points selected for their guns. After each shot, bring your piece back to its present position."

He glared around at the assembled sergents. To a man they grinned back. This gigantic gosse was delightful the way he stormed and ranted with his instructions, and then went ahead and did most of the work himself!

"The English will attack in three lines, as they always do. Be sure that no gun is fired until all three lines are well within range. We don't want to frighten them off; we want to destroy them. Now, every man look out beyond the retrenchment wall." Crosbie lifted his heavy arm and the gunners dutifully turned.

"Immediately in front of the wall is the hundred mètres of cleared ground. That is the terrain of the infantry and the guns on the wall, which the Chevalier Le Mercier will fight. Beyond lies a wide stretch of tangled timber. In no circumstance are you to aim at that obstacle. Just one charge of grape would clear a wide channel through it. And we don't want to make things easier for the English, do we?"

The bellowing agreement from the gunners was proof enough that none misunderstood.

"So, our target area is the space beyond the tangle. Your guns point there now. Keep them aimed so. And don't be too eager. Let them form up before you fire. They'll give you a magnificent target if you will wait. All sergents will watch the space immediately before the retrenchment wall. If too many Englishmen come through to that point, depress your guns and blast them back. One or two rounds should be enough. Afterwards return again to your basic target. Is that understood?" Crosbie paused and a momentary silence fell. "Is that understood?" he repeated. "Answer me!"

The resultant shout rivalled the earlier cheering. Infantrymen on the retrenchment wall turned to goggle as the gunners roared their understanding and admiration. The sergents shut them off after another cheer and herded the crews back to their guns.

Crosbie did not quite appreciate the reason for all the noise, but he was pleased that the men were bright and eager for the coming battle.

"With grape-shot!" he commanded. "Load!"

The crews tailed onto the tackles, pulling the guns back from their apertures. Cloth bags of powder were rammed securely down the muzzles with thick felt wads to hold them in place. Nets of grape-shot followed, solidly tamped home. The cannon were run up again and re-sighted by the sergents, who then shoved worms down the touchholes, twisting to pierce the powder bags. They bit off the tips of powder-quills and poured the fine FFFF powder down the vents. The guns were ready now. Sergents lighted linstocks from the tubs of slow-match and held them high for Crosbie's inspection. The young Scot nodded. The crews were good, very fast and sure. He ordered them at ease and walked to the corner of the wall where he could look down at the end of the retrenchment wall where it met the sloping ground leading down to the river. Here was the point of possible danger that Bougainville had mentioned. None of the fort's guns could command the river from their present locations, but Crosbie had his mobile field-mounted gun in reserve. He observed the ground minutely. Nothing to worry about there he considered. Any enemy boat would be under fire for a good hundred mètres. None had a chance of getting through safely.

Idly Crosbie leaned one elbow on the wall, smoothing at the stone with his fingertip. The infantry troops stood ready along the retrenchment. A brisk rattle of musketry sounded from the forest, but only a few soldiers bothered to look over the retrenchment. There would be a long tiresome delay while the English brought up their troops, formed in line of regiments and then drove the French pickets back. The veteran soldiers rested while they could. Some even managed to sleep, open-mouthed in the glaring sun.

The sound of musketry died away. Crosbie spat thickly on the top of the stone wall and then slid his dirk from its sheath. Using spittle as a lubricant, he honed the dark-steel blade carefully, sliding it forward in long arcing thrusts against the soft stone. He concentrated on his minor task until another burst of small-arms fire caught his attention. Quickly he wiped the blade clean and rammed it home.

From the forest beyond, white-uniformed soldiers came running in long easy strides. They would be the sentries. They waved their arms briskly overhead, signalling to their commanders. After a short delay, a single eight-pounder thumped its dull roar from the retrenchment. Advance pickets, an even division of Indian scouts. Canadiens and regular infantry, fell back in good order from the dense wood, stopping to fire at men that were not yet visible from the fort. A fluttering line of birds soared from the forest, flew swiftly over the fort and across to the safety of the farther shore. It took a lot of men to scare the birds away, Crosbie thought vaguely. The entire English army must be only a short distance away.

A snarling burst of rifle fire sounded much louder this time. These were English rifles shooting toward the fort. Far ahead, a white-uniformed soldier crumpled to the ground, lying small and still as a discarded toy. The remainder of the pickets dashed back toward the thick belt of tangled trees. There they threw themselves, flat, firing in ragged volleys as targets offered. One at a time, they rose to dash across the cleared ground toward the cover of the retrenchment. Most of them arrived unharmed, but Crosbie counted at least nine who had to be carried the last few mètres to safety. The cleared space was perilous to cross, as the English would discover in their turn.

From the cover of the shadowed woods, green-uniformed figures moved out stealthily, taking advantage of all the conceal-ment available. They made taunting targets, but Crosbie saw only one fall during all the firing. The English rangers advanced in alternate waves, disconcerting the French pickets who waited for a clear shot. The English were scoring much better than the retreating pickets, but that was only to be expected, Crosbie told himself. Their rifles were far more accurate than French muskets in this sort of skirmishing, but loading a rifle took nearly three times as long as loading a smooth-bore musket. Altogether rifles were a fine weapon for light infantry, though useless, of course, for troops of the line. The rifle was essentially an assassin's weapon. Crosbie felt no personal dislike, but he realized, as did every regular officer, that one cannot assassinate an entire army. If the infantry commanders were given a choice of improve-ments, they would all prefer a new method of increasing the rate of fire, rather than a useless increase of distance and accuracy. And there again, Crosbie thought angrily, comes the question of a new metal. Someone would have to improve the basic material of muskets as well as cannon before rates of fire could be greatly improved. Something resembling good sword-steel, though that of course was far too rare and expensive a substance to use for guns. But someone would have to …

Crosbie's aimless speculation was cut short when the first dim streaks of scarlet appeared against the green foliage of the forest. Along the full width of the promontory, hints of alien color were visible.

The green-coated rangers fell back, retreating through the infantry. Their work was finished when they drove off the pickets. The time for long-distance shooting was done; now the issue lay with musket and bayonet.

Crosbie leaned far forward. Were the English going to attack against the retrenchment? Or was some English officer wise enough to see that he could cut off the fort by advancing a league farther and wheeling his troops into line along the lake? The basic problem of the entire campaign lay here in this tense, steaming moment. Crosbie was soaking wet with sweat that pasted his shirt against his body, and made a soggy mass of his powdered hair. He waited, bent tautly forward. The entire French army waited.

Then forward from the forest marched English serjeants and company drummers, followed by battalion and regimental color-bearers. Directly ahead, Crosbie could see the English Right forming into line, still half obscured by the standing forest and the felled trees. These were provincial troops in blue-and-buff. The Center and Left were a solid blur of scarlet. Drums rattled commands, serjeants shouted, and along the massed line rippled the shimmer of bayonets whipping from their scabbards. The drums rolled softly, insistently, then the beat increased to a light quick-step. The English line advanced.

On open battlefield, this English line was at once the despair and admiration of less disciplined armies. But in the broken ground before Carillon, the rigid rows lost their formation with the first steps, as soldiers detoured around the standing trees, leaped the fallen timber, stumbled and slipped over the soft loamy earth, with its treacherous layer of rotting leaves and pine needles. But they came on, awesome to any eye.

"Steady!" Crosbie shouted. "Stand steady! I will give the command." Obediently, his sergents stepped back from their guns, removing themselves from the terrible temptation of the powder-filled touchholes. They blew on their linstocks, watching Crosbie intently.

On the retrenchment wall, French officers warned their men not to fire. The English drums rolled in brisk rat-a-plan, and soldiers fought across the littered ground. They reached the wide strip of tangled trees and tore at the entwined mass angrily, trying to pull it apart, managing only to reduce its height and density. The English troops climbed through and over the obstacle and halted to re-form their lines, now only a bare hundred mètres from the retrenchment. Crosbie shook his head in warning. The French infantrymen brought their muskets down from the wall, inspected flints and priming pans and laid their pieces forward again, using the rammed earth of the wall as a rest for steady aim.

Crosbie swept his gaze along the waiting troops. A scant half-regiment had been held fifty mètres behind the wall as Montcalm's corps-de-réserve. All the others were in place along the fire-step of the zig-zag wall. Behind each company stood great mounds of ready cartridges, extra ramrods, boxes of sharpened flints and a few stands of spare muskets. The officers stood poised, swords bare in their hands with the points resting lightly against the earth. The Général waited easily in the precise center of the line, just behind Le Mercier.

Looking far forward, Crosbie observed the English reserve troops just coming into view from the wood. His targets were all in sight now. He bent over the wall, watching Le Mercier, who in turn kept his eyes hard on Montcalm, every soldier straining for the signal to fire.

The silence grew almost tangible. Even the English drums had stopped when the drummer boys were sent to the rear of their formations. Scarlet-coated officers swept their swords high; serjeant-majors lifted their silver bound canes. The troops inspected bayonets, then brought their muskets up in the ready position. The English waited stolidly. Not a man moved.

Beside Crosbie a gunner cursed viciously, slashing his hand through the air in nervous irritation.

"Steady!" Crosbie bellowed, as much to himself as the gunners.

Regimental officers strode forward along the English line, commanders raised their swords. The English moved to the attack. All along the French line, warnings hissed. A musket volley now would damage the enemy, but one delayed until it could be delivered at fifty mètres, or even less, could be disastrous.

"Steady!" Crosbie repeated. His sergents passed along the warning. The crews trembled in anticipation. Muttered curses became routine now as the tension mounted.

The English troops marched slowly forward, muskets slanted at measured angles, black gaiters kicking up puffs of dust from the cleared ground, faces hard and cold under straight lines of their hats. Crosbie ran an admiring eye along the wall of men who advanced so determinedly. Without realizing it, he was smiling a tight humorless smile of professional appreciation. What magnificent troops they were! What ... but God in Heaven! Who were those men?

Crosbie lurched far forward from the stone wall, staring with open mouth, his vision blurred with sweat. Mother of God! The precise regiment moved forward, dark blue-and-green kilts swinging gaily from side to side. Below bare knees, knitted plaid cuffs were visible over short gaiters. The scarlet coats of these soldiers were cut off short, barely below the waistline. Blue bonnets with scarlet pompons danced as the men strode forward, following the Lochaber axes of their serjeants. Crosbie stared without belief. Full-draped plaids swirled from wide shoulders, nearly fouling the bayonets of the following line. Crosbie shook his head.

Scots, he muttered to himself. But how could it be? Those men must be English masquerading in Highland regimentals. Surely no Scot would serve the Sassenach. But even as he thought it, Crosbie realized there were Scots aplenty who were ready to take German Georgie's shilling. Abercrombie himself, General of the army, had a good Scottish name. But Crosbie had never before seen Scots massed in the English army. They must have been enlisted within the past few years, he thought dully. Scots! Caledonia invictrix pimping for a German king! Crosbie spat in disgust. They wanted to be English soldiers, did they? They wanted to fight the Sassenach's battles, did they? Let them look around well to see where the English had brought them to die.

The dark sett of the Black Watch plaids glowed gem-like with increasing visibility. Dourly, Crosbie turned away, his wide thin mouth forced to a tight slit of contempt. He faced toward Montcalm again, refusing so much as one more glance toward the renegade Scots who advanced with the English. Bagpipes skirled savagely. Crosbie coughed away a bitter taste.

"Why does he wait?" Crosbie muttered to himself. He gripped the stone wall convulsively. "Why doesn't he fire?"

Montcalm inclined forward from his observation mound. Le Mercier turned, bellowing to his gunners, his command blown to shreds by the first cannon-shot of the battle. The remaining seven guns erupted angrily, spewing out double charges of canister into the close English formations. Half the infantry fired a deadly volley, withering the advancing troops. The second order fired into the smoke while the first stooped to reload.

"Hold your fire!" Crosbie roared. This was the dangerous moment, when he might lose half his effect if his guns were fired too soon. The English reserve was not yet formed. And the English advance was too far forward for his guns to bear successfully. Crosbie moved restlessly along the wall, speaking with a preternatural calm that was entirely manufactured. "Hold your fire!"

On the retrenchment wall, French soldiers fired in steady, orderly volleys. By dividing his troops into two firing orders, Montcalm had assured a constant torrent of musketry. Half his men turned to reload, each man biting out his bullet, ramming home his charge, spitting his bullet into the muzzle and ramming it solidly, all in unison, ready to fire again after the others had fired and knelt on the banquette to reload.

Powder smoke lay in a dense pall forward of the retrenchment, obscuring details. Through the pale haze, Crosbie could see vast windrows of fallen soldiers in scarlet. As he watched, a tall serjeant fell with a long black spear of iron ramrod skewered through his chest. Some over-eager Frenchman had fired too soon, forgetting to remove his ramrod. The English troops plodded forward, muskets still aslant.

"By the bayonet!" Crosbie said aloud. The English were not firing their muskets! Crosbie was willing to bet that they weren't even loaded. Those fools were hoping to storm the retrenchment with bayonets alone. The young Scot shook his head. Abercrombie should be hung for murder, he told himself.

But the English came on, running now, mouths grotesquely gaping, shouting cheers and curses that were smothered by cannon and musketry. The veteran French artillerymen served their pieces from the retrenchment with swift deadly accuracy, each blast scouring a wide swath with nearly two hundred musket balls tearing through the English line.

To the rear, light infantry and ranger units knelt among the trees, firing at the slight targets offered by the French troops whose heads appeared above the retrenchment. And behind them, the reserve troops formed up rapidly to support the attack. Crosbie raised his arm forward, pointing to them. His sergents stepped into position, linstocks poised, watching Crosbie. Two wide-spread scarlet lines of troops moved from the forest, not trying to retain their rigid line-abreast as they strode forward. Crosbie waited. He drew his sword, holding it glinting in the sun overhead. When he could clearly see the entire reserve force, he swept his sword down.

Sergents touched their linstocks to the powder spread over the vents. A shrill hiss of priming powder spat from the twenty-four cannon. The following blast raised a thin spray of stone dust from the fort's walls. Powder smoke drifted quickly downward and Crosbie could observe the effect of his first cannonade. The English reserve had almost vanished. Three of his guns had dug shallow craters in the earth forward of the scarlet line, but even so, the grape-shot they threw had showered a crippling hail of wood splinters into the massed infantry. Crosbie noted which guns would have to be re-laid. The others had done superbly well, he estimated. There was no longer an English reserve. One well-aimed salvo had swept the formations back into the forest. Green-uniformed rangers and blue-and-buff provincials ran from their concealed positions amongst the fallen timber. Bodies lay where they had dropped.

Against the retrenchment wall, the first English troops still grimly advanced. They were doggedly running up the long slope that fell away forward from the earthen wall. Ahead of them lay that sloping glacis, then the tight abattis of sharpened stakes and tangled trees that slanted forward and downward from the wall itself which reared a full three mètres above. There was no hope, none whatever, but they came on steadily, shouting their hoarse, full-throated cheers. Whole platoons were blown to red ruin by Le Mercier's cannon, but still they assaulted fiercely, bayonets glittering in the sun.

Crosbie supervised the reloading of his guns, personally aiming the three that had thrown low. He ran along the length of the wall from gun to gun, checking aim, warning each sergent to wait for his command. His only target had been destroyed with that first salvo, but soon there would be another, better one. And with his guns ready, the young Scot leaned over the wall to see when his turn would come.

The English Right, mostly provincial troops, broke first, the men running back toward the wood, stooping and jittering like elusive hares through the fallen timbers. Crosbie ran to the left side of the wall, tapping the shoulders of six sergents as he passed.

"These six guns only!" he shouted. "At my command!" Again he drew his sword as an aid in signalling. He raised to the tips of his toes, measuring the speed of the retreating provincials. Their blue uniforms merged cleverly with the underbrush, making their numbers hard to estimate. The first few panicked soldiers struggled through the tangle of massed trees and ran to safety in the forest. Crosbie held his sword high, waiting. Following came the bulk of the broken regiments, officers still clutching their useless swords as they ran for cover.

"Tirez!"

The six cannon spat their charges at the retreating troops. Two of them carried high, Crosbie noted. He leaped to correct their aim.

"Rapid fire!" he bellowed.

The six guns were loaded while in their recoil positions, held firm by taut breeching cables, and then run forward again. Crosbie had time to lay only one before his sergent touched his match to the vent. The young Scot ran quickly to the corner of the wall where the smoke would obscure less of the target. Where a full regiment had retreated was nothing now. Those who had lived through the holocaust were safe in the forest, out of sight. The partially cleared ground was littered with the dark-blue of the fallen provincials.

"Cease fire," Crosbie said. He sheathed his sword.

None of the English regulars had yet broken from the action. Now the scarlet tide swept up the glacis, pulling and hauling at the abattis, struggling to yank the tangled stakes free by sheer force. Crosbie saw them die there, looped in strange, dramatic poses as the deadly musket fire poured into them from the wall.

Why don't they withdraw? Crosbie muttered. They can't carry the retrenchment with bayonets alone. A sensible commander would know he couldn't win at all without artillery to prepare the way, but the English might be stupid enough to try again with loaded muskets. At least they needed muskets. Why didn't they withdraw?

Far along the retrenchment, the English Left had almost gained the summit of the earthen wall. As Crosbie watched, two kilted Highlanders leaped down behind the wall. A French officer slumped suddenly, blood spurting from a gash that had nearly chopped off his right arm with one wild swing from a claymore. Neither Highlander had kept his musket, preferring to have both hands free to claw through the abattis. But they had their claymores, those weighty straight-edged broadswords that had carried the day on more than one Scottish battlefield. They laid about them with lusty strokes, and two more officers were run through or chopped before both Scots were shot down by musketry.

For a full hour, the English attack continued with unabated ferocity, Dozens of scarlet-coated soldiers had surmounted the wall in desperate lunges. All lay dead. Muskets grew scorching hot in the hands of the defenders. Around one cannon, four men had been killed when daring soldiers had thrust their bayonets completely through the gun embrasure, using them as spears. But ultimately, the attack failed, as it was doomed to fail.

The English retreated with no visible sign of panic. They withdrew in reasonable order, pursued all the way to the tangled mass of trees by unremitting musketry and canister. More men fell in the retreat than had been killed near the wall.

The English struggled through the dense tangle of trees. And when they reached the second strip of fairly clear ground, they slowed, unreasonably feeling safe now. Crosbie's lips stretched in a wolfish grimace. This was what he had waited for. These troops had not yet experienced a cannonade from Carillon's walls. They weren't even thinking of such a possibility. They had withdrawn beyond musket range and beyond the observation of the cannon that fired from the retrenchment. So they slowed. Their officers tended to gather together in conference.

Crosbie stooped over the nearest gun, traversing it carefully to bear directly on a regimental banner below which a cluster of officers had collected, talking volubly, gesturing with hands that still clenched forgotten swords. He lifted one arm with deliberate emphasis.

"At my command!" he called. "Fire!" he applied the match to the gun he had pointed and leaped quickly aside to observe the result.

The regimental banner was torn to ribbons. Shiny glitters of blasted silk lay in a swirl around four scarlet-clad bodies. The English, those that remained, were running. This unexpected salvo, coming when they had thought themselves momentarily secure, had been ruinous. Regiments broke and ran in panic. Officers screamed for order, found no response, and turned to run themselves.

"Swab out," Crosbie ordered. There wouldn't be a suitable target for some time. He moved along the line of cannon, making sure that each bore was wiped clear of all powder residue and then scrubbed vigorously with the swab. One brief touch of the swab was all one had time for in combat, but a thorough cleansing was always useful if time permitted. Crosbie tapped an elderly bearded sergent on the arm and walked with him toward the staircase.

"I am going outside," he said quietly. "I will probably not be back here. You will take command of the guns. Don't wait when the English come on next time."

"Again?" The sergent goggled at Crosbie.

"Of course they'll come on again," Crosbie snapped. "More than once, probably. We broke them, but we didn't destroy them.

Now listen to me. When the next attack is formed, fire on them at once. Don't wait. We have used our little surprise, so just blast away now. But don't fire after they have advanced beyond the tangled trees. Wait until they withdraw again. And always keep your eyes open for a second formation of reserve troops behind the first. Understand?"

"Yes, monsieur."

"I'll probably be in sight," Crosbie said. "I'm going to fight the field gun. Send a man for me if I'm needed." He slapped the sergent's arm lustily, staggering him slightly. "Can you manage?"

The sergent stiffened, grinning with tobacco-stained teeth. "We will manage gloriously," he boasted. He pivotted and marched off, roaring for the sergents to attend him.

CHAPTER TWENTY NINE

Duncan Crosbie ran quickly down the narrow stone steps and out the west gate. He slowed to a brisk walk through the wide bivouac area. Panting men struggled with massive water butts slung from double harnesses, staggering and slopping water as they stumbled toward the retrenchment. Seeing them, Crosbie was aware of a burning thirst. He hurried toward one swinging cask and dipped a gourd cup full as the men went along. The warm water almost choked him, but he got it down and hastily gulped another. When he came in sight of the wall, he could see that only a skeletal guard remained in place on the fire-step. All the others were resting, slumped wearily in relaxed postures, clamoring for the water-bearers to hurry. Most of their uniform coats were unbuttoned now, the gaily faced collars and cuffs darky soggy with sweat. Company officers moved watchfully along the wall, inspecting flints, ordering careless soldiers to make a change before the next attack.

Captain Bougainville waved at Crosbie, his curved dragoon's sabre dangling from a leather thong knotted about his wrist. He too was showing signs of fatigue now, and the strong heat had wilted his jaunty lace cuffs and neckcloth. He wiped his streaming face with a wilted handkerchief and grinned excitedly. His voice rose with tension.

"Un moment décisif, eh, Duncan?" he called. "That last salvo from the fort was shattering. I leaped to the wall in time to see them running for the forest."

"They'll be back," Crosbie said bluntly. Surely no experienced soldier thought the English had been defeated with only one repulse?

"The fools were mad to assault with the bayonet alone."

"They won't make that mistake again."

Bougainville shrugged. He fished out his flat snuffbox and tapped the lid lightly to loosen the finely powdered tobacco inside before he took a prodigious pinch. He sneezed briskly, smiled and offered the box to Crosbie.

The young Scot shook his head, grinning in spite of himself for there was something charmingly incongruous in the picture Bougainville presented at that moment as he held out the delicate golden box daintily with the curved dragoon's sabre dangling from his wrist and sweat dripping solidly down his fingers. The combination of fop and fighting man was almost ludicrous.

"No, thank you, Louis," he said. "I want to move my gun over to the Left before the next attack comes."

Bougainville nodded. "You will watch the river, eh?"

Crosbie agreed that he would watch the river. He walked off quickly before Bougainville could find something else for him to do.

Crosbie worked his way toward the Right where Chevalier de Lévis commanded. He could see his field-mounted gun emplaced at the extreme end of the wall where the sloping ground gave it a limited field of fire. Lacking an embrasure, that was the best supporting position for the gun. Around it the crew lay idly sprawled.

A thin officer walked slowly back from the retrenchment, swinging his sword lightly, as a dandy carries a walkingstick. He whipped it smartly up, saluting Crosbie. Only then did the young Scot recognize Captain Seamus O'Neill.

"A great day for the Irish, cock," he said in that sharp, toneless voice that Crosbie would have recognized anywhere. "Bad for the Scotties, though. Come to find a bullet, have you?"

O'Neill's normally calm demeanor was only slightly ruffled. His thin nostrils flared constantly, as a stallion's will in moments of fury. Otherwise, Captain O'Neill was untouched by the wild elation of combat.

Crosbie gestured angrily, brushing O'Neill aside as if the officer were an annoying fly. He signalled for his gunnery sergent, not answering O'Neill, unaware of the Irishman's quick rare flush, his abrupt pivot that headed him back toward the Canadien detachment.

The mustachioed sergent levered himself reluctantly to his feet and snapped to attention as Crosbie approached. Crosbie nodded briskly, centering all his attention on the gun. It had been well swabbed since the firing had ceased and the sergent had cannily gathered a mass of stone to brace wheels and trail, limiting any tendency the gun might have to walk back from its proper site. Everything was in order, except that the sergent had not replaced his supplies. A dozen rounds at least had been fired from the mobile magazine Crosbie had made of the old stone-sled. Possibly fifty charges remained, no more than half an hour's rapid firing by a good crew.

"Very good, sergent," Crosbie growled. "Send a man back for new charges. We will want a full supply shortly. Then get some extra men to tail onto the lines. I want this gun moved to the other side of the retrenchment."

"Not so fast, young man," a light voice said in blunt command. "The gun will stay here."

Crosbie whirled, his gaunt face hard and grim. He forced himself to silence when he recognized de Lévis. It was not the moment for a sous-lieutenant to contradict a Brigadier.

"Monsieur," he said politely, his voice thin with restraint, "His Excellency expects this gun to protect his Left flank. An attack along the river is possible now that..."

De Lévis wiped his face with a handkerchief. He, too, wore his sword knotted to his wrist where a mere flick could bring it into his hand. His massive lace jabot had wilted around his neck.

"You may have your strange gun, young man," he said pleasantly. "But not until we know that the English will attack us again. If they decide now to go around, I will have to counterattack. In which case your gun will be more useful with me. Do you agree?"

Crosbie bowed his head, cursing his forgetfulness. De Lévis was completely right. Now, if ever, the advantages of an alternate plan would be obvious to the English command. And unless de Lévis were prepared to attack swiftly, they might drive home a limited attack that could give them control of the lake, cutting off Carillon.

"Certainly, Monsieur le Chevalier," Crosbie said hoarsely. "I will await your orders."

De Lévis waggled his damp handkerchief in the air. "You will not need orders," he smiled. "If the English attack us here, you may site your gun where you think best. We will know the answer in a few minutes."

The few minutes stretched to half an hour, time for Crosbie to re-stock his stone-sled and even to get a few minutes rest in the shade of a low tree where his crew lay relaxed. He could faintly hear the long roll of English drums as the broken formations were being assembled again. Now and again a bugle screeched a strident order, but Crosbie ignored it all until the harsh wild skirl of bagpipes soared from the forest in a driving call to action that brought the young Scot cursing to his feet. He saw Captain O'Neill standing among his Canadiens, pointing his sword forward and shouting. Crosbie leaped to the fire-step for a view of the field.

The cleared ground stretched emptily forward of the wall, dotted with scarlet splotches where the English dead still lay. Then the dense tangle of fallen trees stopped his line of vision, but through the dry and withered foliage, he could glimpse an occasional flicker of bright red as the English units came out of the concealing wood. He quickly pivotted to stare up toward the fort's wall. The muzzles of twenty-seven cannon protruded silently from their embrasures. No man was visible, but as Crosbie looked in a fever of nervous impatience, the entire battery exploded with a sullen unified roar that made the earthen retrenchment tremble with shock.

Crosbie, one finger on his pulse, timed the interval between salvos. Nearly a full minute passed before the guns fired again. Crosbie swore irritably. That was far too slow for experienced crews. The next round followed in better time and the fourth came after only half a minute. That was good practice. The only fear was that the sergent directing the battery might be sacrificing accuracy for a higher rate of fire.

When the company officers began directing the first musketry volleys, Crosbie assumed he was free to take his gun where he pleased. Obviously, the English were making another full-force frontal assault. Crosbie waved, alerting his gun-crew. Extra soldiers heaved on the heavy ropes and the piece sluggishly lurched from its position, trail suspended high and lashed to the top of the stone-sled. The men strained mightily to get the strange vehicle under way, but in a few steps they were taking almost full strides across the level ground behind the retrenchment. Crosbie marched ahead. The English were not coming at a stolid march this time; they were running. Men detailed for the purpose were tearing at the tangled trees while others sprinted through the narrow openings they made, muskets at the carry, bayonets fixed.

By the time Crosbie had passed the Center, the first line of scarlet troops was pouring through the obstacle, formations forgotten in a wild dash against the French line. And they weren't putting their faith in cold steel alone this time. The troops advanced in alternate waves, firing their muskets, slowing to a walk to reload, then running and firing again. The third line of English troops had passed the tangled barrier when Crosbie came to the end of the retrenchment. Here, scattered over the sloping ground that tumbled to the river were white-uniformed Canadien regulars who fired carefully from prone positions, taking the English from the flank. The blue-and-buff provincial troops opposite them were advancing cautiously now, at least half of them directing their musketry toward the concealed Canadiens while the others blazed away at the retrenchment. Crosbie moved back several mètres to find a location for his gun. He had already scooped out a ditch for the trail and lined it with stone by the time the panting gunners brought the cannon into line. Willing hands unhitched the trail, pulled the gun around to face the English and shoved it into position. The sergent's voice sobbed for breath as he shouted loading commands. Crosbie concentrated on aiming the piece. The crew finished loading. The sergent was inserting his worm and spilling the primer quill of powder down the vent.

"We have only that narrow field of fire," Crosbie said, pointing for the sergent's benefit. "We will not be able to traverse very much, merely to elevate for distance. If necessary, we will have to wait for suitable targets."

But no waiting would be necessary yet. The blue-coated provincial regiment ran forward, screaming threats at the concealed regiment of La Sarre whose companies poured steady volleys at them. Men fell and those following merely leaped over them. Wounded soldiers went down briefly, scrambled up again and kept coming, bloody hands gripping their muskets. Crosbie took the linstock from the sergent and blew it to a bright glow. He waved the crew aside, stepped free of the trail and touched the match to the loose grains of primer powder. There was a sharp thin hiss, instantly smothered by the bellowing roar.

The gun was swabbed out and a new powder charge rammed into the bore before Crosbie could observe the effect of the first shot. Then the smoke blew aside and he could see a long wide swath of blue uniforms spread across the ground in contorted postures. Nearly two hundred musket balls tightly concentrated had cut a deadly path through the provincial regiment.

The gunnery sergent waited until the frail metal canister had been rammed home, then prepared his primer again. He moved aside to let Crosbie apply the match, his hairy face wrinkled in puzzlement. Only rarely did officers fire guns themselves and the sergent was not sure just what his job was in such a case. Crosbie handed over the linstock.

"At my signal only, sergent," he warned. "Watch my arm."

The young Scot sprang up to the fire-step. From there he could see the provincial regiment drifting to its own left, still running forward, firing at a good rate, but gradually inclining away from the riverbank where Crosbie's gun waited.

Great snorting discharges shook the wall again and Crosbie knew that the guns were firing from the fort overhead, probably against the English reserve back in the forest. The eight-pounders on the wall were being served rapidly now, in a steady rumble of explosions as each gun was reloaded and run up, independently of the others. The musketry was still rhythmic and controlled, company volleys only for a more steady result.

Crosbie dropped his arm to signal when a company of provincials broke from the charge and turned to run. His waiting gun blew the company to shreds, sending the men reeling back by ones and twos in mad panic. All across the field, the English attack was stumbling to a halt, the soldiers flinching from the murderous fire that poured from the retrenchment. Their own musketry had not been useless—along the wall lay dozens of French soldiers in the stiffened postures of the dead—but the exposed positions of the English gave them small opportunity to compete with the controlled volleys of the French. They broke and ran again, more quickly this time, less than half an hour, Crosbie estimated. Drums rattled swiftly, the three long beats and three short beats of the retreat sounding over and over, recalling the men from the attack. Highland bagpipes shrieked defiance from the English Left, but the men recoiled from the slaughter. Crosbie leaped down from the retrenchment.

"Swab out," he ordered. "Don't reload until I tell you." The soaking swab sizzled like roasting meat as the gunners sloshed it into the bore.

Crosbie went back to the wall, climbed slowly to the top and stood upright. In the short moment he stood exposed, he could see far down the field where retreating soldiers struggled through the tangle of trees. The guns of Carillon blared their massive salvos from the wall. From the retrenchment, Crosbie's view along the river was clear. One glance was sufficient. Crosbie leaped down as a scattered volley of musket balls whizzed overhead. He had made a taunting target that even the retreating English could not ignore. Crosbie laughed in excitement and ran toward his gun.

With the sergent he surveyed the riverbank, seeking the best location and finding it twenty mètres back from the wall a low hillock from which the river was dominated.

"Have the men run the gun back here and place it toward the river."

The sergent nodded without understanding. An insane officer was no rarity in any army and had to be obeyed in any event. Resignedly, the sergent loaded his equipment and moved it back to the site Crosbie had selected. The gun was loaded with round shot and aimed roughly at the middle of the visible stretch of river.

Just as the second English attack had been shorter than the first, so the second delay was shorter than the first. Drums, bugles and bagpipes called the troops into line before Crosbie had emplaced his gun. The young Scot muttered irritably. He wanted his eight-pounder here to command the river. From this site he could not usefully fire at the advancing troops. He echoed his sergent's resigned sigh.

The new attack, the third in as many hours, surged from the forest again and swept over the tangled trees which by now lay scattered in low heaps across the field. This time the rangers and light infantry supported the assault more closely, using their accurate rifles to some effect while the advancing infantry charged across the open ground.

Crosbie saw little of that third attempt. The first whaleboat poked its prow into view just as the English started across the field. The full length of the boat slid into sight, oars dipping silently into the water, muffled with wads of cloth. The oars lifted, dipped once again and just at that moment a second prow moved forward, closely trailing. Crosbie sprang to his gun, whirling the traversing screw excitedly, swinging the muzzle to the left, searching for just the right spot to fire at the lead boat. All the boats would turn and run for cover with that first shot, so the important point was to let as many boats as possible enter the stretch of river commanded by his gun. Then he would have to allow time for two shots at the lead boat, just for safety's sake. That meant he couldn't let the boat come so far forward that it might thrash forward to safety before he could get off that second shot.

"Bring up another charge," he commanded, almost whispering in his nervous excitement. "Be ready to reload fast."

The boats nosed forward, closely packed with men. Each carried a musket with fixed bayonet. Crosbie counted nine boats before the first came into line with his gun. The tenth and eleventh were visible when Crosbie took the linstock from his sergent. He crouched tensely behind the gun, waiting until the boat was broadsides to him, the sights aimed directly at the center, along the waterline. Crosbie touched his match to the vent.

The crew leaped to reload. The lead boat had been torn in two. The sharp ends of the front and rear quarters protruded straight up, shattered sections of oars turned lazily in the air before splashing back into the water.

Crosbie traversed the gun to the right, laying roughly on the second boat while his crew reloaded. But the gun was loaded and aimed in less time than it took the second boat to turn. One bank of oars was aloft, the larboard bank digging to make the sharp pivot in the water. Slowly the stern came around, but by then Crosbie had applied the match to the vent. This time he shouted for grape as the crew reloaded. Solid shot was excellent for shattering boats, but the purpose of gunnery is to destroy soldiers, not boats. And grape would throw a deadly pattern with its half-pound balls spattering among the boat's crew.

The second roundshot hurled a vast curtain of spray that eliminated the view. Crosbie shouted for speed as he strained to see what damage had been done. The shot had fallen short, he realized.

Along the riverbank, an enterprising Canadien officer had turned his men toward the river and their muskets were blazing in irregular bursts at the easy targets presented by the boats. That might delay them long enough for one extra shot, Crosbie hoped. He bent to aim his gun again. This time the closely choked grape shot tore a wide hole in the side of the whaleboat. In the flickering moment before it sank, Crosbie could see the bare strakes of the opposite gunwale. Then the boat was gone. Only a few men lived to struggle in the sluggish current.

"Vite! Vite!" Crosbie shouted. "Quickly, you clumsy louts! One more. One more." He laid the gun hard to the right, spinning the screw fast. He damned his gunners in a sharp rippling mutter that brought grins to the sweating crew.

His cannon roared. The dull explosion sent grape shot spattering into the river. One single ball smacked into the stern of the third boat. Crosbie stared angrily at the vacant stretch of river.

"Only two," he growled. "Bigre! Two boats when we had a dozen to shoot at. By God, you men will spend some time at drill, I can promise you that. Two boats! Why, my aged Grand'mère could reload faster than..." Disgust choked him off. He glared in bewilderment at his gunners who were all grinning widely, delighted with such excellent results. They were good gunners and they knew it. Two boats sunk with only four shots. They grinned at Crosbie until the young Scot turned away in exasperation.

"Reload, round shot," he said heavily. "Keep a sharp watch, sergent. They may try it again. I want to go up to the fort for a moment. Keep the men at it."

The grinning sergent bowed respectfully and he turned to watch the huge young Scot out of sight before he gave any attention to his men.

The third attack had been pushed home more savagely than the previous ones, with dozens of English soldiers surmounting the retrenchment in fierce, suicidal assault. But the retreat was sounded before Crosbie had fired at the last boat. What the English were doing was admirable, splendid, inhumanly courageous, but it was a stupid way to fight a war, Crosbie thought. The end is to win, not to die bravely. All along the wall, French officers spoke together in hushed, awed tones. What they were seeing was historic, worthy of a place with the legends of Sparta. And it was so clearly motivated by an insensate stupidity that no man commanded the words to condemn it adequately.

The French and English dead, heaped behind the retrenchment were almost the same in numbers. The bodies were collected in a row at a safe remove from the wall. Surgeons in blood-streaked white coats worked swiftly, sending the serious casualties back to the fort, but patching most of them where they stood, waiting for another assault from those incredible English.

Crosbie detoured behind the encampment, taking the shortest route to the fort. He leaped up the steps three at a time, arriving on the wall just as the last salvo was fired. When his view was cleared, he could see no English soldiers standing before the forest. Many crumpled uniforms, folded in on themselves like empty scarlet sacks, lay at the base of the trees. The sergent bellowed the cease-fire and came to report to Crosbie.

"I tried to get in a shot at those boats, monsieur," he said apologetically, "but the field of fire was..."

"I know," Crosbie said easily. "That's why I moved the eight-pounder over beside the river. How are you faring here, sergent? Any casualties?"

"Three minor wounds only, sir. The riflemen are firing at us, but the range is too great. No men have been excused from duty."

"Excellent, sergent. I will leave you to it, then." Crosbie headed back toward the retrenchment. His route took him past the Général's command post.

Montcalm stood easily beside the mound he used for observation, his long brass telescope extended in one hand. His heavy coat was off and his servant, Jeannot, was mopping his streaming face with a napkin. Close at hand, shaded by a small tent fly, was a table and chairs. Jeannot retreated there and brought out a long bottle wrapped in damp cloths. He poured a glass of wine for the Général, and another for Captain Bougainville when the captain came back from the retrenchment.

Crosbie could see several staff officers and two regimental commanders under the shade thrown by the Général's tent fly. There, sprawled heavily on the ground was the burly frame of the Chevalier Le Mercier, his neck bared, his coat pushed back, his mottled face an alarming shade of crimson. Crosbie turned toward him immediately, kneeling beside the bulky Canadien. Le Mercier opened one eye and his chest heaved as he struggled for breath.

"This heat! Sacré!" he muttered. "Too much sun prostrates me. I will be recovered in a minute, young man, but you had better make a tour of inspection along the wall for me. One gun on the Right was out of action, I thought. I will..." He closed his eyes, squinting hard and gulping, fighting for air. A colonel laid a damp cloth on his forehead and pulled Crosbie to one side.

"He should stay here and rest," the colonel said quietly. "If you will take his place, he will soon be all right. It is merely the heat."

Crosbie nodded willing agreement. The Chevalier looked like the corpse of an old man. "Tell him to rest easy, monsieur," he said quickly. He turned away toward the retrenchment.

Ammunition parties hurried back and forth. Great quantities of mingled water and wine were carried to the wall and gulped down thirstily, the soldiers standing in place or sitting slumped wearily on the fire-step while the mad English re-formed for still another attack. Not even the most sanguine Frenchman thought they would quit.

Crosbie devoted his complete attention to the cannon along the retrenchment wall. He inspected supplies in the small expense magazines, sent back bags of grapeshot he found near one gun, reproving the sergent as he did so. Grape was far more accurate than canister, but accuracy meant nothing today. The deadly effect of the massed musket balls was far more valuable. One gun's crew had three men dead, all killed by the same daring Englishman who had found the embrasure in the zig-zag wall and had stayed outside it, firing in through the small space, then ducking away to reload, and returning to shoot again. Each of his shots had been fatal, having been fired alongside the cannon into the massed crew. Crosbie sent for replacements from the reserve gunners of the fort. He moved along to the next gun.

This one, the seventh in line, was the gun Le Mercier had thought was out of action. The Chevalier was quite right. The gun had unbushed itself early in the third attack, blowing its vent fitting free in a flat arc toward the rear. The jagged piece of worn metal had neatly extracted a gunner's eye in its flight, excising the eyeball with a surgeon's precision, hardly drawing blood. The wounded man was sent back to the fort and the sergent was laboriously intent upon his work by the time Crosbie came up.

The sergent had fitted a length of twine through the wide aperture left when the fitting had blown free. The twine was teased out the muzzle and threaded through the new fitting. Crosbie watched the sergent tie a deft knot with his dirty scarred fingers. A gunner drew on the twine when the sergent signalled and the new fitting went clattering up through the bore, small end first. The twine was pulled gently up and the fitting slid a short distance into the large vent hole and jammed. The sergent reversed a swab and poked the metal-bound handle into the bore, tapping gently at the wide flange on the base of the fitting to prod it into place. It was tedious, delicate work, to swing the handle just hard enough to rap the flange lightly without knocking the fitting away from its socket. With each tap, the small end of the vent fitting showed more clearly. At length the sergent withdrew his swab handle and straightened with a deep grunt.

"Ready now, sir," he said heavily. "A few shots will seat it tightly."

Crosbie flicked his dirk free and snipped off the twine. The short end with the knot dropped down the tiny aperture of the new fitting. "Swab that out first," he said. "Then load with half charges."

The lunging crew leaped quickly to position. A powder bag was ripped open and a portion of the charge pilled into the bore. It was tamped securely into place with a fibre wad. A canister container followed it. The sergent primed the gun and fired it out the embrasure without troubling to aim.

As the cannon rumbled back on its timber platform, Crosbie could see that the new fitting was almost level with the breech.

"Use the rest of the charge this time," he said. He wanted that gun ready with no more delay.

After the next explosion had rocked the gun back along its inclined platform, the new fitting was as snug as it would ever be, the stout fresh metal showing only a small opening in place of the two-inch wide gap in the breech itself. The sergent stroked a file gently across the fitting to smooth it even with the breech.

"All ready, sir," he grinned, straightening to wipe his straining face with his sleeve.

"Reload," Crosbie said. "Here they come again."

The alert was sounded by the guns from the fort that fired at the scarlet troops as they first appeared from the forest. Again the English came running forward and this time the volume of their musketry was serious, at least half the troops firing company volleys at the retrenchment while the attack was left to the others. Once the wall was successfully stormed, the musketeers could come on in comparative safety, but the vital need was to get a foothold on the wall and the English were focussing every effort on that goal. Three French soldiers fell wounded from the fire-step before Crosbie's gun had a suitable target.

The young Scot knelt to peer through the gun's embrasure, but his vision was so restricted that he rose immediately, jumping to the fire-step impatiently. He glanced over the retrenchment just as the English volleyed at the earthen wall. His cocked hat went sailing from his head, and Crosbie ducked, white-faced.

The sergent retrieved his hat, grinning widely and thrusting one heavy finger through the bullet-hole in the crown. Crosbie settled it firmly on his head, determined to display none of the nervous tremor that was making his muscles tense into cramped knots. God, what foolishness that was! To go peeking like a schoolboy when there was really no need. He forced himself to stoop again, sighting along the breech of the eight-pounder. A stalwart bagpiper marched briskly into view and behind him the Scots came running, screeching battle-cries as fiercely as the pipes. They handled their muskets awkwardly, compared with veteran troops, and most tossed them aside as they neared the wall, relying entirely on their long straight-bladed claymores.

"You may fire now," Crosbie said, holding his tone to a level growl. He watched unmoving, trying not to think of the Highlanders as the sergent brought his linstock down on the new vent. "Rapid fire!" Crosbie shouted as the gun lumbered back in recoil. "Let's see what you can do! Jump, you men!"

The guncrew followed its disciplined ritual, each man moving at just the moment the previous man had finished his job, each motion fitting to the first in rhythmic sequence, seeming slow and deliberate only because of its smooth, measured cadence. The gun was run forward smartly and fired.

When the cannon was back in recoil again, Crosbie looked put the embrasure and almost backed away in surprise. They were just outside! He had stared out into the glaring face of a Highlander! A musket exploded through the opening and Crosbie saw a soldier lurch from the fire-step, blood spouting from a gaping hole in his neck. He was looking at the slain soldier and did not see the Highlander who came diving down from the wall, claymore swinging viciously.

Crosbie had time only to fling his right arm up as the long blade cut at him. He took the steel on his forearm, a glancing blow that sliced into muscle and grated nastily on bone. Crosbie grappled with the Highlander, falling backward to the ground from the force of the charge, seizing the soldier's swordhand by the wrist. The kilted Highlander went mad above him, his eyes staring hotly, grunting in his fury. He bit Crosbie's clutching hand, tried to force his sword up into Crosbie's body. Crosbie could smell the rank stench of sweat and stale beer, and for years afterward remembered the strange gritty feel of the coarse matted hair on the Highlander's wrist as he clenched the sword hand in desperation.

Crosbie's left hand held the claymore's cutting edge away from his stomach. His right hand, dripping blood from the deep slash in his forearm, crept up to the Highlander's neck and fastened there. Crosbie's broad thumb bit into the hollow of the throat. Tensed fingers sank into neck muscles, without volition, for Crosbie's entire attention was focused on the stiff straight blade of the brass-hilted broadsword.

Crosbie was genuinely surprised when the hand suddenly opened and the claymore fell from limp fingers. Then he looked at his other hand and saw that was almost buried in the Highlander's throat. The tongue protruded fatly and the eyes above were bulging and bloodshot, but sightless now. The soldier was dead. Crosbie rolled his body to one side and lunged unsteadily to his feet.

Around him stood a tense ring of French soldiers, two officers with their swords ready, and infantrymen who held their naked bayonets forward, hoping for a chance to stab the Highlander without wounding Crosbie.

Crosbie stooped briefly and picked up the abandoned claymore. It weighed nearly as much as an issue musket, the metal of its blade almost an inch wide across the back; its great basket hilt of polished brass gleamed in the bright sunlight. Crosbie held it lightly, point touching the ground, as a bearded surgeon came running up to him.

When the surgeon attempted to slit the arm of his coat, he bellowed with outrage, and slipped his arm free, letting the heavy coat dangle down his back, suspended only from his left shoulder. That damned cut would heal easily enough but good uniforms don't mend themselves. He sensibly pulled his lace cuff loose and rammed it into his waistcoat pocket. But he was too slow to keep the surgeon from cutting his shirt sleeve all the way to the elbow.

The gash looked worse than it was, Crosbie thought. Bright blood oozed from the long deep cut, but the surgeon merely sluiced it clean with vinegar, threw four deft stitches across the widest part and bound it up in the blood. Crosbie held his teeth clenched hard against the pain. The surgeon flipped a loop of cloth around Crosbie's neck and hung his right arm in it. He pulled the coat loosely up over Crosbie's shoulder and then draped the swordbelt over it, securing the wounded arm snugly against Crosbie's chest, the hand nearly touching the left shoulder. The surgeon nodded, satisfied, and went off to find someone else in need of his services.

Neither Crosbie's fight nor his bandaging had interrupted the steady rate of fire from his cannon. The infantrymen on the wall poured their measured volleys into the attacking English at a controlled rate of four or five shots every minute and at every third volley, the eight-pounders added their blasts of canister. A long limp rank of dead and wounded lay behind the wall. Only the most daring English soldiers had surmounted the retrenchment, and all of them had died. Again the drums frantically rolled the retreat. Crosbie wiped his filthy face and picked up the claymore again; using it as a walking stick, he backed to a slanting stump and sat wearily, feeling an odd, sickly pulse beating in his head and a great smothering dizziness that seemed to well up from the ground in thunderous tides. He closed his eyes and a red haze swam in front of him. He could still see vividly the ghastly expression of the Highlander, teeth bared, eyes wild with battle lust. His hair had been solidly black where the powder had been knocked off, but his eyes were a brilliant, furious blue. One of those black Scots with a strain of wild Pictish blood, probably. More likely a Borderer than a Highlander, he told himself. But nothing was any good. He must try not to think of him. The man was an enemy, out for blood. Now he was dead and that was the end of it.

Crosbie pushed himself to his feet when the next attack came. He marched in wobbling strides along the wall, spending some time with each guncrew. And later he could recall nothing of the attack, or of those that followed. The English could be killed, but they could not be daunted. The last attack came with the same violent, confident ferocity as the first, the troops not intimidated by the necessity of leaping over the dead bodies of their comrades. But it could not go on forever.

Crosbie forced himself to stay on his feet, knowing that if he were to sit now, he would never be able to get up again. He roamed in slow, stumbling strides behind the guns and the sergents watched him carefully. The huge young Scot had become a symbol to them. They delighted in his alternate dour silences and extravagant, energetic explosions. What would have invoked surliness and mutinous growls coming from another officer, took on a hilarious, cheerful aspect when it came from Crosbie. They served their guns with the speedy rhythm that their gigantic young officer demanded of them. As a result, Crosbie found little that required his attention and even when his mind blurred with pain and dizziness, he knew he was not shirking his duty.

Another attack and another repulse and Crosbie felt a cooling breeze on his damp back, a clamminess that followed the heat of the day. The sun was probably lower, he thought, and he wheeled to look. The sun was indeed lower, glowing almost directly into his eyes, low to the west. It would blind the gunners, Crosbie judged. I'll have to...

Men were leaving the wall now by platoons, less than half of the army still in place. They staggered a few steps and threw themselves to the ground. Droves stumbled toward the row of latrines beside the encampment. Others carried the water butts along the retrenchment for those who had to wait. Crosbie noticed that even his gunners were leaving their posts, all without permission from him. Angrily he pushed away from the sapling he was using for support, bellowing for the nearest sergent with a hoarse roar that made his head throb with sickening waves of pain.

"Duncan, my friend, how did you weather the day?"

Crosbie turned with the pressure of Bougainville's hand.

"Ah, forgive me, Duncan. I did not know," the captain said. "I, too, as you can see." Bougainville grinned, pointing to a fat bandage encircling his left leg. "A mere scratch, however. Poor de Bourlamaque was rather seriously wounded. He will recover, but not for some time."

Crosbie nodded. He closed his eyes to mere slits. That way the pain seemed less. "That's all?"

"The gallant de Lévis has two gaping holes in his best hat, but no more. And the Général was not touched, God be thanked."

"You... you talk as if it's... over."

"And so it is," Bougainville insisted. "There is not daylight enough to mount another assault. And even the English must be weary of the slaughter. They have probably lost a thousand dead at the very least, and twice that number wounded. No army can endure such casualties."

"And we?" Crosbie asked in a voice that croaked.

"I don't know," Bougainville said. "About one hundred dead, I think. So we may assume another two hundred wounded, I suppose. A far happier result, but with our limited numbers, we cannot afford even that. Now come with me, Duncan. We'll find a bottle of wine and ..."

Crosbie brushed the suggestion away irritably, not realizing that he had swung the captured claymore dangerously close to Bougainville's head.

"I will have to see that sergent and ..." His voice faded slowly to silence. He glanced with vague, filmed eyes at his friend. Then, briefly, his eyes flared with alarm. The lids dropped shut and slowly, Crosbie's massive frame relaxed, slumping first to his knees, then with the loss of all control, crashing full length to the ground.

CHAPTER THIRTY

Awareness returned to Crosbie with waves of dull pain. He opened his eyes slowly, squinting even though the room was very dim. He recognized the familiar outline of his window and without turning his head he knew he had been carried back inside the fort and stretched on his narrow cot.

Denis glanced up, wide-eyed, from his crouching posture on the stone floor. The boy smiled hesitantly, his lips trembling. He rose in a quick scramble and ran out into the corridor. Crosbie could hear his heavy shoes clumping down the stone hallway. Denis had left behind a blood-stained napkin. Seeing it lying against the bare floor made Crosbie feel inexpressibly sad.

When the door opened again, Crosbie was sitting up unsteadily. He wore only his uniform breeches and the shredded remnants of a shirt. His slashed arm had been rebandaged skillfully, strapped snugly across his chest and padded thickly with rough cloth that felt like strouding.

He turned to glance up at Bougainville. A sickening dizziness blurred his vision, but it receded gradually as he fought for control.

"Evening, Louis," he said in a thick tone. He cleared his throat roughly. "Had a nap. What's the situation now? I guess the English won't do anything tonight?"

"No," Bougainville agreed, lifting his head in soft laughter. "No, I think the English will do nothing tonight. All is serene."

Crosbie drew in a long experimental breath and was relieved when no stabbing pain struck at him. "Why the laughter?" he growled. He gripped the back of a chair and levered himself erect.

"It is not tonight, Duncan," Bougainville smiled. "It is tomorrow night. You have had a long sleep, not a short nap."

"Good God," Crosbie groaned. "What happened?"

"Not a thing," Bougainville said pleasantly. He came closer to Crosbie ready to support the young Scot if he should stagger. "We passed a night of great tension, even the Général remaining at his post. But there was no attack. At full daylight we moved a regiment forward to reconnoitre and found the English gone. During the night they had marched two or three leagues back to their landing place and embarked again. They must be far down the lake by this time. They ran, Duncan. It is beyond belief, but they ran!"

Crosbie closed his eyes to reduce the swimming sensation in his head. "You are right, Louis," he muttered. "It is incredible. Why…"

Bougainville shrugged happily. "Who can say why? Panic seized them, obviously. They ran away and Carillon is safe for the time, possibly for the entire campaign. You should have seen the stores they abandoned in their haste. Hundreds of barrels of provisions, most of their baggage. And all along the road we found shoes stuck in the mud where the frantic English had left them as they ran. They ran out of their shoes!"

"It is senseless," Crosbie said in an unbelieving tone. "How many men did Abercrombie lose?"

"You may say roughly that each army lost ten percentum of its force in killed and wounded. But Abercrombie still has a monumental army, you must realize, twenty thousand at least. Why he retreated no man can say. He panicked. That much is clear. For the rest, let us burn a small candle and give thanks."

"Amen," Crosbie said fervently. He took three hesitant strides toward the wall, finding his head reasonably clear now, though his legs had a ludicrous tendency to wobble.

"You were merely exhausted, the surgeon said. After a rest, he insisted, you would be perfectly recovered, except for the gash in your arm. How do you feel?"

"Hungry."

Bougainville laughed. "Your Denis is down at the kitchen now for soup. And he will bring a can of hot water. You must make yourself presentable, Duncan. There will be a council within the hour."

"I don't feel like celebrating, Louis," Crosbie objected.

"It is no celebration," Bougainville said bluntly. "I cannot speak until the Général addresses the council, but I can assure you this will be no mere celebration. Rigaud brought serious news with him."

"Rigaud," Crosbie said dully. He remembered that Rigaud was bringing something else, too. The hard-voiced Irishman O'Neill had warned him of this. Rigaud had brought a warrant for Crosbie's arrest. But why didn't Louis Bougainville say anything about that?

"The Governor's brother," Bougainville went on easily, "brought reinforcements, Duncan. Thousands of splendid Canadiens and Indians. They arrived too late to fight, which is a pity, for they are all extremely valiant. They will tell you so themselves. The Général has refused to receive Rigaud, although he did accept the dispatches. Truly, I believe that Montcalm has completely lost patience with the Governor's entire family, starting with the noble Marquis himself and descending to the least grandchild. But, we will see, Duncan. Come to my room when you are ready. And be swift, my friend."

But it was nearly an hour before Crosbie was lightly fed, shaved and dressed. He stood with his hand on the doorknob, looking at Denis. The boy was toying with the great claymore Crosbie had captured. The broadsword was far too heavy for him, but he contrived to swing it clumsily with both hands. The boy's thin face had been wan and fearful, but its expression had grown more cheerful when Denis had realized that Crosbie was only lightly wounded. But what would be his future if Crosbie were court-martialled, as would probably happen? Well, Denis could remain with the army. No civil authority could reach him there. But life could be miserable for an enlisted soldier with no friends to help him.

"Denis," he said softly.

"Oui, monsieur?"

"If I am not back here before morning, I want you to go to Captain Bougainville. Take all your kit with you and pack my things carefully. Tell the captain that I want you to serve as his orderly until I send for you. Do you understand?"

Denis nodded. His eyes were wide with sudden alarm, but something in Crosbie's voice warned him against asking questions.

"Duncan ..." The boy looked quickly away, hiding his face.

"Don't worry, Denis," Crosbie said with a false joviality that fooled neither of them, but helped to make pretense possible. "I may have to leave for a time. You do as I say, eh?"

The boy nodded silently, unable to look directly at Crosbie.

"Then show me," Crosbie said gently. "What way is that for a soldier to acknowledge an order?"

Denis brought both hands into line with the seams of his breeches and lifted his head, pulling his chin stiffly back. Tears stood hot and bright in his eyes, his treacherous nose twitched nervously, but his voice trembled only slightly, "Oui, monsieur!" His heels clicked together with a resounding crack.

Crosbie stood irresolutely in the doorway. After a long silent moment, he went out, closing the door softly behind him.

He marched along the corridor toward Bougainville's room with his chin high. Whatever lay before him would require every degree of restraint and fortitude he possessed. It would only weaken his determination to worry about the possible variations. No matter what came, it would be unpleasant, at best.

There was no way out. O'Neill had said that. Crosbie rapped on Bougainville's door and pushed it back.

The captain sat in a soft chair reading a slim book balanced on his knee. He was fully dressed except for his coat, his wig gleaming, his uniform immaculate as always. He glanced up and smiled at Crosbie.

"Ah, Duncan, come and view my souvenirs," he called amiably, gesturing toward a mound of leather-bound books on his bed. "It was my duty to examine all the papers left behind by our despairing enemy. The books were an unexpected profit. Won't you choose one for yourself?"

"Thank you, Louis," Crosbie said absently.

"I assume you read English as well as you speak it," Bougainville said easily. "Take your choice. The classics, Vegetius, Plutarch, Seutonius in Latin, and Thucydides in Greek. The remainder are in English. An inept translation of La Fontaine's Fables which I have been looking through, a novel called Robinson Crusoe, the poems of Shakespeare, and even an Englished version of the King of Prussia's Regulations. No English officer has troubled his mind with that, eh?"

Bougainville shrugged into his snug white coat. "But here, my friend. I have a most particular souvenir for you. Something to go with that massive broadsword you captured." Bougainville opened the paneled door of an armoire and brought out a colorful tangled mass, dropping it onto the bed near Crosbie. "Can you play one of those things?"

Crosbie lifted the bagpipes curiously. He clamped the bag under his good arm, letting the drones drop against his shoulder. The chanter pipe fell into place for his fingers and the mouthpiece was so balanced that it inclined back only a short distance from his lips. Crosbie blew forcefully into the mouthpiece, inflating the bag easily. He squeezed his elbow against it, blowing steadily to maintain an even pressure, holding all the stops of the chanter pipe that he could reach with only one hand. A wild discordant screech blared through the small room.

"Thank you, Louis," Crosbie said. He stroked his hand over the taut plaid bag, feeling the harsh tartan wool scratch his fingers in that old familiar sensation. "I haven't touched a pibroch since I was a boy. Thank you."

Bougainville waved a hand airily. "And regard this, if you will." He swung a hairy white goatskin pouch from a hook and draped it over one shoulder for Crosbie's inspection. The long silky white hair was inset with three black tufts.

"A sporran," Crosbie said. "A carryall pouch the Scots use. But it isn't worn over the shoulder, Louis."

Bougainville put the sporran back on its hook and grinned broadly. "I know how it is worn, my friend," he laughed. "I also saw those fierce Highlanders as they charged us. I shall use the pouch with pleasure, but I shall not emulate them. Imagine wearing this immense object dangling in such a position. Preposterous! One would be in a constant state of agitation."

Bougainville threw open the door and escorted Crosbie from his room. The Scot paused a moment to drop the bagpipes onto the bed. Another time he would have been delighted to have them, but now he had no interest beyond that decent minimum required by good manners. He bowed to Bougainville and went out into the hall.

CHAPTER THIRTY ONE

The large council room was hushed. Officers stood in tight groups, expectantly glancing around when anyone entered. On the wall between two windows hung Montcalm's map, brilliantly lighted by the bank of candles on his table. Crosbie and Bougainville joined the other staff officers at the rear of the room.

Clustered near the door stood a group Crosbie did not recognize. In their center he made out the hard-lined face of Monsieur Rigaud de Vaudreuil, the Governor's brother. Crosbie looked away quickly. Those men would be the newly arrived Canadiens, he assumed, the reinforcements who had timed their arrival precisely to miss the battle. Those who wore uniform displayed the facings of the troupes de la marine; the rest were dressed in fanciful versions of partisan clothing, with bleached, beaded doeskin shirts above thin silk breeches, beaded bands decorating their hats. Captain Seamus O'Neill leaned casually against the wall, his usually immaculate uniform stained and torn from rough usage during the battle.

The door opened without warning and the Général entered, followed by the Chevalier de Lévis and Estére who promptly prepared to take notes. Montcalm stood with his back to his staff, facing the waiting officers. He did not look like a victorious général, not at all. Judging only by his tense, drawn expression, one would guess that he had been defeated. A chill of apprehension crept into Crosbie's mind.

"Gentlemen," Montcalm said sharply. "This is the first council since our victory, so I wish to compliment all of you on your magnificent conduct. The regiments deserve every praise I can offer. Their behavior reflects the highest honor on themselves and their officers. They are true French soldiers. I would say more, but there is no higher compliment in my power."

A pleased mutter ran through the room and then died away. Montcalm's voice was low and quiet, slightly weary, as though only through serious effort could he make it audible.

"The army, the two-small army of the King, has beaten the enemy. Our victory at Carillon will take its place in the long list of battle honors won by the regiments of France. Tomorrow a Te Deum will be sung in celebration, and our victorious dead will be interred with the full honors they have nobly earned."

The Général glanced around the room briefly and then dropped his gaze to a slip of heavy paper that crackled in his fingers. Crosbie could see that Montcalm's hand was trembling slightly.

"I must now report to you the news that our fortress at Louisbourg will by this time have been surrendered to the English. The fortress commander, the Chevalier de Drucour, has sent his aide, Captain Johnstone, with this tragic warning."

The assembled officers gasped almost in unison. Most of them lifted their heads to stare at the map visible beyond Montcalm. The impregnable fortress at Louisbourg had once before been lost, and regained only at a ruinous price. Its guns guarded the finest harbor of Canada and whoever controlled Louisbourg controlled the St. Lawrence. The bastion of Canada was isolated now; the great central position of Quebec and Montreal no longer had a supply and communication route to France. Single vessels might run the blockade, but the vast fleets that were Canada's lifeline would never be able to slip through. The stunned expression on every face proved clearly that there was no need for the Général to explain what the loss of Louisbourg would mean to Canada.

"You gentlemen will have noticed that our force has been increased," the Général said in a dry tone. "Nearly a thousand men have already arrived and a further two thousand are en route. Monsieur Rigaud commands this welcome addition."

Montcalm's satirical comment brought slight flushes to the faces of the newcomers, but none interrupted him.

"Monsieur Rigaud also conveyed orders from His Excellency, the King's Governor. I am required to pursue Abercrombie, as far as Albany if necessary, and destroy his army."

The Général dropped the sheet of paper onto the table in front of Estére. He looked up again, his face tight, his lips pulled back hard over his teeth.

"I am compelled to assume that His Excellency has not yet heard of the fall of Louisbourg, or hàs not had time to evaluate its meaning. The army will remain at Carillon. The defenses will be strengthened. We will not advance."

Excited comments sputtered from the officers, who knew that Montcalm had previously ignored orders from the Governor, but had never before heard the Général flout them in open council. From the cluster near the door, the Governor's brother shouldered through and placed himself truculently in front of Montcalm.

"Monsieur, I must warn you that His Excellency's orders are explicit. They allow no latitude."

"I have read the orders, Monsieur Rigaud," Montcalm said coldly.

"Do you question His Excellency's authority to direct your campaign?" Rigaud demanded hotly, his full throat bulging above his tight neckcloth.

"At the moment," Montcalm said heavily, "His Excellency is empowered to set the objectives of my operations. I, however, command the army."

"Exactly," Rigaud snapped in a rising, triumphant voice. "So you admit you cannot countermand your orders."

"I will delay execution of the orders," Montcalm amended in a cold, bored tone. "I am sure His Excellency will want to reconsider his decision."

BART SPICER

"And I am sure he will not!" Rigaud's voice made his statement a flat challenge.

"You are mistaken, monsieur," Montcalm said, controlling himself with visible effort. "His Excellency does not realize the gravity of the situation. My troops here are the sole defense of Canada. I cannot be a général now. I must be a cautious banker, investing the lives of my soldiers for the good of France. They cannot be thrown away on audacious assaults. Had you been here with us earlier, monsieur, you would have seen how foolhardy that can be. When Louisbourg was surrendered, we lost more than five thousand soldiers, in addition to the fortress itself. We will not make a stand at duQuesne, so there remains only the Carillon line of defenses to keep the English from Quebec and Montreal. I have now three thousand soldiers. Where will I find replacements when they are killed?"

"You forget the Canadiens!" Rigaud exploded.

"No, monsieur," Montcalm said heatedly, "I do not forget the Canadiens. Nor the Indians. Where were they when Abercrombie attacked? You did great service for France that day, monsieur. You stayed away. Should I remind you of your campaign last winter? It is still fresh in your mind, monsieur? You took sixteen hundred men against Fort William Henry that was held by a scant three hundred English regulars. That campaign was also ordered by His Excellency over my objection. Why did it fail? Was the Governor at fault, monsieur? Or were you?"

Rigaud stepped back, his reddened face distended with rage. Everyone present knew what a fiasco he had made of his campaign and what anger the French officers had felt when this swaggering clown was named to command their troops. Independently, the Canadiens moved closer together at the far end of the room, leaving the French officers alone near the Général.

Montcalm waited a long moment for the irate Rigaud to speak. When he did not, the Général said in a strained voice,

"Your Canadien troops, regular and militia, are very useful, monsieur. But they are not trained or equipped to stand against English regulars. No sensible man could expect it. We must think of them as auxiliaries, not as troops of the line."

Rigaud drew himself erect in a haughty movement. "I must warn you, monsieur," he almost snarled, "every word you have said will be reported to His Excellency."

"I will do that myself," Montcalm said coldly. "It is time for clear speaking, I agree. Now gentlemen, let us pass to this other matter." Montcalm stretched out a hand to take a paper that Estére held ready for him. The Général turned his head slightly. "Monsieur Crosbie!"

Duncan Crosbie stiffened to attention.

"Yesterday I commended the Chevalier Le Mercier for the excellent artillery support his guns furnished to our defense. His opinion, in which I concur, is that much of the credit is rightfully due to your energy and resourcefulness. Your wounds bear eloquent witness to the honorable part you took in the battle. In my order of the day for tomorrow, you will be promoted to the brevet rank of Captain."

Before Crosbie could close his gaping jaw, the Général swung to confront Rigaud. The folded paper in his hand rustled crisply as he spoke.

"You have reminded me, monsieur, that I alone command this army. Monsieur Crosbie's promotion is my answer to this infamous document you have presented. Its accusations are dismissed with the contempt they deserve. Monsieur Crosbie is not subject to the authority of His Excellency, your noble brother, nor is any other soldier of France. I hope you will make that adequately clear in your report."

Montcalm tossed the paper disdainfully toward Estére.

"The council is adjourned," he said bluntly. "Thank you, gentlemen."

Every officer burned to ask questions, to make comments. But the Général's dismissal was flat and final. Montcalm pivotted on his heel, glaring at Crosbie.

"Come with me," he snapped. "You too, Louis."

He strode quickly into his private chamber and slammed the door explosively.

"You besotted young fool," he growled in cold fury. "For two years those Canadien scoundrels have been trying to implicate my officers in their thievery. They want to smear my staff with their dirt. And you, you reckless great idiot, you gave them their chance. I should let the Governor throw you into jail. It would teach you nothing—I am convinced you have no mind whatever—but it would at least be suitable punishment for your unbelievable stupidity."

Crosbie's face flared with a painful flush. He could think of nothing to say. The Général was right.

Montcalm raged. "You and you alone gave the Canadiens their greatest weapon against me. They can now claim that their thievery is a mere peccadillo compared to the behavior of my own staff. And what am I to say?"

The Général stood balanced on the balls of his feet, glaring up at the young Scot.

"You can say that I..."

"Be silent!" Montcalm roared. "Do you think I need explanations? Didn't they try the same trick with Louis last year? But you, you enormous, complacent clown, you were duped! You accepted their favors, you joined their drunken mob of thieves and murderers. You, alone..." Montcalm's voice choked off. With a sudden, contemptuous gesture, he turned away, as if he could no longer endure the sight of Crosbie's stricken face.

Crosbie pulled in a deep breath. He had been feeling very sorry for himself. He had already recognized his error, admitted to himself his own criminal stupidity, but he had never before considered the harm he had done to his Général. Now his juvenile arrogance withered at the thought. At this moment, when Montcalm was threatened on every side, it remained for Crosbie to bring an additional burden for him to carry. The young Scot's hands clenched into tight fists. His chin came up and he stared directly at Montcalm's back, ready now in his own mind to accept without complaint whatever Montcalm planned for him.

"Louis," Montcalm said heavily, without turning around, "do you know Monsieur duMaine?"

"The Sieur duMaine, mon général," Bougainville corrected. "Yes, I have met him."

Crosbie masked his surprise at the even-voiced conversation that followed Montcalm's roaring blast a few minutes earlier.

"I am sending you to the Governor at Quebec with my report. You will carry my answer to his orders. Also another letter which you will deliver only under certain conditions which I will explain later. I want you to take Monsieur Crosbie with you. He is to be quartered on the Sieur duMaine until further orders from me. Is that clear?"

"Perfectly clear, Excellency," Bougainville said readily.

Montcalm heaved a sigh and turned to look for a long moment at Bougainville. "I think it may be perfectly clear to you," he said in a wondering tone. "Your mother must have been a gypsy, Louis. Take this gigantic idiot and go away somewhere. I will send for you later. Plan to leave at dawn tomorrow."

Crosbie said nothing. He understood nothing, but his face now showed no sign of the fiery truculence he had felt earlier. If this was his punishment, then he would accept it and if God gave him the strength, he would be cheerful about it.

Montcalm banged the back of his hand lightly at Crosbie's chest in a rapid tattoo. "You are every kind of a fool, young man," he scowled. "But you are a good soldier, too good to be sacrificed to these rascals who want your scalp. Those guns sang a pretty tune when the English came at us. You did better than I'd hoped for. That's why I promoted you, and I'll see that a permanent commission is found for you. Now go with Louis and try to restrain your ardor for a short time. Good day, gentlemen."

Bougainville bowed promptly and pulled the door open.

"May I..." Crosbie fumbled for words.

"I understand your regret," Montcalm said. "I share it."

Crosbie bowed and followed Bougainville.

When they were alone, Bougainville stopped Crosbie. "That was one of Montcalm's celebrated bourrasques," he said quietly. "As an outburst it compared poorly with the blasts he has delivered to the Governor himself. Do not be down-hearted, Duncan."

"I'm not down-hearted, Louis," Crosbie said glumly. "It was far less than I deserved."

"Was it, indeed?" Bougainville said thoughtfully. "Well, no matter. Remember to be very discreet when you are with the Sieur duMaine, Duncan. He is an old friend of the Général."

"But who is the man?" Crosbie demanded helplessly.

"He is one of Canada's seigneurs. His estate is not far from Quebec."

"Quebec!" Crosbie halted in mid-stride. "Quebec? But what about the campaign, Louis?"

"Softly," Bougainville said. "Softly, my friend. As to the campaign, it is likely that you have seen the last battle of this season. Unless Ambercrombie attacks again, there will be no more fighting. And if I know the English, they will spend the rest of the good weather trying to fix the blame for their recent disaster. It will be too late for campaigning by the time they select a new commander. And we will not move against them; you heard the Général."

"But Quebec," Crosbie said angrily. "It's...exile. Why does he..."

"Can't you guess, Duncan?" Bougainville glanced warily at Crosbie. "Come to my quarters," he went on hurriedly. "This cannot be discussed so publicly."

Crosbie's bewilderment continued as he trailed Bougainville along the corridor. Mystery upon mystery, he thought irritably, until the simplest statement takes on an air of dark intrigue.

"Monsieur!" Bougainville said sharply as he opened his door. His hand behind his back waggled caution to Crosbie. Someone was in Bougainville's room.

"Your pardon, monsieur." A short thin-faced officer came unhurriedly to his feet. He replaced the bagpipes on the bed and smiled easily at Bougainville. "I was told you could assign me quarters." His brisk voice died away as he stared at Crosbie who stood glowering in the doorway, taking up the entire aperture with his huge body, his red hair gleaming like a beacon in the dark corridor. "Naomh Aindrea!" he murmured softly in the soft Gaelic of the border Scots. "Can it be Duncan Mohr? Or his ghost? Surely there'll never be two ... Your name is Crosbie, monsieur?"

"Duncan Crosbie, sir," the young Scot said with a suspicious frown. "And you ..."

"My apologies again," the stranger said briskly. "I am Captain Johnstone. But if you are Duncan Mohr's son, you will call me Jamie, as he did."

"Duncan Mohr," Crosbie echoed softly. He hadn't heard that name since his boyhood days. Big Duncan. Great Duncan. Duncan Mohr, the biggest and strongest of the stalwarts who fought for their Prince against the German usurper, who had the English on the run until that dark day at Derby when Lord George Murray betrayed them and sent them reeling back toward Scotland and that darker day at Culloden. Duncan Mohr, the Prince's champion, who was killed only after he seen his Prince to safety. Crosbie stared blankly at the small dapper stranger.

"Duncan Mohr saved my life at Prestonpans," the Captain said. "I did not know he had a son, but I recognized you the moment I ..."

"You will forgive my interruption, monsieur," Bougainville said crisply. "I am sure you have much to say to Captain Crosbie. But how may I serve you? A billet, I think you said?"

"A bed for tonight, please," the stranger said pleasantly. "I am returning to Quebec tomorrow. The Governor wishes to hear the details of our fight at Louisbourg."

"Of course," Bougainville said with a faint meaningless smile. "You were aide to Monsieur de Drucour, were you not? If you will walk down this corridor a few steps you will see an empty room with the door standing open."

"Thank you, monsieur."

The sudden unexplained animosity that smoldered between Bougainville and Johnstone was obvious to Crosbie.

Bougainville closed the door crisply and banged his fist hard against the wall.

"God blast that man," he muttered.

"What..."

"He ran!" Bougainville exploded. "How do you think we knew about Louisbourg? He brought the news. Somehow he convinced Drucour he should be sent to safety. Five thousand men, they had, and the best system of defenses mortal man could devise. They threw them all away and that smiling, little man comes to us with the news. I would sooner have killed myself than..."

"Softly, softly," Crosbie said, aping Bougainville's own tone.

Bougainville swallowed heavily. "All right, Duncan," he said, forcing a bleak smile. He shrugged and made a dismissing gesture with one hand. "What did we come here for? I've forgotten."

Crosbie had not forgotten. "You were going to tell me why..."

"Ah, yes," Bougainville broke in. "Why the Général was sending you to safety."

"Safety?"

"Think of it as safety and the reason comes clear."

"Safety? How could I be safer anywhere than I would be right here? If the Général wants to keep me out of jail, why doesn't he let me stay where he can see what happens, so he can control..."

"That is exactly the point." Bougainville pulled off his coat and hung it tidily on a peg. "I am guessing, you must understand, Duncan. We know the Général will not surrender you to the Governor. And we know that you would be safest here at Carillon. So what reason could the Général have for sending you to live quietly on a secluded seigneury? What would account for that, Duncan?"

"I don't know, Louis. I couldn't guess."

Bougainville glanced sharply at Crosbie. "I suspect you could, Duncan, but I will say the words. Montcalm is going to resign. When he does, he will not be able to protect you. De Lévis is in line to succeed him and de Lévis is related to the Governor's family. And there you are." He spread his hands.

"You really believe that?" Crosbie's hoarse voice was almost a whisper.

Bougainville nodded. "I have seen it coming for a long time. And this is the appropriate moment, I would judge. The English can make no further advance against Carillon this year, so Montcalm could not be criticized for leaving at a moment of crisis. But the decisive battles will come next year and by then, there must be a unified command for Canada. Now is the time for Montcalm to demand a free hand. I think that is what the Général plans to do."

"I can't..." Crosbie gulped nervously.

"I have been very indiscreet, Duncan," Bougainville said quietly. "You must not repeat what I have said. Not to anyone. Now pack your kit. Come have dinner with me this afternoon. But get out now, please. I have much to do before I can leave here." Bougainville tapped Crosbie's arm lightly. "And don't worry, Duncan."

CHAPTER THIRTY TWO

The small brig swooped up the lake under all plain sail, heeling slightly in the quartering breeze. Duncan Crosbie sat rigidly on the deck near the forepeak where he could be alone.

Behind him in the narrow waist of the ship, Denis perched cross-legged, cobbling together the torn uniform Crosbie had worn in battle. The boy had finished packing all of Crosbie's gear by the time the morose young Scot had returned to his room in the fort. Crosbie had found him crouched in a dark corner, jabbing the captured claymore at the stone floor, cursing savagely. But whatever strong vows he had sworn, whatever dread apprehensions had plagued him, the boy now seemed fully recovered, Crosbie thought. He had not once referred to that fearful time he had spent alone at Carillon.

Crosbie shifted his right arm higher in its sling and pushed the scabbarded dirk out of the way. The pain of his wound was a constant dull ache now, nothing he could not endure. Under the brig, water foamed and chuckled, and the constant motion of the ship made the horizon seem to rise and fall in drowsy rhythm. Now there was nothing visible but the bright sky. Then, as the brig nosed down, the tips of the jagged hills came into view and later, the dark green of the mainland forests. The sun was hot, almost tangible, against Crosbie's back.

"Hot today," a deep voice said behind him. "Don't believe Canada had Spring this year. Just Winter and Summer. It was snowing in Louisbourg the day I left. And that only two weeks ago."

Crosbie turned his head and squinted against the sun to look up at Johnstone. The Scottish captain wore a meticulously neat uniform with a small periwig that had been chosen with a clever eye to complement Johnstone's small precise features. By contrast, Crosbie felt like a grubby boy caught dabbling in the mud. He dragged his elderly coat snugly over his bandaged arm.

"Louisbourg," Crosbie echoed. "Was it ... bad?"

"Aye," Johnstone said heavily, in a resounding voice that seemed too big for his slight frame. "Aye, it was bad. Our Général de Drucour was a gormless dreamer. Our Admiral was a coward, afraid to fight the English navy. Our Intendant was a greedy thief. Between them they lost Louisbourg."

Crosbie made a non-committal sound. He rubbed a broad thumb over the wolf's head engraved in his dirk.

"And you'd never credit the gunnery, my boy," Johnstone said with sombre emphasis. "Two hundred and fifty cannon on the walls and hardly a gunner who could reload. Twelve battleships with five hundred guns on board sunk in the harbor without firing a shot. And the stores of food and gunpowder the Intendant said he bought for the garrison simply never existed, except on his records. Greedy as a mandarin, Prevost. A provincial Intendant gets rich; everyone expects that. But Prevost was a blatant rogue. Och, they betrayed us, Duncan. A new kind of betrayal, distinctively French."

"You held out for a long time," Crosbie said quietly.

Johnstone shrugged. "The English won. That's all that matters now. Amherst has sent Monckton looting and burning through the Gaspé with orders to 'destroy the vermin who are settled there.' I saw that order myself, and I know Monckton. The dirty Sassenach will relish the job."

The slender captain leaned against the railing; only his white-skinned knuckles gripping his swordhilt betrayed the inner tension he fought to control. He forced a thin smile and abruptly shifted into Gaelic. "And how do you enjoy your life among the French?"

Crosbie turned to avoid the direct sunlight. "It is the only life I know," he said uncertainly.

"Ah, yes," Johnstone murmured. "You'd have been a mere babe during the '45, eh? Yes, France would not be the strange land to you, I suppose. Many of us find it difficult."

"And you, monsieur?" Crosbie asked politely.

Johnstone stared down soberly at the sprawling figure of the young Scot. "I could hope to be Jamie with the son of an old friend."

Crosbie flushed brightly. "I...I'm sorry, sir," he said with sharp embarrassment.

"Nonsense. But I hope we'll be friends, Duncan."

"Willingly...Jamie," Crosbie said hesitantly.

Their speech was now an odd mixture of Gaelic and English. A passing sailor glared at them with suspicious curiosity as he walked by. Johnstone snorted.

"The Gaelic is curious, but the English is anathema. That combination is the French reaction to most Scots." He let himself down to the deck beside Crosbie, squaring his gold-buckled shoes neatly before him. "You have not felt the distrust that comes to most Scots. Since John Law swindled the whole nation, Frenchmen have come to suspect all of us. Now a Scot is lucky to be treated as an unwelcome guest. But you seem to have escaped that fate. Your rank is quite unusual, considering your age, even among favored gentlemen."

"I am only brevetted a captain," Crosbie said, somehow unwilling to accept Johnstone's compliment. "And that since yesterday."

"Of course. I heard the Général. Even so, it is remarkable. You've done very well, Duncan."

"I've been fortunate," Crosbie agreed.

"I suppose that's true," Johnstone said in a deep voice full of admiration. "But I doubt if it's the whole truth. One day we shall see you nominated to the Order of St. Louis, eh? How would it sound? Duncan, le Chevalier de Crosbie?" Johnstone laughed in a low pleasant rumble.

The young Scot fidgetted. The name sounded clumsy and just a little silly, he thought. But the honorific "de" that signified nobility was a basic requirement if he hoped to rise as high as lieutenant-colonel. Duncan de Crosbie made one's tongue stumble, but it would be his name eventually, if all went well.

Johnstone stroked his chin and dusted his finger fastidiously. "Few young officers have your luck. Even fewer Scots. But bad as our lot sometimes is with the French, I know we could never endure life in Scotland these days." The amiable sheen faded from his pale eyes and he blinked twice, rapidly. "I saw them die in front of Louisbourg," he said hoarsely, "die by the hundreds, with their plaids smeared and torn in the mud, and the pipers skirling until they were killed, too." His long-fingered hands locked together in a hard grip. "What is it like in Scotland if clansmen will serve the English king? Hell must be pleasant by comparison."

"I have heard that Cumberland…" Crosbie began diffidently, slightly surprised by the growing fervor of Johnstone's voice.

"Billy the Butcher," Johnstone growled. "Aye, you heard aright, Duncan. Cumberland scourged the Highlands, killing and burning, bribing Scots to betray their own people. But I never thought to see the kilts swinging along to an English drumbeat. The tartan is proscribed in Scotland now, and the bagpipe has been outlawed as an instrument of war. Only in the English army can a Scot wear his proper clothes, or hear his own music. What is it now, only twelve or thirteen years since we fought for The Prince in Scotland. And already clansmen are serving the Sassenach, dying for him. I saw them die, Duncan."

"Aye," Crosbie said quietly, touching his slashed right arm. "So did I. They brought the Black Watch against us at Carillon."

Johnstone nodded, his eyes focussed gloomily on the horizon. "It was the Frasers at Louisbourg. They stormed ashore, led by that rat-faced Brigadier Wolfe who was one of Cumberland's pets in the Highlands. He enjoyed burning Scotland and now he enjoys sending his Highland troops to destruction, even though they fight for him. But it…it was hard to shoot at them, Duncan. Did you…"

"Yes," Crosbie said bluntly. He glared at Johnstone, silently challenging his sentimentality. The troops of the English army were the enemy, no matter what uniform they wore. He would fiercely have contested the point; the more fiercely because he dreaded remembering what he had felt when he had directed his cannon against the Scots attacking Carillon.

"Ah," Johnstone murmured in a deep, musing tone. "But then, you were not at Culloden." He laughed suddenly, a surprised laughter that held a note of uncertainty. "I look at you and I forget you are not Duncan Mohr. You look very much like your father. He saved my life at Prestonpans. Did I tell you that?" Without giving Crosbie time to answer, he went on quietly, "He was a giant, one of The Prince's great champions. He and Gillies MacBean and Alasdair and Gentle Lochiel. But it was Duncan Mohr we honored above all. And so did The Prince. Do you know how you come to wear that dirk on your belt?"

Crosbie felt for the jeweled hilt. The dirk had been a part of him so long, it seemed there had never been a time when he hadn't worn it. Even as a boy, he had…

"Duncan Mohr carried The Prince to safety at Culloden," Johnstone said in a harsh growling voice. "Seven gaping wounds he had, but he carried Charlie back before he fell, carving a path through English flesh. And when he dropped, the dirk was in his great hand. The Prince took it and himself brought it to your lady mother when he returned to France."

Crosbie swallowed heavily. He hadn't known. His mother, who lived such a short time after her husband's death, had left Crosbie no account of the dirk.

"And the slogan engraved around the seal," Johnstone said: "That was engraved at The Prince's command, to honor Duncan Mohr. We all heard him shout it just before he fell. Even now, the memory brings a desolation to me. But it gave us new spirit then to hear that great man, like an ancient Fian warrior, roaring, 'Come, wolves of war, here stands a Crosbie!' I saw the dirk in Paris, before The Prince returned it to you. He read out that terrible war-cry in a voice we could hardly hear. And he said, 'It is the true test of a man, that he stand as steadfast in defeat as he does in victory.' We all knew he was speaking of himself as well as Duncan Mohr." Johnstone turned to look directly at Crosbie. "It is a heavy responsibility for you, Duncan."

The young Scot touched the engraving gently. He closed his eyes and slowly he nodded.

CHAPTER THIRTY THREE

The high sharp prow of the demi-canot swerved across the current, making the long limber craft bend alarmingly. To the left, dim and half-lost in the river mist, the glittering spire of Quebec's Cathedral loomed over the city, three leagues upriver. Their passage had been secretive, and no one had seen the slender canot slip past in the ghostly haze.

Safely beyond the city, Le Singe led his crew in a cheerfully noisy song. Paddles lifted and fell with the strongly accented beat. Denis dragged his hand in the icy river, flicking water up against the gunwale. In the bow, Bougainville sat at ease, legs folded under him in an odalisque's pose. The canot bored swiftly through the mist, approaching a wide stretch of tidal marsh that grew rank with weeds down to the waterline. Great clouds of birds rose in panicked flight, dipping almost to the river before their wings caught hold and sent them soaring high overhead.

Directly ahead, Crosbie could see a quick-running narrow river that met the St. Lawrence in a deep indentation of the north bank. On his right was a shimmery dazzle from moist slate roofs, but the houses of the village were obscured in the mist that was as solid as wood-smoke, tingling with saltiness. The canot shot up the smaller river and swerved sharply toward a log landing. Le Singe shouted a command and the bowman leaned out to catch a piling, bringing the canot snugly against the wharf. Bougainville let out a grateful sigh that exploded in the stillness.

"What great luck," he exulted. "A swifter passage than I could have hoped for, and all the way, this fine gloomy fog. You will disappear, Duncan. You will be swallowed up by the mist, lost to man forever."

Crosbie nodded somberly. Since they had left Captain Johnstone at Trois Rivières and joined Le Singe and his voyageurs, their movement had been shielded by the river mist. But Bougainville's pleasure in his own cleverness had blinded him to the fact that Crosbie deeply resented the necessity for sneaking downriver like a runaway servant.

Bougainville leaped to the landing. Denis and Le Singe unloaded Crosbie's baggage while others dragged the half-paralyzed young Scot from the canot and rubbed life into his cramped legs.

When Crosbie was able to walk, Bougainville took his arm and pulled him aside. "I have told the boy," he said quietly, "but I had best tell you, too. It would be wise if Denis made no reference to his previous life. You understand. He comes here as your servant, a soldier of the King. And we do not want the habitants gossiping when they come to market, do we?"

"All right, Louis," Crosbie growled. "We will be discreet."

"How you detest intrigue," Bougainville smiled. "Yet you have a talent for it, Duncan. You are a very sly dog, when it comes to the point."

Crosbie made a vague gesture. He thoroughly hated this evasive behavior. Nothing could make him like it. He accepted it only as due punishment, imposed by the Général, for his stupidity.

"Let's get on, Louis," he said heavily. "Is the Sieur du-Maine expecting us?"

"No, certainly not. How could he? But I have a letter from the Général and a private word for his ear. We will be welcome, Duncan. You will see. Here along the river is the village of Beauport, which is part of the seigneury. We are going to the manor which is beyond on the hill."

Pale sunlight brightened the way as Crosbie set out for the cobbled road that ran toward the small village. Bougainville kept pace beside him and young Denis boisterously supervised the voyageurs who carried Crosbie's baggage.

The small cavalcade filled along the lane through Beau-port, past the high stone gristmill that had originally been the prime defense against Iroquois attack, past the low white church whose gilt-decorated steeple was the highest point in the village. Small slate-roofed houses sat in precise plots with herb gardens and rose bushes beside each door. Grape clusters hung dusty white and purple against the shiny, poisonous green of their arbors. Fruit trees were beginning to sag with the weight of ripening fruit and many had their branches propped. Beyond the village stretched fields of grain and vegetables, rocky pasture land and small lush meadows, carefully marked by stone fences. Bright red smocks made speckles of color in the distance where men were already at work.

Women peered from open doorways, children waved in cheerful welcome. Bougainville frowned at the attention. He urged Crosbie aside as a door opened and two men came out of the last house. The first strode slowly to the fence where an aged white horse was tethered. The second, a priest in dusty black robes, paused in the door, speaking to someone out of sight. Bougainville led the party in a wide arc to pass, then slowed hesitantly, peering at the man near the horse.

"Surely that is the seigneur?" he muttered.

The burly, wide-shouldered man glanced up, squinting, then smiled widely, whipping off his wide-brimmed floppy hat.

"Bienvenu, Monsieur Bougainville," he called. He pushed his horse aside and swept his hat low, stirring a cloud of dust from the road. Bougainville and Crosbie stopped and bowed in response.

"You have come to visit? Excellent! Forgive me for one moment." He turned briskly and went back to the house to say something to the priest. Then he untied his horse and joined Bougainville and Crosbie in the road.

"My apologies, gentlemen," he said soberly. "Poor Madame Arnaud. Only this morning we learned that her son had been killed at Louisbourg. Our curé wanted me with him when he broke the news. The poor woman is alone now. A houseful of children once, and a good husband. Now nothing. An empty house and a large farm she cannot manage by herself." He shook his head. One hand gripped Bougainville's arm above the elbow. "But what sort of welcome is this? We are not always sad at Beauport. It is good to see you, Louis. And your enormous friend. I hope you can stay for a long visit this time."

"Gently, monsieur," Bougainville laughed. "You overwhelm us. Let me present my friend, monsieur le capitaine Crosbie of the artillery. Le Sieur duMaine, Duncan."

"Your servant, monsieur," Crosbie said.

"Yours, sir. Yours. Welcome to Beauport." He moved closer to stare up at Crosbie. "A proper giant of a soldier, isn't he, Louis? God, what fear you must strike in English hearts! But such maigeur! We will have to fatten you up, Monsieur Crosbie. Like a Christmas goose, eh? Or, I know what young soldiers like. Fat beef, venison pie, raspberry tarts and buckets of my best wine, isn't that so? We will put some meat on that vast frame of yours, I can promise you."

"You are very kind," Crosbie muttered uncertainly. The short prancing rotund man with his exciteable, voluble speech was not quite his idea of a grand seigneur, even a Canadien seigneur. He was a cheerful sight with his round beaming face, full of good living and high spirits. There was no pomp about the Sieur duMaine. He wore a long-tailed coat while his farmers wore smocks, but coat and smock were alike made from the same dull red cloth favored in Quebec. His breeches were rough leather and his boots little better than Indian moccasins. DuMaine tucked his broad brown hand under Crosbie's left elbow and eased him toward the manor house, hauling his mare behind by the reins.

"We only just heard about the battle at Carillon, Louis," he said excitedly. "A fast courier brought the news. What a Général we have! He defeats thirty thousand English with only a handful of stout hearted fellows like you. The greatest battle in the history of the New World! I must hear the details. All the news."

Bougainville laughed softly. "It was a great victory, sir, but you make it sound like Thermopylae. For the facts, let me give you Monsieur Crosbie. He was brevetted Captain for his valor at Carillon."

"Indeed? Indeed! None but heroes enter my house, eh? Splendid! My sincere congratulations, Monsieur Crosbie."

"Gently, sir, you will embarrass him," Bougainville laughed. "He is a very tender-skinned fellow. You observe his reddened ears. Ecossais et gentilhomme, as the saying goes, brave as Hector, resourceful as Ulysses, but he blushes like a girl. We must tread lightly with this breed, monsieur, or they become paralyzed with confusion."

"There speaks the jealous tongue," duMaine chortled, several chins wagging in pleasure. "I can tell you, Monsieur Crosbie, I know this Louis Bougainville. Greedy for glory, he is. He envies your prowess, that is obvious. I suggest we leave him – to simmer with frustration while you tell me of that glorious day at Carillon."

Duncan Crosbie laughed and for once self-consciousness did not plague him. This short and happy little man was very much to his liking; no matter how wildly he talked there was genuine good feeling in him and Crosbie responded to it with an abrupt explosion that abundantly illustrated how silent and lonely his life had been previously. The young Scot's harsh raucous laughter almost shocked Bougainville. The Sieur duMaine glanced up wonderingly at Crosbie.

The boy is intense, the seigneur thought. He has a zealot's expression much of the time. A man dedicated to an idea. DuMaine could recognize the symptoms. Often the idea in such a young man would be venery or greed or ruinous ambition, but in Duncan Crosbie's rigid, competent countenance, he sensed a finer quality. This was the sort of man who fought Crusades, who died for an ideal, who sacrificed comfort and happiness to a single conviction. A perfectionist, in short, and a dangerous man.

"I recognize you now," he said quietly. "For months the Indians hereabouts talked of nothing but the young giant who defeated their champion. You are Devil's-Hair. We know of you, monsieur." DuMaine chuckled at Crosbie's blank expression. "You did not know your Indian name? Watch how respectful the Hurons are when you pass by. They know you well." DuMaine nodded soberly at the young Scot. "I deeply regret my son did not live to serve with your Général," he said heavily. "That was my plan and knowing the splendid training he has given his son, the young Comte, I am doubly sorry. We were boys together, you may know. I am the only man in Canada who calls him Louis-Joseph, and the only one who can talk to him of Nîmes and his château of Candiac. But he is no longer the boy I knew. This Louis-Joseph is a great général. A large page in history waits for him. And I ... I am a man of the soil at heart. We are not the same, any more, neither of us, but we are friends and always will be."

Bougainville murmured something and in his brief confusion, he brought out a folded paper, grateful for a chance to shift to a less emotion-laden subject.

DuMaine handed his reins to Bougainville. Then he took the paper, flipped it open and read its message quickly.

"I did not need this," he said, ramming the note into a pocket. "You have come to visit, and all of Louis-Joseph's young gentlemen are welcome here. But I am pleased that you thought of me at this moment. It is serious?"

"Yes, very serious," Bougainville agreed soberly.

"There is something left unsaid?" DuMaine's deeply shadowed eyes glinted with speculation.

"There is ... something," Bougainville said with an unusual hesitancy. "Something may become necessary and ... ah, bigre! Surely I may confide in you. The Général may find it impossible to retain his command. I carry a letter of resignation to the Governor which I will present under certain conditions. That is the situation. Possibly I may be able to return that letter to the Général. I hope so, but ..."

"Yes. I see." DuMaine rubbed his florid jaw with a hand that rasped across the dry skin. "These are bad days for Canada. If Frontenac were alive, he would hang both Vaudreuil and Bigot. I see much of them. I am capitaine de milice for my seigneury, so I know what they are doing. Thieving, whining jackals! They will destroy Canada if they are not stopped soon." DuMaine's cheerful wind-burned face was a sombre hard mask. "Louis-Joseph is right. This is the time. The King must be made to listen."

"That is the next step," Bougainville said. He smiled tightly. "You have a talent for intrigue, monsieur."

DuMaine snorted contemptuously. "Intrigue? Pah! Simple intelligence, my dear boy, requires that the matter be taken to France. Who will go? You?"

"If it comes to the point," Bougainville said.

"It would be well to force the issue," duMaine said bluntly.

"I believe the Général is of the same mind," Bougainville said mildly.

"Excellent. Excellent. I am glad he considers me an ally. There is a group here, you may know, Les Honnêtes Gens, the men of honor, who have joined together to appeal to the King against these scoundrels. But our petitions are never heeded in Paris."

"They will be now," Bougainville said brusquely.

"I believe they will if Louis-Joseph is prepared to raise the issue himself. Well, young gentlemen, let's go sample my new wine. It is still young, but it promises to become a lovely fragrant vintage, if we do not drink it all first."

"I must return, almost at once, monsieur. It is imperative."
Bougainville relinquished duMaine's reins. "I will come and ..."

"You will come and have some wine. Then you may return,
though I hate to see you leave so soon." He prodded Crosbie forward and pulled his horse along, staying on foot himself to honor
his guests.

They walked slowly up the cobbled lane arm in arm,
warm with sunlight and friendliness, even the sophisticated
Bougainville finding himself unable to resist duMaine's expansive, genial roars. It was altogether charming, Bougainville
thought happily. The Sieur duMaine would have been a striking success in the salons of Paris. A pity he had ever left France,
but fortunate for Crosbie just now. The seigneury of Beau-port
offered the young Scot a sturdy refuge.

CHAPTER THIRTY FOUR

In his later years, Duncan Crosbie would remember his stay at Beauport as the first completely happy and irresponsible time of his life. His assigned duty was fully accomplished by remaining within the seigneury boundaries, without causing curiosity or comment. That was easily managed, thanks to the Sieur duMaine.

Beauport's seigneur was constantly surprising to Crosbie. He maintained no elaborate pretensions, but he was a great lord, even when he worked beside his habitants in the fields and flopped to the plowed earth to eat and drink with them, singing and joking with the same rude taste in bucolic humor. He was both friend and master. Somehow the two were kept separate, yet merged when there was need, as in the case of Duncan Crosbie. It was enough for the tenants to know that the seigneur wished no gossip about his huge young guest who was to be addressed merely as Monsieur Crosbie and never with any reference to military rank. The same applied to Denis.

DuMaine was Captain of Militia for his district. Captain was the highest rank, reserved for seigneurs or retired commanders of distinction. A seigneur raised his company, its size dependent upon the number of habitants on his estate, for every able-bodied man was enrolled in the militia as a matter of course. When gathered together, militia units were commanded by the King's Governor or an officer designated by him. Such commanders relied entirely on the seigneurs for their support.

Many of Canada's seigneurs wrapped themselves in a feudal pomp that would have aroused resentment even in France. The

Sieur duMaine was a great lord when required to be, but most of the time he was a master farmer who led his men resourcefully, knowing as much as the wisest, working as hard as the strongest and always maintaining an even cheerfulness that Crosbie tried to emulate.

To Denis, as well as to Crosbie, Beauport offered a new and more pleasant life. The boy was billeted in the village where the thoughtful curé had quickly seized the opportunity to distract the Widow Arnaud from her grief. Billeting Denis in the Arnaud house gave the boy a taste of happiness and offered welcome occupation to the widow. And the boy was a useful member of the household as well. After reporting dutifully each morning to Crosbie, Denis kicked off his military boots and ran barefoot, clothed only in a boy's short breeches and a tattered smock, to tend the fields belonging to the Arnaud family. A watchful seigneur sent some of his men when the occasion warranted and Denis learned to ditch fields, to build roads, to bridge the rushing streams, and to till the fertile land. The mysterious nose-bleeds were forgotten now, lost somewhere in the normal busy life of a young boy who feels himself both safe and content.

For Crosbie there was little he could do until his slashed arm had fully healed. Each day he walked the riverbank boundaries of the seigneury, occasionally exploring inland toward the mountains. Weeks later when his arm was free of its sling, Crosbie remembered the bagpipes. He hid the pibroch under his cloak and walked downstream for a full league to sit beside the roaring cataract of the Montmorenci whose thunderous crashing drowned his first feeble efforts at skirling. There, with no one to hear, Crosbie blew diligently, dimly recalling boyhood lessons, forcing his stiffened fingers to span the holes of the chanter pipe, exposing and covering the stops in a broken rhythm that was probably excellent exercise for his arm that had grown flabby in its sling. But he soon forgot about that in the growing pleasure that came with mastery. In those days of late Summer he had no worries to torment him, no self-conscious concern with his awkward shyness, no straining for advancement. His duty was to remain where he was; no more. The bagpipes were the only challenge in his placid life.

On the day that he considered himself adept, he marched back toward the seigneury, skirling every marching tune he could bring to mind. The day was blustery, the wind striking in gusts from the river, smelling crisp and sweet with the clear hint of too-early Winter. Crosbie's fringed hunting-shirt, made for him at Beauport, was no garment for warmth, nor were the thin Huron moccasins on his feet. But high delight in his new accomplishment helped him ignore the faint chill. The savage shriek of the pipes echoed far up the Beauport river.

Down from the manor came Denis and the seigneur's young daughter, Aimée, running with flailing arms in quick leaps, the girl's long unbound hair flowing free behind her. She was still child enough to enjoy the excitement of a race and she called high challenging cries to Denis as they ran. Her friendship is good for Denis, Crosbie thought; she makes him remember that he is only a child, too, and childhood is a happy time.

Crosbie straightened to his full height and marched regally up the cobbled lane to meet them, the drones towering high overhead, their tartan ribbons fluttering in the brisk wind. The pipes shrilled the marching chorus of All The Blue Bonnets Came Over The Border. Both youngsters squealed delightedly, clutching at Crosbie's arms.

"More, more!" Aimée demanded.

Crosbie rippled a lilting chorus, then let the mouthpiece fall free and chanted the refrain for them:

"So over the heather,
We'll dance together,
All in the mornin' airlie.
With heart and hand,
We'll take our stand,

For who'll be King but Charlie?"

With one repetition, the song was learned. Crosbie inflated the bag again, sounded the note, and led off, knees lifting high, followed by Denis and Aimée, singing the Jacobite childrens' song in thin, excited voices.

The Sieur duMaine came curiously to the doorway, beaming widely when he saw the children. Gay, pretty little Aimée was greatly loved and spoiled as the daughter of this household, not only by her father, but also by the seigneur's invalid mother. The beloved son who was now dead had never been mentioned to Crosbie beyond that first brief identification of the subject of a portrait that hung in the drawing-room. The picture was hung in the place of honor, but the boy's name was never spoken.

In fact, Crosbie realized that very few confidences had been offered by duMaine, for all his expansive friendliness. Beneath his outgoing manner, duMaine disguised a deep-rooted, unexpected reticence. As he paraded up the hill with Aimée hanging to one arm and Denis dancing and singing beside them, Crosbie was oddly aware of how little he knew of his host.

Crosbie circled before the door, prancing high as a piper should, regretting the missing kilts and sporran that should have been bouncing with every stride. He blared out a final skirling chorus, then expelled a long ludicrous squeal from the bag and bowed with mock solemnity. Aimée screamed for more until her scandalized nurse came running to capture her. She propelled the girl briskly inside, complaints soaring high. Denis stood looking after her for a long moment before remembering that Madame Arnaud would be expecting him home. He made hasty adieux and scampered away down the hill.

The seigneur, too, had applauded lustily. "Bravo!" he called out. "That was most stirring, monsieur, I thought we were under attack. I give you my oath. I nearly alerted the militia."

Crosbie smiled ruefully. "I hope you never hear the pipes played by the enemy," he said soberly. "I am sorry if..."

"Nonsense, my boy, it was delightful. Startling to French ears, but thoroughly charming, I insist. I had been hoping you might return soon, though. I have news. Come inside. We will have time for a coup d'appétit before dinner."

DuMaine's cheerful demeanor faded to sobriety as he stepped aside to let Crosbie enter. The young Scot dropped his pipes on a settle in the hallway. DuMaine preceded him, turning left into the diningroom, crossing the scarlet, patterned rug to the wide buffet against the far wall. A long table stretched across the center, set with rigidly spaced couverts of napkin, plate, silver goblet, wine glass, fork and spoon. Two branching candlesticks from the silversmiths of Cap Tourmente held pale green scented tapers. DuMaine ran his finger along a row of flint-glass decanters, selected one and hooked two small glasses between his fingers. Crosbie moved into the room, turning as he entered to face the small rosewood stand with its bowl of rose-water that was always present. He dipped his hands briefly, wiped them on the napkin and then accepted his glass from the seigneur.

"A votre santé, monsieur," he said politely. He sniffed with a pretense of enjoyment. DuMaine's stock of liqueurs was far more extensive than Crosbie's simple tastes warranted. Most of them were unknown to him, and almost all were too sweet for his palate, though he never said so. This one seemed faintly familiar with its bitter-almond scent and it was warm and pleasantly thick in his throat.

The seigneur lifted his glass without drinking. His eyes were sombre, shaded by lowered brows, "I give you a different toast, monsieur," he said heavily. "To my old friend, Louis-Joseph, Général le Marquis de Montcalm." He tossed the drink down with a flip of his thick wrist.

Crosbie finished his small glass and set it down carefully on the table. He drew in a deep breath and held it until his pulse pounded solidly in his throat.

"He has resigned?" he asked hoarsely. Even though he had long expected it, the news came as a shock. It seemed a portent of much worse to follow.

DuMaine nodded soberly. "The Governor has just announced it," he said. "The Chevalier de Lévis commands now."

"But what about..."

"Louis-Joseph remains in Quebec, still occupying his appartement in the Château. He sees no one." Suddenly the seigneur sighed, a thin piping sound that was oddly childish. "I must go to him. Possibly an old friend..." He lifted one hand in an unfinished gesture of helplessness.

Crosbie looked at him, wishing he could think of something to say. His hands clenched tightly together. Montcalm seemed to be the only man capable of defending Canada. Possibly de Lévis would be equally good, but no one could be sure. And if Bigot and the Governor were left unopposed, there would be little in Canada worth saving.

Before he could say anything, Crosbie heard the sliding door of the salon move back. Quick footsteps crossed the hall.

"Papá! Are you deserting us? Grand'mère is already..." The light, brisk—and above all, familiar—voice broke off abruptly. "Oh! It is Monsieur Crosbie!"

"Eh?" duMaine snorted. "You have met my daughter, my older daughter, have you? I did not know..."

Céleste grinned impishly at Crosbie. "Monsieur Crosbie and I are friends of long standing."

Crosbie thought there was a hint of genuine welcome in her tone. He swallowed heavily. "Yes..." he said warily, not daring to place too much hope in the pleasure he thought Céleste displayed at seeing him at Beauport. He hardly recognized Céleste. The splendid gowns, the brilliant gems, the elaborate coiffe-poudre were all absent now. She wore a simple billowing frock of sprigged green silk and her long lustrous dark hair fell softly unhampered down her back, waving from her temples, in the fashion of an unmarried girl at home. At home! She was the sei-gneur's daughter, sister to gay little Aimée. And Beauport, where Duncan Crosbie had found an undreamed-of peace and well-being, Beauport was Céleste's home.

"A comedy of errors," duMaine was saying mildly. "We have treated Monsieur Crosbie merely as a guest. I did not know he was a friend of…"

"He knows me only as Mademoiselle Céleste, the dutiful lady-in-waiting to the Comtesse de Boyer," Céleste smiled.

"Comtesse de Diable!" duMaine spat contemptuously. "We can all be thankful that odious masquerade is ended for you."

"Masquerade?" Crosbie muttered the word in confusion, How could he have been so incurious, so centered in his own problems, as to give no real thought to the life and background of this girl whose dancing green eyes had disturbed him since the moment they met?

DuMaine put down his glass with a sharp crack. "My girl took that opportunity to reach the Ministry of Marine," he said with a sharp note of disgust. "Our group, Les Honnêtes Gens, could get no response from Paris. Our petitions were ignored. But when Céleste went to France with Bigot's vile sister, she found all doors open to her. That is why Monsieur Tremais was sent to investigate Bigot's corruption. Though what good Tremais has done, no one can say. A dry little stick of a man. But no matter what he does, this is the end for Céleste. I'll have her at home where she belongs, not in that swine's Palace."

Céleste winked at Crosbie's reddened face. "Papá is so dra-matic," she said softly.

"Dramatic, am I?" duMaine bellowed. "Who corrupted my son until he preferred to kill himself before…" Choking rage smothered his words into incoherence, but his hatred was deadly obvious; no words were needed.

Céleste touched her father's hand in a swift gesture of sym-pathy. This young girl, apparently as demure and ingenuous as any provincial jeune fille, bore small resemblance to the companion of the Comtesse, but Crosbie was now able to understand her as he had never done before. Her seeming indifference and contempt when he had been bemused by the Comtesse, dazzled by the Palace splendor, made clear sense now. And her elliptical warning when they had first discovered common ground, when Céleste had mentioned a ruined young man, that was clear also. Even the whole romantic nonsense of spying on the Intendant's corrupt circle was understandable, though it remained fantastic.

"I have brought you a message from …" Céleste spoke to distract her father, but Crosbie interrupted almost at once.

"Messages?" he demanded sharply. "You knew I was here?"

Céleste laughed easily. "Of course. All Quebec—including the Intendant—knows where you are. Louis Bougainville was astounded when the Comtesse mentioned it to him, but I quieted his fears."

"Did you now!" Crosbie said with evident exasperation. "And possibly you'd be good enough to quiet mine?"

Céleste indicated her father with a brief decisive motion. "The Sieur duMaine." she said lightly. "He is your surety. Even the Governor would hesitate to offend a grand seigneur. You are perfectly safe while you remain his guest."

Her chin went up with pride and Crosbie goggled in mingled admiration and irritation. What she said might be true. But surely, not even duMaine could …

"The town-major has had a warrant to arrest you for some weeks now," Céleste said sharply. "You have not seen him here?"

"I should think not!" duMaine growled. "I'd set the dogs on him. And anyway, Joannès is no fool. He would never …"

"Of course not," Céleste agreed. "So you see, Monsieur Crosbie. Are your fears lessened?"

Crosbie smiled grimly. He shrugged and made a sketchy bow. "I hope my enemies are as confused as I," he said.

"They are far more frightened, I can assure you," Céleste said bluntly. "Monsieur Tremais can be most ... disquieting when he chooses and ..."

"Tremais!" DuMaine's broad contempt distorted his wide mouth. "That dry stick. A small man of small affairs. He couldn't frighten a nervous child. That man ..."

"He can be very forceful," Céleste insisted. "You may not be frightened by him, Papá, but Monsieur Bigot is frightened, and so is the Comtesse."

DuMaine shrugged his shoulders and let her comment stand without challenge. Céleste was no flighty child. She saw what there was to see. If she said Tremais was a man of hidden force, then she might well be right. The seigneur knew his daughter and respected her opinion.

"You were saying about the Grand'mère," he suggested, with a wry smile for Crosbie.

"Oh! I nearly forgot. Seeing Monsieur Crosbie ... Grand'mère wishes an apéritif. There is time?"

"We will make time," duMaine laughed. He poured a meagre flow of liqueur into a fresh glass. "I will take it in. You are ready, Céleste?"

He left before Céleste could answer. Her fingers stroked lightly over the tablecloth, pinching the soft linen into aimless pleats. Her eyes followed the shadowed lines of the cloth, purposely avoiding Crosbie's gaze. "The Grand'mère is very fond of her apéritif," she said in a voice that wavered slightly. "She is very old and has only a few ..."

"Céleste ..." Crosbie shifted hesitantly, feeling awkward and self-conscious. His face flushed hotly. "Céleste, I ..."

"Oh, Duncan," she whispered. Her deep upthrust breasts pushed hard against her bodice. She put both hands gently on his shoulders. "Oh, Duncan, I have missed you. I was so worried ..."

Crosbie's throat tightened painfully. His hands touched with infinite caution at her waist. "I'm ... here now," he said in a thick voice that sounded enormously foolish to his ears. Why did he persist in being such a gormless lout when he got close to Céleste?

As naturally as if she'd done it a thousand times, Céleste moved into his arms, gripping him in a warmly close embrace. He could smell faintly a soft, intoxicating scent. Roses, was it? The hard lines of his mouth softened against hers.

"Céleste, Céleste," he murmured in a voice muffled against her soft lustrous hair. Just the sound of her name was suddenly a song. He drew her closer, mildly surprised at the solid muscles that tensed along her back; for all her civilized grace, Céleste had none of the softness of fashionable ladies.

"Duncan, I cannot breathe!"

She leaned back in the circle of his arms, looking up with wonderment bright in her green eyes. She could see that Crosbie's gaunt face had lost its youthful roundness and had taken on the planes and angles of maturity. Harsh lines were already grooved around his mouth and eyes, but they smoothed away as her fingers traced them softly.

"The war … Carillon … you have changed, Duncan," she said. "You are not really the same …"

Crosbie tilted her small firm chin higher and kissed her lightly, gaily. The war and Carillon were far away just now. "Not so great a fool, you mean?" he asked, recalling their last stormy meeting when Céleste had been convinced that he was not only a fool but a villain.

She remembered, too. The flood of color to her cheeks told him that. Then the green eyes sparkled. "Not a fool at all, Duncan," she murmured. "Oh, not at all …"

The sudden light gaiety of Crosbie's spirits exploded in a burst of warm laughter. Dazedly, he thought, I'm a happy man. For the first time in my life, I know I'm happy.

"There's a legend among the Scots," he said softly, "about the green-eyed maiden in the green dress who seeks among the heather for a mortal lad. Once he kisses her, he's enslaved for life. They sing a song of her but I cannot recall the words very well. 'And her gown was green about her. And her skin was white as milk.' And now I've kissed the Green Dancer, I'm no more a free man."

"Oh, Duncan, such a pretty tale! Will you play me the song on your barbarous pipes?" Céleste's eyes darkened with mischief, but her fingers closed warmly on Crosbie's big hand.

"It's no song for the pipes," Crosbie smiled. "A lute, perhaps. A rebeck or a violin. A harpsichord. Not the pipes."

"And you..."

The seigneur's low rumbling laughter cut her off abruptly. She stepped back a short pace from Crosbie. DuMaine came slowly into the room, holding his left arm high with his mother's frail hand resting on his wrist in regal fashion. The small, bright-eyed old woman glanced sharply at Céleste, then at Crosbie. One translucent eyelid flickered in the faintest wink imaginable.

"It is time for dinner," she announced in a firm, thin voice. "Other things must wait." Her mouth pursed as she restrained a smile that twinkled in her eyes.

Crosbie stepped back, composing himself, and sweeping his hand low in a respectful bow. He knew how to wait, he believed. But looking at Céleste, he hoped the waiting would be none too long.

CHAPTER THIRTY FIVE

With the approach of Autumn, the slow-paced rhythm of life on the Beauport seigneury increased sharply. Men and women alike raced to complete their preparations before the first frost. In Canada, death by starvation was always a very real threat, for the colony produced barely enough food for survival in the best of years. In time of war, with most of the men away with the army, both planting and harvesting suffered. Nearly three hundred people lived on the seigneury of Beauport, exclusive of the Hurons, and each had his assigned duty to the seigneur, as well as the work on his own plot of ground.

Animals were slaughtered and the meat preserved against the Winter. Fat was boiled down, some of it used to preserve the game birds that hunters were killing by the wagonload, and some mixed with the lye that had been collected in leaching barrels, and used to make soap. The pungent reek of that boiling mixture floated strong and tenaciously over the seigneury. At night candles were molded, or laboriously dipped while the men busied themselves with repairing damaged tools or making new ones.

Little remained to be done in the fields now that the corn had been cut and shocked. Great lumbering wains rolled out to collect the ears that were husked by furiously working crews. Here Duncan Crosbie found that his immense, untrained muscles were no value to him, though he managed to keep up with the habitants by great exertion. He lived long weary hours, tumbling heavily into bed after a futile attempt to remain alert during dinner. He was poor company, but not even Céleste noticed; like

everyone else, she was pushed to the point of collapse as the seigneury rushed to prepare for Winter.

Denis and the other young boys smoked the hives to stu-
pefy the bees while they removed the honeycombs. The honey
was rendered, stored in birchbark tubs, and the beeswax clarified
and stacked for market. These were among Beauport's few money
crops and extreme care was taken in preparing them. The gristmill rumbled steadily as the harvest grain flowed between the
stones. A seventeenth part of each habitant's crop went to the seigneur as a part of the minimal rent paid for the land. The rhythmic crash of the looms could be heard throughout Beauport. The
sweet sickening stench of fermenting grapes contested with the
harsher smells of boiling soap. The last family laundering was
concluded now and entire fields blossomed with white as the
women prepared their household linens for the Winter when no
washing would be possible.

The economic status of Canadian farmers had never concerned Duncan Crosbie before and he found it difficult to understand the peculiar laws that governed the colony. A farmer might
sell his surplus produce at market, but only to an ultimate con-
sumer; the Intendant alone was permitted to act as middleman.
And in critical times, the Intendant was empowered to fix prices
and to confiscate farm produce at that price. As a result, few
farmers troubled to raise a surplus of anything.

The Intendant's great power was designed to stabilize the
colony, but its effect was to permit an era of corruption that
threatened to destroy Canada. The Sieur duMaine's bitter reaction was shared by most of the colony's seigneurs, those lords
who were master-farmers as well as landed gentry.

He and Crosbie leaned over the barnyard fence, watching a red-
faced woman who sat plucking a squawking goose which she held
clamped hard between her stout legs, its ferocious beak hooded
with buckskin. Soft fluffy bits of down floated loosely. DuMaine
plucked a drifting curl from the air and rubbed it against his nose.

"...these ridiculous laws," he was saying with savage calm, "give Bigot the power to wreck us all. In the years I have lived here, I have broken dozens every week. And every seigneur does the same. We have laws governing the number of windows permitted in a house, also the number of chimneys. Also fines for bachelors and unmarried girls. Brutal punishment for unlicensed fur trapping. All unenforceable, but still legally in effect. You can see what a fearful weapon this situation gives to Bigot."

DuMaine squinted up at Crosbie's weary face, wondering if the young Scot was attending him.

Crosbie nodded quickly, pretending an alertness he was far from feeling. "He applies the laws against his enemies, eh?" he suggested in a voice thinned by a smothered yawn.

"Exactly," duMaine said eagerly. "When he is with me, Bigot laughs at these outmoded regulations. He knows I breed an unlawful number of horse and sheep, but he says nothing. But the threat remains, always. And with others less fortunate..." duMaine shrugged. "I cannot understand them. The common folk of Canada, the habitants, the villagers, the city people, none of them seem to understand that Bigot is ruining all of us. Of course, Bigot has one great advantage."

"Sir?"

"He is Canadien-born. Both he and the Governor. That one simple fact carries great weight with all Canadiens. And no sensible man can dispute that Bigot is a charming rascal. God knows I have felt it myself often enough. When he first came here, I expected much from him. A man of the people, obviously, with all the faults of his low birth, but with the ability of Richelieu himself, and a quality of warmth and charm that made every man his friend on sight. Bigot could have carried Canada to greatness. Instead he has chosen to destroy the colony, to steal enormous sums so that he will be able to buy titles and honors when he returns to France."

DuMaine's indignation tightened his voice. Then, abruptly, he yawned heavily, almost groaning. "Dear God, we are a sorry pair," he said. "Would you like to go dye-hunting this afternoon? You must be mightily disenchanted with farmer's work by this time."

"Dye-hunting?" Crosbie straightened from the railing.

"We make our own cloth, and dye it ourselves," duMaine said easily. "The dull red color is most popular in this province, as you have probably noticed. It is almost a uniform. Some we stain a dark blue, as is the preference in Montreal. White lichen and tormentil for the red; dock root, sundew, bitter vetch for blue. This is the responsibility of Céleste. She has supervised the making of dyes since she was a little girl."

Slowly, Crosbie's gaunt face relaxed into a wide smile. Now he understood what the seigneur was offering. A properly authorized holiday with Céleste, without chaperones. In the past few weeks he had never once been alone with her. Usually they met only at meals. DuMaine's suggestion was accompanied by a quizzical stare, and Crosbie masked his elation as he agreed that dye-hunting would be an interesting change.

Céleste carried a light Indian basket woven of sweet-smelling grass and she brought a sharp trowel for digging. She wore a long loosely hooded cloak of that dull crimson wool that Crosbie now recognized as Quebec's favorite. He wrapped his great tarpaulin cloak around him, clapped on his hat and ran quickly down the path to join her.

Crosbie lifted the basket from her arm and grinned at her solemn surprise.

"The Sieur duMaine has sent me as military escort," he laughed. "I shall guard the rear while you engage the bitter vetch in mortal combat."

Céleste smiled at him soberly, her eyebrows knotted in a puzzled expression. "You are very gay today," she said with a questioning note in her voice.

"A holiday," Crosbie agreed. "I feel like a poor, bullied cadet again, free for just one day."

"But..." Céleste made a sharp gesture with her free hand, then tucked it smoothly under Crosbie's elbow. "I quite forgot. You fell asleep at the table last night before Papá could tell you about Fort Frontenac. For a moment I could not understand how..."

Crosbie stopped in mid-stride, his momentary gaiety gone suddenly. Fort Frontenac? He tried to remember where that was, what importance it held in Canada's defenses.

"The English raided Fort Frontenac," Céleste said quickly, answering the question before Crosbie could speak. "It was only a raid, but they remained long enough to burn the fort, destroying nearly sixty cannon and an immense amount of supplies and furs. It was a dreadful loss, but worst is the way it has shaken the Indians. They have lost confidence in our government now. And that can be serious."

Crosbie frowned. What a peculiar girl she was, he thought vaguely. Females weren't supposed to be interested in military matters, not to the extent of worrying about lost cannon and damaged morale. But Céleste was no ordinary girl; he had realized that before, but it was easy to forget when she dazzled you with those great shining eyes. Anything was easy to forget at such a time.

He lifted one hand in a helpless gesture. "I don't even know where Fort Frontenac is," he said mildly. "A western fort?"

"It guards the St. Lawrence at Lake Ontario," Céleste said crisply. "Of course you know of it. Frontenac is the gateway to the west. How else can supplies and men go to Fort Niagara or duQuesne, unless we hold..."

"Softly," Crosbie urged. "Softly. I had forgotten the name. I understand the importance. But surely it isn't so critical? The fort can be rebuilt. A few supplies lost won't ruin us. And I imagine we are sending raids against the English, too."

"Oh, Duncan! Sometimes you are so..." Céleste whirled angrily away from Crosbie, looking out over the broad river toward Quebec. She brushed her hair smoothly back with that soft feminine gesture that always charmed Crosbie.

"Céleste, I..."

"I was thinking of Montcalm, sitting idly in the Château while a fool commands his army." She turned to glance at Crosbie and her voice was strained, sharp with reproach. "You are on his staff. How can you remain here when Montcalm is..."

Heavily, Crosbie backed away to lean against the low stone wall that bordered a field. He said mildly, "I am obeying orders given me by the Général himself."

"But he was only protecting you!" she protested. "Now he needs... oh, won't you understand, Duncan? I was in Quebec yesterday. Montcalm would not see me. He spends his time alone. Only the Bishop comes to his appartement. The Governor, the Intendant, and all their hideous friends are frightened, but they still pretend to scorn Montcalm. They laugh at him! It is insufferable."

"Aye," Crosbie agreed stiffly. "It is that." He put Céleste's gay little basket safely on the stone wall. Without thinking, his big hand found the hilt of his dirk. His thumb rubbed harshly across the Crosbie signet. "Do you think I could help him?"

Céleste lifted both hands helplessly. "I don't know, Duncan. I am... bouleversée. Papá does not understand. He thinks it is good policy for Montcalm to remain in seclusion, and it may be, but it cannot be good policy for Montcalm himself. He is lonely and he must be bitter, Duncan. Even Louis Bougainville is away on some mysterious errand. He is alone, Duncan."

The young Scot nodded gloomily. He stared down at the hard ground between his shoes. "He finished his last bottle of crème de Noyeau at Carillon," he said thoughtfully. "Possibly your father could spare a bottle from his cellar. I could take it to the Général."

Duncan Crosbie understood what he was saying. He would be disobeying Montcalm's explicit order if he went to Quebec. He would be in danger of arrest. But he would accept the risk if it would help Montcalm—and please Céleste. He knew what it was to be alone. All his life he had been alone. He had never even had a good friend until he had come to Canada. And now, looking soberly into Céleste's shining eyes, he could see the end of all loneliness. He drew in a long painful breath.

Céleste's eyes lifted to him. Her lips murmured silently under Crosbie's. He held her gently. A wild high pulse beat a deafening cadence in his head.

"I was wrong," Céleste whispered. "You should not go. I forgot .. "

Crosbie's hard searching mouth sealed her lips again and the protest was not spoken. After a long silent moment, Crosbie straightened slowly. "When I see the Général tomorrow..." he paused, then repeated the words with the greatest care, as if they were part of a solemn vow, something sacred which you could never forswear. "When I see the Général tomorrow, I shall ask him to approach your father for me. Surely the seigneur will not deny an old friend like Montcalm?"

Céleste's eyes were bright, sparkling with excitement and something that might be tears. "You are such a solemn soul, Duncan. To say such things and always with that melancholy expression."

She snatched up her bright Indian basket and ran swiftly down the road. Slowly Crosbie followed, dimly recalling the tune of The Green Dancer and trying to whistle it as he followed the racing girl. The pale Autumn sun was low against the western mountains now and the light shone directly in his eyes, almost blinding him. The light ... and something else.

CHAPTER THIRTY SIX

At dinner that night it was a restless eager young man who sat poking with slight interest at his food, making polite conversation with the Sieur duMaine and his aged mother, and stealing swift surreptitious glances at Céleste who sat opposite him.

Crosbie looked toward duMaine, wondering what the seigneur would say when he was asked to give his daughter to a penniless soldier. If Général Montcalm, or even Louis Bougainville were to intercede, the seigneur might not object too strenuously. But he would certainly demand that Crosbie match Céleste's dowry, franc for franc. And how could he possibly do that? Helplessly, he glanced at Céleste, smiling to see the fleeting flush that tinged her face.

The wise, knowing expression of the Grand'mère sharpened with understanding. She had been amused and tolerant so far, Crosbie realized. As reigning dowager of Beauport, she exercised an influence that was all the more effective because of its unobtrusiveness. By now she would have decided about him, Crosbie felt sure. A brief, wild resentment made his hands curl hard as he considered how much of his life was controlled by people beyond his reach. Hardly anything remained in his own hands. The Grand'mère signaled Céleste, rose and swept from the room, leaving him alone with duMaine.

The seigneur and Crosbie rose with the ladies. DuMaine presented a small fluted decanter and two matching thimble-glasses. He filled the glasses and slid one toward Crosbie.

"Your very good health, sir," Crosbie said. As he sipped gingerly at the oily liquid, he remembered to ask the seigneur for a bottle of crème de Noyeau for the Général.

"A bottle!" the seigneur snorted. "You will take him a full keg. You should have told me before. I have enjoyed the finest liqueurs when I visited Louis-Joseph at Candiac. I would be pleased to repay a small part of that pleasure. A full keg, young man, nothing less. But should you be going to Quebec? I thought you..."

Crosbie shrugged. No, he shouldn't be going to Quebec. In fact, he was specifically ordered not to go. And it was hard to remember now why he had so easily fallen in with Céleste's suggestion. What could he do for Montcalm? Possibly the Général felt some degree of friendship for him, but not the same warm affection he felt for Louis Bougainville. But he was committed. So he would get someone to paddle him to Lower Town, and then he would climb up the steep hill in darkness, hoping to elude the town-major's guard, and reach the Château unobserved. Surely he would be recognized by the sentries. Then the return trip might well be impossible. As he thought of it, Crosbie became increasingly aware of his foolishness in going, but he could not retract now.

"I will not stay long," he said lightly. "If you could let me take a canot, or a..."

"Yes, yes," duMaine said sleepily. "As you wish. You will find whaleboats at the landing on the river. Tell the men I sent you. And remember! A full keg, no less."

DuMaine pushed himself to his feet and lifted one hand in drowsy farewell. Crosbie could hear his slow steady footsteps retreating down the hallway.

Crosbie selected a long clay pipe from a rack against the wall, tamped it full of coarsely chopped tobacco and lit it with a coal from the fireplace. The acrid smoke made him choke. So far he had never discovered the charm of smoking, but with each attempt, he thought it might come to him. Certainly every

Canadien smoked constantly; stubby pipes were as much a part of their attire as their heavy wooden clogs. Maybe they used a milder tobacco, he thought vaguely, but that was hardly likely, for the seigneur would surely have the best available. Crosbie went out to the hall and opened the outer door. A pipe seemed less offensive in the open air. He spat a gobbet of saliva and then strolled out into the frosted garden.

The manor house was quiet behind him, only a few dim lights still visible. With another long strenuous day ahead, everyone was in bed. Crosbie walked slowly, feeling a welcome tiredness, thinking vaguely of sleep, but drifting immediately to thoughts of Céleste, and then finding that all weariness was gone as a pulsing excitement built within him. The Grand'mère and duMaine might have serious objections to a poor Scot for son-in-law. But he would fight them. By God, for such a prize as Céleste, any man would...

Dry stalks crackled under a padding foot. Crosbie froze warily in position. A wandering animal probably, or maybe...

Crosbie clamped a wide thumb over the glowing bowl of his pipe. He listened intently, gradually crouching as an instinctive alarm shouted caution in his mind. Low against the ground he searched the dark sky for a meaningful silhouette. Nothing moved. Crosbie breathed softly, keeping his mouth open, not shifting position. Behind him, a thin whisper of cloth rasping against a dry twig. Swiftly, Crosbie pivotted and as he moved, he caught a choking noseful of smoke from his pipe. He sneezed briefly and threw the pipe with an angry gesture, sending a long streamer of sparks through the darkness.

Against the high rectangle of candlelight from the open doorway, he saw a figure, running lightly forward. And from behind him came the swift crisp sounds of hard shoes crunching over the frosted earth.

"Up, Beauport!" Crosbie roared. He flicked his long dirk free of its scabbard. "Beauport!"

He swirled to his left, stumbling over the hard mounds of forgotten flowerbeds. Far away was the stone wall ringing the pasture. If he reached it, then his rear would have protection and he would not be surrounded. He ran hard, head down, legs driving hard for traction over the broken ground.

A sword blade whistled close to his head, missing him by a perilous margin. Crosbie ducked, abandoning all thought of reaching the wall. He swerved, still crouched tightly. The nearest assailant stumbled past him in his eagerness, but the second had time to counter Crosbie's evasion. The man hurled himself through the air, reaching forward with a wide blade that curled slightly like a naval cutlass, glinting in the dark.

Crosbie lunged forward under the slash of the blade, his left hand groping for the sword hilt, his right stabbing upward in a hard thrust with the searching point of his dirk. His dark-steel blade ripped through cloth, into flesh. It jammed tightly, the jeweled guard thudding against the man's ribs. Crosbie used both hands to throw the man away from him, heaving mightily with a surge that ripped a sleeve free of his coat. Without waiting to see how badly the man was wounded, Crosbie scuttled aside with an awkward, crab-like motion that carried him around in a long silent circle.

Darkness masked all movement, but sounds carried with a brilliant clarity to Crosbie's sharpened senses. Lights appeared in the windows of the manor house. The soft radiance from the open doorway was blocked by the stocky figure of the Sieur duMaine, now loosely garbed in a flowing nightgown, with his rapier naked in his hand. The seigneur held aloft a five-branched candelabrum and bellowed irritably for Crosbie.

The young Scot could hear low moans coming from his left. That would be the man he had blooded, he assumed. Another man was prowling lightly to the right, moving cautiously, probing the darkness with his cutlass. But there had been three of them in all. Where was the third? Crosbie watched tautly, his dirk held well forward, staying down close to the ground where an approaching assailant could not see him against the sky.

DuMaine stormed forward, roaring for Crosbie, swishing his delicate blade nastily through the air. A wide flickering circle of light surrounded him. Crosbie did not move. His attackers could not afford to wait, but he could. When duMaine reached him with those candles, they could stand off any pair of clumsy swordsmen. But Crosbie maintained a sensible silence as duMaine raged across the garden. He watched on the outer rim of the candles' glow, knowing the men skulking nearby would either retreat or make their last desperate attack when the light picked them up.

The circle of candlelight touched his extended arm momentarily. Rushing feet pounded toward him. Crosbie scrambled around, drawing his long legs under him in a tight crouch. This man was alone, he realized. Sharp splinters of reflected light dazzled him as the cutlass swung overhead. Crosbie backed cautiously. Only one man. Where was the other?

Then duMaine shouted hoarsely, a tone full of furious triumph. He had found the third man. Swiftly Crosbie lunged to his feet, no longer fearful of attack from his rear. He flipped his dirk up along his wrist and snapped it forward in a long, measured swing of his arm. In two mètres, the dirk would completely rotate once with the motion of throwing. But maybe he had thrown too late. Maybe the man was too close when ...

The swordsman screamed as Crosbie hurled the dirk. He ducked his head, but kept running forward, holding his left arm across his face as he charged. The dirk spun through the air. Crosbie saw that it would not turn far enough to present its point to his attacker. He lunged forward, leaving his feet in a long reaching dive, his large hands extended hungrily. The cutlass swung down.

Crosbie crashed into the swordsman. His hands touched the man's waist briefly and darted upward fiercely. One great fist clenched around the man's throat desperately, Crosbie fumbled for the swordarm. Then he realized that his man was not struggling. He lay limply on the hard ground beneath Crosbie, his cutlass gone somewhere in the darkness.

DuMaine came running, rapier held ready.

"You captured one of them? Good. Splendid. Mine ran when I pinked him, the…"

Crosbie pushed himself up and got to his feet unsteadily. DuMaine's candles showed him his dirk lying just beyond the unconscious man and he stooped to pick it up, sliding it absently into his scabbard. He hooked one finger through the guard of the abandoned cutlass, then gripped a handful of coat and heaved his assailant erect, holding him easily where his face would be visible. An enormous dark welt swelled on his forehead. Crosbie smiled grimly. The dirk's point had missed, but the heavy jeweled hilt had smacked home. The man had been senseless before he had touched him.

"Do you know this scoundrel, monsieur?" duMaine growled. Crosbie shook his head.

DuMaine thrust an arrogant thumb under the man's chin, tilting it up roughly. "I know him," he said. "A drunken boatman. I hired him once for a few weeks, but he was no good." He let the head drop forward again. DuMaine swung around to look at his lighted house. "What did they want here? Why should he attack me?"

Crosbie heaved the unconscious figure high and draped it over one shoulder. "It wasn't you," he said bluntly.

DuMaine trailed him slowly toward the house. "Do you think these assassins came to kill you, monsieur?" he asked sharply.

Crosbie answered in a harsh tone, not pausing in his swift strides. "I don't know, of course," he said. "But I can be recognized, monsieur. People do not confuse me with other men. These salauds were waiting in the garden for me."

"Yes, that is so," duMaine growled. "But how could they know you would walk in the dark tonight? Have you ever before…"

"Not since the harvest began," Crosbie said. He stopped abruptly and swung around. "So, how did they know? No one knew. Even I didn't know. Which means they must have been here every night, possibly for weeks, waiting their chance. That is a nasty thought, monsieur."

DuMaine nodded soberly, dripping heated wax onto his hand and flicking it away irritably. "Yes," he said somberly. "Duncan, my boy, let us say nothing of this to the ladies, eh? Why disturb them to no purpose?"

"Of course," Crosbie said promptly.

DuMaine stared long and tightly at the gaunt young Scot. Then, deliberately, he nodded once with evident approval. He stepped out smartly toward the cluster of shadowed figures that waited silently in the lighted doorway. Slowly Crosbie followed, barely noticing the weight of the unconscious man over his shoulder as he tried to find the meaning of this new and frightening problem.

Three armed men waiting night after night merely to kill him. If that were the true picture, then his death was desperately necessary for someone. In his life he had never offended anyone grievously enough to justify killing. He had certainly offended the Comtesse and her brother, the Intendant, when he eluded the trap they had set for him. Did that warrant murder? He couldn't judge. So far he had been a gullible idiot, an easy dupe for clever people who needed a scape-goat. Now it was time he served warning that Duncan Crosbie was a pliable boy no longer. He did not know who had sent those assassins tonight, but he was positive that the decision to send them had been approved by the Comtesse or her brother. They thought he would let himself be killed, did they? They had expected him to accept the blame for the swindle of the Britannia, too. Apparently, they would never learn the truth about Duncan Crosbie.

It was time he taught them the first lesson.

His face was bleak with determination as he trailed the Sieur duMaine into the house, carrying the limp body of a hired killer who had already learned the lesson, though a bit too late.

CHAPTER THIRTY SEVEN

Duncan Crosbie paced restlessly up and down the stout stone wharf along the Beauport river. From his position he could see the massive loom of Quebec to the west, the spires of churches clearly outlined against the reddened sky. It was still too early for him to leave. He did not dare reach Quebec before full dark.

A cold blast of wind lifted his cocked hat and he snatched at it. His red hair was heavily powdered and he knew the wild wind would strip the powder off unless he kept it covered. Possibly he was silly to wear his dress uniform. The Sieur duMaine had offered ill-fitting habitant's clothing for a disguise, but Crosbie had refused. He'd wear the King's uniform, and wear it properly with his best gold buttons and gold swordhilt, unpaid for, but magnificent. He'd feel foolish enough if the town-major arrested him, without the added handicap of a rustic disguise that would make him look a clown.

Briskly, he swung a long arm, directing the boatmen to their places. He dropped lightly to his seat in the prow and pulled his cloak high to ward off the vagrant splashes that might mar his fine uniform. He sat hunched low, glowering silently as the grinning crew centered oars in the tholes and pushed off from the wharf.

Even against the hard current of the great river, these men made excellent progress. Dourly, Crosbie gave them full credit. He pointed one finger at the stone quay below the Market Square of Lower Town and the steersman brought the long whaleboat smoothly to a halt beside the steps.

"Wait here," Crosbie growled. "No matter how long. And stay sober." He tossed the heavy keg up on his shoulder and jumped to the wharf. He jammed his hat hard down on his forehead and strode off quickly through the empty Market Square and up the zig-zag path leading to Upper Town.

Light seeped through windows of glass and scraped horn, making the footing easy for Crosbie. A lovely radiance bathed the street, cast by stained-glass windows of the churches lining the roadway. Crosbie paused at the Great Square of St. Louis, keeping in the shadows until his breath returned to its normal rhythm. It would never do to appear before the Général panting like a frightened courier. He struck out boldly across the square, heading straight for the Château entrance where two sentries stood immobile between flaring torches.

Both bayoneted muskets snapped down to bar the entrance. Crosbie halted just outside the wavering light and swept his cloak back with one hand. The gold buttons blazed against his scarlet facings, and his best lace jabot shimmered in the dimness. He glared silently at the sentries until both straightened to a proper stiffness and slapped their muskets in salute.

He passed between them with a casual nod. Inside, he detoured to the rear staircase and descended to the kitchen. He ducked to enter the enormous pantry, smiling affably to the steward and easing the heavy keg from his shoulder.

"For His Excellency," Crosbie said pleasantly. "Will you decant some now? I want to take it to him right away."

"Immediately, monsieur." The steward leaped for a bung starter. When the keg was broached, he placed a fine glass decanter on the floor, balanced a silver strainer in its mouth and rotated the keg gently. A thin, controlled trickle of milky liqueur flowed exactly into the strainer, not a drop splashing free.

"Very well done," Crosbie said, striving for a casual tone. "Now store the keg with the Général's supplies. I'll take the decanter." A green-baize door at the rear of the pantry let onto a narrow corridor used by servants. It had been Crosbie's goal when he entered the Château. Any normal route would have brought him face to face with other officers, but going this way, he might not be seen.

Crosbie tossed his cloak back from his shoulders, took off his hat and clamped it under his elbow. He held the decanter lightly by the neck. The corridor felt clammy, made of smooth stone that was cold and faintly greasy to touch. Crosbie tapped softly on the last door and pushed it open.

There was no one in the small serving pantry that adjoined the Général's appartement. Crosbie could hear the low murmur of voices coming from another room. He dropped his cloak and hat on a chair, took a lacquer tray from a shelf and arranged two glasses and the decanter on it. He carried the loaded tray out of the pantry.

The Général sat back comfortably in a quilted black dressing gown, his cropped head covered with a pleated white silk handkerchief knotted rakishly at the corners. He held a slim book with one finger marking his place and balanced a long-stemmed pipe between his teeth, talking around the bit. At one side stood the bent figure of old Jeannot, Montcalm's body-servant, whose deft fingers had once shaved Crosbie. Jeannot stiffened when Crosbie's shadow fell across him. Montcalm turned as he observed Jeannot's expression.

The Général's face showed no alarm. After a brief moment of inspection, he lifted one shaggy eyebrow in a quizzical stare.

"Very well, Jeannot," he said quietly. "Take yourself off to bed, old friend. I will need nothing more tonight."

"Good night, Your Excellency," Jeannot murmured. He backed into Montcalm's bedroom, closely watching Crosbie until he was out of sight.

Crosbie stood fidgeting in mild embarrassment, waiting for the Général to say something.

"You have brought that for me?" Montcalm asked lightly, using the bit of his pipe to point at the tray Crosbie was holding.

"Yes, mon général," Crosbie said eagerly. "Crème de Noyeau. The Sieur duMaine has sent you a keg with his affectionate compliments." He placed the tray on the table beside Montcalm. He pulled the stopper and poured a glassful. "The Seigneur hopes…"

"I know what Raoul duMaine hopes," Montcalm said blandly. "Pour a glass for yourself, monsieur. Then pull a chair close and tell me what brings you here, against my express orders."

Clumsily, Crosbie poured a second glass. He retreated to a corner for a chair and brought it out to face the Général's. He seated himself rigidly and leaned forward to take his glass.

"I came to bring the crème de Noyeau, mon général," he said evenly.

Montcalm lifted his glass and took a brief sip, pursing his mouth appreciatively. "Very good indeed," he said amiably. "I wonder where Raoul finds the almonds? He makes this at Beauport? Well, no matter. It is his secret. Now, Monsieur Crosbie, will you answer my question?" Lazily, Montcalm lifted one hand, cutting off Crosbie before he could speak. "I am sure you came to deliver the keg. I accept that. But I hope you have a sounder motive for disobeying my orders?"

Crosbie sipped from his glass, rolling the oily liqueur over his tongue as Montcalm had done. Yes, he had a sounder motive, several of them. He looked squarely at Montcalm, wondering if he dared speak frankly. The Général did not seem greatly changed, Crosbie thought. He had the same brisk, healthy coloring, the same crisp, confident voice, and even his alert, half amused attitude toward Crosbie was the same. He certainly looked nothing like a disgraced Général sulking in a dark and deserted tent. There was no tragic Grecian note about Montcalm.

"I had hoped to persuade you to approach the Sieur duMaine in my behalf, sir," he said quietly, hiding the nervousness that threatened to close his throat. "Mademoiselle Céleste and I…"

Montcalm chuckled. He held his pipe to the candle flame briefly and puffed out fat ribbons of smoke. "I cannot promise," he said pleasantly. "It is a serious matter. I hope you realize how serious. But I will consider it." He poked the tip of his little finger at the glowing tobacco. "You could have written me, monsieur, even on such a subject. Was that your only reason for coming?"

"The Sieur duMaine and...and Mademoiselle Céleste were...concerned, sir," Crosbie said lamely. "We have all heard alarming reports."

Abruptly, Montcalm snorted. "Yes, I have heard them, too. And you actually came here just to inspect me, monsieur? Haven't you heard that the town-major holds a warrant for your arrest?"

Crosbie put down his glass and folded both large hands. "Yes, sir, I heard," he said bleakly in a tone that rose in spite of his efforts at control. "Hasn't Monsieur Tremais done anything yet? He gave me to understand there was nothing to worry about. That was before I went to Carillon. It has been months now, and I am still blamed for..."

Montcalm lifted his hand casually, shutting off the harsh flood of protest from Crosbie. "Monsieur Tremais will return to France very soon. His conclusions will be published here before he leaves; which is all the more reason for you to remain in seclusion, young man. If you are caught, the Intend-and might very well ship you off to France before anyone knew where you were. It could be years before you were freed. Coming here was immensely foolish."

"Three men tried to kill me last night," Crosbie burst out heatedly.

The hard furious words lay in the air like smoke, masking all minor concerns. Montcalm's broad muscular face tightened as he brought his lips firmly together. Knots of muscle sprang into prominence along his jawline. His eyes were nearly hidden in shadow. Carefully he put down his pipe, closed his book and dropped it into the chair beside his leg.

"Tell me, Captain," he said briefly.

In short blunt phrases, Crosbie outlined the events of the previous night. When he mentioned finding the unconscious man had died, Montcalm heaved a soft, painful sigh.

"Then you don't actually know that it was you the men were attacking, do you?"

"Sir, it isn't possible to mistake me for anyone else," Crosbie said simply.

"At night?" Montcalm objected. "In the dark? Nonsense. What motive could they have for wanting you dead?"

"I assume they were paid, mon général," Crosbie said testily.

"And what motive impelled their principal to pay them for your death?" Montcalm insisted.

Crosbie shook his head. In his mind, he could guess the answer, but once he mentioned it to the Général, the matter would be taken from his control. He had had enough of that. From now on, he would keep the reins in his own hands.

Montcalm stared intently at Crosbie's dour countenance. When he realized that the young Scot had no answer for him, he smiled thinly. "These scoundrels have often attacked seigneuries before, Captain," he said lightly. "Especially at harvest when the habitants are too weary to keep alert. I think you need look for no other motive. Now, before you make your secret way back to Beauport, tell me how life has been for you. I see few people these days. Now that Louis is in Montreal, I have only Estére for company."

Crosbie grinned with relief. He plunged into an account of his trials with the pibroch, bringing a ringing snort of laughter from the Général as he explained that he had been forced to hide near Montmorenci Falls while practicing to muffle the hideous noise he had made. He was slightly surprised that Montcalm put him through a detailed catechism about the daily routine of Beauport, and was even more surprised to discover that he actually understood much of what he had seen, how one problem related to another, how the ratio of pasturage to tillage was adjusted according to the number of animals, why the various fields were apportioned as they were, how the independent efforts of the habitants all served to contribute to the complex economy that constituted Beauport seigneury.

"How I envy Raoul," Montcalm said softly, sitting back and taking up his pipe again. "I, too, am a farmer, you know. I invested quite heavily in olives at Candiac, just before I left. We have even installed a new oil press. So do we struggle to find a profit. I would give a great deal to ..."

The Général's voice dwindled. He sniffed at his drink, staring blindly across the room, lost in some wellspring of memory. Crosbie turned his head, inspecting the bric-à-brac scattered along a buffet, trying not to break in on the Général's thought. Montcalm's wigs were arrayed against the wall, each on its own stand. One was a towering court wig, full-bottomed and curly, in the fashion of an earlier day, but the others were smail, neat military wigs, made of white horsehair and designed to fit snugly against the head, reaching barely to the ears. An open case held curling irons, combs and long draw-strings, all the tools needed to maintain the Général's wigs in proper order. A large tobacco box was centered before the wigs, with several well-used clay pipes alongside, and one gaudy Indian redstone pipe with a feathered stem fitted with a bleached bone mouthpiece. At the far end was a bulbous glass dome that sheltered a formal display of wax-dipped flowers, pensées these were, dark violet and white cat-faces that seemed to glow by candlelight. Montcalm stirred in his chair and Crosbie straightened attentively.

"You have been making yourself useful, I trust," the Général inquired casually.

Crosbie smiled, thinking of his aching muscles, the blistered hands that had come from laboring at Beauport.

"Yes, I can see you have," Montcalm said with an answering smile. "Well, I have something else for you now." He aimed his pipe at a cabinet behind Crosbie. "I have what maps have been compiled of the riverbank from Quebec to Montmorenci Falls.

None are complete or accurate. I want you to go with them and mark well the fields of fire for artillery from every elevation. You may again play the part of attacker and advise me how the English will storm such a position."

Crosbie nodded silently, a welter of confused thoughts racing through his mind The northern bank of the St. Lawrence would form a strong defensive line, he could see. Flanked by the St. Charles and the Montmorenci, the position could be assaulted only from the front. The land rose sharply from the river and then levelled off in a series of fertile terraces until the mountains were reached. Except for the swift mountain rivers that cut through the area, there was no impediment to a strong defense. But another consideration distracted Crosbie. Montcalm had resigned. He commanded nothing, yet he spoke as if he still held the reins. It was de Lévis who should be making plans. Did that mean that Montcalm intended to...

The Général shrugged. "It will be a long Winter," he said ambiguously. "Many things will change. Louis Bougainville goes to France with Monsieur Tremais very soon. The decision will be made in Paris, but we must do what we can to prepare, no matter who will eventually be given the ultimate responsibility. You understand, young man?"

Crosbie nodded again, not speaking. He had never before realized that Montcalm himself might also be just as much at the mercy of outside interference as Crosbie had ever been. With that brief insight, the young Scot came close to understanding the real basis of Montcalm's genius.

"Ah, well," the Général sighed, "the campaign is nearly finished for this year. The English have already entered Winter quarters at Louisbourg. Abercrombie's army will not be able to move until Spring. Only Brigadier Forbes remains in the field, marching against Fort duQuesne. Winter comes slowly so far to the south, but possibly Forbes will also be halted by the weather. If so, the situation next Spring will be that which exists at this moment."

"I heard of Fort Frontenac…" Crosbie began in a diffident tone. Somehow he could never accustom himself to discussing strategy with his Général as lightly as he might have with Louis Bougainville.

"Yes," Montcalm said more sharply. "There was no excuse for that. Frontenac's destruction is a blow, though mostly to our prestige. It is not critical. However, Fort Niagara and our posts in the Ohio country are going to live on half rations this Winter. Nothing that happens in the west will seriously injure us. We must look to the bastion, to Quebec and Montreal. Here lies the meaning of this war. We can endure without Louisbourg. We can live without Fort duQuesne or Niagara, as long as we do not lose the bastion. That is why we fought at Carillon, not that we need Lake Champlain, but that losing the lake would give the English an easy approach to Montreal and Quebec."

Montcalm's thin, sober tone seemed to stir echoes from the shadowed corners of the room. Crosbie felt a cold prickle along his spine.

"Will we, then, fight here at Quebec next year, mon général? Or will we …"

Montcalm shrugged. "One fights where the enemy attacks," he said wearily. "I must wait here and respond as they offer battle. You may be sure I will never fight at Quebec or Montreal if it is possible to fight somewhere else. Everything rests with the English. The initiative is theirs. They have the choice of three routes. They have already tried to come north by way of Lake Champlain, and failed. They are still trying the western route by way of duQuesne and Niagara. That issue is not yet determined. They were successful only in the east, against Louisbourg. So they may well decide to ascend the St. Lawrence in their advance against Quebec. If they do, we must be ready. I hope, fervently, that they will not realize all the advantages of the river route."

"Is it really so much easier, sir?"

"Immensely so, for a large army," Montcalm said positively. "Only by water can a commander conveniently move the supplies he must carry with him. His men can reach the area of battle still rested and full of zeal. Only the river route is truly dangerous for us."

Montcalm bit on his pipestem with an air of finality. He smiled again at Crosbie, but this time the young Scot understood it was merely a formal, polite smile of dismissal. He rose willingly.

"I shall send Louis with instructions for you, Captain," the Général said slowly. "I do not want you to leave Beauport again without my permission. The order is clear?"

"Yes, sir," Crosbie said calmly.

"Tell Raoul duMaine and his charming daughter that I am in good health and reasonably good spirits. The situation is unpleasant, but you will probably hear of many changes here before next Spring. I will give serious thought to your request, you may be sure, but I am not yet sure what I should do about sponsoring your suit for Mademoiselle Céleste. But do not despair. Now get back, young man, and spend a happy Winter at Beauport." The Général came to his feet in a smooth motion and put his hand on Crosbie's shoulder. "Take no more chances, Captain. I will want you with me next year."

The young Scot backed away and bowed formally. He walked toward the pantry doorway again and was stopped when the Général spoke his name. He glanced over his shoulder.

Montcalm stood with his glass lifted to his nose. "My thanks to Raoul for this excellent liqueur, monsieur. Do not forget."

"I won't forget, mon général," Crosbie said. He bowed again and went out.

Through the bleak cold corridors under the Château, Crosbie walked with slow, almost aimless strides, twisting and turning plans in his mind. He knew what it was he hoped to accomplish this night. But exactly how to proceed was a question that required careful planning. He was halfway across the windswept Great Square before a possible solution occurred to him. The weak link, he muttered softly. Always strike at the weak link.

CHAPTER THIRTY EIGHT

With quickening strides, Crosbie headed toward the steep hill. Quebec's streets were nearly deserted now and only an occasional light filtered dimly from the darkened houses. Good people were in bed by this time; only drunken roisters remained abroad after ten at night. Crosbie smiled grimly as he turned down the mountain street. A sleeping city suited his mood perfectly—and his plans.

He passed a shuffling priest, head low, hands locked together in the wide sleeves of his black robe. The Jesuit moved almost silently up the hill, nodding vaguely when Crosbie stepped aside to let him have the easier footing. During that brief pause. Crosbie heard the sibilant rasp of footsteps descending the hill behind him. He took a few cautious steps forward, listening intently, knowing that any single soldier from the town-major's guard could ruin his plans. He didn't intend to let anyone arrest him. Warily, he ducked into a shadowed doorway. Up the hill was a misty figure, almost running. Crosbie could see the white coat with darker facings as the slight hurrying figure came closer. He watched closely for a moment, then stepped out into the cobbled street again and called out,

"Very well, Denis. Come forward."

The boy halted abruptly, half turning as if he meant to run for cover. Then his thin shoulders slumped and he moved slowly toward Crosbie.

"Well?" Crosbie demanded harshly.

"You ... you walked too fast," Denis complained.

"Don't blither, boy. Why are you here?"

Denis shrugged. "Mademoiselle Céleste," he said unwillingly. "She sent me."

"To watch me?"

"No, Duncan!" Denis's voice rose high and cracked with tension. "Just to see if you got into trouble. Then I was to tell her, so she could ..."

Crosbie's grim countenance relaxed in a quick grin. "Thank you, Denis," he said. "But there is nothing for you to ..." A flashing notion struck him silent for a moment. Then he grinned broadly. "Yes, there is something you can do." He clapped the boy's shoulder an amiable clout that sent him staggering. "You're a soldier! I had quite forgotten. You can go anywhere and never be noticed. Just one more soldier in a city full of soldiers. Yes, by God, that's it!"

He pulled the reluctant boy along with him, turning again toward the Lower Town.

"Denis," he said urgently, "I must find out where Captain O'Neill is at this moment. His quarters are in the Intendant's Palace, but I don't want to go there unless I know he's home. Do you understand?"

"No, Duncan," Denis objected. "And Mademoiselle Céleste said I should ..."

"Never mind that now," Crosbie insisted. "Run straight to the Palace. Tell the guards you have a message for Captain O'Neill. They'll tell you where to find him. Then come tell me."

"But where ..."

"I'll wait at the Lion d'Or," Crosbie said with growing confidence. "No one there cares about the town-major. I can wait safely in the common room until you come. And if Captain O'Neill is away, you find out where. I want to see him. Clear?"

"Yes, but Duncan, I don't ..."

"Soldat!"

Denis's heels cracked together smartly. "Oui, monsieur," he said dutifully.

"I'll be waiting. Now, run!"

Impelled by Crosbie's hand, the boy was off like the wind, rounding the corner beyond the Lion d'Or with his cloak fluttering wildly behind him.

Crosbie let out a sigh of pure relief. He hadn't had the least idea how to locate O'Neill, but Denis's unexpected appearance had solved all that. He had thought briefly of going to the Palace himself, but he would have been arrested the moment he showed his face.

The young Scot strolled slowly downhill toward the tavern. Dear foolish Céleste, he thought suddenly. How like her it was to send young Denis to see what would happen to him. Except for the boy's bad luck, Crosbie would never have known she had interfered. Yet if Crosbie had been apprehended, all the great influence of Beauport would have been wheeled into position to rescue him. Crosbie was still smiling as he pushed open the tavern door and stepped inside.

The low wide room reeked of tallow dips, roasted meat and rank tobacco. For a moment Crosbie could see nothing through the smoke haze.

"But there he stands!"

A raucous voice boomed from the fireplace. Crosbie squinted through the murky atmosphere.

"Devil's-Hair, that's what the Indians call him. What did I say? Did you ever see so much hard meat on one man?"

Le Singe pushed away from the circular table beside the fire and leaped to seize Crosbie's hand, wringing it fiercely while he bellowed full-throated admiration.

"He threw me," the voyageur chief roared. "I swear on my mother's memory. He threw me bodily. Up to that beam. I hung like a monkey. Le Singe, that's me! And this is the wolf who gave me the name." He surveyed Crosbie briefly, then turned again to his audience. "Too bad he's all powdered like a dandy. You never saw hair like a blazing flame before."

"For God's sake," Crosbie muttered in disgust. "Le Singe, you can't..."

"Bow to the lads, Devil's-Hair," Le Singe demanded drunkenly. "They didn't believe me. They said no man like you ever existed. But here you are. Let them see you, man. Bow to the lads. Northwoodsmen, they are, every mother's son of them. They know what a real man should look like."

Crosbie shrugged off his voluminous cloak, lifted his hat and tossed both to a chair. Even in a hazy light of the tavern, he was a startling sight. The sombre blue of his uniform was a perfect background for scarlet facings, silver lace and gold buttons. Nervously, the young Scot fingered the hilt of his jeweled dirk. Low mutters drifted from the table crammed with voyageurs.

"Le Singe," Crosbie said in a low, insistent tone, "no one can know I am here. You've already done the damage. Now you'll have to make the repairs."

Le Singe rubbed a broad grimy thumb along his nose. "The guard?" he asked with a worldly-wise grin that slanted across his heavy bearded face.

"The guard," Crosbie agreed quietly.

"Mother of God, what have you been doing? Stealing Bigot's young carrots, eh? No matter. Come along."

He grasped Crosbie's elbow with forceful amiability and shoved the young Scot forward. "Messieurs!" he bellowed. "Permit me to present Devil's-Hair, monsieur le brevet-capitaine Crosbie."

Crosbie glowered, but he retained presence of mind enough to make a polite leg and sweep his hand low to the filthy floor. A howl of delight went up from the crowded table.

"Monsieur Crosbie is not in Quebec," Le Singe went on in a confidential shout, sliding his finger along his bulbous nose and winking significantly. "He rests at Beauport, the honored guest of the grand seigneur. And the town-major's guard would arrest him like a shot if they found him here. Does everyone understand?"

Generally the table murmured agreement. A snaggle-toothed swarthy man with a twisted back and a villainous scowl left his seat and swept his red stocking-cap low, aping Crosbie's bow. "A distinct pleasure, monsieur," he said in a high affected tone. "You are invisible, are you? But I can see you. And the town-major would pay…"

Le Singe hit the hunchback solidly in the belly. The smirking voyageur gasped heavily and reeled back toward the table. A burly member of the crew reached out and clipped him hard under the ear, sending him staggering forward again.

"That is Pierre," Le Singe said quietly in Crosbie's ear. "Too much wine makes him crazy. Now, you deal with him also. It is best."

The hunchback lurched against Crosbie and now he held a short, thick-bladed sailor's knife in one hand. Automatically, Crosbie slashed downward with his fist, clubbing the knife aside. The knife stabbed toward him and Crosbie twisted away, catching the wrist in one large fist. The hunchback snarled in fury, struggling against the restraint. Crosbie snatched at his other wrist.

Pierre kicked out savagely at Crosbie, his moccasins drumming a tattoo against Crosbie's legs, straining to strike home at his crotch. Crosbie half turned, taking both wrists in one fist. Then he spun in a tight circle, hauling the spitting voyageur around him, legs extended. Crosbie stooped quickly, caught one thrashing ankle and straightened, lifting the hunchback easily overhead.

He stalked deliberately, silently, toward the smoking fireplace. There he leaned forward, slamming the squirming hunchback up against the stone chimney, holding him high.

The table of roistering voyageurs roared approval. Le Singe grinned up at Crosbie.

"Shall I roast him, or just hang him to smoke?" Crosbie asked, his chest heaving.

"Hang him high!" Le Singe demanded. "Let's have another monkey in the crew. Throw him up! Throw him!"

Crosbie stepped back. He lowered the man's legs slightly, shifted to the right, then lunged forward again with a mighty thrust upward, shooting the kicking hunchback high toward the ceiling rafters. The snarling hunchback fended himself away from the beams, gathered his legs tidily under him and landed on the floor like a cat, still clutching the short-bladed knife tightly in his hand. And it was a cat-like sound he made as he spat at Crosbie, his snaggle-toothed mouth distorted with fury.

Le Singe stepped briskly forward and took a billet of wood from the bin. He swung it full-armed, cracking Pierre under the ear. The hunchback crumpled slowly to the floor.

"That Pierre," Le Singe said mildly. "He goes crazy. No sense of humor. He always wants to make trouble." He stirred the unconscious voyageur with a casual foot. "He will be all right when he wakes up," he told Crosbie.

The voyageurs swarmed eagerly around Crosbie, none of them taller than Le Singe whose head barely reached Crosbie's shoulder. But all were wide, brawny men, gaudily clad in scarlet wool and belted leather, all hairy and swarthy skinned and all as gay and noisy as a troop of cavalry. They banged Crosbie's back admirably, offered him beakers of rum or brandy. Le Singe shoved them aside, asserting a command that none disputed. He ushered Crosbie regally to a chair at the circular table and stepped back, gazing around, beaming with delight.

"Did I not tell you?" he roared. "Did I not? This is the man!"

It was nearly an hour before Denis returned to the Lion d'Or and long before then, Crosbie had been compelled to refuse many drinks. Whole bottles were furnished for his consumption by the drunken voyageurs who assumed his drinking capacity was proportionately as large as his muscles. Crosbie sipped cautiously from a wooden piggin of poor brandy and accepted a blackened pipe from Le Singe, wanting neither but eager to keep the voyageur chief in a friendly humor. He joined in three raucous choruses of Auprès de ma blonde, and pretended to sing along with them when they shifted to a heavily cadenced rowing song he did not know. But always he kept one eye on the front door.

Le Singe and his crew were off for the Détroit at dawn and this would be their last carouse until the following Spring. Crosbie squirmed in a ferment of restlessness but he let his expression show nothing of his impatience.

He leaped swiftly from his chair when he saw Denis push back the heavy tavern door and peer timidly inside. The boy grinned when he recognized Crosbie.

"I found him, Duncan! I found him!"

"Softly," Crosbie cautioned. "Where is he?"

"He dines with Monsieur Colbert, the guard said. At Monsieur Colbert's house."

"Good. And where is that?"

"But, I …" Denis took off his hat slowly and turned it round and round in nervous fingers, purposely averting his eyes.

He didn't know, Crosbie realized. For a brief moment, his hands tightened in anger, then, seeing the look on the boy's face, he brought a thin smile to his lips. "Never mind, Denis. I can find out. Someone will …"

"I can tell you, my friend," Le Singe growled. "You plan to visit Monsieur Colbert's house?"

Crosbie nodded silently.

"So that tale about the town-major's guard was just a bit of sport with Le Singe, was it? Pretending to be …"

"What are you saying?" Crosbie demanded.

Le Singe leered. "What do you take me for? You are running from the town-major, but you go to visit Colbert who always has two guards outside his house, night and day. Don't I carry dispatches for that skinny slab of misery? Don't I go to his house? Don't I ..."

"Guards," Crosbie said thoughtfully, picking the one pertinate word from Le Singe's tirade. "Two guards."

Le Singe shoved his pipe angrily into his mouth and clamped down hard on the stem. He removed it and spat out bits of splintered clay. "You didn't know that? You didn't ..."

"I didn't know about the guards, my friend," Crosbie said quietly. "Please keep your voice down. I want to talk to a man who is at Colbert's house tonight. What is the best way to enter unobserved?"

"There is no way," Le Singe said flatly. "No way at all. Colbert's house is in the rue du Parloir, jammed between two others. There is only a front and back entrance and both are guarded."

Crosbie nodded. The problem was clear enough. He would have to ...

"Remove the guards," Le Singe said as if he had read Crosbie's mind. "You will need help for that." He gestured briefly at the crowded table. "You have enough."

"But, I couldn't ask you to ..."

Le Singe shrugged. "Why not? We have nothing to do until dawn. Let me see. Six would be more than enough. Only two guards and three servants at the most. Yes, six would be ..."

Crosbie would need help if he hoped to enter Colbert's house without being arrested. But helping him would be a terrible risk for Le Singe and his crew.

"What if you are seen?" he asked bluntly.

"Who cares?" Le Singe laughed. "We leave for the Détroit tomorrow. And by Spring when we return, they will have forgotten all about it. Monsieur Colbert is going to Paris, you know. I doubt if he will return soon. There is no risk."

Le Singe selected five fairly sober voyageurs and dragged them to a corner near the door where he whispered sibilant instructions that carried clearly to Crosbie's ear. Crosbie pulled on his cloak and took Denis's arm.

"You will come with me," he said softly. "I want you to wait outside the house. If I am detained, make your way to the boat and return to Beauport. Tell the Sieur duMaine what has happened. Do you understand?"

"But, Duncan, couldn't I..."

"No! You stay with Le Singe and see that he is discreet. We do not want the neighbors to call the guard, do we?"

"Oh, I see. Yes, Duncan, I will take care of that." Denis squared his shoulders and smiled with solemn assurance. "Depend on me."

"I do, Denis," Crosbie said, grinning with a sense of rising excitement. "I do."

CHAPTER THIRTY NINE

Le Singe and his men padded soft-footed as Indians up the long winding street to Upper Town, staying well ahead of Crosbie. They ran quickly across the great plaza of St. Louis. Crosbie and Denis followed more sedately, strolling casually like two soldiers on their weary way home after a long night's bout with wine and cards. Le Singe divided his forces at the far corner. Crosbie followed the voyageur chief when he turned into the narrow shadowed rue du Parloir. He held Denis to a slow pace to allow Le Singe time to dispose of the sentry posted outside Colbert's front door.

Crosbie stopped at the corner for a long moment, then went slowly down the cobbled street, keeping cautiously to the crowned center of the pavé. Several of the houses showed dim, screened lights within, though most were completely darkened. Crosbie could hear no indication of struggle. He walked softly, straining to listen. He almost passed Colbert's house.

"A pleasant evening, Your Honor," a brandy-thickened voice called pleasantly. "Does the Captain ..."

"No names!" Le Singe hissed quietly. "This is the door, monsieur. A servant will come when you knock. Silence him and the rest is easy."

The thick chest of the voyageur chief made a solid shadow against the white door. Lightly Crosbie tapped his shoulder in thanks. Then he lifted the bronze knocker and let it fall, hearing the metallic clangor echo through the narrow street.

Long moments passed silently. Crosbie waited impatiently. A nervous hand fumbled with a chain, then a bolt was pulled back and the door opened inward.

A thin-faced, elderly servant peered out, holding a twin-branched candlestick aloft. His stringy wig was awry and his bald skull and his eyes were moist and pinkly rimmed. Softly, he belched and lifted one hand uncertainly to pat his loose-lipped mouth.

Before the man could speak, Crosbie reached in with one hand and plucked him out by the back of his neck, hurling him into the street where one of Le Singe's men gagged him without a sound.

"Very good, monsieur," Le Singe murmured. "Just one moment now until Georges... ah, there he is," he said, pointing a broad finger. "See him wave from the corner? The guard at the rear door is quiet now. In you go, monsieur. Have your little talk. No one will get out of the house. We'll wait here."

"Thank you, my friend," Crosbie went inside and closed the door. He picked up the candlestick that the servant had dropped and put it on a low table. He was standing in a small vestibule whose inner door stood open upon an empty salon. Double-doors, partially ajar, led to the dining room where lights blazed from candles and a fireplace. Softly, Crosbie crossed the carpet toward the sliding doors.

Through the crack in the doorway, he could see into the lighted dining room. Immediately opposite was a wide bank of curtained windows with cushioned benches along their whole length where one might sprawl comfortably and look out upon the small garden behind the house. And directly centered on the windows hung a large gilt mirror of rococo design that reflected in miniature the darkly gleaming table around which three men sat slumped. A bright array of glasses marched along the glossy wood, interspaced among a drunkard's rank of empty bottles and decanters, some lying on their sides like forgotten duckpins.

Of the three present, Crosbie could see only the man he wanted: Captain Seamus O'Neill who sat facing the door, his shoulders low in the fragile gilt chair. He stared blindly, silently, at an empty bottle, his long white fingers revolving a half-full glass aimlessly. The other two sat too far from the door for Crosbie's angle of vision. One was seen only as a pair of legs with bedraggled silk stockings and gold-buckled shoes. The other was a pair of dusty scarred leather boots with empty brass sockets where spurs had once been screwed. Beside them a battered pewter snuffbox lay abandoned amidst its powdery contents.

Behind Crosbie, a clock chimed in pretty tinkling notes, making the young Scot jump nervously. At the sound, Captain O'Neill lifted his head slowly, scratched at his neck where his neckcloth chafed him, and yawned. His mouth was agape when Crosbie slid the doors apart and slammed them quickly behind him.

At O'Neill's right sat Michel Colbert, the knife-thin Canadien whose chin was sunk low in a mass of lace. He snored delicately, nostrils fluttering. Opposite him was a tall gloomy-looking man with a blue jaw and lank black hair, a stranger to Crosbie. And stranger by far was the uniform he wore, a dingy, threadbare set of regimentals with grease spots and stains over its buff facings, but no matter how grubby, clearly the uniform of English provincial troops. The man was a major and he seemed oddly relaxed for an Englishman in Canada, sitting awkwardly at ease, bony elbows propped on the fine table, holding a wineglass just under his hooked nose and sniffing at it with his eyes closed as if trying to memorize the bouquet. Obviously, he was a paroled prisoner, one with too much rank to be troubled by curfew regulations. His face was long and thin, darkly sallow as though from illness, and with his closely set eyes, gave him a strong resemblance to an ill-tended horse.

"Christ deliver us," O'Neill muttered drunkenly, his voice slurred, but just as flat and uninflected as ever. "It can't be our brave Crosbie?"

Colbert snored easily, not stirring, but the English major turned his head, propping it with his folded hands, and stared numbly at Crosbie, his eyes almost crossing as he tried to focus on the young Scot.

Duncan Crosbie drew himself up to his full height, realizing that his unexpected entrance had startled O'Neill and given him a momentary advantage. He hoped he had wit enough to capitalize on it before the Irish captain regained his composure.

"I've come for you, O'Neill," he said with a tight edge to his voice. "You didn't expect to see me alive, did you?"

He moved behind the lanky Englishman just as the major lurched back in his chair and started to rise. Crosbie's heavy hand slammed down on his narrow shoulder, ramming him low in his chair. "Stay where you are, sir," he growled.

Crosbie stretched forward suddenly, clutching O'Neill's collar and hauling the Irishman to his feet. His face reddened slowly with the constriction but he did not struggle. He let Crosbie support him while he drew in deep, desperate gulps of air. His eyes were still filmed, his mind befuddled, but he continued to breathe rapidly, so obviously trying to regain a semblance of sobriety that Crosbie felt a moment's sympathy for him. Even now, O'Neill betrayed no trace of fear, and unless Crosbie could manage to frighten him, his mission would be a hopeless failure. But how could you scare a man like O'Neill?

"Come with me." Crosbie lifted him to the tips of his toes, as he turned brusquely toward the door.

Why doesn't he say something, Crosbie wondered. O'Neill's silent struggle to achieve self-control was somehow ominous to Crosbie's mind. He was far too hardened a scoundrel to break under minor pressure and the huge young Scot felt a sudden twinge of uncertainty. How could he scare the man?

"Major Stowell!" O'Neill gasped in a thin squeak.

Sensing movement behind him, Crosbie whirled, keeping his grip on O'Neill's collar. The back of his broad hand cracked sharply on the Englishman's cheekbone, bringing a bright tinge of color to his sallow face. The major stumbled back to his chair. The hand that had fumbled for his sword crept slowly back to the table-top as the major locked glances with the infuriated young Scot.

"You cain't…" he muttered. "Why Christ in the mountain, man, you cain't just…"

"This man is a murderer, major," Crosbie said in a voice that almost snarled. "Do you want to interfere again?"

Reluctantly, the major shook his head. He wiped the back of his hand across his mouth. A greasy lock of hair fell ropily down his face. "…s'a gennelman," he said firmly with drunken insistence. "Gotta… gotta chal… chal… gotta fight 'im right. Dool. That's it. Dool. Gennelman cain't just…"

"Duel!" Crosbie snorted. "One challenges equals, major, not filth like this… this…" In his incoherent anger, Crosbie shook O'Neill as a housewife shakes a dirty carpet. The Irishman's head wobbled precariously forward and back.

"Dool," the major repeated in his high whining voice.

O'Neill recovered his balance, holding with one hand to Crosbie's shoulder. "Le' me down," he said in a vague mumble. "Le' me down, sir." His hand tapped at Crosbie's arm. "I… I didn't…"

Now, Crosbie asked himself, is this the moment? Will he tell me what happened? Is he frightened enough?

He wheeled on O'Neill, pulling him forward to meet his left hand that swung brutally through the air. The hardened palm smacked O'Neill's face with a sharp impact. Crosbie hurled the Irish captain back in his chair, towering over him, both hands close to his exposed throat.

"Don't lie to me, damn you," Crosbie growled furiously. "Your man didn't die before he talked. I know you sent him to Beauport to kill me. Why do you think I came directly here?"

There it was, Crosbie thought. His entire future riding one cast of the dice. If he had guessed right, O'Neill should now have real reason to be terrified of the deadly retribution standing over him. But if he were wrong, if O'Neill had not…

Crosbie watched O'Neill's hands. If he were wrong, then O'Neill would attack; he was sure of that. O'Neill would grab for the Crosbie dirk that dangled so temptingly close, or he would strike out with his fists. But if Crosbie were right, then O'Neill was already feeling the frozen wariness of fear. And a fearful man was always a timid man, always. O'Neill's hands rose in a light, fluttery motion, then with great deliberation, locked together tightly in his lap. Crosbie felt a welling surge of exultation. He was right! O'Neill had sent those skulkers to Beauport. Or he knew who had sent them, which amounted to the same thing.

Keeping his eyes hard on O'Neill, Crosbie backed to the table and sat on the edge, facing the Irish captain. He drew his dark-steel dirk, and very slowly, stretched his arm forward until the point was resting precisely between O'Neill's eyes, lightly pricking the skin.

"You… you can't…"

"That's what your English friend told me," Crosbie said quietly. "But you're wrong, O'Neill. I can. And I will." All the strong force of his hatred, his months of worry and apprehension, were clear in his cold harsh tone. At that moment, even Crosbie did not know whether he meant to kill O'Neill. "Believe me. I will."

Crosbie's dirk broke the skin at the bridge of O'Neill's nose, but the Irishman did not stir. His pale eyes were wide and staring, with fright peering out like a secret enemy, betraying his effort to control himself. His throat worked convulsively. His pale thin lips moved soundlessly.

"You made a mistake in sending those men to Beauport, O'Neill," Crosbie said in a quiet, confidential growl. "That made the seigneur angry. You didn't think of that, did you? The Sieur duMaine is furious. Do you think Bigot would try to protect you if duMaine wants your head? You know he won't. Don't you?" He prodded lightly with the dirk. "Don't you, O'Neill?"

"Bigot," O'Neill muttered hoarsely. "Not me. Bigot … I didn't …"

Crosbie pulled his lips back in a tight grimace. "I have the dog," he said, trying to keep his voice level and assured. "I'll take the master, if I can. Do you want to trade, O'Neill?"

"Let … let me …" O'Neill shifted one hand as if to lever himself upright.

"No." The dirk broke the skin again in a tiny gash. A hairline of bright blood moved slowly down O'Neill's high thin nose. "Stay where you are," Crosbie demanded. "Did Bigot tell you to send those men to Beauport?"

"Yes," O'Neill gasped hoarsely. "The Comtesse … her idea …"

"Will you swear to that? Will you swear before duMaine?"

O'Neill swallowed heavily, his neck bent back at a cramped angle. "He'd have me killed. Bigot would …"

"And I'll kill you if you don't," Crosbie promised softly. "I'm here and Bigot is there. Which will you choose?"

"All … all right," O'Neill gasped. "Let me … up."

Crosbie sat back abruptly. He pulled his dirk back and balanced it on his knee, holding the point aimed directly at O'Neill's throat. He tossed the Irish captain a wadded, wine-soaked handkerchief. "Wipe your face."

O'Neill rubbed the cloth vigorously over his forehead. He leaned forward and pulled in long slow painful breaths. His eyes remained fixed in mesmeric fascination on the jeweled hilt of Crosbie's long-bladed dirk.

"You … you can't fight Bigot," he said in a flat, slurred tone.

"I can try." Crosbie shifted the blade slightly. "Why did he want me killed?"

O'Neill glanced up sharply, a bright curiosity knotting his thin sleek eyebrows. "You don't … you don't know?"

Crosbie moved the blade nearer. "Don't fence with me, O'Neill," he growled. "Why?"

The Irishman shrugged. His eyes flickered left toward Major Stowell, then returned to Crosbie.

Crosbie realized he was sitting with his back to the Englishman and Colbert. He slipped quickly from the table and circled O'Neill's chair. Then he spun the chair around. In that way he could keep all three men under his eye, though neither of the others represented a serious threat. Colbert still snored thinly in sodden stupor and Major Stowell was held in a glassy-eyed trance, listening carefully with a dark, thoughtful frown, but not moving.

"Why?" Crosbie repeated insistently.

"Dead you are not likely to offer a defense," O'Neill muttered. "Why else?"

"Defense? Defense against what? Is it still the Britannia swindle?"

"Still the Britannia," O'Neill agreed heavily. He fingered the slight nick between his eyes, not looking at Crosbie.

"But Tremais knows..." Crosbie began irritably. Then he clamped his mouth firmly shut. Monsieur Tremais knew the truth, but possibly Bigot did not know that. Very likely Tremais had said nothing. There was no profit in telling O'Neill anything he didn't know already.

"Tremais," O'Neill said dully. "He believes what he has been told. But he hasn't seen the paper you signed. Not yet."

"What paper?" Crosbie demanded harshly.

"The Comtesse has it," O'Neill said. "The whole plan for the Brittania swindle. You're caught, cock. Caught dead. It's your plan, signed in your own fist. You don't have a chance to deny it."

Crosbie stared at the Irish captain. O'Neill had recovered much of his assurance and control. Drunkenness still blurred his mind, but O'Neill was not the dazed, timorous man he had been only moments earlier.

The paper, Crosbie thought. What paper could... And he remembered in a blazing flare of memory. He had signed something the Comtesse had told him was an agreement to invest. He hadn't read it; hadn't even looked at it. Who would, with the Comtesse standing beside him like Venus Arisen, and her gilded swan-bed only a few steps away beyond an open door? That might be the paper O'Neill mentioned. And for all Crosbie knew, it might have been a confession to murder.

"Yes," he said thickly. "Bigot is clever, isn't he?"

"Too clever for you, cock," O'Neill said with growing assurance. "You're done."

Crosbie stretched out one finger and tilted O'Neill's head back. "Possibly so," he said quietly. "You too, O'Neill."

Even with his head grotesquely angled, O'Neill managed a thin, contemptuous smile. "Do you think Bigot will let anyone place charges against me, cock? You'd best worry about yourself. There'll be town-major's guards here any minute. Then you'll be..."

Crosbie's quick smile was enough to make O'Neill break off his sure statement. He frowned in momentary concern.

"Yes," Crosbie agreed. "Have you just thought about them? Where are your guards, O'Neill? I've been here half an hour. What happened to the guards? And Colbert's servant?"

O'Neill forced a casual shrug. "Well, it doesn't matter. You'll never get out of the city."

"But you won't know, O'Neill," Crosbie said softly. "You'll be dead by then. You didn't think I was going to bring you to trial, did you? I've been nine shapes of idiot lately, but even I know that Bigot could easily get you free." He brought his dirk up slowly, candlelight winking viciously on the jeweled guard. "I came for you. O'Neill. I said I would trade you for Bigot. But I won't trade for nothing."

"I...I..." O'Neill coughed solidly, wiping his distorted mouth with his handkerchief. "I remember our last trade," he said.

Crosbie laughed in a rough, barking explosion. "I remember too," he said. "I paid what you demanded, O'Neill. Too bad there wasn't any money left. I gave it back. Or didn't you know that?"

O'Neill nodded. "Tremais has it," he said in a flat, cold tone.

"It's your choice," Crosbie said bluntly. "That paper you mentioned. Where is it?"

"In the name of God, Crosbie! I couldn't get that! The Comtesse has it in her appartement. I've never even been inside."

I've been inside that room, Crosbie thought. And I know just where the paper would be, too. In that big ormolu box on top of her desk. The box with the huge keyhole. If I could get inside that room...

"You'll help me get it," he said roughly. "Wait where you are. Don't try to leave this room."

Crosbie straightened quickly. He sheathed his dirk and moved briskly around the table. He pulled the sliding doors apart and left them open while he went to the front door.

"Le Singe," he called quietly.

The bearded voyageur materialized from the darkness. Crosbie took his arm.

"I want two men to stay here," he said slowly. "They can come inside and wait. The rest will come with me."

"Come where, monsieur?"

"Captain O'Neill is taking me to the Intendant's Palace," Crosbie said in a bright, angry voice. "He doesn't know it yet, but we're going together."

CHAPTER FORTY

It was a strange, silent procession that halted in the shadows beyond the Intendant's Palace. Captain Seamus O'Neill was in the lead, with each arm draped around the neck of a burly voyageur, apparently being supported on his tipsy journey home, actually with both hands gripped immovably tight. A short distance behind Duncan Crosbie strolled to join them, with Le Singe and young Denis on either side. Two swaggering Canadiens of Le Singe's crew formed the rear guard.

Crosbie took Denis's arm and walked with him a few steps aside from the others. "I have an assignment for you, Denis," he said softly.

The boy nodded eagerly.

"Run to the wharf below the Market Square and find the Beauport boatmen. Have them row to the Palace landing on the St. Charles and wait for me there. Stay with them. Oars in the water. Each man at his post. Be ready to leave quickly. I may be running. Understand?"

"Oui, monsieur!" The boy dashed off down the cobbled road, his heavy army shoes rousing sleepy echoes in the night-time stillness.

Crosbie rejoined Le Singe and moved to a safe distance for a whispered conference.

"Watch Captain O'Neill closely," he said in a tight voice. "Don't let him get away and above all, don't let him cry out."

"Yes," Le Singe growled. "I can manage that. But how will you control him when you get inside? He could signal..."

Crosbie stooped to bring his mouth close to Le Singe's ear. "He isn't going inside. He thinks he is, but I merely want him to persuade the sentry to open the garden wicket. I'll handle the sentry. You grab O'Neill immediately. Is that clear?"

The voyageur chief ducked his head quickly, stifling a low, rumbling chuckle.

"Be sure you hold him," Crosbie went on. "We'll cross to the gate just after midnight when the guard changes. I don't think the patrol sergent will come to inspect the post before I return, but if he does ..."

Le Singe made a significant gesture with one hand and Crosbie nodded grimly.

"And when I come back, you must be ready to leave. Where is your canot? At the Market Square wharf?"

"Yes, monsieur."

"Very well. I'll turn and go toward the Palace landing where my boat will be waiting. You and your men run toward the Market Square. Then if I'm pursued closely, the chase will be divided. You might also make a little noise, if you will."

"It will be my pleasure, monsieur," Le Singe said gaily.

"And what about the men you left at Colbert's house?" Crosbie asked.

"They are to wait one hour, then lock everyone in the cellar and return to the Lion d'Or. All is arranged."

"Then everything is ready." Crosbie dropped his hand solidly on Le Singe's thick shoulder. "My thanks, friend."

"No thanks," Le Singe insisted roughly. "I've never had such a night. And don't worry about us. No guard is going to catch us. You go do your desperate work, captain. And we will pray for you while you are in that den of adders."

The two voyageurs had lowered O'Neill's arms, but they stood beside the Irishman, ready to throttle him if he tried to run or shout. Crosbie glanced at O'Neill's bitterly twisted expression and he almost chuckled aloud.

He felt a swelling surge of self-confidence, a sureness that seldom came so strongly to him. Ever since he had returned to Colbert's dining room and found O'Neill working desperately to open a rear window, he had been positive that the captain would try to give the alarm when he entered the Intendant's Palace with Crosbie. Crosbie had let him think they were going in together. But O'Neill's work would be finished the moment he had served as judas goat in getting the gate open. Then O'Neill would find out how foolish his plans were.

Crosbie did not question his sureness. He had overborne O'Neill earlier that night. Granted that the Irish scoundrel had been fuzzy-brained with drink, Crosbie had won nonetheless, and even such a minor triumph was a heady draught. The moment he had decided to take matters into his own hands, his future had immediately become brighter.

Crosbie drew a long confident breath. He had to get inside that Palace, make his way safely to the Comtesse's appartement, find the spurious document she had hidden, and then retreat, all without creating alarm. The Comtesse slipped her lovers in through the garden entrance. That thought brought Crosbie a twinge of angry self-contempt; he had been a fool, and the Comtesse had earned her right to laugh at him. But tonight he could use that very gate to gain his entry, for the sentries there would not be surprised at any unusual message whispered through the barred wicket. Nor would the sentries posted along the way to the Comtesse's suite be as suspicious as others, for they must have seen quite a few silent, hooded figures creeping through the passages.

From where he stood, Crosbie could dimly see the stiffly erect sentries posted outside the main entrance of the Palace. When they were relieved by a second pair, he knew it was time to start for the garden wicket. He nudged O'Neill.

"A trade, remember?" he said grimly. "I don't want you trying to signal the guards when we get inside."

O'Neill nodded silently, his pale perfect features set in a sullen mask. He and his guards trailed Crosbie down the cobbled street, turned the corner and marched directly toward the narrow barred wicket that opened into the Palace garden.

Le Singe's men released O'Neill's arm and ran silently to positions on either side of the wicket, concealed by the shadows. Crosbie and Le Singe remained beside O'Neill until the Irishman had tapped at the heavy gate. Then Crosbie slid forward, crouching low out of sight, and Le Singe moved to O'Neill's rear, standing just beyond the ring of watery light cast by the sentry's lantern.

"Captain O'Neill!" the sentry said in a dull voice.

"Open the gate, fool," O'Neill said in his flat cold tone.

"But, monsieur, I am not supposed to …"

"Open the gate," O'Neill commanded. "Do you want me to have you flogged through the streets? Open, I say!"

The pale blur of the sentry's face vanished from the opening. After a long moment, they could hear the soft clank of a chain dropping. Then a metal bar slid along its keepers and the gate was swung inward.

Crosbie and Le Singe sprang in perfect unison. The young Scot's long arm reached through the gateway, seized the sentry's collar and jerked him suddenly forward, off balance. As he stumbled out to the street, Crosbie hit him precisely behind the ear with the heavy hilt of his dirk. The soldier collapsed with a muffled sigh. Le Singe had his left arm looped tightly around O'Neill's neck, effectively choking off any attempt to call out. O'Neill's fingers tore with desperate fury at Le Singe's thick arm and his face was darkly murderous.

"Ease off for a moment," Crosbie said quietly. He dragged the sentry out to the street and propped him against the wall.

"He wants to fight me," Le Singe growled.

"No, Captain O'Neill doesn't want to fight," Crosbie said easily. "Do you, captain?"

O'Neill glared in silent hatred. Le Singe's arm had relaxed enough to let him breathe, but the bulging forearm remained in place, able to choke him again if he moved. Only the Irishman's cold pale eyes showed his rage.

"You will stay here," Crosbie said to him. "I'll let you go free later, if I find what I'm looking for. Le Singe, have one man stay at the gate with the sentry, in case he wakes up. Let the others stand just inside the gate. Close it, but leave the bolt off. And keep alert for the patrol sergent."

He flipped the wide collar of his cloak high to mask his face as he slipped through the gate. A graveled path crunched noisily underfoot and Crosbie shifted aside to walk on the hard ground. He tried to move with bent knees and a stoop to disguise his unusual height.

When he had entered this way previously, a plump elderly maid had met him at the gate and conducted him into the Palace and along the narrow dank corridors to the Comtesse's apartement. Then there had been no guard stationed at the door to the Palace itself, and those in the corridors had discreetly looked away. He could expect no such good fortune this time.

The entrance from the garden was a double set of glassed doors, heavily shielded with velvet hangings. Moving with infinite caution, Crosbie pressed down the handle of the door. When the latch was free, he could feel that the door was unbolted. He went inside with a rush, flickering his dirk into his hand as he moved.

A torch-shaped lamp hung against the stone wall flickered as the light wind whipped at its flame. Thick ominous shadows leaped and danced along the corridor, but no one was in sight. Silently Crosbie closed the door. He slipped down the corridor until he was in a dimly lighted space between two lamps. Still he could see no one. Surely some sort of guard was stationed at that garden door, he thought.

A heightened wariness slowed him as he moved softly along the stone floor toward the staircase that would lead him up to the

Comtesse's floor. He climbed slowly, keeping to the inside and peering up at every step. Two black shoes waited at the head of the stairs, facing away. Crosbie's gaze moved upwards, observing the coarse thread stockings, the rough uniform breeches and coat. Here, then, was the first sentry he would have to pass. And it would be far wiser to walk confidently by than to fight. Crosbie gripped his dirk tensely under cover of his cloak. He kept his head bent low, his collar high and purposely he stamped up the stairs, making no effort to be quiet. He heard shoes rasp against the stone floor above him. Then a musket butt was grounded with a soft grating sound. Crosbie moved stolidly up, not looking beyond his feet.

The sentry had shifted, he noticed, when he reached the head of the stairs. Now he stood stiffly against the wall. Crosbie did not turn his head. Stiffly, he stalked straight forward, down the narrow hallway, knowing that the sentry would not stop him unless something made him suspicious. If he should recognize Crosbie, then there would surely be a challenge. And soon.

Crosbie's back ached with tension. A space between his shoulderblades prickled with strain. But he did not pause. A bend in the corridor would soon take him out of the sentry's vision. Only a few more steps. His hand cramped agonizingly around the hilt of his dirk. Just to the corner, and then down to the end of the hallway. That was all that remained of his perilous route, but it seemed as long as the distance to Carillon.

He permitted himself a soft sigh when he rounded the bend of the corridor, but he walked silently and quickly to the wide, oak-paneled door at the end. He bent forward with his ear to the door for a long moment, standing in the full glaring light of a flaring torch beside the door. He could hear nothing. His breath was coming quick, almost deafening with its dry rasp in his throat.

Softly, he rotated the silver knob, feeling it move easily with his pressure. This door opened into the Comtesse's salon. Crosbie thanked his favorite saints that he would not have to enter the Comtesse's bedroom. He eased the door back and slipped through, leaving it slightly ajar so the corridor light would help him find the desk.

It was a delicate piece of work, lovingly constructed of polished fruit-woods, enameled panels and gilt medallions, that stood by itself between two windows with its matching chair in front. Crosbie tiptoed swiftly across the floor and snatched up the large domed box that was visible on the desk. He retreated immediately to the path of light near the door and knelt with the box. He used the point of his dirk to force the lock, sliding the blade under the lid. With a determined twist, he tore the lock free of the frail wood. The sharp tearing sound froze him tensely in position. This would be the worst possible moment to be caught, he realized. But if he could just find that paper...

He tipped the box, seeing papers cascade to the floor. After them came a small lady's pistol that landed with a soft thud on the carpet. A thin silver arrow inlaid along the barrel reflected the dim light. Crosbie pushed it aside and feverishly pawed through the papers. He didn't try to read any of them, merely to spread them open, searching for his own bold signature. As he worked swiftly through them, he became aware that this was a collection of financial documents. Enormous figures leaped in strong relief from each paper. Crosbie smiled grimly. If his were not here, he might still have found a treasure that the Comtesse would pay heavily to recover, even to the point of surrendering the spurious document she had tricked him into signing. But there it was! His own youthfully extravagant scrawl below a carefully engrossed series of paragraphs.

The new source of light did not draw his attention at first. He saw only the paper and his face was close to the floor in his attempt to read it in the flickering torchlight. But he did hear the sharply indrawn breath behind him. Swiftly he scooped the small pistol into his pocket. One hand clenched tightly around the stiff paper, wadding it into a tight mass. Without rising, he slewed around on the floor, dirk held high and ready. His legs tensed for a lunge.

The Comtesse held her candelabra high overhead, the light flooding her jewel-box salon with a soft lambent glow. She stared incredulously at Crosbie, her eyes wide and bright with alarm, frozen immovably in shock.

Between them stood a chair covered in golden velvet and over its back was a beautifully embroidered coat in blue satin. Its gold buttons reflected candlelight in sharp dazzling splinters. The coat was a magnificent, extravagant thing, entirely suitable to a lady of the Comtesse's wealth and distinction. But it wasn't a lady's coat, Crosbie realized in that tense moment. From it was draped the shimmering blue watered-silk ribbon of the Order of St. Louis. Crosbie glanced up sharply at the Comtesse.

She was struck silent, terrified. One slim hand crept up to her mouth, pressing hard against her soft lips. It wasn't Crosbie that had frightened her. He was suddenly sure that she had not come into the salon because of any noise he had made. But what was it, then? She was too obviously surprised and panicked. Had she come in for that elegant coat with the pale blue ribbon? Come to take it into her bedroom, and then seen Crosbie? Was that it? Did she have a...

That was the only possible answer. There was a man in the Comtesse's bedroom, one of the rare men honored with the Order of St. Louis. And that decoration narrowed the list so that anyone might guess who was...

Crosbie straightened slowly. A wild surge of soundless laughter tore at him. He was caught. But he had found what he had come for. He could see just one way out, one possibility of leaving safely.

"Good evening, dear Comtesse," he said in a quiet, soothing tone. He moved closer to the golden velvet chair and stretched his left arm forward, holding the crumpled paper. "Will you light this for me, please?"

As if in a trance, the Comtesse lowered the triple candlestick briefly so that Crosbie could light the paper.

"What..." she tried to whisper. A terrible spasm caught her voice. Her throat strained with effort, making strong cords stand out hard against her soft pale skin.

Crosbie held his improvised torch up carefully, turning it to let it burn thoroughly.

"Only for this," he said softly. "A paper I signed by mistake. An error, dear lady, wasn't it?"

"But you... you can't..."

The note of desperation in the Comtesse's trembling voice brought a smile from the young Scot.

He released the remaining scrap of paper and watched it drift toward the floor where it burned itself to a whisper of ash. Crosbie shifted his shoe and ground the ash into nothing.

Then, with a slow deliberate movement, he crooked one finger under the blue silk ribbon and lifted it high. He brought it up to his nose with a dandified gesture and sniffed audibly, raising his eyebrows.

"I wonder if I know him?" He watched tightly as the Comtesse's eyes narrowed with alarm. "His Excellency, the King's Governor, who has a very jealous wife? Or the Chevalier de..." He let his voice dwindle quietly as he backed toward the door, still holding the ribbon.

The Comtesse clutched at the empty air in an imploring gesture, her eyes seeing only the ribbon in Crosbie's hand, her lips stretched tautly in a torment of apprehension. The young Scot bowed slightly, draped the ribbon over the knob of the door and stepped out into the hall, swinging the door crisply shut behind him.

He ran as softly as he could to the bend of the corridor, then compelled himself to slow to a sedate amble as he passed into view of the sentry posted at the staircase. Nothing was ever harder for him than that measured, laborious march. He clenched his teeth painfully and held the Crosbie dirk ready under his cloak. He passed the sentry, keeping his head low. Then he stepped down to the first tread, the beginning of the trip to the ground floor. When his foot finally touched the final step, he lunged forward in a swift sprint toward the garden door. He ripped open the door and leaped through, hearing a hoarse muffled shout somewhere behind him.

His heart thundered wildly as he ran through the deserted garden. His shoes crunched over the gravel, rousing sharp echoes from the garden walls as noisy as a galloping team of horses. Voices rose louder and more intense behind him now, and above them soared a high, infuriated female tone that almost shrieked. Crosbie grinned tightly. The Comtesse, he thought. I wonder what she told the sentry?

Le Singe's man saw him coming and swung the gate open. Crosbie skidded to a halt just outside, fighting to catch his breath.

The voyageur chief stood poised for retreat. His four men were now safely outside in the street, lost in shadow. Le Singe alone remained in sight, one great arm still locked hard around O'Neill's throat.

"Success, mon ami?" Le Singe roared, obviously delighted that the time for silence had passed.

"Yes, thanks to you," Crosbie panted. He pointed his dirk at O'Neill. "Can you take this carrion a short distance from here before you let him go?"

"Let him go!" Le Singe's voice flared in sudden anger.

"Yes," Crosbie said. He grinned at Le Singe's dark frown. "We'll let him live to receive Bigot's thanks for this night's work, eh?"

Le Singe chuckled abruptly. He gestured briefly and two men came from the darkness to seize O'Neill's arms. Le Singe relaxed his constricting grip on the Irishman's neck.

O'Neill straightened, lifting his chin. His smooth perfect features were coldly outlined in the faint light. He stood erect, making no effort to free himself and his voice was held to a low, harsh uninflected tone that gave peculiar emphasis to what he said. His face was utterly expressionless, his eyes coldly impassive as a lizard's.

"I won't kill you, cock," he murmured with quiet sureness. "I'll let you live, too. But you won't want to live when I'm finished with you. I'll ruin everything you ever ..."

Le Singe sputtered with quick fury. One movement of his wide hand was enough to send his two men dashing into the darkened street. The quiet, malignant Irishman was forced to run swiftly between them. A brisk clatter of hard footsteps drowned O'Neill's last comment, but the thorough viciousness of his intent was so clearly evident that Crosbie shivered suddenly.

Bellowing voices roared out orders in the garden behind them. Crosbie clapped Le Singe's shoulder in farewell.

"Again, my thanks," he said soberly. "Now, run, my friend. I'll see you again when you return."

"Good night, monsieur. More amusing than the comédie, wasn't it?" Le Singe swaggered into the street and strolled away into the shadow, whistling shrilly between his teeth.

Crosbie turned toward the river and ran with long easy strides. He was hidden by darkness and almost beyond hearing when the guard spilled furiously into the street in pursuit.

At the Palace boat landing, he slowed to a brisk walk, moving out to the end of the piling and dropping lightly down into the waiting whaleboat.

"Ready for bed, Denis?" he grinned. "Let's go home to Beauport, shall we?"

CHAPTER FORTY ONE

Not until Louis Bougainville came to Beauport nearly a week later did Crosbie learn what had followed as a result of his midnight invasion of the Intendant's Palace.

Bougainville had appeared just as the family was going in to dinner, so no private conversation was possible until late in the evening when the two friends walked out into the frost-blighted garden for a breath of air before retiring. Then, and only then, did Bougainville betray the wild hilarity that almost choked him.

"They are insane with rage, Duncan," he sputtered, "stark, raving mad, I tell you. What happened, no one knows, but God, what a plethora of unlikely rumors. The Comtesse is prostrate with the vapors. Apparently some hulking scoundrel assaulted a sentry, forced his way to her appartement, and was then frightened away when she went to investigate. Nothing was stolen, we are told. The King's Governor, no less a personage, mind you, is talking of posting a reward for the man's apprehension, but one hears that the Intendant wishes the matter forgotten. But the Governor is splendid in his wrath, like an Old Testament King." Bougainville closed one eye comically. "I wonder why?" he inquired blandly.

"I could guess," Crosbie said slowly, thinking of that blue ribbon that had dangled from a chair in the Comtesse's salon. Among his many honors, the Governor had received the Order of St. Louis. What a lurid scandal it would have been if...

"No," Bougainville snapped. "Don't guess. You couldn't possibly have anything to add to the official reports. Idle rumors may enliven an evening's conversation, but able young officers gain only a loss of reputation by spreading them."

Bougainville rubbed his chin thoughtfully, keeping his eyes hard on Crosbie. "I should tell you," he added quietly, "that Le Singe did not get away at dawn as he had planned. One of his drunken crew had been impounded by the town-major's guard and I was summoned to effect his release. As we waited, Le Singe told me an odd story. Very drôle, it was, too. The Général was charmed when I repeated it to him. But we both realized it was merely a clever story of the imagination. You follow me?"

Crosbie nodded soberly. Bougainville's warning was broad. The affair had become a joke. One of those fantastic tales that become more garbled with each repetition. And that was fortunate for Crosbie. There would be no official reprisal, though Crosbie knew a private punishment was being planned for him. He forced a strained smile.

"Something very strange happened also at Monsieur Colbert's house that same night," Bougainville said in an amiable, gossipy tone. "Poor Colbert slept through it all, apparently, so he is unable to provide a coherent explanation of how he came to be locked in his own cellar. He is extremely angry, though he is not sure why. Captain O'Neill is even more furious, in his contained manner. His eyes promise death and his mouth twists into a smile at the joke. He is a gentleman to watch, Duncan."

Crosbie made a noncommittal sound deep in his throat.

"Exactly so," Bougainville agreed. "Mysterious, isn't it? One must assume in spite of the denial, that something important was actually removed from the Comtesse's appartement, for that gracious lady and her brother, the Intendant, later cancelled an appointment to meet with Monsieur Tremais. Do you recall Tremais?"

"I remember him," Crosbie said quietly.

"Of course. Well, it seemed that the Comtesse and Monsieur Bigot had promised to show Monsieur Tremais certain evidence that would prove their complete innocence in the swindle concerning the prize-ship Brittania. When they did not appear, Monsieur Tremais was forced to the unpleasant conviction that the evidence did not exist, if it ever had."

"It did, in a fashion," Crosbie said softly, almost to himself.

"A pity," Bougainville said smoothly. "Monsieur Tremais would be appalled to hear that. You know that gentleman's passion for truth. I think we will spare his sensibilities and not tell him. He is content with his present opinion."

"And that is..."

Bougainville shrugged easily. "I suppose I may tell you. It will be announced tomorrow. Monsieur Tremais will fine the syndicate involved in the Brittania affair a total of two million francs. Immense, eh? And that is only the beginning. What odds will you offer that Monsieur Bigot and his lovely sister will manage to find some dupe to shoulder the blame, even at this late date? It will be Cadet, or another of his creatures who poses as the major culprit."

"But it won't be me," Crosbie said. "Two million francs!" He whistled thinly.

Bougainville grinned. "There is no longer a warrant outstanding against you. It was recalled yesterday. Monsieur Tremais's findings regarding the Brittania will place the blame where it properly belongs. And the charge about Denis was patently absurd. The owner of the boy's indenture is a Frenchman who would have to appear personally in Canada if he wanted to sue you. So the charge is dismissed. However, the Général wants you to remain here quietly, as before. Legally, you are free, but neither Bigot nor the Comtesse is finished with you. And before I forget, Monsieur Tremais wanted me to tell you that he will deposit to your credit with the Banque de Paris, the sum of four thousand francs. He says you will understand what it is for."

Crosbie nodded. That was the amount he had won gambling at the Intendant's Palace, the sum he had later invested in the Brittania. And Tremais was scrupulous about returning it.

"Good," Bougainville went on. "The Général has instructed me to find a permanent commission as Captain for you. Four thousand may be sufficient. Shall I use that money?"

"Yes, please, Louis." Crosbie smiled with a hard, humorless grimace, wondering what Bigot would think if he knew that he had furnished the money for Crosbie's new commission.

"Leave it to me," Bougainville said. "I am already so weighted with private errands that I doubt if I will have time to attend to my work."

"And what is your work, Louis? To persuade the King…"

Bougainville broke in sharply. "Do not speculate, Duncan. However, I can tell you that I have been given the task of arranging the betrothal of the Général's son, the young Comte de Montcalm. That, you may be sure, the Général regards as among my primary duties."

"Yes." Crosbie eyed Bougainville closely. He forced himself to wait.

Bougainville's smile was more sober now. "His Excellency told me of your request for his help with the Sieur duMaine. He mentioned you very pleasantly, indeed with a certain wry affection."

"But he refused?"

"No, Duncan, not exactly that, but…"

"He won't help me?"

"Listen to me quietly, Duncan, and try not to interrupt. The Général is thinking of you as well as his old friend, duMaine. He feels that the Sieur duMaine would object so strongly that even his representations would not help you. And that would close the door permanently. But if you…"

"What, Louis?" Crosbie growled.

"First let me repeat what the Général said of duMaine, for it will help you understand. This problem might not exist if the seigneur's son were still alive. DuMaine's hopes were centered upon the boy, Montcalm says. Now, he must look to his daughter to bring into his family a young man qualified to assume the duties of seigneur." Bougainville glanced up calmly. "I think you have been here at Beauport long enough to realize what that entails, eh?"

Crosbie nodded in bleak silence.

"That, His Excellency believes, would be the most serious obstacle to duMaine's approval. The Général is speaking of a friend of his boyhood, you must remember. He knows duMaine thoroughly, so his advice is doubly valuable."

"Yes. What advice?"

"Just to wait, Duncan. Stay here through the Winter and during that time, bend every effort to ingratiate yourself with the seigneur and with the Grand'mère who exercises great influence over him. Let him see you as you truly are, Duncan. The growing regard will..."

"I am no courtier," Crosbie growled.

"Nonsense," Bougainville said, pleasantly forceful. "You give yourself no credit, Duncan. Clearly Mademoiselle Céleste is enchanted. Even I can see this, so we must assume that duMaine and the Grand'mère are equally as clever. They do not object and that is greatly in your favor. I assume Mademoiselle Céleste is...ah...willing?"

Crosbie smiled abruptly. "Yes," he said quietly.

"Of course. And many a father, Duncan, must settle for a less desirable son-in-law than you would make. Do not be depressed. See it for what it really is. A delay, nothing more. A space of time during which the Sieur duMaine will come to admire and respect you, as your friends already do."

Crosbie snorted lightly. "Louis, you..."

"Listen to me, Duncan," Bougainville insisted. "A man of your years is no sound judge of himself. You were a great gawky boy when you arrived in Quebec, fearful of society, timid with superiors, almost ridiculously aggressive when sensitive honor was affronted. You have grown since coming to Canada. Your mind is beginning to establish control over your great muscles. You have found your way through a really frightening dilemma, which might well have ruined you. You have taken the first painful steps on the road toward becoming a complete human being. It's not a process that ever stops. There is much more ahead of you, Duncan."

Crosbie stared, bewildered by Bougainville's solemn exposition. He had begun to make the transition from boy to man. That much he knew for himself.

"What does it amount to, Louis?" he asked in a voice that strained for a casual tone.

Bougainville looked at him soberly. "Don't think that the Sieur duMaine sees Duncan Crosbie the boy when he looks at you. He knows you as a young officer, an outstanding soldier promoted by the Général he respects above all men. So he sees a man, Duncan. He likes what he sees, as does the Grand-'mère who will have much to say when the question is finally decided. I watched them at dinner tonight. Both of them have noticed the strong attraction between you and Mademoiselle Céleste. And neither disapproves." Bougainville smiled at Crosbie's intent frown. "Think of what I have said. And compel yourself to patience."

"If you say so, Louis," Crosbie said wearily. "I suppose ... it's probably best." He shook himself quickly, trying to throw off the dour depression that darkened his spirit. "When do you leave? Soon?"

"In two or three days," Bougainville said in a normal tone. "It rests with Monsieur Tremais. The frigate is ready now. Tremais will levy his two million franc fine and we will depart. Monsieur Colbert will travel with us, I have heard, so I may be able to discover just what happened in his house that mysterious night last week."

"Colbert? He is going with you? Why?"

"He isn't going with us. He will merely travel on the same ship. There is a difference. And we are not ... compatible, you know. Colbert probably goes to take Bigot's explanation, his defense to the Ministry."

"Bigot's defense," Crosbie muttered. "But when Tremais makes his announcement and assesses the fine, isn't that the end of it?"

Bougainville laughed harshly. "You are naïf, my friend. Tremais holds the King's power in Canada, but in Paris he could be superseded. If the Ministry chooses to intervene, or if Bigot's bribes to Madame de Pompadour are so large that she feels she must do something to earn her profit, then Tremais's decisions may be set aside. It is unlikely, however. Tremais has a firm reputation for probity. I doubt if anyone has ever won a retraction from him. And this fine of two million is only the start, you must understand. Tremais plans to return to Quebec with a horde of competent investigators. His estimate is that Bigot and his coterie have stolen nearly forty-five millions in the past two years."

Crosbie grunted.

"Stupendous, isn't it? No wonder they can afford to buy Pompadour's favor. But the end is in sight, Duncan. I would not give Bigot or the Governor another full year in office."

"I hope you are right," Crosbie said sincerely. "I wish you luck, Louis."

"I will need it. What the future holds for Canada, not God alone could tell. But we will soon be able to live here without thieves in the government. There is a new day coming, Duncan. Wait till next year. We can still save Canada. Bigot and the Governor are actually terrified, you know. They have sent the most beseeching sort of pleas to Paris. The situation is desperate indeed, but it would be helped greatly if we could get rid of Bigot. Then if we can get the troops and equipment we need..."

"Do you really hope..."

"Pray, Duncan," Bougainville said somberly. "Pray very hard. There is still a chance."

CHAPTER FORTY TWO

A wave of panic swept over the colony when the Governor issued a belated announcement of the surrender of Fort duQuesne. The Winter was already well advanced in Canada and everyone had assumed that the English campaign creeping westward across Pennsylvania province had been forced to halt long ago, frozen in the grip of weather. So it was doubly shocking to learn that Brigadier Forbes had pushed on inexorably, denying his own agonizing, mortal illness, driving his men and himself without rest, carving a road through a trackless wilderness and over ruinous mountains, fighting the French scouting parties, their Indian allies, and his own compatriots in Philadelphia who kept him short of every vital necessity. But the sick, dying Brigadier had won through to the fort that commanded the entire Ohio valley. The subsequent surrender came with the sickening shock of lightning smashing down from a clear sky.

No one had expected the French to defend duQuesne against formal attack, but all had believed Forbes had been halted short of his goal. Only later did Canadiens hear of the long months of clever negotiation that Forbes had conducted through his officers and Moravian missionaries to woo the Indian allies from the French. They cajoled, bribed, and bullied; and they won. The hapless few French soldiers had evacuated the fort without a contest.

To Duncan Crosbie, as to every soldier, the news came with numbing impact. The prospect for French control in the New World had never been darker. Of the military position, one could say that the Left had been shattered when the fortress of Louisbourg fell; the Right had nearly been obliterated with the destructive raid on Fort Frontenac and now the loss of duQuesne's commanding position. Only the Center had been held successfully at Carillon. The bastion of Canada remained inviolate. And so did the great province of La Louisiane and the Mississippi valley enclaves that could be supported from the Détroit. But the English were on the Ohio now, and the southern shores of Lake Ontario and Lake Erie would be almost defenseless against them. Oswego, Niagara, Presqu'Isle, Venango, Le Boeuf, and how many other forts were now imperilled? Crosbie listed the positions in his mind. He remembered with a flash of total recollection, the first view he had been given of the French situation. That had been in Bougainville's office when the Général's aide had locked his two hands together, thumbs linked, to illustrate the basic problems. Both of Bougainville's hands had been chopped off, Crosbie thought darkly. Only the linked thumbs remained. The stupidest child could see that only desperate measures could save Canada now.

The past year in America had been bad for the French, the worst in the long tireless contest with England for domination of the New World. But what of Europe, Crosbie wondered; was there encouragement at home to offset American losses? India had been lost more than a year ago when du-Pliex had found the brilliant young Clive too subtle and daring for his limited talents. On the continent of Europe itself, not a single victory marked France's war. Frederick of Prussia, fighting alone against the assembled might of the great nations, supported by English money, had held his own with only minor difficulty. The three female rulers of Europe—Maria Theresa of Austria, Elisabeth of Russia, and Pompadour, actual monarch of France—had hurled their combined armies against the Prussian king time after time, often entrapping his smaller force, sometimes defeating him, but always the elusive, dedicated Frederick had wormed his way free and struck again to scatter his enemies.

In all the world, France could look only at Canada with pride. Of France's générals, Montcalm alone had won. The victory at Carillon against Abercrombie's vastly superior army was the one single triumph France could celebrate.

In the seigneury of Beauport, the defeat at duQuesne had a startling effect. Now, during the Winter, men had time to think and debate in small, hushed groups, growling with bewildered anger. The women seemed universally apprehensive. The war had taken a giant's stride closer to their lives. They saw their children threatened now where before the terrors of battle had been far removed. Everything was different now. The parish church at Beauport was always filled at Mass. In a normal year, the collection of tithes presented a chronic problem, but now the dîmes flowed in with no need for reminders. And in the great manor house that lay high above the village on its snow-shrouded hilltop, the atmosphere was much the same—worried, unbelieving, shocked.

The Sieur duMaine bellowed for his carriage to be mounted on snow-runners and he set off upriver toward Quebec, galloping his magnificent team along the smooth highway afforded by the frozen St. Lawrence.

Céleste and her young sister spent long hours in the ornamental salon of the Grand'mère, and Crosbie saw her rarely, except for mealtimes. The young Scot strapped on a long pair of snow racquets and stalked gloomily around the borders of the seigneury.

He had been assigned a job by the Général and he tried to tell himself that he was inspecting sites of artillery emplacements, but he moved with his head low, seeing little. For once in his self-conscious life, Crosbie was more concerned with another's reactions. All Canada would be thinking of the same man, he thought, speculating whether Montcalm would return to command.

The Général was closely identified with the future of Canada. He had come here less than three years ago to take command after the fumbling Baron Dieskau had been defeated by the English. Then, too, Canada's fortunes had been balanced on a knife-edge. But Montcalm promptly seized the initiative, staving off defeat, driving the English into a defensive posture. It was a determined, personally ambitious Général who had come to Canada, but the years of desperate struggle had somehow altered Montcalm's basic motivation. He was more eager now for victory than ever, but he fought to guard Canada as he would have fought for his home at Candiac, for he had become a part of the New World. Those born in Canada were already developing as a new breed of man, divorced in vital ways from any Frenchman. No man could live among them without feeling the new quality that lived in Canada.

Duncan Crosbie shook his head briskly and turned to stride directly into the hard wind. He was drifting into sentimentality. True, there was a different element that marked the men of Canada but it wasn't without its faults. Much of the blame for Canada's present peril rested squarely with the colonists who refused to defend their homes with their full vigor. Unless these men of the New World fought with Old World fervor, they would never live to enjoy the new wonders of Canada.

As Crosbie stamped along his lonely route, he wished for someone to talk to. Louis Bougainville was now somewhere in a racing frigate bound for Le Hâvre, dodging English men-of-war in the grey, ice-clogged Atlantic. Brother Mathieu was making his fraternal visits at the Détroit, or possibly another post even more removed. He still had Denis, but Denis was a small boy who looked at Crosbie with admiration and utter confidence; misgivings could never be admitted to him. And while the Sieur duMaine was a gentleman of experience and judgment, Crosbie had recently developed a peculiar inability to talk to him openly. Of course, he was trying to make a good impression on Céleste's father, and he therefore tended to avoid controversy whenever he could, and offer his opinion with unusual diffidence when he could not. The bridle on his tongue effectively choked off communication.

But above all the people he knew, just at this moment, Crosbie would rather have had his father available for consultation. Duncan Mohr had lived through a time much like this when he had retreated with his Prince from their most advanced position at Derby to the heather moor of Culloden. Duncan Mohr had tasted defeat; he had lived with defeat, and died in defeat. His counsel would be worth having, for his only son had seen that first dark shadow and he would never again be free in his own mind to dream of victory without remembering this moment.

Crosbie walked himself to trembling exhaustion, his long legs stiffened with the awkward gait enforced by the snow-racquets. And for another two days he walked, restlessly unable to sit quietly. When he was very tired he did not think, and his thoughts had no charm these days.

The Sieur duMaine returned, leading a straggling procession of habitants, torches flaring high in the still cold night. Crosbie heard the exultant din from his bed and he leaped to the window, pulling on his cloak against the freezing blasts that found their way into the snuggest room. When he recognized the carriage, he went promptly toward the fireplace of the salon and heaped a scoop of coals onto the banked fire. The room was pleasantly warm by the time duMaine entered.

Outside, the cheering habitants moved slowly away toward the stable with the carriage.

DuMaine dropped his heavy cloak and kicked off his long fur moccasins. He nodded silently to Crosbie and held his cold-reddened hands to the fire. He turned to present his rear to the blaze and then Crosbie could see the deeply etched lines that forced the solid shoulders into a sagging arc of depression.

Crosbie went into the dining room where he took two glasses and a bottle of cognac from the buffet. DuMaine managed a weary grunt. He stood nursing the tiny glass in one hand, staring blankly at Crosbie.

The young Scot stood waiting. He felt, with a pleasant anticipation, that he knew the reason for the cheering he had heard, but there was an added enjoyment in waiting until duMaine was ready to tell him.

The seigneur's eyes were dull. "He is back," he said in a barely audible tone. "Montcalm has taken command again."

Thank God, Crosbie thought silently. But why did duMaine look at him with that measuring stare, searching for something, and seeming all the sadder for what he saw.

"You, too?" duMaine asked heavily. "You felt that edge of fear too, did you? You wanted someone to protect you. And now you rejoice that a strong man again has command of Canada's future?" DuMaine let himself down wearily into the chair. He sighed from deep within his chest.

"There is something more?" Crosbie asked quietly. "Something I don't have wit enough to see for myself?"

DuMaine shrugged. "Why should you? I have spent the past thirty hours trying to persuade our group, Les Honnêtes Gens, that we should tell Louis-Joseph to stand firm. But even they ..." DuMaine lifted one hand and let it fall in a resigned gesture. "So, we too added our asinine support to the mob. Montcalm understood it was foolish. He, at least, retains a clarity of mind, if no one else does. But the pressure was too great, the panic was too real. Too many men were actually in tears through imagining that the English were but two steps beyond the door. No," duMaine sighed, "there is no reason why you should ..."

"Even now," Crosbie admitted, "I don't understand."

"Fichtre!" duMaine exploded. He swung forward in the chair, his deep fatigue forgotten. His eyes shone with the light of battle. "Everything we have done, my colleagues and I, has been aimed at ridding Canada of the insane thieves who govern us. Vaudreuil and Bigot knew what we were doing and they managed to thwart us at every step. But now! Now we had them! The King knows what it means when a général like Louis-Joseph resigns his command. Montcalm would have been given complete control, if the King had been forced to concede that much to get him back. Montcalm, the only victorious commander of the French army. Why, he could have anything. But not now. Why should the King grant anything when Montcalm has already returned to duty?" DuMaine shrugged and slumped back again in his chair. "So Vaudreuil will remain in his invidious position, able to hamper Louis-Joseph at any time. It will be the ruin of all of us."

"But possibly the King won't know, monsieur," Crosbie suggested. "Until Spring, no ships can ..."

"Pah! Already five messengers have left Quebec to travel overland. They will find some naval vessel skulking from the English in a hidden covert where the ice has not formed too thickly. The King will know before the month is out, certainly before Louis Bougainville is due to return. No, we have been beaten. Louis-Joseph sees this, too. We tried, though. God knows how desperately we tried to make them see reason. And the strange thing was that we had Monsieur Bigot as an ally. He, too, objected to Montcalm resuming command."

"Why?"

"Who knows?" duMaine muttered. "The scoundrel has some scoundrel's motive, but no honest man can fathom his tortuous mind. It is disquieting, though, to find oneself aligned with Bigot on any subject. However, the panicky citizens, even the Governor himself, screamed so loudly that we were drowned out. They prevailed. One would not have been surprised if Vaudreuil had been a little unwilling, since the Chevalier de Lévis who commands in Montcalm's place, is a family connection. But the Governor gave de Lévis no thought whatever. He screamed for Montcalm loudest of all."

"Yes," Crosbie said slowly. "I can see. People are very frightened, monsieur. Merely knowing that Montcalm is back will do much to quiet their fears. And certainly preparations for our next campaign will go better when the people support a commander they respect.

"There is that," duMaine agreed judiciously. "And it is the only point in favor of Montcalm's return. Well, the decision has been made. Now, we should ..."

DuMaine's heavy slow voice dwindled to silence. He cocked his head alertly to one side. Then he smiled, a weary smile that rose wearily to a wide grin. "The girls are coming to welcome their Papá," he said happily. "Let us not mention the grim side of the news, eh? Since everyone else is delighted, let's not spoil their pleasure. They will take it as a present for Christmas, a gift from God, and I suppose it will make for a joyous season."

"Certainly, monsieur," Crosbie said readily. He put his glass down and pushed up to his feet. He turned with duMaine to face the open door.

CHAPTER FORTY THREE

Montcalm's return to command was the Christmas present that all Canada treasured. Earlier fears were abandoned in the merry bustle of preparing for the holiday. The priests lauded the beneficence of a terrible but loving God; the Governor reminded Canadiens of the majesty of Louis XV, and in every home the thought of Montcalm brought ease and confidence.

There was no peace, or any hope of peace in the reasonable future; the overtones of a long and bitter war were everywhere. Hardly a household existed that did not have at least one soldier billeted with the family. And the five francs a day allowance for each soldier that had once been a pleasant little windfall of ready cash was now in many cases the difference between starvation and a bare livelihood. Even among the seigneuries, Beauport's situation was unusually fortunate, with its bulging granaries, storerooms, barns and cellars packed with food enough and to spare for its three hundred people. Basically, farmers fared well in time of famine, but in Canada with the Intendant's guard always searching for surplus food, even a man with his own fields and garden ran the risk of hunger. And for city-folk, the Winter was simply perilous. Every day that passed brought Spring closer, but starvation marched with an equal speed. Flour was now two hundred francs the barrel whenever it was offered for sale. Most of the cattle and many of the horses had gone for food. Generally people lived on stores of salt cod, eked out with meagre additions from the King's stores. These rations, purchased by the King through his Intendant, were meant to be furnished at no cost, but Monsieur Bigot could never forego a possible profit. Large quantities were smuggled from his warehouses and sold illegally throughout Canda, still in containers clearly marked with the King's cipher. The great storehouse in Quebec was universally called La Friponne—The Cheat—by every hungry citizen of the town.

No ships would arrive with supplies from France until the ice went out of the river. The birds and the fish would return no earlier. No game larger than an occasional hare had been seen for many weeks within a day's march of Quebec.

But Christmas came as a joyous season. Families dug into their dwindling stores for feasts that would surely mean hunger in the future. Fifty people might dine in regal splendor each night at the Intendant's Palace, the Chevalier de Lévis might give bi-weekly balls that rivalled the magnificence of Versailles, but a Christmas feast for most Canadiens required the ultimate expenditure of ingenuity and resources. French officers in the junior ranks found their pay too little to buy food and they formed the pleasant habit of walking or riding through the countryside to present themselves as amiable dinner guests wherever they were welcomed. It was these gentlemen who brought home to Duncan Crosbie the meaning of hunger. All of them were men of some worth as men are reckoned; some were wealthy when they were in France; most were of the minor nobility, petits-maîtres who found army life preferable to stagnation on crowded, provincial estates. But all of them during that hard Winter were reduced to such miserable tricks merely to obtain a decent meal. Not one blamed his King. All spoke warmly of Montcalm. But the growing hatred and contempt for the Governor and his thieving Intendant had by Christmastime reached a peak of fury that none troubled to hide. Public announcement of Tremais's heavy fine did little to lower Bigot's prestige; it was already at the lowest possible point. Very commonly, the ritualistic toast to the King's health was followed by one calling confusion upon the heads of Vaudreuil and Bigot.

But Christmas was a merry season. How the Canadiens managed to rise to such a celebration, Duncan Crosbie could not fathom, but his admiration grew as he watched.

Beauport was the center of a constant round of visits and parties. The habitants of the parish found nothing objectionable in the Sieur duMaine's modest display. It was accepted that a grand seigneur would live in a world removed from the petty vicissitudes of his tenants, and they took a certain pride in knowing that Beauport stood firmly among the great seigneuries of Canada. But Beauport's people had food. It might have been very different, Crosbie realized, if starvation had seemed imminent.

Christmas Day arrived after a stormy night full of blowing snow. The slate-grey morning sky lightened with the sun and on Beauport's hill, the bright unearthly sound of the children's choir rose in soft brilliance.

"Noël nouvelet, Noël chantons ici;
Dévotes gens, crions à Dieu merci,
Chantons Noël pour le Roi nouvelet,
Noël nouvelet, Noël chantons ici!"

From the gaily decked salon of the manor house came the thin piping tones of the seigneur's youngest daughter and Denis, softly singing along with the choristers. Crosbie walked lightly to the doorway and peered inside.

The salon was a blaze of color, with silken ribbons and gold and silver decorations. A miniature crèche with the Magi grouped around it, stood in the center of the chimney piece, with a billowing canopy of pale silk gauze above it. Aimée sat beside the boy, their heads together as they sang, almost to themselves, keeping reasonable unison with the faint, muted notes of the village singers. Small gilded sabots, empty now, lay abandoned beside them, and each held a double handful of sweetmeats and decorated cookies. But the gift, the modern reminder of the first gifts brought to the Child, was carefully placed aside, still wrapped and be-rib-boned. This would be opened only when the family was present.

Crosbie leaned in the doorway, anxious not to disturb the children, but unwilling to move away. There was nothing quite like a Christmas morning to bring one's childhood flooding back to the mind. Every sentimental memory, long buried, wells from a forgotten reservoir and even the oldest man feels at least a minor twinge. The delicious agony of anticipation is never quite duplicated at any other time.

A slim hand touched Crosbie's arm and he turned, eyes blank with memory. He smiled vaguely at Céleste, then more warmly as alertness returned.

"The children?" she asked in a whisper.

Crosbie nodded. He took her arm and walked into the dining room. The long table was laid for breakfast and pitchers of cider and milk, loaves of bread and bottles of the seigneur's favorite white wine were spaced amongst the plates. Crosbie slid the doors half shut behind them.

"I didn't want to …" He made a vague gesture, indicating the salon.

"I know," Céleste said softly. "I used to watch them on Christmas morning. Such a wonderful time for children. And you, Duncan, were you remembering a smaller Duncan?"

Crosbie grinned, bending so that his lips touched her gleaming dark hair. "I never could sing very well."

She laughed quietly, deep in her throat, and moved closer to him. She raised her lips to be kissed and he bent lower. They clung together, body seeking body under the clothes, a surge of excitement in their blood. Her breasts were pressed flat against his chest and he could feel the wild pounding beat of her heart.

"Oh, Duncan," she gasped. "Oh, my darling, bon jour de Noël, my dear."

"May it be a good day," Crosbie murmured.

They kissed again, urgently, their eyes closed against a blinding brightness, moving for that brief moment into a private, hidden world.

Céleste pushed herself away, both hands moving up instinctively to adjust her hair.

Crosbie drew in a long, decisive breath. For weeks now, they had been alone for only a few minutes at a time. And he had done his best, he assured himself, done his very best to control the swift passion that leaped into furious demanding life whenever he touched Céleste. And he had tried to make an amiable impression on the Sieur duMaine. It wasn't likely that additional time would alter that impression. Why not put it to the test? Today. Christmas should be the perfect day. Even the crustiest father melts with sentiment for his family on Christmas Day.

"Duncan, what makes your eyes shine so fiercely?" Céleste whispered. "Do you..."

Crosbie stepped back warily in a quick lithe stride, glancing over Céleste's dark head. "Good morning, monsieur," he said, bowing slightly.

"Ah, monsieur, bon jour de Noël," duMaine rumbled. He patted Céleste absently on the shoulder. "My dear, you run and help the Grand'mère. She insists on joining us for breakfast. Hurry. We must not be late this morning."

Céleste kissed her father's cheek in a fleeting caress and turned toward the open door.

DuMaine poured wine. He held a glass toward the young Scot.

Silently they sipped and silently they smiled the vacant meaningless morning smiles of men engrossed in serious thought. Now? Crosbie wondered. No, not just yet. The seigneur's sombre expression seemed to indicate an inward focus that Crosbie did not want to break. DuMaine's normally exuberant, almost boisterous behavior was altered to a quiet distraction, as if Christmas demanded a solemn reverence of demeanour. And the seigneur's absent-minded attitude endured throughout breakfast, despite the bright, excited conversation of the aged Grand'mère who was making an early appearance for the first time that year. The blithe, lighthearted chirping of her thin voice rose like birdsong in the quiet room. But eventually even she began to feel the oppressive weight of duMaine's sobriety.

"Raoul," she asked softly, "you are not well?"

DuMaine glanced up quickly, blinking his eyes. He glanced briefly at Crosbie, then forced a thin smile to his tense lips. "No, no," he said gruffly, "I am very well. I was... thinking..."

"You were thinking most of the night," the Grand'mère said with some asperity. "If it was your footsteps I heard..."

DuMaine shrugged. He broke off a piece of crusty bread and slowly crumbled it to bits in his thick fingers. "I was thinking," he repeated stolidly. "This is the season for thinking. It came to my mind that no man can look forward with confidence to..." His heavy, dull voice died away for a moment. "People do not develop as one might expect. As one might hope." He shrugged again, his thick shoulders moving with resignation.

DuMaine's mother reached out to pat her son's hand gently. "It is time for the carriage, Raoul. We must not be late."

"Yes," duMaine agreed.

He escorted his party to the waiting carriage and directed the coachman to the village. The children drove ahead in a covered pony-cart mounted on runners. During the brief journey, no one spoke. Céleste pretended a deep interest in her ivory-bound breviary. The Grand'mère perched bird-like on the forward seat, her tiny hand nestled in the crook of duMaine's arm, her bright eyes contemplating Crosbie with an amused intensity.

Even the vociferous gaiety of the habitants outside the church did nothing to lighten duMaine's spirits. He settled his group in their proper places and dropped wearily beside them, staring blindly forward, not even stirring when the choir filed in.

DuMaine's sombre reverie infected Crosbie with uneasy concern. That brief moment of determination he had felt early was gone now and the young Scot no longer felt sure that this would be a good day to trouble the seigneur with personal matters. He sat rigidly attentive to the curé, trying to ignore the warmth and soft pressure of Céleste's body beside him.

Possibly Bougainville's advice was best, after all. Advice from mature men of sound judgment could certainly be followed without loss of self-respect, he told himself. He drifted into vague, colorful imaginings of a world that would be based upon Céleste, how they would live, and where. Would she greatly mind leaving Canada? No soldier could be sure where his duty would take him. Possibly she...

"Dominus vobiscum ... Et cum spiritu tuo ..."

Crosbie put away the happy speculations and knelt beside duMaine, seeing the seigneur remained lost in his mournful dreams. The small church seemed suddenly cold and damp.

"Qui tollis peccata mundi ..."

Céleste brushed against his arm and the young Scot's tension left him in a swift rise of confidence. The future wasn't blighted merely because the Sieur duMaine was sorrowful on Christmas morning. There would be other days.

"Miserere nobis ..."

This was not a proper moment for worrying at one's personal problems. Surely a man might, on this Day, devote his thoughts to wider concerns; adopt, if only for a brief moment, the selfless outlook of a true Christian. Crosbie rebuked himself mentally in severe terms, not realizing that his arm had moved closer to rest firmly against Céleste's. He would concentrate on his friends, and wish them well in the coming year.

"Ita missa est ..."

Bougainville, for example, battered by a Winter sea, eager for the first sight of France. And surely dreading the moment when he would present himself to the Ministry to begin the mission that might determine the future of Canada. With so much on his shoulders, Bougainville would surely welcome the good wishes, the prayers, of his friends.

And Montcalm. He must be kneeling now, knowing that when he rose, Canada would rise with him. Whatever came to Montcalm this year would come to Canada, and that knowledge would long since have destroyed a lesser man.

"Deo gratias..."

They rose from their prayers, surprising Crosbie whose mind was still on Montcalm. He struggled to get his long legs unwound. The Grand'mère moved briskly into the aisle, passing duMaine with a brief warm pat on his cheek. Céleste followed and Crosbie trailed her, wondering at duMaine who sat unmoving.

The curé met them near the door, bowing low over the Grand'mère's hand. He assisted the ladies into the carriage while Crosbie herded Denis and Aimée into their pony cart. When Crosbie climbed into the carriage and sat beside Céleste, the footman swung the door closed and signalled the driver.

"But your father..." Crosbie began.

Céleste touched his hand quickly. "Papá remains," she said quietly. "He always remains on Christmas Day."

Crosbie nodded, not understanding. He glanced across at the tiny figure of the Grand'mère who was watching him tightly, her small bright eyes sparkling now with unshed tears.

"It was on Christmas," the old lady said tiredly, "on Christmas morning as we left for church that Raoul was told about his son."

His son, Crosbie thought. The rapscallion boy who had been caught in some scandal and had killed himself. That was a fine present for Christmas, wasn't it? No wonder duMaine had to force himself to speak at all. No wonder his mind dwelt upon the subject of young men who never developed as their parents had hoped. His own son. And he had been gazing steadily at Crosbie all the time he spoke. And thinking... what?

"I'm sorry," Crosbie said heavily. And thank God, he thought, that I didn't approach duMaine this morning. Even if he has a moderate opinion of me, he would dislike me today, possibly even hate me because I'm alive and here, with some prospects, while his son has been buried in unhallowed ground in some remote outpost, disgraced and betrayed.

Duncan Crosbie shivered. The high brilliant tones of children's laughter sounded like thin mockery in the still clear morning.

CHAPTER FORTY FOUR

Tranquility and a degree of gaiety returned gradually to Beauport, for duMaine was not a man who could long remain quiet or sorrowful. His natural high spirits were clearly in evidence by the turn of the year, on le jour de l'an, when the ignoleux came to serenade the manor house, and the rooms were crammed to overflowing with the noisy, dancing crowds of friends who streamed through all day long. As Christmas had been the solemn religious celebration restricted to the family circle, New Year's Day was for friends, and it was full of bustle and roaring good feeling.

Duncan Crosbie determined not to approach Celeste's father until he could be sure the result would be favorable, for if he were refused, he would feel compelled to leave Beauport and that prospect was too disturbing to consider.

This day was the time for gifts, and Crosbie had spent the few louis d'or he still possessed. The cut-steel buckles given to Denis were probably his greatest success, he suspected, but the major sum had gone for a magnificently illustrated volume of La Fontaine's animal fables. This had been designed for Céleste, but at the last moment, Crosbie wisely reconsidered, for the book was obviously too valuable for a casual token on the jour de l'an. Instead, he presented it to the Grand'mère, seeing in the old lady's twinkling eyes that she understood him exactly. Candies for Aimée, a box of fine Brazilian snuff for the seigneur, and a tiny silver pin shaped like a rosebud for Céleste. The silver rose was also a trifle too personal, perhaps, but the seigneur offered no objection.

DuMaine presented Denis with a doeskin shirt embroidered by the Hurons with fantastic designs. And his gift of an emerald ring to Céleste so outshadowed Crosbie's that everyone was put in an excellent humor. But his present to Crosbie was so magnificent that the young Scot felt a momentary suspicion—and elation. For such a present surely carried a meaning beyond its mere value in money. It was a long polished wooden case that had once contained a matched pair of pistols, complete with all the tools needed for molding perfect bullets. Only one silver-butted pistol remained in the case; the other cavity in the pale velvet lining was empty.

"My son," duMaine said in a forcibly cheerful tone, "took only one pistol with him. I regret the set is incomplete, but ..."

"It is ... splendid," Crosbie said slowly. He lifted the long pistol from its case. It was even finer than he had realized. He could see the blunt serration of raised lands inside the double barrels. This, then, was one of the rare rifled pistols, a ruinously expensive weapon that many senior officers could not afford to own. With it, he could fire two shots at a target beyond musket range and be sure of two perfect hits. He eased back the curled hammers and tested the trigger pull. "I ... I've never had such a ..."

DuMaine's heavy hand slammed between his shoulder-blades. "It is a good pistol," he growled. "A soldier should own it. And you will do it justice, I know." He hurried out to greet another carriage-load of guests that had swept up the long hill from the village.

Crosbie replaced the pistol in its case and shut the lid carefully. His big hand trembled slightly. He glanced up at Céleste.

Celeste turned to pick up a small packet from the table. "For your safety," she whispered, "with my love, Duncan."

A thin silver medallion dangled from a frail chain. Crosbie held it high to see the device. On the medal, lightning streaks crashed about a tower where a frightened girl was imprisoned. Storm lashed the shoreline below. Crosbie smiled grimly. He slipped the chain over his head and slipped the medal down under his collar.

"Sainte Barbara," he said quietly. "You know about artillery-men, do you?"

"Only you, Duncan," she smiled. "It is your patron saint, isn't it?"

Crosbie nodded and his gaunt face softened into a slow smile. "She was imprisoned by her pagan father. The storm was sent to avenge her. So Barbara has become Saint of the tempest, and Saint of all gunners. She will protect me well."

Céleste smiled, a wisely secret smile. The new arrivals spilled noisily into the salon and all privacy was shattered in the merry confusion.

During a brief hiatus between guests, duMaine drew Crosbie aside, handing him a folded paper.

"Monsieur de Borgia was kind enough to bring this," he smiled. "It must be your invitation to Louis-Joseph's ball. I have received mine. It will be a great occasion."

Crosbie cracked the seal and flipped the paper open. His Excellency, the Marquis de Montcalm-Gozon de Saint Véran beseeched the pleasure of Monsieur le brevet-capitaine Duncan Crosbie...

An addendum in a broad, clear hand filled the lower corner and Crosbie's gaze skipped down.

"Present yourself at my appartement one hour early." The scribbled "M" below was signature enough. Crosbie folded the paper again and tried to smile casually.

"I'm not much of a dancer," he sighed. "And that's the firm truth. I can't even manage a gigue voleuse."

DuMaine chuckled happily. "You have damned yourself, my boy," he bellowed. "You're ruined, utterly. I cannot dance well, either, but I will never confess it. You will soon learn that nothing delights the ladies more than prodding a clumsy fellow through the intricacies of the dance. Céleste!"

DuMaine wheeled away abruptly, seizing Celeste's arm and bending to whisper hoarsely in her ear. Céleste glanced up and Crosbie saw her grin wickedly, imps of mischief dancing in her eyes.

The remainder of that day, and long hours of subsequent days were devoted to Crosbie's instruction. New arrivals were enchanted with the awkward young victim. Such a splendid clumsy sight he was, much like a waltzing bear, and how comical he was lurching through the lightsome pattern of l'harle-quinade.

A stately minuet was easily within reach of any man with poise enough to stand erect. But le chinoise or la matelote demanded rigid training, a sure ear for rhythm and precise balance. Duncan Crosbie abandoned his efforts a dozen times each hour. But Céleste or one of her laughing friends dragged him in red confusion to the center again. Someone tinkled at the upright harp or kept time with the violin while Crosbie was pulled and hauled through the figures of the dance.

A month earlier, Crosbie would have been in a blind rage, eager to fight the first grinning man he saw. Even now he had to keep his mouth clamped hard, but self-control was no longer so difficult. He even managed a shrug of secret resignation for Denis who stared pop-eyed at him in unbelieving wonderment.

"Au clair de la lune,
Mon ami Pierrot,"

An accomplished musician had taken the chair at the harp and the salon's attention was mercifully diverted from Crosbie's clumsy dancing. The young Scot sank gratefully to a couch beside Céleste.

"I'm hardly a Pierrot," he complained softly, touching a handkerchief to his damp forehead.

Céleste patted his hand swiftly, her full lips pinched in to stifle the laughter that stared brightly from her eyes.

"You are reprieved," she whispered. "Until later. Now give attention. Monsieur de Borgia is a splendid harpist."

CHAPTER FORTY FIVE

Duncan Crosbie sprinted across the wind-swept square of St. Louis, holding his tricorne in place with one hand, using his left to keep his small sword from tripping him up as he ran. He slowed to a stop beside the sentries at the Château and adjusted his dress uniform.

He threw back his cloak and marched stiffly in through the main entrance, confident that no man could challenge his right to be there. The last time he had entered the Château, there had been a warrant outstanding and he had been fair game for anyone. But since then he had been vindicated, the warrant withdrawn. Now as a King's officer and aide to the commanding général, not even the Governor could offend him with impunity.

In the Général's anteroom, Crosbie slipped off his cloak and draped it over a chair. He clamped his cocked hat under his left elbow. A quick glance in the mirror assured him that his powdered hair lay in proper smoothness. He waited for the orderly to signal.

Stiffly he went through the doorway. The Général was lying sprawled in a chair, his head bent unnaturally far back, chin tilted to meet Jeannot's razor that slid crisply along his exposed throat. Crosbie stamped with precision to a position in front of the Général and swept his hat low to the floor in salute.

"Be at ease, monsieur," Montcalm muttered, his voice distorted by his constricted throat. "On the buffet is something to drink. Please serve yourself. Hurry, Jeannot, I cannot..."

The Général's voice dwindled as Jeannot tweaked his nose aside and scraped swiftly down his upper lip. A few deft strokes, a swipe with a drenched napkin, a quick pat of powder, and Jeannot stepped back. "The poll, mon général?" he asked quietly.

Montcalm patted his hand against the top of his head several times to judge the length of the dense black stubble that lay smooth as a beaver's pelt. Then he smiled with evident relief. "Another week or so, Jeannot," he said pleasantly. He held his arms high as the servant slipped a voluminous frilled shirt over his head and slipped around behind him to tuck in the tails and lace the waistband of his black breeches.

The Général would be all in black tonight, Crosbie noted. A black velvet coat laced with silver hung outside the armoire, and Jeannot was already helping Montcalm into a tight black silk waistcoat with a long row of diamond-and-onyx buttons. Fine black silk hose were pulled tight and Jeannot's quick fingers cinched the diamond knee buckles. He knelt to clip diamond-mounted buckles onto Montcalm's black shoes. All that destroyed the black-and-white unity were the red-lacquered heels of the Général's shoes, but those heels were restricted by official fiat to the nobility, and any man whose position warranted red heels wore them no matter how unsuitable they might be. Montcalm adjusted the silver-lace spill at his throat, pulled down the lace cuffs at each wrist. He waved away the coat Jeannot was holding ready.

"Not yet, Jeannot," he murmured. "That coat is death's own weight. Get me a glass of wine first."

Montcalm accepted a glass from Jeannot and lifted it, inclining politely toward Crosbie.

"À votre santé, monsieur."

Crosbie bowed. Montcalm has lost weight, he thought casually. The lines were deeper around his eyes and mouth. And no wonder.

The Général put down his glass and smiled thinly at Crosbie.

"You are looking very well, Monsieur Crosbie," he said amiably. "The holiday season is gay at Beauport?"

"Very much so, mon général," Crosbie agreed stiffly.

"I wish I might have..." Montcalm lifted one hand and let it fall. "Well..." He drew in a slow breath. "Tonight I will receive my guests in the ballroom with my staff officers ranked behind me. It will be an official occasion, you realize. When all the guests have arrived, the staff will be free to join the dancing."

Montcalm let out his breath in a faint sigh. "But not you, monsieur."

Crosbie lifted his chin. "Sir?" His voice was quiet, inquiring rather than challenging.

Montcalm shrugged. "Pour yourself a glass of wine, young man," he said pleasantly. "And a taste for me."

Crosbie put down his hat and reached for the decanter. He filled two glasses and carried one to the Général.

"Tonight I am making a gesture," Montcalm said lightly. "Certain... officials... will be displeased to see you standing with me. But those... gentlemen must learn that I will not be subject to their whims." He lifted his glass and sniffed the bouquet lightly. "However, I have no wish to offer open insult, so you will depart from the ballroom at the earliest moment. I will not explain my attitude to these... officials, but I felt you warranted an explanation. I am not displeased with you... not very much," he amended with a faint smile, "but I cannot..."

"I understand, mon général," Crosbie broke in abruptly.

"Possibly you do," Montcalm said mildly. "I hope so. This is the sort of problem I usually assign to my good Louis. I am rather lost without him."

"We all miss him, sir," Crosbie agreed.

"Yes." Montcalm sighed heavily. "Ah, well. You understand, do you?"

"Yes, sir," Crosbie said firmly. He raised his glass high. "Vive notre Général," he chanted in a quiet, steady tone.

Montcalm flushed slightly. Then he threw back his head and roared abruptly with heavy laughter that rumbled hard in his throat. "You … you …" he choked briefly. He leaned on the table to steady himself. "For a moment I almost thought Bougainville had returned. This is just the sort of ridiculous …" Montcalm gestured vaguely. He lifted his glass and sipped from his slowly, rolling the wine over his tongue, staring absently at a dark corner of the room.

How very alike they are, Crosbie thought suddenly. They might almost be brothers, Montcalm and Bougainville. They even look much the same, both stocky and solid, with full muscular faces. The Général was a volatile Languedocian, while Bougainville had the sure subtlety of a born Parisien, but the difference was more one of comportment than temperament. It must be that strange mutuality that made Bougainville so valuable to Montcalm, so much so that the Général could even trust him to find a wife for his eldest son.

Something of his thoughts must have shown in his face, for Montcalm glanced at him sharply, then asked, "Louis has told you of my attitude toward Raoul duMaine and his …"

"Yes, sir." Crosbie put down his empty glass and drew his shoulders squarely back.

"And how does it go? This waiting?"

"Not too badly, mon général. Probably it is best, I have come to think. If the Sieur duMaine comes gradually to accept …"

"Yes," Montcalm said sharply. "Yes, that would be best. You will remain there until the next campaign, at least. Take all that time, monsieur. Then come to me again and we will see. I know this is hard for you to accept, but … well, do not despair, eh?"

"Never, mon général."

"Splendid! Now go wait with my other young gentlemen in the ballroom. I will be down shortly. Oh, yes, another thing."

"Sir?"

"Captain Johnstone, a countryman of yours, is giving a small dinner party tonight. He wants you to attend, if it is convenient."

Crosbie laughed. He clamped his hat with his elbow and chuckled at the Général's quizzical expression.

"It will be convenient, mon général," he said. "Thank you. Luckily I find myself at liberty this evening."

"Luckily," Montcalm agreed with a broad smile. He nodded as Crosbie bowed himself from the room.

In the interim of delay, fidgetting in the chilly ballroom with the rest of the staff, Crosbie wondered whether the dinner party that Johnstone was giving had actually been planned by Johnstone—or Montcalm. A new facet of Montcalm's personality had been briefly glimpsed and Crosbie realized that the Général might very well have arranged with Johnstone to organize such a party merely to save Crosbie further embarrassment. An invitation to Montcalm's ball was probably the most avidly sought-after item in the long brilliant season. Merely to be present was a high compliment and Crosbie understood that Montcalm was ignoring wise counsel when he invited Crosbie to attend with the staff. He would not be allowed to mingle with the guests, but Crosbie had wit enough to see that the restriction was as much for his protection as any other's. As the Général had said, it was a compromise that would gratify no one. Crosbie was determined to show no least sign of displeasure. The Général had complimented him. Let it go at that.

Behind him the purple curtains of the musician's gallery were drawn aside and the orchestra struck up softly. Servants padded through the immense ballroom of the Château, building up the fires that did little to warm the vast room. Hundreds of long white tapers blazed from crystal-and-gilt chandeliers over-head and long ranks of fragile chairs had been pushed into place along the walls. Tables draped in embroidered linen were being loaded with dozens of bottles, hundreds of glasses, for casual refreshment. Beside Crosbie, the wizened face of Estére smiled up, distorted by a huge mouthful of pastry the secretary had snatched from a table in the dining room. Estére choked down his pastry just as the Général entered through the wide doorway. Staff officers bowed in rigid precision and Montcalm smiled, lifting a casual hand.

"Not so grim, gentlemen," he said. "The ordeal will be brief."

The Général posted himself two strides forward of his staff just as the first guests came through the entrance. A chamberlain bellowed names that soon began to blur in Crosbie's mind. With the staff, he bowed incessantly to the lords and ladies of Canada, his eyes looking but not seeing the bold eyes and bare shoulders of the ladies, or the exquisite coats, the sparkling decorations, the red-rimmed, jaundiced eyes of the gentlemen who were excessively weary after a long and tiring social season. The bright jewels and dazzling smiles grew dim and indistinct, and Crosbie went through his polite motions like a puppet, disinterested and unthinking. The Général's list had been limited to the élite, obviously, but Canada had hell's own amount of élite, Crosbie realized.

Only Céleste's arrival brought his blurring vision into focus again. She was enchanting, Crosbie thought. By far the most radiantly beautiful woman present. Her pale shoulders rose warm and marble-smooth from a cup of emerald velvet. Crosbie winked over Montcalm's shoulder and fought to keep from grinning as he noticed Céleste flush rosily. The added color heightened her beauty noticeably and Montcalm lingered a trifle longer over her hand than duty required. The Sieur du-Maine paused for a word with the Général, then escorted Céleste down the ballroom.

The orchestra sounded particularly fine to Crosbie now and for a brief, over-confident moment, he felt sure that he would have cut an admirable figure if he had been allowed to ask Céleste to dance. Not that he was adept, but he could have managed well enough to justify staying so close to Céleste. He nudged Estére and bent to whisper in his ear.

"Will you seek out Mademoiselle duMaine afterward and tell her the Général has sent me on an errand? I may not return in time to dance. Will you tell her?"

"While we are dancing," Estére whispered, "I may mention you in passing. Very briefly." The wizened little man cocked an eyebrow comically and gazed blandly at the ceiling.

Crosbie submerged the sudden urge to kick him. He bowed again and again, letting the sightless glaze settle again over his eyes, seeing people as targets for bowing, nothing more.

His Excellency, Monsieur l'Intendant was announced with a blare from the chamberlain that brought even Crosbie to attention. The ballroom was almost quiet as Monsieur Bigot led his magnificent sister toward Montcalm. The Comtesse was at her finest in Bourbon white and gold that set off her bold beauty to perfection. She swept low in a curtsey to the Général, took his hand to rise and lifted her eyes, staring directly at Crosbie. Her gasp was controlled quickly, but no one near her could have missed it.

The Intendant bowed in frigid response to Montcalm's greeting. He held out his arm for his sister's hand.

"The Général has a well-deserved reputation for audacity," he said in a harsh voice. His eyes passed smoothly along the faces of Montcalm's staff. He moved away with his sister and Estére let out a soft sighing breath.

Only a few guests were impolite enough to arrive after the Intendant, but all were careful to come inside before the King's Governor entered the ballroom. Officially, the Marquis de Vaudreuil was the King in Canada, and his appearance was officially the beginning moment of the ball. Montcalm bent low in final greeting, kissing the hand of the Governor's lady with obvious pleasure. More because she was the last, Crosbie suspected, than any joy Montcalm found in her peevish expression. The young Scot bent with the others, equally relieved. This infernal bowing was actually fatiguing, if carried to extremes.

Montcalm reached back and tapped Crosbie's arm. Crosbie inclined forward.

"You may leave now, monsieur," the Général said softly. "You will find Monsieur Johnstone in the Chevalier de Lévis's quarters."

"Very good, Excellency," Crosbie murmured. "Good night."

Montcalm nodded. He stepped forward politely, offering his arm to the Governor's lady. As the Général moved away, Crosbie slipped from the rank of staff officers and turned quickly through the open door, sure that no one had noticed his departure while Montcalm was leading his procession down the length of the ballroom.

Crosbie passed the state dining room and stepped briefly inside to snatch a cold squab from a huge platter. Chewing hungrily, he climbed the stairs, threading through narrow corridors, pausing twice to get new directions from sentries posted along the route. He dropped the stripped carcase of the fowl into a flowerpot and rapped briskly on a closed door.

A servant opened and bowed him inside. The young Scot strode briskly forward. A sudden uproar blasted from the inner room, a shouting, raucous chorus bellowed in ragged unison. Crosbie entered a wide, half-furnished room that contained little more than a vast dining table and a considerable number of mismatched chairs, all of them occupied.

"Duncan, my boy! Welcome!"

Johnstone, his thin face flushed to a bright scarlet from wine, heaved himself unsteadily to his feet, propping himself with one hand on the polished table, stretching the other toward Crosbie. The young Scot took his hand silently, smiling.

"Gentlemen!" Johnstone shouted. He banged the table with a heavy-based decanter. "Gentlemen! Pray silence!" Twice more he pounded the table, bellowing for attention.

Crosbie glanced along the circle of reddened faces, holding a stiff and awkward smile on his lips. The company stretched the gamut of commissioned rank from an elderly colonel to a downy-cheeked subaltern, whose eyes stared glassily with drunkenness. But all of them had a superficial similarity, something rather like a family resemblance, which was disconcerting to Crosbie.

Slowly, the noisy table quieted for Johnstone, who proceeded to identify them. But the names! Crosbie blinked with mild surprise.

Dillon. MacDonald. Murray. Fenwick. Chisholm. Gordon. Ewen. Casey, Llewellyn. O'Roark. MacBean. MacGillivray. Another MacDonald. And still another. Names that lived in Ireland, Wales, Scotland, those fiercely independent lands now forcibly united with the English.

"Brevet-Captain Duncan Crosbie," Johnstone announced, flourishing his hand vaguely under Crosbie's nose. "And who here will say that Duncan Mohr died at Culloden?"

An approving bellow soared amiably from the guests. A stoop-shouldered captain of infantry with a great unpowdered mop of brindled hair falling into his eyes lurched from his seat and stumbled forward to seize Crosbie's arm. Red-rimmed eyes glared hotly at Crosbie. "By Heaven, Jamie, you are right. The very image, isn't he?" The captain pulled a chair to the table for Crosbie and then dropped heavily down beside him.

Crosbie swallowed heavily. "You ... you knew him?"

"Knew him? I should say I knew him! Oh, I was only a lad, then, not one of the four champions, but I was with Alasdair when he came to Borradale to welcome the Prince to Scotland. Standing beside that boy Prince was Duncan Mohr. Aye, Duncan Mohr was a man, my boy. You've the look, I'll not deny, and the size, but something lacks, nothing much, but something lived in Duncan Mohr that mortal man does not command by size or strength or even bravery. He was ..."

Johnstone leaned far over the table, resting his elbow on the board, propping his head on his hand and beaming at Crosbie. "Captain MacGillivray wears the white cockade which the Prince himself gave him after Prestonpans, Duncan. Do not be misled by false modesty."

The red-faced captain flushed to a high scarlet, then laughed in a brisk light tenor that crackled like musketry in the distance. "Ah, we were all heroes then, Jamie. Not weary pensioners, eh? Prestonpans was our first battle for Charlie. Duncan Mohr carried him through the surf from the duTellier and the clans rallied to him. What a time that was, eh, Jamie?"

"There was Culloden." Johnstone insisted. "They died there, the champions and the men who followed them. Alasdair, Gillies MacBean, Keppoch and Scothouse..."

"But not The Boy..." MacGillivray said soberly.

"Thanks to Duncan Mohr," Johnstone agreed. "The Prince charged, and his tartan coat and the white cockade on his blue bonnet made him a prime target. But Duncan Mohr caught him as his horse was shot and this last of The Prince's champions carried The Boy from the field, fighting through a ring of Hessians. There were seven great wounds spouting his life's blood onto Scotland's soil, but Duncan Mohr lived to carry Tearlach to safety before he died."

MacGillivray sighed heavily, turning his shaggy head to look at the cluster of drunken roisterers about the table.

"I wonder what we are doing here, Jamie," he growled in a thick tone. "We should be in church this moment, asking forgiveness that we have lived when such men are dead. I cannot..." He slashed his hand viciously through the air. "I have no heart for this. By your leave, Jamie."

MacGillivray struggled unsteadily to his feet. His maimed hand rested hard on Crosbie's shoulder.

"The ghosts are standing at your shoulder tonight, young Duncan. You should not be buried here with these lost men and their memories." His hand pressed on Crosbie's shoulder. Then the shock-headed captain turned abruptly and almost ran, stumbling, from the room.

"Poor Gordie," Johnstone said with alcoholic intensity. "The old days ... the old ..."

"All ... all these gentlemen are ..." Crosbie gestured at the revellers around Johnstone's table.

"Most of them served with The Prince. After Culloden, we ran from Scotland, those of us who could run. The ones Cumberland caught, he hung in London. They were drawn and quartered and their heads mounted on the city's walls. We went to France, most of us. The Prince was in France, and Louis was hospitable, at first. So ..." Johnstone smiled and shrugged in light dismissal. "We come together sometimes and we are Scots again and we curse the English and then we go back to our empty lives again."

Crosbie toyed with a crumpled white satin cockade that lay on the table before MacGillivray's chair.

"Do you still ... hope?" he asked in a voice that sounded hollow to his ears.

"We still hope," Johnstone said softly. "Hope ... and dream."

"It was Culloden," Crosbie said abruptly, "that made me choose to serve in the artillery. There was not a single gunner with the entire Scottish army," Crosbie went on. "I read all the reports and some gentlemen who had lived through the '45 told me about it when I was a boy. How the clans were shattered before they could come to grips with Cumberland and his Hessians. So, I ..."

"Of course, of course," Johnstone smiled. "But there was more to it than just guns, my boy. We might have won if we had been given a little time to rest, and food enough for our men. God, what we might have done, if ..."

Inwardly, Crosbie shrugged. Johnstone was beyond reach. This gathering was a wailing session for lost glories. No breath of cold reality could pierce the romantic barricades in such a mind. Crosbie stared at Johnstone, his young gaunt face held impassive. This man, he thought, had actually been there. He had seen and endured that awful day at Culloden. And all it taught him was...a dream. There was more to be learned, for a man with eyes to see honestly. Culloden had been the end of primitive warfare.

Crosbie reached for the nearest decanter, filling his glass again and offering the bottle to Johnstone. A slim, long-fingered hand stretched over his shoulder to intercept it.

"I'll just have a taste of that," a hard flat voice said briskly. "To toast your King, Jamie, and to ..."

Crosbie twisted sharply in his chair, glaring over his shoulder. His instantaneous anger was no more complete than O'Neill's surprise.

The Irish captain stepped swiftly back, the long-necked decanter forgotten in his hand. After a frozen moment, he turned to Johnstone, his face tight with strain, but with no tinge of emotion in his low, uninflected voice.

"Damn you, Johnstone," he said. "Why did you invite me if you knew ..."

Slowly Crosbie rose from his chair. One broad thumb slid to touch the Crosbie signet imbedded in the hilt of his dirk.

"You'll mind your tongue here, sir," he said quietly. "If you think you've any quarrel with me, we'll settle it decently. Do you wish to call me out, captain?"

The young Scot bent forward at the waist, bringing his truculent scowl closer to O'Neill's calm, white face.

Johnstone drew a sharp breath. "No, Duncan!" he said hoarsely. "You must not. O'Neill's a rare swordsman ..."

Crosbie remembered what Montcalm had said about O'Neill and his sly trickery with the blade. It didn't seem to matter just now.

"Do you, sir?" he demanded harshly.

Abruptly O'Neill lurched away. He slammed the decanter hard on a small table near the door and left the room swiftly, his footsteps soundless on the bare floor.

Crosbie sank back in his seat. He picked up his small glass with fingers that trembled slightly. A cold trickle of whiskey dampened his hand as he gulped.

"What's wrong with O'Neill?" Johnstone asked unsteadily. "I never saw him back away from a fight before."

"A private matter, Jamie," Crosbie growled. "It should never have been brought to your table. My apologies."

CHAPTER FORTY SIX

Spring came late to Canada in 1759. Winter had gripped the land so fiercely that all life seemed frozen.

At Beauport, there was constant work, though its pace was slower. The Sieur duMaine and his habitants laid cobbled roads, raised stone walls, clawed drainage canals through frozen marshland, bridged the streams that darted in small ravines across the seigneury.

The first touch of warmth swept from the west. Gradually the river ice lost its firmness and depth. Ragged cracks showed across its surface.

The great sky-darkening flights of wildfowl were slow to return, but as the harsh Winter dragged to a close, no man complained of the tardy Spring. For the new season would bring death, as surely as it would bring life. The warmer days that eased the earth enough for a plow, that brought new grass and incredible flowers, would also bring the English.

But Canada had many times repulsed the fiercest attacks the English could mount. Montcalm, victorious so many times against overwhelming odds, had become the talisman of Canada.

Food had been reduced to the point of peril early in the year. Stringent rationing kept the townsfolk barely alive. The growing numbers of refugees from the Gaspé peninsula, burned out by marauding Englishmen, brought an added burden. The very young and the very old died with frightening ease. Platoons of Canadien regulars scoured the farms for hoarded food, which the Intendant then sold at a scoundrel's price. Bigot and his coterie made enormous profits, but some of the food did reach the desperate people of Canada, though its price was ruinous.

The first fleet up the St. Lawrence after the ice went out would surely be the annual convoy from France bringing food and stores to Canada. The Commissaire-Général knew how vitally that fleet was needed, for he had been sent to France with urgent pleas from Bigot and de Vaudreuil.

So the coming of Spring that year was anticipated with both dread and hope.

The rank and file of Montcalm's regular troops were fed and housed, but the officers were left to fend for themselves. All were heavily in debt to local merchants, for all prices had increased so much that even a senior colonel's pay would not buy the mere necessities. The depressing effect among the junior officers was apparent in the surveying teams which Montcalm sent along the St. Lawrence. These were composed of several officers of the Corps du Génie and an escort of infantry which averaged almost one officer to each two soldiers. The engineers had come to do their work, but the infantry officers had seized their opportunity to get into the countryside to find decent food and a warm bed.

Duncan Crosbie accompanied the surveyors to plot emplacements for Montcalm's artillery. He then crossed the St. Lawrence and assumed the role of attacker. Quebec was vulnerable from one point, he learned. The city could be dominated by guns emplaced on the heights of Pointe Lévi, directly south across the river.

Save for that danger, Quebec was safe, Crosbie judged. He spent long careful hours with his charts and scales, going out time after time with his enormous brass dispart sights to make sure of the fields of fire from various points. But it was true. Quebec was safe. A resourceful commander who was both clever and patient, could hold it against the finest assault troops ever formed. The heights of Pointe Lévi offered a position from which the city might be damaged, possibly even destroyed. But the military meaning of the terrain was absolute: Montcalm's position was impregnable.

The Montmorenci River might be crossed by a determined enemy, but the cost could be made prohibitive. The St. Lawrence shoreline west from the Montmorenci was low-lying marshland and tidal flats that could be perfectly dominated by artillery. If the entry to the St. Charles River were blocked by a heavy log boom and bridged to permit easy communication, then the French position would be solidly established to the city itself. West of Quebec, the high and forbidding escarpment of solid rock ran for leagues, making a wellnigh impassible barrier, even if the English were able to penetrate so far to the west. Crosbie considered the possibility that the enemy might slip past the city batteries. But the prospect was outrageous. The great St. Lawrence was a mighty river until it touched Quebec. But upstream from there, it narrowed to a slight channel that was completely dominated by the guns of Quebec. If the English were somehow to force their way west of the city, then every artillery officer should certainly be hung for incompetence—if not treason.

Crosbie drafted a tentative report for the Général and packed his papers away.

Each afternoon thin watery sunlight destroyed another layer of ice until enormous floes broke free to move with slow, inexorable purpose with the current. The fast mountain streams flowed clear and crystalline, sparkling with a dazzling purity that everyone had forgotten. Harsh rivulets appeared across the earth as new channels were gouged by the melting snow. The birds returned, in scattered flocks at first, then in black clouds that thundered across the river.

Crosbie chopped musket balls into tiny shards to make birdshot and he took his fusil each day as he walked slowly along the marshland that bordered the great river. A shot that did not bring down at least three ducks was considered wasted, for the birds would not swerve from any danger.

Denis went with him one day, pleased and proud when his shots brought down wildfowl that he could carry home to the Widow Arnaud. The boy looked well-fed and content, Crosbie thought.

"You're happy in the Arnaud house?" he asked abruptly.

Denis bent to pick up a second duck, then he stood straight again and smiled a wide smile.

"Very happy, Duncan," he said. "Madame Arnaud could not be more kind if I were her own son." The smiling face grew serious. "She misses him so, her son. She talks to me about him all the time. 'Robin was quick and clever, like you, Denis. He always brought home the first ducks and fish in the Spring, too.' I try to help a little, to do the things Robin would have done if he had not been killed."

The boy turned away as he dropped the duck into his game-bag. He was growing, Crosbie thought suddenly. Before his eyes, the boy was growing into a man's shape. There wasn't just affection and remembered pleasure in his voice when he spoke of the Widow Arnaud. There was more. The beginning of responsibility, and Crosbie was pleased to hear it.

Soon the Winter was gone, but the ice receded with infuriating slowness. The ice-locked ships frozen at anchor before the city were broken free of their Winter moorings and they sailed in long cautious arcs about the ship basin, airing their stored sails and retraining crews grown slovenly through long inactivity. No ship had yet left the city, though it was common knowledge that urgent despatches had been prepared by the Governor and by Montcalm. Sizable wagers were laid about the departure date of the first ship to slip downstream and test the virtue of the English blockade off the mouth of the St. Lawrence.

But it was not an east-bound ship that first passed the seigneury of Beauport. The high slatting topsails of a rakish frigate crept gradually out of the morning mist, beating upstream. The fluttering white ensign at the fore-peak proclaimed her French.

A swarm of small boats set off from both sides of the river, from the settlements of the Île d'Orléans and from Quebec, all packed with screaming, cheering Frenchmen saluting the first arrival of the new year.

Duncan Crosbie dressed himself quickly in presentable uniform and ran from the house. Only one whaleboat remained of the fleet usually moored at the Beauport landing and that was already fully manned, ready to shove off. Crosbie's angry bellow held the bowman just long enough for the young Scot to gallop down the wharf and leap aboard. The weighted boat danced lightly across the high water with the steersman shifting direction adeptly to avoid floating ice. Why they were so desperately anxious to reach the frigate, no man could have explained. It was traditional that one greeted the first ship with suitable enthusiasm.

But Crosbie knew why he had hurried. It had nothing to do with ceremonious ritual. Louis Bougainville would be aboard the first ship from France. And with him would arrive the future of Canada. The decision had long since been made, but in all the province, only Captain Bougainville knew what it was. Duncan Crosbie burned with impatience to hear the answer. Crosbie urged the oarsmen to a quicker pace.

Dozens of small craft hovered like dragonflies about the frigate. Crosbie gestured sharply, directing the man at the steering oar to lay him alongside. As the whaleboat scraped along the frigate's hull, he stood erect, held one arm high imperiously, signalling for attention. Blankly startled faces peered down from the weather-deck railing. Crosbie shouted furiously, his tone of insistent command clear to every man on board the frigate. A fat tangle of rope dropped from the rail, unravelling into a woven rope ladder as it fell. A strident voice screamed from the rail, but Crosbie ignored it as he measured the shifting gap between him and the frail ladder. He smacked his hat hard down on his head and launched himself toward the ladder, scrambling upward the moment his hands and feet made contact. The first few rungs were incredibly difficult, for the tumblehome of the French shipwrights had given the frigate a fat bulge just above the point where Crosbie seized the ladder. But once he had reached the outer limit, the remaining distance was comparatively easy. He swung over the railing and waved his thanks to the whaleboat crew.

Angrily impatient orders crackled from exasperated officers as the frigate gathered way again. A fussily self-important lieutenant presented himself to Crosbie at the railing, his smooth red cheeks quivering with restrained fury.

"Your authority, monsieur," he snapped.

"Sir?" Crosbie asked.

"Your authority for halting this vessel," the lieutenant demanded tartly. "The captain insists..."

Crosbie drew himself to his full height, staring incredulously down his nose at the ship's officer. "My compliments to your captain," he drawled. "I am Brevet-Captain Crosbie, aide to His Excellency the Marquis de Montcalm, come to welcome Monsieur Bougainville."

Crosbie lifted his bushy eyebrows. What he had said was complete nonsense, of course, but nonsense was the only useful weapon against pomposity. The lieutenant's crisp asperity wilted into confusion.

"Of course, monsieur. The captain is pleased, of course... any small courtesy..." He swallowed heavily. "Monsieur Bougainville shares the captain's cabin. Will you accompany me, monsieur?"

Crosbie bowed. The lieutenant bowed. He ushered Crosbie toward the quarterdeck, managing somehow to bow at each alternate step. Crosbie rigidly suppressed the surging hilarity that reddened his face. He held himself sternly impassive, as comported with the lieutenant's opinion of a Général's aide.

The lieutenant swung open a narrow door and clattered down the dark staircase. Crosbie followed slowly, feeling for each step with a cautious toe. A stinking lamp overhead showed the lieutenant's rotund shadow as he rapped timidly on a closed door. He knocked once more, then bowed himself aside.

"Yes," a muffled voice called. "Enter, please."

"Thank you, lieutenant," Crosbie said, turning the knob. "And my most distinguished thanks to your captain."

"Charmed... most..." the lieutenant stammered.

Crosbie pressed down the latch and went inside.

A stocky figure in a white uniform was bent over an open trunk, back to the door, energetically pressing down a mass of clothing that was obviously too bulky for the available space.

"It won't go in," Crosbie said lightly. "You can't..."

He caught sight of heavily fringed gold epaulets and his mouth clamped shut with an audible snap.

"My... my apologies, colonel. I was looking for... Good God! Louis!" In a dazed gesture, Crosbie managed to knock off his hat. He stooped, fumbling for it, but not taking his eyes from the incredible figure before him. "What in hell are you doing... in a..."

He straightened awkwardly with his hat and banged it against his leg. "A colonel, Louis? Really?"

Bougainville perched lightly on the rim of his open trunk. "Duncan! How good to see a friend again. Colonel?" He laughed. "Yes, a colonel. Also this. You hadn't noticed?"

Bougainville's finger flipped a pale blue ribbon that slanted diagonally across his coat, then drifted up to tap at the jeweled star pinned above it.

Crosbie cleared his throat roughly. "Dear God," he murmured. "Colonel le Chevalier de Bougainville. I'd best kneel, hadn't I?"

Bougainville smoothed the ribbon of the Order of St. Louis and glanced up, frowning faintly.

"Don't be foolish, Duncan. I remain Louis Bougainville, as ever. These trappings are a compliment to Montcalm, not to me.

They are ... in a measure ..." He lifted one hand and let it drop expressively.

"What are you saying, colonel?" Crosbie asked.

Bougainville's grim expression broke with the swift amused grin that Crosbie remembered best. "My name is Louis," he insisted mildly. "Colonel le Chevalier de Bougainville has been sent back to Montcalm as a substitute for a regiment. The Général gets a colonel, but no troops. I have brought him a trunkful of substitutes, Duncan." Bougainville drew in a long slow breath and the light amused expression dropped away completely as he glanced sharply at Crosbie. "He is well? Everything is all right?"

"As always, Louis," Crosbie said readily. "Montcalm is ..." he shrugged easily. "Montcalm. You know. You heard he resumed command?"

Bougainville nodded. "It was a mistake," he said bluntly. "Why?"

"People were frightened, Louis," Crosbie said quietly. "After Frontenac and duQuesne, they panicked."

"But not Montcalm?"

"Certainly not Montcalm," Crosbie smiled. "You know better, Louis."

Bougainville sighed heavily. "Yes, I know him, Duncan."

"What did you mean about the substitutes?" Crosbie asked sharply curious.

Bougainville waggled his head ponderously from side to side. One hand lifted to rub distractedly over his forehead.

"Duncan, I honestly don't think I could explain twice. I have been rehearsing ... I spent the morning ... God, I've spent the past three weeks ... trying to find words to explain to the Général. I just don't know ..."

Bougainville slipped from the trunk and straightened. He adjusted his uniform coat with nervous hands. He strode away from Crosbie. He paused at the stern windows, resting one arm on a long cannon.

"I have some things for the Général," he said. "Papers that weigh more than a musket. Books. Letters. And something... special. You come with me, Duncan. You can be my assistant for this day. Does a colonel warrant an aide, I wonder? No matter. You come along. Then you can hear what I have to tell the Général."

Crosbie nodded. "You are worried, Louis?" he asked. "It's something really bad?"

Bougainville spun on one heel. His mouth opened swiftly, but the angry words were choked off before they escaped. He merely nodded.

After a long quiet moment, he said, "You come with me, Duncan. I am worried. I detest what I must do."

CHAPTER FORTY SEVEN

Four drummer boys formed a rigid line at the entrance to the Château, rattling a salute to Bougainville. A solid double row of curious but silent officers formed an aisle for the colonel and Crosbie as they moved briskly through Montcalm's anteroom, into the short hallway and along it toward the guarded door to the Général's office. As always, the watchful Estére moved quickly to alert the Général.

Crosbie deposited Bougainville's trunk of records on a convenient table. He pivoted swiftly as the door opened. "Your Excellency!"

"Louis, you are... Good God! You are a colonel! My sincere felicitations, Louis. And what is this?" Montcalm grinned broadly as his hand stretched forward to touch at Bougainville's blue ribbon. The same hand was pulled back and one finger flipped the silken band that slanted across the Général's coat. "So we are brothers. Welcome, monsieur le Chevalier. Welcome back."

"Thank you, mon général," Bougainville said hesitantly.

Montcalm pulled him into a quick embrace, his hands thumping briefly on Bougainville's back.

"And welcome, Colonel de Bougainville," he said, stepping back.

"You have a colonel," Bougainville said in a strained voice. "A colonel, but no regiment."

The Général placed both hands behind him and leaned heavily on the rim of his wide table. "Is it ..."

"Yes, sir," Bougainville said. He nodded soberly, his eyes hard on the Général. "A compliment. A number of compliments. A few long cannon. A handful of gunners and sergents and four cadet artillery officers. Some supplies. And…" Bougainville turned suddenly, his face white with tension. He bent swiftly to the trunk and lifted out a carefully rolled bundle wrapped in black cloth. He stripped away the covering and turned back to Montcalm. "And this, mon général."

Bougainville held aloft a darkly magnificent embroidered Général's coat. Crosbie inspected it in vain for significance. Then Montcalm snorted heavily. He took the coat from Bougainville and held it at arm's length.

"A lieutenant-général now, am I?" His hands bunched convulsively, wadding the beautiful coat. He glanced down at the gold-embroidered collar that stood starkly upright. "God damn them," he whispered hoarsely. His hands relaxed and the coat fell to the floor. Montcalm pivotted deliberately and walked around the table. He seated himself slowly and leaned forward, propped on both elbows.

"You saw BelleIsle, surely," he asked softly. "This isn't his answer, this gaudy coat. I can't believe that."

"No," Bougainville said heavily. "Not BelleIsle's."

"Of course not," Montcalm insisted. "BelleIsle is a Marshal of France, as well as Minister of War. He wouldn't…" Abruptly he leaned back and lifted both hands. He smiled up at Bougainville. "No more of this dreariness, Louis. What of my family? The bethrothal…"

"Went off perfectly," Bougainville said soberly. "The young Comte has found himself a lovely bride. And, on the practical side, she commands a great fortune. Your lady's letters will give you complete details. And…" Bougainville paused. He lifted his hands in a helpless gesture and let them fall.

"Yes, Louis?" The Général settled back with a wide, confident smile, as though Bougainville's excellent report of his family had completely erased the frightening meaning of the King's reaction.

"I was already on board," Bougainville burst out abruptly. "The captain couldn't wait and I knew you expected me back as soon …"

"What …" Montcalm's dark eyebrows drew closer together in a faint frown of concentration.

"A townsman from Nîmes, mon général," Bougainville said in a tone of harsh distress. "The man had heard just before he left and he told me …"

"Yes," Montcalm said impatiently.

"One of your daughters," Bougainville said heavily. "Dead."

Montcalm's hands dropped to the table, moved together into a tight grip that whitened slowly. His lips disappeared in a hard slit. Briefly, he nodded. "I have four daughters, Louis," he said in a low steady voice.

Bougainville turned his head and Crosbie could see the tears standing hard in them. "I don't know, sir," he said simply. "The man hadn't thought to ask. One of Montcalm's daughters. That is all he knew. The ship was due to sail. And Nîmes was so far away."

Montcalm lifted one hand to cut off Bougainville's explanation. For a long silent moment he stared blindly at the inkwell before him. "It must have been poor Mirète," he whispered hoarsely. "For a long time, we thought she would not live. She was a tiny baby. Frail. You know how some babies are. Very frail. But she did live. And I loved her best of all." The Général placed his hands carefully on the silver inkwell, seeming to gain quietness from its smooth texture. "We had ten children in all," he said in a voice that no man was meant to hear. "Only six lived. We never expected Mirète to live. Angélique and I … we never expected …"

The Général's voice died away softly. Crosbie shifted his weight nervously. A hasty glare from Bougainville froze him in position.

"I had a brother," the Général murmured. "Mièrete was like him. She had the same way of seeing through problems that perplexed normal men. To her, they weren't problems. She saw the answer, the human answer, as soon as she saw the problem. Maybe she … maybe my brother … maybe …"

Montcalm rose swiftly. He turned away from the table, kicking his chair back. Three steps brought him to the inner doorway. He went quickly through and the carved panel slammed behind him.

Crosbie turned to speak to Bougainville. His mouth opened. The questioning words were on his tongue. But one look at Bougainville's agonized expression and he could not speak.

How very much alike they are, he thought. The same person, really. You cannot wound one without making the other bleed. Louis Bougainville's sorrow was as apparent as the tears that filled his eyes. And Duncan Crosbie bowed his head to stare silently at the figured carpet, thinking the harsh bitter thoughts that come to every man when he watches a friend suffering and feels unable to help him.

Bougainville stood unmoving, not lifting a hand to wipe away the tears that were now trickling down his face.

After a quiet moment, Crosbie pulled his handkerchief from his sleeve and held it up before Bougainville. The colonel blinked his eyes rapidly, grinned briefly, and took the cloth square. His face was dry, his eyes only slightly reddened by the time the Général returned.

And whatever Montcalm felt, whatever tragic hurt, he had left behind him in his private room. When he sat down again behind his table, he was a man completely in command of himself, able even to smile reassuringly at Bougainville.

"Thank you, Louis," he said quietly. He drew in a slow breath and nodded. "Lieutenant-Général de Montcalm. Colonel le Chevalier de Bougainville. No other bribes?"

"Yes, mon général," Bougainville said heavily. "Major-Général de Lévis. Brigadier-Général de Bourlamaque. And the Grand Cross of the Order of St. Louis for the Governor."

Montcalm grinned suddenly in a tight grimace. "They must be worried." He glanced up with bright intensity at Crosbie. "And nothing for our giant?"

Bougainville laughed, a quick, painful explosion that seemed to tear involuntarily from him. "No longer merely a brevet-capitaine, Excellency. Duncan has been a permanent captain for three months. I do not recall the regiment, but I did find the commission. And I saved him a thousand francs on the price."

Montcalm responded with three rattling bursts of laughter that were totally without humor. "We are all to be congratulated then," he growled angrily. His hands locked tightly around the silver inkwell. "And no men whatever?"

"Some four hundred," Bougainville said heavily. "All untrained recruits we can use to bring the regiments up to strength. Sixty technicians, so-called. Engineers, gunners, sappers. And a shipload of powder and lead, with a few long cannon for Duncan to use against the ducks. I suspect they are too elderly for anything else."

Montcalm nodded slowly, his eyes fixed blindly on the inkwell. "That's all?"

"Yes, mon général."

Montcalm gradually rose to his feet. He swirled abruptly and his arm lashed out. His silver inkwell crashed against the wall, throwing ink and splinters of glass, and the battered silver shell across the carpet. Then Montcalm sat again, sedately folding his hands together. The ugly tension around his mouth seemed to have eased slightly, Crosbie thought.

"I hope you insulted someone, Louis," Montcalm said mildly.

"Afterward, sir," Bougainville said in a tone that aped Montcalm's, "afterward, I insulted almost everyone, save

Madame de Pompadour, who managed to avoid me. I dare say the Minister of Marine felt the most offended."

"Splendid," Montcalm said evenly. "De Berryer is a dog who needs nothing so much as a kick in the ribs. Did you insult him seriously?"

"Not sufficiently for that gentleman to offer a challenge," Bougainville said apologetically.

"A pity. And what was Monsieur de Berryer's stupid opinion of our troubles here?"

Bougainville shifted lightly. "The Minister felt that having a crisis in Europe makes it impossible to have a crisis in Canada. Two crises, apparently, would be inartistic. As I recall, he told me that a wise man does not concern himself with the stables when his house is on fire."

Montcalm nodded soberly. "That is de Berryer," he said admiringly. "Few men can reach such heights of asininity. And what was your insulting reply, Louis?"

"I was more irreverent than insulting, I regret to say, mon général. I merely observed that no one could possibly accuse him of talking like a horse."

Montcalm glanced up sharply, long thin lines of strain gouged deeply in his face. Suddenly he chuckled. The low quiet rumbling sound increased to genuine laughter and he lurched back, roaring with a savage intensity.

As the Général's outburst dwindled, Bougainville moved nearer to the big table.

"I should emphasize, mon général," he said sharply, "that the King's ministers are agreed in giving you clear preference over the Marquis de Vaudreuil in all matters pertaining to war. The Governor cannot..."

Montcalm shook his head slowly. The abrupt, nearly hysterical laughter left no trace of humor in his expression. "It is without meaning," he said dully. "The Governor will decide for himself what constitutes a matter pertaining to war. No, command in this colony will remain hydra-headed and confused, as ever. I should never have resumed ..." He shrugged angrily. "It is too late to talk of that. What was the situation when you left Paris?"

"Desperate," Bougainville said quietly. "The Prussians and the English will attack everywhere next year."

"And what have our enemies in mind for us in Canada?" Montcalm drummed his fingers nervously on the table. "Do you have any information?"

"Yes. The English Prime Minister, Mr. Pitt, called one of Amherst's Brigadiers to England to form a new army. That was Wolfe. He had been promoted to Major-General. I gathered all the information I could about him..." Bougainville chewed the inside of his cheek, frowning as he tried to remember.

"I met him years ago in Paris," Montcalm said easily. "He was a colonel then. A long-necked, rat-faced gentleman, as tall as our gigantic Crosbie, but without flesh on his bones. And his hair is red, too, though not the hideous blaze of Crosbie's. A most singular fellow, quite as odd in appearance as the great Condé."

"That is Wolfe," Bougainville said readily. "His reputation among soldiers is equally odd. He is ruthless, as we know from his destruction in the Gaspé country. Also, he is thought to be slightly mad. He is excitable as a Gascon, illogical and unstable. His only tactic seems to be the impetuous attack, so ..."

Montcalm smiled grimly. "Yes," he agreed quickly, "we may be able to entice him to destroy himself. Your information is very welcome, Louis, though a little frightening. An impetuous madman may sometimes conquer merely because his actions cannot be anticipated."

Bougainville shrugged. "Quem Deus vult perdere, prius dementat," he said in an oddly precise tone.

The Général snorted. "If only God would assure me that He planned to destroy Wolfe, I would need nothing more." He stared fixedly at his locked hands. "And how large an army will he have, do you know?"

"Only through rumor, sir, which is surely exaggerated. I heard he will have fifty thousand."

"And we have what?" Montcalm said quietly. "Three thousand troops of the line. As many Canadien regulars and fifteen thousand worthless militia." He drew in a deep, shuddery breath. "And what are my orders?"

"BelleIsle wants you to avoid battle, if you can," Bougainville said flatly. "He says it is impossible to find enough troops to give you an equality with the English, therefore he is sending you none, for fear that any he sent would be intercepted by the blockading English fleet. Excellent logic, isn't it? I corrected the Minister's faulty reasoning, but I could not change his opinion. However, Marshal BelleIsle is a sane commander. He asks you merely to retain a foothold in Canada."

Bougainville broke off when Montcalm banged his double fist furiously on the table.

"They all have great faith in you, mon général," Bougainville insisted. "BelleIsle told me you will surely have your baton by next year."

"God in Heaven!" Montcalm whispered savagely. He lifted his head quickly. Then his harsh frown softened as he looked at Bougainville. "Thank you, Louis. No more for now. I will read the despatches. I am pleased to have you back. And delighted with your promotion. Now go unpack your gear and let our good Crosbie tell you all the gossip. Come have dinner with me and bring your report then. Now, go away, Louis. I want to write a letter before the ship sails for France."

"You will…" Bougainville hesitated.

Voices lifted high with sharp command outside Montcalm's office.

"All is well, Louis," the Général said vaguely. "We will all find our graves under the ruins of this miserable colony, but we have expected that."

Running footsteps pounded along the hallway. A rapid tattoo sounded on the door and Estére slipped inside without waiting for an answer.

"A fleet, Excellency!" he panted. "Eighteen sail. The lookout on Cap Diamant reports…" the wizened little secretary gasped for breath.

Montcalm glanced up sharply, turning to Bougainville with wild surmise. "Could it be the English?"

Bougainville lifted his hands. "It is too early. We would have been warned. It must be the supply convoy."

Montcalm nodded agreement. English ships would be compelled to feel their way up the unmarked river, giving plenty of time for warning to reach Montcalm. This fleet must be Cadet's supply ships.

But were they? The Général moistened his lips briefly.

"Estére," he said calmly. "Send to Cap Diamant again. See if…"

"I have done that, Excellency," Estére said quickly. "The town is in a panic. The sailors on the frigate spread news of the huge English army sailing for Canada. People are already running out of the west gate."

"Stop them! Alert the guards at once. Close every gate. See to it, Estére. We cannot let…"

Hard knuckles rapped on the door. Estére reached out to pull it open.

A panting sentry stood stiffly outside. "French, Monsieur Estére," he gasped. "The ensign they fly is French. It is the supply convoy!"

"Thank you," Estére closed the door softly, turning to Montcalm with a light shrug. "My apologies, Excellency. I thought… Fichtre! I thought nothing. We are all nervous as old women these days."

"Please remain so," Montcalm smiled. "We can ill afford complacency now." He settled back gingerly in his chair. "Monsieur Cadet and his ships surprised us. But he has taught us a lesson, eh? Call a council of commanders for this evening, Estére. I will want a courier ready to ride to Montreal with despatches for the Governor and Monsieur de Lévis. Within an hour."

Estére bowed. He left the room quickly, chewing his lip.

"Louis, draft a brief report for de Lévis. I want him to concentrate his regiments and embark them for Quebec immediately. He is authorized to confiscate boats if necessary. His Canadien regulars are to be sent to de Bourlamaque at Carillon. So we will need a second report for him. He can expect nothing more. Tell him clearly. And advise both gentlemen of their promotions. I will write to the Governor myself. You know how much time you have?"

Bougainville grinned hugely and the hard strained lines of his face were wiped away with quick excitement. "Within the hour, mon général," he said briskly.

"Monsieur Crosbie, where is your artillery report?"

"At Beauport, mon général."

"You may have two hours to get it to me," the Général snapped. "Now jump, both of you!"

CHAPTER FORTY EIGHT

The brief panic that followed the arrival of the supply convoy was all the impetus Montcalm needed to arouse the Canadiens. Quebec was quickly organized for seige. The long-awaited fleet had brought food and equipment for the colony, but no more ships could be expected until the English had been driven from Canada. From this day forward, any sail seen to the eastward would be English. The river was closed to the French.

Montcalm's energetic response caught the popular imagination. Even the immediate mustering of the militia caused no disturbance and that was unexpected, for the volatile Canadiens had long made Muster Day the scene of riotous protest. And this year the call had come so early that the Spring plowing had barely been started. Another starvation season was certain if all the able-bodied men were called to arms before the fields were planted. But, if the men did not go, there might be no future at all for Canadiens.

The King's Governor arrived at Quebec, accompanied by the Chevalier de Lévis. Both were closeted with Montcalm for long hours. His Excellency, the Intendant, was summoned from his château in the mountains. Every hour new boatloads of French regulars from Montreal disembarked at Lower Town and marched through crowded streets to their barracks. The first hastily assembled units of the militia were put to work unloading the supply convoy. The remainder, directed by Montcalm's engineers, erected two great fortified bridgeheads facing each other across the St. Charles, just upriver from the Intendant's Palace.

Between these massive works would be strung a bridge of whale-boats. But the bridge itself was left unfinished until all the ships had been unloaded. Later the lightened vessels would be towed up the shallow river where they would be safe from attack.

The French naval frigates at anchor below Quebec were the object of harsh debate, but no remonstrance from Montcalm or the Governor could induce their commanders to leave the safety of Quebec's batteries for the perils of the lower river where the English lay in wait.

To the Brigadier de Bourlamaque at Carillon were sent several engineers and four newly arrived artillery officers. And with them went orders requiring de Bourlamaque to avoid battle until every expedient had been exhausted. In the coming campaign, the French army at Carillon would again be outnumbered at least ten to one, but no man could expect the English to repeat their stupidity of the previous year. The enemy force marching against Canada from the south would be led by Amherst himself and Sir Jeffrey was a cautious general, ever fearful of entrapment. De Bourlamaque's entire duty would be accomplished if he delayed Amherst; no one hoped for more.

Within the city itself, normal routine ground slowly to a halt as the townspeople prepared to leave. Nuns evacuated their convent schools to the suburb of St. Roch, safely beyond possible artillery range. Within a few short days, only uniformed soldiers could be seen on the streets—the French regulars who assembled each morning in the Great Square of St. Louis, and the thousand elderly men and young boys of the city's permanent garrison.

Montcalm spent the daylight hours in the saddle, inspecting every aspect of his command. His staff accompanied him always, which meant that the huge volume of reports and returns had to be dealt with at night. As a result no man slept enough and tempers sharpened.

The Governor urged a spirited attack on all fronts. Montcalm made little attempt to conceal his contempt for such infantile tactics. The Général presented a detailed programme, which called for blocking both the St. Charles and St. Lawrence with heavy log booms, and fortifying both banks, forming something of an open circle into which the English would be allowed to enter to destruction. De Vaudreuil distrusted Montcalm's plan as he distrusted Montcalm himself. He could not veto the Général's concept in its entirety, but he could impede it and this he proceeded to do. He agreed that the army would be allowed to fortify the north bank, but not the south. The proposed division of forces offended the Governor's sense of military propriety. The fact that Montcalm had been given supreme authority in military matters meant little without the Governor's approval and the Intendant's assistance.

Montcalm's engineers had mapped the proposed lines of defense and the Général threw his entire force along the northern bank, intending to complete those fortifications first and then move to the southern line after the Governor had come to his senses. Three thousand French regulars stripped to the waist in the chilly June breeze and dug like moles from Quebec eastward, gouging an interlocking series of retrenchments in the moist earth, following the ridge that ran for nearly three leagues to the great cataract of Montmorenci. Gradually the army shifted its base from the city to the new position.

As the strategic debate continued, Montcalm's staff gave up all private existence. They were extensions of the Général's will, nothing more. Even de Bougainville, Colonel and Chevalier though he was, slipped smoothly back into his post as chief of Montcalm's personal staff. The wizened, tireless Estére kissed his Canadienne sweetheart farewell and immured himself within the bleak walls of the Château, growing daily paler and thinner as he struggled to make order from the vast stack of reports and indentures needed to control an army in the field. And Duncan Crosbie, in three full weeks, spent only one night at Beauport and that in such a fog of weariness that he nearly dropped off to sleep before he had managed a private moment with Céleste.

The Sieur duMaine drilled his militiamen by day, but still contrived somehow to plow and plant his normal acreage. Young Denis, though officially a regular soldier, was assigned by Crosbie to assist the seigneur and the boy, by virtue of his experience at Carillon, served usefully as a caporal in duMaine's company.

When the first frenzy of preparation had passed, Duncan Crosbie was able to concentrate most of his attention on artillery problems. The choleric Chevalier Le Mercier returned and together he and Crosbie trained the two companies of gunners that had been raised in the city. The cannon lining Quebec's walls, more than one hundred of them, had almost passed their usefulness, but the massive guns that glowered eastward from the six major batteries were in the best condition the colony's resources could afford. All of Crosbie's earlier recommendations had been put into effect. Le Mercier's admiration, born in battle at Carillon, had not diminished. He remained a trusted member of the Intendant's clutch of scoundrels, but he was also a soldier. His fortune increased to staggering proportions through the brisk sale of draft animals—most of them nonexistent—to the army, but the red-faced, swaggering ex-sergent refused to allow Bigot's hatred to turn him against Duncan Crosbie. And when the huge young Scot brought to his attention the useless frigates swinging at anchor below Quebec, it was Le Mercier who braved the storm of outraged naval protest, who demanded, and ultimately received, permission to dismantle the ships and emplace their guns where they might be most effective.

It required all of Le Mercier's persuasive power before the Governor could be induced to impound the naval armament and send the ships upriver to safety near Montreal. When the frigates had been anchored, there were a thousand trained gunners freed for assignment in Quebec. These were pressed into service to man the floating batteries of twelve guns each that Duncan Crosbie stationed along the curving line of tidal flats from Quebec to the Montmorenci. When the floating platforms had been kedged into place, Crosbie felt that he had done everything in his power. Any soldier might feel a shiver of apprehension when he looked at the crumbling wall that guarded Quebec's western approaches. Here centuries of sound planning and hard work had been nullified by thieving officials. The wall was a poor joke. Even its hundred guns were nearly worthless.

From his position atop Cap Diamant, the entire French line was visible to Duncan Crosbie. A thin arcing series of retrenchments marked the position along the ridge, and far distant, the white-washed buildings of Beauport were dazzling in the afternoon sun. The rising ground beyond the village was studded solidly with regularly spaced white tents.

A few merchant ships were visible beyond the completed bridge of boats across the St. Charles. A boom of chained logs was secured downstream of the bridge to protect against a ramming ship-of-war, and two dismasted hulks with their cannon still in place wallowed in the current just behind the heavy boom. Cannon had already been sited in the hornworks that guarded both ends of the bridge.

Crosbie pivoted briefly to survey the towering Heights of Pointe Lévi that lay only fifteen hundred mètres south of the city, within easy cannon shot. Unless Montcalm could persuade the Governor to let him fortify that commanding ground, enemy artillery could be emplaced there to batter Quebec to rubble.

Crosbie settled his hat squarely on his head and leaped from the parapet. His concern was to site his guns and fight them efficiently. Strategic problems were the jealous province of Généraux and Governors. Though why that idiotic Governor failed to appreciate Quebec's danger, Crosbie could not fathom. He clenched his teeth hard in restraint and strode across the Great Square toward the Château.

He threaded his way brusquely through the Général's ante-room, and paused in the hallway to thrust his head inside Estére's cubicle. He raised his eyebrows in silent inquiry.

Estére glanced up, his eyes hooded with concentration. His pale narrow face seemed almost fleshless in the vague candlelight.

"Duncan," he said quickly. "Several things for you."

Crosbie sat beside the table, dropping his hat to the floor and stretching his long legs. He drew in a deep breath and let it out in a gaping yawn.

"Tired?" Estére rubbed his bony forehead with a hand stippled with splotches of ink.

Crosbie shrugged and forced his mouth shut. "Sorry," he said. "What is it?"

Estére shifted papers on his table and slid a folded sheet toward Crosbie.

"I intercepted this report before it reached His Excellency," he said in a mild voice. "I think you'll want to reconsider it."

With one finger, Crosbie flipped the sheet flat. He leaned forward to scan the first few lines. Then he glanced up, frowning slightly. "The gunpowder inventory. Yes, I remember it. Is something wrong?"

"I don't wish to carp, Duncan," the secretary said easily, "but the figures given are not accurate. You list one hundred barrels of gunpowder stored at the Intendant's Palace and three hundred in the St. Louis magazine."

"Yes?"

"Those four hundred barrels do not exist, Duncan. Louis has seen both magazines. Neither has more than a few barrels on hand."

"But, I had those figures from ..."

Estére waited patiently. His thin mouth tightened.

"... from Le Mercier," Crosbie said after a pause to collect his thoughts. "Are you sure Louis didn't ..."

Estére shrugged. "He says not, Duncan. Possibly you'd best inspect yourself."

Crosbie nodded grimly, fighting down a sudden flare of anger. He folded the inventory and slipped it into a pocket. "I'll inspect," he said, grimly quiet. "Thank you. Anything else?"

"Those cannon you want," Estére said vaguely, rummaging again through a clutter of papers. "The ones mounted on the Palace ramparts. What..."

"Twenty-five of them," Crosbie said briskly. "Fine, light brass..."

"Yes, yes," Estére broke in. "Well, you can't have them. Monsieur de Ramesay refuses to part with them."

"But what does de Ramesay..."

"He is the King's Lieutenant for Quebec," Estére said. "He is responsible for the city's safety and he insists he must keep the cannon."

"That dough-headed fool," Crosbie said slowly, his voice shaking with fury. "Those guns are mounted on the Palace wall. And the Palace is in St. Roch. There'll never be a target for those guns unless the English take Quebec. I need them." He drew his legs under him and half rose, leaning eagerly forward with his arms on Estére's table. "Listen to me. Those guns are only half the weight of iron guns the same calibre. I could mount them on..."

"You can't have them," Estére said bluntly. He shrugged and turned one hand eloquently, palm up. "The Intendant supports de Ramesay, so you may as well forget about them. Now what do you want to do about the Braddock cannon?"

"The what?"

"The guns captured from General Braddock at Fort duQuesne," Estére said patiently. "They've been rafted down from Montreal. Here's the list. They're at the Lower Town wharf, I believe."

"Oh, yes." Crosbie took the list from Estére. "These are intended for the Heights of Pointe Lévi."

"That's another item you can dismiss," Estére said in a brittle tone. "There won't be any artillery on the Heights. Not French artillery, at any rate."

Crosbie looked up sharply, dread suspicion clear in his eyes. "We can't protect the city unless..."

"Please, Duncan." Estére lifted a hand in quick protest. "Please. The debate is over. The Général knows he will get no help from the Governor. There won't be any troops on the southern bank at all, and no artillery."

Crosbie sighed softly. "It's the end of Quebec," he said in an odd, flat tone. "Doesn't the Governor see..."

"The Governor has other plans," Estére said with a tinge of bitterness. "He intends to destroy the enemy before he can disembark. Therefore, we need not worry about the Heights."

Crosbie nodded. That sounded like the Governor. "And how will he manage it? Frighten them to death?"

"Fire-ships," Estére snorted. "Haven't you seen them a-building? Eight fire-ships manned by gallant naval officers who have never yet closed with the enemy. But, timid as they are, they will contrive to destroy Wolfe and all his army. The Governor himself told me so."

"Fire-ships," Crosbie repeated in an unbelieving voice. "What are they? Ships set afire and drifted toward the enemy fleet? Is that the idea?"

"Some such notion. Our intrepid sailors, however, will sail them directly against the English ships before setting them afire. There will be eight of them, at a total cost of more than a million francs."

Crosbie glanced sharply at Estére.

"Yes, Duncan. One million francs. Most of it will go to the Intendant and his friends. Would you like to know how they got possession of the ships?"

"I could guess. Bigot confiscated the ships and sold them to the Governor at a slight profit."

"Half a million profit," Estére agreed. He shook his head slowly. "We are neglecting great opportunities, Duncan. With a little enterprise, we could be rich in a week's time." He sighed and rolled his eyes in comic resignation. "Well, I mustn't keep you, Duncan. His Excellency wants to see you. I'll tell the Général you're here."

Crosbie slumped in his seat as Estére went through the door into Montcalm's office. The folded paper in his pocket crackled thinly as he shifted. The gunpowder inventory, he remembered. What a ridiculous fool he would have looked if that report had reached the Général. Now, at least, he could correct it to reflect the true status. And this time, he would place no reliance on anything Le Mercier told him. Crosbie's hard fingers locked tightly in a convulsive grip. Le Mercier had much to answer for.

Crosbie shoved up to his feet and smoothed his coat before moving to the door Estére was holding open for him. He clamped his hat under his elbow and bowed formally to his Général.

The Chevalier de Lévis and three senior colonels sat in a tight circle facing a nervous young naval lieutenant who was leaning over a series of navigation charts spread across the Général's table. Montcalm stood at one side, wearily attentive as the young sailor ran his finger along the river channel below Quebec. The Général glanced up as Crosbie entered, and nodded briefly.

"Please continue, gentlemen," he said in a thick voice. He moved slowly toward Crosbie. Long days of sustained tension had carved heavy grooves like scars around his tensely held mouth. He walked stiffly toward the high windows that overlooked the ship basin and stood staring at the detailed map of Canada that was pinned to the wall between the windows.

"Estére has told you of the decision?" he demanded in a harsh, brittle tone. He did not look at Crosbie.

"Yes, mon général."

"All available artillery is to be emplaced along the retrenchment line. The command will be separated into three brigades. See that each headquarters has at least one battery for close defense. And I want you to survey the west bank of the Montmorenci very carefully tomorrow. That will be our Left flank and I want it well covered. Is that clear?"

"Perfectly, sir," Crosbie said automatically. When the Général used that tight, bitter voice, a quick obedience was the only possible response.

"You may order the gunners to move the cannon into place along the main line, but I will want to approve your plan for protecting the Montmorenci flank before you site the artillery."

"Yes, sir," Crosbie said.

The Général looked sharply at Crosbie. "There will be action enough for all very soon now. The grenadier companies at Louisbourg loaded their equipment on board transports four days ago, I am informed, so they must expect Wolfe's fleet to arrive at any moment." Montcalm stared tightly at Crosbie's sombre expression and he smiled faintly. "How long has it been since you were last at Beauport, my boy?"

"Uh...several days, sir," Crosbie hesitated, trying to remember. "It must be a week."

"Then you will not be sorry to return today, eh?" The Général smiled, a darting grin that was gone almost before it became evident. "I think you might arrive in time for dinner, if you hurried."

"Yes, sir," Crosbie said in a questioning tone.

Montcalm locked his hands behind his back and rocked slowly to and fro. "All regimental headquarters will be established in the field tomorrow. I will make my headquarters at Beauport. I want you to advise the Sieur duMaine."

"Yes, sir," Crosbie said.

"And tell Raoul duMaine to hide all his valuables and to make a careful inventory of everything left behind. A copy of that inventory should be given to Estére."

"Yes, sir. And the family?"

"Family?" Montcalm frowned quickly. "Hasn't the old lady been removed yet? Or the girls?" He sliced his hand sharply through the air. "No matter. They must be sent to a safe place. See to it. Tell Raoul I will assign his company to an area from which he will be able to keep watch on his seigneury."

Crosbie said he understood and he half smiled as he spoke, realizing that even now, in the press of constant work, Montcalm had spared time to consider his old friend. Beauport would fare better than any seigneury within the army area, for Montcalm himself would be on hand to discourage the looting and wanton destruction that invariably followed when troops bivouacked in the field. And by assigning duMaine's militiamen to a neighboring post, Montcalm gave the seigneur a chance to till and harvest his crops, if the military situation permitted.

"My compliments to the Sieur duMaine. Tell him I look forward to seeing him soon." Montcalm slid a finger under the tight drawstring of his wig and scratched briefly. "Off with you. Oh, and take my black gelding, please. Give him a good run each way. He is getting fat with indolence."

Crosbie bowed and retreated through the open door. The Général had returned to the map table before Crosbie was out of sight.

Montcalm's fine black was a noble horse that moved on springy fetlocks in a long and tireless stride along the cobbled streets of the city and out over the bridge of boats that spanned the St. Charles. Crosbie clamped his knees hard and kept a firm hand on the reins as the big gelding pranced and tossed his head restively.

Troops encamped all along the ridge using the firm roadway as a drillground, and Crosbie was never able to gallop the Général's horse more than a few strides before he was forced to pull him in to avoid a clumsy squad floundering under a sergent's wrath.

Crosbie held the gelding to a fast walk as he crossed the short bridge over the Beauport river and approached the village. There

in the smooth road, a complete company of white-coated infantrymen was formed in a precise, three-deep line facing habitants
who stood watching.

The big eager horse fought against the bit, tossing his head
high and spattering froth. Crosbie forced him to quietness and dismounted. He gripped the reins close to the bit and walked the horse
sedately behind the infantry formation. He stopped when a second
horse strode from between two low stone houses. He glanced up.

"Duncan, my boy," the Sieur duMaine smiled broadly. "How
glad I am to see you. Will you be able to stay for a visit this time?"

"Good evening, sir," Crosbie said. "I can spend the night,
which is a long visit for these days. How is ... everyone?"

DuMaine chuckled at Crosbie's hesitation. "Everyone is
in excellent spirits. And she will be home soon, I am sure. She
has gone to take some supplies to Mère de Sainte-Claude at the
General Hospital."

Bellowed commands from the roadway smothered the seigneur's heavy voice. Crosbie glanced over his shoulder in time to
see the shouldered muskets of the company swing down smartly
to the poised position. A second command and every hammer
was pulled back to half-cock. The muskets were balanced at the
present as each soldier extracted a cartridge, white arms with
green cuffs dipping and rising in perfect unison. The charge was
poured into the mouth of each piece and the muskets primed,
all movement rhythmically following the chanted orders of the
sergents. Long whippy iron ramrods flashed in the sun as musket
charges were rammed securely home. The entire company swept
muskets to the return and the assembled villagers sighed in perfect contentment at the precision of the movement. A young,
bored officer sauntered out. At his command, the three rigid
lines of his company aimed their muskets high and fired out over
the river. The three platoon volleys exploded with commendable
unison as each line fired in turn. Crosbie nodded with professional appreciation and turned back to the seigneur.

Montcalm's nervous horse stamped and reared in alarm. The young Scot drew the snorting horse close and stroked his nose with a strong soothing motion.

"I'm none too sure of this beast," he explained to duMaine. "He is the Général's favorite and he hasn't been exercised enough lately."

"A fine horse," duMaine said with a musing stare. "But you are wise to walk him." Courteously, he swung down from his saddle and joined Crosbie. "Aimée is somewhere in that crowd with young Denis, but we won't wait for them. I imagine you're more than ready for a bottle of something, eh?"

Crosbie nodded happily. He led the way up the long hill toward the familiar white house.

"How does everyone feel in Quebec, Duncan? Confident, eh?"

Crosbie nodded. "I would say so, sir. The Général most of all."

"Ah." DuMaine let out a long satisfied breath. "Splendid. I have wanted to ask him how matters were progressing, but I hated to ..."

"Of course," Crosbie said readily. "You will have ample opportunity soon, sir. The Général plans to make his headquarters at Beauport. He should arrive in two or three days. I have been sent ahead to alert you."

DuMaine handed his reins to a smocked habitant who came running from the stables, and signalled for Crosbie to do the same. He waited until the man was out of hearing before he spoke.

"I had a cold chill for a moment," he confessed heavily. "Already the soldiers here have stripped many of my timber fences and chopped some of my fruit trees for fire-wood." He shrugged and lifted his hands in resignation. "But what does Beauport matter?"

"The seigneury will be safer with the Général here than it would be otherwise," Crosbie insisted. "You know the troops are all on their best behavior when they are under his eye. And he did tell me to be sure that you prepared an inventory of everything..."

"Nonsense," duMaine broke in. He forced a jovial smile to his lips and held it there until it became genuine. "Who counts a minor loss when he is threatened with death? That is the choice, is it not?" He urged Crosbie toward the diningroom where he kept his supply of decanters.

"Papá?" a light voice called. "Is that you, Papá?"

DuMaine wheeled toward the drawing room. "Céleste, my dear," he rumbled. "I thought you were still in... ah, my apologies, Monsieur Tremais. I could not see you in the darkness. Céleste, why don't you light some candles?"

Crosbie trailed duMaine into the drawingroom and stood silently just inside the doorway until Céleste had kindled a candlelighter and circled the room, touching it to the candelabra. She caught sight of his immobile bulk as she turned and a small, startled cry escaped her parted lips.

"Oh! Duncan. What a surprise."

"Captain Crosbie has come for dinner," the seigneur interrupted in a cheerful bellow. "And, Monsieur Tremais, I hope you... Ah, but forgive me again. I have not presented Captain Crosbie..."

"The captain and I are old friends," Tremais said in a precise voice. "I am delighted to see you looking so well, sir." He thrust forward a thin leg and bowed over it in a delicate swift motion like a hen bobbing for corn.

Crosbie returned the formality. "And I, sir," he said, determined not to be outdone in politeness, "have been delighted with everything I have heard of your work here. There will be even more, I trust?"

"You may be sure of that," Tremais said dryly. "I have even now come to ask if Mademoiselle Céleste can..."

"Monsieur," Céleste broke in with nervous insistence, "may I offer you some refreshment?"

"Thank you," Tremais said in a surprised tone. He would have added something further, but duMaine's heavy voice rose over his lighter tones.

"What was it you came to ask my daughter, monsieur?" The voice was politely demanding.

"Nothing of importance, Papá," Céleste said quickly. She gestured toward Crosbie, her eyes alone betraying a certain nervous excitement as she tried to distract the seigneur. "Now, don't you think our guests..."

"Céleste!" DuMaine's voice deepened.

The young girl shrugged resignedly. "You know perfectly well," she said with sharp clarity.

The seigneur turned and advanced until his face was close to Tremais's. "Monsieur," he snapped, "I have ordered my daughter to take no further part in any trickery or masquerade."

"My dear sir!" Tremais protested.

"Dieu de Dieu!" duMaine bellowed. "I don't care what you wanted, monsieur. I know you have done valuable work. But I refuse to permit my daughter..."

"Papá!" Céleste almost wailed, her face rosy with suppressed annoyance. Her hand touched lightly at duMaine's angry brow. "Monsieur Tremais asked me if I could recall the details of certain things that occurred in the past. I had already informed him of your attitude."

"Very well," the seigneur grumbled. He bowed stiffly to Tremais. "I intended no offense, sir."

"You have offered none, monsieur," Tremais said briskly, dismissing the incident with a casual shrug. "Now, I fear I must leave. I have engaged my boatmen only until six o'clock. If Mademoiselle Céleste can walk a few steps with me, I am sure she can tell me all I need to know."

DuMaine bustled Tremais into his long cloak and his huge cocked hat. He handed him his stick and even stood in the doorway, smiling tightly as the King's investigator and Céleste walked slowly away from the manor. But he was still flushed with anger when he returned to Crosbie in the drawingroom.

"Now, let's have that drink, my boy. I cannot fathom why I am always such an unmannerly boor with that poor dry stick of a man. I simply cannot learn to like him."

Crosbie nodded cautiously. Tremais was far more than a poor dry stick, but Crosbie was unwilling to contest any issue with Céleste's father, if he could avoid it. He accepted a large glass of brandy and sipped from it gratefully, letting the pleasurable silence build until duMaine himself changed the subject.

"Will you please be sure to tell Louis-Joseph how pleased I am to offer Beauport's hospitality to him and his staff? I will see that all is ready when he arrives."

"And the family?" Crosbie urged gently.

"My mother leaves for Montreal with the girls in the morning. All is ready."

"The Général will assign your company to a post nearby," Crosbie said. "So, if you have any free time, you will be able to spend it at Beauport."

Both men turned as the outer door opened again and Céleste came in. She went directly into the drawingroom without glancing toward the two men who stood before the sideboard across the hall. Crosbie glanced uneasily at duMaine. The seigneur returned his gaze blankly, then shrugged. Feminine vagaries were an old story to him.

"I must see to ... something in the stables," he said hurriedly. "You will excuse me, Duncan."

Crosbie bowed stiffly as the seigneur stamped busily from the room. A door slammed crisply and before the echo had died away, Crosbie was across the hallway.

Inside the drawingroom, he stopped abruptly. Céleste stood at a window, holding back the glossy lute-string hangings and staring fixedly out at the village. Probably watching Tremais,

Crosbie guessed. He cleared his throat lightly. Céleste stepped back quickly and let the curtain fall into place.

"Duncan..." she murmured. Then she laughed in a bright rippling tone. "You are always surprising me today."

"Were you so deep in thought that you had forgotten I was here?" Crosbie asked mildly, choking back the quick resentment that flared in his mind.

"No! Oh, no, my dear. I do not forget you, ever." Céleste moved toward him smiling, holding out both hands to him.

Crosbie took her hands awkwardly. They were slightly cold and they trembled in his grasp. "Tremais," he said abruptly. "He has disturbed you. What was it he wanted you to do?"

She looked up at him for a long moment and there was no brightness in her green eyes now, only a dark, shadowed glint.

"What did he ask you—or tell you?" Crosbie insisted.

"Some things I cannot tell you, Duncan," Céleste said softly. "Some..." she shrugged. "Some you will soon hear in any case. Monsieur Tremais told me that Bigot has issued some eighty million francs in ordonnances beyond the amount he was authorized to issue. Eighty million francs! While good people in Canada, people like Madame Arnaud and the other habitants in Beauport, go hungry!" Céleste's hands were no longer cold in his grasp, but they still trembled. With anger now, Crosbie knew.

"The vast amount of Bigot's thievery may be news," Crosbie said. "The fact of his thievery is not. Tremais must have told you more than that."

Again Céleste was silent for a thoughtful moment. Then she said flatly, "If there was more, I cannot tell you, Duncan. Is it not enough to know how Bigot and his people rob and betray..." her voice hesitated oddly over that word, then repeated it firmly, "yes, betray their own country. My country, too, my home."

Why was she so determined, Crosbie wondered in near-exasperation. How could Tremais's investigations make her forget that he was standing before her, that long lonely days had passed since the last time they had been alone together?

"Do you mean, that in spite of what you told your father, you are going to help Tremais again, endanger yourself again?" he asked sharply.

Céleste drew her hands from his, turned and went to stand at the window. Her voice came to him muffled and remote. She did not answer him directly.

"Canada has a score to settle with Bigot," she said. "So have I."

Crosbie moved toward her, stopped and made a helpless gesture with his outstretched hands. He could not argue with Céleste. Something about her—something as hard as steel for all her loveliness and warmth—told him that arguments and urgings would go unheeded. But he could not endure the thought of danger coming close to her.

After a long moment, he remembered something.

"Wait," he said, his voice almost harsh. "I will be back immediately. I have something to give you, something you must keep with you always in these ... these spyings for Tremais."

She was still standing at the window when he returned. He took her right hand and placed in it a heavy object that glittered coldly where the light struck it. Céleste stared, then lifted wondering eyes to Crosbie.

"A pistol!" she breathed, half startled, almost amused. One finger traced an inlay of silver along the steel barrel, a silver arrow.

"Carry it with you always," Crosbie said. "It is not a foolish joke. If you will play spy, you must face the possibility of danger."

Céleste smiled. "So small and ... elegant," she said. "It looks like a lady's toy."

Crosbie remembered where he had first seen the pistol that now lay in Céleste's slender hand. It would never do to tell Céleste that he had carried it from the Comtesse de Boyer's salon to prevent her from shooting him in the back as he ran silently down the Palace corridor. No, it was not a story for Céleste's ears, not that part of it. He bent to kiss her gently.

"No," he said. "It is not a toy, and it has never belonged to a lady..." his tone stressed the world lightly, "until now." Céleste lifted her lips to be kissed again and Duncan Crosbie forgot everything else. Her mouth was cool, in a child's tight-lipped kiss that softened gradually into a woman's eager searching.

Outside in the lowering dusk rose the clatter of last-minute activity. Once the seigneur's bull-heavy voice roared in exasperation. But Duncan Crosbie and Céleste were, for that brief moment, lost in a secret world. They heard nothing. They did not move even when duMaine's footsteps pounded heavily toward the door.

Suddenly Crosbie stiffened. The roseate film lifted from his mind. He wheeled quickly. The seigneur was running toward the house and that alone warranted unusual response.

"Duncan! Duncan!" duMaine bellowed. Drowning the hoarse volume of his voice came the sharp sullen roar of a signal gun from the riverbank. The alarm was quickly repeated along the line of French retrenchments.

Crosbie leaped for the door, completely forgetting Céleste for a flickering moment. He stopped short, one hand braced on the lintel, and glanced back. Céleste seemed to droop. Her hands fell limply at her side. Then she smiled brightly for him as their eyes met.

"Forgive me," he said softly, "I..."

"Go, Duncan," she answered quickly.

DuMaine's boots thundered in the hallway. "Duncan! It's the English! Pierre saw the mastheads. Hundreds of ships! All English!"

CHAPTER FORTY NINE

The English fleet included fewer than fifty ships-of-war, but totaled nearly three hundred sail in all, of which most were troop transports. But no accurate count of their number could be made that first night. The highest point of vantage in the neighborhood was the spire of Beauport's stone church, but only a hazy glimpse of varnished spars and slender mastheads was visible when Duncan Crosbie scrambled up the narrow staircase to the church tower. In the gathering twilight, the enemy fleet was almost hidden, but white naval ensigns fluttered mistily even when the masts were invisible.

A scattered rattle of musketry crackled faintly across the water from the Île d'Orléans. DuMaine nudged Crosbie when he spied the white froth churned high by desperate oarsmen who drove their escape boats madly across the wide channel to safety at Beauport.

Crosbie followed the seigneur down to the village and stood beside him silently as voluble, frightened habitants chattered of the English marines who had driven them from their homes at bayonet-point. French officers, equally excited, clustered tightly around the refugees, hurling a torrent of detailed questions that even an experienced général could not have answered. All along the solid line of the French encampment, platoon campfires blazed high and nervous soldiers gave up all thought of sleep as they gathered to discuss the enemy in hushed voices.

This was a tensely exciting moment. The enemy had finally come to offer battle, but there was no reason for alarm, Crosbie told himself firmly. Thousands of English troops would have to be disembarked with their heavy equipment. Enemy commanders would have to make their plans for attack. That could take weeks. There was no need to hurry, Crosbie insisted silently. But a wild fierce pulse pounded strongly in his temple.

Within an hour, galloping couriers were thundering along the road, back and forth from the city. And Duncan Crosbie had to leap desperately to keep from being run down when a gilded carriage with pennons flying and outriders clearing the way went hurtling by dangerously in the night. Crosbie recognized the Chevalier de Lévis. As second-in-command, he had been assigned the most vulnerable position on the Left. The Chevalier obviously intended to assume his command before the English could possibly launch an attack against his troops. Crosbie turned back to the milling crowd to find the seigneur. If de Lévis had raced to his headquarters, certainly Montcalm would not be far behind.

Crosbie was still on the fringe of the densely packed mob when he recognized the rotund, sober face of old Jeannot, the Général's servant. Jeannot sat wearily slumped on top of a heavily loaded cart drawn by a plodding horse.

"Captain Crosbie!" he shouted. He made a gesture with both hands as if dumping something into Crosbie's grasp. "You must make them clear a way for me to the Général's headquarters. Tomorrow morning he will be ..."

"Yes," Crosbie said. "Slowly, my friend. The Général comes here tomorrow?"

"In the morning," Jeannot shouted, almost screaming. "Can't you understand? Early, he comes. And I must have ..."

"Softly, softly," Crosbie said with a smothered laugh.

The huge young Scot leaned his great weight against the packed crowd, using his hooked hands to clear a path. Many men growled in momentary anger, but none objected further after a glimpse of Crosbie's bulk. He tapped duMaine's shoulder, gestured toward Jeannot, and assisted the seigneur through the shouting mob that still surged around the refugees from Île d'Orléans.

"The Général's servant is here, sir," Crosbie said, bellowing to make himself heard above the noise. "Could you have someone show him ..."

DuMaine shook his head excitedly. "No, no, I will take him up myself. I must tell Céleste. And the Grand'mère and Aimée will have to hurry. Come, my boy."

"I must return to Quebec," Crosbie broke in. "May I take one of your boats?"

"If you can find a crew," duMaine said. He glanced around. "I don't know ..."

"I'll find them," Crosbie said quickly. "Now, here is Jeannot, the Général's personal valet. W'll you show him ..."

As if he were gratified at being given something definite to do, the seigneur quickly took control of the situation, clearing a path for Jeannot's cart and impressing several habitants to assist in unloading.

Crosbie again struggled through the crowd, heading toward the landing along the river. An excited boatman volunteered to take him to Quebec. The man was visibly frightened as he rowed swiftly down the river, incessantly watching the ghostly masts of the enemy ships against the sky and leaving an erratic wake behind him.

Crosbie ran swiftly up the long zig-zag street to Upper Town, slowing as he moved through the Great Square.

The Général's large office was quiet. Montcalm sat in full dress uniform behind his big table. Louis de Bougainville stood with his back to the windows, hands locked tightly together, staring in moody silence at the floor between his shoes. The Général smiled as Crosbie bowed in the doorway.

"Come in, Duncan," he called amiably. "I want you with me tonight. I may have a target for that great knife you wear."

His voice was almost gay, Crosbie thought. Automatically, his right hand touched at his dirk, the thumb rubbing lightly over the carnelian seal set in the hilt. He glanced quickly at de Bougainville in time to see him look up with a tight frown.

"Sir," he said in sudden intensity, "you cannot..."

"Nonsense, Louis," Montcalm said, shrugging easily. "We may need protection if our good Governor has his rascals with him. And our Crosbie is surely a match for..."

De Bougainville sighed. He offered a quirky smile as a greeting to Crosbie. Then he dropped his gaze to the floor again.

"The Governor has graciously granted me an audience this evening," Montcalm said to Crosbie. "Louis feels this is no time to create further animosity. We should conciliate those thieving, lying..."

A murmur from de Bougainville was enough to interrupt the Général. He smiled, a tight, bleak grimace that held no humor. "Well, we shall see. Come along, gentlemen. Normally, I would allow the Governor to wait longer, but tonight we have much to do."

Montcalm clapped on his huge plumed hat and strode briskly toward the door, which Estére leaped to open. Crosbie fell in beside de Bougainville. His lifted eyebrows posed a question which Louis shrugged aside.

The wizened little Estére, carrying a fat roll of charts under one arm, ran to take his place behind them as they marched through the gloomy, resounding corridors of the immense Château, halting time after time to allow sentries to throw open still another set of guarded doors. Ultimately they were ushered into the Governor's chamber.

Montcalm had used the word "audience" to describe his appointment with the Governor, and in truth, the term was justified, for this vast room was clearly designed as an audience chamber, lacking only a king and royal retinue. Although a dozen people were standing at the far end, it seemed deserted.

The Intendant, Monsieur François Bigot, detached himself from the group and moved forward, bowing casually in response to Montcalm's formal salute. He was dressed ornately, as always, in a pink satin coat over pale blue smallclothes.

"The Governor regrets he will be unable to attend," Bigot said with a pleasant smile. "I have been fully empowered to take his place on this occasion." A humorously mocked eyebrow indicated Monsieur Bigot's conviction of his ability to replace the Governor on any occasion.

He acknowledged Montcalm's presentation of his staff with supercilious bows, his smile vanishing entirely as he looked at Crosbie. He raised his right arm stiffly out from his side and his imperious, flashing-eyed sister came forward to rest her hand on his wrist. She studiously avoided glancing toward Crosbie. Montcalm bowed politely, then waited silently for the Comtesse to remove herself. Two beautifully uniformed young lieutenants slid heavily carved chairs out from the wall. Bigot seated the Comtesse and himself. A third chair was belatedly produced for Montcalm, but delayed just long enough to indicate the Intendant's condescension. Montcalm waited, his face stiff with outrage, small hard knots of muscle visible along his jaw.

Louis de Bougainville shifted to the Général's right and Estére, unperturbed as ever, took position on the left where his charts would be readily available. Crosbie stood rigidly, directly behind the chair, staring hard at the bright cluster of gaudy coats at the end of the room. The watchful faces were a featureless blur at first, but gradually recognition grew. Most were the same politely vacuous faces that were always displayed at official functions, but poised at one side, ostentatiously apart, was the thin, impassive mask of Captain Seamus O'Neill, his pale cold eyes looking blandly at Crosbie. No flicker of emotion disturbed the expressionless gaze that held Crosbie's eyes with a lizard's pitiless glare. The young Scot felt a coldness move along his spine. He looked away when the Intendant sat forward tensely in his chair.

"The Governor has informed me," Bigot said in a quick voice that quivered with inward excitement, "that all seven fire-ships will be completed tomorrow. I felt you would be delighted to know that we are prepared to destroy the enemy before he can land his troops."

Montcalm nodded. "Most gratifying," he said evenly.

"The Governor has drawn up a plan, mon général," the Intendant went on, his voice rising with tension. "We will launch the fire-ships in conjunction with an attack by the army against the English units that may have landed. The floating batteries will later be towed close to the Île d'Orléans to support our assault in its final stages. Now what do you think of that!" Bigot sat back. His soft hands locked together in his lap and his chin lifted high as he beamed at the Général.

"Very ingenious," Montcalm said equably. "His Excellency and you, monsieur, have shown clever imagination."

Bigot glanced in momentary bewilderment toward the Comtesse, then turned again to Montcalm. "Is that all you have to say, monsieur?" he demanded. "Surely such a plan requires a more forceful response."

"From me?" the Général inquired blandly.

"Indeed from you, monsieur." The Intendant's voice rose high with sharp insistence.

"I must congratulate you, sir. The plan shows a daring spirit worthy of a true son of France." Montcalm spoke with a slow precision that betrayed no hint of personal opinion. "I must, however, decline the part you have intended for me."

"But..." The Intendant stiffened. A dangerous anger pulled his wide mouth down at the corners. After a fleeting glance at the Comtesse, he cleared his throat. "I speak for the Governor," he said, "in demanding that you join in this attack, monsieur."

"With all due respect to His Excellency, I must decline."

"Then the Governor will take the militia and Canadien regulars and lead them himself against..."

"All troops, including the militia, are under my sole command, monsieur," Montcalm said sharply. "Please remind His Excellency of that fact."

"But you have ten thousand militia," Bigot said.

"I have eleven thousand, most of them untrained," Montcalm said in cold arrogance. "I will retain them all."

The Comtesse shifted irritably in her chair and her brother turned to look at her for a long, meaningful moment.

"Do you plan to allow the enemy to land unopposed?" Bigot asked stiffly.

Montcalm's shoulders tensed. "I must remind you, monsieur, that the Governor's orders have already cancelled two opportunities to strike the enemy. My plan to fortify Cap Tourmente and to emplace artillery on the Île d'Orléans."

"The Governor insists that a military force should never be divided. He says it is the first lesson taught a cadet."

"I am no cadet, monsieur," Montcalm said coldly. "I will explain once more why I oppose your fire-ships. Please attend me. First, it is a criminal waste of our meagre stock of gunpowder and explosive shells. But more important, it is doomed to fail. The launching of fire-ships is the most intricate and dangerous maneuver in naval warfare. An incredible degree of skill and good luck is necessary to bring the ships anywhere near the enemy. And a suicidal bravery is also required. Your naval officers have neither, as we both know very well. At Louisbourg, the navy refused to fight, even when the enemy was outnumbered. Here we saw the frigate commanders skulk upriver long before the enemy appeared. I repeat," Montcalm said heavily, "we cannot afford the waste of ammunition. And we do not have men of sufficient training and bravery to carry out the mission. I remain opposed."

"The Governor insists you attack," Bigot said sharply. "Attack, mon général. Do you know what that means? Attack!"

Crosbie's chin rose in angry response and he could hear Louis de Bougainville mutter quietly. The Général was straighter, stiffer.

"The responsibility is mine alone, monsieur," he said in barely controlled fury.

After another silent consultation with his sister, the Intendant swung back to Montcalm. "Just what are your plans, sir?" he demanded. "How do you intend to defeat the enemy?"

"I will not defeat him," Montcalm snapped impatiently. "I do not play the part of Hannibal in this campaign. I am cast in the rôle of Fabius. I will force General Wolfe to defeat himself."

The Comtesse sniffed audible contempt and her brother sneered dramatically at Montcalm. He lifted one soft hand as if to mask his expression and in so doing, merely emphasized it. The Comtesse leaned forward in sudden decision. Her voice was sharp and brittle in the quiet room. "Wars are won by attack, monsieur, not by running from the enemy."

Montcalm turned to look directly at the Comtesse. He stared at her silently, bowed slightly and returned to the Intendant.

The Comtesse slapped both jeweled hands smartly against the arms of her chair. "I spoke to you, mon général," she almost spat.

"Madame," the Général said heavily, "with due respect, permit me to have the honor to say that ladies ought not to talk war."

The Comtesse's gasp was echoed by the watchful courtiers who lounged behind her. She gripped hard at her chair and her thin, mobile face tightened to a shrewish mask. "Général, I insist that you …"

"Madame!" Montcalm's parade-ground rasp over-rode her lighter voice. "With due respect, permit me to have the honor to say that if Madame de Montcalm were here and heard me talking war with Monsieur Bigot, she would remain silent."

The Intendant came to his feet briskly. There was a sly look of satisfaction in his eyes, Crosbie thought. But why? Pleasure at his sister's discomfiture? Or had the entire interview gone just the way he had planned? Bigot stretched out his hand to his sister. "You will hear from the Governor, mon général," he said in a harsh tone. "This audience is dismissed."

Montcalm rose and his farewells came from clenched teeth. "Monsieur," he said, bowing politely. "Madame la Comtesse." His staff backed away as the Général saluted the Intendant's sister. Montcalm put on his plumed hat as he turned away. His face was hard and cold. His heels rang sharply on the bare floor. He held his mouth angrily closed as he stalked through the door.

Estére scurried ahead to make sure that no inattentive sentry delayed the infuriated Général. On the long trip back to his office, Montcalm said nothing. De Bougainville chewed his inner cheek, looking at Crosbie thoughtfully. Inside his private room again, the Général dashed his ornate hat to the table and whirled on de Bougainville.

"And I suppose you will say it was possible to conciliate that imbecile, eh?" Hot fury choked the words in Montcalm's throat.

"No, sir," Louis de Bougainville said. "I could not have contained myself as long as you did. The Intendant deliberately set out to provoke you. And to present himself as the valiant champion of Canada. I wonder who it was he hoped to convince. But..." he shrugged. "In a long campaign, we will need the Governor's support. There is no point in alienating him and his Intendant, if it can be avoided."

Montcalm seated himself wearily and held his head in both hands. He was silent for a long moment. Then he spoke, his voice muffled. "You are right, Louis. We must placate the fools somehow. Any suggestions?"

De Bougainville slid the roll of charts from Estére's grip. He extracted one and spread it across the Général's table. "The bulk of the militia will be massed on the Right. We have assigned a number of able officers under Captain Dumas to command them. We might offer the Governor titular command of the Right. He could harm nothing."

Crosbie leaned over de Bougainville's shoulder, seeing his finger trace the position of the French Right, from its flank on the city, to its eastern boundary where it joined the Center which would be commanded directly by Montcalm.

The Général lifted his head. He glanced casually at the chart and nodded. "See to it, Louis," he said tonelessly.

"I will, sir," de Bougainville said quietly.

Montcalm's eyes fastened blankly on Crosbie, then gradually focussed with growing interest. He half smiled at the huge young Scot who towered in the doorway.

"I will go to Beauport tonight," he said abruptly. "Louis, you move the headquarters in the morning. Duncan can come with me now." He rose with quick decision. "Yes, I'll go to Beauport now. I want to see the troops. I've spent too much time in Quebec lately."

The Général strode to the door, flung it open and shouted for Estére. Crosbie glanced silently at de Bougainville.

"He is all right, Duncan," Louis said in a soft whisper. "It has been a trying period, but the waiting is over now. Go with him."

CHAPTER FIFTY

The next morning Duncan Crosbie awakened early, seeing grey light on the walls of his room at Beauport and hearing the wild lashing fury of a storm that blew gustily from the west.

Crosbie stretched lazily, then suddenly remembered that the English fleet was lying at anchor off the Île d'Orléans. In one swift lunge he was out of bed, thrusting his chilled feet into Indian moccasins. He scrubbed his face in cold water and pulled on his clothes hastily, fingers trembling with urgency.

Guiltily he wondered if he might have overslept this morning, even though he knew from experience that he was seldom able to lie abed after the first light. But last night had been a late one by any standard, for he had accompanied the Général to Beauport and their progress had been one long triumphal march from Quebec to the manor, with the road lined thickly by cheering soldiers who fired their muskets in a reckless feu-de-joie as if they had already conquered General Wolfe and his huge English army. And Montcalm, with that instinctive feeling for the common soldier that marks every fine commander, had dallied endlessly, responding with bows, pausing to salute old comrades in arms, taking time to visit every regimental headquarters along the way and drink at least one toast to Wolfe's confusion. Montcalm, for all his volatile explosiveness, was a well-loved commander. The self-appointed escort that followed him to Beauport must have numbered half the regular troops of the army.

Aroused by the cheering soldiers, the Sieur duMaine had awakened in time to greet them. He had come outside, bypassing a loaded wagon and his high gilded carriage that stood ready before the door. Crosbie recalled that the ladies of the seigneur's family were planning to leave for Montreal in the morning. And he had not yet had an opportunity to say farewell to Céleste.

Eagerly, he had looked inside the drawingroom, hopeful that Céleste might have come to welcome the Général. But the seigneur had ushered them both to their rooms with affectionate brusqueness. Crosbie had paused to assist the Général with his tight boots and had then gone to his own room, to lie awake nervously until a welcome sleep had seized upon him at last.

His last waking thought had been a determination to arrange a private moment with Céleste before the carriage took her off to safety at Montreal. And as he pulled on his shirt in the morning, he remembered in complete detail just how he had planned to arrange that meeting.

He rammed his bulky shirt tails into his breeches and snatched up his shaving canister. He moved briskly toward the kitchen. In the hallway he could hear a faint murmur of heavy masculine voices speaking softly as men will when they know people are still sleeping, but rising now and then in forgetfulness. Warily, Crosbie tapped on the kitchen door before he entered.

Inside, Montcalm sat in his customary morning deshabillé, his cropped head covered with a knotted silk handkerchief. In both hands he nursed a steaming mug of coffee, leaning forward across the kitchen table, smiling lazily at Jeannot, who stood at the sideboard, slicing a long loaf of fresh bread.

"Ah, Duncan," the Général said pleasantly. "Come join us. A miserable morning, eh?"

"Yes, sir," Crosbie said. "Especially for the English."

Montcalm chuckled. He slid a second chair forward for Crosbie. "Monsieur Wolfe came to my mind also when I saw the rain. I do not envy him this morning." He poured a second mug of coffee and pushed it toward Crosbie. "I was saying to Jeannot that..."

Cautious footsteps clattered in the hallway outside, and the mellow clank of spurs echoed each stride. A gloved fist tapped lightly on the half open door.

"Louis!" Montcalm rose briskly from his chair and moved around the table. He pounded his hand against de Bougainville's shoulder, sending a spray of moisture into the air each time he touched his aide's dripping cloak. "What a surprise to see you so early, my boy."

Louis de Bougainville opened the clasp of his cloak and let it drop to the floor. He peeled back his sopping hat and handed it to Jeannot. His uniform was damp around the collars and cuffs, with the linen wrinkled and sagging. He bowed sketchily to the Général and wearily accepted the coffee that Jeannot offered him.

"It is not early, Your Excellency," he said in a thick tone. "I can assure you, sir, it is not early. It is, rather, devilishly late for a man of my retiring disposition."

Montcalm laughed easily and gently pushed de Bougainville to a chair. Crosbie seated himself after the Général had taken his place again.

"Up all night, were you? Carousing, I suppose? Ah, you reckless young..."

"I am a careful old man, as Your Excellency well knows," de Bougainville said dolefully. "I have spent a strenuous night with the Governor, the Intendant, and an endless number and variety of young gentlemen..." He sipped briefly from the mug of coffee. "...and young ladies. At least, the Governor said they were ladies. I would not care to be so positive on my own authority. Incidentally, I considered it part of my duty to join the gentlemen at the Intendant's gaming table. I lost some fifty louis. Do you suppose I could be reimbursed for..."

"Certainly not," Montcalm insisted with mock-solemnity. "That is a small price to pay for keeping evil associations." He turned to Crosbie and cocked one eyebrow. "The moral is clear to you also, I hope?"

"Perfectly, sir," Crosbie smiled stiffly. How in God's name, he wondered, would he be able to see Céleste alone, if the Général wanted him as escort today. He fidgeted anxiously.

"In any event," de Bougainville said quietly, "the Governor is no longer furious with the army. Somehow he has convinced himself that your refusal to attack is merely a decision of the moment. He fully expects you to change your mind soon. And he realizes that he should not subject you to additional pressure during these trying days." He leaned slowly back in his chair and sighed heavily. "The man is an idiot. And Bigot is no better. Do you know that our worthy Intendant is going to join the Governor in the field today? Yes, these stalwarts will be on hand every day to cheer the troops. Of course, they will dine at the Palace and sleep there, probably, but they will lend the weight of their inspiring presences at ..."

"Excellent," Montcalm broke in. "Go to bed, Louis."

De Bougainville shook his head determinedly. "The Governor is going to visit you this morning. To view the enemy, he told me. And also, to tell you that he will launch the first fire-ships tonight. There will be no English army tomorrow, so I'd best stay awake to see the end of the war."

Montcalm snorted. "Go to bed," he said flatly. "Duncan will be sufficient company for this morning. I will be back at mid-day." He turned briskly to Crosbie. "In ten minutes, monsieur?"

"Yes, sir." Crosbie gulped his coffee hastily. He filled his shaving canister from Jeannot's supply, snatched a chunk of bread and carried both back to his room.

He shaved in frantic haste, and threw on his uniform with hands that seemed to fumble stupidly. He slid his dirk into position, snatched his hat and cloak and almost ran along the hallway toward Céleste's room. Outside, he lifted his hand with determination, then hesitated. His knotted fist poised in mid-air. After a brief, cowardly moment, it fell to his side. What if the Sieur duMaine were to hear him? Or the Général? What if Céleste cried out in alarm?

Crosbie clamped his teeth in painful tension. And what if, he repeated to himself, what if he left without seeing Céleste, and never saw her again? Which would be worse? Swiftly, before he had time to reconsider, he tapped softly on the door.

There was almost no delay. The latch clicked and the door swung open. Céleste came into the hallway and closed the door softly behind her.

"Duncan," she whispered. "I was coming to …"

"My dear, I was afraid …"

Both stopped in mid-sentence. Both began again, in unison. Crosbie broke the momentary deadlock when he touched her shoulder gently. She moved into his arms with no hesitation. Crosbie kissed her upraised lips with a soft pressure. Only after a long warm moment did she push herself away.

"Duncan," she smiled. "Do not be so urgent, my dear." Céleste lifted her hand to her hair and only then did Crosbie notice that she was fully dressed in one of the crisp, demure morning frocks she wore for housekeeping duties. "Now, take me to the Général. I must see that he has a proper breakfast."

Crosbie laughed in helpless bewilderment. "The Général has breakfasted long ago, my dearest," he said in an uneven tone. "He will leave in a few minutes and I … I must go with him. I probably won't be back before you leave for Montreal and I hoped …" His inane, stumbling words brought a high flush to his face and he fell silent.

"Leave?" Céleste said lightly. She looked closely at Crosbie, seeing with a woman's bright magic what it was that disturbed him so deeply. "But, my darling Duncan, I am not leaving. Only the Grand'mère and Aimée. I stay here. Papa has permitted me to help Mère de Sainte-Claude at the General Hospital." With infinite gentleness, she touched his mouth with a cool finger that stroked away the bitter tension. "I will be here, my dear."

In a swift surge of thankfulness, Crosbie lifted her hand to his lips.

"I've been a fool," he muttered.

"A lovable fool," Céleste agreed, smiling. "Now go quickly, if you must. I will be here, my dear."

Crosbie moved away slowly. Then, abruptly, he turned and ran toward the door, almost leaping in high elation. He buckled his tarpaulin cloak tightly at the neck and stepped outside, pausing to unhook the cocks of his hat.

At the doorway, young Denis stood draped to his feet in a sodden cloak, holding the reins of two bay geldings that fretted nervously at the hard, driving rain.

"Good morning, Denis," Crosbie grinned. He hadn't seen Denis very often in the past few weeks. "How are you, my boy? And how is the kindly Madame Arnaud?"

"We are well, Duncan," the boy said soberly. "As well as most at such a time."

Something in the boy's tone was disturbing. He looked thinner, too. Crosbie frowned thoughtfully. "What is it?" he asked abruptly. "What's troubling you?"

Denis traced a pattern in the wet earth with the toe of one boot. "It is nothing," he muttered. Then he raised his eyes to Crosbie and the young Scot saw a look of frustration and bewilderment there. "Madame Arnaud's sister and her three children are with us now," he said. "They are refugees from the English. Two of the babies are sick with fever. Their father was killed."

Crosbie nodded sympathetically. It was not an unusual story these days, he thought gloomily.

Denis swallowed hard. "They are hungry," he went on, "half-starved. There is so little food. I hunt and fish for them, but it is not enough. Of course, I have my rations, too, but there is never enough. What money Madame Arnaud had has gone to buy food. But, Duncan, it buys so little!"

Crosbie's lips tightened. Bigot and his scavengers, he thought. Making ever-growing fortunes from the hunger of Canada's people. Even the well-run seigneury of Beauport was suffering. He asked the boy if the seigneur could not help.

"He helps, Duncan." Denis said. "But he has so many people. We cannot ask for more than our share. And there are five of us in the house now, not two." He smiled with determined cheerfulness. "You must not worry. We will manage."

"We'll have to do something," Crosbie said heavily.

He stiffened as the door opened behind him. The Général stood in the entrance, his back turned as he gave last-minute instructions to Jeannot. Then he pulled on his floppy hat, latched his cloak, and joined Crosbie in the rain. Denis flicked protecting cloths from the saddles of both horses. Crosbie took the reins from Denis and paused to look at the boy. Denis grinned widely. Duncan Crosbie smacked him gently on the shoulder with one heavy fist. He eased his great weight carefully up and swung into place. Then he touched his spurs and his fractious mount lunged after Montcalm.

The Général dropped unheralded into company areas, rain streaming from his hot and cloak. He never once allowed a guard to pass him without a proper exchange of challenge and countersign. Company officers were summoned by frightened couriers. Montcalm strode through the mud down the rows of company tents with chilling rain blowing hard under his cloak, seeing everything. One company commander, absent when the echoes of the réveille bugle had died away, was relieved on the spot.

There seemed to be no limit to the Général's savage energy as he swept along the full three leagues of the retrenchment. He gave the impression of being everywhere at once. Soldiers standing lazy and sleepy-eyed at first formation would see their Général sitting his tall bay gelding, watching their officers intently. And those same soldiers, after a route march into the hills to practice assault evolutions, would find the Général waiting for them, his full muscular face hard with concentration, his eyes fierce and determined. And no man thought of slighting his duty, for Montcalm was certain to see him and equally certain to scourge him with the full force of a blazing fury.

At mid-morning, even the great muscles of Duncan Crosbie were beginning to feel the strain, but Montcalm seemed to gain added spirit from his endlessly exacting inspections. But even he sighed gratefully when he and Crosbie swung down from their saddles and handed the horses over to the sentry who stood guard before Beauport's church.

"We've inspected almost everything else," Montcalm said with a quick smile. "Shall we now have a look at Monsieur Wolfe?"

Crosbie stepped under the shelter of the porte-cochère and banged his soggy hat against a post. Abruptly he sneezed and looked up in mild alarm. "The middle of Summer," he growled, "and the. rain is falling like ice."

The Général laughed pleasantly. "It is nearly July. We have already passed the season of Summer. Here in Canada, Winter comes before August, I suspect. What an abominable climate."

He slid his telescope from a saddle compartment and climbed rapidly up the narrow staircase. The Général's sharp voice blazed angrily at two young lieutenants he found lounging in the bell-tower, languidly eyeing the British fleet. Crosbie stepped aside to let the chastened pair escaped the Général's baleful glare.

Montcalm slipped the guards from his telescope, slid it out to its full length and aimed it at the Île d'Orléans. With his naked eye, Crosbie could see well enough, considering that all visibility was seriously hampered by the slanting rain that churned the river into froth. A forest of denuded masts stood in stark pattern beyond the island. There seemed to be no activity that Crosbie could make out.

"I have been reminded a thousand times lately," the Général said in a casual tone, "of the miraculous salvation of Quebec some fifty years ago. An English fleet entered the river then, and was destroyed by a great storm. Many people have been praying for a repetition. I have little hope that..." the Général grunted abruptly and fell silent. His hand adjusted the eye-piece of his glass more precisely. "Ah-hah!" he breathed with satisfaction. "Not a second miracle, but..."

"Sir?" Crosbie stood on tiptoe in vain effort to see more clearly.

"Two wrecked whaleboats," the Général said. "They have clearly been abandoned. And one, two, three, four, five flat-boats. All damaged. That will put an extra spoke in Monsieur Wolfe's wheel. And if there has been that much destruction that we can see, there must be more that is out of sight. Possibly even to the ships themselves."

"Will that be much handicap, sir?"

Montcalm turned quickly, frowning. Then he shrugged. "No, certainly not. But all soldiers are superstitious, you realize. An evil omen can have a serious effect among troops. But it is no set-back to a sensible commander." He returned to his careful inspection of the island. Then he pushed his telescope together and screwed on the guard-caps again. "De Lévis says they have some fifty warships. How many guns would you say they carried?"

"Most navies average forty guns, I believe," Crosbie said easily. "Unless the English have an unusual proportion of smaller ships, they must have some two thousand cannon on the river."

Montcalm made a brief noncommittal sound deep in his throat. He gestured for Crosbie to precede him down the staircase.

"A pity the storm did not come up to expectations. I wonder if the Governor's fire-ships will be any more successful?" And the Général laughed softly, almost to himself, as if he had remembered an old, private joke.

CHAPTER FIFTY ONE

It was a gay party that crowded the small square belfry of Beauport's church that evening. The Marquis de Vaudreuil had invited Montcalm and his staff to join his victory celebration. And since the outcome could not be questioned, the festivities began even before the fire-ships left their moorings in the St. Charles basin. Bottles of wine circulated freely, with the gentlemen acting as wine stewards since the tower was too cramped to admit servants.

When the Général, closely followed by Colonel de Bougainville and Captain Crosbie, had reached the church entrance, he had found the yard tightly patrolled by two full companies of Canadien regulars, every man dressed in the fantastically rich uniforms that Crosbie had noticed earlier at the Palace.

Lesser courtiers blocked the narrow staircase, pushing with polite ruthlessness for a view from one of the tiny windows that pierced the tower. On the upper landing, the Chevalier Le Mercier, huge and choleric, barred the way to all but favored guests.

The Général moved briskly forward to bow to the Governor and his aides followed. Then, their duty accomplished, de Bougainville and Crosbie mingled with the excited, chattering company. The bleak walls and simple windows of the tower had been patriotically draped in white and gold bunting and huge masses of scented wax candles blazed from makeshift chandeliers, stirring bright dazzles of reflected light from the jewels and enameled orders of the ladies in court dresses complete to trains and panaches. Most of the men were in dress uniform and even the Governor had restrained his taste for the exotic and tonight was wearing a simple coat of stone-grey velvet with great clusters of gold lace cunningly arranged to simulate a Général's uniform.

Duncan Crosbie backed skillfully through the press of elegant people around the Governor. He stretched out one large hand and tapped Le Mercier's shoulder with peremptory insistence.

"A word with you, monsieur," he said in a confidential growl.

Le Mercier grinned widely. He gulped the remainder of his wine and deposited the glass on the railing. "I am always at your service, my good friend," he said heavily. "How may I serve you?"

Crosbie slipped a folded paper from his pocket and flipped it open. "I prepared an inventory of gunpowder reserves a few days ago," he said in a harsh tone. "You gave me certain information. You recall?" At Le Mercier's nod he went on with barely restrained anger. "Some four hundred barrels of powder you told me were stored at the Palace and in the St. Louis magazine simply do not exist. Can you explain that, monsieur?"

The burly ex-sergent wiped the back of his hand across his mouth and glared blankly at Crosbie. "Do not exist?" he asked in a voice that almost whispered. "This is true?"

"It is true," Crosbie said in cold fury. "Colonel de Bougainville has inspected. How do you ..."

Le Mercier's bewildered gaze lifted from Crosbie's fierce eyes. Slowly, the Chevalier pivotted until he was facing the crowd of twittering courtiers that surrounded de Vaudreuil and Montcalm. "How many barrels in all?" he growled.

"Four hundred," Crosbie snapped.

"One moment. Please wait here." Le Mercier strode forward abruptly, lunging his solid weight against the wall of people in his way.

Crosbie watched intently as Le Mercier fought through the crowd toward a distant corner. Crosbie saw him tap a short, big-wigged man's shoulder and he recognized the flat frog-like features of François Bigot when the man turned to face Le Mercier.

Crosbie could see no more than the back of Le Mercier's head, but Bigot's face was visible and the young Scot stared with growing amazement as Bigot's expression registered first shock, then skepticism, then sorrow, then reassurance in response to Le Mercier's impassioned comment. Crosbie cursed himself for not following Le Mercier. It was clearly obvious that the Chevalier was accusing Bigot either of inventing the very existence of the gunpowder, or of removing it from the magazines. But Bigot's bland assurances, his swift recovery from the initial shock, was complete now. And his glib and practiced explanations were soothing Le Mercier's suspicions. Even Crosbie could see that the burly Chevalier was forgetting his first anger and was now merely bewildered by the turn of events.

When Le Mercier returned after a few minutes and explained that the powder had merely been shifted while the magazines were being inspected for dampness, Crosbie had nothing to say. Tomorrow he would do a careful inspection himself. For the moment there was nothing more he could do. He forced a meaningless apology for troubling the Chevalier.

Le Mercier smiled benignly. "Now, say nothing more of it, my boy. I like to see a soldier who knows his work. If that powder had truly been missing, I can tell you, there would have been complaints from me that even the King would have heard. And now," he said softly, leaning forward, one heavy finger laid along his nose in a confidential gesture, "tell me honestly, what do you think of those fire-ships?"

Crosbie sipped his wine and shrugged. "If they succeed, the idea is magnificent," he said absently.

Le Mercier chuckled. "If they succeed," he roared. "Very good! Oh, that's very good! If they succeed. Do you know who is commanding this desperate venture?" He went on without waiting for Crosbie's reply. "A naval coward named deLouche, a man who has run away every time he has been on the same ocean with the English. My boy," Le Mercier lowered his bull's voice to a thunderous whisper, "my boy, this will be a fiasco! Mark my words."

"I suspect so," Crosbie agreed easily. "But a profitable one, I have heard." He lifted his eyebrows.

"Exactly," Le Mercier said. "One million francs. A tidy sum. I wish now that some of it had come my way. Ah well, I shouldn't complain, I suppose."

"Indeed," Crosbie said noncommittally. "When is this desperate venture scheduled to assault-the English fleet?"

Le Mercier shrugged. "It was scheduled for nine o'clock. Since it is now nearly ten, we must assume that deLouche's belly has again failed him. Speaking for myself, I expect only a pleasant evening spent in amiable company, nothing more. Now, excuse me, my boy. I'll have just a word with Monsieur Cadet before ..."

Crosbie trailed the burly Chevalier into the crowd, heading vaguely for the windows. He could hear the Governor praising Monsieur deLouche's great enthusiasm, his superb dash, his endless courage. Montcalm merely nodded in response and made amiable noises in his throat. Louis de Bougainville stood casually nearby, blandly ogling the extreme decolleté of the gown worn by a bold-eyed beauty who languished in a posture that displayed her outstanding charms to excellent advantage. Crosbie grinned and skirted around the Colonel.

Dozens of naval telescopes had been furnished for the guests and many were in use, though there was as yet no action on the river. Crosbie adjusted an instrument and applied himself to the open window nearby. The broad river was almost obscured by a filmy bank of fog that seemed to drift like a stormcloud just above the water. On the Île d'Orléans, oil-soaked flares mounted on poles a good five mètres high furnished flickering illumination for the English troops who were still unloading their ships.

Only the reflection of their flares could be seen from Beauport and Crosbie soon wearied of the view.

He put the telescope aside and accepted a glass of wine and several small cakes from a tray being passed by an officer he did not know. He found a quiet corner and enjoyed his supper as well as he was able in a roomful of preposterous idiots. A shouted word from an officer posted at the window was the first warning of action. The Governor clapped his hands ceremoniously. He waited for silence, then escorted Montcalm to the window and offered him a telescope.

"A great moment, my dear Général."

"Memorable, indeed," Montcalm said equably, holding his face severely straight. "The fleet is in sight?" He extended his glass and leaned toward the window. Protocol required a decent privacy for the Governor and Montcalm, but everyone in the crowded tower moved constantly forward, shifting slowly but inexorably toward the windows, turning with small cries of apology and vexation to their neighbors, shrugging as if to blame the gentlemen behind, but never stepping aside. Soon Montcalm and de Vaudreuil had a dozen close neighbors, pressing in from all sides.

Crosbie strolled around the blind side of the tower, finding the floor completely clear. He joined de Bougainville who stood in quiet resignation where he had stood before, his eyes following the languid charmer now deserting him for a view of the fire-ships.

"A great moment, my dear Colonel," Crosbie murmured.

De Bougainville grinned suddenly. "Memorable indeed," he echoed. "What utter nonsense! Shall we go downstairs, Duncan? Possibly we can ..."

Crosbie shook his head. "We'd never be able to get down. The stairs are too crowded. Do you think anyone can see at all?"

"The Général will have a good view. We'll make him tell us the details later."

The Governor crowded exultantly from the window where he was leaning out, glass at his eye. "I see them! Four, five ... only five? Ah, doubtless the other two are hidden in the fog. Can you make them out, mon général? There, to the ..."

"They are perfectly clear, Excellency," Montcalm said amiably. "What is the plan? They will first sail around the Île d'Orléans, then fire the ships and ram the English fleet?"

"Exactly, sir, exactly," the Governor cried happily. He pulled his head back inside and lowered his glass. "It will be some time yet before they are in position, then what a sight you will see, mon cher général! A celestial display of pyrotechnics, I promise you. We have loaded those ships with ..."

"Great God!" Montcalm snorted. He leaned forward toward the open window.

The Governor stared for a brief moment, then followed Montcalm. Those fortunate enough to be at the window seemed to gasp in unison, Louis de Bougainville lifted his eyebrows curiously at Crosbie but did not move toward the windows.

Fragmentary comments rose in brief clarity above the incessant chatter. "... two leagues from the island, at the very best!" A smothered word that sounded like "idiots!" drifted to Crosbie's ears. And a young girl slumped in a collapsed heap and had to be assisted to a chair crying "what a dazzling fire!"

Colonel de Bougainville scratched his ear with casual disinterest, "Apparently the fire-ships caught fire," he murmured softly.

"A great pity," Crosbie agreed, forcing his mouth to rigid lines. A wild hilarity sparkled in his eyes. He was able to withstand the temptation only a moment longer, then he walked briskly toward the window. Happily, his unusual height gave him a vantage point. He could see a thin stretch of the river.

There, in a ghastly nimbus, lay a burning ship. Its masts and spars were perfectly outlined in dancing flames and the hull was a solid blazing mass. As Crosbie watched, the prematurely ignited fire-ship drifted downstream and a second came into the narrow space he could observe. This one had only recently been lighted, and tongues of flame were still licking at the masts as if in exploration. The mainsail vanished in a soft explosion of fire, then the flames raced along the entire superstructure of the ship.

The patch of river he was watching must be nearly four kilomètres from the western tip of the Ile d'Orléans. At such a distance, the fire-ships must be an amusing sight for the English.

Another ship drifted crazily by, solidly aflame, with crackling detonations sending great sheets of sparks out over the water. Barrels of pitch or oil exploding, Crosbie suspected. Then the ship spewed fire and smoke like an erupting volcano. Vast rumbling explosions tore the bottom out. Showers of grapeshot and musket balls roared harmlessly over the river. A cannon boomed once with that peculiarly hollow roar that means only one thing to a gunner: the piece was overcharged and had blown itself to shreds. Another rippling series of minor explosions, followed by an oily black cloud of smoke outlined with scarlet flames, then the fire-ship fell into blazing bits scattered across the river bed, drifting downstream, still burning brightly.

Bugles soared in alarm along the French lines. Fainter staccato commands stuttered from English trumpets across on the island. Both forces stood to arms, their commanders completely bewildered by the magnificent, meaningless display on the river.

Crosbie stepped back, his own eyes slightly dazzled. Colonel de Bougainville nudged him and drew him aside, close to the staircase. "Wait here," he said softly. "The Général will want to leave as soon as he can."

The Governor pushed himself slowly from the window. He turned and rested briefly on the sill, his back to the bright flares on the river. His hand opened absently and let the telescope clatter to the floor. Montcalm bent low and spoke quietly in his ear. The Governor glanced up and forced a thin smile.

"Monsieur deLouche is a poltroon," he announced in a quavering tone. "How can an officer do such a thing?" He drew his cupped hand over his forehead and looked up blankly at Montcalm.

Crosbie glanced curiously around the crowded tower. Most of the Governor's guests had moved unobtrusively away from the windows, hiding telescopes behind them, as if to deny that they had witnessed the shameful fiasco. As the press of people shifted, Crosbie had a momentary view of Monsieur Bigot who was whispering in Cadet's ear. The Intendant's face was tautly drawn with restrained humor. He grinned, a brief malicious grimace, then regained control.

De Bougainville nudged Crosbie again and the young Scot returned his attention to the Général in time to see him bow to the Governor and turn away toward the staircase. The evening's entertainment was over. Crosbie cleared the way to the top of the stairs, then stepped aside to let the Général precede him.

Side by side with de Bougainville, Crosbie descended the tower and followed Montcalm out into the yard. Five fiercely burning ships were still visible on the river. The light of the blaze made the village of Beauport as visible as if by moonlight. If those ships had been sailed resolutely among the English fleet, havoc would have been the only possible result. Two ships veered from their drifting courses and Crosbie realized that daring English soldiers had rowed out with grappling lines and were now towing the flaming ships safely away from their fleet. Not even by accident would the Governor's fire-ships damage the enemy.

Montcalm mounted swiftly and spurred his horse up the hill toward the manor. Crosbie kneed his horse close to de Bougainville.

"Louis," he said softly, "did you see Bigot's face just before we left?"

"No. I do not care to look at that face. What was interesting about it?"

"He was laughing," Crosbie said in wonderment. "You'd think he would take such a failure seriously."

"Don't bother about it, Duncan. These people are insane, I am ready to swear. They must be insane."

"I wonder," Crosbie muttered to himself. He urged his horse to a faster trot.

CHAPTER FIFTY TWO

For days, the enemy troops bivouacked on the Île d'Orléans, recovering from their long journey on cramped transports. They ravaged the prosperous island communities and farms, looting the gardens and fields, burning vast quantities of wood in fires that seemed to blaze night and day as the English strove for comfort in the chill of Canadien summer.

The Governor summoned a court of inquiry into Monsieur deLouche's peculiar conduct with the fire-ships. After hours of mutual recriminations, the hearings were dismissed with no result. Montcalm refused to attend the hearings, and he curtly banned the subject as one suitable for his staff officers.

After a week's rest, the English commander aroused himself. In the early morning, a brigade of infantry rowed across the south channel to Pointe Lévi and disembarked. Canadien partisans and their Indian scouts blasted musketry at their closely packed ranks, inflicting severe casualties for their limited number. After a brief skirmish, the partisan force withdrew in good order, and General Wolfe's first brush with his opponent ended in a clear victory for the English, uncontested, but nonetheless a victory.

The following morning, a courier from the Governor brought a proclamation that Wolfe had addressed to the citizens of Canada. It had been posted on the parish church at Pointe Lévi. The English commander ordered all Canadien citizens to remain neutral in the present conflict, promising full protection of property and religion if they did so, but threatening destruction of churches, houses, goods and harvests if they fought beside the French. The Governor attached to the English proclamation a rebuttal in almost equal terms, addressed to the same people, promising the same dire results if they did elect to remain neutral. Montcalm snorted impatiently and threw both papers contemptuously into the fire.

Montcalm went once more to the Governor, pleading for necessary assistance in fortifying the Heights of Pointe Lévi. The enemy was close, but a determined counter-attack could push them back into the river, the Général promised. The Governor refused to consider it. Two days later, Wolfe sent five thousand men across to the Heights opposite Quebec and the chance was lost: The English commander had assured the destruction of the great stone city that dominated the St. Lawrence. The entire force went to work building batteries to protect the artillery that would batter Quebec.

Four batteries of the city's permanent installation were able to bear on the enemy position. Crosbie also wheeled into place on the promontory of Cap Diamant two additional batteries of bomb-throwing mortars. The stubby mortars, barely a mètre from the ground, looking like great bulbous iron baskets, hurled a bomb nearly half a mètre in diamètre. Measurement of the powder charges required an expert judgment, as did the length to which the long tow fuse was cut. A short fuse exploded the missile harmlessly in mid-air; too long a fuse allowed time for the enemy to snuff it out before the bomb was detonated. Duncan Crosbie experimented with careful, finicky calculation to determine the best combination of charge and fuse length.

He traversed the cauldron-like mortar until it was aimed directly at the forward wall of the first parapet being thrown up on the Heights of Pointe Lévi. This was long range for a mortar and accuracy with these guns diminished as the distance increased. He called for three level scoops of powder to be poured into the gaping muzzle and rammed home with a wad of felt. The big shell was inserted carefully until the iron belt swedged around on the bomb casing was resting securely on the step inside the muzzle. Crosbie took a measuring rule and laid it along the fuse. He flicked his dirk from its sheath, cutting the fuse and making a mental note of the length. He signaled the sergeant to prime the mortar and he turned for the smoldering linstock propped handily against the wall. First he applied the match to the bomb fuse, and counted off a full five seconds before applying the match to the mortar. The gun roared.

High over the river the bomb soared, its flight marked by the sparks that flickered from the burning fuse. It seemed to hang for long moments at the apex, then dropped suddenly. Three seconds droned by, then the bomb erupted, throwing a billowing cloud of dust and rock fragments high into the air from a point far beyond the English breastworks. Too much powder, too much fuse, Crosbie told himself.

A second bomb soared perfectly in line, hung at the peak of its trajectory, then seemed to fall straight down. It dropped out of sight beyond the earthworks. Crosbie counted again with patient fury, waiting for the explosion. After a full minute, Crosbie knew it would not detonate. Either the fuse had failed, or enough fuse had remained to allow time for a daring Englishman to slice it off before it could ignite the charge.

He snipped the third fuse a hair shorter. This time the bomb exploded the moment it landed. An enormous section of the unfinished enemy redoubt blew high over the river. There was no protection for the soldiers digging. An entire platoon must have been wiped out with that single bomb, Crosbie estimated with professional interest, judging by the crumpled scraps of scarlet uniform he could see on the torn earth.

He called the sergents to him, demonstrated the length of fuse required, showed them how much powder was needed. He cautioned them to re-lay each mortar after every shot. The battery officer, an elderly lieutenant with one eye covered by a piratical black patch was warned not to waste one of the precious shells unless a suitable target was offered. Then Crosbie stepped back to watch the battery's practice.

Three rounds from each of the four mortars demolished what the enemy had accomplished so far. Across on Pointe Lévi, no enemy soldier save the dead could be seen. Crosbie nodded his approval.

"Very well. Cease fire. Probably you will have no worthwhile target until tomorrow morning, but keep careful watch."

Crosbie left the mortar battery, walking slowly back to the Château battery whose long-range cannon were firing with calculated irregularity in hopes of deranging the enemy's plans and upsetting his troops, even if the shots found no target.

"Stop that nonsense." Crosbie summoned the senior sergent and blasted him angrily. "We can't waste powder and shot like that, sergent," he almost snarled.

"But the Chevalier Le..."

"I don't care what the Chevalier said," Crosbie raged. "Targets of opportunity, yes. But not blind targets. I don't want a single gun fired without good reason. Is that clear?"

The sergent snapped to attention stiffly. "Oui, monsieur."

Through every battery, Crosbie stalked balefully, inspecting every detail with the thoroughness he had learned from Montcalm. In each he asked for the Chevalier Le Mercier and each battery commander sent a courier running for the commandant. But at mid-day, when Crosbie had finished his tour, he had learned only that Le Mercier could not be located. The angry young Scot shrugged with a bitter gesture. Le Mercier was avoiding him, obviously. That meant that he had learned the powder on his inventory actually was missing. For a moment, Crosbie considered visiting the Palace magazine to make sure, but he dismissed the subject at once. There could be no doubt that the powder was missing; probably it had never existed except on the Intendant's records. Vaguely Crosbie remembered that Jamie

Johnstone had told him of just such a savage piece of thievery at Louisbourg during its last days. Thank God, all the rest of the powder was safely in military hands. The supply would be limited, but intelligent supervision could make it stretch for an effective campaign. The strictest orders would have to be despatched at once to all units forbidding casual firing, and restricting all future issue to units commanded by regular officers who could be depended upon to enforce the order. Crosbie headed for the Château where he had left his horse. He would have to tell the Général, and probably write the order himself.

This afternoon he would detail two companies of infantry to move his cannon into position along the Montmorenci flank.

Then ... well, then he might make a trip of inspection to the General Hospital, just to see that everything was progressing satisfactorily. And he might, quite accidentally, see Céleste. Quite suddenly, the day was brighter.

CHAPTER FIFTY THREE

That night, thousands of enemy soldiers, working frantically in the darkness, threw up a serviceable cannon emplacement on the Heights of Pointe Lévi. It was not a redoubt of symmetry or excessive strength, but it was enough.

At dawn, when he jumped to the jutting parapet of Cap Diamant, Duncan Crosbie stared incredulously at the thick rampart, some two mètres high, that had risen magically on the Heights. Narrow slits of embrasures in the earthen wall each held a gaping iron muzzle aimed at Quebec. As he watched, the redoubt vanished in a billowing cloud of grey powder smoke. A wailing banshee's howl whistled in his ear and a terrible wind flung him backward off the parapet. A solid iron shot clanged resoundingly as it struck a metal beaker. Then the cannonball ricocheted, lifting slightly until it buried itself high in the wall of the Citadel. A long line of finely powdered stone sifted from the gaping hole.

Crosbie rubbed his head where he had smacked it in falling behind the parapet. He turned swiftly and ran down to the protected angle of the Great Square where the mortar batteries had been sited.

The lieutenant had already loaded his ranging piece and was ready to fire. He glanced up as Crosbie sprinted into view.

"Carry on, lieutenant," he said crisply.

He wheeled toward the Château battery, inspecting gun-crews and supplies with ruthless energy. Every battery that could be brought to bear against the enemy emplacement was in action soon afterward.

The artillery duel lasted through the long hot day. The few citizens still in the city ran for their lives, arms loaded with hastily gathered treasures. Crosbie spared a moment to give thanks that Céleste was safely ensconced in the General Hospital which lay out of range along the St. Charles.

Though the English gunners could spare few shots for non-military targets, many houses were destroyed, for the city was built closely around the main batteries, and even a near-miss found some sort of building.

By mid-day, three enemy cannon were out of action in the eight-gun battery, all due to the French mortars that were firing slowly but with considerable effectiveness. All through the deafening battle, the full-throated, bull-like roar of the Chevalier Le Mercier soared above the din, exhorting his gunners in extravagant profanity. Crosbie ignored the commandant. Today's work was merely siege warfare at its most rudimentary, the first lesson learned by the novice gunner. Le Mercier could harm nothing with his interference.

Only once did Crosbie notice the Général. Montcalm rode his favorite black, closely followed by de Bougainville and Estére, moving from gun to gun, watching every crew, but offering no comment to Crosbie. Later, the young Scot realized that the silent approval was a compliment. But at the moment, he was too preoccupied to think about it. He saluted absently and went back to the huge brass dispart sights he was using to correct a cannon's aim.

Early in the afternoon the rate of fire from the enemy guns slackened. The mortars from Quebec had held a ring of fire around the enemy, keeping supply parties away. Diminished stocks of powder and shot were being hoarded by the English. Crosbie cursed wearily as he ordered a slower rate of fire from his own guns. He, too, had a supply problem to consider.

At twilight, when lowering dusk made careful sighting difficult, the rate of fire dwindled even more. Duncan Crosbie slumped in exhaustion, feeling the long muscles in his legs quiver as he stretched. Five English cannon had been knocked out of action. He must compliment the guncrews. But Crosbie felt no elation. By morning, those five ruined guns would be replaced. And a second, possibly even a third redoubt would be completed. Tomorrow, with more guns at their disposal, the English would be able to devote their attention seriously to the destruction of the city. And there was nothing Crosbie, or any French soldier, could do to prevent it. Tired as he was, Duncan Crosbie felt a wild, errant pulse beating hard in his head as he thought of the fatuous Governor de Vaudreuil. With one petulant decision, he had demolished Quebec.

Wearily, Crosbie pushed himself erect and walked with stiff, stumbling strides to the Château for his horse. During the hour's ride to Beauport, he wavered often in his saddle, half asleep. He dismounted clumsily and handed the reins to a sentry. He could hear urgent voices in the Sieur duMaine's sitting room which the Général was now using as his office, but he kept walking unsteadily down the hall toward his room. As he pulled on his clothes, he glanced once briefly at himself in the mirror, and not until he was in bed, did his noise-stunned mind register what he had seen. His face was caked with burnt powder, deeply black in the grooves of fair skin, an unhealthy grey film on his forehead. And the carefully powdered red hair had a hard crusty halo of black that framed his face. Duncan Crosbie licked the acrid gunpowder from his lips and fell promptly asleep, still hearing the incessant cannonading in his deafened ears.

By morning his ears were only slightly better. No amount of scrubbing could erase the burnt-powder greyness from his skin. He brushed the black crust away and washed his hair several times. Even so, he had to use the powder dredge lustily before he felt presentable enough to appear at the Général's table.

As had now become routine, Crosbie and the Général were alone at breakfast. The Général was comfortably seated at the table, toying with a wineglass, chatting aimlessly with Jeannot. The young Scot glowered at the sight of his commander who seemed insultingly well rested and alert when Crosbie was sharply aware of his bloodshot eyes, his slightly impaired hearing and his painfully dry throat that merely croaked when he tried to speak. He bowed formally, poured a measure of white wine from the carafe on the table. When he had gulped it down, his momentary resentment vanished entirely and he was able to return Montcalm's smile with genuine pleasure.

"You were busy yesterday," the Général said easily.

"Yes, sir," Crosbie tore off a wedge of warm bread and dipped it in his wine. He bit off a big chunk and chewed hard.

"You returned too late to hear what the Chevalier de Lévis reported, didn't you?" The Général's lifted eyebrows, his faint quirked smile were the only indications of disapproval. No aide would dare to retire without his commander's express permission, so Montcalm was pretending he did not know that Crosbie had sneaked off to bed without reporting his presence.

Crosbie grinned. "I was too tired to hear anything," he agreed. "And I'm still a little deaf."

Montcalm nodded soberly. "It was hot work yesterday."

"And it will be hotter today," Crosbie said. He accepted the coffee Jeannot poured for him.

"Not for you," Montcalm said mildly. "We will leave the city in Monsieur Le Mercier's control today."

"But, sir ..." Crosbie began, choking in his attempt to speak.

"Please," Montcalm said, lifting one hand in command. "It is merely siege-craft. Le Mercier is qualified to deal with it. And do not interrupt me, Duncan. I know about the gunpowder inventory. I know Le Mercier will have to function with limited supplies. The fault is his. And the Intendant's. But I know all that. And I have told Monsieur Tremais. It will interest you to know that Monsieur Tremais is now prepared to request a warrant of arrest for both Monsieur Bigot and our worthy Governor.

Both have become incredibly brazen lately. They have made no attempts to conceal their thefts. Monsieur Tremais has all the evidence he requires."

Crosbie nodded. His first thought concerned Celeste. Now she would not be tempted to interfere with the Intendant's affairs, not if Tremais had all the evidence he had come to find. But the young Scot bit off another chunk of bread and smiled quizzically at the Général.

Montcalm laughed. "Yes, poor Tremais. He has the scoundrels at last. But he can do nothing without authority from Paris. And there is no way for him to communicate with Paris. A pity. But it does brighten the future. If we have a future. Now," Montcalm made an emphatic gesture. "The Chevalier de Lévis has received considerable attention from Monsieur Wolfe. Yesterday the English navy bombarded his position for some hours. I imagine you were too occupied to notice?"

"Yes, sir," Crosbie said.

"A small force of the enemy landed for reconnaissance. That unit remained on the north bank below the cataract, in the village of L'Ange Gardien. And de Lévis, very sensibly, feels that Wolfe will occupy that position with a major force today. I will be there this morning and I want you with me."

"Certainly, mon général," Crosbie agreed.

"Good. And please try to curb your restlessness, Duncan. Really, you fidget too much. If you must do something energetic, take yourself along the Montmorenci flank and see if you can find any of your gunners awake." The Général flicked his hand impatiently. "I will be at the Chevalier's headquarters at réveille. Meet me there."

"I will, sir," Crosbie said gratefully. He snatched an extra chunk of bread and went out, chewing a huge mouthful.

The morning was fresh and cool as Crosbie left the manor. Only the faintest lightening was apparent in the sky, but visibility was clear for a few mètres. A sentry slapped his musket in salute and Crosbie nodded casually. He turned toward the stable, then stopped short.

"Denis?" he called sharply.

"Oui, mon capitaine," the boy shouted. "One moment."

Hoofs clattered in the stableyard and a horse snorted. Denis came slowly into view, riding a shaggy, stunted brown horse hardly larger than a marshland pony, and leading Crosbie's bay gelding. The boy slid awkwardly from his saddle and brought his heels together with a tremendous crash.

"Good morning, Denis," Crosbie smiled. "Where did you find that miniature Rosinante?"

"The Sieur duMaine gave him to me," Denis said swiftly, his tongue almost stuttering in his eagerness. "I told him it was not fitting for me always to stay behind when you went off on duty. And he agreed. So now I have a horse, too, and I will go with you." The boy glanced up sharply, his thin face set hard with determination.

"And what of the good Madame Arnaud?" Crosbie asked. "You have her approval?"

The boy hesitated. "No, sir," he said honestly. "Not exactly. She said she would prefer that I stayed safely at home. But when I told her I would be with you, she said I must decide for myself." Wide eyes searched Crosbie's face. "She sends you thanks for the flour you had delivered to us. Things are a little better now, for the moment. The children are getting well." Denis grinned slightly. "Madame Arnaud hoards the food and issues it like medicine."

"But no one in the house is hungry?" Crosbie asked sharply.

Denis shook his head. "Thanks to you, Duncan. We are all right, for the moment." Then he returned sternly to the matter at hand. "You will let me accompany you? I am not one of these tame old servants, Duncan," he said in a quiet tone. "I am a soldier."

Crosbie stared at the boy silently. Surely he could come to little harm. Briefly, he nodded permission. "You will hold your position two mètres behind me at all times unless I signal you. Clear?"

"Oui, mon capitaine."

Crosbie waited until the boy had scrambled onto his ungainly mount. Then he swung into his saddle and led the way across country toward the Montmorenci. He heard Denis grunting with exertion and he twisted in his saddle to look back. The boy was struggling to sling a fusil across his shoulders and to control his horse at the same time. Crosbie slowed to give him time to catch up.

"Heavily armed, aren't you?" he smiled.

"As regulations require, sir," Denis said stiffly.

"Quite right," Crosbie agreed. "Follow me."

Crosbie found alert guards on duty at every gun he had sited along the Montmorenci. And he rode from one to the other in frowning concentration, deeply suspicious that the guncrews had by now become aware of his early habits and had all made a great point of careful watchfulness during that hour before réveille when Crosbie was most likely to come inspecting. Then he shrugged away the notion with a quick grin. Soldiers alert to their officers' quirks would be equally alert to enemy movement.

He kneed his nervous horse around and headed him toward the St. Lawrence, aiming toward the distant farmhouse that the Chevalier de Lévis had pre-empted for his headquarters.

"Denis," he called softly. "Isn't the Sieur deMaine bivouacked somewhere near here?"

"About half a kilomètre farther, Duncan," Denis said in a sleepy voice. He kicked his sluggish horse to make him trot. "Shall I lead?"

Denis turned toward the high ground that overlooked the Montmorenci, slowing as he rounded a curve. Ahead lay a thicket of dense bushes and beside it was a low stone hut, its dark slate roof glossy with moisture. Denis gestured forward and beat at his horse. Crosbie trotted easily behind the eager boy.

The Beauport militia company was already awake and moving busily. Each small platoon managed its own rations, and Crosbie could see a score of small smokeless fires flickering from the dim scrub-oak forest around the hut. As he and Denis dismounted, an unarmed sentry slouched forward, pulling off his red stocking cap politely and offering to hold the horses. Crosbie restrained his impulse to reprimand the militiaman. The Sieur duMaine bustled from the low hut, puffing noisily on a stubby clay pipe.

"Duncan, my boy," he called. "I thought I heard voices. And good morning to you, Denis. If you hurry inside, you may find that Pierre has some sweet cakes in his box." He patted the boy's back lightly, urging him toward the hut. Then he craned his neck to look directly at Crosbie. "Are you official this morning, Duncan?"

"No, sir, not at all," Crosbie said hastily. "I was passing by and I …"

"And came for a visit, eh? Excellent." He led the young Scot briskly to a pair of chairs set facing a low table. "This is my headquarters. Rather small, but pleasant enough."

Crosbie sat and removed his hat. He stretched his long legs straight out and slumped comfortably. "You are up early here, sir," he said amiably. "Most of the others are still abed."

"It is a theory of mine, Duncan," the seigneur said earnestly. "Militia can never be expected to stand against regular troops, but they will behave far better than anyone expects, if they are handled properly. Now, I have eliminated much of the foolishness the army so dearly loves. We are all farming folk in this community and we keep early hours as a matter of habit. And while my men cannot drill very prettily, they are really very fine troops in this sort of broken country where they have all hunted since they were children. You see?"

"Perfectly, sir," Crosbie smiled. "But I wouldn't let the Chevalier de Lévis hear of your innovations."

DuMaine shrugged casually. "None of those elegant gentle-men visit our humble bivouac, Duncan. You are the first."

"And not a very elegant one, I fear."

The Sieur duMaine inspected Crosbie from powdered head to dusty boots. "Elegant enough, I should say," he stated in a judicious tone. "And how have you been, Duncan? Well, I hope? And have you seen Céleste lately?"

"Quite well, sir. No, I haven't seen Céleste since…two days ago. She was quite busy."

"Ah, yes, she works very hard."

DuMaine copied Crosbie's languid posture, sliding low in his chair. The amiable silence stretched on for a long moment as Duncan Crosbie regarded the seigneur. DuMaine's attitude was exceptionally friendly, but Crosbie searched back through his recent memory and realized that the seigneur had been increasingly pleasant during the past few tense weeks. It might not mean anything, but…

He had been warned to wait. Both the Général and de Bougainville had urged patience. But was it really necessary? Judging by the Sieur duMaine's manner, an application for his daughter would surely not be considered insulting? Crosbie sought for courage to speak openly.

With a sudden surge he lunged from his chair, stood stiffly erect before the seigneur and spoke very quickly, in a loud sharp tone.

"Monsieur, I have the honor to request your daughter's hand." He felt his face blaze fiercely red, but he locked his jaw tensely and glared hard at the seigneur.

The Sieur duMaine turned his head to gaze directly at Crosbie. He smiled faintly, seeing the rigid, frightened young Scot. "I wondered how long it would take you to find the courage to ask me," he said quietly.

"Sir?" Crosbie goggled.

"I talked to Louis-Joseph some time ago," the seigneur said in a mild tone. "He speaks very highly of you, Duncan. Did you know that? And so do I. You have my permission, my boy, provided my daughter is agreeable. And I assume she is."

"Yes, sir."

"Splendid. Now please sit down, Duncan. I cannot forever stretch my neck to look at you. And do not gape so widely. There is no surprise to this, surely? Even my mother knew of it before she left for Montreal. And she wishes me to give you her blessing. I will leave it to her to deliver the kiss." DuMaine puffed heavily at his pipe, then put it aside abruptly. "I ... I am not an emotional man, Duncan. You know that. But these are dangerous times, and I am very pleased to have a son again. You will make a fine seigneur for Beauport. And now I may hope to see a grandson, eh? A new dynasty for Beauport."

"I ... I am a soldier, sir," Crosbie said uncertainly. "I had not thought ..."

"Nonsense, my boy. It is not a matter one decides casually, I quite agree. The time will come when Beauport will be more appealing to you than the army. You will see. And Beauport can wait. So can I. We have both had long practice."

"Thank you," Crosbie said quietly. "I cannot find words to thank you, sir. I think you know ..."

"Yes, I know. After all, I love Céleste, too. And since being despatched to this ridiculous post, I have had much time to think. There is little else to do. We can amuse ourselves watching the English search for the ford, but most of the time we ..."

"What?" Crosbie snapped. "What ford? Across the Montmorenci?"

"Why, yes," duMaine said, opening his eyes wide in surprise. "Is that important? The ford is some thirty mètres upstream."

"But there isn't any ford!" Crosbie growled. "The maps don't show one."

"Ah, those preposterous maps," duMaine snorted.

"But you have actually seen English scouts across the river? How do you know they were looking for the ford?" Crosbie's harsh voice drove insistently over duMaine's milder tones.

"Scouts? Yes, scouts and light infantry, too. And I knew they searched for the crossing because they were probing the river with long poles. They had several renegade Hurons with them, probably warriors who knew the ford existed, but did not know exactly where."

Crosbie grasped duMaine's arm above the wrist with a hard clutch. "Listen to me, sir. This is very important. You must assemble your men as quietly as you can. Take them to the ford and have them conceal themselves, ready to stop any English troops that try to cross. Do you understand what I mean? The English could break our defenses if they find that ford before we can guard it. Why I don't even have a single cannon within range! Now, move your men immediately. I'll ride to headquarters and get a company of regulars to relieve you. But hurry!"

"Duncan, you are serious? This ford is certainly known to …"

"Only to you. And the English!" Crosbie snapped. He ran for his horse. "Hurry!"

The mettlesome gelding welcomed an opportunity to run, even across the broken ground that rimmed the Montmorenci. Crosbie, an indifferent horseman at best, could only clamp his knees hard and try to retain his seat as his mount galloped madly toward de Lévis's headquarters. Thin whippy branches slashed his face and twice he was forced to lean flat along the gelding's neck to keep from being scraped to the ground by low-hanging limbs. The open tilled fields around the headquarters house were a welcome sight. Crosbie touched his spurs lightly and forced another spurt from his willing horse. He dismounted in a swirl of dust, tossed his reins to a surprised sentry and dashed inside.

Jamie Johnstone whirled from a mirror, both hands still tweaking at his tight wig.

"Ah, good morning, Duncan."

"Jamie! There is a crossing over the Montmorenci behind your position. The English know it's there and they have scouts searching for it." Crosbie paused to draw in a long breath.

Johnstone stiffened. His thin eyebrows pulled into a frown. "Come with me," he said thoughtfully. He opened a door into what had once been a large diningroom and led Crosbie toward a map on the opposite wall. Johnstone's finger traced along the Montmorenci. "No ford shown here," he said flatly.

"Damn you, Jamie, don't argue with me. The Sieur du-Maine told me. And he is positive."

"So were the engineers who made this map," Johnstone said. "You want me to inform His Excellency?"

"Who? Montcalm?"

"I was referring to Major-Général the Chevalier de Lévis. He likes the staff to call him ..."

"Yes, yes," Crosbie interrupted savagely. "Quickly, Jamie! Don't waste time."

Johnstone stared silently for a moment, then nodded. "Wait here, Duncan." He went out quickly and closed the door behind him.

Crosbie leaned closer to the military map, scanning it carefully. Not the least sign of low water showed along the entire stretch of river for long kilomètres to the north. And yet the seigneur had been positive. He wheeled impatiently from the map. Where in hell's name was Jamie? What was he ...

"Ridiculous," a sharp voice said with flat finality. "The man is mistaken. There is no ford."

Crosbie lunged to the door and jerked it open, sending it crashing against the inner wall. His forward motion carried him almost into collision with the Chevalier de Lévis.

Montcalm's second-in-command was not the early riser that the Général was. He was dressed only in breeches and shirt, with a knotted handkerchief over his head. A spot of dried lather under his ear made a peculiar rakish contrast with the black beauty patch on his cheek.

"My apologies, monsieur," Crosbie said hurriedly. "But the map is wrong. The Sieur duMaine says..."

De Lévis lifted one hand in languid command. "If you please, captain. You are..."

"Captain Duncan Crosbie, artillery aide to His Excellency," the young Scot said swiftly.

"Of course. I knew I had seen you before. We fought together at Carillon, did we not? I have heard excellent things of you since then."

"You are very kind, sir," Crosbie said in growing desperation. "But the troops..." He gestured excitedly. "I took the liberty of ordering the Sieur duMaine and the Beauport company to guard the ford while I came here. He will need help. There are no cannon within range, and..."

"Gently," de Lévis said in a pleasant tone. "Come join me at breakfast, Monsieur Crosbie, and we will discuss the matter. But do not let these petty provincial nobles disturb you."

"In God's name, sir," Crosbie exploded. "There are enemy troops in those woods this minute."

"Yes, I know. They have been landing all through the night. Very noisily, too. We could hear them above the roar of the cataract, couldn't we, Johnstone?"

"But, sir, I must insist..."

The Chevalier de Lévis rocked back on his heels and glared stiffly up at Crosbie. "I have said there is no ford, monsieur," he said sharply. "Do you question my word?"

"Certainly not, sir. But I do..."

Réveille bugles drowned his protesting voice and also served to cover the sound of footsteps behind him. The first he noticed of Montcalm was the uniformed shoulder that intruded between him and Lévis.

"Good morning, monsieur," the Général said briskly. "Why are you so heated, Duncan?"

Crosbie eagerly poured out his story, emphasizing the seigneur's sureness. The Général listened intently. When Crosbie had finished, he turned again to de Lévis.

"Send two companies immediately. Order all the Montreal militia to concentrate along the Montmorenci line. Keep the regulars in position. Duncan, you go with the troops. Report to me when they reach the ford."

"And the cannon, mon général?" Crosbie urged.

"Time enough for that later," Montcalm said easily. "First make sure the enemy scouts do not force the crossing."

Fortunately the réveille formations were still in place when Crosbie raced to the colonel of Royal Roussillon with the order written by Johnstone for his commander. Despatching two companies took only a moment, since all troops fell in with full field equipment each morning. Crosbie mounted his tiring horse and led the way, forcing the infantry to a quick-time march across the rough terrain.

The snarling clatter of musketry sounded far ahead and Crosbie shouted to the company officers, "Deploy your men as skirmishers!" He galloped forward, unable to restrain himself any longer.

Behind him the heavily laden regulars spread into battle line and sprinted after him, but they were soon outstripped as Crosbie spurred his horse anxiously.

A sharp fire-fight was in progress somewhere to his right and Crosbie leaped from his saddle and dashed down the precipitous slope toward the river, slipping and sliding in his eagerness, unable to see anything through the dense growth of stunted birch and pine that clogged the gorge. He slithered to the level stretch just above the water and ran forward toward the sound of musketry. He almost stumbled over a prostrate soldier in a short scarlet coat, and then was compelled to leap the body of a green-uniformed English ranger.

Above the brisk rattle of the fusillade rose the weird gobbling shriek of an Indian war-cry. Crosbie burst through a low bramble thicket and ahead of him he could see the wide flat crossing over the Montmorenci. Water lashed and gurgled in boiling speed, with no apparent slackness, but the usual depth of the river had obviously shallowed here, for as Crosbie came into view, a Canadien militiaman sprinted across, lifting his feet high, holding his musket overhead to avoid the spray.

Crosbie followed him to the ford, detouring around a huge fallen log. There, just at the crossing, lay the Sieur duMaine, his head supported at an awkward angle by Denis's arm. The boy was struggling to lift the bulky seigneur.

"Leave him alone," Crosbie roared. "Let him down flat, Denis." He dropped to one knee and eased the seigneur to the forest mat, straightening an arm that was bent under his back.

"Don't ... don't shout at the boy," duMaine said in a wavering voice. "He ... saved my life, Duncan. Shot a great hulk of a ..."

"He's a good boy," Crosby agreed quickly. "Where are you hit?"

"Just ... just the arm," duMaine said slowly.

"All right. Don't try to move. What happened here?"

"They found the ford and tried to cross. We stopped them. Gave chase."

"That's foolish," Crosbie snapped. "There's half the English army in those woods. Where's your bugler?"

"Gone ... with the soldiers," duMaine choked. He smiled suddenly. "Very good ... for militia, eh?"

"Excellent," Crosbie said absently. He rose and looked across the wide ford. Not a man in sight, though the sound of musketry was still brisk from the dark woods beyond. Crosbie turned quickly and ran up the embankment. Once on higher ground, he could see the French regulars still trotting forward in line of skirmishers. Crosbie gestured for the leading officer.

"Your trumpeter," he demanded. "Have him blow the recall. Post your men along the forward slope where they can cover the ford."

A gasping bugler stuttered out the recall, the triple notes, thrice repeated.

From the forest beyond the river, came the wobbling notes of a bugle blowing the charge. Crosbie cursed savagely. "Again," he snapped. "Keep blowing."

He slid back down the hill to the seigneur and used his hand-kerchief to bind his arm. It was a simple wound that had not struck bone. "Do you feel all right?" he asked quietly.

"Fine, Duncan," duMaine insisted. "Fine."

Militiamen and Indians began to drift back across the ford, many of them holding aloft ghastly dripping scalps and all of them gobbling the Huron victory cry. They capered exultantly through the shallow water, roaring defiance at the enemy.

"Pretty good … for militiamen," duMaine repeated softly.

"Yes," Crosbie said. "But I wish you'd waited. We could have trapped them all. But you did wonderfully well, sir. You have a fine company."

"Very good," the seigneur said complacently. He struggled to rest his back against the tree. He winked at Denis's solemn face. "And you were best of all, my boy. I'm promoting you to sergent tomorrow. Now, Duncan, do you think we could finish our conversation?"

Crosbie shifted his gaze from across the river. "Sir?"

"About my daughter," duMaine said slyly. "Do you still want to marry her?"

CHAPTER FIFTY FOUR

With a week, almost all of Lower Town was in ruins. English shot and shell had demolished the low stone buildings, creating a vast disorderly rubble along the waterfront.

The viciously intense cannonading had first been countered savagely by the French gunners, but depleted stores of gunpowder soon forced a halt to that. This diminution of French gunnery tempted the English navy to greater daring. During a night when the fog was particularly dense, two frigates and several smaller craft tested the defenses of the St. Lawrence. Running dangerously under heavy sail, the enemy ships sped for the passage to the upper reaches of the river beyond Quebec. The channel narrowed to a mere five hundred mètres and even veteran French pilots would have hesitated to make the passage on a murky night. But the English gamble won. Cannon roared and rumbled from Quebec, but the ships sailed through. A second flank had been turned by Wolfe. A new threat had been added.

Worse than the military danger was the food shortage, caused by English frigates on the river west of Quebec. The besieged city had long depended on shipments of foodstores from the west, from Trois Rivières and Montreal. Those supplies had been sent by boat. With the English navy in command of the major route, the price of bread immediately soared to three francs a loaf, which put it entirely beyond the reach of most people. To the hoards of penniless refugees from the Gaspé were now added the huge numbers of Quebec's citizens, driven from their homes, and dependent upon the Governor for food and shelter. Sickness took a firm hold in the temporary quarters erected in St. Roch. The sparse medicines available at the General Hospital were soon exhausted. The only encouragement lay in the knowledge that epidemics of fever and flux were also ravaging the enemy.

The English force was now divided in three camps, one still on the Île d'Orléans, the second at Pointe Lévi, and the third downstream of the cataract of Montmorenci. Wolfe had shifted his headquarters to the village of L'Ange Gardien, clearly visible to the French.

Every young officer of the French army—and many who should have been wiser—burned to attack the divided enemy posts, sure that a well-delivered thrust would be successful even if the enemy did outnumber them three to one. The pressure mounted from every source, but Montcalm was adamant.

"Let Monsieur Wolfe remain where he is," the Général insisted. "If I attack, he may move someplace where he can do us some harm."

Wolfe had achieved some success, but not enough. Quebec was almost destroyed. The enemy fleet had penetrated the city defense and now sailed unmolested on the upper river. But Montcalm's three-thousand-man force of regulars, his eleven thousand militia, were intact. Whether a building remained standing or not, the French still held the vital military position of Quebec. Montcalm could afford to wait, while every passing day brought a wind that was just a touch colder. Wolfe's time was fast running out. No matter how determined, he would have to withdraw before the river froze. Montcalm could afford to wait. He could afford to do nothing else.

On a crisp July morning with bleak grey storm clouds lying hard against the mountains, Wolfe launched his first massive assault of the campaign. For six endless weeks, the English commander had maneuvered for position without result. Every lure he had dangled had been contemptuously disregarded. And now, as Montcalm had long anticipated, Wolfe was driven to the mad extremity of frontal assault.

Forty cannon had been laboriously rafted to the English camp beyond the Montmorenci and the morning opened thunderously as the guns began preliminary bombardment of de Lévis's line. Three ships-of-war loomed close in-shore, screened in the mist of the river, to add their massive armament to the cannonade. The Général sent Crosbie with orders to de Lévis. No men or guns were to be jeopardized in a duel with the enemy artillery. Crosbie stayed at the Left long enough to make sure that the enemy was merely preparing for an attack which was not yet mounted. Then he returned impatiently to Beauport.

The English were demonstrating along the riverfront, obviously in a deceptive series of movements designed to mask their real objective. Hour after hour, longboats loaded with scarlet-clad troops moved along the river.

Shortly after mid-day, de Bougainville brought in a fresh sheaf of reports. Boatloads of enemy soldiers had embarked from Pointe Lévi. Some had landed at the Montmorenci camp, but most were still hovering on the water. Montcalm nodded as he read through them.

"Béarn and Guienne," he said briefly to de Bougainville. "My compliments to their colonels. The regiments will move to the Left immediately."

But another two hours passed before Montcalm called for his horse, and by that time Duncan Crosbie was in a ferment of nervous apprehension. It was now obvious that the enemy concentration was aimed at the French Left. Montcalm sent couriers calling for his entire force to shift toward de Lévis's position. Only a skeleton defense remained at Right and Center. Then, casually, the Général mounted and trotted easily toward de Lévis's headquarters, trailed by a silently fuming Crosbie.

"Duncan, you may shift three more batteries to this front. And all the mortars available. You may be extravagant with gunpowder, but not until the assault is actually launched."

"Yes, sir," Crosbie almost shouted, enormously relieved to have a clear-cut assignment. He bellowed raucous orders before the Général had dismounted. With a lashing frenzy driving him on, he harried his guncrews until half the French artillery was emplaced along the Left front.

And then more delays. The hours droned by. Crosbie stamped nervously into de Lévis's headquarters and joined the tight knot of regimental officers gathered about the Général.

On the table before him, Montcalm had spread a small-scale map. His thin forefinger swept along the line of tidal marsh that bordered the river.

"Monsieur Wolfe has been ready to attack for the past two hours," the Général said. "It is clear that he is waiting for something he cannot hurry. This." Montcalm's finger tapped at the chart. "The tide will be at its lowest point at five-thirty. The low water at the mouth of the Montmorenci will permit enemy troops to march across. So we may expect the attack at five-thirty, gentlemen. The enemy troops will have to cross some mètres of thick mud. They will make easy targets."

The regimental officers murmured a chorus of understanding. A few asked minor questions, and then the Général sent them back to their posts.

"Your guns are in place, Duncan?" the Général asked sharply. His voice had been held to a quiet, conversational tone as long as the regimental officers had been present, but now that his orders had been given, the Général relaxed his tight control just enough to show a hint of that boiling tension he usually held tightly in check.

"All ready, mon général," Crosbie said, making no effort to hide the excitement he felt. The Général sniffed and offered a thin smile. "I think we will have rain soon."

Crosbie grinned, thinking of the steep embankment up which the enemy would have to climb before reaching the French line. A good soaking rain, and that incline would be too slippery for a goat. So let it rain, the more the better.

With de Bougainville and Estére, Crosbie trailed the energetic Général from the headquarters building out to the brink of the French retrenchment. The three English ships were still firing rapidly, their shot breaking through minor stretches of the fortifications.

Across the cataract of the Montmorenci, half obscured by frothing billows of spray and mist, a brigade of scarlet infantry stood to arms, three thousand magnificently equipped soldiers who awaited the signal to storm the French position. And straight ahead, in a dense pattern, drifted the boats of a second brigade. Crosbie noted the dark green coats of the English rangers, and three boats loaded with soldiers wearing the plumed bonnet of Highland troops. Crosbie was by now accustomed to the sight of Scots fighting with the English, but it still required a positive act of will for him to look upon them as enemies.

A few spatters of rain smacked against the raw earth of the retrenchment. Faint puffs of dust rose with the impact and the troops of both armies gazed up to inspect the sky. The solid outlines of the heavy clouds had been torn by the mountain peaks and a strong wind was pushing them slowly toward the river, with a great sheet of rain falling like a gradually approaching curtain. The French grinned with delight.

Montcalm glanced once more toward the scarlet brigade across the falls.

"They are dead," he said quietly. "The rain has ruined Wolfe."

Signal flags soared to the masthead of a ship and a strident bugle stuttered from the troops beyond the cataract. Enemy boats formed into a solid line along the river, headed toward the French Left. Their oars dipped in unison. And the brigade waiting across the Montmorenci dashed forward in column of threes, bayonetted muskets held high as the soldiers ran through the low water at the mouth of the river.

Boats grounded hard in the deep tidal mud offshore. And the infantry from the Montmorenci camp were also mired as soon as they passed the river.

The massed French army poured a deadly volley at the enemy. The cannon concentrated behind the retrenchment blasted a hail of grape and canister at the English formations.

The first troops to land from the boats were grenadier companies, soldiers selected for exceptional height. Their high mitred caps towered above the rangers who followed close behind. The tall Englishmen were easy targets as they struggled through the broad tract of mud left by the receding river. But they came on without flinching, every third man wounded or killed before they reached firm ground. Their commanders dressed ranks as carefully as if on parade.

Regular, measured volleys of musketry blazed from the French positions, and the tall bronzed soldiers of the grenadier companies crumpled in place, leaving momentary gaps which the serjeants were quick to close. French artillery shifted target, at least half the guns devoting their full attention to the Montmorenci force. The mouth of the river was beaten to thick froth by the cascade of shot.

And the rain struck in earnest. It whipped in gusty torrents over the river, turning the steep embankment into an otter's slide of thin mud. Without waiting any longer, the massed companies of grenadiers made a rush for the French position.

The small square redoubt near the cataract was abandoned hastily, French gunners and infantrymen dashing for the safety of high ground. Crosbie could see them, bare-handed, slipping and sliding, clawing at the embankment and digging deeply for traction as they struggled up the slippery incline.

The riverbank was soon lost in the rain storm. Crosbie could see less than halfway down the slope, but that was far enough to observe the first enemy soldiers surging forward, fighting to maintain their footing. Wounded men tumbled to the slippery embankment and rolled quickly out of sight.

Bombardment on both sides slackened abruptly. The Général wheeled with a frown for Crosbie, then nodded quickly and turned back to the battle. In a rain squall, no gunpowder can be kept dry. Even prepared charges will become damp enough to misfire, and then a cannon becomes clogged with a useless charge which must be carefully extracted. All that is a lengthy process, but the hazard is the same for both sides. There was no point in complaining. Crosbie considered that the army was firing with creditable speed in view of the difficulties. Since there were no complaints from Montcalm, obviously the Général was of the same mind.

Through the murky clouds along the river slope, enemy uniforms gradually changed color as the first companies of grenadiers were shattered by the disciplined resistance of the French. Line companies of infantry pressed home the assault, and behind them came howling formations of kilted Highlanders, wearing the Fraser tartan, Crosbie noted angrily. But no matter how gallantly the English charged, no single soldier surmounted the slippery embankment. This was no longer a battle, but something more like execution. It was no surprise to hear the enemy bugles blaring the retreat. Montcalm jumped down from his vantage point, his muscular face strangely stiff, his eyes hard. He strode silently toward the headquarters building. Estére followed, but Crosbie delayed to see the end of the engagement.

Two deep growling explosions lit the sky briefly from the river front, then tongues of flame leaped high. Both grounded ships had been set fire by the retreating enemy. The massed formations that had crossed the Montmorenci were in full flight back to their camp, columns straggling as the wounded were assisted to the river. Boatloads of infantry waited offshore to cover the retreat as Highlanders, rangers, grenadiers and light infantrymen clambered back through the thick mud to their longboats.

The French militia, unable to resist the tempting opportunity, charged from the retrenchment, dashing precipitously down the incline, bayonets fixed. Indians who had been hiding at the rear seized the chance for safe trophies.

A dozen regular officers were overwhelmed in their attempt to halt the insane rush. Crosbie cursed savagely. He lunged forward, his fists balled furiously, bellowing in incoherent rage. Forward at the retrenchment, Colonel de Bougainville led a disciplined detachment of Royal Roussillon quickly over the slope. Their bayonets and determined expressions drove the maddened militia away from the enemy wounded.

There must have been five hundred English dead and wounded, Crosbie thought. The scarlet uniforms were almost a solid carpet down to the river's edge. Musketry still rattled briskly from the boats lying off-shore and the hard-bitten men of Royal Roussillon drove desperately at the militia, forcing them back up the incline, away from the river. A few slipped past the protecting screen de Bougainville established and single soldiers were sent to apprehend them. A small handful of surgeons and their assistants assembled their equipment and went forward over the retrenchment.

Crosbie ran with great strides, but the need for action was gone before he reached the incline. He slowed and leaped over the retrenchment, both arms swinging wide to maintain his balance on the slope. Then, shouting furiously, he lunged down the bank, his hand fumbling for his dirk as he ran.

Below him, a painted Indian warrior knelt over a wounded Highlander who lay on his face. The Huron had dug his fingers deep into the Scot's hair and pulled it tautly back for his knife just as Crosbie bellowed. The warrior glanced around apprehensively to see Crosbie hurtling toward him. He had time only to release the Highlander and swirl to a crouch before Crosbie was upon him.

The young Scot swept his dirk around in a vicious, threatening arc, forcing the Indian away from the wounded soldier. As the naked warrior turned to run, Crosbie seized his left arm in a hard grip, spinning him over the muddy ground. The Indian stabbed with his scalping knife and Crosbie turned his hip, letting the thrust go harmlessly by. He snatched at the Huron's knife arm and drew it in toward his hip with a hard pull. The arm broke sharply at the elbow with an explosion like a snapped twig.

Duncan Crosbie stood quietly in the pelting rain, looking down at the wounded Highlander who lay with the pale cast of death on his face. The bloodthirsty Huron cringed away, nursing his broken arm, keening a shrill whine of pain that Crosbie did not hear. The young Scot stared closely at the Highland soldier of King George. The man was a serjeant and with his great chest and long legs he was a stalwart figure. A Lochaber axe lay buried in the muddy earth at his side. A big solid hand still grasped the helve.

"A sizeable man, Duncan," Louis de Bougainville said at his shoulder. "Quite as large as you, I should think. That was excellent, what you did with that Indian swine. We will get the wounded to the hospital very soon now. How are you? All right?"

Crosbie did not shift his eyes from the unconscious Highlander. The man was just about his size. And just about his age, he would guess. But there was no other point of similarity. Except you might say they were both professional soldiers, employed by foreign monarchs. Crosbie nodded slowly.

"Yes, I'm all right, Louis. We won a victory, didn't we?"

Colonel de Bougainville scowled. "That maniac, Wolfe," he snarled. "Such generals should be hung. Yes, we won a victory, Duncan. But it was a battle we should never have fought."

Crosbie glanced down at the Fraser plaid across the Highlander's shoulder. "Neither should he," he said softly.

CHAPTER FIFTY FIVE

asically, it was Denis's idea. Only a romantic young boy
would think of such a wildly preposterous...

Duncan Crosbie shrugged angrily. If Louis de Bougainville
had not leaped at the suggestion, nothing more would have been
heard of it.

Denis had joined Crosbie and de Bougainville on the
muddy slope along the river and he too had noted the sharp
resemblance in figure between Crosbie and the wounded
Highlander. Then he had suggested that the uniform would fit
Crosbie well enough to let him walk through the enemy camp
without challenge.

And Louis had quickly added the one point that had decided
Crosbie. The Général had long been disturbed at apparently
illogical movements whenever he had attempted to guess at
Wolfe's future plans. No sensible man could soundly anticipate
the maneuvers of a madman. So any information Crosbie could
obtain would certainly be highly useful. Tonight, after their
disastrous repulse, the English were bound to be in a state of
confusion. The sentries would not be alert as they were normally.
The opportunity was heaven-sent.

Duncan Crosbie had let himself be persuaded.

Now, in the gloominess of his room at Beauport, he looked
down at the Highland uniform, dry and brushed free of mud, that
lay spread across his bed. It would be wrapped in a waterproof
cloth and Crosbie would swim naked across the Montmorenci,
dress himself, and stroll casually through the English camp.

It would be that simple, de Bougainville had insisted. Crosbie glanced up sharply as the door opened behind him.

"Louis, I don't like …"

"Be quiet, Duncan," de Bougainville said sharply. "And conceal that uniform, in God's name. Monsieur Bigot has come to dine with the Général this evening. You mustn't let anyone see …"

"Do you think Bigot would betray me, Louis?" Crosbie snorted.

"I don't know," de Bougainville said soberly. "Hide the uniform, Duncan. I have deposited our wounded Highlander at the General Hospital, but the sisters do not think he will live. However, to add a brighter note, I can tell you that I spoke to Mademoiselle Céleste."

Crosbie smiled. He rolled the Highland uniform tightly in its protective cover and tied it securely. "Yes?"

"My congratulations, Duncan," de Bougainville said warmly. "I told you that patience was the watch-word, didn't I?"

"And you were right," Crosbie conceded. "How did she …"

"She was more beautiful than ever, but very distressed until I could assure her that you were perfectly safe. She will tell you herself how happy that makes her, Duncan. She and her father are dining with the Chevalier de Lévis. They will stop here on the way back to Quebec."

"But I …" Crosbie gestured toward the rolled uniform.

"You will be back in time, Duncan. I have been thinking that it would be best to go early, before the night-time sentries are posted. The guards will be tired, and not very alert."

Crosbie drew in a deep breath. "Now, you mean?"

"Now. I have horses saddled. I thought I would go with you and wait at de Lévis's headquarters. That would be more convenient for you, eh? And I can take your uniform with me."

"All right, Louis. Let's get it over."

Silently, they left the room. Crosbie draped his huge tarpaulin cape over his shoulders and clamped the rolled Highland uniform under his arm. Denis grinned delightedly at the door and Crosbie paused to rub his knuckles across the boy's head for luck.

He and de Bougainville rode slowly toward the Montmorenci, skirting the French encampments. Happily, the rain had stopped earlier, but the evening breeze was sharp and cold. A few mètres from the river, de Bougainville halted near a shadowy clump of scrub oak and wheeled his mount.

Colonel de Bougainville held both horses while Crosbie stripped off his clothes, ramming each folded piece into a saddle-bag. Only when he was completely naked did he remember that he would need some sort of raft for the borrowed uniform. He fumbled blindly over the ground to collect fallen branches, and tore long strips of bark from a tree for bindings. It was a clumsy affair when finished, but it would serve to keep the uniform dry while he swam the river.

Louis de Bougainville groped for Crosbie's hand in the gloom. "Be very careful, Duncan. Don't try to enter the head-quarters and don't ask any questions. Just stroll slowly by and listen to what is being said. I'll be waiting at de Lévis's house. Be watchful that our sentries do not see you coming back. Bonne chance."

"Thank you, Louis," Crosbie backed cautiously down the precipitous gorge, easing his burden through the darkness behind him. At the water's edge, he paused to inspect the opposite bank. Faint flickering reflections of campfires were visible in the distance, but he saw no sign of a sentry. Visibility was very poor in the shadowed gorge with the pale mist rising from the water. Crosbie waded forward, almost gasping as the icy water touched his feet. The river was frigid almost beyond endurance. The worst torture was the need to move slowly to avoid splash-ing, for the slow immersion drew out the torment excruciatingly. Crosbie lowered his clumsy raft to the water and slid in after it, propping his chin on the tangle of branches and kicking silently with his feet under water. He angled toward the far shore, letting the swift current carry him along. He had half a kilomètre to go before he would need to worry about the cataract. And he was on the opposite shore, holding to a willow before he could clearly detect the booming crash of the falls.

He wriggled up from the water and tore open the bundle. He scrubbed himself dry with the Fraser plaid and quickly drew on the Highland uniform. His fingers fumbled with the tiny buckles of the kilt, and he found he had completely forgotten how to knot a rosette bow to keep his knee stockings properly taut. He buttoned the tight short coat and tugged the wristbands of his shirt into frills. He pinned the plaid to his shoulder with the big flat brooch and stood to adjust the bonnet to the required regimental tilt. He rolled his tarpaulin cloak and carried it under his left elbow. Then he eased quietly from his hiding place.

He walked due east, feeling for a path that would take him down to L'Ange Gardien. All through the high wooded ground beyond the river he could see bright fires, and occasionally a short raucous burst of masculine laughter carried to his ears. They seemed strangely spirited for a defeated army, Crosbie thought. He detoured, picking a route that lay between the fires.

A narrow, well packed game trail followed the edge of a gully and Crosbie turned warily right toward the St. Lawrence. From this point, he could expect to meet English troops at any moment. And he must act as if he had a perfect right to be walking here in the dark. He straightened to his full height. He eased the tight band of his bonnet and marched confidently forward.

The frail airy notes of a flute slashed at him suddenly, making him start with alarm. That was The Lilies of France, Crosbie realized. But surely, these were English troops?

A thin harsh voice soared nearby. "Gi' us a song, Ned. Blarst yer pipes clear, laddie, an' gi' us a rare 'un."

"On naught but thet pukey spruce beer? Not bloody likely. A dram o' rum now, and I'll not sye no."

Crosbie strode along in strong easy movements, taking care to mask the sound of his footsteps on the hard earth. He was abreast of a large campfire now, probably a company headquarters, he suspected, judging by the number of non-commissioned officers lounging near the blaze.

The flutist warbled a few more bars of The Lilies of France and a shrill, untrained tenor voice rose stridently through the night:

"Come, each death-doing dog who dares venture his neck,
Come, follow the hero that goes to Quebec;"

Crosbie snorted in quiet contempt. Come follow the hero, he thought. Follow him to your death. The singer paused in mid-flight and his fellows bellowed encouragement. Crosbie passed beyond the edge of firelight, but that sharp tenor pursued him along the path:

"Jump aboard of the transport, and loose every sail,
Pay your debts at the tavern by giving leg-bail;
And ye that love fighting shall soon have enough:
Wolfe commands us, my boys: we shall give them Hot Stuff!"

Endless choruses were happily muted behind him as Duncan Crosbie approached the brow of the riverbank and moved forward with great caution, feeling for firm footing before shifting his weight.

A milling crowd of scarlet-coated soldiers swaggered up from the river toward him and Crosbie immediately broke into a low humming, half singing the ridiculous English version of The Lilies of France. The soldiers streamed past him with no interest. One muttered drunkenly, something about a "bloody murtherin' Scottie," but his voice was carefully pitched to be inaudible to Crosbie.

The small stone village of L'Ange Gardien lay spread out before him, glistening with spray from the booming cataract beside it. Crosbie stepped into the cobbled street and turned casually. An open window nearby looked tempting, but a sentry posted at the corner was too alert. Crosbie moved lightly along the lane between the short double row of buildings.

The rippling sound of Parisien French cascaded from another window and Crosbie halted in sharp suspicion. A second, heavier voice answered in a thick guttural tone, but the language was unmistakably French. Crosbie edged closer. Sentry or no sentry, he had to hear what was being said. He lifted to the tips of his toes for a brief glimpse of the room. There were two men, both in the scarlet and gold of English officers of the line.

"...and, my dear Simon, I cannot think what Monsieur Wolfe had in mind. I know he is not demented, but there are times when I..."

That was a colonel, Crosbie noted, and his French was the quick but heavy, almost Germanic tone of Switzerland. And with that observation, Crosbie relaxed. These were more of the mercenaries employed by the English. Swiss, by the sound of them. And they had probably learned long ago to speak in French if they wished to be private.

Now that his eyes had adjusted to the moisture-laden gloom of the village, Crosbie could see that the yards of all the houses were littered with wounded men, most of them fitfully asleep now, but many moaning with throbbing plan. Louis de Bougainville had estimated five hundred enemy casualties but there seemed to be that many more wounded lying in L'Ange Gardien. Crosbie went along the crowded field behind the houses. He would pretend to be searching for someone, if he were asked to account for his presence. He edged closer to a guarded house, ignoring the posted sentries, angling toward an open door from which a wide beam of light escaped.

He could hear voices, but they were pitched very quietly. He crept closer, half turned away, and almost backing toward the door.

A nastily precise voice almost spat, in sudden clarity, "The word 'decimated' does not imply total destruction, my dear captain. It means that a tenth part has been lost, nothing more."

An unsteady young voice responded with great heat, "Damme, sir, I'm no clerky feller, but I'll say that no army can lose a tenth part of its force and still be fit for attack. Jamie Wolfe lost something more than a battle today. He's a sick man, and now he's lost confidence. We'll not see victory here, sir, and you can lay to that."

"Nonsense," the first man insisted with pedantical sharpness. "Wolfe will pull it out, mark my words."

Crosbie moved past the open doorway and he turned quickly for a glance inside. Two infantry officers sat on either side of a table, leaning toward each other. And between them, sitting with his face toward the door, was a thin-faced sallow officer in a major's dark-blue coat, uniform of an English provincial regiment. Some colonist from York or Pennsylvania or some such place, Crosbie thought. Another stranger come to die for his foreign king. Then Crosbie halted suddenly and turned for a second look. Yes, he knew that face. But where had he seen it before? That long dark face with the greasy-looking dark hair. Where...

The sentry tramped stiffly around the corner and Crosbie drifted unobtrusively down the row of houses. The guard dropped the butt of his musket to the ground and spread his feet comfortably.

Ahead, Crosbie could see the brilliant ensign of England flying over a low, one-storied stone house. Four pair of sentries stood guard, one at each corner. That was likely Wolfe's headquarters, Crosbie told himself. But there was small opportunity for him to enter or even to approach. He moved entirely around the building.

"You there!" a sharp voice barked. "You, serjeant! What are you doing there? Stand where you are!"

Crosbie whirled. A fatly pompous major of infantry stalked toward him. Two of the sentries from the headquarters detail moved briskly out into the field, coming up on either side of the young Scot. Crosbie snapped briskly to attention.

"Sir?"

"What are you doing here?" the major snarled.

"Looking for my captain, sir," Crosbie said in a thick, indefinite tone. "He was wounded this afternoon, and ..."

"Bah! You Highlanders have no right in the army area. You know the General can't stand the sight of you. We've made examples enough, but by God, we'll make another if you insist. Looking for your captain, were you? Malingering is more the truth, I suspect. Or robbing the wounded, eh?"

"Sir, I ..."

"Be silent, you ... you witless savage! Corporal!" The major swung toward one of the sentries. "Escort this dog to the boat landing and see that he leaves for Lévi straight away. Understand? I don't want him moving around where the General might see him. Take him away."

The corporal lowered his fixed bayonet at Crosbie's throat and gestured significantly. The young Scot turned slowly away, his huge hands knotted tightly with restraint. He marched silently in front of the sentry.

He was under no particular suspicion, he realized thankfully. Here, his only crime was to look like a Highlander. Until he reached the Scottish encampment, no one would think him an impostor. But once at Pointe Lévi ...

"The major doesn't like Highlanders," Crosbie said in an amiable growl. "I suppose he must have been at Culloden. eh?"

"Aye," the corporal said with a snarl. "And so was I. Now shut yer gob, or I'll scratch your liver, bucko. I'd as soon kill you as not. I don't like you murderin' rebels no better nor the, major."

Crosbie strode stiffly forward. This contemptuous hatred seemed perfectly routine treatment. The revolt of '45 was nearly fifteen years past, but the bitter reaction was obviously sharp as ever. The Scots were not considered fit to live in the same area as General Wolfe, whose delicate soul might sicken if his queasy eye fell upon a kilt. Good enough to die for German Georgie, but nothing more than that. But death might seem attractive to a Scot after a few years in the English army.

Ahead was the military boat landing, ringed with high flaring torches. Longboats, whaleboats, small craft of every description plied busily in and out of the tiny mooring. A tight line of alert sentries were posted at all the approaches. Crosbie slowed gradually, then pretended to slip on the slimy mud that coated the street cobbles. He hit with a realistic thud that actually jarred his teeth. He moaned in spurious pain and lay crouched on the cold stone. A boot kicked at his back and he twitched with simulated agony.

"'Ere now, you..." The corporal kicked the recumbent Crosbie again, then stooped, hooking one hand under Crosbie's arm and yanking him up to his feet.

Crosbie came up readily, legs gathered tensely under him. He lunged from the ground and snatched the sentry's musket with one deft motion. The corporal's mouth gaped. He started to bellow with outrage. Crosbie grasped the musket-butt, stepped smartly forward and swung at the corporal's head. The brass-bound wooden stock smacked with a soft, sickening impact under his ear. Crosbie caught the unconscious man before he fell and dragged him quickly beyond the reach of the flaring lights at the landing.

If he were caught now, he would probably be shot as a deserter before anyone discovered he was a spy. Crosbie shook out his rolled cloak and pulled it tightly around him to mask the gaudy Highlander uniform. He unbuckled the plaid and let it fall to the earth. Then he snatched up the sentry's tricorne and substituted it for the blue bonnet.

He kept warily to the shadows, walking with long padding strides back through the small village and up the bank again to the lane that paralleled the Montmorenci. Signal flares had been lighted now to guard against surprise attacks and most of the riverbank was bathed in shadowy dusk. Crosbie moved softly up-river about half a kilomètre above the point opposite de Lévis's headquarters before he turned off the path. Sentries were posted in a thin line, each man standing between pole-mounted flares. Crosbie crept down a brush-filled ravine and crashed thunderously through the dried branches that clogged the shallow gully. No one came to investigate, though he waited for long tense moments beside the river.

Carefully, Crosbie stripped off the Highlander's uniform, keeping only the heavy shoes which he wrapped in his cloak. Then he eased again into the icy stream and swam strongly across. He rammed wet feet into the shoes, pulled the clammy cloak about him and climbed briskly up from the gorge. All the way to the headquarters house, he ran with fast jogging strides, swinging his arms, fighting away the chill that seemed to knife through to the bone.

De Lévis's headquarters was just as closely guarded as Wolfe's had been and Crosbie was loath to appear openly in merely his cloak and shoes. He stepped inside the rim of guard-light and bellowed for Colonel de Bougainville. His full-throated roar echoed solidly from the farmhouse. Three sentries turned quickly to intercept him, but their approach was halted when de Bougainville stepped from the doorway, shouting commands. The colonel moved out of sight briefly, then came quickly toward Crosbie, his arms stretched forward, piled high with Crosbie's clothes.

The sentries stood suspiciously watchful as Crosbie snatched his breeches from de Bougainville. He slipped into them hurriedly, pulled on stockings and stepped into his boots. Only then did he open his cloak and reach for his shirt. He had never dressed so quickly before, but the edge of chill in the night breeze had made his teeth chatter uncontrollably.

"Was it necessary to parade so indecently?" de Bougainville asked in mild derision.

"Damn you, Louis, that river was melted snow, and only barely melted at that. I'm frozen."

"What luck, Duncan? Anything important?"

"No," Crosbie said bluntly. "It was a hopeless chance. The sentries were too alert. I was nearly caught for my pains. Now, get me some brandy, Louis. Then I'll tell you all about it."

"I have something even more stimulating for you, Duncan. Had you forgotten that Mademoiselle Céleste is here? I prevailed upon her to wait, though in truth, I wasn't sure when you might return."

"If ever," Crosbie growled. "Thank you, Louis." He moved swiftly toward the lighted doorway, then halted as a small knot of people came outside.

The Sieur duMaine held his arm high to support his daughter's hand. They bowed to the Chevalier de Lévis and his aide, Captain Johnstone. Crosbie came up in time to make his leg to the Chevalier.

DuMaine led Céleste toward the bright, gilded caléche that stood waiting before the stable.

"I had planned to drive Céleste to Beauport to collect medicines and supplies for the Hospital," he said gruffly. "But I am an old man and I have had an exciting day. Can I depend upon you to see her on this errand, Duncan?"

The young Scot choked in gratitude, but he managed to express his assurances. The seigneur kissed his daughter, saluted de Bougainville and Crosbie, and stepped back.

"A great day, my boy," he said in farewell.

"A great day, sir," Crosbie said amiably. A murderous day, a butcher's holiday, but a successful day for the French. He swung into place beside Céleste and took her hand gently. De Bougainville clambered into the driver's seat and gathered the reins.

"Now, Duncan," he said casually, stirring the horse to a sedate amble. "Now, you can tell me what happened to you in the English camp tonight."

Céleste gasped. Her fingers tightened on Crosbie's hand. He was suddenly glad that she had not known of his wild escapade until now.

"Duncan, are you mad?" she demanded unsteadily. "To walk into the enemy camp? You might have been caught and shot for a spy!"

"I was a spy," Crosbie said with a curious lightness, and a smile for the frightened girl. It was good to realize what her fears for him must mean. No one had feared for him for long years. He felt he had come home again. "You spy for your Tremais, my dear. May I not spy for my Général?"

"But, Duncan," Céleste protested, "it is not the same thing at all."

"And why not?" he asked mildly. "Why not?"

Crosbie held her hand comfortingly as he recounted his expedition in quick short sentences. He had seen a large number of wounded. He had heard grumbling among the officers, but the soldiers could still sing around their campfires, so their morale had not been shattered, despite their hideous losses that day. And ... and he had seen a man, a man with a familiar face ...

"Major Stowell!" he said abruptly. "Now I remember! It was at Colbert's house in Quebec, when I went there to find Captain O'Neill. An English major was dining there. The same man. He was a paroled prisoner. Ah, that was bothering me. I couldn't remember what was so familiar about his face. I suppose he managed to escape?"

"He's a scoundrel if he did," de Bougainville snorted. "Paroled prisoners are the Governor's responsibility. I'll ask when we get to Beauport. You have done very well, Duncan. The Général will be pleased, I know."

De Bougainville whipped up the ambling horse and the light calèche rumbled quickly over the cobbled road. Crosbie held Céleste tightly against the lurching motion of the carriage. And in his booming baritone, he sang the defiant song he had heard in the English camp. The first chorus sufficed for the brief journey to Beauport. De Bougainville swung the carriage up the hill and stopped at the entrance.

"I must leave you now," he said with a faint smile. "But if you will wait for me near the door, I'll ask the Governor if he knows how Major Stowell comes to be in the English camp." He touched Crosbie's arm lightly.

"I'm rather curious about the man," Crosbie admitted.

"And I," de Bougainville muttered. He moved quickly toward the headquarters entrance.

Crosbie assisted Céleste to the ground, and let a sleepy attendant lead the horse and carriage to the stables. The sentries at the door looked carefully away as Crosbie and Céleste strolled up and down outside.

"I've met your Major Stowell," Céleste said carefully, almost as if she were straining to be casual. "Last week, at the Hospital. He came with Captain O'Neill. A tall thin man with peculiarly dark skin?"

"That's Stowell," Crosbie said. He heard the strained note in her voice. He knew it carried a meaning, but for the moment, he was sick of hidden meanings. He slipped his arm around her shoulders and moved farther into the darkness, pulling her close to him. "This is Crosbie. Shall we consider Crosbie now?"

Céleste's response was muffled against Crosbie's lips. She pushed quickly away as de Bougainville opened the door, but she did not go far. Her hands stayed warmly in Crosbie's grasp.

They returned to the lighted doorway and went into the hall with de Bougainville.

"Major Stowell escaped a month ago," the colonel said softly. "The Governor thought there was no need to notify the military. So that explains Stowell. Good night, Duncan. The Général wants to see you in the morning. Good night, mademoiselle."

"Good night, Louis," Crosbie said.

De Bougainville returned to the diningroom where Montcalm was entertaining the Governor. Crosbie turned to Céleste.

"Duncan, I am sure I saw Major Stowell only last..."

Crosbie touched her chin lightly and she lifted her lips eagerly. Worries about escaped prisoners vanished.

"We... we came here to collect supplies?" Crosbie asked after a long silence. "Shouldn't we..."

Céleste laughed softly. She led him quickly through the quiet house. She found baskets which Crosbie held while she loaded them with packets of dried herbs, roots, bark, and mysterious looking potions.

"We have so little," she said softly, "and the Hospital needs so many things. There are so many wounded, sick, dying... Will this war ever be over for us, Duncan?"

"No talk of war tonight," he said firmly. "Talk of us, but not war."

Céleste smiled, but there was a hint of sadness in the smile. She went on piling her baskets high. Then she paused and frowning slightly, she consulted a mental list. "Bandages! That's it. Old, soft linen for bandages. Grand'mère sorted things before she left. Now where..."

Neither linen room nor the Grand'mère's salon held the linen that Céleste sought. Crosbie followed quietly, holding a candle high as the girl searched. The young Scot tried his best to be very quiet. If any of the staff had returned to quarters, they were exhausted enough to sleep soundly. Crosbie could not hear a sound in the quiet house, except faint murmurs from the diningroom.

At last they came to Céleste's room. She opened the door and turned to Crosbie with a small gesture of triumph. On a table lay great folded white stacks.

Crosbie put down his candle. Its small flickering flame illuminated the room that had been Céleste's since childhood. It was a dainty, feminine room. Light glinted from silver and crystal and shimmered against a silken carpet. The bed was pale enamel, draped in ruffles. A faint, sweet fragrance filled the room, the flower fragrance that for Crosbie, meant Céleste and no one else, so that he would have known it was her room, even in darkness.

She was looking around thoughtfully, her green eyes enormous in the candlelight, her face soft and lovely as if her thoughts were tender thoughts.

"Someday, when the war is over, Beauport will be truly ours again," she said softly, "and perhaps we can make it as it was when I was a child. Ah, Duncan, it was so lovely then, while my mother still lived, while my brother was at home, before..." She turned swiftly to Crosbie, eyes shining, hands outstretched. "We will be happy here, won't we, my darling?" she asked with sudden passion. "We will have our chance..."

He went to her quickly across the room that was filled with the faint ghost of her perfume. As he took her in his arms he could see that the shining eyes were wet with tears. It almost frightened him, for he could not guess whether she cried for the past or for the future. He only knew that he had never seen her cry before, and that it must not be allowed. "Hush, my dearest," he murmured softly. "Of course we will! Of course..."

Her arms went about him almost fiercely. The forgotten candle was brushed to the floor and snuffed out. And then there was only the thin pale moonlight coming through the curtained window, the pervading flower-sweetness, and the trembling figure of the girl in his arms.

It was no child's kiss she offered him this time, but a woman's kiss, warm, eager, shaken by the swift surge of her emotions. He lifted her and she was light and soft against him. And the last thought that he could remember was a dazed, incredulous, "This isn't real. It can't be real." It had to be a dream—but it was not.

CHAPTER FIFTY SIX

Through all of August, Wolfe's army lay licking its wounds, unable to mount another attack. But from the west and south, the enemy moved closer to the bastion of Canada.

After two weeks of siege, Fort Niagara's under-manned garrison surrendered, despite a last-minute attack by partisans and Indians called hurriedly from the Détroit. The Chevalier de Lévis was assigned eight hundred of Montcalm's troops and sent to Montreal to guard against an approach from the west.

South, at Carillon, the Chevalier de Bourlamaque had held Amherst's great army fixed in position, but eventually he was compelled to withdraw, but not until he had destroyed the fortifications of Carillon and Fort Frédéric. He retreated to the Île aux Noix, that low island that lay like a cork in the bottle at the mouth of Lake Champlain. And there he stayed, fending off the attack that would have ruined Montcalm.

It was Louis de Bougainville who told Crosbie of the loss of Carillon. The young Scot stared silently, remembering Montcalm's great victory the previous year against Abercombie. But, looking at de Bougainville's drawn face, he did not speak of it.

"I remember telling you that Carillon would never again be Ticonderoga," de Bougainville said heavily. "I was wrong. It is Ticonderoga again. And Fort Frédéric is now Crown Point. But Île aux Noix will never become Walnut Isle, please God, or we are lost."

He tapped together a sheaf of papers and rang for his clerk. "No, don't go, Duncan," he said quickly as the young Scot turned toward the door. "Stay and talk until it is time for me to leave."

"Leave?" Crosbie returned to his chair.

"Don't you read the Général's orders?" de Bougainville smiled. "I am to command the troops at Pointe aux Trembles."

Crosbie nodded soberly. The English navy now sailed with comparative ease west of the city and several times they had made small raids along the north bank. Some fifteen hundred troops had been sent to counter the enemy raids. That was a command that warranted a Brigadier. Crosbie whistled softly. "And a promotion?"

De Bougainville shrugged. "I will be acting-Brigadier," he said with an attempt at a casual tone.

"My congratulations, Louis," Crosbie said. "It's a difficult assignment, I imagine."

"Unusual, at any rate," de Bougainville agreed. "The enemy ships sail up and down the river and we have to follow on foot. Men cannot march half as fast as ships can sail. But, with a few permanent guardposts and a great deal of running, we should be able to block them."

"I'm sure you will, Louis," Crosbie said in a voice full of admiration.

Louis de Bougainville smiled grimly. "Pray for an early winter, Duncan. Wolfe is a sick man, I hear, but his Brigadiers will surely insist he do something to break the stalemate. They will have to withdraw before the river freezes, but a few more weeks may mean the end of Canada, even if we are not defeated."

"Yes," Crosbie said soberly. "I've seen the fires, too. Whole parishes have been put to the torch. It's Scotland all over again. Even the churches have been burned."

"The houses, the churches," de Bougainville said bluntly, "are not as important as the harvest. Hundreds of militiamen are deserting every day, hoping to salvage their crops before they rot in the fields. Thousands of arpents are being ruined by the English. How can our people live without food for the winter? Starvation and disease will finish what the enemy began."

Crosbie thought gloomily of the vast untended fields around Beauport, weed-grown now, but dense with ripening grain. The women of the seigneury would manage to harvest some of it, but only a small part.

De Bougainville made a brusque gesture. He slammed the lid of his traveling-desk and rose impatiently. "Your friend, Captain Johnstone, will be recalled to take my place here. He has had much experience, Duncan. I have not yet learned to like him, but I hold him in considerable respect. Good-bye, my friend."

"Bonne chance, Louis."

Crosbie accompanied de Bougainville to the bridge across the St. Charles. Then he rode slowly back to Beauport, feeling a peculiar sadness he could not identify.

With Louis de Bougainville went all the warmth and light-heartedness of Montcalm's headquarters. Captain Johnstone was an able, resourceful aide and he slipped into the routine effortlessly, but he was not de Bougainville. A man of little humor, Johnstone could not cheer the over-worked staff as de Bougainville had, nor could he take his place with Montcalm, making it necessary for the Général to worry about many details he had formerly left entirely to his aide.

Montcalm had grown more nervous, almost explosive, during the last weeks of August. He seemed unable to rest as Wolfe's time drew shorter and shorter. Even during the night, sentries were alert for him, knowing he roamed the retrenchments constantly. Montcalm's full, muscular features had fined down to thin taut planes and his coat hung on him in loose folds. But his energy, his tired watchfulness, never flagged. The younger officers of the staff were soon worn to exhaustion, but the Général showed little sign of strain, though the lines around his eyes were etched more clearly every day.

The depressing atmosphere of the headquarters sent Duncan Crosbie out to spend all his free time with the artillery units encamped along the river. Troops living so long in a static situation tend to become listless with inactivity, and Duncan Crosbie aroused their commanders constantly, insisting upon arduous training maneuvers every day. Gunners and officers alike developed a keen hatred for the gaunt young Scot, but none dared challenge his orders. Day followed day in a long haze of weariness for Crosbie, but he had a growing sense of accomplishment to sustain him.

On the evening he left the Béarn position, the gunners had saluted him with a ragged, undisciplined cheer, a sincere tribute which warmed Crosbie as he rode up the hill toward the headquarters, hunched low against a chill breeze. He smiled thinly in the darkness, thinking how strange it was that men would cheer an officer who pushed them so hard. Actually, he knew, they were cheering themselves and their new competence born of hard work.

He handed his horse over to a groom and stumbled wearily inside, too tired to respond to the sentry's salute. He dropped his hat and cloak and stood for a moment in the warm hallway.

"Monsieur! Monsieur le capitaine Crosbie!"

A pale-faced, weeping woman burst from the drawingroom, both hands stretched out in entreaty toward Crosbie. Behind her, two young officers halted indecisively in the doorway.

"Sir, this woman insisted ..." one began angrily.

"Monsieur, I beg you ..."

Crosbie raised one hand. "One moment," he growled in a heavy voice. He waved the young officers away. "Now, madame," he said quietly. "I know you, don't I? Madame ..."

"I am Madame Arnaud," the woman said swiftly, words tumbling excitedly from her lips. Her hands fastened tightly on Crosbie's lapels, as if she were determined to stay close to him until he had heard her out.

"Gently, madame," he said. He eased Madame Arnaud toward the settle. "Please sit here. And tell me what troubles you?"

"It is not me, monsieur. It is Denis! Denis! They are going to kill him!"

Crosbie stiffened. "Kill him? Who?" All weariness vanished as he leaned forward. "Tell me!"

"My sister came to …"

"Never mind your sister," Crosbie snapped. "What did you mean about Denis?"

Madame Arnaud drew in a deep breath and now that she knew someone would listen, she grew calmer. "It begins with my sister, monsieur. She and her children, three little boys, came to stay with me when the English burned their home. So it was hard to find food for all. What you sent helped us and we were all grateful."

Crosby nodded grimly. No one in Canada had enough food. "Well? Get on, madame," he insisted roughly.

"I opened the cache," she said tightly, "so the babies would have something to eat."

"Yes," Crosbie muttered. Every farmer had a cache where he had hidden a small store of preserved food. No law was stringent enough to eliminate hoarding. "And someone reported you?"

Madame Arnaud nodded, her eyes huge and red-rimmed.

The drawingroom door slammed back and Captain Johnstone burst into the hallway. "Stop this infernal … oh, Duncan. What's happening?"

"Be quiet, Jamie," Crosbie said brusquely. "Go on, madame."

Johnstone looked over Crosbie's shoulder, but all of Madame Arnaud's attention was focussed on the tense young Scot who tried desperately to control a furious impatience.

"And so they came, the Intendant's men. They demanded the food. I … I refused. I called upon God. I showed them the babies. I …" The woman's voice broke on a high, shrill note.

Crosbie seized her hands tightly. "Please, madame. Tell me the rest."

Madame Arnaud swallowed painfully. "Then...then the officer struck me. I fell to the floor. And that was when Denis came home. Just for the night. He is a good boy, monsieur, a good soldier. He came only to ..."

"I know the boy," Crosbie said.

"Denis shouted something terrible and he struck the officer with his musket."

Crosbie froze. A soldier who assaulted an officer could be shot. He did not dare ask Madame Arnaud to go on. Behind him, Johnstone drew in a thin breath.

"The soldiers took Denis away and they said...they said he would be killed. They...they beat him. But Denis was brave, monsieur. He did not flinch. He told me to come for you. And I came."

"That's enough," Crosbie said heavily. He straightened and stared blankly at the wall. His mouth tightened with anger.

"Don't let them kill my boy, monsieur. Don't let them."

"He's my boy, too," Crosbie exploded. "No one is going to kill him."

"Duncan," Johnstone said quickly. "If it was the Intendant's men, they will have taken Denis to the Palace. Shall I ..."

"Yes," Crosbie said quickly. "Will you find out what happened? I'll see the Général."

"No, Duncan. Wait for me. He'll want all the facts. Wait till I get back." Johnstone moved briskly to the door and went out.

Waiting was torture for Crosbie. A dozen times he cursed himself for letting Johnstone ride into Quebec in his place. But Crosbie knew that he could never have gained entry to the Palace. The Intendant would see that all sources of information were closed to him. The young Scot sat rigidly in the hall beside Madame Arnaud, hearing the dry, harsh weeping of the stricken woman, holding himself in tight restraint, his large hands balled into hard fists. He was full of dread.

"They could not have been the Intendant's men," Madame Arnaud said in a wavering tone. "Monsieur Bigot would never employ such wolves. Not Monsieur Bigot. He is Canadien, too. He knows how we all suffer. He would never hurt the boy. He would not..."

Crosbie patted the woman's bowed shoulder until she quieted. His jaw ached from the tension he applied to keep from answering. Always, Bigot used that simple fact, his Canadien birth, to deceive the people who still trusted him. Even now, with proof on every hand, with legal evidence enough to depose and jail him, Bigot retained the faith of the common folk of the colony. Even when he was exposed as a perjurer, a thief of incredible sums, even as a traitor, Bigot would probably be remembered as a man of honor by those Canadiens who never knew him. Crosbie felt a sense of despair, hearing Madame Arnaud's simple defense of such a scoundrel.

Lights were placed throughout the headquarters and work went on without pause. Sentries were changed outside, servants rushed quickly along the hall with dinner trays for the officers who could not leave their desks. Crosbie and Madame Arnaud sat unnoticing, Crosbie in a frozen, stony silence, the woman crying again in hopeless quiet.

His only hope was Montcalm, Crosbie realized. Legally, Denis was guilty of the worst crime a soldier can commit. But he was only a boy. A child, really. Montcalm would never let him die. Crosbie repeated it over and over in his mind. Montcalm would never let him die.

Crosbie came to his feet swiftly when he heard horses clatter up to the house. He pulled open the door.

"Jamie, thank God..."

"Good evening, cock," a level voice said.

Johnstone leaped past Captain O'Neill in a quick lunge, just in time to catch Crosbie's arm. He leaned hard against the furious young Scot. "Don't, Duncan. You fool, let him alone!"

Crosbie stepped back, letting his arms drop. Johnstone pulled him further down the hall out of earshot. "O'Neill was sent by the Intendant, Duncan. Don't touch him or you'll make things worse. Now, let's go in to the Général. Don't say a word until I tell you."

Johnstone ushered O'Neill toward Montcalm's office. The sleek Irish Captain tidied his uniform and sauntered down the hall, a hard smile fixed on his lips. Crosbie offered his arm to Madame Arnaud.

Inside Montcalm's office, he brought a chair for Madame Arnaud and posted himself behind it stiffly, listening as Johnstone explained the problem to the Général. Montcalm heard him through in silence, one hand shielding his tired eyes. Captain O'Neill stood easily, watching Crosbie's immobile face as Johnstone spoke. He bowed gracefully when Montcalm turned to him in obvious inquiry.

"Captain Johnstone has the facts right, mon général," O'Neill said in a flat, toneless voice. "The criminal was arrested and tried. He was sentenced to death, as regulations require. He will be executed tomorrow."

"A quick trial," Montcalm said, speaking for the first time.

"As regulations require," O'Neill said easily. "I can assure Your Excellency that the criminal was given every opportunity to defend himself. I know, for I was presiding officer of the military court."

The Général glanced at Crosbie, just as O'Neill did. The flickering, watchful look told Crosbie more than anything O'Neill had said. Denis was the price O'Neill had exacted for the insults he had suffered from Crosbie. O'Neill twisted one corner of his thin mouth in a contemptuous grimace.

"Your Excellency will agree," O'Neill went on in his hard, uninflected voice, "that such crimes must be punished promptly and severely. Especially in time of war."

"But the extreme provocation," Johnstone said hotly.

Madame Arnaud had remained in her chair silently, her eyes moving between Montcalm and O'Neill. Now she lurched forward, pathetic in her awkwardness, stumbling to her knees before Montcalm's table.

"For the love of Heaven, monsieur!" she cried. "Denis is a little boy! He tried to protect me. That brute of an officer demanded the food that would keep the children alive. He knocked me down! Denis..."

"No such evidence was presented to the court," O'Neill broke in coldly.

"You didn't call the witness," Johnstone snapped.

"Monsieur le général," Madame Arnaud wailed. "Hear me, I pray you. I am on my knees before you. I was once a wife. You sent my husband to Niagara to be killed. I was once a mother. You sent my son to Louisbourg to be killed. Now, my boy Denis, as dear to me as my own son. Will you kill him, too?"

Hard knots of muscle leaped into prominence along Montcalm's jaw. His hands twisted a quill-pen to shreds. "Please, madame," he said in a strained, painful voice that was barely audible. He, too, had lost a child recently, Crosbie remembered— his most-beloved daughter. "Please take your chair. Duncan, help her."

The tall young Scot assisted the weeping, incoherent woman to her seat. He gripped her shoulder with one strong hand, but never for an instant took his eyes from the Général.

Montcalm cleared his throat with a harsh sound. He thrust himself back from his table and rose quickly. He stood glaring at O'Neill. "Was this 'criminal' you tried wearing a uniform?" he snapped.

Hope surged in Crosbie. Of course, he thought, why didn't I think of that? Denis is one of Montcalm's soldiers.

O'Neill nodded, his confidence momentarily shaken by the unexpected question. "Yes, Your Excellency."

"By what right," Montcalm thundered, leaning forward with clenched hands on his table. "By what right do you arrest and try one of the King's soldiers?"

"Why...why..." O'Neill drew himself up stiffly. "One of the Intendant's officers was assaulted by this soldier."

Montcalm's angry voice rose high over O'Neill's lighter tone. "This soldier is mine! I alone am responsible for him. No Intendant has any control over him. Tell your master that for me, monsieur. Captain Johnstone!"

"Sir."

"My compliments to the commander of Béarn. He will furnish you with an armed escort. You will take our soldier from the Intendant's Palace and bring him to me. Is that clear?"

"Sir," O'Neill said quickly, "you cannot..."

The Général drew in a long breath before answering O'Neill's objection, but his expression alone had been enough to silence the Irish captain. As Crosbie watched, Montcalm rose slowly, dominating the quiet room, his shadow monstrously tall against the ceiling, but no taller than Montcalm himself seemed at that moment. The Général's intention was fixed beyond question.

"I can," Montcalm said bluntly. "And I will. Report to me when you return, Captain Johnstone. You are dismissed, Captain O'Neill."

The two officers withdrew silently. Johnstone eased the door shut behind them. Montcalm walked slowly around the table and looked down at the tear-stained face of Madame Arnaud.

"This terrible war," he said quietly. "Sometimes I think we have all gone mad."

Madame Arnaud reached out a timid, pleading hand, touching Montcalm's sleeve gently. "Monsieur le général, you will save him? You won't let them kill my boy?"

Montcalm took her hand in a warm clasp. His eyes glistened as he bowed. "Try not to worry about the boy," he said with quiet reassurance. "I will do all that can be done." He straightened and looked at Crosbie's drawn face. "See this lady home, Duncan."

CHAPTER FIFTY SEVEN

Early in the morning, Duncan Crosbie rode in toward Quebec, weary and depressed after a long sleepless night. He had accompanied Madame Arnaud to her house and waited until she and her sister had put the children to bed, and then discussed with them endlessly the trouble that had come to Denis. Johnstone's infantry escort returning to Beauport had given Crosbie a chance to slip away. He had seen to Denis's requirements, finding food and blankets for the boy and taking them to the guardhouse outside Beauport. The boy seemed dazed, bewildered by what had happened to him, but confident and unworried after he had seen Crosbie. He was far less worried than Crosbie.

Crosbie shook himself awake and reined his horse toward the bridge of boats crossing the St. Charles. Denis's fate lay with Montcalm now. The boy would have to be punished, Crosbie realized, but the Général was not a man who killed children. Crosbie turned uphill toward the Palace Gate, feeling a strong unwillingness to enter the ruined streets.

The thunder of bombardment rumbled constantly from the enemy cannon on the Heights across the river, with only a rare response from Quebec's batteries. Solid shot crashed into stone walls, heavy mortar shells exploded with deafening impact in the narrow streets. The city's permanent garrison kept well out of harm's way in their stout stone barracks, but they had furnished bomb sentinels who were posted at regular intervals to blow bugles or beat drums to warn passers-by off the streets. The raucous, shrill alarm of "Gare la bombe!" swept through the city night and day.

Crosbie left his mount at the gate and walked into the battered city. He held his countenance rigid, striving for the sober, unruffled attitude that marked Montcalm under fire. But, involuntarily, his eyes lifted to scan the skyline above the enemy position.

He heard faintly a loud whoosh, and saw a wide trail of sparks bright against the grey afternoon sky. Almost immediately there came a deep crumping explosion from Lower Town. Another arcing flare of red was followed by another fierce rush of wind. Crosbie could see the falling arc of the shell hanging in the air, the spitting fuse-glow paling as it approached the ground. He leaped for a doorway and turned his face away from the street. A rain of cobblestones followed the blast. Crosbie waited wearily before he stepped out again. A great crater lay deep in the street before him. He skirted around it quickly and walked with lengthening strides up the hill.

It was hard to believe that the English were nearly at the end of their tether when one saw the havoc they continued to work in Quebec.

The shrill bomb-whistle was adequate warning now that Crosbie was adjusted to its meaning. Without looking to the dangerous sky, he dived for cover, slipping down a cellar stairway, tumbling out of control over a dusty mound of crushed stones. He caromed away from a sturdy shoulder and sat up slowly, muttering apologies that were smothered by the ear-shattering blast of a shell exploding close by. A choking cloud of stone dust made Crosbie cough raspingly. He pushed himself erect and looked at the huddled form of the man he had knocked over when he came stumbling down the steps.

"Very sorry, sir," he said inadequately. He peered closer, dimly aware of something wrong, but unsure what it might be. "Can I help you, sir?"

"No, my son," a voice said soberly. "God be with you."

"Mathieu!" Crosbie said in shocked surprise. "Isn't it Brother Mathieu? I can't see clearly in this warren, but I'd swear ..."

"You were always overly free with profanity," Brother Mathieu said sharply. His grey-robed figure became more visible as he moved toward the entrance to the staircase.

"But, Mathieu," Crosbie said uneasily. "Back in Quebec with never a word for old friends? I thought you were still at the Détroit."

"I ... I failed, Duncan," the friar said quietly. "I was sent back with the partisans who returned to lift the siege at Niagara. And I came on here when they were defeated." His thin, shaken voice said more than his words could convey.

A chill edge of apprehension touched Crosbie's mind. "What happened, Mathieu?" he asked as casually as he could manage. "Some difficulty with the Indians?"

He could see the sharp outline of Brother Mathieu's robe now against the dim light. And he noticed the involuntary shudder that shook the heavy shoulders.

"Yes," the friar said thickly. "The Indians. I ... I was constantly afraid, Duncan. They were less than men. You know how they are. Less than men, but somehow more than men, also. Satanic. I was a ... a failure, Duncan. The Indians mocked me. My superiors lost their faith in me."

Crosbie murmured in sympathetic response.

"It was the English prisoners at the Ottawa village that ended my mission. Mere babes, some of them, torn from their homes in the English provinces. The Indians were going to kill them, but I managed to stop them. I ... I stood fast, Duncan."

"I am sure you did, Mathieu."

"Yes, I stood fast. The chieftains listened to me, but the warriors and the women ... my God, the women! They screamed for the slaughter. But I prevailed against them all. I had the power of the Cross and these were all Christian Indians."

"Splendid," Crosbie said absently. He glanced out at the deserted street. It seemed safe to go on, but he could not abandon Brother Mathieu so abruptly. "I think you did very well, Mathieu."

"Very well! Dear God! Very well! Do you know what they did, Duncan? Afterward, after they had listened to me in their solemn meeting, they brought the prisoners to my chapel and let me baptise them. Oh, I was delighted then, I can tell you. I thought I had won. I actually thought I had helped the Ottawa along the path of Godliness. Heaven forgive me."

Crosbie shrugged helplessly. He did not understand what the young friar was saying, but he knew he should not interrupt. He laid one broad hand on the grey-robed shoulder and waited patiently.

"Then ... then, after the baptism, the prisoners were led from my chapel. Straight to the center of the village, to the red-painted post. And they were killed. Every one. Even one babe who was as yet too young to walk. Since their souls were now safe with Jesus, the Indians saw no reason to spare their lives. They were slaughtered, scalped and burned. And the slobbering beasts cut them and ..." Mathieu's voice was strangled by the memory. A painful sound tore from within him.

Crosbie looked at his shaken friend. He felt ashamed and a little sick. Mathieu had actually been compelled to witness one of the ritualistic feasts. No wonder he sounded so horrified. Good God, no wonder!

"So they sent me back. I was too weak, too uncertain in my faith to serve any longer in the wilderness. Out there, priests must be of stronger fibre. Men who can baptise and then ..."

"Yes." Crosbie broke in heavily. "It is revolting, Mathieu. I ... I wish I had ..."

The young friar pulled in a deep shaky breath, fighting for control. Duncan Crosbie maintained his silence, unable to think of a word that was not fatuous or inadequate. His hand gripped hard on Brother Mathieu's shoulder.

"It is all right, Duncan," the friar said softly, as if it were Crosbie who needed comforting. "I am usefully employed here in helping the sick and the wounded. I have little time to think. Except ... except at night."

Crosbie urged his friend out toward the street. In the clear, unflattering light, Brother Mathieu's broad peasant's face seemed insensitive, stolid and unimaginative, until you saw the eyes that burned with memories few men were able to endure. He clasped his hands at his waist and smiled thinly at Crosbie.

"A fortunate meeting, Duncan," he said in the sharp, reproving tones that Crosbie remembered so well. "I was somewhat disturbed by the shelling, I am afraid. You will please forget what I have said?"

"Of course, Mathieu," Crosbie said readily. "Can I ..."

"No," the friar said sharply. "No, I am perfectly all right. I have my duties to perform and I assume that you have yours. I see by your uniform that you have won promotion, so I know you have applied yourself diligently. Continue to do so, Duncan."

Brother Mathieu lifted his cowled head to look at the gutted building beside him. His sombre eyes inspected the long street of broken roof-tops and shell-torn walls. "I know you have little knowledge of holy writings, Duncan," he said with a flicker of his former mild humor, "but you may have been reminded lately of the Lamentations of Jeremiah, as I have. 'How doth the city sit solitary, that was full of people! How is she become as a widow! She that was great among the nations, and a princess among the provinces, how is she become tributary!' Except that Quebec has not yet become tributary, it is strangely applicable, isn't it?" The young friar nodded slowly, then forced a smile as he glanced at Crosbie. "Farewell, Duncan. God be with you." He lifted his hand in brief benediction and then turned abruptly away.

Crosbie stood unmoving, watching his friend out of sight. For a brief moment the friar was outlined sharply against the lowering grey sky that was only slightly lighter in tone than

Brother Mathieu's threadbare robe. A hint of thunder-storm lay buried in the distant clouds. A chill wind whipped through the broken street, blowing billows of smoke and dust.

A shattered city, Crosbie thought dourly, and a shattered man. But if Mathieu could find a way to repair the damage done to him, who dared say that Quebec's future was hopeless?

Crosbie wheeled away and walked up the inclined street, his head low in angry reflections. He moved briskly across the Great Square and turned toward the Château battery. At the high stone rampart, he paused beside a weary, unshaven gunnery sergeant for a look at the cold, slate-colored water below the city. Hundreds of small boats darted around the naval ships near the Île d'Orléans. Several rakish frigates heeled over in the stiff breeze as they moved back and forth before Quebec. A long line of transports stood anchored beyond Pointe Lévi.

"They tell me Wolfe has got most of his army on those ships now," the sergent offered in a sober tone. "They say he's just about ready to up-anchor and sail for England as soon as the river starts to freeze."

Crosbie nodded. For more than a week, the bulk of the English army had been living aboard their transports. Many of the ships had slipped west of the city, threatening a landing there, and forcing Louis de Bougainville to quick-march his troops up and down the long escarpment, following the feints of the enemy. But Crosbie put no faith in the sergent's hopeful rumor. Wolfe had not given up, not yet, Crosbie felt sure. Wolfe was certain to try one more desperate attack before he sailed home to the scorn and humiliation that surely awaited him there. He was commander of nearly thirty thousand soldiers and sailors, picked men every one, and he himself was the most highly regarded flag officer of the army, with a long record of valor and resourcefulness. Yet he had failed against a mere three-thousand-man force buttressed by untrained militia. His artillery might have destroyed Quebec, but he was as far from taking it as ever. No, there would be no future for Wolfe when he returned to England. So, Duncan Crosbie, putting himself in Wolfe's place, knew there would be another attack, for he too would have chosen to lead his army forward in mad assault rather than admit defeat. Wolfe would certainly try once more. Where and when were the only mysteries.

A high shrieking wail rose from beyond the city wall, a snarling, whining chorus of howls. Crosbie glanced at the sergent, frowning thoughtfully.

The sergent's eyes were red-rimmed with fatigue as he returned Crosbie's questioning gaze. He shrugged easily and rubbed at his stubbled throat. "Wolves," he said with cold disinterest. "They are getting bolder now. You hadn't heard them before? They run in packs by the hundreds now, they tell me, right through the city streets."

Crosbie shuddered slightly. He turned abruptly toward the inner magazine, stooping to avoid the low ceiling as he entered. Inside, seated at a rickety table, twirling a half-empty wine glass as he peered near-sightedly at an official-looking document, was the Chevalier Le Mercier. He had removed his coat and torn open his collar. Between the gaping buttons of his waistcoat, shaggy wisps of grey hair protruded. Le Mercier wiped a gunpowder-stained hand across his mouth and blinked as Crosbie loomed in the small entrance, completely blotting out the pale watery daylight.

The young Scot came forward, towering over the Chevalier, his grim stony eyes bright with contempt. He bowed briefly and turned completely around, scanning the small room. Scanty reserves of powder and shot were stacked neatly along the walls. A basket of wine bottles, most of them empty, lay on its side near the door. Crosbie glanced down at Le Mercier.

"His Excellency left his telescope here a few days ago, monsieur," he said in a bleak, formal voice. "Will you be good enough to find it, please?"

"Telescope?" Le Mercier batted his eyes and tried to focus on Crosbie's face. "I haven't seen it. Take him mine, if he needs one. It's beside the door." He cleared his throat with a resounding crash and his eyes clouded with embarrassment as he avoided Crosbie's cold stare.

"I doubt if His Excellency would touch anything of yours, monsieur," Crosbie said. "Will you, please ..."

Le Mercier kept his eyes fixed on the document he held. He pushed a wine bottle toward Crosbie, as if trying to placate the grim young soldier who stood over him with clenched hands.

Slowly, Crosbie swept one arm across the table, dashing the bottle to the floor. It shattered with a sharp crash and a thin stream of white wine ran thickly through the dust toward the open door.

"I'll not drink with you," Crosbie said coldly, "nor even look at you, except as the Général orders me. I wouldn't ..."

He stopped in amazement. A shell wooshed high above the battery and the Chevalier cringed behind the table as the whining note reached a peak and then softened to a whistle that ended soon in a dull crumping explosion. Le Mercier gulped the wine that remained in his glass.

"Thousands of shells," he muttered in a shaky voice. "Thousands. Look here." He rattled the paper he held, turning it around for Crosbie to read. "One of the cadets prepared it. Four thousand barrels of gunpowder, the English have already used against the city. Four thousand! Where do they get it? How could they ..."

"Maybe they got it from you," Crosbie said furiously. "The powder you stole from ..."

"It wasn't stolen." Le Mercier tried to straighten in his chair and hold his head high, but he soon slumped again and dropped his head into his cupped hands. "I didn't steal it," he repeated dully. "It never existed. Bigot never bought it. He just took the money."

"There's no difference," Crosbie said flatly.

Le Mercier dropped his hands and looked up at Crosbie. Bright tears hung in his eyes. "There is a difference," he said with a strange dignity. "I have taken money, yes. A little douceur to sweeten existence in Canada. Everyone did the same. I sold horses that never existed, and reported them dead after a few weeks, and bought still more non-existent horses. What of that? It was only money, I tell you. Never have I...cheated France."

Crosbie averted his eyes. Le Mercier's simple words aroused the beginnings of sympathy in him and he was determined to feel nothing but contempt for Le Mercier and his thieving friends.

"You whine when you're caught," he growled. "A great patriot in your mind, but to anyone else, a thieving, cowardly..."

"No!" Le Mercier knotted his huge hands tightly on the table. "No, I tell you! I am through with them; I have told Bigot that. I would never agree to stealing the army's very flesh and blood. A little money, yes, why not? But not gunpowder and not..."

"You aren't finished with Bigot," Crosbie said flatly. "Monsieur Tremais has evidence enough to send him to the Bastille for the rest of his life. And you, Monsieur Patriot, will go with him."

Le Mercier sighed. He lifted his clenched hands in helpless protest. "No," he said stolidly. "I will not go to the Bastille, no matter how much I deserve it." He looked up sharply at Crosbie. "You think your fine friend Tremais can defeat Bigot? I tell you Bigot has a plan. He will..." The commandant's heavy voice droned to a full stop as he stared blindly at the table.

"He will what?" Crosbie demanded. "Kill Tremais, I suppose? That would be his first idea, I know. But it won't do. Tremais's evidence would reach Paris."

Le Mercier spat his opinion of Tremais's evidence. "You think that evidence will ever reach Paris? You blind young fool! Who will send it? The English?" Le Mercier half rose with the vehemence of his feelings. "Will the English send it, if Bigot gives Canada to them?"

Crosbie's face darkened and grew ugly with sudden hatred. His hand darted up, flicking his dirk from its jeweled scabbard. "How?" he demanded in a hoarse growl. "How will Bigot deliver Canada to the English?"

La Mercier shrugged. "I don't know. I'm not even sure..."

Crosbie laid the point of his dirk against the commandant's throat. "Tell me," he said, quietly savage.

"I don't know!" Le Mercier shrilled. "Kill me, and make an end. I have no stomach for this. I don't know what Bigot is doing. I just got the idea because..."

"Because?" Crosbie insisted.

Le Mercier raised his hand slowly and pushed Crosbie's dirk aside. "I told you, I don't know. Bigot doesn't tell me anything these days. I saw his Captain O'Neill talking to that English prisoner and then the prisoner was supposed to have escaped, but he didn't. Because I have seen him at the Palace since then. And he's coming back from Wolfe's camp again tonight, so I thought..."

Le Mercier's voice rumbled on and Crosbie listened in growing horror. "But how could he?" Crosbie asked in complete bewilderment. "How could Bigot deliver the city? How could he keep Montcalm..."

"I don't know." Le Mercier turned to snatch another bottle of wine from the basket. He drew the cork with his teeth and poured a glassful, his big hands shaking so that the table was drenched with spattering wine. He gulped thirstily. He looked up then, more composed. "I don't know what he plans. I'm not even sure my suspicion is... But it must be! Why else does that Major Stowell make all those trips?"

"Stowell," Crosbie muttered. He remembered Major Stowell, remembered seeing him at a private dinner with O'Neill at Colbert's house; remembered seeing him at the English camp beyond the Montmorenci.

"You'd better tell the Général," Le Mercier said thickly. "I couldn't... couldn't face him. But you tell him. He can find out.

Maybe Tremais knows what's being planned, though I'm sure he doesn't. Or maybe that Mademoiselle Céleste of yours ..."

"Céleste?" Crosbie tensed. The point of his dirk lifted toward Le Mercier again. "What did you say about Céleste?"

"She's spying again," Le Mercier said. "She's been talking to the Palace guards and servants. But Bigot knows what she is doing, and so does the Comtesse. You should hear them speak of her, especially the Comtesse. God, what hatred! So she probably hasn't heard anything, if Bigot knows that she ..."

But she has, Crosbie thought dully. She knows about Major Stowell. She knows he once returned to Quebec after reportedly escaping. And knowing that, she might ...

"Tremais," he said aloud in a harsh voice. "She is doing it for Tremais?"

"I suppose so," Le Mercier said, his eyebrows lifting in surprise. "Don't you know?"

Crosbie put his dirk away with slow deliberation. "You said Stowell is coming to Quebec tonight?"

Le Mercier nodded.

"Where?" Crosbie gritted his teeth to force himself to calm restraint. Every fibre shrieked for furious activity, but he had to stand quietly here and ask simple, sharp questions before he would know enough to make action effective. A booming pulse almost deafened him and he leaned forward to hear Le Mercier's answer.

"At the Palace, or Colbert's house, or ..."

"You aren't sure?" Still that quiet, deadly tone.

"No."

"Do you know where Tremais is living?"

"Tremais?" Le Mercier blinked in concentration. "Tremais. He's at St. Roch, near the Palace. A house there ... The widow Gagnon."

"You stay here," Crosbie snapped. "Is that clear, monsieur le Chevalier? You remain here and you send no messages to anyone.

If you send any warning of any sort, I will return here and kill you. Believe me, monsieur."

Le Mercier swallowed heavily. He nodded. "I...I believe you," he said unsteadily.

Crosbie whirled swiftly to the door, leaping from the battery ramparts in a driving run, angling toward the Palace Gate and St. Roch. Tremais first, he thought savagely. Tremais first, to stop whatever hell's brew Bigot has scheduled. Then Céleste. And if any harm had come to her...Crosbie shook the worry from his mind and thought only of running, unmindful of the bombs and shot that crashed constantly on the ruined buildings of Quebec.

CHAPTER FIFTY EIGHT

Enough light remained to make jagged, shattered walls of the ruined city clear to Crosbie as he ran. Exploding mortar shells from the enemy guns were sending great sheets of brilliant dazzle over the city. The huge Palace Gate was almost invisible. Crosbie stopped, seeing the sentry.

"The widow Gagnon," Crosbie bellowed. "Do you know where her house is?"

"The widow Gagnon?" the sentry repeated slowly. "The house stands just there." A finger pointed at a stone house across the road. "The one with the high windows and ..."

Crosbie turned away without listening to the rest. He leaped briskly up the stone steps and pounded on the door. He banged twice, then rotated the knob and entered. He shouted for Tremais the moment he was inside.

"Good Heavens, young man," a woman's voice complained. "Why can't you ..."

"Yes, who calls me?"

Crosbie heard the second voice coming from the staircase. He swept his hat off in a rudimentary bow for the angry woman standing arms akimbo in a doorway. He dashed quickly up the stairs.

Monsieur Tremais stood calmly on the landing. Behind him, an open door showed a warm, bright room.

"Monsieur Crosbie, what is ..."

Brusquely, Crosbie laid his hand on the small man's chest and pushed him back into his room. He kicked the door shut before he spoke. Words spilled from him in short bursts like musketry, broken only when he drew in a quick breath.

Tremais listened quietly, a slight air of reproof in his manner. His thin lips clamped hard and his eyes glistened. His nostrils flared as Crosbie continued in his fast, breathlessly impatient voice.

"The Chevalier was intoxicated, was he?" Tremais asked sharply.

"Yes. What difference does that make?"

Tremais lifted one hand to quiet Crosbie. "Most of what you have told me, I knew long ago. Only yesterday, I reported to your Général that some attempt might be made to betray the city to the enemy. However, I did not know... Tonight, Le Mercier said? Major Stowell and ..."

"And who?" Crosbie growled.

"Stowell has dealt with Monsieur Colbert for the most part. That I know. Since Le Mercier mentioned Colbert's house as a possible meeting place, I think..." As he spoke, Tremais stripped off a light dressing gown, donned his coat and buckled on a thin-bladed rapier. He clapped on a tightly curled tricorne and took a long black cloak from his closet. "Come with me," he said in a peremptory tone of command.

"Sir?" Crosbie frowned at the sudden order.

"If Stowell comes to Colbert's house tonight, he must be intercepted. Come with me."

Tremais clattered briskly down the stairs and out into the street before Crosbie could catch him. With quick determination, Crosbie snatched the thin man's arm, pulling him to a halt.

"I want to know that Céleste is safe before I ..."

"Nonsense," Tremais said crisply. "She is perfectly well. Thanks to her, I knew about Major Stowell weeks ago. She has done very well indeed. No, do not grumble, young man. I command you in the King's name to assist me. Now hurry."

Tremais swung his long cloak around his shoulders and pulled up the deep, concealing conspirator's hood. He trotted up the dark cobbled street toward Monsieur Colbert's house. Crosbie ran to catch up, then walked more slowly, two of his long strides matching three of Tremais's fast steps.

"And if Stowell comes," Crosbie asked quietly, "don't you think he'll object to being arrested?"

"That is why I want you," Tremais said testily. "I will arrest him. And everyone else present. You will enforce the arrest."

The man's brisk assurance was overwhelming. Crosbie found himself nodding agreement before he even considered the serious fight he might have if Colbert and Stowell had any men with them. Monsieur Tremais trotted eagerly up the street, paused at a corner to squint at the shattered doorways, then darted across to Colbert's house.

Along the slope toward St. Roch, many buildings stood with some resemblance to their original appearance, and Colbert's was one of these. The line of the roof sagged and the upper window frame hung at an impossible angle, but the lower floors seemed to be intact. Tremais ran up the short stairs and tried the door handle.

"Quickly, quickly," he whispered. "Search the house. If no one is here yet, we will wait. But be very sure. And very quick. Now!" He thrust the door back against the foyer wall and jumped in.

Crosbie followed swiftly, his dirk leaping into his hand as he crossed the threshold. He jumped ahead of Tremais and lunged into the salon and beyond it to the curtained diningroom where he had first seen Major Stowell.

Both darkened rooms were empty. Nothing moved. Crosbie halted in mid-stride, listening intently. Behind him, Tremais swished his supple rapier.

The cellar, Crosbie remembered. Le Singe had locked Colbert and Stowell in the cellar for a few hours on his last visit. Crosbie wished Le Singe and some of his stalwart voyageurs were with him now.

"I'll try the cellar," he said softly to Tremais. He heard the investigator murmur something, but he did not stop. Through pantry and kitchen he moved on softly padding feet, letting his dirk inspect all the shadowed corners before he committed himself. The cellar door stood open. Below the darkness was even more forbidding. Crosbie nerved himself and felt for the first step. He went down quickly, knowing he was especially vulnerable as long as he was on the staircase. He strode quickly forward across the stone floor and crashed his shoulder against the far wall. It was a small cubicle, Crosbie realized. His hands patted along the walls, outlining the shape of a locked winebin and open compartments which gave off the odor of long-stored vegetables. He turned back to the stairs.

Overhead, a mortar shell exploded with a resounding blast that shook the solid house. Crosbie leaped up the stairs three at a time, whirled through the kitchen toward the foyer. A choking cloud of stone dust raised by the bomb lay thickly through the building. Not a direct hit, Crosbie guessed, but it had been close.

Running footsteps pounded down the narrow stairs from the upper portion of the house. Crosbie dropped warily to a crouch, peering blindly through the dense pall of dust. Thin bright flames licked at the darkness, flickering dimly, then surging high and sharp. The running figure was starkly outlined in that brief moment before he crashed solidly into Crosbie, sending the young Scot reeling back into the salon. The man was Captain Seamus O'Neill, wig awry and uniform dusty, eyes flaring with panic as he caromed away from Crosbie, steadied himself momentarily at the door, and then ran out into the dark street.

Crosbie came angrily to his feet. He took one swift stride toward the open door before he heard the soft rasping sound from the staircase. Cautiously, he turned, bracing himself. There was no sound for a long moment. Crosbie listened sharply. He leaned forward, feeling for the stairs with his left hand. He climbed silently upward, searching each tread with his fingers before he moved. A soft groan just above him made him jump with nervous response.

"Monsieur ... Monsieur Crosbie," a weak voice called.

That was Tremais! Crosbie rushed up to the landing. A frigid blast of wind struck at his back. Crosbie realized that the bomb had ripped the roof from Colbert's house. Farther down the upper hallway, dark against the dusty floor, he could see a shadowed shape. Holding his dirk poised, Crosbie crept forward. Fire blazed steadily along the shattered roof, illuminating the landing in dazzling flashes.

Crosbie saw the tightly curled outline of Tremais's hat, and then the voluminous cloak spread wide. He knelt and slid his arm gently under Tremais's shoulders. The bomb, he thought, Tremais had been caught by the explosion. Or had he collided with O'Neill, too?

He lifted the scrawny figure, supporting the shoulders. He felt a warm dampness under his hand and he explored until he found a long gash torn in Tremais's scalp, just over one ear. A wide flap hung free. Crosbie pressed it back into place and gathered himself to pick the man up in his arms.

"No," Tremais muttered weakly. "Not me. Get ... get ..."

Crosbie eased him back to the floor. Get what? Tremais struggled to speak, but words choked to incoherent mumbling in his throat. Growing alarm made Crosbie turn completely around, frowning hard as he tried to see clearly through the harsh flickering firelight and the drifting dust.

Farther down the hallway was another dark patch that looked very much as Tremais had from a distance. Was that what he had meant? Crosbie padded along the floor, his dirk ready.

Another of those enormous conspirator's cloaks covered a recumbent figure. Crosbie remembered with a sudden dreadful sureness where he had seen two such cloaks before. In duMaine's warehouse when Tremais and Céleste ...

A harsh cry strangled behind his teeth as Crosbie lunged awkwardly forward, forgetting everything else as he scooped both hands under the wide cloak, then lifted the light-boned figure, and rose to his feet.

A soft silky fan of loosened hair dropped back as the cloak's hood fell away. But Crosbie knew who it was before the face was visible. He had held that figure before, just this closely. His arms were adjusted to that weight, and the scent was dearly familiar to him.

"Céleste," he whispered hoarsely. "Dear God, Céleste!"

He held her close and bent his head, trying to hear a heartbeat. She isn't dead, he told himself calmly. Of course, she isn't dead. She has been hurt. She and Tremais were caught in the bomb explosion. They should be in the hospital. But of course she isn't dead. She can't be.

Crosbie shifted Céleste's weight easily to his left arm, sheathed his dirk and shuffled cautiously along the hall until he reached Tremais. He stooped and hooked his right arm under the small man's waist. Then he stood again, almost without effort, and walked carefully down the littered stairs to the door.

Within five minutes, possibly three, he would have them both in bed at the General Hospital. They would be all right then. Tremais seemed to be unconscious now, but probably he had fainted. And Céleste had merely fainted, too. She would be all right very soon now. Of course Céleste was all right.

She can't be dead. It wasn't possible. She can't be dead.

CHAPTER FIFTY NINE

Behind the General Hospital stretched dense blocks of white army tents being used as temporary quarters for Quebec's refugee population. Hundreds of small children ran free in the grounds, leaping and screaming after a pack of scrawny dogs. Duncan Crosbie shoved back from the high window and turned away to stare at the closed door.

He drew in a long breath and folded his arms patiently. It had been a long trip to the hospital, and carrying two unconscious people had been hard work, even for him, but everything was all right now, he assured himself. Both Céleste and Tremais had been put to bed and competent surgeons were plentiful here. He hadn't been allowed to stay with Céleste and he hadn't wanted to stay with Tremais, so he had been shunted into this cramped cubicle to wait. But it didn't matter. Nothing mattered. He could remember what a frightful shock it had been when he thought Céleste might be dead. God, how clearly he remembered! Even now, the mere thought was enough to make him sicken in his soul. But everything was all right now. He must be patient. He mustn't complain, or ...

The door swung open slowly and Crosbie forced himself to stand still. He watched eagerly as Brother Mathieu's sombre features came into view.

"Well, Mathieu," Crosbie called, almost gaily. "This is your hospital, too, eh? You didn't tell me."

"Yes, Duncan," Brother Mathieu said in a quiet, measured tone. "I work here. I visit the sick, and try to bring comfort to the bereaved ... you know."

"Of course, of course. Glad to see you." Crosbie smiled. "Sit down, Mathieu. I'm just waiting to hear how soon I can take Céleste home. She was ..."

"I know, Duncan," the young friar said heavily. "I was here when you brought her in, with Monsieur Tremais."

"Were you?" Crosbie said absently. "I was too busy to notice. I suppose. That fool Tremais persuaded her to help him again, I suppose you know. She was nearly killed. I can tell you I'll put a stop to such foolishness right this minute. There'll be no more of that for Céleste. Why, she might have been killed!"

"She was, Duncan," Brother Mathieu whispered hoarsely.

Crosbie snorted. "That is what the surgeon said before. Nonsense, Mathieu. A knock on the head, that's all. Tremais is all right, isn't he? A knock on the head isn't fatal, you know. They were both caught in a bomb explosion. Now don't you be tiresome, Mathieu. I'm trying to be patient, but I can endure only so much foolishness."

Brother Mathieu swallowed heavily, keeping his eyes tightly on the over-excited, voluble young Scot. He made his voice come out in quiet smoothness, masking the terrible anguish in his heart. "Won't you have a drink, Duncan?"

"Excellent, Mathieu. Excellent," Crosbie said, rubbing his hands together briskly. He watched with close interest as the young friar brought out a dusty bottle of brandy and poured a small measure for him. He lifted it high and beamed, "I'll need this, you know. And probably a bit more, too. I'll have to explain to the Sieur duMaine that I was stupid enough to let Tremais put Céleste in such a dangerous position. Why, she might have been killed, you realize." He gulped the brandy and held out the glass for more.

"She was killed, Duncan," Brother Mathieu said with no particular emphasis. "She was dead before the bomb exploded, we believe. Anyway, she wasn't hurt by the bomb. Only Tremais. He is all right, as you expected. A bump of the head. He will be able to go home soon. But Céleste was dead before ..."

"Nonsense, Mathieu." Crosbie drank the brandy quickly and slammed the glass to the table. "I told you ... a knock on the head ... she can't be ..." His enormous shoulders slumped suddenly and the wild, frenetic gaiety was wiped clear from his face. His mouth pinched in savagely. "Mathieu," he said in a terrible, choked voice. "Mathieu, she ... Dead, Mathieu?"

"Yes, my son," the friar said solemnly. He approached Crosbie and pushed the stunned young soldier to a chair. Softly Brother Mathieu's hand rested on Crosbie's bowed head as he whispered a gentle prayer.

"She can't be dead, Mathieu," Crosbie said forcefully. "She can't be ..." His voice broke completely then and a great sob tore from his chest. He gripped his face with hard fingers, digging deeply, crying with harsh dry intensity, drawing in short breaths that seemed to strangle him.

Brother Mathieu did not shift. His hand lay easily on Crosbie's head and tears streamed down his face as he listened to the terrible racking sobs. The door opening behind him was a welcome interruption. There was something in Crosbie's eyes that he couldn't bear to see.

Monsieur Tremais limped into the room, clutching his foolish conspirator's cloak about his throat and holding one hand out as if he were carrying something valuable.

"I must thank you, monsieur," he said crisply. "I owe you my life."

Crosbie rose with painful deliberation. His sombre face was streaked with dirt and tears and his eyes were mad, but his lips parted in a strained, humorless grimace that might have been intended for a smile.

Tremais watched with stunned fascination as the young Scot approached him.

"No, Duncan!" Brother Mathieu shrieked suddenly. He sprang quickly to intercept Crosbie. "No!" Over his shoulder, he snapped, "Get out of here, you fool! Do you want to die?"

Tremais's eyes widened with alarm. Involuntarily, he stepped back. Then he stiffened and made himself look straight into Crosbie's maddened eyes. "If Monsieur Crosbie holds me responsible for Mademoiselle Céleste's death, then he will certainly kill me," he said thinly. "But first let me show him this." He thrust his thin clenched fist out toward Crosbie and opened it slowly.

Tremais's utter fearlessness and the momentary distraction were enough to break Crosbie's insane focus. He drew a hand weakly across his forehead and blinked at Tremais. He looked down at the small leaden pellet in his hand. "What is that?" he asked hoarsely.

"A pistol bullet," Tremais said sharply. "The surgeon removed it at my request from ... from ... her."

"A pistol bullet?" Crosbie said in a dazed tone. "But the bomb ... the bomb ..."

"No, Duncan," Brother Mathieu interrupted. "I tried to tell you. She was dead before the bomb hit. I did not know about the pistol, but it was obvious that she was shot to death."

"Shot." Crosbie's voice was dead, without inflection.

"I was struck on the head, Monsieur Crosbie," Tremais said dryly. "But not because of that bomb, either. A man struck me. A slim man in the uniform of the troupes de la marine. He was in the hallway with a pistol in his hand when I went upstairs. A captain with a tight white wig. I did not see his face."

"It doesn't matter, sir," Crosbie said in a flat, quiet voice. "I know who it was. Mathieu, may I ... see her? Just for a moment?"

The young friar hesitated briefly. "You will be all right, Duncan?"

"But, Monsieur, if you know the man," Tremais insisted, "it is your duty to tell me."

Crosbie walked blindly past Tremais and pulled the door open. "Show me the way, Mathieu. I must hurry. I will stay just a moment."

CHAPTER SIXTY

The night was very cold and damp. After a while, the rain came down, softly at first, then harder as the wind seemed to drive it from the mountains. It was icy rain that brought the smell of snow with it.

Crosbie walked slowly. Somewhere he had lost his hat and the rain rinsed all the powder from his hair. The coldness of it felt good on his head, though Crosbie was vaguely pleased to have his tarpaulin cape to button over his coat.

He talked to himself as he walked the deserted streets. At first he was surprised and a little worried to hear that low mumbling voice always in his ears, but he grew accustomed to it, and he paid no more attention to it than he did to the cold rain.

He could hear explosions as shells landed on the shattered city, but even that crashing noise was not enough to make him think of the war, or of the enemy that had been packed tightly back into its transports and was sailing up and down the river, searching for an unguarded place to land. The war had been his life, the part that had required the most thought and energy. But no more. Tonight he had no time to think of war.

In his mind, he had already planned his marriage day in the minutest detail. Céleste had been especially radiant in a shimmering ivory satin gown that had been her Grand-'mère's. And he himself had been quite satisfactory in a new uniform, with a silver-lace neck-cloth Aimée had given him. The Sieur duMaine had been very boisterous. And later he had gotten very drunk and cried a little as he spoke of Céleste. And the Général had amiably guarded his old friend through that trying day. Yes, Crosbie sighed pleasurably, it had been perfectly organized, everything just so, as was only to be expected considering the groom was a staff officer and details were the basis of good staff-work.

And now, Duncan Crosbie, husband and captain of artillery, had to plan his future. Probably Montcalm would be promoted to Marshal during the Winter, and he would certainly offer Crosbie a place on his staff. Céleste would like that. Duty in Paris, even. That might come his way. Then he and Céleste could take their position in society in a minor way, as the Général—the Marshal—would expect. And then, if no campaign offered new opportunities, he could retire in a few years and come back to Beauport. Seigneural duties would, of course, be tiresome after the strenuous work on Montcalm's staff, but he would always have the militia company to keep him occupied. It might be vastly rewarding to see just how efficient a militia company could become with devoted supervision, sound training and plenty of drill. Yes, it would be a good life, rich and satisfying.

"It isn't any good," he said aloud. He heard the voice clearly, heard the words and heard the meaning.

Duncan Crosbie swallowed painfully. He must have been talking for hours, he realized. And walking as well, from the ache in his legs. And none of it had done any good. He had retreated into a dream and the dream had been wonderful, even in the rain. But now it was over. Something had awakened him.

He stopped and lifted his face to the sky, opening his mouth to feel the cool rain in his throat. He was somewhere in St. Roch, he knew, upstream of the Intendant's Palace, in a narrow cobbled street hedged by locked and shuttered houses that shone like dark silver in the rain. The loom of the Palace was visible even at night, and Crosbie walked slowly toward it.

He felt slightly tired, but he was not worried. He was strong enough. His hand felt under his cloak, twisting until it lay coldly against the skin of his chest. His fingers touched the warm medal of Ste. Barbara that Céleste had given him. She should have kept it for herself, he though suddenly.

Céleste had been killed because she had believed in something… something big, something outside Crosbie's understanding. Canada, maybe, or Justice, or … something like that. Crosbie realized that Canada to him was merely another foreign country, as all countries were foreign to an exile. He approved of Justice but not to the point of doing anything to attain it. And in all that he could see a great lack in himself. He had taken terrible risks, but only for advancement, for money or for glory. Never for a starlike ideal such as Céleste had followed. And that made him a small man, for all his immense size, a lesser man even than the fearless, devoted Tremais.

Duncan Crosbie turned at the Palace entrance. He took his hand away from the medal. The sentries moved to halt him in routine challenge. Crosbie swung back his wide cape, unmindful of the rain and gave them a glimpse of his regimentals. They stepped back smartly and stiffened in salute. Crosbie walked slowly inside.

"Monsieur, one moment," a voice said behind him.

In the foyer, Crosbie pivotted, seeing one of the sentries frowning heavily at him from the doorway.

"You are the capitaine Crosbie?" the sentry asked in sharp suspicion. Without waiting for Crosbie's answer, he shouted, "Sergent! Sergent!"

The guardroom door slammed open beside Crosbie. A stout, perfectly uniformed sergent stayed warily back. Slowly, Crosbie turned, shoving his cloak back from his shoulders. He placed his hands deliberately behind his back. Quite obviously the Palace sentries had received strict orders about him. The young Scot forced a confident smile to his grim face.

"His Excellency, Monsieur Bigot will wish to see me," he said easily. "Please present my most distinguished compliments and asked him to give me a moment in privacy."

The sergent hesitated. He glanced swiftly at the sentry and back again to Crosbie.

"I know what orders you were given, sergent," Crosbie said quietly. "They do not apply now, as Monsieur Bigot will tell you." Silently, he hoped Bigot's curiosity would outweigh his hatred.

With infinite slowness, he brought one hand forward and felt for his coat pocket. The glint of a gold coin flashed as he held his hand out toward the sergent. "Please find His Excellency at once, sergent," he said. "I will wait in the ballroom."

The sergent nodded, responding to the tone of assurance and command as he had been trained. He took the coin deftly. "Jean, stay with monsieur le capitaine," he said briskly. "And be alert!" The sergent wheeled and marched smartly down the wide hallway toward the staircase.

Crosbie moved toward the open door to the ballroom, his hands locked behind his back. The young sentry followed cautiously, musket poised. He halted just inside the door, blinking in the bright dazzle of the massed candles that guttered in their crystal and gilt chandeliers.

Earlier that evening, an orchestra had played here. Ladies and gentlemen of Bigot's circle had danced and conversed elegantly. But now they were gone and the vast empty room smelled of dry, forgotten flowers, of stale perfume and spilled wine. Linen-draped tables held the remnants of a lavish supper and the magnificent floor was sadly scarred with the shuffling of a thousand feet. Crosbie took three measured strides inside, turned and waited, looking with unseeing eyes at the watchful sentry, feeling cold and blank within himself, thinking of nothing, waiting for Bigot with a calm certainty that allowed of no misgiving.

His Excellency, the Intendant, arrived with appropriate fanfare, despite the advanced hour. Two sleepy-eyed sentries entered first, followed by the sergent. Then the Palace chamberlain with his silver-tipped staff paused in the doorway, bellowed Bigot's title in a great voice that roused echoes in the empty ballroom.

The sentries flanked Crosbie carefully; the sergent stepped aside and bowed. François Bigot strolled casually inside, his bold-eyed, dazzling sister on his arm.

Bigot's ugly, mottled face was stiffly controlled, only his slightly lifted eyebrows betraying a consciousness of caution. As always, he was dressed in spectacular clothes, a white satin coat sprigged with embroidered roses over pink silk smallclothes. A long purplish wine-stain was smeared down one sleeve. He lifted a scented handkerchief to his wide flat lips as if to pat away a smile of triumph that was spreading across his face. He winked at Crosbie with a bright twinkle that seemed to suggest they were fellow conspirators.

Crosbie bowed with stiff formality; the Comtesse swept low in a mocking curtsey. Bigot stood easily, openly grinning now, tossing a pair of silver dice up and down in one hand, surveying Crosbie with malicious curiosity.

"I granted your request only because it gave me an opportunity to offer my sincere sympathy, monsieur," Bigot said in a low vibrant tone that was almost convincing. "And my dear sister, of course, is eager to add her condolences. A tragic loss. This frightful war. And she was such a dear child. We were both immensely fond of our dear Céleste."

Crosbie inclined his head gravely, ignoring the mocking overtones. "I asked for a moment in privacy," he said bluntly.

"Should I dismiss my guards?" Bigot asked, still grinning. "With such a dangerous fellow as you?" He chuckled quietly at his joke and the Comtesse laughed with tinkling, brittle amusement.

Crosbie's gaunt features indicated no response. "You will not want anyone to hear what I have to say." His tone was positive.

Bigot's smirking grin faded. After a long reflective moment, he moved his head sideways in signal to the sergent. The sentries lowered their muskets and left the ballroom. Bigot waited, one jeweled hand patting his protuberant stomach, smoothing the bright silk of his waist-coat. When the door closed behind the guards, he raised both eyebrows in obvious question.

"I have come for Captain O'Neill," Crosbie said flatly.

"Indeed?" Bigot's eyebrows climbed higher in pretended surprise. "I thought you asked to see me?"

"Yes. I want you to give him to me."

"O'Neill? Oh, I see." Bigot chuckled easily, a vast, satisfied gurgle deep in his throat. "And why do you want him, my good fellow?"

"He killed Céleste." Crosbie's voice was quietly bitter.

"No. No, I cannot believe that," Bigot said sharply. "But even if what you say is true, why should I deliver him to you?"

"Listen to me," Crosbie said patiently. "You will give him to me because you will want to. He is a liability now. He knows about your plot with Major Stowell. He knows a great many things, and if he comes to trial, as he will, he will be tempted to save his skin by trying to involve you. You wouldn't care for that."

"No," Bigot laughed easily. "No, I certainly wouldn't like that. Nor do I like hearing it now."

"Don't interrupt," Crosbie said in deadly seriousness. "Monsieur Tremais can identify Captain O'Neill as the man who murdered Céleste. Tomorrow he will go to the Governor, and O'Neill will be arrested. To stop that, you must kill Tremais, or O'Neill, or both. I can solve the problem and spare you the trouble."

"Indeed?" Bigot glanced sharply at his sister and his mocking humor was completely wiped from his face now. A faint frown made a shadow on his forehead. "How?" he demanded sharply.

"Tell O'Neill to come to this room," Crosbie said. "Just that." He lifted his gaze from Bigot and stared blankly at the wide double-doors. In his mind there was no doubt of Bigot's answer. But the Intendant would probably need some time to reach his decision.

"And," he said quietly, "I will want the keys to all the doors. Have your servants bar every window to this room. Then send O'Neill to me."

Bigot shook his head slowly. "You are a cold-blooded young man, monsieur," he said almost admiringly.

"Yes," Crosbie said.

"You should thank Monsieur Crosbie," the Comtesse said brightly. "He has an audacious mind. I saw that long ago. He solves vexing problems with a single daring stroke of great simplicity, much as Alexander solved the riddle of the Gordian knot. Thank him, François."

Bigot and his sister looked at each other for a long tense moment.

"No," the Intendant said slowly. "I won't thank him. Not yet." He held out his arm for his sister and led her out the door into the hallway.

Crosbie stood unmoving, timelessly patient and sure of himself.

A few minutes later, four servants, obviously men who had just been routed from their beds, came hurriedly into the ballroom. They fixed metal sheathing into place over the windows with the speed of long practice. Before they went away, the oldest man made a tour of the great chamber, locking all the doors and extracting the keys. He inserted an enormous key in the entrance lock and left it there. Then the servants bowed silently and withdrew. Crosbie moved to a position where he would be shielded by the opening door when O'Neill came into the ballroom. He leaned against the wall, crossed his feet and folded his arms stolidly.

He waited with a deadly, unnatural calm.

The guard changed outside the Palace with much noisy ritual. The crash of muskets and the slap of hob-nailed boots stopped eventually and Duncan Crosbie wondered with no least interest what time it was. Probably that was the two o'clock change, but it might just as easily be the four o'clock. He had been blind and numb during that long walk he had taken when he left the hospital.

When Captain O'Neill approached the ballroom, Duncan Crosbie could hear him coming long before he reached the door. He was sauntering, his footsteps uneven almost as if he were dancing down the hallway. He pressed down the latch and sauntered in, one hand holding a lace-bordered handkerchief that smelled violently of rose-water. Duncan Crosbie leaned forward from the wall, placed one large hand precisely between O'Neill's shoulder-blades, and shoved.

The elegant Irishman stumbled headlong, fighting for balance. During the time it took him to recover, Crosbie had locked the door and pocketed the key. He turned soberly toward O'Neill and stalked heavily down the bare scarred floor.

"Crosbie! What are you…" Awareness flared in O'Neill's pale eyes. "My good friend, Bigot. Yes, I see. So that's his game!"

O'Neill bared his teeth in a brief, savage smile. His features tightened to a cold mask of controlled hatred. He stepped warily back to give himself adequate room to draw his rapier. He held it casually, the point touching the floor in front of Crosbie. "That's far enough, cock," he said in a low, hard voice.

Crosbie drew in a long breath and sighed. He had been afraid O'Neill would not fight. He should have known…

O'Neill flicked his blade up in a lunge that made Crosbie slither quickly aside. Crosbie's dirk was in his hand as he moved. Like a snake's tongue, the dark-steel dirk slashed at O'Neill's extended arm, opening a long seam in the perfectly tailored sleeve, but not drawing blood.

O'Neill withdrew briefly to inspect the damage. His eyes were blank, remote. He arched thin black eyebrows and drawled, "Not much chance for you, is there, cock? One lucky slash. That's the end for you."

It did not occur to Crosbie to answer. This was not a duel. He was here simply to destroy Captain Seamus O'Neill and that he would do, even if the sleek, confident Irishman had a dozen long-bladed swords.

O'Neill padded forward lithely, making no sound on the bare floor. He was careful now, though he permitted his lip to curl in mild contempt as he eyed Crosbie's dirk. His rapier darted forward in a dazzling series of swift feints. Crosbie extended his great arm to the utmost and prayed he would be able to parry O'Neill's thrusts. But it was only a matter of time before the clever Captain broke through his guard with another quick lunge.

Crosbie recoiled clumsily, almost slipping on the waxed floor. O'Neill advanced, containing his sharp arrogance, his cold, grave eyes watching Crosbie tightly. Before O'Neill was aware of his intention, Crosbie swept his arm up and lunged, hurling the jeweled dirk. The point stabbed perfectly into its target. The hilt quivered with brilliant reflections from the impact as the blade dug into the floor after piercing O'Neill's shoe. The slender Irishman was pinned solidly in place.

O'Neill shrieked, a thin, startled sound, as the first pain stabbed into his brain. Crosbie watched the agonized twisting of lips in the pale contorted face that was shiny with sweat. O'Neill screamed again, harshly. Then fury swept across his face and he slashed desperately with his rapier. The blade whistled about Crosbie's head and the young Scot stayed outside its arc, waiting his chance.

O'Neill shifted his sword to his left hand, then thrust his right into a wide pocket of his coat. Swiftly, he brought out a small silver-mounted pistol and pulled back the hammer with his thumb. The flat clicking sound alerted Crosbie to his danger. He crouched quickly. But not quickly enough.

The small pistol spat a thin tongue of flame. The explosion seemed to detonate inside Crosbie's head. He fell solidly to the floor, stunned and unbelieving. Above his right ear he felt a vast numbness; nothing more. As his fingers explored the wound, the bright lights of the ballroom winked out and for a brief, frightening moment, Crosbie was blind.

A sudden sharp impact against his chest made him turn his head down and with that movement, his vision returned. On the floor near him was the small, silvered pistol O'Neill had just thrown at him. Crosbie blinked, staring at it until he could see clearly again. The shiny arrows along the slim barrel made the pistol familiar. He remembered the moment he had scooped it up from the floor of the Comtesse's room. And later he had given it to Céleste. Céleste! She had tucked it inside the tiny bag that dangled from her wrist. And now O'Neill had it. And Céleste was dead. Crosbie grunted painfully and pushed himself up from the floor. He looked at O'Neill.

Desperately, the Irish captain balanced himself on his maimed foot and kicked at the glittering dirk. His shoe caught the guard and lifted the blade smoothly up and away in a high glittering arc.

With no change of expression, Crosbie crossed the room slowly to retrieve it. He pocketed the small decorated pistol and stooped for his dirk, pausing to wipe it clean against a tablecloth. The blade shone dully as he turned back.

The Irishman was on one knee. His rapier lay beside him and his stiff fingers fumbled with the gold-buckled shoe on his wounded foot. He tore the flap loose and pushed the shoe off. Then he glanced up to see Crosbie advancing again, blood streaming from the right side of his head, soaking his shirt scarlet in the bright light. O'Neill did not dare take time to bind his foot. Thin smears of blood left a sticky spoor as he retreated, limping swiftly to the far corner.

Crosbie stalked implacably forward, fighting off the waves of dizziness that threatened to blind him again. An icy calm wiped every human expression from his face. O'Neill's habitual pose of detached control cracked completely, leaving no trace of the contemptuously fearless man he had pretended to be.

Fat, bitter tears rolled down his smooth cheeks. The cold grave face was contorted with pain and ... could it be fear, Crosbie wondered.

"No," O'Neill said in a quiet, placatory voice. "No, that's enough, Crosbie. Damn you, I'm hurt. I can't..." His eyes widened as he saw Crosbie advancing with slow, unhurried strides. "No, I tell you! I'll... I'll... Crosbie, you can have Bigot! I'll give you Bigot! And the Comtesse, too! I know how to do it, Crosbie. Trust me. I tell you, I know. I can do it, Crosbie. You don't want me, you want Bigot. Crosbie, listen to me!"

His voice rose high and snapped on a shrill note. He sobbed wildly and he shrieked for Crosbie to stop, just to stop for a moment and talk. Only for a moment. Crosbie's heavy shoes rasped quietly across the bare floor.

O'Neill turned swiftly, searching for escape. He screamed with pain when he put his weight on his wounded foot. As he swung back to the approaching Crosbie, he swept his hand forward, lashing the air blindly with his rapier.

Crosbie halted, grunting with pain as savage waves pounded on his head. Cold beads of sweat stood strong on his forehead. He had no time to waste now. He turned from O'Neill and snatched a padded linen cloth from a table nearby. Quickly he wrapped it solidly around his left arm from hand to shoulder, leaving a long corner dangling. Then he advanced again, his dirk balanced lightly in his right hand, his eyes coldly intent on the crouching O'Neill. He offered his swathed left arm to the Irishman's rapier.

O'Neill had backed completely into the corner and his eyes flared with panic. "I didn't mean to kill her," he babbled. "I thought... in that great hooded cloak, I thought it was another of Tremais's ..." O'Neill stumbled aside, glaring at the inexorable young Scot, mouthing frightened obscenities in a fast, incoherent mumble. His smooth chin was flecked with spittle.

As Crosbie came nearer, O'Neill launched himself forward with a high, despairing cry. His thin blade stabbed at Crosbie. The young Scot swept his left arm wide, feeling the cutting edge of the rapier slice into the cloth guarding his arm. Then he stepped in close. The dirk struck solidly home and O'Neill gasped. He sagged slowly, looking blindly into Crosbie's eyes as he died.

Crosbie watched the body of Céleste's murderer slide off his blade. He felt nothing. No pain, no happiness, no pride in vengeance. Only the coldness that now seemed a permanent part of him.

Crosbie looked down at O'Neill's huddled body. I've executed a murderer, he thought. He killed Céleste and now he is dead. This is justice then, by any standard. I thought I would feel better when it was done, but I don't feel anything. That is very strange, he told himself. I should feel something.

He turned toward the distant door. And he walked alone down the long deserted room, hearing only the echo of his heels on the bare floor.

CHAPTER SIXTY ONE

Duncan Crosbie paused at the ballroom door to strip the padded cloth from his arm. He caught a glimpse of himself in a mirror. Blood glistened moistly all down the right side of his face. Clumsily, he soaked the cloth in wine and wiped away the worst of it. He wadded a napkin and held it against the wound while he clapped his hat on tightly to hold the makeshift bandage in place. He knew that scalp wounds always bled profusely and he was not worried, but a painful dizziness and an impaired vision were disturbing.

He unlocked the door and stalked with unsteady strides down the hallway and out of the Palace, ignoring the stares of servants and sentries.

He moved cautiously down the stone staircase to the street. The rain had stopped long ago and it was full daylight now. The sudden brightness struck under his eyelids, almost blinding him. He turned toward the St. Charles, then stopped as a column of jogging infantrymen came swiftly across the bridge and slowed for the steep climb up to the ruined city. They kept formation very well, their muskets precisely aslope, intervals exact, even when they came down to quick-time. But what were they doing here? Crosbie stared with professional curiosity. Those troops were Languedoc. They belonged in position along the Center retrenchment. Then why were they . . .

He pushed through a rapidly swelling crowd that lined the street. Galloping horses alerted the townsfolk and they retreated hastily, leaving Crosbie alone beside the marching soldiers. He glanced up, frowning heavily as he tried to make his eyes focus. Horses pounded directly toward him.

One of that troop was Captain Jamie Johnstone, Crosbie noted, riding at a breakneck pace over the cobbles. Jamie was too clever a horseman to run his mount on such footing unless he had excellent reason. Crosbie swung his arm up in a peremptory signal. Johnstone reined his horse down to a bone-racking trot and then halted.

"Duncan, where in the name of hell have you been? The Général is wild! Where ..."

Crosbie looked up, steadying himself with one hand on Johnstone's saddle. "I've been ... busy, Jamie," he said in a thick voice. He coughed to clear his throat. "What's happened? Where are you ..."

"The English, damn you!" Johnstone shouted hoarsely. "They landed on the Plains of Abraham last night! Their whole army!"

Crosbie shivered in the sharp wind. His hands felt curiously weak as he gripped the saddle tightly. He was aware of a painful, pulsing surge in his head. "Let me ride, Jamie," he said heavily. "I can't ..."

"Duncan!" Johnstone swung to the ground and braced his hand under Crosbie's arm. "What's happened to you? Your head is covered with blood! Were you fighting?"

Crosbie pushed him away. "Don't trouble, Jamie. Help me up." He lifted one foot, waited until Johnstone stooped with cupped hands. He pulled himself laboriously up into the saddle. He sat stiffly, trying to ignore the waves of dizziness that blurred his vision. Johnstone leaped up easily behind him and reached past to gather up the reins.

"The Général is outside the St. Louis Gate. The regiments are forming in line of battle beyond the city. I think we're going to fight them, Duncan."

"Yes," Crosbie said in a vague mumble. Long slow tremors of feverish pain pulled at his muscles in rhythmic pulsations.

He heard the harsh, sullen intensity of enemy bombardment through a haze of distortion. Probably the English ships had sailed close-in to add their guns to the cannonade. The sheer volume of sound set Crosbie's nerves jangling.

He was forced to hang onto the saddle grimly with both hands. Each stride of the rough-walking horse sent waves of pain through his head. Johnstone talked constantly, excitedly, but Crosbie heard none of it.

They rode uphill outside the city wall, passing the St. Jean Gate where crowds of Quebec's refugees huddled apprehensively. The horse trotted on toward the St. Louis Gate and Crosbie strained to fight off a growing dizziness. Hot, knifing pain stabbed from his wound, concentrating with blinding force just behind his eyes. His muscles quivered as he struggled for control.

Roughly Johnstone kicked his mount into a lumbering canter and turned him in at the great overhanging portal of the St. Louis Gate.

"There'll be a surgeon stationed here, Duncan," he said quietly. "You'll need some attention before ..."

Johnstone's voice drifted into silence, Crosbie thought. He felt the slender Captain clutch tightly at his arm and vaguely, he wondered why Jamie was gripping him so hard. Then Crosbie hit the ground solidly, landing heavily on his side with a thudding impact that drove all consciousness from him.

He came alert minutes later with the surgeon's arm under his shoulders and a beaker of sour-smelling brandy held to his lips. He sipped cautiously, choked, but forced the spirit down his dry throat.

He was braced against the crumbling stone of the city wall, legs stretched full length. His face had been washed clean and a great wad of bandage covered his head like a turban. He pushed away the brandy and struggled to rise.

"The first casualty of the day," the surgeon said with bright nervousness. "You had best lie quiet, young man. That wound will be very painful. The bullet scraped along your skull and ..."

Crosbie staggered as he came to his feet. He propped one arm unsteadily against the wall, hanging his head until the first dizziness passed. The pain was already a solid fact. It did not come and go in waves as before, but swept over him with a deep agonizing ache that seemed to have no specific source, but to be in total command of his body. He drew in long gasping breaths. He could feel cold sweat on his face, icy in the chill wind.

"Here," the surgeon said briskly. "If you will be a fool, take this." He held out a small black tablet and offered Crosbie the brandy to wash it down. He watched the young Scot swallow his medicine and he smiled tightly. "Opium," he said. "Here are several more pills. Take them if the pain grows worse."

Crosbie nodded his thanks. His throat closed when he tried to speak. He gulped hard several times and managed to mutter his gratitude, but his voice seemed to come from far away, dimly.

The surgeon dropped the opium pills in Crosbie's pocket. He watched Crosbie walk carefully toward the gate, measuring each step with extreme caution.

Canadien regulars swarmed in undisciplined groups through the gate. Crosbie joined them until he was outside the wall, then stepped aside for a clear view of the field.

Some six hundred mètres forward, along a low ridge, the line of French infantry was strung from the edge of the St. Lawrence escarpment almost to the slope of the St. Charles valley. A perilously thin line to Crosbie's eye, but one that thickened each minute as new units came running up and were assigned their places.

Crosbie strode slowly out, feeling a shaft of pain in his head every time his bootheels struck the hard earth. But gradually the pain subsided to the point of endurance, thanks to the surgeon's black pill.

Montcalm and three senior colonels came into view as Crosbie topped the low ridge. He turned toward them, then stopped to stare across the flat plain at the enemy. A narrow red line stretched endlessly, with high-flying battleflags to mark the regiments. Crosbie's gaze swept along the English ranks. They were as thin as the French, he estimated. But in the distance, thick scarlet knots of massed companies were coming into position. It was to be a race as well as a fight, Crosbie realized, and the faster army would be the stronger when the battle was joined. Obviously Wolfe would not be able to bring his entire force into action unless he was given most of the day. Crosbie moved along the ridge toward his Général.

He held back, seeing the colonels and Montcalm were in serious discussion. He stared unbelievingly at the Général who sat his favorite black gelding with an easy seat. Montcalm was in full-dress uniform, and over his lieutenant-général's embroidered coat was a silver-inlaid black cuirasse that completely covered his chest and back. The horse pawed nervously and Montcalm pulled him down gently, sitting tall against the brightening sky. Pale sunlight glinted from his beautiful, archaic armor. What could that be, Crosbie wondered, a memento of earlier days, or might it be a symbol of fear, of foreboding? Crosbie had never seen the cuirasse before and looking at it now brought a cold shiver to his spine. He moved a few steps to the right, putting himself inside the Général's range of vision.

"Duncan," the Général called sharply. He reined his mount away from the colonels and walked the big horse toward Crosbie. "Where have you ..." His harsh voice broke off when he observed the bandaged head, the torn shirt soaked brownish-red with blood. "Are you fit for duty?" he asked quietly.

"Perfectly fit, sir," Crosbie said promptly.

The Général nodded. "I hope you are. We will say more of this later. Have you seen your young friend today?"

"Denis?" Crosbie asked. "No, sir. Is he all right? Did ..."

"He is free," Montcalm said with a hint of a smile. "I sent for you, but ..." The Général shrugged. "I was compelled to punish him, you understand. I dismissed him from the King's service. The Sieur duMaine immediately enrolled the boy in the Beauport militia. Raoul will see that he keeps clear of Monsieur Bigot." The Général looked down at Crosbie and his tired eyes glinted with genuine pleasure. "He is a very nice young boy, that Denis. We had a long talk. I could not see him come to harm. When all this is finished, and we go back to France, we will leave the future of this land to such boys. I am glad you brought him to my attention, Duncan."

"Yes, sir," Crosbie said in a vague tone. "Thank you, mon général."

Montcalm dismissed his thanks with an amiable gesture. "Stay close to me, Duncan. I will have work for you when I see what Monsieur Wolfe decides to do."

Crosbie drew himself erect and blinked to clear his eyes. "And the artillery, sir?" he asked briskly. "Where will the guns be emplaced?"

The Général smiled, a brief humorless grimace. "I don't know. Wait here, Duncan. I have sent Estére to Monsieur de Ramesay for the Palace cannon."

"Very good, sir," Crosbie said in a brisk tone that was designed to mask his painful dizziness. The Palace wall held twenty-five brass guns. Only six-pounders, but good enough against troops massed in the open. With twenty-five small cannon, Crosbie could destroy that English line before the enemy could advance to musket-range. He lowered his head and closed his eyes briefly. The waves of hot pain had begun to pound at him again and Crosbie wavered uncertainly. A hand fumbled for the pills the surgeon had given him. Quickly, he crunched two between his teeth and waited stolidly until the narcotic dulled the pain again. He looked up in time to see Estére pull his elderly mount to a halt and salute the Général.

"Only three, sir," Estére cried in a high, taut voice.

Crosbie smiled inwardly. Even Estére was not proof against the excitement and tension of impending battle. Even Estére, the imperturbable, could feel...

"De Ramesay will give us only three, mon général," Estére said with bitter clarity. "The Governor and the Intendant are there with him now, and they agree we should have only three guns."

Dear God! Crosbie sucked in a quick breath. Three guns only, out of the hundreds at Quebec? Only three guns against the whole English army?

"They will serve," Montcalm said briskly. He waved away the problem. "We will take the bayonet to them today, Estére."

He is very strange today, Crosbie thought. I would hardly have recognized him. The voice is much higher and tighter. And he-behaves as if this is merely a pleasant outing in the Bois. Does he really think...

"Duncan," Montcalm said crisply. "You will have three cannon. I want to see brisk work today, my boy. Emplace them at the Center where you see my standard. You may open fire when the guns are ready."

"Yes, sir," Crosbie said vaguely. He steadied himself momentarily. He drew in a long breath and held it until the pain had completely left him.

Only much later, when he tried to remember as clearly as he could, did he realize that this was his last truly conscious moment of the day. The loss of Céleste, the long furious night, and his wound were enough to disturb any mind, but the opium pills he had taken to smother the pain had served to separate him thoroughly from all reality. He had functioned well that day. He was told so, and events seemed to bear it out, but the little that he could recall came to him in short tableaux, as lightning flashes will illuminate a night scene for one flickering instant, before darkness drops again, blacker and more impenetrable than before.

He could recall with startling clarity the sight of Montcalm, commandingly tall on his restless black, and the bright energy of the Général as he prepared for battle. He could not recall what guncrews had served his three fieldpieces, not how efficient they had been.

Many accounts were written later and Crosbie read them all avidly, trying to identify himself with that disastrous battle. But it remained always for him as dim as a legendary Grecian conflict, except that he knew the people involved.

Much later he heard of Captain de Vergor, who had commanded the one-hundred-man guard post that blocked the Anse-au-Foulon, and how that treacherous, slovenly officer had permitted most of his detachment to go home to harvest their fields, provided they agreed to get in the Captain's crop later. Captain de Vergor was captured fast asleep by the daring Highlanders who scaled the precipitous path and opened the narrow route to the English. During the night, five thousand troops, the bulk of Wolfe's effectives, had made their way up the declivity.

English ships had laid a withering hail of bombardment on the city. Other vessels had threatened Louis de Bougainville's command above Camp Rouge, some seven leagues from Quebec, keeping his force, now increased to two thousand men, safely in check until it was too late for him to come to Montcalm's support, though by forced marching, he arrived before noon and launched a swift assault against the English flank.

The Governor and the Intendant remained throughout the day safely in the hornworks guarding the St. Charles bridge. And with him, the Governor kept the major portion of the militia. The regiment of Royal Roussillon, encamped some three leagues from Quebec, had managed to come onto the field in time to fight, but the militia, stationed just beyond the wall, could not manage to move in time.

Basically, it was a battle of the regular forces. Five French regiments of the line against ten of the English. Montcalm's force was aided also by units of Canadien regulars and militia from Quebec, Trois Rivières and Montreal, as well as small partisan units that sniped from the flanks, but their men were simply not trained for such formal combat in which blocks of infantry advanced in a determined line, firing rigidly controlled platoon volleys as they moved, until the proper distance was ultimately reached at which the bayonet charge was launched. No, it was a regular's battle, and Duncan Crosbie in his wandering memory, could often hear the thin hoarse cheering of the hard-bitten veterans of Oswego, William Henry and Carillon as they saluted their Général outside Quebec.

Somehow the English artillerymen had managed to muscle a six-pounder up the steep cliff in time to bring it into action against the French attack. Grape and canister had torn savagely into Royal Roussillon as that regiment came into line. But the English infantry held its fire until the French were well within musket range. Along the double rank of scarlet coats, officers moved briskly back and forth, cautioning their men and behind them, with his own fusil primed and cocked, stood their tall, nervous commander, watching the high, stark silhouette of Montcalm as he waved his men forward. The disciplined English troops endured several irregular volleys from the Canadien regulars without flinching.

Montcalm led his army forward gallantly, but Duncan Crosbie was then urging his gunners into a faster rate of fire and he did not observe the advance until the Canadiens loosed their first volley in defiance of orders. The Canadiens, accustomed to partisan fighting, threw themselves to the ground to reload, and for one wild moment, Crosbie thought they had been wiped out to the man. The French regulars advanced steadily, firing as they marched, but now both their flanks were uncovered when the Canadiens fell far behind. Most of the Canadiens stayed where they were, firing desultorily but with good effect from their prone positions some one hundred mètres from the English lines, which was extreme range for muskets.

A sharp spiny ridge ran from the English line toward the French advance, and the regulars drifted to either side, dividing themselves into two separate units, both with exposed flanks. Officers ran along the lines, shouting to bring them into a single formation again, but by then the steady English volley rang out.

Far to the rear, Duncan Crosbie thought a large field piece had been brought into action against the French, so unified was that first volley. He looked up dazedly to see the French waver. A second volley, a wild cheering charge, led by kilted Highlanders with their bagpipes skirling stridently, and the French broke. First the poorly disciplined Languedoc regiment fell back in confusion, further exposing the remaining units. Highland claymores flashed in the dull sunlight. And English bugles shrilled the charge. Hit from front and flank alike, the French infantry fell back, at first in reasonable order, despite their broken files. But in the confused mêlée, men panicked and the entire army fled in straggling masses back toward Quebec.

It was this mad flight that remained as Duncan Crosbie's clearest recollection of the battle on the Plains of Abraham. The tangled, desperate confusion of retreating soldiers, wildeyed, bellowing hoarsely. And towering above all, fighting to control his restive mount, was Montcalm, sword in hand, who vainly tried to stem the tide of defeat. The Général's horse backed into one of Crosbie's guns, stumbled and almost fell before Montcalm could swing him safely around. And then followed the last sharp picture in Crosbie's memory: the brief, hardly noticeable lurch when the Général sagged in his saddle. Crosbie could hear the leather creak as Montcalm fought for balance.

Crosbie reached with one hand to brace the Général. And then the massed, overwhelming flood of retreat swept them back toward the city gates, the Général reeling, but able to maintain his seat with Crosbie to support him. The huge young Scot lay, half draped, over the gelding's back, holding Montcalm with a savage clutch. Both of Crosbie's legs dragged along beside the horse, but the weary young Scot was beyond pain just then.

Only the Canadiens, regular and militia, remained to slow the English charge. They lay prone on both flanks and poured a withering musketry at the advancing enemy, and stoutly maintained it until the broken French regulars were safely off the field.

But that first surging rush had carried Montcalm and Crosbie in through the St. Louis Gate. The panicked crowd opened for the Général's horse. Crosbie let it drag him until someone seized the reins. Then he let go and slid to the ground in a heap.

"Oh, my God," someone shrieked in Crosbie's ear. "Oh, my God, the Général is dead!"

Crosbie tried to shake his head. "No," he thought when the words would not come from his lips, "no, not the Général. Céleste is dead. Not the Général, too."

CHAPTER SIXTY TWO

And Montcalm was not dead, not until the afternoon of the next day. He lived long enough to know that the battle for Quebec, and for all of Canada, had been lost beyond question, that in winning, the English commander, Wolfe, had also been mortally wounded on the field and had since died. But the most bitter knowledge was for him to learn that Quebec lay almost deserted as his army fled toward the mountains in broken disorder. A handful of English could have taken the city that first day, but they delayed, fortifying the battlefield, and energetic French officers rallied the regulars and brought them back to their duty. But not until their Général had died in silent, savage bitterness.

It fell again to Brother Mathieu to bring the news to Duncan Crosbie, and the young friar spoke in a voice that quavered with a dreadful sense of loss. But not until some days later was Crosbie able to understand what had happened.

In his confused mind, the two worst days of his life had merged into a single hateful fact. From the moment he had left the hospital knowing that Céleste had been killed, until he woke up in bed at the General Hospital with Brother Mathieu leaning solicitously over him, Duncan Crosbie had been insane. He accepted that fact, as he accepted the fact that he had red hair. For that space of time, he had been a madman. The execution of Captain O'Neill had been part of that brief insanity, though even now Duncan Crosbie could make no apologies. Now he would proceed differently, but the end result would most certainly have been the same.

Nearly a week after the battle, Duncan Crosbie lay half asleep in Brother Mathieu's own tiny cell at the crowded hospital. On his naked chest hung the bright medal of Ste. Barbara and his thin fingers plucked aimlessly at it, lifting it and letting it drop against his skin with a solid coldness. His head was swathed in clean dressings and now the throbbing pain was not too bad as long as he remembered to lie still. Somehow he had received a slight wound along his side from an English musket ball, which the surgeon had discovered at the hospital. That was healing adequately, too, but from both of them, Crosbie had lost so much blood that he remained weak and listless, dull and dispirited, even with Denis and the Sieur duMaine who came daily to visit him.

DuMaine's was one of the few units remaining devotedly on guard at the city's walls. When the Governor fled, he took with him the Canadiens who would still accept his orders. And safely in his retinue were the Intendant and his band of thieves. But a few remained to relieve the strain on the demoralized regular regiments. The enemy lay calmly waiting outside the walls, bombarding the besieged city relentlessly, and blockading all food shipments to the beleaguered defenders. Already supplies were at a perilous low; many people had not eaten since the day of the battle, and there was no relief in sight. Colonel de Bougainville managed to slip a few boatloads of food past the blockade, and his polyglot army harassed the enemy constantly, with slight effect.

The King's Lieutenant for Quebec, and the town major were now the senior governmental officials in the city and they were desperately worried men. Counsel was sharply divided on the basic question of further resistance, but the outcome seemed inevitable.

Crosbie lay quietly, staring with mesmeric fascination at the tallow dip that flickered across the room, throwing grotesque patterns on the wall. The hospital was very still now, except for the muffled groans from the wounded men who were lying in the corridors. Knuckles rapped softly on the door and it moved back.

Brother Mathieu padded in silently and stood aside to let a second cowled Récollet friar precede him. Crosbie lifted his head curiously and bit his lip to stifle the cry that rose in his throat from the sudden pain of moving. He fell back on the pillow and blinked in dull resignation at the ceiling.

"Be very quiet, Duncan," Brother Mathieu said in a tense whisper. "I have brought you a visitor." He gestured to the second friar and then retreated to the door, blocking it with his frayed sandal.

The other friar shoved back his deep cowl and smiled at Crosbie, moving close to the bed so that his face was clearly visible to the young Scot.

"Louis?" Crosbie's voice was a thin croak. It couldn't be Louis de Bougainville, he thought. Louis was commanding the army outside the city. He hadn't been captured, surely? Or surrendered? Crosbie shoved himself back and struggled to prop his head against the wall. "Louis?"

"The same Louis," de Bougainville said mildly. "I am sorry to see you in such pain, my dear friend. I had hoped..." He shrugged and sat slowly on the edge of Crosbie's bed. "I knew you were wounded, but I thought you might be able to ... to come with me. Heaven knows I need a good artillery officer, Duncan."

"I can't walk, Louis. I ..."

"I know, Duncan. Don't distress yourself."

"But you are still fighting, though?" Crosbie tried to make his voice carry a lively interest, but even in his ears it rang flat and toneless.

"Yes, we still fight, Duncan." Colonel de Bougainville sighed and rubbed his tired eyes with the heels of both hands.

"Tell me frankly, Louis," Crosbie said as forcefully as he could. He propped himself on one arm to see de Bougainville more clearly. "Is there still a chance?"

De Bougainville turned his eyes toward the floor. His chest lifted once with a deep breath. "I don't know, Duncan. Honestly. The reason for my visit to Quebec today was to attend a council-of-war. I was too late. The city has already accepted the enemy's terms. The articles have been signed, with the Governor's agreement. Quebec will surrender in the morning. I was too late. But they would not have listened to me anyway, Duncan. Maybe it is best, to surrender before ..."

"No," Crosbie said flatly. A brisk hard note crept into his voice and his eyes seemed to glint. "You could lead the army out, Louis. You could break through the enemy, and ..."

"Yes, something could be done," Louis de Bougainville said softly. "But the army has no heart for such an effort. The battle ... ruined us, Duncan. Most of the best officers were killed, as well as the Général. It was Montcalm's death that destroyed our last hope. Now there is hardly a man in Quebec with the will to fight further. It is over for Quebec, Duncan. That is why I came for you, to take you with me, if I could."

"I don't understand you, Louis," Crosbie frowned. "I told you I can't ..."

"Yes, I know. But I thought ..." de Bougainville sighed again, softly. "One of the articles of surrender, Duncan, calls for the immediate repatriation of all soldiers in Quebec. They will be sent back to France very soon, the officers within the week."

A dark blue vein knotted in Crosbie's forehead. A wild pulse lifted the knot. Large muscles of his jaw bulged in painful relief. "I'm coming with you, Louis," he said bluntly. "I won't stay here and ..."

De Bougainville shook his head. "No, Duncan. I can't carry you. We would have to crawl for hours up the St. Charles valley to get clear of the English. It is out of the question."

Crosbie glared at the weary colonel. He was suddenly struck again with the close resemblance Louis bore to Montcalm. He, too, had lost weight until his uniform draped loosely from his shoulders, and the same fine sharp lines were etched deeply in his tired face. And the eyes, something about the eyes ...

"Forgive me, Duncan. I should not have mentioned it." De Bougainville lifted one hand and let it fall. "I have talked to everyone about the battle, my friend. I have been trying to understand what happened, and why it happened."

Crosbie leaned against the wall and closed his eyes.

The colonel's voice went on, quietly insistent. "Why did he attack? Why did he conduct a brilliant defensive campaign for long patient months and then, on almost the last day, throw it all away on a mad gamble? Why did he attack, Duncan?"

"I don't know," the young Scot said in a hollow voice. "Jamie Johnstone said the Général thought Wolfe had only a portion of his troops in line of battle, so ..."

"No," de Bougainville said emphatically. "No, they were all visible to him. He hadn't lost his ability to count. No, that explains nothing, Duncan. We could have manned the city walls and compelled the enemy to attack us. Why didn't we?"

"Not those walls, Louis," Crosbie protested. "I inspected them and I can tell you they wouldn't keep out a determined assault for more than a few minutes."

"Very well," de Bougainville shrugged. "But why fight with only a part of his troops? Why didn't the Général send a regiment and herd all the Canadiens into the battle line? Why didn't he force de Ramesay to send every gun from the Palace walls?"

"About the guns I don't know, Louis. With only a dozen, I could have ruined the English line. And certainly the rest of the Canadien regulars would have been useful, I would think. But there is something else, Louis, something you haven't considered. Possibly you didn't know."

"Know what, Duncan?"

"Monsieur Tremais brought all his evidence to the Général some days before the battle. So Montcalm knew that Bigot was making arrangements to betray the city, hoping that proof of his thievery would be lost in the confusion afterward. That was the situation. Then, early one morning, the Général finds that the English have reached the Plains of Abraham, past a guarded outpost without an alarm being given. Don't you think the Général would suspect that was the first step toward betraying Quebec? Don't you think he would prefer to take the troops he trusted most and fight a battle that he might possibly have won, rather than give Bigot a further opportunity to betray us all?"

De Bougainville stared at Crosbie in sombre silence. After a long thoughtful moment, he nodded gloomily. "That is how he would have reacted, I agree." With a savage gesture, he banged his fist against the wall. "God, I wish I had been with him. If only he'd waited for me to come up. I could have stopped him."

Crosbie opened his eyes and looked at de Bougainville. The colonel had both hands locked fiercely together, controlling himself with visible effort. He spoke in a low, shaky tone.

"He was a great man, Duncan, a splendid soldier. He loved the army as he loved his home, and he was a brilliant commander. But he was not a patient man. He was audacious by nature and he truly detested the niggling, cautious defense he was forced to adopt here. He burned to attack. That is the real answer, I believe. For months, the Governor screamed for an assault and Montcalm denied him. You know how angrily he refused. He denied himself at the same time. I knew that. Often, during the long siege, he spoke longingly of Candiac. He planned new enterprises for his estate. But I think he knew then that he would never see his home again. He used to tell me that war is the graveyard of the Montcalms. He was a quick-tempered, valiant man, as you know, Duncan. But of late he had become more quiet, almost fatalistic. I do not believe he expected to live. Like Dürer's knight, Death walked always at his side. Possibly he welcomed it—at the end."

De Bougainville's voice choked off abruptly. He swallowed heavily.

"Don't, Louis," Crosbie said quietly. He reached out to touch his friend's shoulder. "Tell me, Louis, what does it actually mean, losing Quebec? Is it the end? Or will you be able to stand against..."

The colonel straightened and drew in a long shuddery breath. "Until Spring, Duncan, we can hold out. De Lévis, de Bourlamaque and I can confuse the enemy enough, I think. But when the snow melts again, Amherst will surely move north. Wolfe's army will advance toward Montreal. And we will either retreat to the Détroit or fight a battle we cannot hope to win. That is the future, Duncan."

"Could Quebec have held out longer?" Crosbie demanded in a harsh tone.

De Bougainville glanced sharply at the angry young Scot and he smiled with bitter understanding. "The city was doomed when Montcalm was killed. I know what prompted your question. It doesn't matter now, Duncan. Bigot had no opportunity to betray the city. Quebec was lost in combat. I have heard that the Governor was prepared to surrender all of Canada, but obviously, wiser counsel prevailed. But you may believe this, Duncan: If any overtures were made to the English, I will discover that fact. I have made arrangements for Monsieur Tremais to send his documents back to Paris. And Monsieur Bigot will most certainly end his days in the Bastille, together with the other shameless scoundrels who have looted Canada. Trust me for that, Duncan. Bigot and the Governor will learn what it is to suffer."

"I trust you, Louis," Crosbie said. And he smiled at the hard sureness in the colonel's voice.

"Now, I must go, Duncan." De Bougainville rose. He stood looking down at Crosbie. "I cannot bring myself to speak of... of Mademoiselle Céleste. I know what she meant to you. I offer you my sympathy. I... I was shocked—and I was very pleased—to hear of Captain O'Neill's punishment."

"Thank you, Louis," Crosbie said heavily.

De Bougainville lifted his shoulders and let them drop wearily. "I wish I could command the Général's eloquence. I cannot say what is in my heart. You have lost terribly, Duncan. But you have gained much, too. I think you will see that one day. We may talk of it again. In France. Some time."

"Yes." Crosbie's voice was dull, without resonance. "Goodbye, Louis. Bonne chance."

"Adieu, Duncan."

CHAPTER SIXTY THREE

The cart creaked and groaned, lurching as it rolled onto the shattered wharf. Duncan Crosbie lay flat on a stretcher in the cart-bed, with twenty other wounded officers beside him. The long painful trip from the hospital had taken hours, the cart stopping often as endless lines of marching troops clogged the littered streets of Quebec. English soldiers paraded through the gates with flutes, drums and bagpipes blaring lustily, and the slow, dispirited columns of French infantry marched silently to their barracks to wait for their turn to board the ships for France. But the officers, considered the more dangerous element, were being embarked immediately. The cartloads of wounded had rumbled from the hospital since dawn, even during three hours of icy rain, and now, in the middle of a bleak and cheerless afternoon, Duncan Crosbie's turn had come. His ancient cart ground to a complaining halt on the stone quay. Overhead, Crosbie could make out the yardarms of a mainmast. The ship had been moored alongside the quay to make the loading easier. He watched as sailors speedily attached a rope sling to the first stretcher and signalled to the ship. Blocks squealed, the thick rope tightened, and slowly the stretcher lifted straight up, and swung dizzily through the air toward the ship's deck. Crosbie closed his eyes and shivered in the cold sunlight.

He thought wryly of his arrival at Quebec, of the cheerful bustle, the excited crowds. Today he had not seen a single person on the long tiring trip to the dock, except for the blank, impassive faces of his captors who had lined the streets silently guarding against any last-minute dash for freedom. They had been very busy, the English, in the few days since Quebec had surrendered. And they would have to be busier still if they hoped to evacuate all the French army before the river froze.

Another stretcher was swayed up and out toward the ship. Crosbie followed it with his eyes until it dropped from view. He turned his head away and as he did, a red-silk cap popped over the side of the cart and a thin voice shrieked, "Here he is! I found him!"

"Denis?" Crosbie croaked. He coughed his throat clear and forced a smile.

The boy clambered busily inside and perched on the side of the cart. He waved his arm to someone out of sight. A moment later, the round, weathered countenance of the Sieur duMaine rose over the side.

"Good boy, Denis," the seigneur said, patting the boy's narrow back. He flipped open a high fleecy stack of blankets and bent to tuck them warmly around Crosbie's shivering frame. Then he extracted a fat leather flask and slipped it down beside the young Scot. He smiled warmly. "A touch of crème de Noyeau. For ... for old times. You know."

"I know," Crosbie said thickly. The Général's favorite, he thought. I'd rather have anything else than that.

"We have been hunting all day, Duncan," the boy said seriously. "I inspected every wagon that came on the wharf, and ..."

Crosbie examined the boy, not listening to what he was saying. He wore a thick woolen smock, high leather boots and leggings. No trace of uniform. He glanced at the seigneur, the question clear in his eyes.

"I burned that damned white coat myself," duMaine said harshly. "He's Canadien-born and he'll stay in Canada."

"At Beauport?"

"With me," the seigneur said. He smoothed the blankets around Crosbie's neck, and added softly. "It is the boy's home, Duncan. You may rely on that."

"Good. Thank you, sir. I was ..."

"Yes, I understand. The boy will be all right. He will stay where he belongs. And ... and you, Duncan. Beauport is your home, too, if you will come. Won't you be able to return after the war is ..."

Crosbie turned his face away and closed his eyes tightly. "No." His voice was savagely quiet. "I ... I could not abide ..."

DuMaine's hand closed tightly on his shoulder. The presence of Celeste was very clear to both of them, but neither could mention her name. "I understand, Duncan," he said gently. "But one day, maybe ..." His voice dwindled slowly. He took his hand away and sat back to let the English sailors attach the sling to the stretcher beside Crosbie's. Denis watched the intricate process with a boy's rapt fascination, but the seigneur's sombre gaze never left Crosbie's haggard face.

"We will miss you, Duncan," he murmured. "Come back, if ... if you can, my boy."

"Yes, sir," Crosbie said, holding every muscle rigid in the terrible effort to contain himself. Hopeless tears burned behind his eyes and he fought to keep them there. "It will be strange ... now ... in Quebec."

"I suppose it will," duMaine said with a peculiar questioning tone. "Especially at first, but ..." He glanced briefly at the occupied city. "I wonder if the English will seem any more foreign to us than the French?"

Crosbie almost smiled, remembering the seigneur's fierce defense of everything French. But whether he was trying to convince himself or not, his new attitude was certainly the wisest, in view of the great changes that lay in store for Canada.

"I will miss Beauport," he said, knowing the seigneur wanted to hear him say that. "And my friends."

"The land will be there, Duncan. And the church. And the people. We will go on living. Somehow. And so will you, though it may not seem likely to you just now. Please write, Duncan, if you will not return. I will follow your future with deep concern."

Crosbie snorted quietly. "What future?" he muttered in a tired voice.

DuMaine smiled and again his broad hand touched Crosbie's shoulder. "The voyage home will see you well again, my boy. You will walk ashore at Le Hâvre, and then the future will be worth thinking about, eh? Somewhere, someone is always fighting a war, particularly we French. There is always a future for a good soldier."

Crosbie lay still, barely breathing. DuMaine looked up at the lowering sling that would be connected to Crosbie's stretcher. He moved to the side of the cart as the bustling sailors slid the rope under Crosbie's litter.

Denis stood stiffly, his cap in hand. His soft boots made a dull thump as he tried valiantly to crack his heels together. "Adieu, mon capitaine," he said in a thin sharp voice that threatened to break.

"Adieu, Denis," Crosbie smiled. "Good-bye, sir. Make my farewells to … everyone … for me, please. Good-bye."

The sling tightened, lifted, and Crosbie rose swiftly out of the cart. Tarred hands guided his stretcher to the main deck. A piercing tenor voice shouted an order and alert seamen jumped to cast off the lines that moored the ship to the quay. In a matter of minutes, the vessel had eased away from the stone landing. From his position, Crosbie had a clear view of the topmen as they scrambled aloft to set the vast sails. Slowly the ship moved out into the wide basin below Quebec, then heeled slightly as it made for the channel.

The ship glided smoothly away from the city, out from under the dark cold shadow cast by the great rock. Crosbie turned his head to look at the shattered black outline of the Cathedral spire against the bleak sky.

As the wind veered, the transport heeled slightly, coming about on the opposite tack. The deck tilted and Crosbie's stretcher slid to the railing. Between the stubby gilt posts that supported the railing, he caught a glimpse of the steeple at Beauport. A thin beam of winter sunlight flashed a sparkle from the cross at the top. Céleste was there, he thought. Directly beneath that tower where he had stood with Montcalm to watch the English sail against Quebec. And now it was Céleste's tower and he could never think of it as anything else. As he watched, the vagrant brightness vanished, as if it had been purposely snuffed out.

The transport levelled onto its course and Crosbie stared overhead at the leaden grey sky. Dimly he could make out the brilliant colors of the English ensign fluttering from the masthead. Then Duncan Crosbie closed his eyes. There was nothing more to see.

AUTHOR'S NOTE

For nearly a year, the remnant of the French army held off Amherst's overwhelming force. Ultimately the three Chevaliers, de Lévis, de Bourlamaque, de Bougainville, were trapped at Montreal. The Marquis de Vaudreuil promptly surrendered all of Canada.

In accordance with the terms of the capitulation, the French military officers and the chief civil officials were sent to France. The moment they arrived, the thieves who had looted Canada were imprisoned in the Bastille. The Marquis de Vaudreuil, Bigot, Cadet, Péan, Bréard, Varin, Le Mercier, Penisseault, Maurin, Corpron and lesser rascals were tried in 1761. All attempted to clear themselves by informing on the others. Bigot was sentenced to lifelong exile and a fine of one-and-a-half million francs. Cadet was banished from Paris for nine years and fined six million. The others were fined and all were held in prison until they paid. De Vaudreuil was acquitted for lack of specific evidence.

Montcalm's second-in-command, the Chevalier de Lévis, eventually became a Marshal of France, but Louis-Antoine de Bougainville, restless to the end, resigned his commission. Later he made a voyage of exploration around the world. He organized the settlement of the Falkland Islands. During the American Revolution, we see him serving as commander of the Guerriere, a naval captain in the fleet of Admiral Comte d'Estaing.

England's great explorer, Captain James Cook, was sailing master of a frigate off Quebec. His were the first dependable charts made of the St. Lawrence approaches.

In many ways, the long struggle for Canada can be seen as a rehearsal for the American Revolution. Sir William Howe, commander of the British army from Boston to Philadelphia, served as a young regimental commander under Wolfe at Louisbourg and Quebec. His brother Richard, who succeeded to the title when George, Lord Howe was killed before Carillon, commanded the British fleet during the Revolution. Wolfe's quartermaster, Sir Guy Carleton, was the defender of Quebec when the Americans attacked in 1775.

All of the trained officers with the American forces were seasoned in the Canadian campaigns. Among the Major Generals were Charles Lee, a young Grenadier officer who was wounded at Carillon and at Niagara; Israel Putnam, Major of Rangers who was captured outside Carillon; Richard Montgomery, a Lieutenant with Amherst, later killed in 1775 during the assault on Quebec; John Stark, Lieutenant of Rangers who later won the Battle of Bennington against a detachment of Burgoyne's army; Arthur St. Clair, a young Ensign at Quebec and later America's unluckiest commander; Philip Schuyler who served as a Captain under Abercrombie at Carillon. And of course, George Washington, who at the Half-King's camp, fired the first shot of the war that was to end French influence in the New World.

Made in the USA
Middletown, DE
29 January 2021